SHADOWMAN

NYLA K.

Paperback ISBN: 979-8-9869189-8-3

Cover Design by Ashes & Vellichor
Cover Model: Hong Phi Filler

Interior formatting by Champagne Book Design
Proofreading services by Nice Girl Naughty Edits

Shadowman

Alabaster Penitentiary, Volume 5

For three years, I've resided in Alabaster Penitentiary. Surrounded by the same faces, day in and day out, the deranged souls I now call my *friends*. We eat our meals together, shower together… *Hell, we even fool around on occasion.*

Still, after all that, not one of them truly *knows* me.

It's my fault. I'm a withdrawn hoarder of secrets. A *shadowman*, dwelling on the sidelines, damned to this pit of despair for reasons I still can't accept.

Being the outsider in a group of weirdos isn't always fun. After all, if no one sees me, do I even exist?

Okay, let's not go there.

I'm resenting my permanent sidekick status when a distraction arrives. A *newcomer*—tall, mysterious, and severely beautiful, with black hair and violet eyes. His abrupt arrival has my prison pals suspicious. But not me. I'm instantly intrigued by that peculiar gaze following me like nothing has before.

He actually *sees* me. And it's intoxicating.

Trevel Fenwick could be an ally. Maybe he could be… *more.*

My body sure seems to think so. But the brighter he lights me up, the deeper he slips into the shadows himself.

What is this striking stranger hiding behind that charming accent and penetrating stare? Why is his need to seek revenge so strong? And can we fight past our demons enough to become *real* partners in crime?

When a brutal storm ravages Alabaster Isle, we're left sifting through the rubble. The fences are down. Stress cracks in the foundation, secrets escape, fragile loyalties tested. But the war is far from over…

In fact, it's only just begun.

To imaginary friends.

FOREWORD

Alexa, play Back In The Saddle, or Guess Who's Back, or Back In Black, or Back to liiifeee, back to reality…

Okay, you get the point. **WE'RE BACK, INMATES!**

Going back again, back to the Pen to see our friends!

Can't stop, too excited. I *swear*, many of you thought this day would never come… But alas! It's here. *Two years* of waiting, and Byron Kang is *finally* ready to make his debut as the star of the show!

Before we dive in, I just need to warn you about a couple of things…

First, as I tend to mention at the beginning of most of my books, *specifically* when it comes to this series, ***this is NOT your typical romance book.*** This ***is not*** your typical dark romance series. If you've made it this far, you're probably aware that the Alabaster Pen books are done… a bit differently.

Not only is this thing the *size* of two books (at least), but it essentially has two plot lines in one story. There's the romance plot, and then the Alabaster Penitentiary plot, which is the overarching storyline we've been following since *Distorted*. Both parts intertwine to form one behemoth of a book. Just to give you an idea of what I mean, Byron and Trevel don't even meet each other until literally more than ten chapters in.

No, I'm not kidding.

This is very atypical of romance, and I know some readers probably hate it (*I know I do lol*). But I say again, this is ***not*** an average romance book. We have a ton of ground to cover before the finale; secrets to be revealed, backstory, action, drama, and suspense to experience, a relationship to build and a found family to fall even more in love with. That's what this book is all about, and trust me when I tell you… We're only just getting started.

Next, I need to mention something very important. We all know that *darkness* in romance is subjective. I consider this series to have varying levels of darkness. Some of the books are light gray, others are pretty dang close to pitch black. And some have pitch-black moments scattered in between the gray—I think that's this book.

There are moments that get pretty heavy, the heaviest of which comes as part of Trevel's backstory. Now, I'm a big proponent of listing content warnings separately, making them easily accessible to anyone who might need them, without risking spoilers for those who don't. At the bottom of this page, you will find the link to my content warnings page for *Shadowman* (a scannable QR code for paperback readers). That said, I need to mention one thing first, just to ensure that there are no harmful surprises.

Trevel Fenwick is an extremely troubled character in a lot of ways. The things that he does, and endures, early in the book, could definitely make some readers uncomfortable. If you are someone who struggles with reading about addiction and drug use in books, check the content warnings.

This book does contain the death of a trans character. Trust me when I tell you, it was not done in vain, nor is it something I decided to do just to be shocking. It's been a part of the storyline since Book 3, and because it's a part of Trevel's backstory, now is the time when it comes up. If you feel that this might be harmful for you to read, please check the content warnings (I have provided more information there on how you can skip the chapter if need be.)

There are resources listed at the end of all my books, and linked via the content warnings page. Please please please, I'm begging you… Do what's best for yourself as a reader and as a person. Take your mental health and wellbeing seriously, and protect yourself above all else. If you're even a little concerned about reading dark material, check the warnings, and use your best judgements.

This is a fictional series. Much of what you read here is dramatized for entertainment purposes; *however*, there are facets that can tie into the real world or feel like real life. I promise you that nothing in this book is intended to harm anyone. But it could, unintentionally, so please be sure to do your due diligence.

Alright… Are we *ready*? Are we *set…?*

The storm clouds are darkening, warriors… Fences are down.

Time to run. ;)

Find content warnings here: https://authornylak.com/shadowman-content-warning

Scan for content warnings

PREVIOUSLY ON ALABASTER ISLE

A recap of events from volumes 1-4 in chronological order

(Please note, some events happen on the same day/within days of each other. Others are separated by weeks/months. EBook locations are estimated.)

Backstories:

John "Velle" Chevelle - Joyless eBook location 1618 (paperback page 89) + Chapter 18
Joy Jameson - Joyless loc. 1218 & 3581 (page 66, 200) + Chapter 9
Kellan Kemper - Distorted loc. 5949 & 6640 (pages 341 & 381)
Lexington "Luthor" Deon - Fragments Chapters 2 & 8
Warren "Ren" Xavier - Fragments Prologue + Chapters 3 & 9
Dascha "Dash" Reznikov - Distorted Chapters 10 & 27 + loc. 6997 (page 402)

Byron Kang arrives in Alabaster Penitentiary as Luthor and Ren's "relationship" ends - **Fragments loc. 5257 (page 272)**

Luthor gets a new cellmate (Henry Landon), Ren discovers the "proxy" with Velle, and Parker Freeman gets sick - **Fragments loc. 5508 (page 286)**

Felix Darcey (aka "The Carver") is caught and brought to Alabaster Penitentiary (Backstory) - **Brainwashed (Chapter 32)**
Felix sets his sights on Kieran O'Malley - **Brainwashed Prologue**

Harley "Rook" Samuels backstory - **Joyless Chapter 26**
Rook begins working for Manuel Blanco (The Warden of Alabaster Penitentiary, aka "The Ivory") and Kemper is acting weird about a newspaper - **Joyless loc. 345 (page 16)**
Felix Darcey kills his cellmate, Ivan Wilkerson - **Brainwashed loc. 581 (page 26)**
Velle goes to tell the Warden about it, and someone is under his desk - **Joyless Chapter 4**
Joy and Byron (the cell phone is mentioned again) - **Joyless loc. 1185 (page 64)**

New inmate coming (and mention of Governor Russo) - **Joyless loc. 1779 (page 97)**, **Fragments loc. 426 (page 17)**
Dash arrives at Alabaster Penitentiary and his head is shaved - **Distorted loc. 329 (page 15)**
Kellan Kemper quits - **Joyless loc. 1848 (page 99)**
Ren & Byron interact, then Kieran O'Malley is brought to The East Wing - **Fragments loc. 896 (page 41)**

Warren Xavier (aka Ren) introduces us all to the "proxy job" - **Distorted loc. 1510 (page 83)**, **Joyless loc. 2289 (page 77, Fragments loc. 1263 (page 63)**

Guards' partying (Jasper & Hancock first hookup) - **Joyless loc. 2432 (page 137)**

The Ivory informs everyone that a world-renowned doctor is coming to study The Carver - **Joyless loc. 2259 (page 125), Brainwashed loc. 1170 (page 59)**
Dr. Lemuel Love's backstory: **Chapter 3, Chapter 7, & loc. 5908 (page 311)**

Joy Jameson is watching out for Dash, and delivering things to him on behalf of Kellan Kemper - **Joyless loc. 2655 (page 148)**

The Ivory warns Rook about Ren - **Joyless loc. 2771 (page 155)**
Rook loses Dash in the East - **Joyless loc. 2879 (page 160)**

Storms plague Alabaster Isle, and Luthor is brought in to help fix a glitch in the servers - **Distorted loc. 2579 (page 146), Fragments loc. 2494 (page 128)**

A power outage prompts some very salacious activity - **Distorted loc. 2705 (page 153)**

Velle & The Ivory - **Joyless loc. 3651, 6419, & 6755 (pages 204, 360 & 381)**

Velle is suspicious of The Ivory selling to his mom. Goes for a ride with Harley on his Harley (an anniversary gift) - **Joyless loc. 4619 (page 260)**

Ren and Dash are sent to solitary for fighting, where Ren hears interesting sounds - **Distorted loc. 3714 & 3750 (pages 208 & 213**) + Luthor, Ren & Byron hook-up - **Fragments loc. 4120 (page 211**)

Luthor uncovers something interesting about Dash - **Fragments loc. 4424 (page 228)**

Dr. Love & the East Wing "doctors" - **Brainwashed loc. 2805 (page 147)**

(**Free bonus short - The Control Room/tinyurl.com/APControlRoom**)

Dash freaks out and is sent to The East - **Distorted loc. 4965 (page 284), Joyless loc. 5176 (page 290), Fragments loc. 4711 (page 243)**
Dr. Love gives Felix Darcey the keys to the cells, and Felix kills O'Malley (using a special knife he found), then sets Dash free - **Brainwashed loc. 3040 (page 159)**
Dash escapes - **Distorted loc. 5159 (page 294)**
Velle is punished by The Ivory - **Joyless loc. 5395 (page 304)**
Velle burying more bodies - **Joyless loc. 5572 (page 313)**

Lem has dinner with The Ivory - **Brainwashed loc. 4062 (page 215)**

Rook talks to Luthor, Ren, and Kang about Dash, then a meeting is held wherein The Ivory kills Steve Islo with the butterfly knife (The lockdown starts) - **Joyless loc. 5864 (page 330)**
Kang confronts Darcey about killing O'Malley - **Brainwashed loc. 4993 (page 262)**
Velle is confiscating things on behalf of the Warden - **Joyless loc. 6160 (page 348)**, + Ren's connections - **Fragments loc. 5895 (page 305)**
Dash calls Luthor, realizes the truth about Officer Kemper - **Distorted loc. 5500 (page 314), Fragments loc. 6252 (page 325)**
Dash arrives in Tulum and meets the real Kellan Kemper - **Distorted loc. 5611 (page 323)**

Velle's mom dies and he leaves the island - **Joyless loc. 6517 (page 366)**
Lem has drinks with The Ivory in the mansion and meets his assistant, Yari - **Brainwashed loc. 6093 (page 320)**
Velle, Joy, and Rook confront one of The Ivory's dealers - **Joyless loc. 6655 (page 375)**

Velle, Rook, and Joy return (Velle's confrontation with The Ivory) - **Joyless loc. 7065 (page 398)**

Kemper confesses the truth to Dash - **Distorted loc. 6889 (page 395)**

Velle cashes in on his deal with Ren - **Fragments loc. 6603 (page 344)**

Kemper anonymously reports the location of Dash's mom, then The Ivory calls - **Distorted loc. 7371 (page 423)**

Lem leaves to deal with Trevel (His P.I. friend) - **Brainwashed Chapter 31**
Felix Darcey is left in the care of Doctors Templeton and Hassan - **Brainwashed loc. 7069 (page 369)**
Lem returns in time to save him - **Brainwashed loc. 7702 (page 407)**
Felix gets a bedroom - **Brainwashed loc. 7867 (page 415)**

Lem & The Ivory talk about Trevel, and there's tension between him and Velle - **Brainwashed loc. 8131 (page 430)**
Kemper calls Joy - **Joyless loc. 7224 (page 406)**

(Patreon bonus scene - Rook, Velle, and Joy go to visit her parents www.patreon.com/posts/96718413?collection=256259)

Dash calls Joy and the guys - **Fragments loc. 7127 (page 372), Distorted loc. 7449 (page 428)**

Rook's family visits the mansion, and Rook talks to his dad about digging up dirt on Manuel Blanco - **Joyless loc. 7366 (page 421)**

Lem & Velle come to an understanding - **Joyless loc. 7593 (page 429)**
Rook, Velle, and Joy help Felix and Lem dispose of Templeton's body, Trevel Fenwick arrives, and Lem lies to Felix - **Brainwashed loc. 8227 (page 435), Fragments loc. 7512 (page 391)**

Felix is invited to speak with Dash on the phone - **Brainwashed loc. 8435 (page 446)**

Byron calls Luthor & Ren out - **Fragments loc. 7763 (page 407)**
The "new regime" takes over - **Fragments loc. 7880 (page 411)**

(Patreon bonus scene - Felix & Lem's holiday fun time amidst the chaos www.patreon.com/posts/76603897?collection=256259)

"The Storm" - **Brainwashed loc. 8543 (page 452)**
Luthor gets LOIS 2.0 working - **Fragments loc. 8018 (page 418)**
The Ivory reveals to Ren that he was "Mask Daddy", then a mysterious voice is heard just before the fall - **Fragments loc. 8408 (page 439)**
Fireworks: Luthor and Ren escape - **Fragments loc. 8588 (page 452)**
They find each other in California - **Fragments loc. 9128 (page 480)**
Meet up with Cyrus, Colson and Tauren *(Double-edged)* - **Fragments loc. 9394 (page 493)**

(Patreon Crossover Story - The Vacation, Chapter 8 shows what Dash & Kemper have been up to in the meantime... www.patreon.com/posts/99293259?collection=408552)

Luthor speaks to Trevel on the phone - **Fragments loc. 9863 (page 518)**

PLAYLIST

Listen to the full playlist on Spotify!

Heathens - Rivals
Can You Feel My Heart - Bring Me The Horizon
Swallowed - Bush
DISCONNECTED - Chase Atlantic
Numb - Sleep Theory
Fire In My Head - Two Feet
Lipgloss and Letdown - A Static Lullaby
Mind Games - Sickick
CONCRETE JUNGLE - Bad Omens
Nightcall - Kavinksy
Figure You Out - VOILÀ
Dark Matter - Rivals
Poet - Bastille
HUSH - Ari Abdul
Uncomfortably Numb - Arrows In Action
The Walls - Chase Atlantic
Undisclosed Desires - Musc
The Drug In Me Is You - Falling In Reverse
Let It Bleed - The Used
MATCH MADE IN HELL - Dutch Melrose
sugar honey ice & tea - Bring Me The Horizon
i know (faded) - Ex Habit
love or chemistry - nothing,nowhere.
Therapy - VOILÀ
Chokehold - Sleep Token
Noise and Kisses - The Used

Off The Edge - VOILÀ, LUNA AURA
Put You Through Me - Arrows In Action
Zombie - YUNGBLUD
Moonlit - Rivals
Addicted To You - Huddy
indigo - mgk
I NEVER EXISTED - Chase Atlantic
Partners in Crime - Set It Off, Ash Costello
Renegade - Kavinsky, Cautious Clay
Crimson and Clover - Joan Jett & the Blackhearts
Spitting Off The Edge of the World - Yeah Yeah Yeahs
Burning Down The House - The Used
iris - mgk, Julia Wolf

"Anger clouds the mind. Turned inward, it is an unconquerable enemy."

—Master Splinter

PROLOGUE

Byron

FEEL HEAVILY, OR FEEL NOTHING AT ALL.

Those are the two wildly different sides of mys personality. Sometimes I'm empty. *Dead* inside. Lost like a shadow, existing only as a silent, lurking piece of someone else.

Other times, my heart races so fast, and my chest cinches so tight, I think my ribs could snap. My mind captures a thought; traps it the way a child traps a butterfly in a jar, to ogle with wide eyes while it flutters about… *Before it ultimately dies from lack of oxygen because they forgot to poke air-holes.*

Do I resent being like this?

Yes. Of fucking course I do.

It's not exactly *fun* to live each day not knowing how I'll feel the next. If I'll be stewing in a silent ache of emotions that make me want to scream and punch the wall until my knuckles are bloodied to the bone…

Or if I'll be a corpse.

But the thing is, no one knows about any of it. These are things that rest beneath my surface. And nobody ever gets that deep.

The world is full of narcissists. Human beings are inherently self-involved, which certainly enabled me when I was free. Before I got locked up, I adored how engrossed people were in their own bullshit.

Made it real easy for me to slink around undetected.

But here, in *Alabaster Penitentiary*, I find the lack of attention sort of... vexing.

I'm not saying I want everyone to be focused on me all the time, or even most of the time. It'd drive me nuts. But there are certain moments when I feel like I could slit my throat in the middle of this cafeteria, and no one would bat an eye.

Do they even see me?

Or am I still *completely... invisible?*

Lifting my gaze from the plate of slop in front of me, I watch my friends. Luthor is talking about this device he's been working on for months. His body is turned, facing Ren, which would indicate that he's really only speaking to him. Not me.

And Ren is smiling—as he does when he's looking at Luthor. Full attention given, only occasionally breaking eye contact to watch Luthor's lips move.

Pouring over him curiously, I study Ren's face. Sparkling eyes the color of a bright blue sky, pointed nose, curved lips forming their signature smirk and framed by pretty-boy dimples. Jawline sharp, dusted in a dark stubble. *Almost time for a shave.*

Down my gaze travels, over the slope of his neck to his wide shoulders, biceps and torso plump with muscles you can't see when they're hidden by his shirt. But I know they're there.

One of his long arms is extended slightly, and I lean forward to see where his hand is, though I don't really need to. I already know it's resting possessively on Luthor's thigh, subtly grazing up and down.

Because Luthor *belongs* to Ren. He always has, even when he was acting like he didn't.

It didn't matter that Ren cheated on him. I knew from the moment it happened he would fall back under the spell of Warren Xavier. It was only a matter of time before they were like this. *Attached*, in a state of constant fawning and obsessive desire that borders on psychotic.

Luthor's a genius—*literally*. The kid is so smart, he could probably work for NASA, or become the next Steve Jobs—if he wasn't locked away in concrete hell, that is.

So forgive me for harboring some resentment over his stupidity when it comes to our friend Ren.

Not that I think it's stupid for someone to want Ren... A lot of people do. I just feel like it was obvious Luthor would go back, and him claiming he wouldn't drove me a little nuts.

Maybe it's none of my business… I mean, it is *their* relationship. They can go about it however they want. *Obnoxiously codependent… Fine. That's their prerogative.*

But I've been caught in the middle of their toxic shit many times over the years, which is why I sometimes feel trapped on this hellish carnival ride with them.

For me, it was unintentional. But I think for them—especially for Ren—it was very deliberate. It's just the way he is, I suppose. Another selfish soul with a one-track mind, compulsively aimed in only one direction.

Still, that doesn't make it any less infuriating.

Deciding I need to get up and move for a second before I explode, I stand with my tray. Luthor's eyes fling to me, and he tilts his head, as if he's about to ask where I'm going. But then Ren picks up one of Luthor's hands, affectionately playing with his fingers.

Attention effectively drawn back.

Rolling my eyes, I clench my jaw while stomping away from the table. My brain is pinging receptors of many vivid emotions, all of which are bothering me immensely as I sullenly dump my food into the trash, tossing my empty tray into the pile with a huff.

This is all just so *annoying*. The way I'm filled to the brim with chaotic things that have no business being inside me. The itchy discomfort of feeling like I'm a child again, standing in the corner…

Watching. Always just… watching.

Luthor is one of the very, *very* few people in this world I actually trust. I'd go as far as to call him my *brother*, which may be kind of weird, considering recent events. Nonetheless, he's been my friend since the moment I got here, and I don't like resenting him for things beyond his control. After all, it's not his fault his naivety and general sweetness made him easy prey for someone like Ren.

Glancing back over at the table, I scoff internally at their heart-eyes and hushed conversations.

Ren's such a jealous weirdo.

He had the nerve to imply that *I* might have a *thing* for Luthor. The other day, in the showers… He was messing with me about it. And he couldn't possibly be more misguided.

I mean, where would he even get that from??

Sure, Luthor and I messed around a tiny bit. Just once. But I've also been consistently fucking Ren on and off pretty much since I got here, so it's really not a big deal.

Plus, he was *there!* With me and Luthor. *He* orchestrated the whole thing, as he tends to. One of his *brilliant schemes* to lure Luthor back in, using me as a pawn in his damn sexual games.

I guess I could just tell him to fuck off when he suggests it... But it's very important to me that they understand how little I care.

I'm *not* gay. I'm not interested in men sexually. I never have been...

Yes, we're in prison, and the options here are severely limited. Understandably, your hand gets old real quick. If someone's offering, I'll take it, because a mouth is just a mouth. A hole is just a hole, no matter how surprisingly good it feels. *Maybe some more than others...*

Whatever. The point is, it *doesn't matter.* Their mess isn't mine, and fooling around with them is just another way to pass the time in this boring fucking place.

Luthor is still just my friend, and I could fuck Ren a million more times without feeling a goddamn thing. And more to the point, now that he and Luthor are screwing, it's all irrelevant. Because I assume that means he doesn't need to use me anymore...

Which is *fine. Since, you know, I never cared in the first place.*

Ren got what he wanted, and he'll probably never even think about all the stuff we did together ever again. *So... good.*

I'm not thinking about it either.

Inside, my stomach is twisting and wrenching. Probably because I barely ate and I'm perpetually starving. A burn is making its way up my throat as I reluctantly wander back toward the table, dreading it and pretending I'm not. But I don't get more than a step or two before someone appears in my peripheral.

My face shifts, and I peer up at the figure now standing right beside me. It's the new guy... 102.

His irises shine down at me, and I'm instantly held still, just like when he came up to us the other day. It was the first time I saw him, this new inmate who popped up seemingly out of nowhere, with his peculiar eyes the shade of indigo. They're practically purple. *Very odd.*

And he clearly isn't shy with eye contact.

"Hi again," he hums quietly. I just blink at the lurching character; tall and slim, with messy black hair and a British accent. "You're Kang... right?"

I nod slowly, eyes flicking to my table, checking on my friends like a reflex. Ren wasn't shy about his distrust for this person when we met him in the showers. But he's one to talk... Ren's a pretty untrustworthy motherfucker himself.

Either way, it's irrelevant. *Because he's not paying attention to me, anyway.*

"Byron," I murmur to the Brit. "Your name is..."

"Trevel," he answers, though it was on the tip of my tongue. A unique name, for sure. "Trevel Fenwick. Newest addition to this bloody nightmare."

I huff a small breath that's usually as close to a laugh as you'll get from me. I'm not one for flagrant laughter. *Not many things are all that funny.*

Unsure of what to say to the guy, or why he decided to come up to me in the first place, I simply stand still and portray my standard indifference.

"So, how long have you been here?" he asks me, interested, or at least pretending to be.

"Well, I'm #62," I tell him in a bored tone, though the way his intense violet gaze is zeroed in on my face brings an inexplicable need to fidget. "If that gives you an idea."

His head tilts curiously. "That must be a couple of years, then? At least?"

I nod again, pulse picking up, because his accent reminds me of someone... Someone who meant a great deal to me.

I don't like it.

Trevel isn't put off by my surly silence. He lets out an exhale, unusual eyes drifting over to Luthor and Ren. "Those are your mates?"

I swallow hard. "Yes."

Pursing his lips, he offers a curt bob of his head. "I hope I haven't offended them somehow. The dark-haired one seemed to think I was up to no good when we met. Though, I can't say it's the first time someone's assumed that about me at first glance."

His shoulders move subtly, a rumbly noise coming from his throat. A very modest chuckle, like mine.

"That's just Ren. It's how he is. He's crazy protective..." My voice trails before I add, "Of Luthor."

Trevel shifts his gaze back to me, cocking a dark brow. "Only him?" My lips part, but he goes on, "I recall him moving you away from me as well..."

I can't help the scoff that puffs out of me. "Oh, yea. He'll definitely act like he's being a loyal friend. But really, he's just trying to control everything."

And manipulate me.

"You don't strike me as the type to be controlled," Trevel says, almost curiously.

The comment makes me feel strange, but I push past it and remember myself. "I'm not," I grunt, catching a brief twitch of his lips. "But he bosses me around like I'm just some lovable sidekick. And yet when it comes to standing up for our friend who was *murdered*, he shrugs it off."

Shaking my head, I feel the palpable rise of heated anger in my veins when thinking about what happened to my cellmate… Before *and* after his death.

Trevel's forehead lines, orbs of deep purple cast down at me. "Your friend was murdered?"

"Yea," I sigh. "By this preppy little shithead who calls himself *The Carver*. And now my *friends* are befriending the psycho. Inviting him to sit with us and shit, like it didn't even fucking happen. Totally spitting on our friend's grave."

This little tangent is spewing out on its own, but I barely even care. Because now that I'm saying the words out loud again, I'm fuming on behalf of Kieran O'Malley, someone who meant a lot to me. *Clearly, a lot more than he meant to Ren.*

Something in Trevel's face has shifted. His already severe features have gone dark, a bit of mayhem in his eyes. It's pretty alarming.

But before I can try to inch away from it, he reaches out and places a hand on my shoulder. I flinch, startled by his touch. But he keeps it intact and leans in closer.

"Loyalty is everything," he whispers. Chills sheet my flesh. "I'm sorry about your friend."

Frozen, I stare up at him, forcing myself to croak, "Thank you."

Trevel's chin dips, lips moving too close to my ear. "You might like the taste of revenge." Warm breath brushes my skin, and my teeth set, gut flipping upside down. "I know I do. It's quite… *sweet*. Like honey."

My throat is so dry I can barely gulp as his hand sweeps off my shoulder, grazing down my back before it leaves my body. I only have one full second to stammer until the guards bark that it's about time to leave. My eyes flick toward them, and when they return to Trevel, he's already walking away.

What the hell was that?

My mind is cycling through his words as Luthor and Ren walk over to me. Confusion traces the fingerprints I can still feel on my shoulder.

We leave the cafeteria. And it's as we're walking that my gaze also wanders… cautiously to the mysterious stranger with the violet eyes. I'm unable to rid myself of this sensation, one I haven't felt in a very long time.

He can actually see me, can't he?

A fellow man in the shadows, perhaps.

CHAPTER ONE

Trevel

3 months earlier...

"WHAT DO YOU THINK IT MEANS?"

I hate when he asks me that. *As if he isn't fully aware of what it means already.*

But he wants *me* to say it. Not even to find out if I'm smart enough to be on his shared wavelength… He knows that I am.

He wants to hear me say the words.

Pausing—for dramatic effect—I give him a taste of his own medicine. I wish I could say that it causes even the tiniest reaction from him, but it doesn't. *The bloke's like stone.* "I think it means that I wish I'd killed my parents."

Dr. Love stares at me for a moment, giving me that blank robot-gaze, penetrating in its rigidness. He taps his pen on his notebook. Twice. I try not to notice it because I rather enjoy holding his eyes. It makes me feel like less of a head-case patient to one of the best clinical psychiatrists in the country.

Finally, he speaks, after a few heavy seconds that hang in the air like smoke. "How do you feel about the fact that you didn't?"

I shrug, bored. Noncommittal.

He's not buying it.

Releasing a slow breath, I shift in my seat. "Maybe a tad edgy.

Knowing they're still out there… Living. *Breathing*… when they don't deserve to be."

The amber in his eyes lights up a bit. It's dazzling to witness, and even more captivating to know that *I* made it happen.

"How do you know they're still alive? Have you checked?" he asks curiously, with the accompanied head tilt and everything.

"Well, *no*," I huff. He gives me a look. "But I can tell they are. If they were dead, I'd feel it. In my bones…"

He blinks, as if he finds this notion ridiculous. And of course he does. He's a doctor; a researcher, a *scientist*. Things must always be black and white, a factual explanation for everything. *It's his one weakness.*

Dr. Love sits back, crossing his left ankle over his right knee. It lifts his tailored dress slacks enough that I can see his socks. Navy blue to match his button-down shirt. He's not the type of bloke to wear socks with fancy patterns or comical depictions on them, as if one's socks are an expression of their personality. The Wall Street bankers in their Tom Ford suits, wearing socks with designs from *Game of Thrones* or *Stranger Things* to prove they're more than what meets the immediate eye.

Hey, I'm not a boring corporate wanker! Look at my socks. That's Patrick from SpongeBob*!*

Although, if we're being honest, Dr. Love's humorless dress socks might be exactly that. A look into his *Post Raisin Bran* personality, and a proud one, at that. He has no hidden eccentricities to show when his pants ride up.

He's an organic individual. What you see is what you get. And what you *see* is a stoic, unsmiling enemy of the cheerful *robot*-person, whose only joy is derived from cracking open the skulls of deranged human beings like myself and poking around inside. *Figuratively, of course.*

Still… he makes it look good.

My eyes travel up from the drab sock, getting lost in how well his slacks fit the obviously muscular shape of his legs. The same goes for his torso… Sometimes it looks like his clothes are painted onto his body. As if he stands naked in his closet every morning and, like a tanning booth, has his expensive attire sprayed onto the curves and slopes of hardened definition that he undoubtedly works quite hard to craft.

And I'm drooling.

"Trevel," he says my name the way he's been saying it for the last three years; like he's my *doctor* and I'm his *patient. That's all.*

He's only with me because he's being paid to be, and thus any flutters that may occur when hearing him speak my name are completely one-sided and foolish.

I jump, startled out of the way I was ogling him—*hopefully not too blatantly.* "Hm?"

His eyes narrow. "I asked if you've thought any more about what we discussed."

"Right." I clear my throat. "No, not really."

"And why not?"

"Because I just…" I pause to consider *another* way to explain this to him, since it doesn't seem to be registering. "I don't want to scare her away."

Dr. Love appears surprised by what I'm saying. As much as he's able, anyway. *Maybe fifteen percent.* "Do you think what you have with Alice is that fickle?"

Yes. "No… Not necessarily." My jaw tightens a bit, and I look down. "But we're only still getting to know one another."

"Isn't sharing things like this a part of that?" he asks pointedly.

"I would say revealing my inner monster is more three-month anniversary material, don't you think?" My lips quirk, and for all of his robotic tendencies, I get the reaction I've been craving. The most minor change to his face, from stone-serious to mildly amused.

It has me *flying.*

He scribbles something in his notebook before glancing back up at me. "I see you're no longer referring to Alice as 'they/them.' That's new."

I nod. "She's decided to use pronouns that make her more comfortable."

"Good. I'm sure that's helpful for her."

"It is." My mind reflects to a few months ago, when I first met Alice. "She said that she was using 'they/them' in the early stages of her transition, but that she's always wanted 'she.' I'm happy to give her whatever makes her feel happy and respected."

He stares at me for a moment before asserting, "This relationship is clearly growing more serious for you, Trevel." *Uh-huh… and?* "It's interesting to me that you have no problem accepting Alice and supporting her emotionally, but when it comes to opening up yourself, you're afraid she won't accept you."

My head tips back and I stare at the ceiling. "That's not the same thing."

"I believe it is." The gruffness in his voice causes my chin to drop, our eyes meeting once more. "This is a part of you, Trevel. This is who you are. If you ever want to move forward in your personal relationships, you'll need to let people see the real you."

My stomach twists into a knot as I blink at him. "What if she hates it? What if she… runs screaming?"

Honestly, who wouldn't?

He gives me a bit of a patronizing look that reminds me of Riverwoods. *White walls, fluorescent lights, little paper cups full of pills and the gurneys with the straps…* "If someone isn't willing to accept you for who you are, then they're not the right person for you."

Sighing harshly, I rub my eyes. We've been having this conversation for nearly a year, since I left Riverwoods—the psychiatric facility I'd been confined to following… my crimes.

Dr. Lemuel Love, PhD, has been my doctor for long enough to know pretty much everything there is to know about me. He knows all about what I've done, what I've experienced, and who I am as a result of those things.

He knows *exactly* how fucked up I am; how broken and jaded inside. And he's also seen how far I've come. From lashing out in the early days at Riverwoods—screaming and crying and throwing fits—to existing as a productive member of society. *More or less.*

I have a job that I enjoy, a small apartment here in downtown Atlanta that's more than enough for just me, and a few acquaintances, though more often than not, I choose to spend time alone. That is, until Alice.

Part of me thinks I liked Alice more *before* we started dating. Another part of me thinks that's an excuse.

Because of how well Dr. Love knows me, he's more than aware of how much stock I put into finding love. Then again, that's also the most obvious thing about me. I never had love growing up, so I search desperately for it now as an adult.

It's so axiomatic, it borders on cliché.

The difficult part comes with the idea of a *real* relationship. Something more than just the superficial. It's human nature to hide our faults in order to get people to like us… But to Dr. Love's point, is that sustainable?

Do I really want a relationship with someone I have to hide things from? Would my partner want that?

I think we all know the answer to these questions, which is why my doctor won't let it go. But still… when I consider the darkness that lurks in the corners of my mind…

Scream.

Thud.

Pain.

Slap slap slap.

Tears.

Slice.

Twist, drag.

Blood. Everywhere.

"In all honesty, this could be the reason you're hesitating so much when it comes to getting physical with Alice," he goes on, yanking me, almost brutally, out of the depths of my thoughts. "You feel like you're being dishonest."

I swallow thickly. "I've had physical relationships with people since Riverwoods..." My voice trails, though I don't mean for it to. So I roll my eyes to seem extra adamant. "It's not like I tell people I meet on Tinder about all my issues before sleeping with them."

"Those relationships are strictly physical," he counters. "Correct me if I'm wrong, but with Alice, it's different, is it not?" *When are you ever wrong, Dr. Genius?* I nod hesitantly. "You've been invested in making this relationship work for weeks, despite not having been physical yet."

Petulantly, I pout. "We've done *some* things..."

"And in showing your support for Alice with her struggles," he goes on, ignoring my stubborn little comment, "comforting her through her family troubles, being an ear and a shoulder for her, you've aided in her bringing down her walls." He stares at me for a moment before murmuring, "What about yours?"

Fucking hell... The bloke is good.

Sometimes I resent it. How he's able to make the things I grapple with seem so cut-and-dry. But then I remember that he has my best interests at heart. He's been the only one on my side for years...

He's the *only* one who knows the real me.

Maybe I like that fact...

In lieu of accidentally blurting this out, or making some face that allows him to read me, I look down at my hands, wringing them in my lap. "I suppose I could... speak to her about it."

Dr. Love nods in agreement. "But just so we're clear, Trevel, in no way do I think you *need* to tell Alice about your past, your condition, or your fears in order to get physical with her. I don't believe you owe her anything, especially if she's as eager to be physical as you've said." I release a breath and nod, relieved. "That said, I do believe you owe it to yourself. Something is holding you back. Fear of hurting her is only the surface of it."

My head is swirling with his words. All of these thoughts that make me question myself...

Who am I?

What does it all mean?

Will I ever *move on?? Or has this tortured madness been baked into me too deep?*

Dr. Love taps his pen against his full bottom lip.

"Maybe I'll tell Alice I prefer to go to bed alone," I croak, watching his mouth. "So that if we do… something… I won't be worried about wigging out on her in my sleep."

"Sure." Dr. Love nods. "Just find a way to word it that doesn't make it sound like you're kicking her out after sex." His mouth pulls the faintest of smirks.

But still, it's there. And it's breathtaking.

A small laugh puffs out of me, my chest all warm and fuzzy as he glances at the wall behind me.

"We're out of time for today." He slaps his notebook shut.

Standing, I ignore the familiar sting in my chest I tend to feel when our sessions are over. It's entirely nonsensical, anyway. "Cracking, as always. See you next week?"

Dr. Love stares at me for a moment, something peculiar flashing in his striking amber eyes. But it's gone in a blink as he nods. "It's a date."

Those three words are on my mind for the rest of the evening.

All throughout the ten-minute walk to my favorite sushi spot, the fifteen minutes that I wait for my food to be prepared, then the five-minute walk to my apartment. The whole time I'm enjoying my eel and sweet potato roll while watching *What We Do In The Shadows*, chuckling at the hijinks of Laszlo, Nandor, and Colin Robinson. While I'm relaxing on my chaise lounge, adjacent to my bed because I live in a studio, writing and thinking. When I begin to yawn and decide it's time for sleep. During the entirety of my nighttime routine, and even when I climb into bed…

They're in my brain. Flickering like the flame of a candle I refuse to blow out. Three words, out of the whole lot, hold me captive.

It's a date.

My weekend kicks off like any other. I work a full day on Saturday, texting with Alice here and there.

Weekends are always busy at Zen—the yoga studio and relaxation spa where I work. I've been a yoga instructor here for about nine months.

I was surprised when they hired me, being that the only experience I had was leading our yoga class at Riverwoods. But they gave me a chance, and I'm grateful. Even more so that they promoted me a couple of months ago to part-time masseur, because massage therapists certainly make more than yoga instructors, what with the tips and all.

I'd taken a few massage classes to pass the time, so I decided to throw my hat into the ring as a sort of *fill-in*, in case someone called out sick. A week later, they were giving me clients and allowing me to bring in my own.

The money is good, and I enjoy what I do, but the city is expensive. Outside of Zen, I tend to pick up odd jobs here and there for extra cash. Tomorrow, I'm walking dogs, next weekend I'm house-sitting for a woman in my building, and in two weeks, I have a gig filling in as a teacher for a poetry writing workshop at the local community center.

None of these things pay in private islands, but I'm sure if I keep flitting around, using my skills and my charms wherever I can, I'll find enough work to support myself. I've been doing it my whole life…

Finding ways to get by. *Surviving*.

By the end of my Bikram class Saturday evening, I've agreed to meet Alice for dinner at some Korean barbecue place she's been dying to try. Scuttling my way back home, I'm showered, dressed, and ready for a date in under an hour.

Inside the restaurant, I spot her right away, sitting at the bar. She's wearing a red dress that looks great with her tanned complexion and heels that accentuate her long legs, dirty blonde hair blown out and flowing like a sumptuous mane.

She's *stunning*, and honestly, I often find it hard to understand why she's chosen to date *me*… After all, we're very different people.

Alice is from Colombia. She moved to the States with her twin brother, Andres, when they were children, after their parents died tragically. Apparently, they had family here, but they weren't very accepting of Alice, being that she's known she was transgender since she was young. She had to quit school to get a job to support herself after moving out on her own. But as soon as she was able, she got her GED, put herself through cosmetology school, and even began studying to become a social worker.

Despite her complicated upbringing, Alice Alvarez is a force. She doesn't let things get her down. In fact, she manages to rise above pretty much everything the world throws her way.

Simply put, she slays.

And that's not to say I've let life beat me down, because I, too, had a complicated upbringing. Not that it's a contest, but I think I've had the most fucked-up life of anyone I know, *including* Alice. The shit I've been through brought me to where I am today, and all things considered, I think I'm doing great. But I wouldn't say I'm crushing it, like Alice is.

She inspires me. Dr. Love is right… I want this relationship to work out, because Alice Alvarez is the most brilliant person I've ever met.

Unfortunately for me, I'm not certain I have what it takes to hold on to her.

She's way too good for me.

"Why hello, beautiful stranger," Alice croons to me as I step up to her side, kissing her cheek.

"Hello, angel." I grin back. "You look lovely, as always."

She smirks, showing off the little diamond studs in her dimples. "I ordered you a fancy drink, but you took too long, so I drank it." She gestures to the empty glasses.

I chuckle, then tease, "You know I have to be fashionably late. If I can't make a grand entrance, what's the point in showing up at all?"

Giggling, she tosses her hair over her shoulder. "So you're just *never* going to get a car?"

I shrug casually. "Why do I need a car? I have perfectly functional legs."

"Or you're afraid to learn to drive…" she mutters, grinning.

I slap my hand over her mouth. "That's enough out of you."

She's laughing beneath my palm, shoving me off of her. "Ugh! Lipstick, you cretin!"

"Sorry, sorry." I assess her mouth. "Still perfect."

She hops off of her seat, taking me by the arm as we follow a hostess to our table. Peeking down at Alice, I can't help remembering how we met…

How I followed her around for a good three weeks before she finally noticed me and asked *me* out.

My personal belief is that she finds odd behavior charming. It's something that happens a lot. People are too trusting. *If I met myself, I'd be rather wary of me.*

Even so, I'm glad that Alice wasn't creeped out or repulsed by the lurking emo giant who kept popping up everywhere she was. So far, she's shown it to be the opposite. I think she *wants* to be much closer than we are, and I'm the one always putting on the brakes.

"Going into any relationship, after what's happened to you, and what you've

done, will be extremely difficult… There's no real way to know if your nightmares will manifest themselves into a reality…"

Dr. Love's words ring in my brain as I sit down to a nice meal with Alice. My *girlfriend…?*

Granted, we've only been dating a few weeks and have had no conversations about exclusivity. I know *I'm* not seeing anyone else right now, but I wouldn't expect her to tie herself down to me. Especially when I feel as though I'm only giving her little bits of myself.

"So Andres has been badgering me again," Alice tells me while we pick at some appetizers.

"For what?"

"Money, I think." She licks some sauce off of her fingertip. "I mean, he didn't say it outright, but I can tell something's off with him."

I peer at her. "You think he's using again?"

Alice shrugs; her attempt at seeming unaffected. But I can tell the idea of her twin brother falling back into old habits hurts her greatly. "I know I'm not supposed to enable him, but it's hard. He's all I have, you know?"

I nod, though I have zero experience with how it feels to watch a family member struggling. I have no family, no one close enough to even be considered *family adjacent*.

On the other side of that, when I struggled in the past with my own issues, I had no one to turn to for help. It was just me and the streets of Manhattan…

In that spirit, I give her all I have to offer on the subject. "If I'd had a sister like you, my life might have ended up very different…" It comes out wistful and reminiscent, because now I'm actually wondering what would've happened if someone *had* been around for me to lean on back then.

Alice slides her hand over mine on the table. I glance down at it, admiring her fingers, slender with perfectly manicured nails painted shimmery black. Her skin color is a contrast to mine because of how pale I am, though we both have tattoos. *I like the way our hands look together.*

Lifting my eyes to hers, I find her watching me closely. It's worrying. I have absolutely no idea what she sees when she's looking at me.

I feel like I'm constantly on edge, wondering if being with Alice is the right thing, for *her*.

I know it's right for me, because I care about her greatly, and I want nothing more than to be a permanent fixture in her life. But I just can't rid myself of the constant fear that simply being with me is going to cause her harm.

Why, though?? I don't think I would hurt her... I'd certainly never intend to.

"It might not be your choice, mate," the voice rumbles in my brain, and I close my eyes briefly, ignoring it.

Go away. Not now.

"Is everything alright?" Alice asks, and I blink at her, swallowing.

"Mhm." I force a grin. "Perfect now."

She smiles as I lift her hand to my lips, pressing a kiss on her butterfly tattoo.

"Tell me about your day, angel."

It's Monday at three, and I'm back at the office of Dr. Lemuel Love, PhD.

I arrived early and wound up pacing outside his building for twenty minutes. I wish I could say this was the first time it's happened, but it's not. I look forward to my sessions with Dr. Love, so much so that sometimes it's all I can think about leading up to my appointment.

I hate to say it, but I rely on him. For comfort, solace, support, and insight. Ever since Riverwoods, when he would show up twice a week and sit in the therapy office with me, in the common area, or even in my room—if it was one of those times I was going nuts and requiring constant supervision.

The staff would advise him against coming in with me, but he'd do it anyway. He isn't afraid of killers, that's for sure. *No one's going to tell Lemuel Love who he can and can't sit near.*

Over the years, he's become my constant. *And cards on the table, I do happen to find him unbearably beautiful.*

I mean, how could you not?? He's stunning, masculine perfection with just the right amount of detachment; that bored, slightly cold and grumbly persona calling to anyone with Daddy issues like a bloody siren song.

But more than anything, I love that he knows everything about me and is *still here*. It almost seems as if he cherishes me. Strictly as a patient, but still. I think he does. I think working with me gives him some satisfaction, and that causes me bunches of complicated feelings I refuse to ever disclose to him.

Knee bouncing rapidly while I wait impatiently, I check the clock on the wall.

Hm... It's five minutes past three. That's odd. Dr. Love is never late. For anything.

Squirming in my seat, I think back to the other night, with Alice…

After dinner, she insisted on driving me home, even though the restaurant was less than a ten-minute walk. I was nervous that it was just an excuse for her to come up, and naturally, it was.

When the goodnight *kiss* started fogging up her car windows, I reluctantly invited her upstairs. My nerves were at the forefront of my mind, but I also hadn't gotten laid in, like, a month, so I was trying not to overthink it.

Calm down, I kept telling myself. *This is what you both want.*

"Are we still taking things slow?" Alice asked, pushing me backward on my bed.

No, my dick said, loudly. *Fast fast fast.*

"Um…" was all I could get out before her mouth was mauling mine.

Clothes started coming off, and my worried thoughts were fading away. It was *fine*. We were going to have sex, and I was sure it would be amazing. Surely, if I could manage it without hurting the random Tinder hookups, then I could pull it off with Alice.

She's *perfect*.

With my dick in her mouth, I was in an instant daze. This was happening. I was going to fuck her, and then… we would be a couple. We'd be in a *real* relationship…

The first one I've ever had

"But you're incapable of giving love, Trevel," the voice told me. *"You only know how to be used."*

My chest constricted as I turned my face, slowly to the left, locking our eyes. My teeth ground together. "You'd *love* to watch that again, wouldn't you?"

Alice pulled her warm, wet mouth off of my cock. "Huh?"

Glancing down at her, I swallowed. "Nothing. That f-feels… good."

She grinned, climbing back up my body. "Fuck me, stranger."

"Trevel, Dr. Love will see you now!"

I startle at the sound of Dr. Love's secretary, jumping up from my seat while trying to seem normal.

For someone who had it off with their girlfriend, you're awfully twitchy.

Making my way to Dr. Love's office, I'm still reeling. Alice and I *finally* had sex, and it was great. No one hurt anyone. We both survived. And much to my own surprise and delight, she opted not to stay the night without me even having to bring it up, sparing me that awkward *I hope I don't scream and punch you in the face at night* conversation.

I'm excited to tell Dr. Love all of this. Not that it should matter how my shrink feels about me sleeping with someone. But to me, it does. I want to see if he's chuffed for me. If he's proud, or satisfied… Or jealous.

Right. That would never happen in a zillion years. It's tapped to even think about it.

But I can't help it. My interest in Dr. Love have blurred over the years, from my doctor, to my confidante, to my friend and protector… *To a chap I have confusing sexual feelings for, apparently.*

I'm not *trying* to have them. They're just there.

I'm well aware that he's straighter than a straight line, and far too professional to ever even *entertain* an attraction to a patient. But that doesn't stop my deranged mind from hanging on every interaction, as if it's desperate for one to blossom into something *more.*

But what's even more disturbing is that I just took things to the next level with my girlfriend, and yet I can't stop obsessively thinking about my doctor.

Let's just chalk it up to the constant flailing confusion of being bi/pan.

"Happy Monday," I chatter to my hot doctor on my way inside his office, cringing because I sound like a twit.

Sidling over to the small couch, I take a seat.

"Hello, Trevel," he says in his usual brogue. And for once, he's not fiddling with his notebook. In fact, there's no notebook at all. "How have you been?"

"Fine." I shake my head. "I mean, good. *Well.*"

Take a breath, you knob, and tell him your news.

I'm actually jittering with eagerness, anticipation brimming for any way he could react to what I'm about to say.

Just as my lips are parting, he speaks, "That's good to hear. Because I have some news."

My lashes flutter, everything inside me going still, as if someone pressed pause.

He *has news? He's never shared anything with me before…*

"Oh…?" My brows lift, and I find myself shivering in wait.

"I've accepted a job offer," Dr. Love says, far too casually when I'm not even breathing. "In New York."

He folds his hands in his lap, just *looking* at me while my insides crumble. Blasé. Unaffected. *Careless.*

"This will be our last session, Trevel."

CHAPTER TWO

Byron

R*AINDROPS…*

Quivers seize my body.

I'm on the outside, looking in. Peering through the glass, between plump, wet beads that are falling all around me. One tumbles over my trembling lips…

"P-please…"

Moisture is soaking through my clothes, and my hair, in the chill of a saturated spring evening in Manhattan.

"Please… s-stop…"

My eyes, fixed on firm hands gripping her thighs, fall shut, and I exhale. The breath that leaves me is shaky. From the cold…

I'm sure that's it.

"God, gorgeous, you're everything…" I groan.

"N-no…"

My hands glide up long arms, to the wrists held together by plastic.

"You… feel… so… good…"

Frantic movements jerk me awake. Lids springing open, I gasp. And like an instinct, my hand flies to my chest, pawing desperately at the ache, behind my ribs, amplified by the aggressive banging of my heart.

"Fook yeh!" Belligerent words roar from above me. The thrashing is really rocking the bed around, as it does. But if that hadn't woken me up, his screams would've done the trick.

Puffing out a breath of hopeless irritation, attempting to steady myself after my *own* fucked-up dream, I slam my pillow over my head. It doesn't help much with anything, since he's flailing like he's drowning up there.

That's the magic of bunk beds… When one moves, they both move.

Good times.

"Timmy! What're yeh doing?!"

"Yo… bro!" I whip my pillow away and bark at him. "Mellow. It's just a dream—"

"Fook 'em all! Yer all gonna pay!" O'Malley wails, something clearly fucked up happening in his unconscious mind.

Someone up the row yells at him to *shut the fuck up*, but I know it's pointless. You have to just let him ride it out, which is unfortunate for me more than anyone else, since I have to share a cell, and a rickety bed-frame, with this chaos.

I'm used to it by now, though. Kieran O'Malley's been my cellmate for almost a year, and honestly, his night terrors are the tip of the goddamn iceberg. Just one of the many, let's call them *eccentricities*, he possesses that make living with him nonstop unhinged fuckery around every corner.

It's sorta like living with an abusive, alcoholic stepdad… *You never know what to expect, but at least the constant unease keeps you on your toes.*

Tonight's episode is a bit higher on the Richter scale of his issues, which is good, in a way, because it's distracting me from what *I* was experiencing in dreamland—probably not as atrocious as his, but still fucking painful. The more inmates are woken up by his shouting, the more noise echoes through the row, and eventually, one of the guards shows up.

"O'Malley, I swear to fucking God…" Linetti growls as he storms over to our cell. "Everyone, shut the fuck up!"

"Don't bother," I hiss, launching out of bed. "I got this."

Grabbing O'Malley by the ankles, I drag him off of the top bunk. You'd think his body crashing onto the concrete from several feet in the air would wake him up, but it doesn't quite do the trick. He's still freaking the fuck out, wriggling around as I straddle him, attempting to hold him down. He manages to knee me in the kidney, and now I'm fucking pissed.

"Okay, fuck this shit," I growl.

It's the middle of the night. I'm tired, and grouchy, and I can still smell the rain… *Feel* it falling over me, cooling my stiflingly hot skin…

"I didn't do it! Yer a liar!" O'Malley chokes. "Get off!"

He's really struggling beneath me, fighting to get me off of him, and it's working up with the images in my head; blinding me in a haze of agonizing nostalgia.

"Stop fighting!" I snarl and smack him hard across the face. "You *asked for this...*"

I smack him again, and I think it wakes him up. But it's too fucking late now...

I'm already gone.

Next thing I know, I'm choking him, and he's punching me, and Linetti is stomping inside our cell to rip us apart.

Just another night in Alabaster Pen.

"You need to tighten yer grip," O'Malley breathes, once Linetti is gone and everything's back to normal. "I been choked harder by my ninety-year-old grandmum on her deathbed."

I huff and spit some blood into the sink. "Funny. How's that handprint on your face feel?"

He's visibly trying to smother his grin as he works his jaw. "You slap like a girl, too."

"Your mom didn't complain when I was leaving that same mark on her ass," I snicker.

"Fook off." He chuckles as he hoists himself back up into his bed.

I crash onto mine. "Sweet dreams, Shamrockstar."

"Fook off twice."

And he's one of my closest friends.

Some might say O'Malley and I have a dysfunctional relationship. But I *defy you* to show me a relationship in prison that *isn't* dysfunctional. After all, we're the most morally corrupt, heinous criminals in the country—or even the world—locked up together in concrete hell. *It's not exactly a fifth-grade sleepover.*

Instead of pillow fights and braiding each other's hair, we get tattoos and try to kill each other. As far as the guards are concerned, as long as no one dies, it's a good night. And I'd have to agree. *What's a little harmless bloodshed between friends?*

Scrapping with O'Malley is helpful in at least one way... It puts me out like a light. No more gnawing dreams.

Yup. Everything's back to normal.

The endless cycle of nothingness continues.

The next morning, we're being herded to the cafeteria like half-dead cattle when someone breathes by my ear, "Wait till you peep what I've got stashed in my pants."

My teeth grind together, stifling any potential reaction that will encourage him. "That might be your worst line yet."

"As much as I know you'd love some of this breakfast *sausage*, that's not what I meant," Ren whispers, smirking as he links his arm with mine.

I scowl at him. "What are you so chipper about?"

"Oh, muffin…" His bright smile widens. "Just you wait."

He winks at me, and I pretend not to notice the vast dimples, or the way his dark hair is growing out, or just how disgustingly *perfect* his smile is. *I mean, who looks like that in prison?? It's fucking unreasonable.*

More to the point, the *characteristics* of Warren Xavier are needling me in the chest right now. And I hate it.

Ren is *also* one of my best friends—definitely more so than O'Malley. I don't want to feel resentment when I look at him. But lately, it seems to be popping up more than usual, and it's aggravating me to no end.

In an effort to ignore it, and him, I focus on the rest of our crew. Luthor and O'Malley are shuffling, lifelessly, side-by-side. And now, when I peek at Ren, his blue gaze is stuck on Luthor, turning more intense than it is when he's looking at anyone else.

That's standard. Nothing new here.

Ren's obsessed with Luthor, and Luthor's acting like he's unaffected by it. Of course, I know it won't last, but I guess I appreciate how fervently my pal Lex is clutching that protective shield to his chest.

Too bad it'll never work against the emotional warfare of Warren Xavier.

The four of us move through the chow line to grab our food, then meander to our usual table. The moment we sit down, Luthor is slouched forward, practically falling asleep in his stale Eggo waffles.

"Tired?" O'Malley asks with his mouth full, and I smirk when Luthor whips a scathing glare in his direction.

"You could say that," he seethes.

I can't help but huff. *He's such a baby when he doesn't get his rest.*

Suddenly, Ren is scooting in way too close to me. He's practically on my lap. "Byron… check this out."

Peering right, I give him a bemused look. It's too early for this kind of enthusiasm. But then I notice him reaching into his pants, and my brows zip.

"Dude, please tell me you're not about to whip your dick out at the table." I sigh admonishingly. "We talked about this…"

Ren rolls his eyes. "Just shut up and look."

Glancing down, I'm fully expecting to see his junk, because this is *Ren* we're talking about. *Wouldn't be the first time...*

But I'm surprised when, instead, I find a cellphone tucked into the waistband of his fitted black Calvis.

"Where the shit did you get that??" I gasp as quietly as possible, subtly scanning the room to make sure no one's looking.

"Who cares?" he hums, grinning with pride, but somehow making it look flirtatiously sinister. "Wanna touch it?"

I can't even make myself scoff at his foolishness right now. I'm too busy lusting.

Cellphones in Alabaster Pen are like Bigfoot. You figure they could be around, *maybe*, but you never see them. I've been here for years, and I've never come across one myself. It's one thing that even the most skilled *canoodler* can't usually weasel out of the guards.

But then we all know Warren Xavier lives for a challenge.

"What're you two nellies whispering about over there?" O'Malley leans over the table to sneak a peek. "Comparing yer flutes again?"

Luthor perks up, though he's clearly trying to downplay his interest as he peeks under the table. Both his and O'Malley's eyes go wide when they see what Ren has.

"Yo, put that away!" Luthor whispers nervously. "If Velle finds out, you're fucking toast. Automatic trip to solitary..."

"He's right," I mumble, then bite my lip.

Because as much as I know I shouldn't care, that device holds oh-so-many possibilities...

I wonder if I could use it to—

I blink hard.

"Please." Ren flips his hand in the air. "I can handle him."

"Of course you can." Luthor rolls his eyes.

A ghost of unease flashes in Ren's bright blue eyes, but as always, he covers it up quickly, turning to me. "Take it."

"Now??" I grunt. "Why me?"

"You wanna use it, don't you...?" He cocks a brow.

"I mean... *yea*," I mutter. And now my brain is whirling around all the things I could do with that janky old iPhone. "Does it work?"

Ren nods. He checks once more that the coast is clear, then slips the phone out of his undies and into mine. *Literally*. Just stuffs his hand into my pants. *The dude has no boundaries.*

"Fuckin A..." I grumble, adjusting the phone, and my dick. "Jesus, Ren..."

"Fair warning, when it comes time for checks, you might need to... ya know..." He lifts his dark brows at me. My gaze narrows, and he makes a fisting motion with his hands.

The look I'm giving him is one of pure horror. "That's disturbing. The thing's like... four inches wide."

"Oh, right. You've never gaped it before," Ren sighs casually.

I can feel the way my face has contorted in even more appall.

"Ren..." Luthor scolds, rubbing his eyes.

"*Fine*, I guess you could just clutch it between your cheeks." Ren grins. "Do the ol' credit card swipe."

"Fookin' nutter," O'Malley laughs.

I can't help cracking a tiny smile. It's disturbed, but still... With Ren, it's virtually impossible not to fall into the web of his charms, in one way or another.

Swallowing hard, I try to eat my food, though I'm now acutely aware of this piece of deadly contraband resting on top of my dick. They're not exaggerating the risks. Velle would have an utter conniption if he found it. *And the Warden...*

A chill runs through me.

I'm not sure if the benefit outweighs the consequences on this one. But when I think about what I could do with a cellphone, my toes wiggle in my shoes. It's the closest thing to *freedom* in here. The *only* opportunity for contact with the outside world...

Plus, I'm *good* at keeping secrets. *Better than any of them.*

After breakfast, everyone else is brought to the showers. But not us. *'Cause we're special.*

Someone grabs me by the arm, and I know who it is right away. *Smallest hands of any guard on this island. Not to mention, the distinctly female scent you don't get from anyone else in the general vicinity...*

"Let's go, homie," Joy says, dragging me along while snapping at Luthor, Ren, and O'Malley to keep up. "I'm in the mood—"

"To get your ass kicked?" I cut her off with a smirk.

"I was gonna say to make you eat shit," she teases. "But that's the spirit. I like your confidence."

I chuckle at her wise-assery while the five of us make the trek down to the basement.

I won't go as far as to say I get *preferential treatment* in here, because

I certainly deal with enough bullshit to understand my place on the food chain. But rec time is one thing I'm incredibly grateful for, and I think it's safe to say, none of us would get it if it weren't for Joy Jameson.

Joy and I bonded right away when I got here. I don't know that it's just because we're both Korean, but that didn't hurt. We also have similar backgrounds, though her family loves and supports her, and mine is… well, the opposite of that. But because of our heritage, we have things in common that I'm not sure anyone else here would fully understand. That, and we've both been super into Tae Kwon Do since we were kids.

We're even close in age. In fact, I think it's safe to say that if she'd grown up in New York rather than Boston, Joy Jameson definitely would've been my girlfriend.

Or, at the very least, she would've been someone I devoted my *attention* to.

Once in the basement rec room, we all scatter about, heading for our respective areas. Luthor and Ren grab the basketball, yelling at O'Malley, who's more interested in the rickety old set of dumbbells, to *stop fucking around* and join them.

But Joy and I have our own routine. We're immediately wrapping our knuckles and feet, getting ready to spar. The only problem is that I'm highly aware of the cellphone hidden in my pants. *I won't be able to fight with it in there.*

Waiting for Joy to turn around, I quickly stuff it in between a stack of old mats no one uses.

"Come on, *jeonsa*!" she calls to me, and I jaunt over, putting the phone out of my mind for now. "Let's dance!"

I've gotta say, I *love* this. Still, every time I practice Tae Kwon Do, in any form—even just fucking around with Joy—it feels like home. I feel centered, *calm*. I can block out all the bullshit of a prison sentence I still struggle with every day, though I pretend not to, and just move.

Breathe. Advance. Swing, left, swing right. Kick.

"That's excellent! Look at you go!" I hear the familiar voice of my grandfather in my brain, his deep voice sounding almost regal with the accent. *"You'll be Master material, yet. My grandson, the warrior."*

In his hayday, my grandfather studied Tae Kwon Do under one of the most famous Grandmasters in the world. When I was coming up, a confused pre-teen, raging inside and searching for an outlet, it was him who got me into a program. And he stuck by me the whole time. Unlike my father…

Rafe Byron Jr. was my mother's father, and he was my favorite person in the world. Born and raised in London, his work as a very successful journalist brought him to New York, where he spent the remaining years of his life. When I was two, he got sick, and my family moved from South Korea to be closer to him.

Rafe battled cancer for years. He was a tough son of a bitch, and I'm a hundred percent certain that *he* made me the man I am today—flaws, *secrets*, and all.

I used to call him Master Splinter—like from *Teenage Mutant Ninja Turtles*. Sure, he didn't teach me Tae Kwon Do, but he was *my* master. Caring and patient, smart and cunning. He was an all-out awesome fucking guy, and he raised my mother to be the same way. Which is why I'll never understand how she chose someone like my father to marry.

"Headstrong isn't a very good quality, adeul*,"* my father said to me, shortly after Grandfather died. *"When you are difficult, you are a project... You will not find a career or a wife behaving this way."*

Yea. Great way to encourage a boy on the cusp of becoming a man, grieving over the loss of the only supportive person in his life while struggling to figure himself out.

No wonder I spent so much of my life after that lurking in the shadows...

"Come at me, bro!" Joy huffs, out of breath, because I've been playing her defensively. Wearing her out. *It's a tactic of mine.*

She launches a few more hits at my face, and I block every single one. We've been going at this for a bit, and I can tell she's getting tired. That's when I make my move.

Kick, kick, jab jab jab, then spin and wham! Kick to the head!

And she's down!

Of course, we're not beating the shit out of each other or anything. It's not about that. But we also agreed when we started doing this to never hold back. It's not in either of our natures.

Once she's on the ground, I pin her down, breathing heavily with a triumphant grin on my lips. I'm man enough to admit she beats me more than I beat her. But that just makes moments like these all the more satisfying.

"I *win, jagiya,*" I murmur, hovering over her.

We're both panting, chests jumping up and down, exposed skin flushed and a little sweaty. It becomes painfully obvious in a split second that my dick is jamming into her, and not that it's rock solid or anything, but it's certainly *alive.*

Joy's pupils dilate, and she licks her lip, glancing across the room at the guys, who are still messing around with their own activities. "Get off me, inmate."

Her raspy little growl gives my dick a stir. I lean in closer. "Or what?"

She arches up. "Meet me around the corner in two minutes."

That's all I needed to hear.

Rolling off of her, I watch as she hops to her feet, removing the tape while skipping toward the locker room off the main area. I sit up, head spinning, checking on the guys myself.

It's not news that Joy and I hook up from time to time. It usually happens down here, too, because she's not one to let her sexual escapades be known to the rest of the prison, especially when it comes to fooling around with an inmate.

The guards hook up with the inmates here. It's just a fact. Some do it more than others, but the thing is that they're all *men*. Joy is the only female, so naturally, there's extreme interest in getting at her, knowing she's literally the only option for sex without crossing over into gay territory.

But unfortunately for every straight prisoner *other* than me, Joy Jameson is off-limits. She pointedly does not hook up with inmates. I'm the one and only exception to that rule, which makes me feel even more pretty and special.

If I were to guess why, I'd think it's because she knows I'm well-versed in the premises of both keeping it strictly physical and keeping my mouth shut—*when it's not feasting on her pussy, I mean.* Even Joy's other half—her partner in crime and her ex, John Chevelle—hasn't so much as shot me an evil look pertaining to me messing around with his *Cherry*. Of course, he knows. It's widely understood that Joy and Velle pretty much share a brain. But I also think Velle, more than anyone on this island, treats sex like the ultimate show of power.

Joy throwing me a bone, on *her* terms, makes me less of a threat.

I'm not exactly sure that's true, but at the end of the day, I'd never do anything to fuck Joy over. She's another one of my closest friends, like Luthor, Ren, and O'Malley. I trust her implicitly.

Moseying over to the locker room doorway, I'm trying to be as subtle as possible, whistling like I'm not doing anything sneaky. *Just casually walking into this private area, following the sounds of running water. Nothing to see here…*

Joy is already in one of the showers, and I have to pause and gulp because she's naked and dripping wet… And her body is *insane*.

We've fucked before, but we don't usually have sex. Her rule is that *if I beat her, I eat her.* You'd think it'd be the other way around, but no. Eating her out is my prize, because I never get to do it anymore.

I'm surrounded by dick. *Dick dick dick, everywhere. Dick and ass. That's it.*

Spending some time with tits and pussy is a welcome treat.

In seconds, I'm naked too, joining her in the shower. It's a bit dirtier down here than the showers upstairs, so you have to be careful where you step, but no matter. Right now, I'm more focused on getting us both off; making this good, but more importantly, making it quick. She can't exactly leave the others alone for long. Though, I'm sure Velle knows every inch of what's happening down here and is more than prepared to crack skulls if anything goes sideways.

I start out kissing Joy's mouth and neck, licking up her sweat mixed with the cool water, because it tastes good. Next, I'm at her tits, savoring them because, *goddamn*, it's been *way* too long. And lastly, the main course; her sweet little pussy.

There are many sensations flooding my body when I do this, things I never thought I'd feel while eating a girl out. It's crazy to me how different it starts to feel, because of how rare it is… It's like the whole time is spent hurdling through all the ways this is *different* from the other sex I have here. The other details I hold close to my chest.

Maybe that's why I enjoy hooking up with Joy so much. There's no risk of getting swept up in memories, like there is with Ren. With Joy, I can be the old Byron again.

It reminds me of simpler times.

Only five minutes with my tongue putting in mad work, and she's clenching her thighs around my head, yanking my hair so hard it hurts. I like it.

When she's done coming, and all gushy, I hold her up against the wall with her legs around my waist and rub my dick up and down through her wetness.

"Where should I come?" I whisper out fast and hoarse, fisting my cock and beating it rough.

"Come on my tits," she breathes.

"Fuck yea," I growl, succumbing to the sensation. Stroking faster and faster.

Closing my eyes… Seeing tear-stained cheeks and a waiting mouth.

Shit…

I force my eyes open. *Shit shit shit…*

And then I'm coming, shooting all over her perky tits, biting my lip to keep the desperate hums in.

"That was awesome," Joy sighs as I put her down, immediately washing up.

"Mhm…" I gulp.

Yea, it was. It felt great, because orgasms always do. And it was hot. *Duh.*

It's… comforting with Joy. Like being a musician on a comeback tour. There's something satisfying about going back to your roots.

Fooling around with females is my original repertoire.

Shaking off the weird feelings bogging me down, I get redressed, then follow Joy back into the rec room. If the guys noticed us disappearing together for ten minutes, they know better than to comment on it. Especially in front of Joy.

I'm certain she'd give them a nice bonk with her billy club.

"Alright, maggots." She claps her hands together, austerity shifted carefully back into place. "Time to go. Chop chop."

I hang back just enough, lingering by the mats where I stashed the cellphone. Tugging it out quickly, I check the screen. It has full service down here, which is a minor miracle. Without another moment of thought, I stuff it back where it was, scurrying after the others. Keeping it hidden down here seems much safer than carrying it around with me or keeping it in my cell.

As we make the long-ass journey back up to general population, I get a shove in the side from my cellmate.

"Where'd yeh put it?" O'Malley asks. I lift a brow, and he gives me a look. "You know…" He holds his hand up to his face, making the international gesture for talking on the phone.

Eyes on Joy, I whisper, "I left it down there. Tucked between those old mats up against the back wall."

He nods, but says nothing.

I'm not too worried about it. O'Malley's a freaking nutjob, but he's still one of my best friends in this place. I trust him.

That might be a loaded statement, but we'll see how things play out.

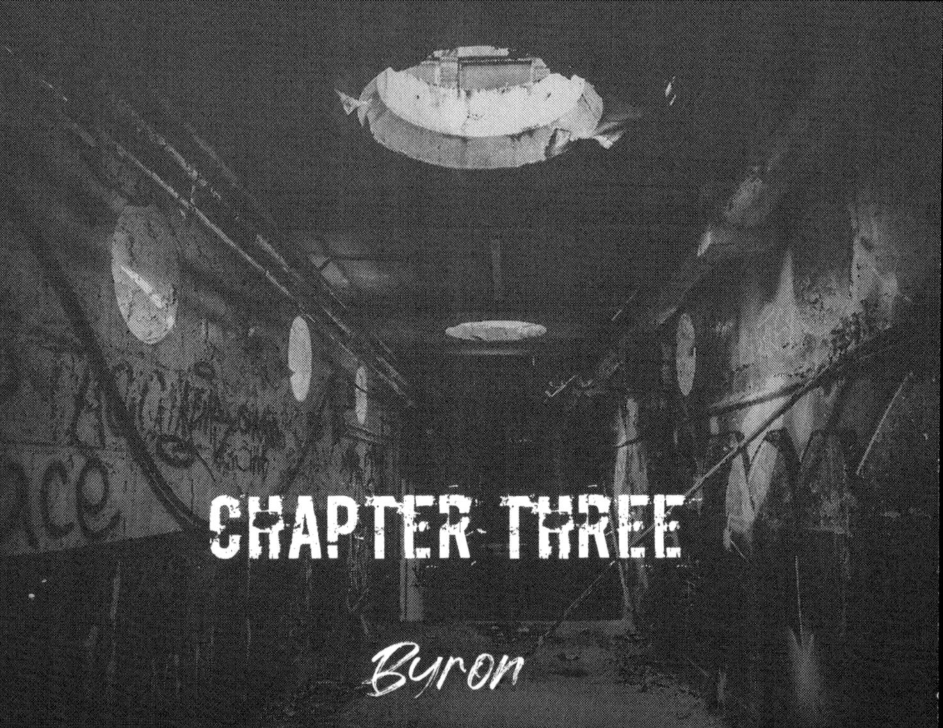

CHAPTER THREE

Byron

MY GRANDFATHER USED TO SAY, *"OUR SECRETS ARE JUST AS SIGNIFICANT A PART of who we are as anything else. The role we allow them to play in our lives is entirely up to us."*

I always found that interesting.

From a young age, we're taught not to keep secrets. That it's harmful and hurtful, and that keeping a secret is essentially holding on to our inner shame. But as I got older—the more truths I began to keep to myself—the more I discovered that secrets don't automatically equal guilt. At least, they don't *have* to.

Everyone keeps secrets. If you say you don't, you're a liar. Not a single one of us has shared every single aspect of our lives with someone else. *Think about it. There have to be at least one or two things you've never told anyone before.*

Why be ashamed of that? It's our right as human beings to keep things to ourselves. Whether it's a thought, or something you did, or something about yourself you choose not to divulge…

Imagine how crazy it would be if our minds were on permanent display, like an episode of *Black Mirror*. It would be a violation of our inherent privacy.

Not to mention, *secret* doesn't have to mean something only *you* know. Sometimes you can come together with your fellow man to keep a secret from someone else. Might sound fucked up, but in a way, it's a form of bonding.

Remember, *I Know What You Did Last Summer?*

Sorta like that.

That's the kind of secret that *Quiet Night* is.

Quiet Night was the name given to a weekly meeting of guards and prisoners in the basement rec room. Long story short, it's like a cockfight, only with prisoners. Organized by a few of the guards and kept heavily hidden from everyone else on the island.

Sounds like a secret society within an already mystery-shrouded prison, right? Sort of... Except that we're not equal, because the guards oversee it and they place bets, make money, and threaten to kill us if we ever tell anyone. *Like a more intense version of* Fight Club.

The inmates who fight get a say in whether we want to participate, but let's not act like saying no, backing out, or giving off even the slightest whiff of judgement won't put a giant bullseye on your back. Still, for the most part, us *Night Fighters* agree to do it because we're bored, angry, and we enjoy the act of both fucking people up and getting fucked up in return.

O'Malley and I are part of it, though I only choose to go down every so often. *When I need it.* O'Malley, on the other hand, would be down there *every* damn night if he could.

The dude loves fighting, and not in the same *professional* way that I do. Never in my life have I seen someone take on dudes three times his size, and get his ass beat with such masochistic glee... *He's like a schizophrenic Chihuahua.*

It's actually pretty alarming. *But then I like to fight, myself, so who am I to say anything?*

Yes, O'Malley has more issues than *Time* magazine, and *yes*, he should probably be on serious medication and constant surveillance from some kind of medical professional. But in Alabaster Penitentiary, things like that don't matter. His obvious problems aren't seen as a liability, but rather something to exploit for personal gain.

That might be the one truly *honest* thing about this place... We're all fucked the hell up. At least in here, we're celebrated for our issues, rather than condemned for them.

Unless, of course, we're talking about the East Wing. But that's a whole other side to this sentence I don't want to think about right now.

A select few of the guards got together and started *Quiet Night*. It's never been confirmed, but if I were to guess, I'd say they call it that because when we're down in the basement, pummeling each other in the face, Gen-pop gets much quieter. That and the guards use it as a *code phrase* of sorts to let us know when it's on.

"We're gonna have a quiet night *tonight, got it?"*

"Let's make it a quiet night *for once, inmate."*

That sorta thing.

Truth be told, I'm not even sure if Velle knows; that's how *hush-hush* the whole thing is. Part of me assumes Velle knows about literally everything that happens within these walls, because he *is* the Warden's top dog; his henchman, his eternally loyal second in command. It's his job to have eyes everywhere, just like the Warden does.

So he *must* know... *Right?*

Still, I can't be absolutely certain. Velle's never shown his face in the rec room for a *Quiet Night*, and the guards who organize it seem to go to great lengths to keep any mention of it away from him. But just because he doesn't participate, doesn't mean he's not aware of what's going on. *Same goes for The Ivory...*

I'm positive the Warden knows about *Quiet Night*. But he's not going to say anything, because that's the name of his game. To let us *think* we're getting away with things... Meanwhile, he's standing over us all, pulling the strings, goddamn puppet master that he is.

First rule of Quiet Night is you never, ever talk about it.

See what I mean?

It must be around three o'clock in the morning, though I'd have no idea. I haven't looked at a clock in ages. But despite the haphazard schedule and lack of windows in this place, your body's internal clock adjusts. And after a while, you start to work off of that.

We're in the basement—a group of deranged criminals and the equally feral men in charge—where we have been for hours. And I just kicked the shit out of Nieves, on a mat, surrounded by a circle of cheering guards and prisoners.

It was a decent fight. He got a few licks in, and I can feel my right eye swelling already. My knees are wobbly, skin raw, various sore muscles. But I won.

Linetti and Brenner, two of the guards who host *Quiet Night*, are counting their winnings on the side, while one prisoner, Cooper, drags Nieves off the mat, leaving a trail of blood as he goes.

He'll be fine.

"Ayo, walk it off, papi," grumbles Lucas, a guard who lost money.

Serves him right for betting against me. I'm undefeated, bitch.

"Rub some dirt on it. You'll live," Brenner adds, unsurprisingly unsympathetic. "Who's up next?"

Linetti checks the writing on his hand. "Uh, let's see… We got Hammond up against… Oh, shit." He chuckles. "O'Malley. Good luck, sport." He shoots Hammond a look, who understandably appears worried.

O'Malley isn't *undefeated* per se, but even his losses feel like a win, because of how brutal and fucking crazy he is.

I'm swiping blood away from my eyebrow as O'Malley slaps me on the side. I wince from the tenderness after being punched there probably a dozen times.

"No mercy," he says to me, grinning and sticking out his tongue.

"No surrender." I grab him roughly by the shoulders, shoving him toward the circle.

He jogs onto the mat like a psychopathic Connor McGregor, beating his chest and yelling out nonsense, threatening everyone who boos him.

Hammond has a good foot on O'Malley in height—the dude is barely five-six—and probably at least fifty pounds in muscle. He's a big guy. But size doesn't mean dick in fighting, especially under prison rules.

Anything goes.

No holds fucking barred.

The shouts, whistles, and taunts are amplified when Brenner calls out, *"Fight!"*

I'm often surprised no one can hear us down here. For as huge as this place is, and all the thick concrete everywhere, the noise still really travels.

Running fingers from my brow, over my eye and onto my cheekbone, I shiver at the sensation of *pain*; the throbbing ache with its own heartbeat.

I like it. I don't know why, but I do.

I'm not a total masochist. *At least I don't think I am…* But ever since I was thrown into Alabaster Pen without an ounce of warning, I've become more and more invested in pain. Really anything that allows me to *feel*, whether it's sex, or fighting… Shallow acts for my body to endure, to remind me I'm *not* just an empty husk.

The thing is, it wasn't Alabaster Penitentiary that made me this way…

I've felt invisible for as long as I can remember. Since I was a child standing in the corner.

I don't like to complain about my childhood, because I know some people have it so much worse than me, but still, I don't remember ever being happy with anyone other than my grandfather. Certainly not my father.

Tae Jin Kang is the epitome of a hard ass. Stone-cold, reserved and perpetually indifferent. I suppose he loves us… my mother, my sister, and me. Because he *has* to. But he never truly cared for my grandfather, or New York; that much was clear. As far as he was concerned, he came to America as an obligation, and as soon as my grandfather was dead, he could pack up and head back to Seoul—*after collecting my mother's hefty inheritance, of course.*

Unfortunately for him, Rafe Byron Jr. held on for as long as he could. He passed away on my thirteenth birthday. It was the last time I cried. *I also haven't celebrated a birthday since.*

By that time, we were already settled in Manhattan, living in the penthouse that belonged to my grandfather. He left it to my mother and me when he died. Naturally, my father wanted to sell the place and move back to Korea, but he needed my signature to do so, even though I was a child. It was a stipulation of the estate. And I refused to sign.

That sure as shit didn't make father dearest like me any more.

Maybe that's why my dad has always despised me so much… I remind him of his father-in-law, who never saw him as a good enough man to raise his grandchildren, or support his beloved daughter.

Rafe was the only member of my family who ever understood me; he was the *only* person who even tried. And with him gone, I felt even more invisible. My grandfather had died, but *I* was the one who felt like a ghost…

Maybe that's why I love to fight so much. Why I love the pain and the secrets… The darkness. Because it's all I have left.

It's the only thing that keeps me breathing anymore. Living day to day, basking in the darkness, without becoming too much of a vampire. That's what my friends are for, I guess. They keep me up, keep me rooted in the present. That's the tightrope you must walk in a life sentence… Staying fully in the *right now.*

No thinking about the future. And *never* any dwelling on the past.

Watching O'Malley run around Hammond and jump up onto his back like a damn spider monkey, I'm releasing tiny bubbles of soft laughter. He's just such a loon. *Mucho loco.* But still… He's my friend. And having friends in here is key.

Maybe it's weird to say I didn't have many friends until I came to prison, but it's sort of true. I had acquaintances, but no one I would consider as close to me as Luthor, Ren, and O'Malley are. I think that's a prison thing, too. When you're stuck in the same place, with boredom following you around every corner like a shadow, your best bet for survival is to be part of a group.

I struggled with it at first... How *much* to trust these people. But at the end of the day, I think I trust them as much as they trust me. We'll call it seventy-five percent. Because I'm sure they're keeping things from me. Just like I'm *definitely* keeping things from them.

Maybe not the same kinds of things... Or as many.

Grabbing one of the cloths they have lying around for us to clean up with, I dunk it into the bucket of water, holding it up to my eye. The cold feels good and will help with the bruising and swelling.

After a *Quiet Night*, I always wonder if Luthor or Ren will ask questions. But that's the beauty of this whole operation... Prison fights are a part of daily life. No one bats an eye when somebody shows up with fresh wounds.

There are orderlies from the East Wing in on it. They take a cut from the guards, and if a fighter gets badly injured, they fix him up—*as best they can, anyway.* It doesn't happen often, but it does happen.

I'm still watching O'Malley scratch and bite Hammond while I think about Ren...

I'm surprised that he, of all people, hasn't found out about this yet. He's the official *Gossip Guy* of Alabaster Pen. He has this uncanny ability to find things out around here.

But then, I guess he doesn't know *everything*...

My throat feels thick as my mind rushes with images, like a slideshow of all my secrets flickering behind my open eyes.

I wonder what he'd think if he found out...

Eyes gliding left, I peek at the stack of mats where I hid the cellphone the other day. I still haven't had a chance to use it, and I *really* want to. I'm contemplating how risky it would be to grab it now and sneak into the locker room real quick while everyone is distracted...

But loud cheers and bellows reclaim my attention.

"You little fuck!" Brenner shoves O'Malley back.

"Want some, yeh lazy cuck?" O'Malley shouts up at Brenner, getting back in his face.

I didn't see what happened, or why *they're* fighting now, rather than O'Malley and Hammond, but honestly, it could've been anything. We all know O'Malley has a short fuse, and Brenner is a prick of epic proportions, so they tend to be at each other's throats.

"Fucking *fight*, you worthless toad, or I'll mash you into the ground myself," Brenner snarls.

Linetti stomps in closer. I can't tell if he's going to separate them or join in.

O'Malley steps back, his classic move, wherein he makes you think he's backing down, and then *bam!* He slaps Brenner in the face.

It doesn't look like it was hard, but Brenner is fuming at the disrespect, and O'Malley is laughing like a damn Looney Tune. Before Brenner can even react, he's already running back over to Hammond, instantly launching blows at his face and body.

Everyone is cheering and screaming. It's mental. Hammond is bleeding, and Linetti and Brenner are just watching, because as much as I'm sure they want to take O'Malley out right now, they want *money* more, and I'm pretty sure they bet on him to win.

Which he does, sweeping Hammond's legs out from under him, then kicking him in the face until the dude finally taps out.

Wild Quiet Night, man.

A little while later, the fights are done, and the guards are cleaning up and getting ready to clear out. They have to get us all back up to Gen-pop before the morning crew of guards shows up for the shift change. Lucas is cuffing inmates while Linetti and Brenner are counting their winnings and talking shit, so I figure it's the perfect opportunity to at least check on the cellphone while they're all preoccupied.

Casually inching over to the stack of mats, I reach in between for the phone. Only it's not there.

My panic is immediate. I'm feeling around, searching for it while simultaneously making sure no one's looking, and *praying* I just forgot exactly where I put it.

"Yo, what the fuck?!" I hear Brenner bark, and I freeze. He's stalking over to O'Malley. "What the fuck is that??"

Motherfucker…

O'Malley has the cellphone. He's holding it up, trying to be subtle—*the way a fucking gunshot is subtle*—while clearly recording Brenner and Linetti with the cash in their hands.

Oh, great. This is just fucking perfect.

I distance myself, because I'm not going down for his stupidity. *It wasn't even his to play with! Goddamnit!*

"Smile for the camera, pretty boy," O'Malley mocks them, backing up as Brenner and Linetti come at him.

"Get everyone back upstairs *now!*" Linetti orders Lucas.

And I'm just shaking my head as I'm cuffed and shoved out of the rec room along with the others, stealing one last glimpse of my friend, the lunatic, being tackled to the ground.

Well, fuck. There goes that idea.

CHAPTER FOUR

Byron's Book of Secrets

"Every villain has an origin story . . ."

Stalking gets a bad rep.

Following someone doesn't always mean you intend to harm them. I've never hurt anybody. I just find it easier to get to know people when they don't know you're getting to know them.

It's more genuine, I think. Watching someone without them knowing you're there is the best way to find out who they *really* are. Because people do a lot of things they normally wouldn't when they think no one's looking, and that's the point.

Like birdwatching. *Observe the creature in its most natural habitat, and you'll catch the subtle nuances that make them unique.*

Stalking is an art form. And I'm good at it.

Or maybe I'm just good at fading into the background, who knows.

New York City is a great place to slink around unseen.

I was born in Seoul, but by all accounts, I'm a *New Yorker*. The city is an extraordinary place. Bustling with life and chaos, grim and guile. For someone like me, it's a haven of resounding solitude. The perfect place to be surrounded by people and yet completely alone. The perfect place to be *invisible*.

That's exactly how I met my *ex*.

By some minor miracle, I'd actually graduated from Bronx Community College. Nothing fancy, but I got my bachelor's degree in Exercise Science & Kinesiology, basically preparing for some sort of job as a personal trainer. My main interest has always been fighting; Tae Kwon Do, to be exact. Working out is my favorite hobby, but moving into adulthood, I got super into various forms of mixed martial arts. I just wasn't sure if I wanted to be a fighter, or a coach, instructor, something along those lines.

Either way, graduating was quite the feat, since I wasn't

that into school. I like to learn, but the physical act of being in class wasn't for me. By the end, I was doing most of my classes online.

Mulling over what to do next, I took a job delivering for DoorDash. I had a Kawasaki Ninja street bike that was my pride and joy—his name was *Raphael*, after my favorite Ninja Turtle—so I figured the delivery thing was a no-brainer. An easy way to make my own money while I was still living with my parents, to rely on them as little as possible.

Any time spent out of the house was a good thing too Avoiding their constant lectures was in my best interest.

My sister, Jaelyn, had gotten married the year before and moved back to Seoul with her husband. The way my parents had practically thrown her a parade for something as simple and stupid as *falling in love* was a constant point of inner contention for me. I just didn't understand why getting married and settling down was such a big deal.

That's not to say I was a *bachelor* or anything. I rarely dated, and sure, when I did, it was mostly casual. But it's not like I was some out-of-control horn-dog, sleeping around all the livelong day. As far as my parents were concerned, if I didn't bring a girl home to meet them as a potential future bride, it wasn't worth knowing about.

Just another thing that made me feel unseen in their eyes.

To my father, it was all about legacy. *Family* meant carrying on our name, as some self-appeasing form of immortality. I didn't care about carrying on our name, though, nor did I care about having someone to come home to. I couldn't see liking anyone enough to share my life with them, because my life was *mine* and mine alone.

And yet, because I'm a *person*, not a robot, they'd somehow gotten under my skin. I'd steadily begun to wonder about companionship. *Partnership*. I wondered if there was anyone out there I might mesh well enough with to sustain an actual relationship Or at least enough to bring home and present as my girlfriend.

Maybe then my parents would see *me* as a real person. Maybe then I might *exist* to them.

The first time I saw Rey was at the restaurant where she worked. This Korean place called Red Bird. I went in to pick up someone's takeout order, and she was up at the hostess stand, on the phone.

I think noticing her was inevitable. I'm sure a lot of

people noticed her She was absolutely stunning. Bronzed complexion, light brown hair all silky smooth and running down her shoulders. She had gorgeous eyes, with long, dark lashes—possibly fake, but who cares—and full lips, glossed over and sparkly.

Still, I think what inevitably hooked me was her smile

She had the phone wedged between her ear and shoulder while she tapped the screen of an iPad, most likely taking a customer's order. I stepped up to where the bags of takeout were sitting, checking for mine. But all the while, I couldn't stop watching her.

She was clearly busy, and I felt a bit like a weirdo just standing there, staring at her, out in the open. I had no problem watching people; we know this. But I preferred to do it from somewhere they couldn't *see me.*

I felt vulnerable. And I didn't know how to process it. I grabbed the bag of food, ready to get the hell out of there. But then, the girl glanced at me. Her eyes popped up from the iPad screen. They locked with mine.

And she smiled.

It was bright, luminous, and just for *me.* There was no one else around At least, no one close enough that I could be mistaking their smile for my own.

She was smiling at *me*, in a way that felt flirtatious. Interested.

Maybe it could be her I thought. *Maybe she could fill the void.*

Time sped back up, and I forced myself to turn away and leave. Because when you're like me, you don't just ask a pretty girl out the first time she smiles at you. That's foolhardy. That's like buying electronics without reading the reviews first, or moving to a city before you've even visited.

No, no. That was too far out of my comfort-zone.

Instead, I finished out the rest of my deliveries, went back to Red Bird, and just watched.

I spent about a week watching the girl—from across the street, or around the corner. I drove up and down that block more times than I could even count, just to catch a glimpse of *Rey.* I got to know her from afar, and once I felt confident enough, I began inching in closer.

Sometimes I would follow her to Starbucks, or to the park on her breaks. I listened to a lot of her conversations—that's how I found out she lived alone. And naturally, the next thing I knew, I was following her home.

Like I said, I'm not offended by the S-word.

I know what you're thinking "*But Byron, how will you ever know if someone wants you around if you don't let them* know *you're there?"*

That's part of this story. We'll get there.

Weeks of following Rey around had led me to believe that she could be my perfect mate. She was just the right combination of introverted extrovert. She wasn't a wild party girl, but she knew how to have fun. She was sweet and caring, but also tough when she needed to be. She would bring leftovers from the restaurant to the homeless people up the block and stop to give tourists directions. At the same time, she had no problem cursing people out when the situation called for it and flipping them off in the typical New Yorker, *I'm walking here!* fashion.

She was a beautiful, independent woman who might enjoy some male attention—when *she* wants it, of course. And the cherry on top was that she was Korean. *See, Mom and Dad?? I listen.*

I was smitten already; a great spot to be in before your first date even happens. All I had to do was decide on how to make first contact.

I obsessed about it for days, I won't lie. Debating whether I should ask her out at the restaurant, or accidentally bump into her somewhere else. Admittedly, asking girls out wasn't my strong suit. I was much better at following people around and dating them in my mind. But that wasn't good enough this time. I needed to suck it up if I wanted this girl to *actually* be in my life. *For real.*

One night, I just so happened to be dropping off a DoorDash order on her block when I saw her coming out of 14th Street station. She was walking right toward me.

My heart crawled up into my throat so fast, I coughed. *This was it.*

Tugging my helmet off of my head, I let out a breath, watching in my peripheral as she grew closer. And just as she approached me, I turned, and we made eye contact.

She slowed down. "Oh hey!" She smiled, and I smiled back.

"Hi," I said casually, narrowing my gaze, because I had to at least *pretend* I didn't instantly recognize her.

"Red Bird," she chirped. "I've seen you in there before picking up orders."

"Ah, right." I nodded, playing the part as I pushed my hair away from my forehead. "Small world."

"That's Manhattan for you." She chuckled, then bit her lip. "I'm Rey, by the way."

Of course I knew that from looking at her mail. "Nice to meet you, Rey." I grinned, laying on the charm, though my palms were sweaty as fuck. "I'm Byron."

"Very nice to meet you, Byron." Her eyes did a satisfying glide up and down me, and the interest was blatant. Safe to say, the bike was working in my favor. "So burning the midnight oil?"

I chuckled. Forced, but I didn't mind. "Gotta make that money, right?"

"Unfortunately," she sighed, clutching her coat.

"You live around here?" I asked, knowing exactly where she lived.

She nodded and bit her lip again. "Just up the block."

"Well, that settles it then." I hopped off my bike. "Looks like I'm walking you home."

She giggled, a flirtatious sound I'd heard numerous times while listening to her on the phone. But still, this one was different. Because it was for *me*.

I walked her to her apartment, and we chatted back and forth. It was casual enough, but the whole time, all I could think was that *this girl* was going to be my girlfriend. My first *real* girlfriend. Not a high school experiment in losing my virginity, or a Tinder hookup, or a crush living exclusively in my fantasies. An honest to God *relationship* I could bring home to my parents, to prove that I was capable of being someone they were proud of.

In hindsight, I was getting ahead of myself, but in that moment, I didn't see it. I saw everything else Handholding, and smiles. Double-dates and holidays. Moving boxes, and rings, and white dresses, and sonograms

All the *important* things that made up a conventional happily ever after. Whether I'd seen *myself* having them or not.

"This is me," Rey said when we stopped in front of her building.

And I used the elaborate scenes in my head as motivation to choke out the words, "Can I see you again?"

Her head slanted curiously. "Are you done seeing me now?"

My brow furrowed in confusion, because honestly, I hadn't expected that. But before I could even process it enough to respond, she grabbed me by the hand and tugged me along, inside her apartment.

Now, let me start by saying that sex before even a first date was not part of my initial plan. Truthfully, I thought I'd have to work for it a lot harder than I did, being that we didn't technically know each other at all. That said, I'm still a guy, and turning down sex with a beautiful woman is not a skillset many of us possess.

So while that wasn't how I'd anticipated my first night with Rey going, it was still amazing, and I couldn't find it in myself to be disappointed. Relationships begin with one-night stands all the time. It's not common, but it *does* happen. I wasn't worried about it.

I definitely should've been. But again hindsight is 20/20.

After we fucked—hard and dirty, thus solidifying my desire to lock this girl down—Rey and I exchanged numbers and agreed to get together for an actual date. I left her apartment walking on a damn cloud.

I was *ecstatic*. Not just because I'd gotten laid for the first time in a few months, but because I could feel the connection already. It was solid, something tangible I could reach out and grab. *Finally*, things were coming together.

Not that I wanted to put so much stock in a relationship as the thing to make me feel less like a zombie shuffling through my mundane existence But I couldn't help how good it felt to finally *have* something. *Someone*.

A person to be on *my* side for once. That partner in crime I was secretly yearning for.

I waited a few days to call her, so as not to seem too eager. And we made plans to get dinner Saturday night. I was as excited as I was nervous.

Saturday night came, and we had dinner, followed by more sex. I felt like everything was falling into place. Rey was *perfect*, and I could really see myself settling with her.

Settling *down* with her, I mean.

I used to think people in relationships were suckers. Unhappy with themselves and desperate to find someone to make them feel good when the rest of life was shit. To me, it seemed inherently selfish to put that burden on somebody. To rely on someone else to fix you.

But for all of my insecurities and uncertainties—the giant gaping hole inside myself I could never seem to fill, no matter what I did—I *knew* that the locust of my identity revolved around desiring connection I could never seem to find. My family didn't understand me Shit, I barely understood myself.

I spent the next week texting with Rey, trying to make plans to see her again, because I was already addicted and ready to move full speed ahead on making the fantasies a reality. Sure, I liked her, and the sex was fire. But more than anything, I suddenly had a purpose. Something that made me visible.

Rey was busy with work and school, but we made time to see each other when we could. *Okay I* made time to see her. She was becoming a bit elusive, but I refused to let it sway me. I was determined to look past every single red flag she tossed up and see only the future I'd concocted in my mind.

Unfortunately, it was becoming increasingly difficult to get her on the phone. Even our texts were dwindling, and I was frustrated. She was my *girlfriend*, I was sure of it. But she was dodging me, and I just didn't understand *why*.

I swear to God, I paced for a full day. I just couldn't fathom why *I* felt all these deep, longing things, and all she wanted was to fuck. I mean, I wanted to fuck too. Of course I did. But I didn't want to *just* fuck, because that was basic shit.

I could fuck anyone. I wanted Rey for *more* than that.

The more I obsessed over it, the more unhinged I became. I *hated* the idea of losing the good, stable thing before I even had the chance to show it off. If I wanted to keep this relationship, I'd need to take matters into my own hands.

It was late, well after midnight. And it was raining, so not many people were out walking the streets. I left my bike up the block and walked to her building. And when no one was looking, I climbed the fire escape.

Cards on the table, it wasn't the first time I'd done it. So I knew it was secure.

There was a window that looked right into her bedroom, and I knew how to keep myself hidden enough to peek inside. I just wanted to *see* her. To look at her. Find out what she could *possibly* be doing that was more important than returning her alleged boyfriend's calls.

By the time I got onto her fire escape, my hoodie was soaked through. Raindrops were tumbling from my hair down my face as I crept up to her window and peered inside. My heart shattered to pieces in an instant.

Actions have consequences. That's what people need to understand.

We come to a fork in the road, choose a direction. And that choice is directly responsible for where we end up.

Do we sometimes imagine what might have happened if we'd gone the other way? Sure. It's normal to wonder. But ultimately, there's no going back.

That was the night everything changed for me

Because Rey was fucking some guy in her bed.

Some fucking prick was putting his dick in *my* girlfriend's pussy on the other side of that window. And I was just standing, in the pouring rain, *watching* it happen.

Invisible. *Nothing more than a shadow in the dark.*

The events of that night brought me here. I didn't know it at the time, but *that moment* was my fork in the road

Peering through a window on Jane Street in the rain, I unknowingly chose a path that led me to a concrete tomb in the middle of the ocean.

That was the first time I laid eyes on Michelangelo Russo

But the thing is, I'm not sure I regret it.

CHAPTER FIVE

Trevel

FOR MY SIXTH BIRTHDAY, MY PARENTS GAVE ME A STUFFED BEAR.

Now, I should preface this by saying that receiving gifts in our household was a rarity. There were no presents, wrapped up in colorful paper under a twinkling Christmas tree. No toys accompanied by balloons and sugary confections to celebrate another year on this planet.

The *things* I got from my parents weren't fun. I'd come to expect nothing more than torment; scars, both physical and emotional.

So when I got the teddy bear, my first thought wasn't that I was probably technically too old for a stuffed animal, nor was it the normal unenthused reaction of a child receiving a basic birthday gift.

My first *actual* thought was, *What's the catch?*

Because I wouldn't put it past my father to hand me a toy, only to smack me upside the head the moment I accepted it.

But when he *didn't* do that, my next reaction was one much sadder. I hugged him.

I was *grateful* for receiving my first gift—at *six* bloody years old—in that cheap, poorly made hunk of polyester. So blindingly *ecstatic* that I'd actually been given something other than bruises and pain. In my undeveloped mind, I'm sure I interpreted the gift as a symbol of love. Which of course, it was not.

But I didn't know that then.

At the time, I was happy. Before that, if I'd wanted to play, I had to pretend. Make up games to entertain myself while sadly looking on at the kids in school who'd carry around their favorite toys, slumping in defeat when I'd see the commercials on television. *Action figure this* and *Barbie's Dream that*. Shiny plastic with smiling faces to match those of the lucky children who received them.

Naturally, I was jealous, but even that felt like too strong of an emotion most of the time. Usually, I was just numb.

That is, until that faithful day, when *finally*, I got a toy.

Every blow after was softened because, at long last, I had a *friend*.

If my parents had known *anything* about me, or bothered to show even the slightest bit of interest in their only child—the way parents are supposed to—they would've known that six-year-olds rarely play with stuffed teddy bears, and I was actually quite big on the *Teenage Mutant Ninja Turtles*. They were my favorites. But since my parents decided to gift me a raggedy bear, that honestly might have been stolen from some other poor kid, I had to, once again, use my imagination.

I found a scrap of blue material and cut out two eyeholes to make his mask, tied two plastic utensils to his back, and *voila!*

Leonardo was born.

I took that bear everywhere with me. It wasn't long before he was even rattier; worn and torn, ripped and tattered from overuse. But I didn't care. He was my best friend.

My *only* friend.

I wasn't allowed much time with my mates from school. My parents isolated me, for reasons that are quite obvious now. But at the time, it was difficult. I was a lonely little weirdo, which didn't get better when I began talking to a stuffed bear.

Still, none of it mattered. *Nothing* did. My life was a dark, devastating place. Leo was there for me, as much as he could be, anyway. And all I wanted, the *one thing* I would wish for late at night, cowering in my bedroom, was for him to come alive.

I wished he was *real*. I *needed* him to be.

And then one day… he was.

"This won't end well…"

"You sound rather unsupportive for my alleged *best friend* of nearly twenty years," I mutter through gritted teeth.

Leo falls into step beside me while we walk home from the market. *"Don't be snippy. I am your best friend, which is why I'm looking out for your best interests. As always."*

"Right. Or maybe you're jealous." I stop at a crosswalk, peering at him. "Because you feel like Alice is stealing me away from you."

He scoffs. *"That's preposterous."*

"Is it?" I lift a brow at his jagged face, only partially hidden by the blue mask. "You know, I'm beginning to think you *don't* really want what's best for me..."

I take a step forward, but he grabs me by the shirt, stopping me from walking into oncoming traffic.

"You were saying?" He sneers.

I roll my eyes. "Bugger off."

We keep walking, arguing back and forth, all the way back to my flat. I recognize that my sanity is wearing thin. You might think I'm oblivious to it, but on the contrary.

I've always been rather self-aware, and *yes*, I know how that sounds coming from someone who's having a full-blown conversation with an imaginary bear. But the fact remains.

I'm not psychotic. I'm not schizophrenic. *If I were, I'm sure Dr. Love would have picked up on it.*

I'm fully aware that the creepy bear I've been talking to since I was a child isn't *real*. I believe him to be more of a coping mechanism for extreme trauma and chronic loneliness. And yes, that's a lot sadder than if I *were* clinically unwell. But the truth is, I enjoy having him around.

Leo is my imaginary friend. A version of my old teddy bear I had as a kid. Sadly, I lost the toy when I ran away from home at eleven. I was devastated, until one day, like magic, Leo showed up. Large and maybe a bit frightening to look at. But to *me*, he was perfect.

He was my friend, imaginary or not. A manifestation of exactly what I needed, who popped up *exactly* when I needed him.

He's been around ever since, and I'm afraid I'm too attached to let him go at this point. He was always *here*, even when I was still taking my meds, which is all the proof I need that seeing and hearing him doesn't mean I'm in some fit of untreated psychosis.

I suppose my past is only one part of what someone would need to accept if they were going to enter a real relationship with me...

"And what about the other day at work?" Leo goes on as we enter the apartment. I sigh, tossing my keys onto the table. *Just because he's my lifelong imaginary friend doesn't mean he's not fully exhausting sometimes. "If I didn't care about your well-being, would I have warned you about that perverted client?"*

"Yea, some good it did me..." I toss the bag of cheap processed food—the only kind I can afford now—onto the counter, then stagger to the couch, plopping down with an exhausted sigh. "I lost the best job I've ever had. The *only* real job I've ever had… Now what am I going to do for money??"

He's quiet for a moment before sitting down by my side. *"You can't expect me to do all your thinking for you, mate."*

Rolling my eyes, I lean back, staring up at the ceiling. "What do you think Dr. Love is doing right now?"

"Pfft. Who needs him." Leo fiddles with his rusty ninjatos. *"Big, fancy shrink with his fancy new job in New York… Good riddance. You're better off."*

I'm not sure that I agree, but I nod anyway, suddenly so very tired. I wish like hell I could just close my eyes and get some rest… But it won't happen. I end up sitting on the couch for hours, just staring. Until eventually, I get up and pace around my apartment, pretending to clean, when really, I think I'm making more of a mess.

The next thing I know, it's nine-thirty in the morning. I have no idea where the time went, but I have to get ready for my appointment with the replacement doctor.

The cheap Dr. Love knock-off.

Please. That guy is nothing like Dr. Love. He doesn't even have dreadlocks!

Just another affable old fool acting like he gets it, when he hasn't the slightest bloody clue. Charlatans.

Making my way to his office, I'm stewing all the while. Things have really fallen apart for me since Dr. Love left, though I refuse to admit it. I *hate* to give him that much credit, since dropping me as a client was as easy for him as tossing something into the garbage. Either way, I think it's evident that I've been better…

I lost my job. A job I truly enjoyed, by the way. I think they could tell something was up with me, but I convinced myself it was nothing. Still, I was showing up later and later, more and more disheveled. And then one day, this massage client came in who reminded me of someone from my past.

Let's just say, it didn't go over well. And now I'm unemployed and falling detrimentally behind on my bills.

I'm also off my prescribed medication and back to self-medicating. Bonkers how easily it happened, too. I haven't used drugs since before I was arrested, which was nearly eight years ago at this point. And yet the moment things get rough, I slip right back into it, as easily as breathing. Imagine, all that clean time down the drain…

I didn't realize I was such a junkie.

"Dr. Callahan will see you now," the cheerful girl at the desk says, barely thirty seconds after I arrive.

"What's she have to be so chipper about?" Leo grunts, and I hold my hand up to him.

"Stay out here."

I know he's pouting, but I don't care. Dealing with Callahan is annoying enough without Leo in the room commenting on everything and distracting me.

Striding into his office, I close the door behind me, placing him immediately. My new *doctor.*

Ugh. I suppose I should get used to him.

In my initial naivety, I thought Dr. Love might return after a few weeks. I held out some hope that he'd be back when he finished his special job in New York—which was apparently *so* important that he left his whole life here in Atlanta behind. Foolishly, I inferred—when he was breaking up with me—that it was a *temporary* position.

But it's been two whole months. And I'm stuck with Dr. Callahan, the dopey prick who, despite coming *highly recommended* by Dr. Love, is entirely too much of a *shrink*.

He's a dime-store therapist, when Dr. Love was the real deal, a true behavioral psychiatrist.

It's like going from Debussy to the *Titanic* soundtrack.

"Trevel, good to see you." Callahan smiles, gesturing for me to take a seat.

I look at the seat and frown, opting to pace around his office instead.

"Um… how are you feeling?" he asks, already sounding like he's out of his element. It's accurate.

He is, and he has been since his *colleague* dumped me into his lap.

"Fucktastic," I grumble.

Callahan is quiet for a moment before continuing, "Are you… sure you're alright? You seem on edge…"

"Why would I be *on edge*, Doctor?" I glare down at him. "Because I'm a ticking time-bomb, walking around waiting to go *kaboom*??"

"What…" He pauses to clear his throat. "What do you mean by that?"

"Oh, nothing…" I mumble, poking at things on his bookshelf.

"Have you been taking your medication?" he asks.

"Yes," I lie.

"Are you… sure?"

My face slopes in his direction. He's staring at me. "Do I seem like an idiot?"

His face freezes in perplexity. "No…"

"Good. Because I'm not," I grunt. "I know the difference between taking medication and not taking it."

"Right…" He sounds nervous. *I kind of like it.* He clears his throat again. "How's work?"

Turning away from him, I pick up a book, flipping through the pages. "I got fired."

"I'm sorry to hear that."

"Are you?" I peer at him.

He nods. "Yes… I know you enjoyed that job. Would you like to tell me what—"

"You know what?" I slap the book shut. "Maybe I *am* on edge. I've been on edge since I was handed off to you, like something inconsequential. Like a pen, or a shopping bag… or a goddamn biscuit that's been in your backpack for two years!"

"I'm not sure I—"

"I *told* that self-righteous robot what would happen if he tossed me aside," I growl, storming around with my fists in my hair. My emotions are skyrocketing, and I'm still not entirely sure *why*. It's like my thoughts are going haywire, bouncing back and forth so fast I can't keep track of which way I'm going. "*I matter*, do you understand that?? I'm a bloody *human* fucking *being* with feelings and problems and deep, festering emotional wounds—I *will not* be *ignored!*"

Callahan looks like he's about to shit himself. He has no earthly clue how to deal with me right now, and truth be told, neither do I. I don't know if anything he or anyone else could say or do to me right now would help how I'm feeling. I'm angry and stressed. I'm keyed-up and confused, and… tired.

So tired.

I'm sleep-deprived and depressed and pissed the fuck off at the world. So many things are happening inside me, I want either to explode or lie down. Or explode, *then* lie down.

Maybe you should take your fucking meds, wanker.

No. I don't need those things. I need more drugs. I need…

Alice.

Stomping toward the door, I'm reaching for the handle when Dr. Callahan jumps up. "Trevel! Wait… Where are you going??"

I take a breath with my hand on the knob, chin tipping in his direction. "Anything I do, from here on out… is his fault."

Sucking in a deep breath, I lift my hand, knocking *one, two, three* times on the door. I peer left, then right, shifting my weight back and forth, fiddling with the rings on my fingers.

I haven't slept in a while. I'm not certain how long it's been…

When did I sniff that shit that tasted like dirt with Andres? At least a few days ago…

Every noise has me flinching, until finally the door opens.

"Hey…" Alice says, her smile strained.

I'm trying not to notice the concern in her eyes.

Pushing my way inside, I sniff. "Hey. Is your brother here?"

She doesn't answer me, and when I spin to face her, she's standing there with her arms folded over her chest. I lift a questioning brow, and she sighs. "No. He's out with Tommy."

"Who?" I rub my eyes.

"You know, the busboy from the restaurant."

"Oh… right." I have no idea who she's talking about, but it doesn't matter.

I can't think. I feel itchy and twitchy, and I was *really* hoping he'd be here so I could grab something to sort me out.

Fuck fuck fuck. What am I gonna do now??

"Trevel… are you alri—"

"Do you know when he'll be back?" I ask before she can go there, pacing circles around her living room.

I hear her sighing some more. "No. I don't. Listen, I don't like you hanging out with him. He's a bad influence."

Pausing my movements, I peek at her.

"Who made her the Queen of England?"

"Shut up," I rumble at Leo. Alice's face falls. She looks upset, and I squeeze my eyes shut in a hard blink. "Sorry, love. I'm just… stressed. It's not a big deal… I have everything under control."

Stepping up to her, I take her face in my hands, forcing her to look up at me. *She's much shorter without those killer heels she loves to wear.*

"I'm worried about you," she hums, her tone slithering its way inside my chest, in between the cracks and jagged pieces, wrapping around my decomposing heart. "You've been acting different the last few weeks… I'm not sure what happened, but I just hope you're not, like, getting hooked on that shit, or—"

"Baby, I'm *fine*, I promise," I tell her in the most assuring voice I can manage when I know bloody well it's bullshit. I'm hanging on by a goddamn thread. "I can stop whenever I want."

She gives me a look, but I ignore it, leaning in to kiss her lips softly, hoping to distract her from how obvious it is that I'm lying through my teeth. Unfortunately for both of us, it works. And the next thing I know, we're in her bedroom, tearing off each other's clothes.

Because despite how terrible I've been feeling for the last few months—since I was *abandoned* by the only person who's ever truly understood me—there's still one thing in my life that puts me at ease. Something that settles me better than the drugs…

She peeks up at me, deep brown eyes framed by long, dark lashes, sparkling with hope; the purest potential I've seen in them since that first day, when I finally worked up the courage to let her see me. After weeks of following her around, just *watching* her in fascination; such a beautiful creature, brokenness worn on the outside, like a badge of honor. I've been drawn to her since the moment I laid eyes on her, like a moth to her brightly burning flame.

That *she* asked *me* out was an undeserved miracle, because she's entirely too good for me. But now that I have her, I *should* do whatever it takes to keep her. Rip out my own heart to keep her smiling. I feel infinitely stupid for ever fearing getting closer to her… Though I know in my heart she's stupid for getting close to *me*.

I don't want to hurt her… She's perfect.

She tames the evil inside me. She's the antidote to every bit of my darkness.

If ever there was a moment to tell her about my past, it would be now. She deserves to know the truth, to understand why I've been struggling. That there's a reason when I pull away or act distant, and it has absolutely nothing to do with her.

I think she might be the only person left to help me overcome it… After the one who left me high and dry.

"What if she leaves too?" I blink. *"You're damaged, Trevel."*

Ultimately, I know he's right. So I keep myself hidden, for her sake and mine.

Alice and I get dressed, and despite not getting the drugs I came for,

I'm still floating on a dopamine cloud. I'm sure I can overcome the evil inside me… And I don't need medication or therapy or *Dr. Love* to do it.

I just need her. A real partner in my corner.

But of course, my joy doesn't last long. It takes barely a half-hour for the orgasm-high to fully wear off, and the next thing I know, I'm wound the hell up again and back to obsessing over my need for some serious narcotic assistance. I'm happy to be spending time with Alice, surely, I am… But in the back of my mind, I know the longer I hang out here, the more likely her brother will eventually show up. And then I can get my fix.

Fidgeting on the couch, I'm flicking through television channels, so quickly, there's no way to tell which programs I'm passing. I'm just… doing it. In a trance, pressing the button over and over *and over and over and over and—*

"Baby, what's wrong?" Alice's melodious voice slinks into my ear at my side while I click click click on her remote, staring mindlessly at the screen. "Talk to me."

Finally, I stop. My face slants slowly in her direction, and I blink at her beautiful, worried face.

She's worried about me. She *cares*… for *me*.

My lips part.

"Don't do it," Leo warns from across the room where he's smoking a cigarette, watching me. *"I'm begging you…"*

"I'm in therapy," I confess, just a sliver of truth. A small piece… It's all I'm comfortable giving.

I shoot Leo a look. He's sighing out of relief. *Chuffed, are we, mate??*

Alice grins, taking my jaw in her hands. "Babe, that's what you were worried about telling me? I would never judge anyone for seeking help. Shit, I've been in therapy since I was, like, fourteen…"

"It's just… It's a bit more complicated than that…" I rumble nervously. "Dr. Love—my psychiatrist—was something else. He was… like a breath of fresh air. So very different from all the others. He took pride in his work. In treating me. He actually… cared." I stop and shake my head. "At least, I thought he did."

"What happened to him?" Alice's voice squeaks, full of intrigue. Compassion and wonder. "You're speaking about him in past tense…"

My jaw tightens, and I scowl while Leo rolls his eyes. "Six weeks ago, he up and decided he was leaving. Pawned me off to some hack, and now he's gone. The only person who's ever known the real me…" I blink at Alice, and she back at me. "Until you, I mean."

Her lashes flutter. Her wide eyes sparkle at me. She looks pleased…

I just wish it wasn't tainted by the lies, and all of my *many* secrets.

Shifting in my seat, I cover my face with my hands. "I have issues, Alice. Lots of them. If I were you, I would run screaming—"

The words I'm grumbling into my palms are cut short when she takes my hands in hers and pulls them away. I peek at her, sincerely bewildered by the way she's gazing at me, holding my hands tight. She's not running away… In fact, she's leaning in closer.

"My beautiful stranger…" she sighs over my mouth, her forehead dropping to rest on mine. "Thank you for telling me."

She's not afraid.

I can't believe it. She's not *scared* of me…

"She should be…"

I'm about to shoot him a glare when the door flings open. Alice and I pull apart as her brother stomps inside, followed by a guy I think I've seen before.

"Look at these two lovebirds," Andres snorts, an air of hostility about him. He always has it, and I'm unclear if it's just part of who he is, or if it's something reserved for me.

Giving me a look I can't read, he cocks his head to the side. Then he reaches into his pocket, pulling out a small ball of plastic filled with light brown powder. "I've got what you want."

It's odd how fast my mouth is watering, the tremble in my limbs changing from something pure to something mischievously sinister in seconds flat.

Eyes following the friend, I watch as he slumps down on the adjacent chair, dumping out a different-looking substance onto the coffee table. He begins fiddling with it, cutting it up into lines with what looks like his driver's license.

Andres snaps his fingers in front of my face. "So whaddya think, loverboy? Want me to sort you out?"

He smirks, much more devilish than his sister, though it's painfully apparent that they're twins. Not identical, but still. The resemblance is there for sure, despite Alice's femininity in her angles and Andres's ruggedness. Honestly, he's a bit scary. Aggressive and brash, with a darkness in his eyes, unlike his sister, who's all light.

Andres is just such a *man*. I wish I didn't find it as attractive as I do…

Either way, that doesn't matter. I just want the drugs. That's it.

Despite how good it feels to have Alice, someone beautiful, smart and kind, who loves me… I'm still broken. Overflowing with bad things she doesn't know about. Things I don't want to feel anymore.

I need to shut it up… All the noise.

I want to be numb again.

"Andres." Alice says his name admonishingly. She seems like the older sibling, though they're the exact same age. "It's not a good time."

"It's always a good time to get high," the friend says, sticking a rolled-up bill into his nose and leaning forward to snort a line of whatever he's doing. Whipping his head back, he sniffs and wipes his nose before turning to Alice. "Want some?"

What's he doing…? I might want some of that…

"I'm all set. Thanks," she mutters, clearly annoyed.

"Come on, Sis," Andres goads. "Live a little."

She aims an irritated glare up at him before turning to me, still showing me that empathy and care she was giving me moments ago, before the dope fiends showed up. "Baby, I'm not sure it's a good idea…" Her brows lift, like she wants me to understand the point she's trying to get across.

Of course she's right. Getting high is a crutch, and a dangerous one, at that. But I'm in a downward spiral that feels too good to ruin with rational thinking or consequences.

"It won't help," Alice says softly, only to me.

"I have to agree with the bird on this one," Leo meddles.

My eyes flick to him before returning to my girlfriend. I pinch her chin between my fingers. "I think it will." Placing a chaste kiss on her frown, I stand up. "Don't worry, gorgeous. I'll be fine. I always am."

The last thing I see is her sad smile. *My angel…*

Unfortunately, the devil is much more tempting.

I follow Andres into the loo. I'm not really sure why… I assume it's because we're going to shoot it, and this is where he prefers to do that. But I'm behaving like such a raving junkie, I'm sure I'd follow him out onto a ledge at this point.

Inside, with the door closed, he turns to face me. But says nothing.

I lift a questioning brow. "Well?"

"*Well* yourself," he snaps, gently. "I'm assuming you have no money…" I swallow hard. "So… you know how this works."

I sigh and roll my eyes. "*Fine.* But remember our deal…" I drop to my knees and start opening his pants. "She never finds out."

"You're such a good boyfriend to my sister," he croons sarcastically, grinning down at me while I pull his dick out.

"Fuck off," I grunt. And then I'm sucking.

But it's *fine*. It doesn't mean anything.

I love Alice; I know that. This is just something I do, usually as a form of currency. I suppose I can admit that it *also* happens because I'm a terribly destructive person who can't seem to resist hot, toxic fuckboy dick.

What can I say? I have a *deeply* rooted need to self-sabotage.

I was raised keeping secrets. And despite knowing how good it feels to tell the truth from time to time, I find myself chasing it down… The high that comes from hiding things. *Doing fucked-up shit and keeping it from people on purpose.*

I wish I wasn't like this, but I can't help it. It's an addiction, stronger than any of my others.

Knowing that my girlfriend—someone who *loves* and *cares* for me—is on the other side of that door, while I'm in here with her brother's fist in my hair and his cock jamming at my tonsils… It's a delectable ache, and the more I try to thwart it, the more I *crave* it.

Even Dr. Love, as much as he used to advocate for me, knew that I was incapable of *truly* changing who I am. I could pretend I was getting better all I wanted, but deep down, I always knew it was pointless.

I'm a monster. Plain and simple.

I don't believe I would hurt Alice *physically*. But clearly, I am more than capable of slaughtering her emotionally.

Regret weaves through my extremities, but it's too late for all that. Because her twin brother is coming in my mouth, holding my head in place so I have no choice but to swallow.

When he's done, I stand up on shaky legs, and he sighs, tucking himself away. "Fuck yea… That mouth is fucking lethal."

Pushing me up against the sink, he kisses me, and I'm a little confused. I've been under the impression that Andres is straight, and he simply learned from a few minor stints in prison that when it comes to getting off, all mouths essentially feel the same. But now he's biting on my lips and tonguing my tongue, and it feels… different.

Worse, because I'm certain that if it keeps growing like this, Alice will eventually find out. And she'll be crushed.

I have to put my obsessing on pause, though, because Andres has stopped kissing me and is now taking out needles and tying up my arm.

The devil twin shoots me up, whispering wicked words in my ear… Touching me all over while my eyes roll back.

And I fall, willingly, into the depths of evil.

CHAPTER SIX

Byron

SHOCKINGLY, O'MALLEY ONLY GOT ONE DAY IN SOLITARY FOR THE CELLPHONE incident. Still, the second he comes shuffling back into our shared cell, it's apparent that it was a pretty shitty one.

But I don't feel bad for him. *Not even slightly.*

That was all *his* doing. *He* made the executive decision to taunt Brenner and his butt-buddy Linetti, knowing full well that they're both extremely short-tempered assholes who get off on watching inmates suffer. *And*, he did so while also exposing the cellphone that Ren went out of his way to get and give to *me*. It was his choice to be stupid, and he should have to deal with the consequences of his actions.

Not to mention, he put us all at risk. Because the guards aren't as dumb as they look. They know O'Malley doesn't exactly have the wherewithal to procure a cellphone himself. So who are they going to look at?

His stupid friends.

This is the exact shit I voice to him as soon as he returns.

"What the fuck is your problem, anyway?" I bark at him, pacing around the cell while he just sits on my bunk, hands folded in his lap like he's being scolded by a parent. "I mean, are you just *that* fucking certifiable??" He shrugs, and I stop, bending to line our faces. "No... You're *selfish*, that's what you are."

He frowns. "That ain't—"

"Not only did you lose something we hadn't even had the chance to use yet," I cut him off, "something we *never* fucking get in here... But you also put us, your *friends*, at risk! I swear to God, it's like you don't care about us at all."

"Yo, mate, it's not like that..." he mutters, finally seeming remorseful.

"Yes, it is," I huff firmly, straightening and running my fingers through my hair. "I would *never* do something like that to you."

"Aw, yea, big brother Byron is fookin' *perfect*!" he growls. "Must be nice to be a goddamn celebrity in prison! You, Luthor, Ren... yer all the fookin' golden boys. Meanwhile, yer tapped fookin' friend is the black sheep! The one everybody hates..." He grabs two fistfuls of his hair and starts yanking it visibly hard. Hard enough to rip it out. Smacking himself in the face over and over. "No one understands... I know I'm a worthless screwup, alright?? I *know* that... Yeh don't have to rub it in!"

Staring at him, I watch his little meltdown closely, feeling the tiniest twinge of empathy. I know I'm not responsible for the way he feels. He's a tornado of destruction, and he should have to deal with that, like the rest of us do.

At the same time, I understand where he's coming from...

I was the black sheep of my family. The *disappointment*. I felt unseen in my own home, like he did. Granted, I never would've thought to harm any of them because of it, especially if I'd had a younger sibling, like O'Malley did...

I've never actually thought about killing someone in a way that wasn't completely abstract. *Certainly not an innocent child. It's unfathomable.*

But still, the reason I've bonded with Kieran is the rest of it. Being perpetually invisible.

And what he doesn't understand is that I *still* feel that way now. Even here, with the occasional attention from Joy, and the inmates who sorta look up to me. With Luthor and Ren...

I'm still in the shadows. Begging to be pulled out.

Sighing out hard, I plop down next to him. "You know I'm not like that. I feel left out all the time..."

With them.

I don't say the words, because I hate how they make me sound, to myself more than anything. Like I'm a whiny third wheel, a desperate, dejected prop in their epic, toxic love story. But that doesn't stop me from feeling it sometimes. *Okay, most of the time.*

Always a supporting role... Never a lead.

When's it gonna be my turn?

Kieran looks up at me, nodding, as if he understands. "You know I didn't tell 'em anything, yeah? About the phone… where it came from."

I nod in response. I know he wouldn't do that. But it doesn't matter.

"Did they even ask you where you got it…?"

He balks a bit, shaking his head.

Exactly. They don't need to ask because they already know.

"I guess we'll just have to wait and see what happens," I mutter, choosing to change the subject. I'd rather not stress about something I can't control. "How was solitary?"

He snorts. "Fookin' great. On my way back, I saw that preppy little creep… The *Carver.*"

"Felix Darcey?" My brows zip.

The infamous serial killer has been here for a couple of months, but we don't see him much. They started keeping him isolated, since pandemonium tends to break out any time he's around the rest of us.

Well, the crazier of us.

"Yeah. Got himself a cellmate," O'Malley huffs.

Now I'm even more surprised. "Really?"

He nods. "Yeh know that new preck who came in the other day, then disappeared? Big, dumb-lookin' fook…"

"Oh, yea…" I hum, thinking back to seeing the guy for two seconds, then never seeing him again. "His name's Wilkerson. I just assumed he switched groups."

O'Malley shakes his head. "He's in a cushy, private cell with preppy boy. I heard the little nutter went on a hunger strike or some shit, demanding a cellmate. Velle must've caved."

A breath puffs from my lips. "Well, that… sounds like a bad idea."

But it doesn't necessarily surprise me. Felix Darcey is a hot commodity in Manuel Blanco's collection of twisted trophies. *Makes sense that they'd give in to his every spoiled demand.*

O'Malley laughs. "Put me in with him… I'll fook 'im up. That boy ain't shit."

He jumps up and starts bouncing around, play-boxing while talking shit about The Carver. And I'm just shaking my head.

I dunno… You can never be sure what's inside someone else's mind, right? The kinds of secrets we hold…

Kieran O'Malley wears his issues on his sleeve. That's one way of doing it, I guess. But I know for a fact there are certain things he refuses to talk about. Like his crimes, for example.

What he did to his little brother…

I'm sure Felix Darcey has done similar shit. He wouldn't be here if he hadn't.

Crazy doesn't always *look* crazy.

Thoughts are cluttering my mind, and I don't like it. I need to get them out. Unfortunately, O'Malley is still prancing around, ranting about nonsense, and I don't want to risk going for my secret stash spot while he's awake. He's fucking nosy, and while I don't mind sharing my toothpaste or the occasional cigarette with him, there's *one* hidden item I can't have him—or anyone else, for that matter—finding.

The sudden, clunking footsteps indicative of a correctional officer up the row pause my swirling secrets. Officer Hancock comes strutting over, then stops in front of our cell.

Odd… We're supposed to be in for the night.

"On your feet, 62," he says vacantly, then barks at O'Malley, "You… Over there. Hug the wall."

I gape at him before glancing at O'Malley, who looks just as uneasy as I'm sure I do.

"What is this?" O'Malley places his palms flat on the opposite wall while I stand up slowly. "I just got back!"

"I don't care about you," Hancock breathes out, like he's already exhausted by the sheer act of talking to us. He nods at me. "Turn around."

What the hell??

Rather than arguing, I do as he says, despite my internal unease. There's no point in fighting it. I'm most likely going to solitary, or to The Box… *Somewhere they can torture me because of that goddamn cellphone.*

Still, I make sure to shoot O'Malley one last *this is your fault* look while Hancock cuffs me and drags me away. In his defense, he does appear pretty guilty. But that won't save me from whatever the fuck they're about to do.

Nervous chills are rushing across my skin, and I can't help it. As hard a shell as I try to build up around myself, it's no use. This place has a way of breaking through even the sturdiest of barriers.

I've been here for nearly three years. Sometimes I feel like I've spent that time turning myself to stone. Other times, I'm just as scared, lonely, and sad as I was the day I woke up strapped to that chair…

"Wait a minute…" I mumble. Mostly to myself, since I know Herby Hancock doesn't care what I have to say. "We're not going down…"

"No talking, inmate," he growls, unsurprisingly.

But this is weird…

Why are we going… up?

Why are we crossing over... to the West Wing?

For some reason, this is causing me to shake even harder. I expected solitary, the East, The Box. I expected *torture*. As far as I know, none of that happens on the west side of the prison.

You'd think heading in the opposite direction of misery would be comforting, but it's not. Not even a little.

Inmates rarely come over here. Because it's where *he* is...

Hancock brings me up some stairs—*actual fucking stairs!* There are no stairs anywhere else in the Pen. It's bizarre as hell, made even stranger by the fact that there actually *are* stairs. Just not on our side, apparently.

God, this building is like The Labyrinth meets Kubrick meets fucking M.C. Escher.

It's insane how much higher up I feel just from walking upstairs for the first time in three years. The altitude is making me high.

Hm, that's funny.

Hancock stops me in front of a door, silencing everything in my head. He knocks, and I'm just standing, *shivering*, in place, with my hands cuffed behind my back.

I'm sure I know who's on the other side of this door... *But I don't wanna think about it.*

"Come," the voice calls, and my teeth set, a long breath leaving my lungs.

Fuck.

The door opens, and I'm shoved through, into the middle of a wide-open space. Before me is a window displaying the ocean, barely illuminated by the setting sun. A desk, large and richly brown—something like mahogany.

And of course, The Ivory. Sitting behind it, his gaze focused on the screen of a MacBook.

He's not even paying attention to me, but I'm fidgeting in place, feeling like I'm on display. The room isn't huge, but it's big enough that everything feels especially spread apart right now. There's nowhere to hide.

"You want me to take the cuffs off, sir?" Hancock asks, startling me when his voice breaks through the silence. *I forgot he was there for a second.*

"That'll be all, Officer," The Ivory sings, deliberately ignoring the question while making a condescending *shoo* motion with his hand.

I peer over my shoulder at Hancock while he scowls and storms off, closing the door behind him.

Shit... He's gone.

My face slowly tilts back in the Warden's direction, and I gulp.

Why am I here?

What does he want??

Questions litter my brain while I stand still and wait for him to say or do something. It feels like an hour before he finally sighs and closes the laptop, folding his hands on top of it.

Then he locks his black eyes on mine, and his mouth quirks. "How are you, Byron?"

I swallow another lump, mouth dry as a bone. "Um… fine."

His eyes narrow into slits, a threatening look if I've ever seen one. I shift awkwardly.

"Thank you for asking. H-how are you…?"

He makes a small noise, not quite a chuckle. More of a puff of air accompanied by a smirk. He cocks his head. "I have to say, I'd be a lot better if you hadn't stashed a cellphone in the basement rec room…"

Well, fuck me. That's it.

I'm completely screwed.

Allowing myself a moment to sift through various responses, I watch him cautiously as he blinks up at me from his fancy-looking desk chair. "I don't—"

"Come here, please," he cuts me off with a stern command. I don't want to. And my feet know that, refusing to take a step. But he hisses, "That wasn't a request, inmate."

The look on his face is causing a stiffness to take over my body, nerves bunching up, keeping me tense. But I have no choice but to obey him. I mean, what's the alternative?

He's in charge. There's no free will here.

I'm at the mercy of Manuel Blanco.

Stepping over to his desk, I stop right in front of it, by the two chairs he has on this side. But he's not satisfied. I can tell just from the way he's glaring at me wordlessly. So I keep walking, taking tentative steps, while still moving briskly enough that he doesn't yell at me for taking too long.

Now, I'm on his side of the desk, standing before him while he sits. He swivels his chair, peering up at me, displaying a more contented expression.

"There you go," he chirps, slapping his hands down on his knees. I flinch. "That wasn't so hard, was it?"

"What am I doing here?" I blurt out the question, a bit more hostile than I meant to sound.

But the wondering is stressing me out. I don't like feeling vulnerable like this. I hate it, in fact.

Obviously, *he* likes it. It's why he does stuff like this… Plays this cat-and-mouse game. Toying with you before he sinks his teeth in.

I'd rather he just snap my neck and get it over with.

Naturally, he stays quiet for way too long before finally responding, "I wanted to check in with you. About the cellphone." He sits back in his chair. "Who were you planning to contact?"

He asks the question as if he already knows, and it turns my stomach. *Because I'm sure he does.*

"No one," I mutter. "I wanted to play *Candy Crush.*"

This time, he actually laughs. Even so, it's a low, growly, *I can't believe your audacity* sort of sound.

"Byron, you seem to forget that I've always given you the benefit of the doubt." He lifts a light eyebrow, and I gulp. "Never once have I interfered in your affairs, or held you accountable, despite your often questionable choices…"

"Like what?" I seethe defensively. It just comes out, like the quip of a petulant child.

But he gives me an obvious look that has me shrinking into myself. "I can only hope you know what you're doing." He sighs. "I'd hate to see such potential squandered on some pretty blue eyes and a brilliantly deceptive mouth."

Now my jaw is clenched so tightly, my teeth are aching. "I have no idea what you're talking about…"

The Ivory shakes his head admonishingly, giving me that *tsk-tsk* bullshit. Heated shame is rushing up my neck, and it's pissing me the fuck off. "I know it feels good in the moment, but he'll never be your Michelangelo…"

In an instant, I'm set ablaze. His words, the match on my puddle of kerosene.

Launching at him, I lean in close, hovering over him while my chest heaves with rage. If my hands weren't cuffed behind my back, I'd be grabbing him by the throat. Undoubtedly a terrible idea, but I can't help it. I'm fast-fuming.

"You don't get to say that name to me," I snarl. "I'm done playing games. I'd rather you just slit my throat and be done with it."

The Ivory is entirely unaffected by my threatening stance. *Of course.*

If anything, it's just entertaining him more. Straightening, he inches his face up to mine, holding me still with those black irises.

"My sweet Byron," he whispers over my mouth. "Where's the fun in that?"

In a snap, he grabs me by the shoulders and shoves me to my knees. I crash onto the floor with a wince, but I don't have time to register the pain because *his* hand is around *my* throat.

"I cannot *believe* how ungrateful you're being," he hisses, long fingers digging into me. "Do you know that I believed you from day one, Byron? I saw the truth in you when no one else did, and this is the thanks I get?!" His tone is taking on a maniacal volume as his grip tightens, cutting off my air supply. "You should be *bowing* at my feet, you little shit. We're done playing when *I say* we're done *fucking playing.*"

Having him in my face, saying these words, is infinitely more terrifying than him choking me. He's not loud by any means, and yet he's roaring at me like a malicious beast. I know he could tear me to shreds with his bare hands, and he'd probably love to do it.

But Manuel Blanco's weapon of choice has been, and always will be, his ability to get inside your head…

And turn it into his personal playground.

The fear, the way my pulse is rapping frantically beneath his palm, the deranged twinkle in his obsidian eyes… On my knees while evil bares its teeth right in front of my face. It sends an unexpected lightning bolt through my insides.

I don't understand it, not one single fucking bit. But my skin is balmy, and my lips are quivering.

"I'm… s-sorry," I croak, blinking a hazy gaze up at him.

His grip loosens slightly, as if I've uttered the magic words. And he growls, "Say it again."

"I'm so sorry," I breathe. He loosens more. "Sir…"

A hum rumbles from within his throat, dark eyes falling to my mouth.

I feel like I've been strung up by my feet. My blood is rushing, fire burning me from the inside out, flushing my entire body until I'm sweating.

I can't believe this is happening to me again…

"Why do you insist on testing my patience, inmate?" He finally releases my throat, sliding his fingers to cup my jaw. "You know how much worse I can make things for you…"

I don't really know what he's talking about. It barely even seems like he's talking to me…

And yet, I nod. Rippling with fear, but also some bizarre heat. "I know."

"Is it because you... like it?" Fingertips brush over my bottom lip.

I can't move, let alone speak. There's *no way* I can admit this out loud... *Because it's fucking crazy.*

The Ivory moves back a bit, reclining in his chair as he gazes down at me curiously, still touching my mouth. "You don't have to say it, I suppose..." He sighs. "But you will stay down there until some part of you gives me what I want."

Blinking up at him, I'm buzzing from head to toe. Shivering and shaking, my head is spinning off of my body with a whirlwind of memories... A collection of secrets at the forefront of my consciousness.

And this time, when his fingers trace the seam of my lips, they part. And I let him stuff them inside.

Fuck...

My mind sighs as my body unfurls. Like it's *finally* being fed after far too long wasting away in captivity.

In an instant, I'm lost. Wandering through the darkest mist of my deepest, most confusing desires. I suck on his fingers, *desperately*, my cock already rock hard and visible. But I don't care.

Whatever. I'm done fighting.

This is always how it happens... It keeps bubbling, rising to the surface until it inevitably boils over, and I just... overflow.

"Mmm... I knew you wanted it, *pajarito*," he croons, thrusting his fingers in and out of my mouth, rhythmically slow. I have no clue what that word means, but my mouth is sloppy wet, and I'm fucking *crumbling*. "There's no point in running. I'll always *catch* you."

H-huh...?

"Mm-mm," I object, shaking my head. Though it's obvious bullshit because my dick is straining against the flimsy material of my jumpsuit pants and I'm sucking hungrily on his fingers like a needy slut.

He rumbles, one of those chuckle sounds, tugging them out carefully. I whimper, and he faux pouts. "You might be my favorite of all the damaged souls in this place, you know that?"

"Why?" I whisper, dazed and burning with shame. "Because I'm easy prey...?"

"Oh, far from it, my angry boy." He soothes me with a soft touch, threading fingers through my hair. Then he yanks it, hard, and I mewl from the delicious pain. "Your brokenness is your best quality."

The rationality in my brain knows that none of this falsified praise is real. He's using me, toying with me for his own sick amusement. I'm not stupid.

But the cold hard truth is that ever since the moment that got me locked up here—the night I gave in to my truth and lost my life for it—I've been *begging* for a reason to feel again. Searching for my next secret.

Anything to get me as high as he did.

The Ivory tugs me closer by my hair, while his other hand works on his belt. "Show me your *sorrow*, shadow creature."

I barely even recognize where I am, or what I'm doing anymore. All I know is that my mouth is filling with saliva as he pulls out a very, *very* long dick...

And shoves it between my waiting lips.

Taking it with a startled grunt, my cock instantly leaks in my pants. The sensation of smooth flesh covering a deliciously hard object resting on my tongue has my eyes rolling back in my head. And before I can overthink it, I'm bobbing. Sucking and *chasing*, while reacquainting myself with this action.

It's been a while—*not that long*—but it comes back to me quickly, like muscle memory. Relaxing my throat, I let him slide back, gagging a little, but gulping all the same. The taste of salt and clean, soft flesh wrapped around a thick, solid shaft curls my toes and throbs my balls.

I swear to God, I could have a full blown orgasm just from this. Or a million little ones, either way.

I don't get it. I don't fucking *understand* this *need*, and I never have. But I'm also not trying to think about anything right now.

No labels, no consequences.

No fighting.

Just fucking.

"Greedy boy," The Ivory purrs while fucking in and out of my mouth. I catch a spurt on my tongue, and I groan, sucking it all out and swallowing as he growls, "*Hungry* boy..."

Suddenly, there's a knock at the door. And every single thing I was just feeling is stomped out in an instant of fast, petrified regret.

Oh God, oh Jesus... Who is that??

They're gonna see me in here. They're gonna know, and they're gonna tell someone.

Everyone is going to find out what I do, who I am, what I am.

My secrets will all be exposed, and then I'll just be...

Out in the open.

Bright lights shining in my face.

I'm frozen, dick still in my mouth, just gawking up at him with wide, watery eyes, asking a wordless question. *What do I do??* Followed by a silent plea. *Please please please, don't let them know…*

The Warden swallows visibly. Then he scoots forward in his chair, removing himself from my mouth while shoving me underneath his desk with his legs.

"Come in," he calls to whomever is knocking.

I'm terrified. Shaking so hard, my body is spasming. But I press my lips together and keep absolutely still. Staring at The Ivory's dick while someone enters his office.

Jesus fucking Christ, what am I doing??

Whose life is this?!

The Warden tucks himself away—though it doesn't seem to *want* to go away, a fact I'm not trying to think about right now—zipping up his fly with someone in his office. It's fucking whacked. I have no goddamn clue what's happening, but I'm radiating two very different things…

Explicit fear, and illicit thrill.

"Never you mind what's happening in here, Officer," he says to the person. Even from under his desk, I can hear a faint smirk in his voice. "How can I help you?"

But then I zero in on his words. *Clearly, the person is suspicious of something… And why wouldn't they be?? He literally just zipped up in front of them.*

My limbs are jittering from nerves *and* the pain of being cuffed behind my back for so long, but I'm trying to hold them steady, to keep the cuffs from making noise.

"Wilkerson's dead. Darcey," the deep male brogue speaks, and I recognize it instantly.

It's Velle. *Fuck.*

Fuck fuckity fucking fuck!

He's the last person I'd ever want to find out about this!

Side note: Darcey killed Wilkerson already??

Damn, the kid works quick.

Holding my breath, I watch as The Ivory's hands rest on his knees, and he leans back in his chair, obviously not fazed by his shirt still being untucked and his belt being open.

"Do you know what I'm going to say, Jonathan?" He speaks so casually, so polished and engaging… I have to stop from answering him myself.

"Ivan Wilkerson was a waste of space, yes, but the fact remains. No one can know about this. Do you understand?"

Obviously, he's not talking to me. But that sure is a purposeful thing to say when there's literally another person in the room and they both know it.

"So you'll have to take care of it." He continues firmly. "Yourself."

The room is silent for a moment, while I'm trembling, crouched under this goddamn desk, scared as hell of making a peep.

"I don't want to do it again..." Velle whispers, soft and more vulnerable than I could ever imagine him sounding.

"But you must, Jonathan," The Ivory counters. "You're the only one I can trust to do so."

This is nuts. This conversation I'm overhearing is almost as insane as the fact that I'm under the Warden's desk right now, jaw sore from sucking his giant, evil dick.

It wouldn't take a genius to decode what they're sort of dancing around here.

Wilkerson's dead. No one can know. You have to take care of it.

All signs point to The Ivory making Velle dispose of the body.

But Velle said... *I don't want to do it again.* Meaning, he's done it before.

My spine stiffens. *How many times? How many bodies??*

How often has Velle taken care of *something for him?*

My guess would be a lot.

I don't have time to obsess over it any further, though. Because the Warden is slowly lowering his zipper once more.

Um... what?

Reaching forward, he grasps my jaw, tugging me back to his cock. And just like before, the hesitation is minimal. I give in easily and welcome him back into my mouth.

I mean... I'm already down here...

Might as well ride this wicked locomotive straight to hell.

Easing myself in between his legs for a better position, I pick up where I left off, losing myself in blowing him. Bobbing up and down beneath his desk, slurping on the Warden's thick cock while *John fucking Chevelle*, Head Correctional Officer of Alabaster Pen and one of Manuel Blanco's most loyal pets, is standing right on the other side of this sturdy wooden structure.

Watching...? I assume he is. I haven't heard him move.

And the idea that he might be... intrigued by this little show, or maybe even *aroused* by it, has me pulsing even more precum into my already damp boxers.

I'm out of my fucking mind. Practically in outer space. This is so intense; I feel like I could come and cry and collapse all at once. In fact, there are tears streaming down my cheeks, and now my dick won't stop leaking. My mouth is overflowing with saliva, helping me to suck sloppily. It's probably loud, but I can barely hear anything over the rush of blood in my ears.

"I know you'll handle it, Jonathan. Because you're strong… and capable…" The Warden goes on speaking, but his voice is echoey and muffled, being drowned out by the sounds of messy wet suction and my soft, eager little secret slut breaths.

He sounds sinister. In my head, he's Satan.

And I'm on my knees, cuffed, under his desk… Sucking on the wicked dick of Lucifer. *The fallen angel.*

His fingers caress my face gently as he croons, "You're just what I need, you know that, right?"

I nod frantically, sucking almost mercilessly on his big cock, sticking my tongue out to cradle the shaft, trying like hell to throat him deep enough to lick his balls.

Am I doing well for you?

Are you enjoying this?

Use my mouth… Fuck, *please pour cum down my fucking throat, evil Daddy.*

"Good boy," he praises, and I fucking break.

Cum begins throbbing uncontrollably from my cock, soaking the entire inside of my boxers. It feels like I'm melting into a puddle, just trying to breathe through my nose and not openly weep on him while he asks Velle, "Will that be all, Officer?"

Velle mumbles a weak, "Yes, sir." Then I hear him stomping away, leaving and closing the door behind him.

My sucking has slowed way down, but I'm still on it, basking in the high of what just happened. A wave of vitality washes over me, unlike anything I've ever felt. A fullness, *completion*, but also control. I've never felt so powerful… It's wild.

This… is what Ren feels.

This is what he *felt.*

The Ivory scoots back just enough to gaze down at me. His dark eyes are glittering with ravenous desire.

"This is an exceptional mouth," he rasps, swiping a wetness from my cheek with his thumb. "You nearly had me spilling into you while he was standing right there."

Please please please please please…

More.

"Keep going, wicked boy," he whispers, closing his eyes and reclining in his chair. "I'm sending you back with a belly full of cum."

In this moment, I'm watching myself from outside the glass…

Through the window, I see myself, sucking the cock of a villain. I'm gazing with eyes widened in disbelief.

I see *myself* in the bedroom with the dark-haired stranger. He's on top of *me*, pushing *my* legs open…

What the fuck…?

God, fuck me…

The Ivory stiffens, his lids growing visibly heavy. He bites his lip. *It's…* so *pink.*

Then he lets out a sweet, breathy grunt before his long cock bursts, and he spills hot cum into my throat. It's pulsing in waves, and I'm gulping them back, swallowing and sucking, so far outside of myself, I'm not sure I'll ever make it back.

Of course, I do. It only takes a few moments for the high to wear off. And a thick bout of nausea overtakes me, smothering me like a weighted blanket.

"Shush," The Ivory says, still petting me as he pulls his softening dick away and tucks it back into his pants. "Calm now. No need to panic."

My head is shaking back and forth. I'm *freaking out*, on the verge of a massive anxiety attack.

I just want to get out of here.

Let me out…

I want… out.

Crawling out from under his desk, I go to stand, wobbling so bad I nearly fall down. He stands before me, steadying me with his hands on my waist.

"D-don't t-touch me," I stammer, lightheaded. "Just let me… out."

"Byron, look at me," he snaps, grasping my face. I blink over and over to stop unwanted tears from bursting out of my eye sockets.

I don't understand… what that was.

Who am I??

What am I doing??

What… am I?

"Fuck off," I growl at him. "You… forced me to do that."

He rolls his eyes. "Don't be boring. You sucked my dick, Byron. And you loved it. You came all over yourself, and do you know why?"

Because I'm fucking sick too…

"Because you're *hungry*," he rumbles, eyes set on mine while I tremble and fight for breath. "You've been starved, and I fed you. Simple as that."

I bite my lip.

"It's okay to want in secret. It's okay to play in secret, to unleash in secret… To *let go* in secret. Just remember that who you are in the shadows is also who you are in the light." He leans in and presses a soft kiss on my lower lip. It's so unexpected, it stops my shivers, like the snap of a hypnotist's fingers. "And who you are… is *my* property."

Another knock at the door has me squirming again.

"Come in," he says with the brush of his thumb over my lip.

He steps away from me just as Hancock comes trudging into his office. I'm not even sure how he knew to show up right now, but I'm too busy gawking at the Warden and praying to whoever wants to listen that no one notices the huge wet spot on my pants.

"Bring Mr. Kang to solitary," the Warden says to Hancock, smirking at me. "He needs some time alone with his thoughts."

You… fucking… monster.

CHAPTER SEVEN

Byron's Book of Secrets

"Ghost Rider"

Here's the thing about conformity To a certain extent, it's primal. Part of human nature is to bond with your fellow species.

Animals do it. They flock, or pack, tribe or clowder. And while human beings are evolved enough to value individual identity, we *still* possess this baser instinct to bond with others. To be *accepted* by the group.

Even though I knew I'd never be like my mother and father, or my sister and her husband, I still found myself on the outside looking in Wondering if maybe there was some way I could make them accept me, even just a little.

That was why my relationship with Rey was so important. Being with her made me a real person. Not only in my family's eyes, but in my own too. It was like I'd finally found something that brought me out of the shadows.

A relationship with a beautiful girl, one who I could bring home to my family. It was just what I needed. For that reason more than anything else, I *could not* accept that Rey was sleeping with someone else. It just didn't fit the picture I'd created of us in my head.

As far as I was concerned, everything had been *fine* until she started fucking that guy.

I mean, who even was that asshole?? Where did he come from??

I was in an emotional tailspin. It was insufferable. I had to do something. I needed to know *more*.

So I fell into my default mode and went back to following her. All of my spare time was spent watching Rey, stewing in frustrated consternation. The obsession had become stronger than my feelings for her ever were, and that only served to piss me off more.

Then one night, when I was outside watching her window from the street, someone familiar showed up. It was *the guy*.

That *asshole* who'd been fucking my girlfriend. The one who ruined *everything*.

I watched him enter her building, barely waiting two minutes before I was climbing up her fire escape to spy on them through her bedroom window again.

He looked to be about my age. White guy, maybe twenty-three to twenty-five, with dark hair and these pretty-boy dimples I just wanted to smash repeatedly with my fists.

Not ten minutes into him arriving, they were already getting naked. I could barely fucking see, I was so irate.

This is what she was blowing me off for? Mediocre sex with some random fuckboy?

Really, Rey?? Him??

What the fuck is so special about him?!

I watched them with every muscle in my body stiffening. I didn't exactly want to see what they were doing together, but I couldn't make my eyes look away from his hands on her. The way he pushed her legs apart and tore open the condom wrapper with his teeth before rolling it onto his

Fuck, I felt sick. I was dizzy and sweaty, and I had to grip the railing to make sure I didn't fall off the goddamn fire escape.

Who are you? I wondered, jaw clamped as I watched his hips move, pumping his cock into her, over and over and *over*.

Lost in a haze of strife and internal doubt, I couldn't move. My breathing shallowed, though my heart was leaping up my throat. I wanted to leave, but I *couldn't*. I was in some sort of trance, physically unable to drag my eyes away from the prick who'd stolen my girlfriend. The pretty boy with the chiseled body and the silky hair *Ruining* my *life* without a care in the world.

The next thing I knew, they were done, and he was leaving.

Pfftt. Pathetic. I lasted like four times longer.

Snapping out of it, I made a quick decision to climb down from the fire escape and jog over to my bike. As soon as the fucker came out of her building, without a moment's hesitation, I followed him.

He drove a black Mercedes AMG I'm sure that made him feel superior to a lot of people. Having a car, especially a nice one, is a flex in New York City, due to how expensive it is. He was probably some rich boy, a theory that was confirmed when he drove that thing all the way up to Harlem and parked it in front of a townhouse. He hopped out of the car and went inside, like the obvious narcissist he was.

As if I wasn't smoldering enough already, when I strolled

inconspicuously over to his car, I found it parked in front of a sign that read *City Government Permit Parking Only.*

What the fuck?? Either he works for the city, or he's so entitled that he just parks wherever

But sure enough, there was a *City of New York Gov* parking pass sticker on the inside of his windshield. Plus, he had special license plates.

Bemused, I peered at his building. *Who the hell was this guy?* He didn't look old enough to be working for the government Unless he was an intern? Or maybe someone from the mayor's office?

I was beyond confused and *itching* for details. The dude clearly had money, and some sort of important job, two things I didn't. We were comfortable because of my grandfather, but that didn't exactly equal townhouses on St. Nicholas Ave.

A ping on my phone snapped me out of my thoughts. It was an alert for a DoorDash order in my area. One *Michelangelo Russo* had ordered from the Just Salad on Columbus, to be delivered to—

I blinked at the address on the screen, my gaze lifting to the building before me.

119 St. Nicholas and 126th.

Well, I'll be a monkey's uncle

My lips twitched with a pure, serendipitous thrill as I accepted the delivery order.

The entire way to pick up the food, my head was swirling. I wasn't *positive* that the person I was about to deliver to was *the guy.* It seemed too good to be true. Still, even getting into the building would be helpful. I began concocting a story, making up things to say in the event that there was a doorman or something.

With Michelangelo's crispy chicken poblano in tow, I whipped Raph back into Harlem, all the while fizzling with nervous excitement. I couldn't stop wondering if this could be him Michelangelo. I really hoped it wasn't. The fuckface who'd been screwing my girlfriend didn't deserve a cool name like *Michelangelo.*

The silliest of the Ninja Turtles, but an integral part of the team. *He's a party dude. Can't blame him for being the jester of the group.*

Scoffing at my thoughts, I turned onto his block, contemplating what I would do if it *was* him. Would I confront him for sleeping with Rey? Maybe punch him in the face?

I wasn't sure, but I was allowing the adrenaline to fuel me. It felt good. Something about this was a hell of a lot more exciting than my usual stalking game. Maybe it was the idea of revenge

Sucking in a breath, I grabbed the takeout bag and stomped up the stoop. When I checked the intercom system at the door, it had only one name *Russo.*

Son of a bitch He owns the whole place?? How??

Lifting the visor on my helmet, I pressed the call button. And the next thing I knew, the door was buzzing. I pushed through the front door, stopping at a second. A thin pane of glass allowed me to see inside the extremely fancy apartment of opulent decor and wide-open space. Just a *massive* townhouse, indicative of old New York. Old money.

That toolbag can't possibly own this place.

But sure enough, there he was. Padding over, barefoot and bare-chested, wearing only gray sweatpants, his dark hair the same manner of tousled it had been when he left Rey's.

My teeth ground together as he pulled open the door, wrath clouding my brain and tightening muscles all over my body. I felt pretty confident that I might attack him

Until he smiled.

"Hey, thanks so much," the dude rumbled politely.

His voice was deep and sort of raspy, those few words spoken in the tone and perfect diction of an actor on Broadway or something. He certainly looked the part

Blinking myself out of whatever had just frozen me solid, I extended the arm holding his food, and he took it. Our eyes met through the small opening in my helmet, and it was the strangest, most insane thing I'd ever felt As if my lungs were shriveling.

All the air just *whooshed* right out of me.

His head cocked, and it took me a moment to realize I was still holding the bag. His blue eyes fell to my hand, fingertips exposed by my fingerless gloves.

"Sorry," I croaked, barely audible as I released the bag quickly.

He chuckled, then hummed teasingly, "No harm, Ghost Rider." The dimples were even more intense up close. "Have a good night."

What the fuck is wrong with you?? I remember thinking to myself. *Do something! Call him out! Judo kick him in the face!*

But I just cleared my throat and muttered, "You too."

Then spun and stormed out of his stupid townhouse, kicking myself for being such a fucking loser. I totally bitched out. And I hated myself for it.

Waiting until my bike's engine roared to life, I growled out loud. "What the hell was that?!"

What a goddamn waste! You were supposed to fuck him up! He screwed your girlfriend and all you can do is stare at the guy?!

Pathetic.

Needless to say, I didn't sleep well that night. All I could think about was *Michelangelo Russo* The dude who'd stolen Rey from me and then had the nerve to *smile* in my face like everything was fucking *fine*. Like he wasn't some rich daddy's boy living in a two-story townhouse, ordering food and looking like *that* and giving me stupid fucking nicknames.

Who does that??

He didn't know me. We weren't pals. As far as he knew, I didn't exist, and that was what carried me into the next few weeks.

By all accounts, I was done following Rey. I'd moved on to her blue-eyed fuckboy.

Unfortunately, stalking Michelangelo was infinitely more frustrating than anything I'd experienced with Rey, or anyone else, for that matter. He was *impossible* to get a read on. Every time I thought I'd figured him out in some way, he'd switch things up and throw a wrench in my judgements.

As it turned out, he wasn't dating Rey at all. They never crossed paths again the entire time I spent watching him. He did, however, go out to bars and flirt with *other* girls—which only verified Rey's casual hookup persona. Because of this, I assumed Michelangelo was just another rich Tinder fuckboy in Manhattan, sleeping with girls left and right.

But it didn't really happen that way. For all the girls I saw him hit on, he never brought any home. I followed him on one Tinder date, and it went about the same way it had with Rey. He went home with her, they fucked quick—*less than ten minutes*—and then he left.

Yes, I watched. Grow up.

So he *wasn't* a playboy. And as much as I wanted him to be, he wasn't an arrogant jerk either. In fact, a lot of the qualities that had drawn me to Rey were also popping up as I watched Michelangelo. He stopped to give money and food to homeless people, as well as help tourists with directions—*patiently*, I might add. He volunteered work with inner-city kids and helped old ladies carry their groceries. He paid for the coffee of whomever was behind him in line *every time* he went to Starbucks.

He spent a lot of time in the gym, but not in a douchey way, like his friends did. Rather, he simply enjoyed staying in shape and keeping active. Like *me*.

Most of the time when he went out with people, he'd find excuses to break away from the herd. And when he'd sit alone, gazing at his phone screen as our generation does, he wouldn't be scrolling Instagram or TikTok Usually, he'd be reading. Sometimes it seemed like he was playing a game, though I could never see which one. I desperately wanted it to be *Call of Duty* or something stupid like that. *Anything* to make him less unique, and more like the shallow, predictable *dudebro* he was *supposed* to be.

Knowing him, it was probably Pokemon *fucking* Go.

As it would happen, Michelangelo Russo was a rare and remarkable aberration. His personality just didn't fit. And it made me despise him all the more.

No one who looks like that, with that kind of money, and such an obvious plutocratic pedigree, is ever so genuine. So thoughtful, interesting and sweet.

Ugh.

I couldn't stand how unpredictable he was. How *cool* he was. And the craziest part was that the more I watched him, the more addicted I became to watching him. It made no sense

I should've stopped once I found out he had no interest in dating Rey, but I didn't. I *couldn't*. Without even realizing it, I'd become obsessed.

I *hated* him, I knew I did. That was the one and only reason I was still stalking him. It had to be. Because if not, then *why?*

One night, as I sat outside a community theater for hours while he was in there, it dawned on me I hadn't even *thought* about Rey in almost a week.

This whole thing was supposed to be about her. If it wasn't, then *what the fuck was I doing??*

My emotions were running high. The void *Rey* was supposed to fill had somehow been filled by *this fucking guy*. And it confused me so deeply, I began to simmer, on the verge of a rage blackout. I followed him home, where I sat stubbornly and waited for that golden opportunity to present itself. I was making this happen tonight. *No more bullshit.*

I was going to flip Michelangelo Russo upside-fucking-down.

It took a while, though not as long as you'd think. Eventually, his name popped up on DoorDash, and I had my *in*. I got his food and brought it to him, just like the last time. Only this time, I had a more concrete plan.

You know what they say about making plans, right?

He came to the door in just his joggers again, showing off that damn perfectly sculpted eight-pack covered in smooth, unmarked olive skin. I swallowed roughly, forcing myself to look anywhere else. He was holding a stack of papers as he jaunted over, and I managed to sneak a peek at them It looked like a script.

So he *was* an actor. Or at least he was trying to be. *The community theater thing makes sense now*

"Hey, again," he murmured as I handed him the takeout bag. He tilted his head, a curious gleam in his ocean eyes. "You ever take that helmet off?"

"Sometimes " I grumbled stupidly, and he chuckled. My jaw ticked while my stomach flipped, and I cleared my throat to distract myself from it. "Rehearsing?" I nodded to the papers in his hand.

"*Auditioning*," he corrected in a humbled, almost self-deprecating tone. As if he didn't think he was good enough for whatever he was doing, but he was going to do it, anyway.

I could relate *But damn him for once again being so real.*

"For what?" I asked, though not sure *why*.

He peeked at me, our eyes connecting through the open visor of my helmet. "*Little Shop of Horrors*."

"Cool," I breathed. "Well I hope you get it."

What are you doing?? Why would you say that??

He smiled bright, perfectly straight white teeth on display. "Thanks, Ghost Rider."

"Mhm " I turned away before I could implicate myself anymore.

I heard him hum, "Goodnight," behind me, but I was more focused on the tape I'd subtly slipped over the door mechanism.

I wandered around for a couple of hours, waiting for him to go to sleep, all the while wondering what in the hell I was even doing. I was being driven by something else entirely, something I didn't understand, but that filled me with an almost thrilling sense of mortality.

Usually, my stalking was just harmless fun. Some might call it weird, or creepy—or *illegal*—and all of those things would be accurate. But I'd gotten used to doing it over the years. I was comfortable with it. It *comforted* me.

I've always been the quiet kid. The kid with only a handful of friends, but who preferred being alone. None of my friends really knew me, but it was okay. Because I was better at being in the shadows, anyway. *Still am.*

But something about Michelangelo had a very real hold on me. I just hoped, for my sanity's sake, that breaking in and breaking *him* would break the spell.

When the lights turned off in his townhouse, I went back and crept inside quietly. Stealth, like a cat burglar or a jewel thief. Helmet off, but still protected by my face mask, just in case.

Adrenaline had my pulse popping as I wandered farther inside. The rush I got from doing this was unlike *anything* I'd felt before. Being inside someone's space without them knowing It got me so much higher than simply *watching* ever had.

Chills of excitement wove through my limbs while I snuck around a corner, peeking left and right, listening for any noise. He seemed to live alone, which was still odd to me. The place was *enormous*—at least one visible set of stairs leading to another floor. And the decor wasn't what you'd expect of a twenty-something Broadway kid. It looked like they'd used John Gotti's decorator.

In his sitting room, I went for some framed photos on the mantle. And right there, front and center, was the explanation for all of it.

It was Michelangelo smiling, standing in between an older couple who were clearly his parents. I recognized them immediately.

Michelangelo *Russo*. As in Antonio *Russo*. The Governor of New York.

Michelangelo is Governor Russo's son.

"Holy fucking shit " I whispered, an instant ball of dread forming in my gut.

I'd just broken into the governor's home. I was standing in the *Governor of New York's* fucking living room, after having stalked his son incessantly for almost a month.

My first instinct was to flee. To run the fuck out of there and never look back—it certainly would've been the *smart* thing to do. But instead, I took a moment to breathe and think.

Clearly, this wasn't Governor Russo's primary residence. I was pretty sure I remembered hearing that he lived in Long Island somewhere. This was most likely just his place in the city he used occasionally. Where his *son* lived, like the entitled, wealthy-as-fuck son of a politician he undoubtedly was.

Despite how fucking nuts this revelation was, I couldn't deny that I felt powerful. I was standing in Governor Russo's home, amongst his personal belongings With his son sleeping right above my head. My heart was beating faster than it had in years, and the need to chase that feeling was unrelenting.

So, rather than slinking out of there with my tail between my legs, I made my way upstairs. On a mission, with one objective.

The place was eerily quiet. It was so big, darkness shrouding me from all angles. I truly was a shadowman, drifting a long corridor to follow a light at the end.

The dull glow coming from what I imagined was Michelangelo's bedroom lured me closer, until I was just outside, limbs jittering with nervous electricity. When I peered through the crack in the doorway, I spotted him right away. Lying in his bed

Naked. Eyes closed, with his dick in his fist.

What the fuck.

Swallowing became impossible. My breathing instantly sped up, and I had to focus on keeping it quiet. I was so caught off-guard, I didn't know what to do with myself. For a few heavy seconds, I was stuck. Just *staring*, eyes gliding over the curves and contours of his body on display, bathed in blue light from the TV across the room. Which I then realized was playing porn

Gay porn.

Jesus Christ What in the holiest of fucks?!

It was muted, so all I could hear were his breaths and my blood rushing in my ears. I *wanted* to leave. But just like when I watched him with Rey, I couldn't. I couldn't move.

Because I didn't want to?

It made no sense. I wasn't interested in men. I wasn't *attracted* to what I was seeing. At least, I didn't think I was

I was stunned. That was it. It was a *surprise*.

Just another thing I hadn't expected from him.

"What the—" The sound of his gasp stiffened my spine, causing me to jump.

He'd spotted me. *Fuck*, he was looking *right fucking at me*. Eyes wide with shock and fear.

My heart leapt up into my throat, the brain-fog lifting fast as my thoughts raced frantically for action.

God, what do I do Run away? Hide? Storm in there and attack him?

In theory, that had been my plan—more or less—but now that it was actually *happening*, I was horrified.

Before I could panic any further, though, Michelangelo propped himself up on his elbows, his features having smoothed out a bit.

"What are you d-doing here?" He stuttered with obvious uncertainty. And yet, he made no moves to escape the stranger who'd broken into his home. He did nothing to cover himself up or hide the graphic gay porn playing on the TV.

He just stared at me, face flushed, erection resting on his abs.

I said nothing. How could I? *What* would I even say??

The humility of the situation had me sweating beneath my clothes. The fact that I was standing there, as a *straight man*, peeking into the bedroom of another man who was naked and giving me some strange look I couldn't read It made me dizzy. I felt like I might pass out, my heart was hammering so fast.

I forced my feet to step back, but he called out softly, "Wait "

It stopped me once more, dead in my tracks. Woozy and trembling, I stared at him, and he at me. With our eyes locked, I wondered if he knew it was me

Ghost Rider.

"You should stay." Michelangelo reclined, gazing up at me from the bed. His fingers skimmed back down the length of his body in a teasing manner. Slowly *taunting.*

My stomach rolled in confusion.

Stay? A masked stranger breaks into his house, and he wanted him to stay??

"Why ?" I growled, my voice low and grungy, disguised by the tension in my chest.

"What if I tell someone you were here?" His fingers continued to brush his skin, purposely moving around his erection. "My father's a very important man I'm sure he'd stop at nothing to find out who broke into his home and harassed his son." He cocked his head. "It's in your best interest to make sure I keep quiet."

There was no more oxygen in the room. Everything around me felt hot and muggy with temptation. I couldn't remember where I was, who I was, what I was doing It had all gone blank.

I was just gazing, transfixed. As if I'd inadvertently opened the door to Eden. And the serpent was right there with a shiny red apple, offering me a bite.

I wasn't gay, or bi. I'd never considered the notion, because even *considering* it frightened me. I was already such a disappointment to my father I could only imagine how much more he'd hate me if I started dating dudes.

No, I couldn't be queer. That wasn't what this was.

My obsessive interest in Michelangelo wasn't about wanting him. At least I didn't think it was. In that moment, I couldn't remember why I was there.

All I knew was that I was vibrating. I couldn't think of

a time when I'd felt this Blood pumping, skin burning with illicit desire. *He* made that happen.

He could see In the shadows, he fucking *saw me.*

Michelangelo bit his lip, eyelids drooping as he slowly wrapped his fist around his thick shaft, working back up to a slow stroke. The sight of him, writhing in his bed, touching himself and *goading* me with it, brought on even headier sensations. A jolt between my legs, suffocation in my chest and tingles raining in the pit of my stomach.

It made me angry.

"Stop doing that," I barked at him quietly, praying he wouldn't catch the tremor in my voice.

"Make me," he whispered. It sounded like a hoarse plea.

I pushed into the room, stalking over to his bed. "I said stop," I snarled, and he peeked up at me. "Or I'll fuckin' kill you."

His eyes rolled back, and he arched up to me, dick leaking onto his abs. "Oh, fuck yea," he moaned softly, squirming in his palpable state of arousal.

I blinked down at him, swallowing a mouthful of saliva.

He likes this ?

The notion had me dropping my knees onto the bed. I hovered over him, grabbing him by the throat. "This is your secret, isn't it?"

His lashes fluttered over a lust-drunk gaze, aimed right at me. Cheeks blushed pink, lips shivering, pupils blown out I swear to God, he looked *mesmerized*, mesmerizing me in return.

"No one knows not even Daddy that the prince of New York is just a needy little slut."

"Mmf *please* " he mewled.

"Please what?"

"Don't hurt me." The deep blue in his eyes glimmered at me, and I was fucking gone.

His hands reached up to my waist, holding on to me before the fingers on his right hand crept between my legs. It wasn't until he cupped my cock that I realized how fucking hard I was.

Growling, I grabbed his hands fast, pinning them above his head. All rational thinking had gone out the window.

This is how I hurt him.

"You're not gonna say a word about this, got it?" I held his wrists down with one hand while the other scrambled down, hastily, to open my zipper.

My hands were shaking, chest heaving. I was jittery and a little scared Actually, I was terrified. But I was hard, *so* fucking hard I was aching. I knew it meant something I'd never let myself deal with, but I was too unleashed to care.

"*Fuck*, give me a reason not to " he whined gruffly, spreading his legs beneath me.

It was so sexy, I felt precum wetting my boxers.

God, what am I doing ?

I got my dick out of my pants, and he groaned, lifting his hips up to mine, like he wanted to feel my cock on his. But I was just out of reach.

Dipping my hips, I dragged my hot, heavy erection up his chest, brushing his warm flesh with my slippery wet head. Part of me wanted to spread him open and fuck him in half But that need was scary as shit. I'd never felt it before The desire to sink into a man. It was making it hard to breathe.

So instead, I knelt over him, holding him down forcefully with my body weight. "I have a way of keeping you quiet," I purred, and he swallowed visibly, nervous, but not enough to stop him from parting his lips.

He was scared. But he liked it. It was a goddamn *revelation.*

Without another moment of thought, I shoved my cock down Michelangelo Russo's throat. I fucked his face deep while he choked and cried, and for a moment, I wondered if I really was assaulting him But then he came all over himself, hands-free. From nothing more than me riding his gag-reflex.

It split me down the middle. I came like a roar of thunder, fisting his dark hair, holding him in place so he had no choice but to swallow my every aching drop.

And when I finally returned from outer space and pulled out of his mouth, he curled up with a satisfied hum.

"Feel free to break in again Ghost Rider."

CHAPTER EIGHT

Trevel

APPARENTLY, I BLACKED OUT. OR FELL ASLEEP. *SAME THING?*

That was some strong shit…

When my eyelids flutter open, I'm in Alice's bed. She's nestled up by my side, her back to me. I watch her for a moment in the dark, hoping she's not terribly upset with me for getting high. Praying to sweet Satan that if—or *when*—she eventually finds out that I've somehow wound up, on occasion, with her brother's dick in my mouth, she won't hate me forever.

Lifting my hand, I gently brush my fingers through her silky soft hair. I let out a sigh, about to wrap my arm around her waist. But a rustling across the room stops me.

I'm groggy, movements slowed as I glance up at the shadowed frame creeping over to the bed. I only notice that it's Andres when he doesn't stop and slinks into the bed right next to me. It's a queen, so technically, there would be room for the three of us, but he's instantly sort of wrapped around me.

"What are you doing?" I whisper, peeking at Alice. She hasn't moved.

Her brother kisses me on the mouth, then the jaw, moving his lips to my ear. "I want more."

"You're tapped," I hum, as quietly as possible. My adrenaline is giving me chills, mixing with the warm and fuzzies of the drugs. It feels good, but I don't want it to.

This is so fucked up.

Andres rolls me over a bit, settling in behind me and rubbing his erection on my ass. I'm just now realizing I'm in only my underwear. "But I got so hard out there thinking about you…" He breathes, biting my shoulder as his hands slink down to grip and squeeze. "Let me inside. Just once, pretty boy."

Fucking hell… This is so bad.

I'm shivering and mentally scolding myself for it. My cock is already stiff from what's happening, and how *wrong* it is. But when Andres reaches around and starts rubbing it, I'm falling apart.

This is a new low, even for me. It's one thing to suck my girlfriend's brother off for drugs once in a while. But letting him fuck me in her bed while she's asleep *right next to us??*

Alright, this isn't working much to talk me out of it.

I try looking around for Leo as a voice of reason, but of course, he's conveniently absent.

Figures. He worships chaos and loves when I behave like a wild animal. *Rather uncharacteristic of the real Leonardo, just saying.*

Andres is already pulling my underwear down, not waiting for verbal consent, which, let's be honest, doesn't seem quite like his thing. But I'm also not stopping him, or fighting him off, so…

I'm the worst person in the world. And I'm going to get off so bloody hard…

Squirming as he spits generously into his hand, I truly hate myself. *I swear to Lucifer*, I do. Because despite how purely abhorrent this behavior is, I'm quaking for it. I haven't bottomed in *so* long… It's been at least a year, maybe more, since my last venture onto Grindr. I think it's safe to say, based on how my body is reacting, I missed it.

In the interest of making this quick—or being impatient to fuck without concern for my feelings—Andres simply pushes his cock between my ass and starts nudging. The spit-lube is there, but it's not much. Yet it's clear that I'm just as needy, because only a few more seconds of panting and shoving, and he's inside me.

"Fuuuuck yea," he groans, *quietly*, but still.

My heavy lids are on his sister—my *girlfriend*. Her back is still to us, so I take a moment to close my eyes and whimper at the sensational burn and stretch.

"Shhh," I scold him, and myself, a louder purr sneaking from my lips when he begins stroking.

"Quiet, pretty boy. My sister will hear." He covers my mouth with his hand, fucking slow and deep while licking and sucking on my earlobe.

This is fucking ludicrous…

I must still be high, because everything feels so infinitely *spectacular*. I'm smart enough to know it's smoke and mirrors, but still… It doesn't stop me from drowning in this bad wrong terribly *treacherous* thing I'm doing.

Andres is fucking me harder, rocking the bed far too much. But Alice still hasn't so much as shifted.

Something flickers on the edge of my consciousness…

"Is this how you fuck her?" he growls in my ear, pumping between my cheeks. "Push into her tight hole in the dark and ride it deep?" I whine at his words, and the way his dick is grazing my prostate. "Must be nice to come in her as much as you want, huh?" *Fuck fuck fuck…* "And I bet she knows you're just as needy for it. That her darling boyfriend wants *his* little pussy filled with cum too…"

Bollocks. Can't… hold… back.

I fist the sheets as my dick shoots almost painfully into the bed, all the while staring at my girlfriend's back.

She still hasn't moved… Why hasn't she moved?

God, I'm coming so… bloody… hard.

"Don't worry, pretty boy. Daddy's here to breed you like you need it."

His words are rippling through my brain, desires and memories tangling into a mess, until I can't tell what's what anymore.

"That's it…"

"Oh yea, baby. That's it."

"Take it…"

"Take it," Andres groans out loud—*way* too fucking loud—hips bucking as he comes in me. "Take this load like a good boy…"

"Fuckin' hell…" I cry behind his hand, the agony of what I'm seeing in my head somehow mixing with the pleasure, springing tears to my eyes.

He's barely done, but I'm reaching for Alice.

Something isn't right. Something is—

"Alice??" I grab her shoulder.

She's stiff.

My stomach claws viciously up my throat as I roll her over. And my heart comes to a full stop when I see her eyes…

They're open.

And her lips are blue.

No… wait.

What??

"Yo, what the fuck?!" Andres pulls out of me and jumps back.

Sitting up, I'm in a fog. It's not registering. This doesn't feel real.

What the bloody hell is going on??

"Alice… Baby??" I shake her, hesitantly sliding my hand up to check her pulse.

It's not there. *It's not bloody there!*

And she's ice-cold.

"What did you do?!" Andres shouts. I whip my face in his direction. "You killed my sister!"

"*What??*" I gasp, shivering so hard my teeth are chattering. "No, I… There's no way…"

I didn't. I *couldn't* have.

Covering my face with my hands, I rub and dig my fingers into my eyes. *No. No no no no no. This isn't happening. I didn't do this.*

Smacking myself hard on the cheek, I growl, "Wake up."

"You sick fuck!" Andres hisses. "You killed her and then let me come in here and fuck you right next to her?? Knowing she was dead the whole time?!"

Standing up fast, I lunge at him, grabbing him by the throat. "Lower your fucking voice," I snarl in his face, towering over him with my height and a pure, horrified rage. "I did *not* kill your sister! I'm in love with her! This has to be some mistake… Something happened, or—"

"Bullshit. You're a fucking junkie psycho," he spits. "You were so out of it, you wouldn't know what happened!"

My head tilts, and I blink. Something about this isn't adding up.

There's no way I killed her. I couldn't have.

My lower lip trembles, pressure building in my skull as I release him.

I'm off my meds…

The nightmares…

Dr. Love's words ring through my brain. *"There's no way to know… You may have been… born this way."*

Rushing back to the bed, I crash down next to Alice, wrapping her stiff body in my arms. "Baby… *please*. Tell me I didn't do this… I didn't *mean* to…" Sputtering for breath, I'm shaking so hard I'm nearly convulsing. "P-please… C-come b-back, b-baby."

Fuck, this is it. I'm going back to prison.

And real prison, this time. Not juvenile detention. I'm going away for the rest of my life…

Remembering Andres, I turn to find him jumping into his clothes and sneaking out of the room. I dart after him, coming to a confused halt in the living room.

His friend is still here, passed out on the couch. Andres is shaking him.

"Yo, T, wake up, man," he says frantically. "She's dead. You gotta bounce."

My brows zip together, a stunned fury filling me fast. I stalk over to them, and Andres peers up at me, looking nervous.

"*What…?*" It's the only word I can produce.

I think I'm in shock.

Andres slaps his friend across the face, and he finally wakes up.

"What the hell, bro??" the dude grumbles, half-conscious.

"We gotta leave, man," Andres says, too calmly for someone whose twin sister is dead in the next room. "Alice is dead. This asshole fuckin' killed her, and we need to get outta here before the cops show up."

The guy—*I can't remember his bloody name*—sits up fast, eyes widening. "Shit, man, you didn't call 'em, did you??"

Andres is glaring at me, purposely not answering. I'm assuming he didn't call them.

"What… happened?" I croak, scared and heartbroken and *angry*… Fucking angrier than I've ever been before.

"I swear, it was an accident!" the friend shouts, and Andres backhands him across the face again.

"Shut the fuck up!" he barks at the guy. "Don't say another word! Just fuckin' bounce. Now!"

Everything around me feels swimmy. The air is heavy with tension and confusion and… death.

Without a second thought, I tackle Andres to the ground, wrestling him until I'm on top with my hands around his throat.

"What did you do?!" I roar in his face.

"Me?? You fuckin killed her!" he chokes out. But he's not very convincing, and now I have no clue what to think.

I blink hard, shaking my head. "I don't think I did…"

Glancing up at the sound of footsteps, I watch the friend scrambling for the door, whipping it open and running for his life.

Probably a smart move.

"You don't know what's going on," Andres wheezes. "You're just a worthless junkie cockslut who was never good enough for my sister!"

Lifting him, I bring his head down quick, bashing his skull on the floor. It stuns him, and he groans.

"Shut the fuck up!" I thunder, tightening my hands around his throat. "I wouldn't hurt Alice! I loved her!" I bash his head again. "I *love* her!" And again. And again.

And again.

Until *crack!* His skull splits, blood instantly pouring out of him.

I'm gasping, panting and heaving, crying and crying and *crying*. I can't see. I can't *breathe*… I can't…

I just… *can't* believe it.

"I love her…" I sob.

And she's gone.

This can't be real.

"Nicely done, mate." The familiar voice settles me down. I sniffle, my tear-stained gaze lifting slowly to where Leo is leaning up against the wall, smoking. *"Now… Let's get this cleaned up, shall we?"*

"Snap out of it, man."

"No… No… No no… no no no." I'm shuddering, down to my bones. Sick to my stomach. I've already thrown up twice. "This isn't happening. This isn't happening."

"Hey!" Leo shouts at me, grabbing me by the face until I'm forced to stop mumbling and sniffling. *"Pull yourself together."*

"I c-can't…" I whimper, cowering as he glares at me; dark, sinister eyes behind a tattered blue mask. "She's g-gone. I… k-killed her."

"Trevel, look at me." His voice is deep, commanding. *"I need you to wade through the drug-fog and harness every bit of your mental capacity right now."*

Blinking at him, I sniff, "What does that… m-mean?"

"You know what it means," he says firmly. "Think, *Trevel."*

My head goes back to swaying. Lips shivering, breaths labored. "I don't… I don't know what… h-happened."

"Yes, *you do,"* he snaps. *"Think."*

Pulling a long inhale, I attempt to steady my heart rate, glancing at Andres Alvarez, dead on the floor. There's a pool of blood around his head.

"I killed him," I whisper.

"Yea… And??"

My eyes move to the doorway to Alice's bedroom. I whine an

aggrieved sound. "She's dead. My *Alice…*" Tears slip from my eyes once more. "She was the love of my life… and now she's just… gone."

The feeling of Leo's grip on my face loosens. His furry hands slip down onto my shoulders. *"I am sorry, mate. She was a good girl."*

Flinging a glare in his direction, my eyes harden. "Why didn't you stop me?! You *wanted* me to kill her, didn't you??"

His look of sympathy returns to one of frustration. *"No. Wrong. You will* not *blame this on me…"*

I let out a breath and rub my eyes. "I miss her already…"

"Go…" His voice echoes, more of an internal command as I scramble to my feet and dart into Alice's room.

I freeze when I see her still lying on her bed. And I want nothing more than to crumble to bits on the floor and die with her. But I force myself closer. At the edge of her bed, I look her over, attempting to find any sign of what might have happened.

There's no blood. No strangulation marks around her throat…

How else would I have killed her? Maybe I… smothered her with a pillow?

My heart is cracked in half inside my chest, barely pumping enough evil black sludge to keep me alive.

I'm damaged, man. Broken. A complete and utter monster.

I was in the bed next to her… Panting like a whore for her asshole twin brother while she was lying dead *right next to me?! What kind of person does that??*

"An evil one," Leo says from the doorway. I aim a tearful glower at him. *"No, Trevel, you're not a good person. But that doesn't mean you* killed *your girlfriend. Now fucking* focus."

"Why can't you just tell me what happened…?" I whine, exhausted and devastated, angry and scared. Guilty. And confused.

Very fucking confused.

"You know I can't do that," he hums, voice fading once more.

Shaking myself out of the grief and despair—as much as I can—I crawl tentatively onto the bed, taking a closer look. I touch her neck…

Aside from being cold, it feels normal. I check her pillows for makeup, and I check myself for scratches that could allude to a struggle. I see nothing.

Lifting Alice's hand in mine, I brush my fingertips along her skin, still so supple, despite the early signs of rigger-mortis. I bite my lip. "Baby, I'm so sorry…" My fingers run up her arm, cherishing her one last time.

But then they stop… when I notice a small mark on her inner elbow. I recognize it immediately.

"A track mark…?" I whisper, puzzled, blinking for a solid thirty seconds before checking my own arm.

I have the same mark. It's from Andres shooting me up earlier. Just a tiny, reddened bump. Nothing more than a swollen dot from where the needle injected the poison into my vein…

But why would Alice have one too?? She doesn't do drugs like that…

"Remember, *Trevel…*"

Closing my eyes, I think hard, *deep*, searching my mind for any memories from earlier…

Andres shot me up, and I sort of collapsed into him. The feeling is… indescribable. *Like a wave of soft ecstasy. A blanket of tranquility that folds you up and carries you in weightless perfection.*

I tend to black out a bit when I shoot it, which is why I prefer not to do it that way often. I don't like to waste the high lying around like a zombie.

Maybe that's why Andres chose that method tonight…

Because he wanted me out of commission.

This thought sparks a recollection… The sensation of being carried. Someone was carrying me…

Andres helped me out of the bathroom and into the living room.

Alice's voice…

"Oh my God, what did you do to him??" She rushed over, taking me from him. I can *feel* her touching me… I *remember* her arm around my waist and her lips kissing my neck. *"Trevel, baby, are you alright??"*

"I told her goodnight…" I whisper now. *I remember getting those words out.*

"Okay, goodnight, beautiful stranger," she'd chuckled. Hearing it in my head breaks my withered heart into even smaller, jagged pieces.

Then she helped me into the bedroom, lying me down in her bed. After that, it's all darkness. My memories are of a dark room… *Her bedroom.* That's it.

Running my fingers up into my hair, I grip it hard and pull. "Think think *think*. Come on!"

Voices…

I hear them… Slowly, they come back into focus.

They were speaking in the living room. I'm not sure I could hear what they were saying, though.

"Focus," Leo insists. *"What were they saying? Listen to them…"*

"I don't... *know*," I groan hopelessly. "The next thing I remember was waking up with Alice next to me... But when did she come into bed? And how did she get that mark??"

"You know you want to try it..." Leo says. But his voice doesn't sound like him.

It sounds... like Andres.

"You know you want to try it, Sis," he said to Alice. *"There's a reason loverboy in there is so obsessed with this shit."*

"Because he's hurting," Alice clapped back. *"He's suffering with his own shit, and you're preying on that."*

"Don't be so dramatic," Andres huffed.

"You wanna talk about dramatic*?"* she muttered, her tone accusatory. *"Let's talk about why you find it necessary to take my boyfriend into the bathroom alone to do drugs..."*

"Maybe they're fucking," someone chuckled. *I think it was the friend.*

"Yea right." Andres growled. *"I ain't no homo."*

"Real mature," Alice grunted. *"Honestly, I wouldn't put it past you..."*

"Wouldn't put what *past me??"* Andres snapped.

"Fucking around with my boyfriend behind my back," she went on, sounding angry, but also not all that shocked. *"You've always been jealous of me... Always trying to steal my stuff."*

Quiet. Tense silence, for a few beats before...

"Fuck off, Alex*,"* Andres hissed.

Then things got *loud.*

Slap! "How dare you fucking call me that!" Alice hissed. *Shuffling. "Do you have any idea how much that hurts?? For my own twin brother to disrespect me like that?!"*

More sounds... Banging and thudding. Yelling and cursing.

"Get off me!"

"Fuck you, you bitch!"

God, I wish I could see *what's happening!*

I *loathe* the idea that I was lying in the next room, *rotting* like a piece of trash while the woman I love was fighting those pricks. Rage is rising inside me again, regret and remorse so strong it's burning up my throat like bile.

If I could revive that cunt just to kill him again, I would.

"And then it got really quiet," Leo says.

"Shit, man... That was fucked up," the friend says in my memories.

"Shut up. Whose side are you on??" Andres barked. *"Gimme the bag of that other shit."*

"Wait… why??" the friend asked nervously.

"Just do it!"

I remember them stomping around, whispering back and forth. I didn't hear it all… But there are flickers.

"… How much?"

"All of it…"

"Make it look like an overdose…"

"… blame that British fuckboy…"

My chest is caving in, blood rushing so loudly in my ears it's drowning out the memories.

This can't be right… There's no fucking way.

They actually shot Alice up with drugs to give her an intentional overdose?? Why would her own brother do that to her??

"You heard him," Leo says. *"He was jealous. He's probably always been jealous of her. That's why he fucked you…"*

"Thanks. That makes me feel so much better." I rub my eyes hard.

Leo shrugs. *"Hey, you're the one who bent over for him."*

"Because he was hot! And an asshole. And I'm a goddamn chaos agent, you know this!" I bark, hating myself so deeply I could vomit. Again.

"But the good news is you *didn't kill her,"* Leo declares, far too chipper for my liking. *"So, you know… silver lining."*

I glower at him. "My girlfriend is *dead!* The only person I've ever truly loved… is fucking dead. And I let her killer fuck me…" I whimper, covering my head with my arms. "*Fuck*, I can't believe I did it again… I'm going to jail."

Curling up into a ball on the bed, I rock myself back and forth.

The memories are coming in clearer now… Now that my high has mostly dissipated and I'm stuck in the purgatory of real fucking life.

Andres and the friend moving Alice into bed with me… The friend grumbling about being fucked *as he shuffled out of the room.*

But Andres stayed. I can feel him staring at us in the dark.

"Sorry it had to be this way, Sis," he'd whispered, running his hand from her over to me.

I remember feeling it, on the edge of my consciousness… My clothes being removed. I knew I hadn't passed out practically naked. *Andres* took off my shirt, then my pants, touching me all the while.

The feeling of being touched and groped… At the time, I'd thought it was a nightmare. But it was *him*.

"Your boyfriend wants to get fucked by a man, Alicita… I could do it right now and he'd probably love *it."*

And the worst part is that he was fucking *right*. I am a pathetic whore who let his girlfriend's brother fuck him right next to her. The whole time, I thought she was sleeping, and it was some forbidden game, when in reality… she was dead. And it was just tragic.

"Alice, I'm so… *so* sorry," I weep, holding her and kissing her shoulder and neck. "I failed you in so many ways. Because I'm… cursed…"

I'm falling into panic once more, memories from deep within who I am resurrecting…

"No… please…" Pain. Rough, throbbing agony.

"Please stop…" Dirt in my face, in my mouth.

I can't breathe.

"Fuck, yea… Shut up and take it."

"Mate, I know you're grieving, but time is of the essence here," Leo rumbles, cutting into the flashes of misery in my brain. *"We've got to get a move on."*

I hate what he's saying. But I know he's right.

Only a moment of wallowing more, and I eventually pull myself together, saying one last goodbye to somebody who may have been my true love… My other piece.

Maybe in another life.

"I'll never forget you, Alice Alvarez," I whisper to her, closing her eyes with a swipe of my fingertips. "I'm sorry I couldn't… be *good* for you."

Stomping out of her bedroom, I sniffle and wipe my eyes, glancing around the apartment. The place is a mess; drugs everywhere, blood… And in the middle of it, a very dead asshole.

I kick Andres's lifeless corpse.

"I can't believe I let him fuck me," I sigh, shaking my head.

"Can't you, though?" Leo snarks, and my jaw tenses.

"Whatever. It wasn't even all that… I barely came." I bite my lip. Leo snorts, and I whip a scowl in his direction. "Don't say a fucking word."

He holds his bear paws up, smirking. *"No judgement."*

"Sod off."

Pacing around the body, I can feel the drugs fizzling out of my system more and more as adrenaline takes over. *Awareness* is turning up my manic state several degrees.

I suppose I should just get the fuck out of here. Leave Atlanta in my rearview and go out on the run… After all, that's what I *should* have done the last time. But I was young. Naïve. *I didn't want to leave New York.* But more than that, I was *proud* of myself. I foolishly thought the punishment would be minimal because of *why* I'd done it, and a minor price to pay for my revenge.

I suppose I'm proud of killing Andres, too… Avenging Alice's death feels like the best parting gift I could give her.

"So Dr. Love was right…" I sigh. "I couldn't stop myself from killing again. All that work I did, the hiding and pretending to be someone else. It was… no use. *This* is who I am. I was—"

"Born this way?" Leo finishes, and I peek at him, shrugging. He rolls his eyes. *"Maybe. But you didn't kill her. That's what matters."*

"I suppose…"

Glancing at the body on the floor, my mind swarms with thoughts of my former doctor… *What would he think about what I've done? Will he find out?*

Could this… bring him back?

"So… What's the plan?" Leo asks impatiently.

Wandering over to the couch, I plop down in front of the coffee table, picking up a rolled bill. Tightening it, I stick it up my nose and snort the drug leftovers. Sniffing and swallowing back the bitter taste, I'm hit with an instant rush; a warm wave of confidence and sharp, swift exhilaration.

When I peek back down at the table, I notice something that sticks out. A driver's license.

Picking it up, I read the name…

Thomas Webber.

My fingers twitch as I read his address, mulling it over. This *plan.*

"Leave a trail of breadcrumbs…" I mumble, my lips sloping into a smirk. "And he'll have to follow it."

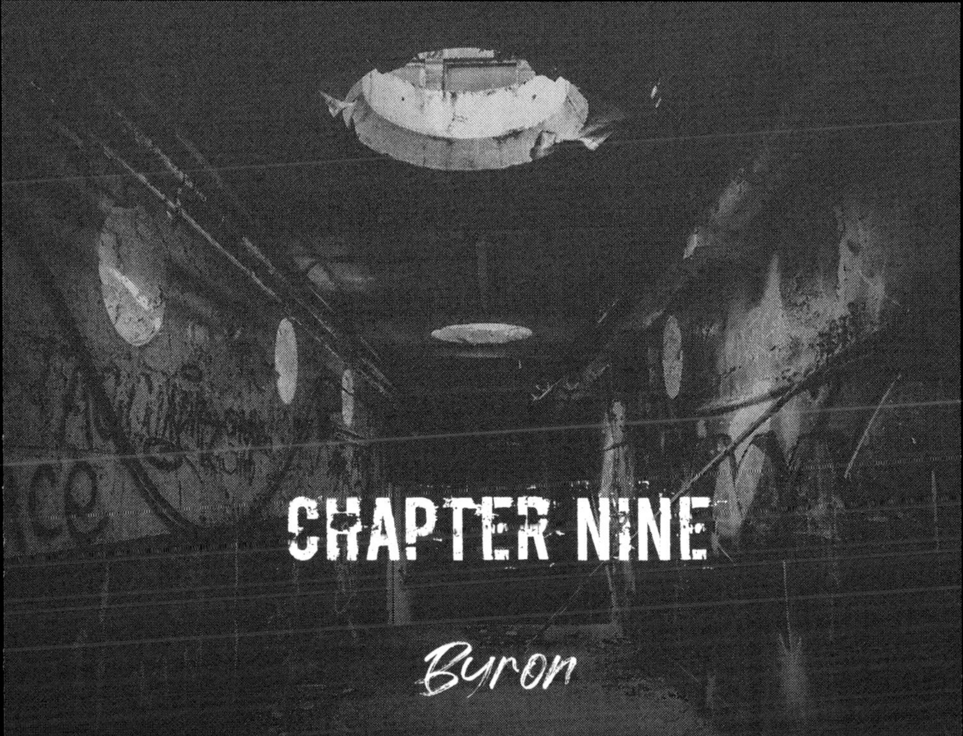

CHAPTER NINE

Byron

I'VE OFTEN FELT THAT ALABASTER PEN MIRRORS MY MOODS. RATIONALLY, I KNOW that's not possible. Things happen on a cosmic scale, and I'm not that important. But if you believe in energy shifts, the moons and the tides and all that crap—*which I'm not sure I do*—then you can understand why I might feel inclined to believe that the constant rollercoaster of highs and lows that is my mental state is directly related to the events of Alabaster Penitentiary.

By my estimation, Kieran O'Malley was ripped out of gen pop roughly two months ago. It was a quiet afternoon in the Pen. We were playing poker, and I was schooling him, which was entertaining on many levels because he's the sorest of sore losers, when out of nowhere, Officer Hancock came strolling into our cell and cuffed me.

My first thought was *not again*… Seriously, the dejà vu was kicking. Fast nerves and dread, and the tiniest flicker of thrill that made me want to throw up, rippled through me.

I did my time in solitary after what happened in the Warden's office. That should've been my lesson learned, right there. No matter how *good* he manipulates you into feeling, there are repercussions when fraternizing with the devil.

At the same time, if Manuel Blanco wants something from you… he's going to get it. Searching for a rhyme or reason will just stress you out.

So I went with Hancock, my stomach churning and my palms

sweating... But we only made it a few feet up the row before he stopped, outside of Ren's cell. I was relieved, until it dawned on me. The same sort of thing was happening...

I was about to be manipulated; used for someone's selfish purposes. And I would go along with it, because my body is *weak*.

That's exactly what happened, too. Ren had Hancock bring me to his cell so that he could beg me to do some proxy shit with him in the showers, in an effort to get Luthor's attention. *Ridiculous.*

He's forever dragging me into their relationship, wedging me in between them because Luthor won't give him the time of day. He uses me as a bridge to get the one he actually wants. It's been *years* and I still can't tell if I should be insulted by it.

I guess I'm not... Since I keep coming when he calls, like a stupid fucking lapdog.

Why do I keep going back?

Am I that desperate to feel needed??

Regardless, it was while I was with Ren that O'Malley was snatched up. We only found out later that he was in the East, though it's still unclear *why*.

He's been to the East Wing before, strapped to things and experimented on, but never for this long. I'm not sure what they expect to gain from him, but then that's not something any of us *criminals* are worthy of knowing.

It's just the Warden. Whatever he says goes, no matter how pointlessly cruel it may seem. *Unnecessary pain is his side-hustle.*

Within the quiet, I can still hear O'Malley shouting as they hauled him away. Like a reflex, my eyes lift to the mattress above me...

"Focus. Head in the game, remember?"

Ren's words replay in my mind, his tone meant to calm me down, while also reminding me of our agreement. The one we all made after Freeman was taken.

Always keep your head in the game, no matter what.

Don't let this place break you.

Because it will, if you let it. We've all seen it happen, more times than we cared to. Luthor's past cellmates—*whether I gave a shit about them or not*—were all overcome by the mayhem and madness of being locked up forever in Alabaster fucking Pen. And now so has O'Malley.

Parker Freeman, Ren's last and only cellmate, wasn't swallowed up by it like the rest were. But still, he lost himself, his soul... *Fuck it, his* life.

We know he's dead. Denying it does nothing for anyone.

He's *gone*, and when it happened, Luthor, Ren, and I made a pact. No matter what they do to us, no matter how hard they try, we'll *never* lose ourselves within the walls of this goddamn crypt. Never lose sight of what's important… *Survival.*

The Ivory can chain our bodies, but he'll never possess our minds.

More memories try to slink in between my defenses, but I block them and *focus* on what's happening now, in this moment. The bland, colorless shuffle out of my cell for some mundane routine.

Will it stay this way? Or will this be another bout of mayhem…?

I guess we'll find out.

Joy and Rook are herding us into the row, and I peek behind me to find Luthor coming my way. By himself, meaning Dash is still in solitary.

I shiver at the thought.

Dash is Luthor's new cellmate, and they've been attached at the hip since his arrival—coincidentally the same day O'Malley disappeared. *See what I mean? It's either nonstop action, or mind-numbing tedium.*

Dash winds up in solitary often. The kid's been in the hole more times in his *two months* here than most of us have in years. One could rationalize that it's because he kicked Velle in the balls within twenty-four hours of his arrival, and he's been paying the price ever since. But honestly, I'm not sure that's the real reason.

It makes more sense that he's an undercover troublemaker… With a tendency to attract unwanted attention.

I'm biting down on the inside of my cheek as Luthor sidles up to me.

"Hey," he grumbles, sounding tired. *Makes sense.*

Ren's been in solitary too, after he and Dash apparently got into some fight with Gage and his homeboys in the showers. I haven't seen Dash since the night the power went out…

Storms have been ravaging the East Coast for weeks, causing frequent power outages. Luthor even had to go down to the East Wing at one point and help them with the servers. That was when he verified that O'Malley *was* alive, although knowing what goes on down there, I'd say simply being *alive* isn't exactly a comfort.

Ren's only been gone a couple of days, but Luthor is clearly worried. He tries to act like he doesn't care, but his demeanor betrays him. You can see it all over his face, in his slumped shoulders and his movements heavy with melancholy.

Luthor is an empath. He can't help it. He carries the burden of what's happening to his friends as if it's happening to him. And when your friends are Ren *and* Dash, keeping up with that concern is like a full-time job.

I can't say I don't understand. I've certainly felt off since my cellmate was taken. *Fortunately, there's no shortage of other crap for me to obsess over.*

Grunting a response to Luthor's greeting, I'm eyeing him in my peripheral. When we reach the end of the row and find Ren's cell still empty, I *feel* him deflate a little more at my side.

"Looks like it's just the two of us," I breathe, then stiffen.

I'm sincerely hoping things aren't going to be awkward after what happened the other night in the hallway...

Not that we did anything *to* each other. *But things were definitely happening in our shared bubble.*

Luthor shows me a small, comforting smile. "You know what that means..."

I cock a brow.

"Bro date."

I can't help the puff of laughter that leaves my lips. *Of course* I'm overthinking it. After all, Luthor and I have a different kind of friendship. We're *fam*, above all else. Something as insignificant as a voyeuristic orgasm couldn't shake our foundation.

Just a couple of bros jerking off watching their other bro swallow some cum. What's the big deal?

In the caf, we get settled at our usual table with our usual trays of slop, digging in without words. It's always quieter when Ren's not around. I like to think I prefer it this way, but I can't deny that something is missing...

After a few minutes of mindless chitchat, I sigh. "You know, we can talk about Ren if you want. I don't mind."

Luthor flashes me a look of vulnerability in between poking at his mac and cheese. "That's not bro date conversation. That's—"

"Girl talk?" I shrug, smirking.

He laughs, then shakes his head. "I don't know, man... He's confusing."

"Uh-huh," I hum in agreement.

"I mean, he let Gage fuck him in half while we were supposed to be..." his voice trails, and I witness him swallow.

"I remember," I say softly, mind littered with memories of that time, three years ago...

The day after I arrived in Hell, my new friend had his heart ripped out and stomped on. And I focused all of my energy on trying to help him through it.

I've gotta say, it was a great distraction.

"But then he gets sent to solitary for kicking the dude's ass?? *Twice*, mind you." He shakes his head. "He's just… too fucking much. But I feel like I'm stuck with him, and the craziest part is that I'm not even mad about it. I love being stuck with him, even though I hate it and he drives me absolutely insane." His green eyes lift to mine. "Hating that you love someone… How messed up is that?"

I blink at him, swallowing down the stuff I wish I could say.

It's not as messed up as you think…

"Listen, you've obviously known Ren longer than I have," I mumble.

"Yea, but you know him too," he cuts in. "Just as well as I do… Maybe more. Because you can see beyond the Ren-daze."

Those words stop me for a second, and I stare at him blankly. *Can I, though?*

I guess he's right… I *do* know Ren. *Really fucking well.*

But why…? Why *do I know him as well as his own fated fucking mate??*

I barely even remember what I was going to say, so I croak, "So then… You know as well as I do that Percy fucking Gage doesn't mean shit to him. Just like Velle doesn't, or Jasper, or Rook… or me."

The way Luthor is looking at me right now has me immediately regretting those words, sinking deep into a hole of *Jesus Christ, why the fuck did I just say that??*

I'm about to start backpedaling, when the center of the goddamn universe himself comes traipsing into the cafeteria.

Jasper is standing by the doorway, having brought him up, but Ren isn't cuffed and he's just beelining over to us like he's on a mission.

I find myself gulping and sitting up straight for some reason.

"Hey," Ren breathes out as he plops into the seat next to Luthor.

"Holy shit… Are you alright?" Luthor asks him right away. "We heard you and Dash were in a fight in the showers…"

"Yea, we sorta took on Gage together." Ren chuckles fondly. "Dash is… He's a really cool guy."

Luthor looks pleased by this statement. He likes when his friends are getting along. *He's sweet like that.*

But now I can't stop thinking about Dash. *In solitary…*

"Look, there's something I need to talk to you about," Ren says to Luthor, an air of dedication to him that's stiffening my muscles for some reason. "And I know you might not want to hear it, but I just need to get this off my chest."

My stomach twists up like a contortionist as I peek at Luthor. His eyes are wide, unnerved, but curious as he nods slowly. "Okay…"

Ren locks his gaze on Luthor's, taking a deep breath, preparing himself to drop a bomb. I'm not breathing. "Lex, I'm… *sorry*." He blinks slowly, posture relaxing a bit, like a ton of bricks just came off of his shoulders.

Ren goes on with his apology, and I just sit across from them, staring. Listening to Ren confess this shit that the rest of us already knew, as if it's some great revelation.

In a way, I guess it is. Because for him to actually admit this stuff and to be *honest*… It's a big deal for our friend, the compulsive liar.

The way they're gazing at only *each other* has me growing uneasy, shifting in my seat.

I shouldn't be here for this…

This is a private relationship conversation. Why am I listening to this?

"So…" Ren clears his throat when he's done with his monologue. "You have the floor. If there's anything you'd like to, um… contribute. To this, uh… dialogue." He's fumbling, and it's kind of adorable.

He has no idea how to have open communication. With *anyone*, really, but especially with someone he has feelings for.

I can relate.

Luthor's lashes flutter. And then he glances at me, a brief, pleading look in his eyes, like he's asking me for help. Like *I'm* a part of this conversation too, and it's confusing as shit.

Here I was, thinking I should quietly slink away and give them space. But now they're both looking at me, as if I have *any* fucking say in what's going on between them. It's weird, and fully verifying of my ongoing, very reluctant involvement in their tumultuous relationship.

I can do nothing more than give Luthor some telepathic advice…

Just be honest.

Clearly, it's a *do as I say, not as I do* type thing.

"I guess I appreciate your apology," Luthor says to him, reticently. "If it's true…"

"It is." Ren nods.

"I like that you're finally acknowledging how batshit psycho you'd be if I did even a fraction of the stuff you do." Luthor goes on, pointedly, slanting his head.

"I was never very good at math, baby." Ren smirks, his hands slinking across the table, going for Luthor's.

It's one of his standard moves. *Distract with physical contact to control the situation and avoid emotional intimacy.*

But Luthor isn't having it. He rolls his eyes, tugging his hands away. "Stop. I'm always the one who has to sit back and watch you doing fucked-up shit. I just wish you knew how that felt for once..."

I'm zoning out again until Luthor says, "Look at you and Kang, for example."

My spine stiffens at mention of my name.

"You guys have sex, in the showers, right in front of me..."

Um... Am I supposed to weigh in?

Lips parting, I can feel heat rushing up my neck into my face.

"I'm pretending it's *you*," Ren whines in defense, and my jaw clenches.

Okay...

Luthor flips up his hand, dismissing Ren's argument. "That's irrelevant. It's *not* me, okay? Everyone knows it isn't. I mean, shit... What if *I* hooked up with Kang in front of you?"

My eyes widen, head slanting at the trajectory of this conversation.

"You think me just saying, *'But baby, I'm thinking of you the whole time,'* would really make you feel any less murdery about it??"

I'm still just gaping at them, frozen in awkwardness. But I have to register that Luthor has a point... One that basically derails Ren's whole *proxy* rationalization.

Sure, he *absolutely* does pretend his proxies are Luthor. *I would know.* But still, it's a weak-ass justification for sexual infidelity.

Ren is squirming, and Luthor is clearly basking in his victory. Until Ren breathes, "*Fine.*" He winces, like he's swallowing something gross. "You can... hook up with Byron. In front of me. And I won't... interfere."

Wait... What?!

For a second, I think I'm hearing things.

There's no way he actually just said that, right?

I mean... He did not *just volunteer* my *body to prove some kind of point...*

Bulging eyes flinging to Luthor, I find the same shocked expression I'm undoubtedly wearing. It's *exactly* the look you'd expect from someone whose boyfriend just told him he wanted to be cuckholded.

"Come again??" I burst into the conversation, because I *cannot* possibly stay quiet for one more second. *This is entirely ridiculous.* "We're doing *what* now??"

As usual, Ren is nothing but casual, his nonchalance weaving me in tight frustration. "You two fool around, and I'll just sit there and take it. So I'll finally know how it feels…"

He's *still* talking only to Luthor. They're literally *arguing*, back and forth, about something that directly involves me… *Without involving me at all!*

What in the actual fuck?!

It's driving me *insane*. I'm still so baffled, I'm not even listening to what they're saying anymore. I'm just sitting, *fuming*, in my seat, rage bubbling up higher and higher.

Typical. This is so fucking typical of the two of them, I swear to God…

Always using me as some kind of bargaining chip, or buffer, or… fucking emotionless sex toy with no thoughts or feelings, here just to help them figure their shit out!

When I hear Luthor's tone shift from appall to as if he's *actually* considering it—*the smart one!*—I have to speak up again.

"*Excuse me?!* Do *I* have a say in this??" I glare at Ren. "Now you're pimping me out to other people, too?? Unbelievable…"

Ren gives me one of those patronizing looks. "No one's forcing you to do anything, Byron." Gaslighting me with that charming fucking tone, like I'm a child and they're my fucking parents. "I'm just saying, I think it might be helpful."

For WHO?!

"Well, shucks. How *romantic…*" I snap sarcastically, my eyes damn near rolling out of my skull. "For *you guys!* I'm glad I can be of service, just offering up dick to whoever needs it for dumbass fucking experiments."

I rake my fingers through my hair, amazed at the *audacity* of these two. That I'm even having this conversation feels completely ludicrous.

But then there's this teeny, tiny flicker in the pit of my stomach… At the notion of being needed. It's fucking psychotic…

But I mean, who else are they turning to for this shit?

Who else has what it takes to sit here and deal with these morons… The patience, and the composure, and the… sexual fluidity? Apparently?

"Dude, it's okay," Luthor scoffs. "This whole conversation is stupid. We're obviously not doing it, so don't worry—"

Oh, now we're not…?

Because you *said so??*

"I'm not worried," I hiss, jaw tight as I glare at him. "What, you think I'm *afraid* to hook up with you?"

Luthor is visibly stupefied. "Uh… no… I don't think you're afraid. I just know that you're not—"

"Not *what?*" I growl, brow cocking. "*Gay??*"

Ren leans in and whispers, "Are you?"

Maybe. "No!" I snap. "But I'm not afraid of touching some dick. I'm not afraid of shit." I launch out of my seat. Furious determination powering my actions. "In fact, let's go. We're doing it. Right now."

Yea. Didn't expect that, did you?!

They share a look of sheer disbelief, and it buzzes through my muscles.

That's right. Your move, bitches.

"Wait, now??" Luthor gasps.

"Yes, *now*," I grunt. A *command.* "I don't care. I'll save your stupid relationship. My dick is like the fucking Red Cross at this point."

The more they protest, the more my stubbornness takes over, until I'm ready to do just about *anything* to prove how fucking casual I am.

This shit doesn't affect me. I'm fine.

I'm so fucking centered, I'm basically magma.

They're *the babies. I'm a sexual Dalai Lama in this bitch.*

They wish *they could be on my level.*

We're doing this. Because they *need* me.

Luthor is fidgeting, making logistical excuses, but I flick my hand in Ren's direction. "Work your *Ren magic*, bro. Have Jasper take us to your cell." Without waiting for them to keep stalling, I grab my tray and storm off, barking at them over my shoulder, "Come on, chop chop! We doing this, or what??"

Dumping my trash, I saunter over to where Jasper is posted up on watch by the door, my head spinning with too many things. But the adrenaline is pumping, clouding me from overthinking, and it's good. *I need it.*

I refuse to stop for one second, because stopping will give me time to second-guess this decision, and I don't want that.

I want to *win.*

This is a game, after all. *Everything* Ren does is a game, using people like chess pieces. Controlling us, pushing us around the board in whichever way will benefit him the most.

Well, guess what, bro?? You exposed your weak spot… Bad move.

He brought this up, and now he deserves to feel all kinds of stupid.

I'm gonna mess around with the love of his goddamn life, and he's gonna sit there and watch it, just like I have to sit back and watch all kinds of shit…

"What do you want, inmate?" Jasper grunts, because I'm just standing here, smirking to myself.

"Ren has a favor to ask you." My grin widens.

Jasper rolls his eyes. "Great…"

Luthor finally gets up, hesitantly stalking over. I whistle and nod at Ren.

Let's go, boss. You wanted this.

Ren's face is the picture of miserable uncertainty as he convinces Jasper—*rather weakly, I might add*—to bring the three of us to his cell. Luthor is nervous, understandably. But he seems like he's ready for it…

Whatever we're about to do together in the name of making his possessive boyfriend jealous.

Much to everyone's surprise, Jasper agrees. We set off walking, back to the row. And every step of the way, my heart is thumping…

We're doing this.

We're doing this.

Wait… Why *are we doing this?*

"Well, that was…" Luthor's voice is raspier than usual as he sighs, "Crazy."

"Uh, yea." I'm vigorously chewing on my lower lip. I can't seem to stop…

Maybe it's because I'm trying not to focus on the salty taste of cum lingering on my tongue.

Cum that just so happens to belong to my two best friends.

It's strange, but I can *feel* Ren's in my stomach, and it's making me all jittery.

He's never been… inside me before.

Gulp.

How did we get here??

It's all a blur, honestly.

I refuse to take responsibility for what just happened.

We're blaming it on Ren. It's all his fault.

"I had fun," Ren chirps, as casual as ever. Permanently missing the awkwardness gene—the part of his brain dedicated to over-analyzing, and the receptors that dip your serotonin back down to normal levels when an orgasm wears off.

He's forever *up*. Never down. It's as fascinating as it is infuriating.

"What else is new?" Luthor grumbles, redressing and fixing himself up while I do the same. I'm much more visibly fidgety, but we won't focus on that right now. "You weren't supposed to be involved, remember?"

"You two weren't doing it right," Ren hums, reaching for Luthor, who yanks away from him. "I had no choice but to step in and sort you out."

I scoff. "Everything's always about you."

He frowns up at me. "What's that supposed to mean?"

"You know damn well what it means," I snap. "You couldn't even let Luthor have his moment of getting back at you without stealing the show." I peek at Luthor. "We should've made him stand outside the bars."

Luth cracks a smile, but Ren is squinting at me. It binds my muscles with unease. I hate when he looks at me like that… It makes me feel like he can read my mind; see right into the vast expanse of secrets I'm keeping locked up in there.

It's the same look I give *him* when I know he's lying.

"Are *you* jealous now, Byron?" He smirks, cocking his head. My jaw clamps. "Because you wanted to be the star this time?"

"No," I huff, sounding way too defensive to my own ear. "I'm not… I don't…"

"Shhh." Ren crawls to the edge of the bed, sticking his finger into the waist of my pants to tug me closer while I wriggle away. "No need to be so defensive, darling. We're all friends here. And sometimes friends suck each other's dicks. It happens."

"You're certifiable." Luthor sighs.

"First and *last* time," I growl with our eyes locked. "I assure you."

He grins wickedly, tongue darting out to flick my lower lip. I grumble out of annoyance and shove him away from me by his throat. He tumbles back onto his bed, chuckling like the blue-eyed spawn of Satan he is.

Stomping and keys jingling most definitely mean Jasper has returned to bring us back where we belong. I'm actually glad. *I need some time to myself right now.*

He doesn't bother cuffing us. Just opens the cell, shooting Luthor and me a bitchy look that says, *Go*. And we do, leaving the memory of a strange, ill-conceived threesome behind where it belongs. With Ren.

The beautiful, chaotic planet around which we all orbit.

"We're good..." Luthor murmurs softly to me as we approach my cell, "Right?"

I glance up to find his light green eyes shimmering with concern.

"It's not weird or anything...?"

"Bro, please." I wave him off while Jasper opens my cell and I step inside. "I already forgot about it."

Luthor smiles, and I give him a small one back, waiting until I'm sure he's out of sight to let it slip off.

He's so caring. Really, *truly*, just the best friend in the whole world, to all of us. *We don't deserve him.* And for a moment, while I'm pacing around my cell, in the aftermath of a gay threesome I think I might have accidentally *started*, I wonder how he'd react if I told him the truth.

Maybe not *all* of it, but at least some.

That actually wasn't my first time sucking a dick, Luthor...

I wasn't completely straight before I got here. I'm not as ice-cold as I try to make it seem.

I've been in love before, I think...

I've done things I'm not proud of, but that I really enjoyed doing in the moment, and I think that's why I keep doing them. Becoming someone else when no one's looking feels... really fucking good.

Being my true self in the dark is what keeps me from losing my mind.

The thing is, I know *Luthor*, of all people, wouldn't judge me. He doesn't judge anyone. He's good like that. Just a supportive, all-around awesome dude who wouldn't bat an eye if I told him I think I'm... something *else*. Something other than what I've been claiming to be.

But it doesn't matter. Because I can't tell him. *I can't tell anyone.*

They wouldn't understand, because I barely understand it myself. And it's no one's business.

Yea. It's no one's goddamn business what I did in the past, or what I choose to do with my free time. Who says friends have to tell each other everything, anyway?? What would that even accomplish?

I *like* having secrets. I like keeping them stashed away deep in the hollowed-out cement box of my heart.

Head. In. The. Game.

Plopping down in my bed, I reach behind the mattress, feeling around for my stash spot. I move the big chunk of concrete aside, stuffing my hand into the wall until I feel leather.

Flipping the pages of my journal, looking for the next free page, I stop on my last entry... And the sheer *enormity* of seeing such intense, staggering *truths* written out on paper has my pulse thumping faster and faster, a chill of dreadful excitement creeping up my spine.

These are things *no one* knows… Things I'd never *dream* of speaking out loud to anyone, not even my best friends. But they're *here*, in this small leather-bound journal that was given to me as a welcome gift.

I still wonder why me… I wonder it every time I hold this book in my hands.

Why would he give this to me, *of all people? What is it about me that warranted such a gift? That warranted a gift* at all…

I didn't have to use it. And for a while, I had no desire to. I've never been a writer, mainly because I never had a story to tell. But after some time passed—*I think around a year or so*—I realized that maybe I *do* have something to say. A lot of somethings, in fact… Piling up inside me, desperate for an escape.

Maybe that's why…

Clearly, they won't be coming out of my mouth. I write in this book because I have to… Otherwise the secrets might eat me alive.

My fingers run over the words on the page. Another secret spilled like droplets of blood…

"Let me touch you," I growled into his ear.

"No."

"That wasn't a request."

Slapping the notebook shut, I take a deep breath, closing my eyes and counting to ten.

Some are obviously worse than others…

Blinking, I look around, reacquainting myself with reality. The good news is that I'm still here, sitting in my cell alone, *not* in some twisted, drug-induced hallucination. The bad news is that my dick is hard from reading that little passage… Which is always confusing.

Hey, whatever, right? As far as I'm concerned, it's like getting a boner from reading fiction.

Hot, slutty, gay fiction…

No big deal.

Except that it's *not* fiction, no matter how desperately I wanted to believe that one instance in particular was a dream. What happened the night the power went out…

Rubbing my eyes, I curl up in bed and allow myself to sink for a moment. *What am I doing, man?? I'm out here acting like a…*

Like…

Jesus Christ, I'm acting like Ren.

Glancing up at the mattress above, I cringe, stomach rolling in disgust with myself. I cover my head with my pillow, growling and whining into it.

I'm severely fucked up. That's the only explanation. And now I'm terrified that my friendships will suffer for this. Denial is all well and good, but it can only work for so long…

Ren's words from earlier replay in my head. *"You're not a wedge, love… You've been keeping us together."*

My heart swells, and I *hate* that it does. I don't want to rely on being a part of *them* to give me validation. Like my only reason for existence in here is to be the stone they step on to get where they need to go.

But if not that, then… *what?*

The warrior, the friend, the proxy, the shadowman…

What's my purpose? Who am I, really??

Regardless, I just *can't* be the prison slut. *We already have one of those.*

But my behaviors tell a different story. The one that's written on those pages.

He ruined me. That's what it is.

Even if it wasn't his fault, he fucking broke *me, and now I have no idea who I am or what I'm doing.*

Emotion builds pressure behind my eyes. At first, I try to fight it. But it's no use.

It's alright… I'm alone again.

All… alone.

I can stop fighting, and no one will know. I can break down, if only right now…

Because in the shadows, no one sees me.

Word around the cellblock is that the storms have finally subsided, and it's actually nice out.

I wouldn't know. None of us have been outside in years at this point. I don't even want to know what my vitamin D levels are at… Probably nonexistent.

There's an abundance of D available in Alabaster Pen… But definitely not the kind you get from sunshine.

Still, I have to give credit where it's due. The mood around here has improved drastically over the last few weeks. Not that it's because we're all sucking each other off all the time, because aside from that one occasion, it hasn't happened again. *And* not only did things not get weird, but it seems like we've found our groove again.

Nothing is perfect, of course. We're in *prison*. But for the most part, everyone is doing okay.

Except for O'Malley. He's still in the East, according to Dash, who saw him last.

Am I worried about my friend? *Sure.* But there's nothing I can do about it. So for right now, I'm just moving along with life in prison, worrying only about the things I can actually control and holding out hope that Kieran will be back at some point. *No more, no less.*

It's time for showers. Wandering out of my cell, I'm looking for my crew, like a reflex. Luthor and Dash are already out in the row, headed my way. But as soon as they're close, I can tell something is up.

Oh, come on…

Please tell me I didn't jinx it.

Luthor seems a bit shiftier than usual. My eyes flick to Dash, who glances up from his shoes, pinning me with a shimmering hazel gaze that sets my teeth on edge.

"I don't want this…"

"Sup," I grumble, swallowing down the tension I need not to be feeling.

But Dash seems infinitely less fidgety than usual. In fact, he's acting more normal than both Luthor and me combined as he chirps, "Hey," offering me a kind smile.

The hunch in my shoulders retreats, and I exhale.

Okay, so… Good.

This is good.

My eyes shift to Luthor, narrowing at the way he's picking invisible lint off his shirt. *But what's up with him now?*

Ignoring it, the three of us putter along, following Jasper and Peters to the showers. Ren isn't in his cell, which automatically sparks some worry in my gut. But I remind myself that Ren kind of does what he wants, and it's not unusual for him to be off trading goods or collecting gossip the way a child collects tickets at an arcade.

Doesn't automatically mean he's off taking his… supplements.

"You got anything for me?" Dash's voice cuts into my thoughts, and I peek at him. He lifts his brows in wait.

I'm momentarily caught off-guard as a slideshow of memories hits my brain. But I shove them all back into the shadows where they belong.

"*Privet, kak dela*?" I say to him slowly, sounding out the words he taught me.

Dash chuckles, beaming. "Not bad, my dude. You're making better progress than me… *Tokki*."

I cackle. "You just called me a rabbit."

He chuckles, forcing a scowl. "That's what I meant to say! It's my nickname for you… Bunny."

Luthor snorts. "Aww! *Bunny*… So cute."

"Nice, dumbasses." I shake my head, my own smile unrelenting.

Whatever weirdness Luthor was dealing with has slipped away. And I can't ignore the way Dash's face is glowing.

If I didn't know any better, I'd say they got some action. Separately, I mean. Not together. Unless…

The moment we step inside the showers, my curious musings are once again cut off. Moans are echoing off the walls.

My stomach drops so fast it's in my shoes. Luthor and I share a look, all of his joy from a moment ago having sunk into a sea of fear.

Racing around the corner, I'm praying that I'm not about to see what I'm expecting to see… I'm dreading it, holding my breath and everything. And Luthor is practically falling down. But we come to a stop when we find the source of the sex noises.

Hancock is fucking Benson up against the opposite wall. My anxiety evaporates, as does Luthor's. I literally hear him exhale as if he just narrowly avoided death.

"What are we watching?" All three of us jump, startled by the voice that just snuck up behind us.

It's Ren. He's fully clothed and standing beside us, also watching Hancock drill into Benson.

Ren tilts his head, eyes lingering on the sight for a couple of extra seconds before murmuring, "Unless you wanna get jizzed on, might I suggest moving to the other side of the wall. That dude Benson can *shoot*… I swear to God, he could hit a target from twenty feet away."

We're all just staring at him until Dash lets out this raspy giggle. Then I snort. Then Luthor cackles. And before I know it, we're all dying.

"Shut up!" Benson yelps, voice choppy from the thrusts jostling him back and forth.

"Yea, some of us are trying to picture Pedro Pascal over here!" Hancock grunts.

"Huh...?" Benson rasps, then groans.

"Let's go," Ren hisses, still laughing. "Now now now!"

We all hustle around the corner, tripping over each other and wheezing, like children. It's fucking hilarious.

Sometimes this place is fun.

The rest of the shower goes on as they tend to, the four of us washing up together, sharing products and ragging on each other. Then we head to the caf for dinner.

"So, how long until you're back in solitary?" Ren teases Dash, picking something out of his instant mashed potatoes. I don't want to know what it was.

Dash rolls his eyes. "Funny."

"I'm just saying..." Ren chuckles. "You spend more time in the hole than the only top at an Ariana Grande concert."

I'm trying not to laugh too hard, and clearly so is Dash, his face flushing as he shifts in his seat.

Luthor glares at Ren, who's snorting as his own joke. "Ren, cut the crap."

"Oh, come on! That was funny," Ren sneers.

"It's fine..." Dash looks like he wants to say something more, but instead, he clears his throat and changes the subject. "Hey, Ren, you think you could give me some ink?"

Ren's laughter cuts out, his face sweeping into pure elation. "Really?!"

Dash smirks and nods, to which Ren squeals, shimmying around in place.

"What made you decide you want one?" Luthor asks Dash.

Dash pushes food around on his plate. "I don't know, it just feels... right." He clears his throat. "I mean, it's something to do, ya know?"

There's something different about him... I can't put my finger on it. He seems much calmer than he has been up until this point.

I don't want to think about what kinds of issues he has... I'm just glad he's feeling better.

Luthor is giving Dash a look, and it reminds me of the way he blushed when we were—*Nope. Not thinking about it.*

That's what the journal is for.

"Let's get you tatted, baby." Ren winks at Dash. Then he points at me. "And you're next."

I shrug. "You know I'm always game, *bra…tishka*?" I look to Dash.

"Almost," he chuckles.

"Get him to teach you Twat-Waffle," Ren whispers to Dash, his eyes on mine. "I need to know how to write it for a thing…"

"First of all, Joy would obviously understand how to read it, and then she would castrate you." I grumble-laugh. "Second of all, there isn't really a 'twat waffle' in Korean. It's more like… vagina pancake."

Ren cackles out loud. "Oh my *God!* Please, B! I'm *begging* you—"

He goes quiet when Joy stomps over, plopping down next to Luthor. He's literally holding his lips together with his fingers. It's killing me.

"Alright. It's done," she says to Luthor, unaware of the ridiculous conversation we were just having, involving Ren's promise to tattoo her in exchange for helping Luthor get his computer parts.

Luthor is instantly bouncing. "Oh goodie oh goodie oh goodie! Thank you, Joyful!"

"Yea, yea," she sighs. "If anyone asks where you got it, what do you say?"

"A spaceship landed, and it—"

"Yea, whatever, I don't care." She grunts. "Just not from me."

"Yes, ma'am." Luthor nods.

Shaking her head, she grumbles under her breath. "Not sure when I became UPS in this bitch, but whatever…" She peeks at Ren. "You owe me some ink."

Ren beams. "You got it, vagina pancake."

Joy lifts a brow, suspiciously unamused, while the four of us try to disguise our laughter.

Her face turns slowly from Ren to Luthor. "Do I wanna know?"

Luthor just shakes his head.

CHAPTER TEN

Trevel

THAILAND IS GOOD FOR ME.

Well, not *good*, but you know…

Bangkok is bustling with action from sunup to sundown, and I'm almost certain their main cultural export is sadness.

It's not a bad thing. I think the people who live here being overly familiar with the clandestine, the perverse and the deceitful, makes it one of the few truly *genuine* places in the world. Granted, I haven't been to many places, but in terms of cities, I like the ones that wear their grit and grime on the *outside*, for all to see.

London's not like that. On the outside, it pretends to be prim and proper. But there's a festering underbelly, just like everywhere else. The hypocrisy makes my eye twitch.

That's not to say I blame London for all of my problems growing up, but I certainly associate it with many of my youthful hardships. I do miss things about it from time to time… Like how lively the city gets in summer. *A good Yorkshire pudding.*

Especially being here, in Bangkok, a place so inherently different—it's liable to make your head spin if you visit here from somewhere like America or England.

Despite missing some of the comforts of the States, Thailand is the perfect place for me to continue living the hedonistic lifestyle to which I've grown accustomed. I can get by pickpocketing, as if I'm twelve years old again—*back to my roots!*—there's heroin on every street corner, and strange, filthy sex is a staple.

In short, I'm living my best destructive-boy life down here, and I couldn't ask for more in terms of a breakaway from the path of *straight and narrow* I was attempting to follow in Atlanta.

I miss Alice. Of course I do. I think about her every day.

But the more I sink into the perversions and debauchery of my current lifestyle, the more I realize we weren't meant to be together. She was just another mask for me to wear… A beautiful one, yes. But my biggest mistake was not listening to my gut.

I always knew she was too good for me—*I was right.* And she paid the ultimate price from getting mixed up with someone as wholly tragic as yours truly.

Am I certain that Andres wouldn't have killed her one way or another if I'd never come along? *No.* But the course laid out by the universe is a mysterious and melancholy one. Something about me slithering into Alice's life disrupted her cosmic flow. Who knows, it could even be a twin thing… My malediction muddied the waters between Alice and Andres. As soon as I started fucking around with them, they both wound up dead.

I'm fine swallowing all the blame. It might even be my *purpose.*

Some more evil to balance out the world's good… Yummy.

Anyway, none of that matters anymore. Because I've been living in Thailand for about three weeks, and every day, I move further and further from the person I was trying like hell to be, and back to who I *am.*

I'm dozing on the cot I call my bed, in this shabby hostel of sorts where I've been crashing. Sweat lines my bare flesh, from the heat of summer and the amorous activities between myself and a lovely young lady named *Moon.*

At least I think that's her name… I've been sky-high since the moment I touched down at Suvarnabhumi, so I wouldn't be the best person to ask for confirmation of anything right about now.

I'm not positive where she even came from. She sort of just appeared out in the hall the other day, and we decided to get high together. Naturally, one thing led to another, and the next thing I knew, we'd been fucking for almost a full day, in more positions than my drug-fueled libido could even stand. And now, I'm sticky and sore, melting into the bed with humidity and hours of sex lingering in the air.

Coming in and out of consciousness, I register her saying

something I don't understand in Thai, slinking out of bed and leaving. I'm almost certain she robbed me, but honestly, it's to be expected. Plus, the way she made me come was more than worth a few *baht* and the last hit of *panda*.

Footsteps that sound clunkier than hers approach my bed, but I'm too fucked up to be concerned or even *look*. I simply flop over onto my stomach and wait for whatever is about to happen to me.

Unfortunately, it's something I don't expect. Which is saying a lot.

"You Trevel Fenwick?" someone asks. A man. Older, with what sounds like some sort of Eastern European accent.

"My name is Tippy McMasters." I chuckle into my pillow. "Now please, either make a deposit or leave me to rot in peace."

The room is quiet for a moment, and I think maybe I was hallucinating the voice. Until I feel a large, meaty hand on my face.

The stranger grabs my chin, hard, yanking it in his direction. I grunt out of displeasure, blinking back grogginess to peek up at him.

"Uh… hi," I grumble while he looks over my face, assessing me. He's not ugly, so I add a sighed, *"Daddy."* His eyes sharpen, and his hand drifts down to my throat. "Ooh, *kinky*," I snicker, then lick my lip. "I should warn you, you're getting, like, sloppy fifths at this point."

The man scoffs, then hauls me to my feet, literally by the throat. *If I could feel anything, I'm sure that would have hurt.*

"Get dressed," he grunts. "You're coming with me."

"Hey, I told you I'd pay the rest later," I slur, yanking out of his hold. "We made a *deal*, remember?" I cock an eyebrow, because while I don't recognize him, it's safe to assume he could be here on behalf of the shady people I've been associating with since I got here.

But he just continues to offer me a bored glare. "I'm not here for money, and I don't care what you've gotten yourself into. Like I said, you're coming with me."

Alright, now I'm confused.

The situation has sobered me up just enough to take in the stranger standing before me. A big, sort of burly white guy, likely in his mid-to-late forties with light blond hair shaved close to his scalp. He's wearing all black, including black leather gloves, glancing at his phone screen in between watching me, rather closely.

Yawning, I rub my eyes. "Yea, I'm not going anywhere. Sorry, mate. Who even are you?"

The man sighs, clearly irritated by my fluttering around naked, defying him and asking questions as opposed to just doing what he says. He tucks his phone away, then reaches behind his back to pull out a pistol, aiming it at my head.

An uneasy laugh puffs from my lips. "Fuckin' hell… *Really?*"

"No games, Trevel," he snaps in a deep, commanding brogue. "The only reason you're not bound and gagged right now is because you coming along willingly makes the flight much easier. But if you'd rather opt to do this the hard way, just know… My only instruction was to bring you in *alive*. They never specified in what condition."

Even more unease awakens inside me, sending a chill up my spine. I peek left at Leo, who shrugs from where he's seated at the rickety kitchen table, flicking away a cockroach.

The utter seriousness of this man, who is clearly not from around here… The gun aimed at my face… His words. It's all turning my stomach.

Flight?

Bring me in…?

They??

I feel myself pale in an instant, nausea from weeks of heavy drug use and not much food or water mixing fast with my nerves. Turning, I hunch over and throw up on the floor next to him.

"Jesus Christ…" the man mutters, frowning.

Pulling in a breath, I straighten, dizzy with my head spinning. "That's better. Now, where were we? Oh, right… *Who* are you?? And what do you want with me?"

"I'm the man who was sent here to fetch you." He speaks evenly, no emotion in his tone or visible on his face. "Now, hurry up and get dressed. Trust me, you don't want me to do it."

I gape for a moment before glancing at the floor. "You're, um… s-standing on my shirt."

The man blinks at me, losing a bit of his disgust and hostility as he peeks down at his feet. Noticing that he is, in fact, standing on my shirt, he moves, allowing me to bend and pick it up, along with the rest of my clothes.

I dress quickly, feeling like I must be having some sort of mental episode. I don't understand anything that's happening. All I know is that while I don't necessarily *care* whether I live or die, if my only two options are to go with this stranger or have my brains blown out, I suppose I'll take the former.

It's like one of those *Choose Your Own Adventure* books. *Go with him and I get to keep reading. Don't go… and the story's over.*

Once my clothes are on, I stand still and stare at him, awaiting his next command. I think he's surprised, and maybe a bit impressed by my compliance, because he asks, "Would you like to freshen up before we go?"

"Oof," I huff, grinning. "Look that bad, do I?"

He's not amused. "Go use the restroom, Trevel. Unless you'd rather do it at the airport."

There it is again… Airport.

Who is this bloke? Where is he taking me??

Shaking it off when I sense the stranger's impatience, I mumble, "The loo is out there," nodding toward the door. "It's a communal… situation."

Sighing again, his jaw sets visibly. He grabs me by the arm and drags me out of the room, then gives me a little shove. "Move. And don't try anything. I will not hesitate to shoot you in the balls."

I cast him a horrified look while scampering toward the bathroom. "A wee bit extreme, don't you think?"

"Not really, no," he grunts, following me inside.

I do my best at cleaning up while this scary ogre of a person is hawk-eyeing me, dunking my head in the sink, gargling mouthwash and using a random toothbrush someone left by the sink.

"My name is Sven, by the way," he says, and I pause.

Blinking at him in the mirror, I spit, then smile. "Trevel Fenwick. Charmed, I'm sure."

He cocks a brow, but says nothing.

"So, Sven…" I use my sweetest tone, batting my eyelashes like Bugs bloody Bunny when he's about to pull one over on Elmer Fudd. "Where, pray tell, are you bringing me? I feel it's within my rights to know that much, don't you think?"

Sven regards me for a moment, dark eyes and a tight jaw holding back answers to my questions. *He's good.*

Finally, he speaks. "Trevel, I'm going to require your absolute cooperation here. We'll be traveling together for an extended period of time, and I must warn you, I'm not one for chit-chat. All you need to know is that you're leaving Thailand forever. From the looks of it, you enjoyed yourself here, but playtime is over. Do you understand?"

A small frown tugs at my lips as I roll my eyes. "Lovely. At least tell me you sprung for first class?"

Naturally, no answer.

The next couple of hours consist of Sven yanking me around and barking clipped orders. From the taxi to the airport and finally onto the plane, it's nothing but, *Move. Don't move. Hurry up. Over here. Stand up. Sit down. Stay still. Eat this. Drink that. No talking.*

I swear, the bloke is a wannabe drill sergeant. *Talk about reluctant travel companions.*

And I still have no idea who sent him, or where we're going; where our final destination will be.

The first plane we board is going to Seoul, but I assume that's just a layover. Which it is.

We spend about four hours in the Seoul airport, and even *that* is exciting for me because I've always wanted to travel here. I make sure to eat what I can stomach—fried chicken and kimchi. I love Korean food, but my appetite isn't exactly flourishing.

"Eat as much as you can," Sven gives another command while we sit in a booth at an airport restaurant. He slides me a bottle of Gatorade. "And drink. I'm assuming you've come down from excessive heroin use before?"

I swallow a gulp of delicious food that's slowly losing its flavor. "Not really..."

He stares at me.

"This is the first time I've ever gone, like... nonstop."

"Oh..." he rumbles, taking on an air of pity, though I can't miss a subtle twinge of amusement in his eyes. "Well, buckle up. You're in for a fun few days."

My mood is plummeting fast. "I've only been using for three weeks straight," I mutter, stubbornly refusing to take accountability for the situation I've put myself in. "And maybe three more weeks before that, on and off."

Sven's lips twitch. "I'm sure you'll be fine then."

Tosser.

Exhaustion is beginning to take over while I gaze out the window, wishing I could see something out there; *anything* in actual Seoul, other than the airport runways. But before I can wallow too much, it's time to go.

Sven drags me to the gate, and we begin boarding our next flight... To JFK.

Fifteen hours.

That's how long the flight is from Seoul to New York. Somehow the trip back to the States from Thailand seems epically longer and more insufferable than the trip there.

I sleep for the majority of it because, as much as I'd rejected the idea of withdrawal, my body *is* crashing. Still, every moment that I'm conscious is spent thinking, *obsessing*, over who could be responsible for this capture.

After all, it's not as if I have rich parents who would send someone to drag me back and force me into rehab. I have no one. I *know* no one...

Well, maybe one person.

And... he does happen to live in New York now.

The more my hazy paranoia rushes over this, the more I attach to it, and the more I convince myself it's true...

That *Dr. Love* is having me delivered to him.

I mean, that must be it. What other explanation could there be??

But now, the most significant question remains... *What is he going to do with me when I get there?*

A large black SUV picks us up at JFK, and we set off to yet *another* location. Nearly three hours in the car and we reach our next stop, which I'm assuming is also not our final destination, based on the fact that it appears to be a ferry dock.

When Sven exits the vehicle, I follow his lead and get out, stretching my arms and inhaling a deep pull of ocean air.

"Where the hell are we?" I ask, knowing bloody well no one will answer me.

"Alright..." Sven sighs as he nods at someone behind me. "This is where I leave you."

"Wait... *what?*" are the last words I get out before a bag is pulled over my head.

In an instant, I'm fighting, struggling against the hold of two men. They slap handcuffs on my wrists, and shackles on my ankles, dragging me a few feet then shoving me into the backseat of a different SUV.

"Oy! Sven! What the fuck is this?!" I shout, wiggling around while they slam the door. "I slept on your shoulder, you manky old fuck! And this is how you play me?? *Ugh!*" I roar, breathing heavily, rage and a sense of betrayal weaving through me.

It's not as if we became *friends* or anything. But still... He could have at least given me a heads-up.

The same bloke who made it his business to feed me so I didn't get sick... Bloody bastard.

I can't see shit. It's all pitch black from the bag, but I can make out voices just outside the vehicle. Suddenly, the front doors open, and I hear people getting into the SUV and starting it up. Then we're moving again.

"What the fuck is going on??" I growl, my limbs instantly growing tired from flailing around.

And the withdrawals are starting. Lovely.

They're all still ignoring me, one of the new male voices speaking from the front seat, "Yari? Yea, lemme talk to El Jefe, *por favor. Gracias.*" He goes quiet for a moment while I struggle pointlessly. "Hey, boss. We got him. *Si*, he's—"

I launch my foot forward, kicking the back of his seat.

"He's alive and kickin'." The man chuckles.

"I swear to God... No. I swear to *Lucifer himself*, I'm going to freak the fuck out if someone doesn't tell me what's going on *right now!*" I holler.

"Shut the fuck up," a different voice scolds from the driver's seat.

"Uh-huh... sure," the other bloke keeps speaking, I'm assuming to someone on the phone. "Your call. Okay, ten-four."

Lying on my side on the leather, I'm defeated. My anger is fading into hopelessness, and it's making me even more tired than I already was.

"Alright, fuckface," the man says, tone much less professional when it's for me. "The boss wants me to tell you he's looking forward to meeting you." I say nothing, and he barks, "*Escúchame*, dipshit! I'm talking to you! I'm gonna need some sign that you're hearing me or you'll get the taser, *comprende*??"

"Who, *me?*" I murmur, smirking beneath my bag.

He growls, "Yes, *you*, Monty Python. Jesus..."

"Ohh, sorry," I croon. "I thought you were still on the phone."

"Jefe is gonna cut out his tongue." The driver chuckles.

"You better watch your tone with the boss," the first bloke concurs. "You're a special delivery. We all know what that means..."

"Clearly, I don't," I mutter. "Who's your boss? Dr. Love...?"

"Who??" The driver grunts.

"What? *No,*" the other one scoffs. "But funny you should mention him... I heard this is all his doing. You are his *thank you* gift, I think."

My head is spinning off my body. "What the bloody hell are you talking about??"

"Yo, asshole... You got any idea where you're off to?" the driver grumbles, voice more oafish than the other one.

"No. That tosser Sven wouldn't tell me fuck-all. So if you lads have any insight to give, I'd be much obliged."

The two of them are quiet for a moment before they burst into laughter.

"*Wow*... alright then." The passenger sighs out his amusement as the other adds, "He's *fucked*."

"Listen closely." The main bloke continues. "You're on your way to *prison*, boy."

"Yea, but not just any prison..." the driver adds, putting in his commentary like a parrot on the first lad's shoulder.

"No sense in sugar-coating it. It's hell on earth. And once you shuffle your ass through those doors, you don't *ever* come out, you got me?"

I'm breaking out in a cold sweat. I'd love to say it's a symptom of coming down, but I think that's currently playing second fiddle to my increasing state of panic.

"Bullshit." I gulp. "They can't just lock me up and throw away the key... This is *America*. Prisons have regulations and... whatnot."

"What don't you get about this ain't no regular prison?" the deeper voice counters.

"It's true. If you're hoping some lawyer or judge... or *Dr. Love* will get you outta this, you'll wanna redirect that mindset. Only way out is in a body bag."

"Well, unless you're—" The driver's words are absorbed by a grunt.

The other man whispers a scolding, "*Callate, idiota*!" Then he returns to me. "You see, the Warden asked for you by name. That's never a good sign. Dr. Love sold you up the river without a paddle..."

"Without a goddamn *boat*..."

"Was probably a no-brainer for him. Anything to stay in the Warden's good graces. And now, well... there's no other way to put it, Brit boy. You're fucked."

"With a capital *fucked*."

Shivering with rage and confusion, my fists ball behind my back. I can't even fathom what I'm hearing. I don't want to believe them… But then what would they get out of lying?

That's why Sven wouldn't tell me shit. That's why we've been traveling for more than twenty-four hours, and why it feels like we're on our way to another bloody *planet* right now.

A place with no federal regulations… A place you can't ever leave.

I assumed Dr. Love would keep tabs on me from wherever he was… *But as it turns out, he wasn't the only one watching.*

Closing my eyes, I give up the fight, physically and mentally. I'm tired of running… Honestly, I'm tired of breathing.

My soul is exhausted.

"So…" I gust, disparaged enough that even my snark feels weak. "What's this *prison* called, anyway?"

CHAPTER ELEVEN

Byron

Sparring by myself isn't an ideal situation.

But sometimes it's all I have.

Things have been fucked up lately, and the isolation of being in this cell alone for most of every day is weighing on me. I never thought I'd say this, but I'm beginning to understand why Luthor is always moping when he loses a cellmate.

Speaking of…

I launch my foot at the pillow I have tied to the bars. My makeshift punching bag.

Dash is gone.

Punch.

O'Malley is dead.

Hit hit hit.

And I'm trying not to obsess over any of it, because all I have are questions and no goddamn answers. It's clouding up my head with so much noise, I've barely slept in days and have been living in a constant state of migraine.

Strike, strike… strike.

Sharp pain sears through my hand, and I realize the pillow fell. I've been hitting metal.

Great.

Guards enter the row. And not that I care about their feelings, but Jasper and Hancock both look equally stressed and exhausted as they gather us all for breakfast. I'm sure the loss of two inmates in twenty-four hours hasn't been easy on any of them...

Come to think of it, I haven't seen Velle in days.

The entire island is on lockdown thanks to this drama, but no one really knows *why*. All we know for sure is that Dash and O'Malley are both gone, in different ways. We have no idea how or why it happened, who's responsible, and what the fuck this means for the rest of us, prisoners and guards alike.

Luthor comes to walk next to me, but neither of us says a word, sharing only a brief, solemn look of mutual unease. When we get to the end of the row, Ren's cell is empty, and a wave of nauseated fear hits me so fast, my legs almost give out. I can feel Luthor having the same reaction.

"Where..." he chokes quietly. "Where is he??"

My mouth just hangs open, and I feel myself reaching for Luthor's hand because I just need *something* to hold on to right now. I need some form of contact to calm me down before I break in half.

No... No no no, we can't lose him too.

Not him...

Just as my mind is slipping into an even darker place than I'm used to, one of the doors at the opposite end of the corridor swings open, and Ren comes traipsing through. Like nothing happened.

Like he didn't just scare the ever-loving shit out of us!

He really needs to stop doing that.

Ren grins and waves while Luthor and I are releasing exhales of mutual relief. His eyes widen at the guards. He turns, and I catch him whispering something into whatever room he just came out of before closing the door tight behind him. Then he scampers over to join the herd, sliding right into place beside Luthor and myself. *Where he belongs.*

Jasper gives him a surly look, but Ren just winks at him.

"Where were you?" I ask, attempting to rein in my emotions.

"You scared the shit out of us," Luthor adds.

"Confidential meeting," Ren murmurs, lowering his voice to a whisper. "I've got details."

Fuck. My stomach creeps back up into my esophagus.

"Spill," I demand. But he holds up his hand.

He doesn't have to speak. I know he's telling me to wait until we get some privacy.

Easier said than done, bro.

In the caf, we grab our trays fast, rushing to our usual table. And once we're settled and away from the prying ears of everyone else, Ren sighs.

"Okay, so… here's what I know." He's watching Luthor closely before his eyes jump to mine. "Felix Darcey killed O'Malley, then set Dash free."

The ignite of rage starts slow, like early crawling flames, while I process those words. But it spreads quickly, absorbing brush and oxygen. Weaving from my gut, into my veins and muscles, until I'm engulfed in an inferno of wrath.

Crackling red splashes in my vision, and my fists clench tight.

That preppy little shit?

He's *the one who killed my friend??*

Luthor's hand drops onto my shoulder, and I flinch. "You okay?"

"Are you sure?" I hiss quietly at Ren, teeth gritted so tightly I can barely articulate. "How do you *know?*"

"I can't tell you," he states evenly. "I have a source, though, and they confirmed it. Darcey got out of his cell in the East and into O'Malley's with a weapon, stabbed the fuck out of him, carved him up, then somehow meandered his way into Dash's cell and let him out."

I'm fucking stunned speechless. Blinding anger of the highest degree is overwhelming the confusion of what I'm hearing.

I knew O'Malley was dead… From the moment we heard the rumor, I just *knew* it was true. And despite Ren's theories, I refused to believe that some self-righteous, narcissistic, wannabe Bundy fucking *fanboy* was the one to take my friend's life—*my friend, the absolute manic terror.*

The fucking Carver *did it. He chose to murder one of my friends and let the other go. Before I had the chance to say goodbye… to either of them.*

"How the fuck did that even happen?" Luthor asks Ren while I'm gripping the edge of the table so hard I might snap a chunk off. "Like just… *how??*"

Ren's quiet for a second. "I'm… not sure."

He's lying.

"So what the fuck *are* you telling us?? Huh?!" I bark.

Ren's eyes widen. "Shh! Simmer down, bitch."

"No. Fuck that!" I roar, jumping to my feet. "You're saying that dweeby psycho twink *somehow* murdered our friend, then set our other friend free?? And it's just like, *'Ah well... Shit happens! Prison's no match for The Carver!'*" I rake my fingers through my hair. "O'Malley didn't deserve to die that way!"

I'm splitting. I can *feel* the stress cracks slithering all throughout my insides. Picking up my tray of food, I whip it at the wall.

These emotions are too intense. The grief, the hopelessness, the regret. I can't process it all.

No. I don't *want* to. Anger is much easier for me to manage. Anger is straightforward, but the rest of this shit is just too... fucking *messy*.

"Kang, it's okay," Luthor stands, trying to talk me down, his eyes shifting nervously. "Just breathe... Head in the—"

But it's too late. I'm overflowing, and it's gotta go somewhere.

I smack his hand away when he tries to touch me, cutting off his attempts at reassurance. "You know Dash is probably dead too, right?? Fucking fish food, bro! They're both gone, you get that?? We're never gonna see them again!"

"Hey!" Joy comes out of nowhere, grabbing me by the shoulders. "You need to calm your ass down."

"Fuck off." I gasp for air, struggling to breathe all of a sudden.

My heart is beating too fast.

I don't need this.

I don't... belong... here.

I think I'm having a panic attack.

Joy quickly drags me away, pulling me out into the hallway while I'm physically fuming, chest huffing and puffing. As soon as we're out of view of everyone else, she lets me go. Lets me pace back and forth like a caged animal, because she knows I need to. She just stands back and watches me, arms folded over her chest.

It's not working to calm me down, though, and I'm sure she knows that too. Eventually, I have to stop, or I'll collapse.

Fuck this.

Fuck every single bit of this fucking place.

With my back up against the wall, I slide down onto the floor until I'm slumped, holding my head in my hands. Just trying to breathe. To focus on just that; the inhales, and the exhales.

Joy plops down next to me, leaning in close. She runs her nails up the nape of my neck, and it's oddly comforting. The touch right now feels good. So good that my stiff muscles eventually ease and my breathing evens out.

"I know he wasn't a… good person." I tremble out the words. Now that the rage is fading off, the other emotions are building up higher in its place. "But he was still my friend. I understood how he felt sometimes… We were both—" I swallow down my words on a painful gulp.

We were both lost.

"I'm sorry, *yeobo*," she hums.

Sniffing, I peek at her. "Do you think Dash made it?"

There's a rare flash of worry in her eyes as she rests her head against mine. And she mutters, barely audibly, "I fucking hope so."

We sit in silence for a while, until Joy finally stands with a sigh, pulling me up by my hand. "You wanna go back? I'll bring you food."

"What about the lockdown…?" I ask, defeated by the metric ton of uncertainty weighing on my shoulders.

"Let him come for me over some goddamn cup-o-noodles." She cracks the smallest smirk, and I mirror it back.

I still have friends here. They're not all gone.

Not yet, anyway…

"Thanks, *aein*."

She rolls her eyes at me, and I chuckle

We walk back to my cell in silence. When we get there, Joy says, "You're more, Byron."

Stepping inside, I turn to meet her gaze between the metal bars. "More than what?"

"You're just… *more*." She taps her knuckles on the steel. Then she wanders off.

A few minutes later, she returns to drop off some food for me. And I eat it alone, in the quiet, with just my thoughts. Ruminating and contemplating… How much *more* I could be if I weren't so convinced I'm less.

The day after I found out the truth about O'Malley's murder, I ran into Felix fucking Darcey in the showers.

I'm not sure who thought it'd be a good idea to bring him up to general population, but clearly, they were misguided.

It took everything in me not to bash his sweet little bespectacled head into the concrete enough times to crack it right open. Fortunately for him, my own best friends stopped me.

Luthor and Ren are… acting weird. I'm not sure what's up with them, but if I were to place a wager, I'd say Luthor is mourning the loss of yet another cellmate—his other best friend, Dash—by being an idiot. And Ren, as usual, is taking advantage of that.

Neither of them seems to care very much about O'Malley being gone. It's all about Dash. And *no*, neither of them was very close with O'Malley, and *yes*, he was a scumbag of a human. But the way I see it, that's irrelevant. We're *all* scumbags in one way or another, and O'Malley, hate him or not, was *our friend*. For a whole fuck of a lot longer than Dash was.

But they just don't care, and it's fucking bothering me more than I'm sure it should. As is the way they've been hanging on each other more excessively than usual.

It's not a sudden shift. *No fucking way.* This has been building for a while… Which is why I can't be too surprised by it. I always knew they'd migrate back to one another. It doesn't matter if Luthor claims they were never actually *together*, and if Ren is physically incapable of being faithful. They're two of the worst gluttons for punishment I've ever met. And I suppose I'm just as bad…

Because here I always am, right beside them. *Still* allowing them to drag me along for the toxic, codependent ride, because they're all I have…

Lying awake, I'm staring up at the mattress of the empty top bunk. Wishing for noise again, but getting nothing but quiet. No screaming nightmares from above my head, no rampant fucking from up the row. It's infinitely less loud than it was only a couple of weeks ago, and you'd *think* that would be a good thing. But instead, it just feels… unsettling.

Like the calm before the storm.

Fingers trailing below my navel, I slip them into my pants to palm my cock. Might as well… *Maybe a quick O will help turn off my brain and get me some shut-eye.*

It's not hard—not yet—but one touch and it slowly starts to fill. It's been weeks since I last got off. With Luthor and Ren… That stupid fucking threesome we had that brought *them* closer and pushed *me* further away.

Good. I don't need any of that shit.

I'm not like them. I don't need a relationship to validate my existence. I'm better off on my own, just like I always knew I would be.

I'm not gay. And Luthor and Ren can get fucking prison married for all I care. It doesn't bother me. I'm fine.

Fisting my dick, I tug it slowly, closing my eyes to let some salacious memories fuel me.

A mouth is just a mouth… A hole is just a hole.

They can feel good and not mean a goddamn thing.

"I'm not… into dudes…" I remember the gravelly words leaving my lips.

"So just pretend," the smooth voice rumbled as he pressed his wet flesh against mine in the showers. *"That's what I'll be doing."*

He dropped to his knees quickly, and before I could protest any further, he was stroking my cock in front of his face. Giving in to temptation almost effortlessly, I'd grabbed a fistful of wet hair, yanking until his blue eyes shined up at me.

There he is…

"W-who will you be… imagining?" I stammered to Ren the first time he sucked my dick.

He ran his hands up my thighs, and I shivered. *"You're gonna be Lex for me, okay?"*

"Whatever…" I sighed as he took my cock into his warm, wicked mouth.

And you'll be… Michelangelo.

It's been weeks since the last time Ren used me as a *proxy*. *Maybe months?*

Since Dash's first day here. Damn…

Shaking it off, I close my eyes and go back to fondling myself.

Whatever. I should be *happy* Ren isn't using me for his immature shit anymore. But my mind won't stop circling back to it, like an annoying song stuck in my head.

Maybe that threesome did exactly what it was supposed to do…

Maybe it got them back together.

My stomach feels like it's full of lead all of a sudden, and I don't know why. Curling into a ball, I absentmindedly tease my cock with my fingers while my chest aches from the inside.

I love being alone… I swear I do.

I don't want someone else doing this for me… I'm not *desperately* craving someone of my own to fawn over. Someone to watch me obsessively the way Ren does Luthor. To touch me and smile at me and whisper things in my ear.

Who fucking needs it?? Not me.

I'm fine on my own because love is for suckers.

But inside the jumbled static of my thoughts, I know why I'm harping on it… Because I lost *my* proxy.

My Michelangelo stand-in.

The next morning, I'm exhausted and irritable. The lack of sleep has been draining me. Not to mention, all of the guards are on a short fuse because of the lockdown. They're not partying or getting laid twenty-four-seven anymore, so to say they're *on edge* would be an understatement bigger than their collective swollen blue-balls.

In the cafeteria, I slouch next to Luthor, struggling not to fall asleep in my eggs. I mumble something to him and Ren, but when neither of them answers or even acknowledges me, I glance up.

They seem oblivious to my presence. Too busy making serious googly eyes at each other to even notice anyone else at the table. Their whispering back and forth wrings out my stomach like a sponge. My eyes fall to their joined hands on top of the table, teasing and toying. I swallow a rough gulp like a mouthful of sand.

It's not just Ren fucking around and Luthor pulling away… This is different. *They're*… different.

They're acting like a fucking *couple*. A real one.

Holy fuck, they had sex.

A weird chill brushes over my whole body, like that first tickle of nausea before you throw up. I don't know why, but I just have the grossest feeling rolling around in my gut, like raw meat in a tumble dryer.

Is this really happening?

Are they really…?

Before I can comment on what I'm piecing together, Joy stomps over to the table and grabs Luthor. Ren and I watch uneasily as she drags him to the other side of the caf, until they're nestled up in the corner, just out of view.

"What the crap?" Ren grunts, worry overwhelming his face and tone. He cranes his neck to get a better look. "What the hell was tha—"

"Did you and Luthor fuck?" I snap. Abandoning all attempts at burying this under my own neuroses.

Ren glances at me, lashes fluttering. "Um… No?"

"Are you asking me or answering me?" My gaze narrows.

"Um… both? No, neither." He falters, then exhales swiftly. "Fuck, I don't know what to say here… I don't want to upset him. You know he's all shy and shit."

His lips slope into a dopey, love-struck grin that he tries biting off while my shoulders drop.

"Holy… fuck," I breathe, like a deflating balloon. "You did. You two finally… had sex."

My mind feels as blank as my face.

Meanwhile, Ren's smile is brighter than the Aurora fucking Borealis as he leans in. "Just don't tell him I told you or anything. I'm sure he's trying to downplay it to make himself feel better."

I swallow even rougher, nodding. Just nodding, over and over. I can't stop. Totally on autopilot right now.

Great. This is… great.

I'm so… happy… for them.

"He's gonna want to keep it casual." Ren sighs, still beaming. Practically floating away. And I'm weighted to my seat. "For now. But he'll get there. I'm confident."

"That's…" I have to stop to clear my throat, because my voice is jagged as fuck. "Great. Good for you guys, I guess."

Ren does one of his dopey puppy-dog looks. "You don't sound happy."

I bite the inside of my cheek and shrug. "I don't care that you and Luthor are banging… Do whatever you want. Just don't come crying to me when shit falls apart again. Or expect me to pick up the pieces. *Again* ."

"Gee, thanks for the vote of confidence." Ren rolls his eyes. "Look, I'm really trying this time, okay? I don't want to screw this up—"

"*Again…*" I say the word for a third time, sounding very salty. *Extra sodium.*

"*Because* I know this is my last shot." He shoots me a serious look to counter my obvious skepticism and blatant inability to be supportive.

Now it's my turn to roll my eyes and gag a response. "Whatever, Ren. I'm happy for you guys because you're my best friends. But after a certain point, it's like… I don't know, I'll believe it when I see it."

Ren is gaping at me, but I can't look at him anymore. My stomach is bunched, and I've completely lost my appetite. I just want to go lie down.

I'm so fucking tired. This one stupid conversation feels like it took years off my life.

Why do I feel like this?

What's wrong with me??

Luthor comes wandering back to the table, slumping down next to me with an aggrieved breath.

"What was all that about?" Ren asks, immediately scooping Luthor's hand back up in his.

I can't stop staring at their tangling fingers while Luthor straightens.

"I just spoke to Dash on the phone. He's... alive."

It's not often that I allow myself to miss things from the outside. That's a habit that'll most definitely drive you nuts in here.

I don't like to wonder what's happening outside these walls. What my parents are doing, how many kids my sister must have, what the big movies and TV shows everyone's loving must be...

Has technology changed drastically? Are the robots uprising yet? Did the Jets finally give up?

Too much uncertainty. I'm better off living in quiet denial, pretending that nothing outside matters or even exists. As far as I'm concerned, this stupid fucking island is the entire world.

Fuck me, that's depressing.

I don't even like to let nostalgia seep in, because we all know that's a slippery slope. But we also know I'm not as good at simply *forgetting* things as I like to pretend I am. My memories are all I have left. *Literally.* I *have* to rely on the past, because the state of my present is growing increasingly bleak.

Luthor and Ren are a couple now—as much as Luthor will allow, anyway. Which basically means they spend every waking minute making me want to barf with their incessant cuteness, but Luthor still refuses to call Ren his *boyfriend*. He's probably just doing it to get a rise out of Ren.

That's what I would do.

Shaking my head, I close my eyes tight before my thoughts make me puke as much as the live rom-com being played out in front of me. When I reopen them, I spot Rook, Joy and Velle across the room, also visibly teasing and flirting.

Something happened between Velle and the Warden. None of us knows exactly what, but the power trio over there left the island together for a few days, and when they came back, they were a *throuple.*

The prison is technically still on lockdown, but Velle is steering the ship. No one's seen Manuel Blanco in a while... I know that should be a relief, but it's not. Sometimes it's better to see the danger than to worry about it hiding around every corner.

Still, nobody else is worrying about it. I swear to God, this place feels more like a couples resort than a fucking prison right now, and not just for *current* inmates and employees...

We started talking to Dash on the phone from wherever he is. It must be somewhere far and secluded, based on how comfortable everyone is with him calling Joy weekly. But the kicker is that he somehow met up with a former AP guard, Kemper, and now they're in some super adorable, squishy, gross relationship too, yucking it up in fugitive heaven.

I wish I was kidding. They've got a house and a dog, and they spend their days fucking, cuddling, and being *free*. While we're still stuck here, living vicariously.

I love Dash, I do. I *swear* I'm happy for him, but I can't help the way hearing him chuckle and sigh on the phone with my other stupidly in love friends every week makes me want to jam concrete in my ears. *Or curl up in bed with my headphones on, blaring A Static Lullaby.*

To top it all off, someone *else* has been venturing out of hiding lately, proving once and for all that his actions have no consequences...

Felix fucking Darcey.

You know, the prick who killed my cellmate and set Dash free.

Thankfully, he doesn't interact with us much, and mostly reigns over the East Wing with his Doctor Daddy. *No joke.* The allegedly world-renowned psychiatrist, who was brought here simply to *study* The Carver, wound up fucking him.

What sort of bullshit is that??

This entire building is made of heart eyes. Almost overnight, they all went from an abstinence-fueled rage to standing outside each other's windows with a boombox.

Hancock and Jasper are vibing in a pretty obvious way, Peters has a bounce in his step... Even Percy Gage, Ren's former obnoxious doofus of a fuckbuddy, has calmed the hell down and stopped harassing people. Word on the street is he started bottoming and now he's a changed man.

Yea. I'm telling you, it's a goddamn epidemic.

Everyone's happy.

Everyone but me.

Which is why I'm doing the exact thing I never let myself do... Wishing I were anywhere but here.

I miss Manhattan. I miss other angry people cursing at each other over some bullshit. I miss the aggressive horns honking and cabbies shouting at bicyclists.

I also miss Google, because right now, I could really use a search-bar…

Can you die from anger?

What's the world record for the longest scowl?

Is being a "hater" ever considered a medical condition?

It's not that I *want* to feel this way. I can't help it. While everyone around me is joyously floating on their cotton candy-flavored rainbow magic carpets, I'm stuck down here on Earth. Chained up in a place that sucks, with no one left to entertain me or distract me from how lonely I am.

My best friends are assholes. Openly chatting about how they like Darcey—*the guy who killed our friend!* Luthor actually waved at the kid the other day when he was up here… Fucking *waved* at him! *Can you believe that shit?!*

Ugh, it really steams my biscuits. Where's the sense of loyalty?? If not for O'Malley, then for me*!*

I'm crunchier than a bag of Fritos, and I'm not trying to be. I hate coming off as *jealous*, but this just stings, like salt in a wound.

I lost all of my friends. O'Malley, Dash, Luthor, Ren, Joy… They're either dead, gone, or *preoccupied*. And it's all thanks to that prissy little shithead Felix Darcey.

So excuse the hell out of me *for not wanting to chill with the guy. He fucked up everything.*

I'm seething while simultaneously cowering inside. And no one cares… Not a single person in this room full of people is worrying about *me*, wondering if *I'm* okay.

"Hey, you want the rest of my juice?" Luthor's voice cuts into my deep wallowing, and I glance up to find him smiling at me.

I release the tiniest bit of hostility and stop feeling sorry for myself for just long enough to shake my head. His smile slips off, and he nods. But because *he* is a good guy, he doesn't stop there.

"You still got that deck of cards?"

I clear my throat, working up the energy to converse with him. He's trying, and I shouldn't blame him for the way I feel. Yes, I'm annoyed with him for siding with Darcey, and I'm disappointed in him for climbing right back up Ren's ass like he has amnesia or something. But he's still my friend, and I should at least try giving him the benefit of the doubt.

"Uh, yea…" I mutter, sounding every bit as unenthused as I am.

"Cool," he chirps. "You should bring it tomorrow. We can play Texas Hold 'Em."

"That game sucks," Ren groans, resting his head on Luthor's shoulder. "Let's play strip poker!"

"Babe… shut up," Luthor grumbles.

I almost crack a smile. But then I remember I'm pissed and force it away.

Resting bitch face: activate.

"What about Blackjack?" Luthor asks me specifically, eagerness on his face.

Now I feel like a child of divorce whose dad is dating someone new and is trying to make up for missing my last however many baseball games by being extra present.

It's the pity, man. I can't stand it.

I don't need anyone's fucking charity.

"It's not fun with only two people," I grunt. "One of us has to be the dealer."

"Well, we could invite someone else to play," he suggests with hopefulness in his green eyes.

"Like who?" I squint at him. He shifts and parts his lips, but I cut him off. "Don't you dare say Darcey."

"I wasn't going to say Darcey…" He frowns. But I can tell he was thinking it. "What about… Simmons?"

"Man, I hate that guy," Ren gripes. "What's up with his laugh?? He sounds like a creepy clown in a haunted maze…"

"Why are you such a downer?" Luthor snaps at him.

But Ren just grins and pinches his cheeks. "We can't all be beautiful, glowing rays of sunshine like you, baby boy."

Luthor's face visibly flushes, and he bites his lip to cover that enamored former-virgin smile he's been rocking lately. My jaw clamps, and I can *feel* the hatred I'm about to spew everywhere. Before it happens, I stand up and grab my tray, unable to help the scoff that flees my lips.

Dumping the rest of my food into the trash, I linger by the doorway, wondering if anyone would even notice if I just walked out…

Glancing left, then right, I inch toward the door.

"Where you think you're going?" Joy scolds, though her lips are slanted into a small smirk.

I sigh. "Nowhere. Are we done in here yet?"

Her brows zip. "You got someplace to be?"

No... Nowhere to be, no one to see...

"I'd just rather be in my cell," I gripe. "It smells like crusty asshole in here."

"You paint a very pleasant word picture, you know that?" She huffs, then nods. "Come on. We're going to showers."

I stay with Joy the whole way there, avoiding walking near Luthor and Ren, because if I get tangled up in their incessant need to hold hands everywhere they go, I might rip their arms off.

I'm all pent-up aggression with nowhere to direct it. We haven't been down to the rec room in forever, and I could really use the exercise. Being able to move around in a space bigger than a ten-by-ten, sparring with Joy...

She probably gets enough cardio now that she has two huge boyfriends.

"What's up with you?" she asks me, smacking her billy club into her palm over and over. "That time of the month again?"

"Fuck off," I mutter, and she chuckles. "I'm just... whatever. It's *prison*. We're supposed to be miserable. Isn't that the point?"

She gives me a look, a studious one that has me feeling exposed. Especially when her eyes shift behind me to Luthor and Ren.

"You know what I think?" She inches closer. "I think you need to get laid."

My eyes spring to hers. Her grin widens, and I scoff, phoning in some cocky overconfidence to avoid feeling like she might be right. "You volunteering your services?"

"Please. You could barely handle what I used to throw your way." She winks. I roll my eyes.

Refusing to admit that on some level, she might be right.

Once we're settled in the showers, I can't help mulling over Joy's words. I know it's not the only reason I'm hating life right now... But it's definitely a side-effect.

Being one of Ren's consistent Luthor-proxies gave me access to semi-regular orgasms. Losing that was a hit to my prison sex life, though I refuse to admit it. *Looks like we're back to my hand, or nada.*

Stepping under the flow of water, I let it wash over my warm skin, peeking right. Remembering a time in this exact location, nearly three years ago...

When I first laid eyes on my very own black-haired, blue-eyed replacement...

A throaty chuckle and a soft whimper drag me out of my memories.

I peer right again, but unlike in my memory, Luthor and Ren are *together*, under one shower head, soaping each other up.

Biting the inside of my cheek so hard I taste blood, I force myself to ignore them.

Ignore how good it looks… How much I want *that.*

Stop it. You're not fucking gay, and you don't need a boyfriend.

Whatever I thought I could've had outside of here is irrelevant. Because *outside* doesn't matter anymore. *Inside* is all we have, and my inside is fucking *empty.*

Alabaster Pen is the world I'm living in. Where a hole is just a hole, fucking is just fucking, and when it's over, it's just… *over.*

I don't need a new pretty boy with dark hair and bright eyes and a killer smile. *I don't need another Michelangelo.*

This heartless fighter will be *just fine* on his own.

CHAPTER TWELVE

Byron's Book of Secrets

"Why so serious?"

The first time I followed someone, I was sixteen.

I was coming home from school after staying late for detention, traveling as slowly as humanly possible because I knew the kind of horrible berating I was about to endure from my father. He did *not* tolerate his children slacking off in school, let alone receiving detention for smoking a cigarette in the bathroom.

Man, you'd think he was Buddha him-fucking-self the way he acts like he's never made a single mistake.

Anyway, it was getting dark, and I was just entering the park when I saw this girl. I could tell right away she'd been crying based on the way she was wiping her eyes and sniffling as she shuffled ahead of me, clutching a backpack over her shoulder.

Naturally, she didn't see me. People rarely did, unless I was directly in their eye-line. It was just this quality I had; this uncanny ability to fall into the background. Call it a symptom of my quietness, or maybe a coping mechanism formed around my desire to be alone and not have to deal with people's constant, nagging questions.

"What's wrong??"

"Why are you so quiet?"

"Is everything okay?"

"Why so serious? Cheer up, kid! It's not all bad!"

Um, yes. Actually, it is.

I swear to God, if one more person told me to smile, I was gonna go all Heath Ledger in *The Dark Knight* on them. *Let's put a smile on that face You know the line.*

Because of how over it I was—the constant, nattering vocal spewage—I had somehow manifested myself into an *actual* shadow. A lurker who could effortlessly fade into the background and just watch.

I didn't mind. In fact, I liked it. *Most of the time*

It could get lonely, or isolating, but I told myself if and when someone came along worth stepping out of the shadows for, I'd do it. And hopefully, they wouldn't look right through me like I was made of cellophane.

The sad girl couldn't have been more than eighteen. She had auburn hair with this cool streak of blonde running down the front. I liked it. It made her look *unique*. So I kept walking behind her, keeping my steps light, so she wouldn't hear me, leaving just enough space between us that if she *did*, she wouldn't think I was some creeper.

And it worked. It worked so well, in fact, that once we got to the exit of the park, I wound up going right, following her, instead of left, toward my house.

There was just something I related to in her energy. She was lonely too, I could tell. *Maybe that was why she'd been crying*

I felt a connection to her. Like a kinship A need to protect. For some reason, I needed to keep following her to wherever she was going, just to make sure she was alright.

I followed her for a while, and not once did she notice me. But it was okay. I didn't mind being her shadow, if it meant neither of us was *alone*.

She eventually went into a building, which I sincerely hoped was her home, but you never know. I remember going back there a few times after that and just waiting outside. Hoping to see her again, maybe happier than last time. But I never did.

It didn't necessarily mean anything That was just life in New York. It's not a small town where everyone knows each other's business. You can't know what's going on with someone unless you're directly involved in their life. And even then we all have secrets.

After that day, I started following people who interested me; people I wanted to know, or observe, or keep an eye on. It was my secret hobby, and I loved that no one knew about it. Keeping the secret was half the fun. *Maybe more.*

Pair sneaking around with keeping a secret, and you've got a recipe for a pure, wicked thrill.

For that reason, I was blissed out beyond all rationale in the weeks leading up to my arrest. Because I'd been keeping a *deliciously* sneaky secret. The kind that's so good you want to bury it within the deepest crevices of yourself to prevent it from ever being discovered, while also fighting the desire to shout it from the rooftops.

Since that first life-obliterating night, I'd been back to

Michelangelo's place four more times. Each visit under the guise of *breaking in* and *assaulting him.* Of course, we both knew that wasn't really what was happening. But we did a pretty damn good job of acting like it was.

I wasn't sure what was wrong with Michelangelo Russo; if there had been something from his past that made him crave the rape fantasies, or if it was just his secret kink. Regardless, I was all the way on board. *No shade whatsoever.* His need to be tied up and degraded by a sexy stranger worked perfectly with my need to *be* that character.

The only slightly confusing part was that we were both *straight*—at least as far as the rest of the world was concerned.

Due to the nature of our weird little arrangement, we didn't talk much, outside of the pure filth that would exit my mouth sometimes when I had him zip-tied to his headboard. Other than *this one*, we weren't exactly swapping secrets, and that meant I hadn't the slightest clue what Michelangelo's *deal* was. But based on the way he behaved sometimes—and the quick, boring sex I'd seen him have with women—I was willing to bet he was gay.

It was none of my business. But I couldn't stop wondering if maybe his father, Governor Russo, was the reason for him keeping his sexuality under wraps. If it were true, I hated that for him Just like I hated it for myself.

I still wasn't sure if I was really bisexual, or just experimenting. All I knew was that every day since Michelangelo had come into my life, I'd been feeling more and more *human.* I finally felt alive and *real.*

Something was working. And that *something* was sneaking into the home of our governor in the middle of the night and having dirty, sweaty, morally ambiguous sex with his son.

I was in no rush to confront my sexuality hang-ups anyway. It wasn't like I could ever come out to my family. They wouldn't get it, especially my father. I refused to think about his reaction, but I knew it wouldn't be acceptance and proudly displayed rainbow garb.

I was better off keeping the secret. For now, it was just good, and I didn't want to ruin it by overthinking. *I'd much rather enjoy the best orgasms of my life, thank you very much.*

That said, I often think back to this time and wonder if it was inevitable

It was a crisp Friday evening in May, and I was at the gym. Hands and feet taped, punching and kicking the bags while my mind flickered through memories of the night before

When I'd crept into his townhouse and up the stairs to find him in the shower

We'd both sort of come into our own with the *act*. He'd gotten better at fighting and pretending he didn't want it, and I'd become better at playing the sadistic monster he wanted me to be. It was enticing, albeit a bit more difficult to subdue him. But I pulled it off, and the next thing I knew, I was in him up to my nuts and he was clenching that hot, quivering pressure around me.

Pausing my blows to catch my breath, I had to peek down and check my pants to make sure I didn't have a visible hard-on from the memories. Sure, I was the only one in the kickboxing studio, but still. I didn't wanna be *that* guy.

I could barely help it, though. I never knew just how fucking *awesome* it'd feel to fuck a guy in the ass. I'd been nervous about it at first, but judging by how he fell apart in my arms, I'd say he was just as into it. If he came in two minutes, then I was convulsing into him approximately twenty seconds later.

I was just so curious to know if this was really all about Michelangelo, or if it had been in me all along—lying dormant and waiting to erupt. I wondered if it had been his first time with a guy too But I didn't have the stomach to ask. Mainly because I didn't like how violent it made me to think about him saying it wasn't.

Practicing my spin-kick, I got lost in the memories of gushy wet tightness and skin slapping

"Fuck, you feel so good "

"Unngghh please. P-please s-stop."

"I don't think you mean that, spoiled little slut Your pretty cock is leaking everywhere. That means you like it "

"N-no "

"Yes "

"No "

"Yes "

"Oh fuck, oh Jesus Ghost Rider I'm gonna c-come."

"Come for me, you greedy bitch. Open that hole up and swallow—"

"Excuse me?" A sudden voice burst into my reverie, startling me into almost toppling over.

It was instantly familiar And when I whipped around, I came face-to-face with the exact scrumptious specimen whose ass I was just remembering coming in.

Michelangelo was there. In the gym. In *my* gym, standing in front of me, blue eyes sparkling, dimples deepening as he grinned at me.

I blinked heavily.

"Sorry. I didn't mean to scare you." The grin grew. So did the dimples.

Fuck me, he's so pretty, I thought. Then scolded myself to act straighter.

"It's fine " I cleared my throat, fidgeting in place.

Did he recognize me? He'd still never seen my face without the mask on. But we'd been fooling around for weeks

Couldn't he tell? Would I??

"I was just wondering if you could show me how to do that." He pointed to my knuckles wrapped in tape.

It took another generous moment for me to break out of the awkwardness of seeing him in a real-world setting—outside of my stalking, or our secret rendezvous. This was really *him* Michelangelo Russo, standing in front of *me*, Byron Kang.

I had nowhere to hide, and it had me feeling all kinds of vulnerable.

"Uh sure," I croaked. He was giving me an intensely curious look, so I spun away and went for the tape. "This your first time?" I balked at my question, stammering, "I mean, um boxing? Or kicking *kickboxing." Jesus, man, get it together.*

He chuckled. I loved the sound when I heard it in secret, but it turned out it was even better when he was knowingly giving it to *me*.

"Uh, yea, you could say that," he answered. "I took karate when I was a kid. Figured I'd get back into it. This'll make good practice, right?"

Swallowing hard, I glanced down at his hand, hoping he'd catch on to what I was too frozen to ask. He didn't, so I had to grab his hand myself, and the contact was *intense*. I caught his pupils dilating, but I clenched my jaw and focused on taping his knuckles.

"So are you trying to defend yourself against someone?" My eyes lifted to his. He smiled again.

"That would be wise, I'm sure " he hummed, brilliant blue gaze falling to my mouth for a split second. "But no. I'm auditioning for a small part in a movie that's super actiony, and I listed *karate* as one of my skills."

My eyebrow cocked, and he laughed.

"I know, typical struggling actor lying on his resume. Anyway, now I have to actually pretend like I know what I'm doing "

"Isn't that acting?" I quipped without even thinking.

He laughed again, a softer, more rumbly one this time, teasing, "Wow If you weren't helping me right now, I'd storm off."

I bit the grin off my lips. "You know, I'm actually a Tae Kwon Do instructor " I flinched. "Sometimes. I mean, I've done it before." *If I focus on wrapping his knuckles, I won't have to see him looking at me like the uncool loser I so clearly am.* "Just saying, if you ever need a trainer, or something "

Despite how hard I was fighting it, my eyes rose to his, and he was just *gazing* at me I didn't want to fixate on what it meant, but I could feel myself drowning in the blue pools of possible interest.

"Thank you," Michelangelo murmured sweetly. "That would Yea. I mean, that would be amazing."

I simply nodded because I didn't know what else to do. My skin was all hot and itchy.

"You seem really familiar." He cocked his head. "Do I know you from somewhere?"

My heart pounded harder. Fortunately, I'd finished wrapping him up because my hands were shaking and I feared he'd feel it. The look on his face was subtle enough, but invested all the same.

There was no way I was imagining this The flirtatious smile and the batting of his eyelashes. How damn *close* he was standing to me. I wasn't crazy. He was affected, and it was blowing up my entire world.

Maybe he *wasn't* afraid of being gay, or bi. Maybe that was just my own shit I was projecting onto him. Because in that moment, he didn't seem scared to be standing so close to another man, touching him and checking him out in public.

Glancing behind him, I watched his friends he'd come in with as they messed around with some boxing gloves and laughed to themselves. Even *they* didn't seem concerned about their friend flirting with a guy out in the open.

And in that moment, I *imagined*

I imagined what it would be like to answer him truthfully. To say, "It's me, baby. Your Ghost Rider." Then cup his sharp jaw and kiss him right there, in front of barely anyone, but still somehow *everyone*.

I imagined how good it would feel to touch his lips with mine—we'd never done it before. I imagined him feeding one of those adorable little chuckles into my mouth, and me smiling back while we kissed deeper and *hungrier* because nothing else in the world mattered.

I even imagined going to his house, *invited*. Watching movies and having dinner, laughing and touching, and so much more kissing Having *real* sex. No mask, no games. Fucking him to pieces because he was *mine*, then falling asleep with his head on my chest and my fingers in his soft hair.

In a matter of seconds, I imagined having a *boyfriend*. But not just any boyfriend *Michelangelo*. The sweet, smiling optimist to my brooding, furious fighter.

But here's an ugly secret for you I was afraid. Petrified, in fact. The idea of doing that, of *having* that made my heart weightless, and that *terrified* me. I couldn't do it.

Turns out, it was me all along. *I* was the one clinging to the shadows.

So I looked away from his face like a scared ass fucking baby, and lied, "Uh, no. Don't think so." Then I backed away, hastily grabbing my stuff. "But I actually have to go. It was good meeting you."

"Wait " he called out after me as I reached the door. And just like that first night in his bedroom, I stopped. "I didn't get your name. For the lessons?"

I peeked at him over my shoulder. "It's Byron Kang."

His lips parted, still with the bright blue confusion and incessant want in his eyes. But I just *couldn't*. I ran off before he could get out another word.

Needless to say, I wanted to punch myself in the face after that whole charade.

I felt like such a fool. Such a goddamn wuss. What the fuck was I so afraid of, anyway? My *parents??*

Who even gives a fuck about those? I mean, I know it's ingrained in me to care what they think, and despite never amounting to a thing in their eyes, I still wanted them to *love me*.

But if they don't now, then that's never going to change.

I knew I deserved to be who I wanted to be, and I knew that blood didn't always mean *family*. I wasn't convinced that it was all about them But I was afraid to deal with anything deeper.

My adrenaline was jacked for *hours* after leaving the gym. By midnight, I realized I had no hope of calming down, but more importantly, I had this gnawing need behind my ribcage I just couldn't ignore.

I had to see him. Whether I could tell him the truth or not, it didn't change how much he'd flipped me upside down. *And after I'd thought I was gonna do it to him*

Racing into Harlem took me ten minutes, and the whole time

I was chuckling to myself *Ghost Rider. What a nerd.* When I got to his townhouse, I rushed up the stoop, using the spare key he'd *accidentally* left lying around for me after our second night together.

I'll admit, I was being a lot less stealthy than usual. Because this time, I wanted him to know I was there. I jogged upstairs to his bedroom, out of breath as I stormed inside. Not from exertion, but from *this*. Whatever this manic sensation of a million crazed butterflies in my stomach was that I couldn't ignore for one more second.

He was sitting in the big chair by the window, in his boxers, smoking a joint. I had to stop and just *stare*. Because he looked like a dream, and I still couldn't figure it out. But right then, I didn't want to.

I only wanted one thing

Striding over, I didn't stop until I was wrapped around him like a vine. Straddling him on the chair, running my hands up his chest, and neck, onto his jaw. Our eyes locked, and I felt it. The mirrored yearning.

I tugged my mask out of the way. And I fucking kissed him.

Because *fuck* being scared.

The sound he made melted me from the inside out; this sexy little whimpering gasp, all jagged and throaty, because he was a *man*, and he had a deep, honey-coated voice that soothed me. My hands were in his hair, and his were on my face, our mouths moving, tongues lashing.

I had to stop to breathe, and when I did, he grinned and whispered, "I knew it was you."

It hurts now It's a pain unlike any other.

Because I still have all of these memories, just as vivid as if they'd happened ten minutes ago.

I remember standing up and bringing him with me, strapped to my body, his legs around my waist. I remember the urgency in our movements as I brought him to the bed and crawled over him.

I remember him purring, "Tie me up, Byron."

And I remember doing it, with his phone charger.

I remember pushing his legs open, just like he'd done to Rey, that night when I watched them from outside her window. Except I went into him bare, because he was *mine*.

I remember fucking him deep, and hard, but slow, kissing him and fisting his big, pink cock between us.

"Fuck me, baby." His rough voice still rings in my ears,

hushed and dripping with lust. "Nothing has ever felt like this *Uhhh*, fuck me there."

"Right here?" I gasped, kissing his jaw, then his neck, biting down on his pulse while I rippled my hips between his thighs. His dick throbbed in my hand, leaking everywhere. "God, gorgeous, you're everything "

"I fucking *love* your big dick in me "

"You love it?" I grunted, and he mewled, nodding fast. "In your sweet, greedy little rich-boy cunt?"

He nodded again, with tears tumbling down his cheeks.

"You like how I fuck what belongs to me?"

"Ohh God oohhfuck! *Fuck fuck fuck* " He was moaning and whimpering, long arms stretched above his head.

He was clamping onto me, and I *loved* how I could read his body already. It made me feel so close to him. Like we were one person.

This was it. This was what I'd wanted all along. And it didn't matter that he was a guy. The hang-ups had all but faded away

My Michelangelo was about to come, and I wanted to come with him. I wanted to fall With him.

Straightening, I grabbed his calves, one in each hand, holding his legs open so I could watch myself fucking the cum out of him.

That was when I heard it.

Seconds sooner and I could've done something. Maybe I could've reacted

But I was too lost in him and his beautiful noises, his intoxicated flush and swollen, pillowy lips, and the way he was *so* damn *beautiful* right at the edge

The thumping footsteps were drowned out by the thumping of my heart. By the time I heard them, it was too late.

"Oh my God! What the *fuck?!*"

It was Antonio Russo. Michelangelo's *father*

Diving into the room, right at me, with some big guy by his side.

In the blink of an eye, it was all over. Me and him, our future, my *life* All crammed back into the dark.

I was tackled to the ground by the large dude while the Governor of New York screamed and cursed at me, kicking me in the ribs and in the stomach.

For what it's worth, Michelangelo was not silent. He was shouting at his father, explaining that we were friends, that he *knew* me. I was fine with him not calling me his boyfriend. We hadn't had that conversation yet, so it made sense.

Whatever, I acknowledge that he was trying to explain. But it didn't matter. Governor Russo didn't want to hear it, and the optics weren't good.

I still had my mask on. It was out of place from the kissing, but still. Antonio Russo didn't see that part, nor did he care to listen to his son's tearful pleading.

"Dad, stop! It was just a game! He *wasn't hurting me!*"

Falling on deaf ears.

I was a masked man, in his home, who'd tied his son up and *raped* him. That was all the governor needed to know.

The barrel of a gun hit me in the back of the skull.

Back in the dark for *real*.

The first time I woke up, I think I was in jail. Or some sort of a holding cell, based on the way noises echoed, how cold it was, and the smell. Something about the smell made me think of a jail cell, though I'd never even been arrested before, so I wasn't sure how I came to that conclusion.

I didn't know how long I'd been out, or where I was exactly. All I knew was that I'd been gagged and hog-tied, and was lying on an extremely uncomfortable surface, with a bag over my head.

I barely remember anything about these few fleeting moments. Mostly, I just felt like I was about to die.

My jaw was already sore from the gag, and the sensation of saliva flowing from the corner of my mouth was driving me nuts. But I got over that quickly enough when I realized I could hear Governor Russo speaking from somewhere in the distance. It sounded like he was arguing with someone on the phone.

"I don't care," he barked. "Listen, listen, listen I don't fucking *care* how abnormal it is. You're taking him, right fucking now. So make whatever preparations you have to and do it immediately."

Eerie silence swept through the cold space while I wriggled around, attempting to fight through whatever was holding me, despite knowing it was pointless.

"You let me worry about that," the governor went on, and I heard footsteps coming my way. "As far as I'm concerned, all you need to know is that a new piece is being added to your collection."

The blood rushing in my ears nearly drowned out the sound of a loud door being opened and someone stomping over to me. Whoever they were, they were strong, because they hauled me to my feet in one aggressive yank, then began dragging me along.

"I'm sure you will." Governor Russo's voice was closer. "It's what you do, after all." And then he whispered by my face, "I've carved out a nice little spot just for you in Hell. Nobody fucks with a Russo. Think about that while you rot for the rest of your miserable existence, *Byron Kang*."

I barely had time to react before I felt a pinch.

The *second* time I woke up, I felt like pure dogshit.

I was groggy as fuck, head too heavy to lift, and my mouth so dry, my first instinct was to panic that they'd cut out my tongue. But as awareness slowly seeped in, I realized it was there, and I was no longer gagged.

When I eventually pried my eyelids open, I saw light. Fluorescent white that blinded me. My head was no longer covered. But when I tried to rub my eyes, I found my wrists secured. And my ankles. And my neck.

Dread arose fast. I tried not to let it, because I knew it would only make things worse, but I couldn't help it. I was strapped down, and the more I blinked the blur out of my vision, it appeared that I was in a padded cell.

The fear climbing up my throat was so thick I felt sick to my stomach I was somewhere very bad, and getting myself out would likely be impossible.

I recall my initial fight instinct, dense and potent enough that in seconds, I was roaring and screaming and rattling whatever bizarre piece of furniture I was strapped to.

"Now, now " A deep voice spoke from somewhere in the room. "Settle down, or you'll hurt yourself."

"Who Who are you??" I croaked. "Who's there?!"

A form appeared at my right, and I struggled to turn my head. Fortunately, he came to stand right in my line of sight, leaning in so I could make him out. He was a tall, white guy, with dark eyes and white hair, dressed in a suit. Assessing me, the way a child observes a bug in a jar.

"Who are you?" I asked again, slowly, growling on each word.

The man grinned. I was momentarily taken aback by how dazzling it was.

"My name"—he reached out to trail his fingers along my jaw.

I tried to flinch away, but it was no use—"is Manuel Blanco. *The Ivory*. And you, dear Byron Kang, are now my property."

I choked on more agitation and started coughing. "What the fuck ??"

The man brushed my hair back with long, slender fingers. Then he straightened, pacing around the room while he spoke. "You were rather out of it when you arrived here, so unfortunately, you didn't get to experience the whole *production*." He waved his hand in the air. "But allow me to explain what you missed. Welcome to Alabaster Penitentiary, your new home for the rest of ever. *I* am the Warden, and *you*, along with everyone else on this island, belong to me."

Home Forever

Warden Island

Alabaster Penitentiary??

Understandably, I started freaking out.

"P-please can you t-take this off m-my neck?" I sputtered, head spinning, vision blurring once more. "I c-can't breathe "

Manuel Blanco sighed, but humored me, unbuckling the strap around my throat. Immediately, I sucked in gulps of air, calming down enough for my pulse to even out.

The Warden lifted a light eyebrow down at my face. "Byron do you know why you're here?"

"No," I barked, an aggressive instinct to fight. Defend and *deny*. But then I closed my eyes in defeat, because it was no use. "I mean, yea I guess I do. But it's not what you think! I didn't do what Governor Russo is saying I did!"

I was pleading with this man *The Ivory*. Some bizarre stranger with a creepy nickname standing before me in a padded room. Confiding in him, like he was my lawyer or some shit. The fucking *warden* of a *penitentiary* As if *he*, of all people, might listen, realize this was all just a big misunderstanding and let me go.

Yea, I was pretty naïve back then.

The Warden simply smirked. "You're our sixty-second inmate here, Byron. That means roughly sixty-one times, I've stood in front of some poor sack of shit and listened to them blather on about how they're *innocent* and they *don't belong here*. 'I was duped! Framed! Made to look guilty by everyone in the world who has it out for li'l ol' *me*.'" His hands clasped together as he openly mocked me.

I was fucking fuming.

"Every *single* excuse, Mr. Kang I've heard them all." He dropped his hands onto my arms where they were strapped to the chair. Hovering over me until his breath was on my lips and I was shivering with fright. "So tell me what makes *you* so different?"

I won't lie; I was scared. But more than even that, I was exhausted, angry, and devastated I felt like nothing mattered anymore. My life was over.

So I used every bit of force I could muster, arched up to him, and hissed, "I fell in love with the governor's son. *That's* how I'm different. So if that's a crime, then I guess fuck it. I deserve to be here. But I wasn't hurting Michelangelo—" I couldn't help but choke on his name and sniffle to cover it up. The Ivory's gaze narrowed. "We'd been hooking up in secret for weeks. His dad caught us, and I guess he thought because it sorta looked like I was " My voice cut out, and I shook my head. "It doesn't matter. He wasn't listening, because he didn't *want* to. He'd rather dispose of me than face the truth His son likes to be tied up and fucked by strangers in masks pretending to assault him."

The room was silent for a moment, nothing but my labored breathing to be heard while this odd, impeccably dressed warden assessed me carefully. I couldn't deny how overwhelming he was to look at, with the black irises and peculiar white hair, and obviously expensive tailored clothes. His attractiveness just gave way to how dangerous it felt to be in his presence.

Finally, he spoke again. It wasn't what I expected. "Are you telling me the truth, Byron?" he asked me calmly, as if he didn't really *need* to, but still, he preferred to do his due diligence.

I nodded slowly, a persistent ache in the now hollow cavity where my heart used to be.

I'm never going to see him again

"Yes " I whispered hoarsely. "But I wish I wasn't."

The Ivory rumbled, "And why's that?"

"Because it won't change anything," I sighed. "I'm never getting out of here am I?"

He shook his head, almost solemnly on my behalf.

I breathed harshly, swallowing back the emotion rising in my throat. "So there you have it. I'm fucked for the rest of my life, all because I fell in love." I bit down hard on the inside of my cheek until I tasted blood. I didn't know why I was confessing this to him when I hadn't even said those words to *myself*. "I should've stayed in the fucking dark."

"No," he rumbled firmly, and I glanced up. "Falling in love is the most exquisite pain, Byron. No matter how deep the cut, how nasty the gash it still feels like *bliss* while you're bleeding out Doesn't it?"

Gazing at him, my eyes remained locked on his face, the sharp contours and severe lines. The deep blackness of his irises holding me still, like large hands squeezing my throat.

I nodded, because it felt good. I didn't understand how or *why*. But it was like comfort. Like *home.*

Slowly, he moved to release me from the straps of the chair without speaking another word, strong fingers brushing my hair once more, petting me gently.

"Relax in here as best you can," he whispered. "I'll send someone to fetch you and show you to your cell."

There was so much I wanted to say, but I knew it was no use. Something about this experience felt final.

Something in the air here felt permanent.

He was wrong about me. I wasn't one to beg for my life or to make excuses. And honestly without Michelangelo, after coming so close to my light, only to be stuffed back into the darkness of the closet What difference did it make if I was locked up or roaming free?

Resigning myself to my situation, I nodded slowly, swallowing a massive lump in my throat.

The Ivory took me by the chin, lifting my face. "I believe you'll do quite well here, Byron Kang. Quiet fury to fuel the fire."

So here I am In prison.

Except there was no trial, no sentencing. No jury of my peers.

I was suddenly just gone. Tossed away, banished from society for being stupid enough to fall in love with someone I couldn't have.

Maybe The Ivory was right. The pain of love certainly felt good in the moment. But every other scrape and bruise was horrendous.

I'm sure I'll never feel real love again. I *can't.* It seems physically impossible now. I hadn't even noticed that I'd fallen for Michelangelo until it was too late. Until he was ripped out of my grip in the most agonizing moment of my life.

That first night in Alabaster Penitentiary, as I curled up

on my flimsy prison mattress, on a bunk bed I fortunately had to myself, I vowed two things

1) I would keep as many secrets as I could hold, store them up inside as my protection against the agony of vulnerability in the *truth*.

And 2) I would never, *ever* fall in love again.

My second day in prison was better. I met Luthor.

It was my first time in the cafeteria, and I was *way* out of my element. I didn't know where to go, and I didn't have it in me to act *hard*. So when I saw him sitting alone and looking kind of sad at a table by himself, I walked over and sat down, like it was nothing.

The kid with the shaved head and green dismay in his eyes peeked up at me, then muttered a weakened, "Sup."

"Hey," I grunted, picking at my disgusting-looking food.

"You new?" he asked, casually interested. Not prying or trying to size me up. Just asking.

I nodded. "Name's Kang. You?"

"Lex," he sniffed. "But everyone here calls me Luthor."

"That's cool," I said, bored. But not because of him. I just had nothing left to feel. "What number are you?"

"35," he hummed.

"Shit " I breathed. "That sounds like a while ago."

He sighed tiredly. "Yea. It was."

"Sorry," I muttered remorsefully. "That was a dick thing to say."

"No, it's fine." He grew a tiny curl to his lips. "Honestly, I appreciate having someone around. My friends are Well, they're not here."

I lifted a brow. "Friends ? As in, other inmates?"

He nodded. "Yea. Usually, we're all together, but lately, we haven't been, and it's just I don't know, it feels even more isolating than normal." He peered at me. "I don't know why I'm saying this to you Probably freaking you out more. My bad."

"I don't mind." I shrugged. "I'm used to being alone."

Picking up my sandwich, I took a bite while Luthor watched me, smirking. As soon as the food touched my tongue, I spit it out.

"Ugh! Gross." I spit more, trying to get the foul taste out of my mouth.

Luthor was chuckling up a storm, like it was the funniest thing ever. I grimaced while pulling apart the sandwich, only to find mold all over the cheese.

"Hey." He sighed out his laughter. "Maybe we can be alone together, huh?"

Like the girl with the auburn hair.

Yea I thought, hopefully. *Alone together sounds pretty good.*

When I returned to my cell after lunch, I found a small, rectangular object on my bed, with a card taped to the top. As I grew closer, I found it to be a journal and a set of pens. Nice ones.

Lifting the card slowly, I read it to myself.

For your secrets.

Signed simply with an *X* at the bottom.

It was from Manuel Blanco, though to this day, I'm not sure how I knew. And as much as I wanted to hate him, for keeping me here when he clearly knew I didn't need to be, I couldn't help the subtle slope to my lips.

Write it down, Byron All of it. To keep it from eating you alive.

Who knows? Maybe someday someone will be worthy of reading it.

CHAPTER THIRTEEN

Trevel

ALABASTER PENITENTIARY.

That's where I am. Where I've been locked away, *naked*, in a cold, dank room with no light—a ten-by-ten box of concrete that smells like dried blood and stale ocean water—for at least a full day.

I think. There's no way of knowing how long I've truly been here, because there are no windows, clocks, or any indication that anyone is *ever* coming to get me.

I must say, this is *much* worse than I expected. I assumed I'd get, at the very least, a cot, some food scraps... *A jumpsuit.*

On the contrary. I arrived and was immediately stripped naked, cavity-searched to the point of being excessive, then thrown into this room to rot. The officers who brought me in weren't being dramatic.

This is no correctional facility.

The discomfort of being naked on a freezing cold, filthy concrete floor, paired with the way my bones are already aching beneath my violent shakes, isn't all that's preventing me from getting rest, though. I'm also stewing in a wrath so potent, I can *smell* it like sulfur and ash.

I saw Dr. Love. In fact, he was the *first* person I saw upon my arrival at Alabaster Penitentiary. When the two officers who'd driven me here yanked the bag off of my head and pulled me out of the SUV, there he was. Standing just a few feet away, dressed in his usual tailored clothes, the sleeves of his dark-blue dress shirt rolled up his muscular forearms. Still and emotionless. *Watching* me, as if nothing had changed.

As if we weren't on an island in the middle of bloody *nowhere*, outside of the foreboding monstrosity he left me for. As if he hadn't chosen to sacrifice me to *this place* for his own selfish purposes based on a few measly murders.

Bloody robot man.

He looks exactly the same. And yet somehow… different.

I can't place my finger on it, but when I came face-to-face with the man who'd been my doctor—my *rock*—for three years, the person responsible for getting me out of Riverwoods and convincing me that *I*, Trevel Fenwick, could lead a *normal* life… I sensed a change in him. His *aura* felt renewed; *enlivened*.

Naturally, it made me sick with rage.

What about working in this devastating place has made him seem more fulfilled than he ever was in his sleek, modern office in downtown Atlanta?

What could possibly be here *that's making him happier than he was back in civilization??*

We exchanged words, though I was seething so hard I can barely remember what I said to him. Still, the look on his face is burned into my brain. The way he stood there, beside three guards—two men and a woman, all of whom were watching me with distinct distrust on their faces—giving me nothing more than his typical brand of impassive, *holier-than thou* attitude.

There was no remorse for bringing me here. *Why would there be??* He's never given a single shred of a *fuck* about what happens to me, and that's clear now more than ever. He didn't deny that he sent Sven to find me and bring me here as some token of his appreciation for *The Warden—whom I still haven't met, by the way.*

If anything, he was gaslighting me into thinking he somehow did this for *my* benefit.

"I'm glad to have you here, though. I think this could be good for you."

My teeth are set, grinding away as I growl into the pitch blackness of this tomb.

This is good *for me, is it, Doctor?? Dying a slow, humiliating death with my bangers out… Locked away like a worthless bloody animal?!*

I'm a volcano of contempt, ready to erupt. And what's worse, I haven't seen Leo since I got here. I'm completely *alone*. Not even an imaginary friend to keep me company anymore.

I swear, if I ever get out of here, I will make it my *life's mission* to destroy Dr. Love. I don't care if it kills me in the process. Revenge is the one thing I'm good at.

Lemuel Love will pay for what he's done to me.

Footsteps steal my attention, and I sit up. There's a lot of *noise* in this place. Even when you're separated from everything else by thick walls of concrete, you can still hear things banging and clanging from somewhere in the distance. Although, this is the first time the stomping and jingling of keys have come this close…

Someone has stopped outside my door. And before I can even prepare myself, it flings open, and I'm being blinded by fluorescent light.

I can't see fuck-all. I'm just cowering, with my hands over my face.

Whoever is there tosses something at me that feels like fabric. "Put those on."

"*God?* Is that You?" I mouth off, because I can't help myself, blinking over and over.

"Pretty much," the male voice rumbles. "Get fucking dressed, 102. *Now.*"

My eyes are slowly adjusting to the light, just enough to make out some clothes on the floor by my feet. Dull gray jumpsuit pants, a white t-shirt, and some basic gray slippers that look like they'll barely fit. I wriggle into everything quickly, attempting to stand, though it takes me a moment. I'm very wobbly.

"Good job," the man growls with patronizing sarcasm.

The more my eyes adjust, the more I begin to really *see* him. He's quite large, and attractive, with dark hair tied back into a tiny man-bun.

Wait a minute… I recognize him. He was one of the blokes standing beside Dr. Love when I arrived.

I blink as he pulls handcuffs off of his holster. "Up against the wall, palms flat. You move, I break your jaw."

Quite the sterling personality on this one.

Doing as he says, I rest my front on the wall, and he immediately stomps up behind me, grabbing my arms and forcefully cuffing them behind my back while I grunt in displeasure. Then he bends and attaches shackles to my ankles. And not that I should be fixating on this, but he smells delicious.

Chalk it up to me smelling nothing but mildew and despair for the last however long.

Spinning me around, he yanks me roughly until I stumble. "Try to keep up, inmate."

Walking in shackles is difficult. I'm trying not to trip, since it seems like the sort of thing that will get me scolded, but I also can't stop myself from ogling the man. *Yes*, he's rather good-looking, in a dark and devious sort of way. Almost the same height as me, which says a lot, being that I'm six-five. Tanned complexion, studs in his eyebrow and nose, and tattoos on nearly every visible plane of flesh that isn't covered by his uniform—an ensemble he wears *shockingly* well, by the way.

Not exactly my *type*, but still... *I can appreciate a Muscle Daddy who could probably snap me in half with his bare hands.*

Sneaking a peek at his name tag, I mumble, "Chevelle..."

His eyes dart to mine, a deep blue that holds my gaze. "That's *Officer Chevelle*, if you know what's good for you."

"Oh, I don't," I reply, teasing, but not really. "Otherwise, I'm sure I would have strangled the bloke who brought me here and left him in the airport bathroom."

Officer Chevelle gives me a look, cocking his pierced eyebrow. But he says nothing, simply continues on, dragging me through long corridors that all look exactly the same. I'm momentarily bewildered by how he clearly knows his way around, despite no signs or distinguishing marks. As if he could be blindfolded and still maneuver himself through these halls effortlessly and just as fast.

Must mean he's been here a while...

He certainly carries himself like someone with a high level of authority, though that could be said of all the guards I've encountered so far. They all behave the way you'd expect of prison guards, especially the type who work in a place like this. Morality doesn't appear to be a requirement of Alabaster Penitentiary.

Still, *Officer Chevelle* has a different vibe. Naturally, I'm intrigued.

Our trek through the long hallways goes on for minutes, until we finally stop in front of a door. The noise is much louder here; booming voices of inmates and guards alike echoing from somewhere nearby. I'm no stranger to such sounds, though it's been a while. But this already feels monumentally different from any prison or institution I've been in. For starters, it feels like this place was built centuries ago.

What is Alabaster Penitentiary? Where did it come from, and why is it here?

Officer Chevelle raps his knuckles on the door twice. And we wait until a voice from inside calls, "Come in."

I'm ushered into a new room, and from one look around, I can see that it has an obviously unique setup. Half of the floor is tiled, with a few drains, as if there were showers at one time. But I don't believe *showering* is what happens in here now…

There's a very distinct smell of bleach invading my senses, and while it's apparent that some cleaning has happened, the grout in between the tiles is permanently stained black; I'm guessing a healthy combination of mold and caked blood.

In the middle of the room are two chairs, facing each other. One of them is empty. And in the other sits a man.

He glances up and simply nods at Officer Chevelle, who's already tugging me closer and shoving me down into the empty seat, across from the stranger. And then he leaves.

My head whips to the door as it's slamming shut. Call it my own naivety, but I was sort of hoping the giant tattooed beast would stay with me. For protection.

I gulp as my gaze slowly creeps back to the man sitting barely three feet from me. We're so close, our knees are practically touching.

"Hello, Trevel…" He greets me by name on a bit of a sigh.

There's a familiarity in his tone, as if he's known of me for a while and is *finally* seeing me face to face. Which is confusing because I don't know this man.

I think I'd remember meeting him…

His appearance can only be described as *unmistakable*. Slim and clearly quite tall, even when seated. Pale skin and dark eyes, with hair as white as snow—though judging by the lines on his face, there's no way he's older than fifty. He's dressed in a three-piece suit, obviously expensive and tailored to an immaculate fit, yet his collar is loosened casually, sleeves rolled up his forearms.

My first guess is that he's the Warden, but then this place is an utter shithole, and he looks… Well, far too pristine to even *be* here.

"I'd like to formally introduce myself." He continues, tone polite, professional. Again, not what you'd expect sitting in a room that resembles a slaughterhouse from a *Texas Chainsaw* movie. "My name is Manuel Blanco, but you can call me The Ivory. I am the Warden of this lovely establishment we call Alabaster Penitentiary." He gestures around the room in a subtly mocking fashion, as if he knows it's foul and he's being cheeky. "On behalf of us all, let me welcome *you*, inmate #102, as our newest arrival."

I can do nothing more than blink. And stare. And blink… and stare.

Honestly, I'm not certain I'm even breathing.

I'm usually rather well-versed in reading people. It's something I learned from living on the streets as long as I did. I pride myself on rarely being surprised by the ways in which human beings behave, but this is throwing me for a loop.

Who is this peculiar, eccentric, well-dressed anime villain of a man?? Why is he here, and most importantly, what on earth does he want with me??

The Warden sits back a bit in his chair, crossing his ankle over his knee. *His socks have little birds on them…* "I'm sure you have many questions bouncing around in that pretty head of yours. Trust me, I have some of my own. So let us get the formalities out of the way before we move forward with the juicy bits. First of all, as I'm sure my men informed you, you are here to stay. Prisoners are sent to me from far and wide, for various reasons. But the one thing you all have in common is that you were hand-selected to reside *here*, as opposed to, say, a federal prison, correctional facility, or rehabilitation center.

"Because of that, you have lost the right to certain freedoms, comforts, protections of the US Constitution, blah blah blah." He waves his hand in the air flippantly. "Suffice it to say, living here may be a shock to your system, but I must ask that you accept it. Get onboard, Trevel, or things can get much worse than they need to be."

Uh… What?!

My lips part to ask him a million questions, but he stares even harder at me, gaze narrowed as his own mouth sets into a firm line. And my voice dries right up.

He tilts his head. "Second of all, please know that I have eyes everywhere, and I don't just mean the guards. But speaking of them, you'll get to know my officers quite well during the course of your time here. They oversee everything…" His voice trails off, and he gets a contemplative darkness to his features. "There are rules to be followed, just like everywhere else. But on this island, the most important of them all is that *I* own *you*."

Those last three words come out slowly pronounced.

He owns *me??*

I think he can tell I want to counter this point, so he uncrosses his legs, sitting up straighter in his seat. "The way you behave has consequences, Trevel. There are repercussions for the things you do… and the people with whom you surround yourself. But I'm sure you've already figured that out..."

Who is he referring to? Dr. Love??

"Look, Mr.... Ivory," I croak, shifting in my seat, the metal from my cuffs clinking behind my back. "I'm not one to claim innocence. In fact, far from it. But—"

The Warden clears his throat, and I stop abruptly. Both feet planted on the floor, he leans in closer to my face. "It is not your turn to speak yet, Trevel Fenwick." I blink and shiver. "I know you think you're here because of Dr. Lemuel Love. And while he was helpful in having you delivered, make no mistake, I could've just as easily gotten you here myself."

"But *why...?*" I manage to croak over the sandpaper in my throat.

He's so close to me. I feel the warmth of his breath on my lips, see the depths of tenebrosity in his eyes; a cavern of black that feels like it could swallow me whole. This man is utterly terrifying, and my entire body is now sheeted in chills.

"The answer to that question is a complicated one, I'm afraid," he whispers over my mouth. Eyes never once leaving mine. "But before I get into it, I need you to answer one for me."

The tingles running through me have seemingly shifted. I can't explain it, but I'm becoming warm beneath my skin, and my heart is racing at an abnormal rate. Something about how *close* he is, the chokehold of his irises and the reverberation of his low, raspy voice soaking into me through his mouth...

I gulp and nod. His eyes dip to my lips. Just a split second, but it causes a strange and confusing throb between my legs.

The Warden cocks his head to the side, like a curious animal. "The young lady you were dating..." he starts, quiet and intense. My brow furrows. "She was a twin, yes?" I'm gaping at him. "And her last name was... *Alvarez?*"

I'm so thrown off by the trajectory of this conversation, I physically can't produce words. But he's staring at me so hard it feels like I'm being strangled.

I nod.

"She had a twin brother...?" he asks, pressing further, voice almost nonexistent. I nod again. "What happened to him?"

My heart is thumping so fast, I'm quaking. I have no idea why he's asking me this, how he knows these things, or why he seems *so* very invested. But I know he's requiring an actual answer on this one, so I manage to cough up the words.

"I killed him."

The mound in his throat dips. As the only movement in the general vicinity, it catches my attention. But then something else moves… His right hand, squeezing into a fist, visibly tight.

Fuck…

When I glance back up at his face, he's wearing the most severe look anyone's ever given me. Agony and rage, anguish and fury, all a breath away from my face. A word away from unleashing.

He looks like he's hanging on by a thread.

"Tell me his name," The Ivory commands; the rumble of a deadly creature. One wrong move, and I'll be torn to shreds. I'm blinking, frozen in baffled mute. He grabs me by the throat and hisses in my face, "*Say it.*"

"A-Andres," I stutter, practically pissing my pants. "Andres Alvarez."

His grip on my throat loosens. In the blink of an eye, his wrath has retreated.

He backs up, just an inch or so, but still. I'm no longer staring into the wide-open jaws of a Great White. Releasing a long exhale, his shoulders drop, and he closes his eyes, visible relief washing over him. And I'm simply *gawking*, even more confused than before.

What in the bloody fuck??

The Ivory's lips curve into a small grin, and he shakes his head. His long fingers are sort of petting my throat, gently caressing me while he chuckles, "Oh, Trevel… Trevel Trevel Trevel…" He laughs a little more. "Do you have any *idea*…?"

He's just laughing to himself now, and I'm gaping in sheer perplexity, *needing* to understand what on earth is happening. "Any idea of… what?"

"No. *No*, of course you don't. How could you?" He jumps up from his seat and begins pacing around me, raking fingers through the silky strands of his white hair. "The universe is… *wow.* I mean, just…" He pauses to make that mind-exploding motion with his hands. "Such a trip, man."

"Um… not to step out of line or anything, sir, but am I supposed to understand a word of what you're saying?" I ask, watching him carefully.

Plopping down on the seat once more, he places his hands on my thighs. "Trevel, I brought you here to kill you." He says it so casually, it almost distracts from the threatening nature of that statement. Paired with how *jubilant* he looks right now, it's a complete one-eighty from how he was glaring at me only moments ago. "Well, *eventually,* you would've died.

But believe me, the things I was planning to do to you… Death would've been a kindness!" He cackles, then sighs out his amusement, dipping his chin. "And you would've begged me for it, Trevel. A plea I would have gleefully disregarded for as long as it felt necessary to me."

I swallow a lump in my throat. "So… you were planning to torture me?"

He nods.

"May I ask… why?"

He smiles, a *real*, bright smile of repose and delight. I don't know him at all, but I can tell it's not something he does often. It's quite pretty… but also rather unnerving.

Giving me a quick once-over, he reaches into his pocket. I stiffen in fear, until he pulls out a set of keys, using them to unlock my cuffs. But rather than doing it behind my back, he wraps his arms around me. An oddly intimate way to remove cuffs. He also smells mouthwatering, and feeling his warm, taut frame surrounding me for even just a few seconds is… interesting.

Once the cuffs are off, I move my arms out of that uncomfortable position, the ease in my muscles allowing me to relax a bit. The Warden takes my wrists in his hands, rubbing them for me. Such a caring gesture…

I swear to God, it's impossible to get a proper read on this bloke.

"I won't bore you with the details." He speaks calmly. "The history and complex, ardent backstory…" *Bollocks. That's what I wanted to hear!* "But essentially, it boils down to vengeance."

"*Vengeance?*" I repeat the word, and he nods.

"*Sì.*" He shakes his head. "Sorry. *Yes.*" His dark eyes glide up to mine. "I heard about your most recent killings. Some misinformation was given to me, and in the heat of the moment…" His words fade and he looks away. "Long story short, it became clear we had the wrong person after you arrived, but I still had to ask you myself. Just to be one-hundred percent certain. And I take *full* responsibility for not properly investigating the situation before dragging you here." Clasping my hands in between his, he locks his eyes onto mine, shimmering to convey full sincerity on this topic. "But you have to understand, I was out of my *mind* with rage, Trevel. In fact, I know *you*, of all people, can empathize."

"I can…?"

He nods. "Everyone thinks you killed your girlfriend. But you didn't, did you?"

Furious despair instantly weaves through my extremities at mention of Alice… And what her despicable brother did to her.

"No," I growl. "I didn't."

The Ivory's eyes are alight with understanding. "You took the lives of the people who *did*… Didn't you?"

I nod, jaw clenching. "Simple death was too merciful for them… Especially that fuck Andres. I wish I could bring him back to life just to slaughter him again… over and over and fucking *over*. For her."

His lips twist into a knowing smirk. "You do understand."

Breathing out steadily, I compose myself, focusing once more on the here and now.

So he's saying he… wanted to kill me? To avenge the death of someone he'd thought I killed?

But who?

He sighs, releasing my hands. "So you see, Trevel, my dear boy… This was all just a big mix-up." Grinning, he gives me a playful smack on the cheek before sitting back, crossing his ankle over his knee again. "And to think, we went through all that trouble to get you here…" He huffs and shakes his head some more. "The parties responsible for winding me up with inaccurate information have been dealt with, don't worry about that. And trust me when I tell you, they'll be fact-checking extra hard the next time they think they hear something about—"

"Wait, if you brought me here by mistake…" My eyes widen, sudden anticipation running through me. "Then I should be free to go!" I gape at him, hopeful and almost pleading with my eyes. He simply cocks his head. "Right…?"

"Trevel…" He pouts, tone patronizing. It's turning my stomach. "Unfortunately, it doesn't work that way."

"Why not??" I bark. "You said it yourself; I didn't do whatever it is you thought I'd done. It was all a misunderstanding!"

"Yes, that's true…"

"So then *why* can't I be set free??"

"Well, even if you hadn't already seen much of our setup here…" he begins with the excuses, but I cut him off.

"I won't tell anyone, I swear—"

"It's a liability I'm not willing to take on." He shuts me down firmly. "This island is kept secret from the general public for good reason. I can't simply let people *leave*…" His eyes grow menacing and he mutters, "I'm dealing with the repercussions of too much of that as it is."

"Who would listen to me, anyway??" I keep trying, scooting in closer to get my point across. "You clearly know about my life, my history."

His gaze narrows, as if maybe I'm getting through to him.

"I'm a degenerate! I'm telling you; *no one* cares about me."

"Trevel, don't be silly." He leans in, putting us nose to nose. "*I* care about you." Closing my eyes, I breathe out of defeat. "You're right, I looked into you quite a bit. And you know what I found? A fighter. A *survivor*. Someone who doesn't take the evil of the world lying down. I respect that." I blink as his head tilts. "In fact, you remind me of someone…"

"So you're not letting me go…?" I mumble.

He shakes his head, grinning wickedly.

Fantastic. So I don't belong here, but I can't leave.

"When you come across an unexpected gift, you don't simply let it scamper off into the night. You keep it close. You *treasure* it." His face is illuminated with sinister sweetness; a praising malfeasance that has every hair on my body standing on end. "And *you* are simply too special to let go." He smirks, and I flinch when he reaches up to brush his fingers through my hair. "I have plans for you, Trevel Fenwick. My shiny… new… toy."

CHAPTER FOURTEEN

Trevel

Getting a proper grasp of how I'm feeling is proving difficult.

By all accounts, I'm fucking fuming. I don't want to be here. I *shouldn't* be here. The Warden flat-out admitted that I didn't need to be locked up in this shabbiest of shabby prisons, miles and miles outside of civilization, but that he's decided to keep me here for his own personal gain. Not that I even understand what he wants from me, but I can already tell he's not the most *transparent* of individuals.

I can't help but wonder if maybe I'm not alone… If there are others like me, who *aren't* the worst criminals ever, rather poor blokes who wound up in the wrong place at the wrong time.

Nonetheless, my mood has flat-lined, and it could be due to the all-time-low dopamine levels. But I'm choosing to believe it's more the fault of The Ivory… and his *pal*, Dr. Love.

As far as I'm concerned, they're both responsible for my current predicament. Though, if we're being candid, I blame Dr. Love *way* more.

Manuel Blanco is just a sociopathic monster. But Dr. Love *isn't*. He's a regular person, a *doctor*; a professional caregiver. And yet he threw me right underneath the bus without a second thought.

That, as far as I'm concerned, is inexcusable.

Despite the unhinged sense of betrayal I'm feeling, thanks to my former psychiatrist, I can't deny that being here isn't all that different from some of the other places I've existed—a sad notion in its own right. Of course, the setting itself is more rundown than even the worst fleabag motel I've squatted in. But I'm not exactly *picky*, nor have I ever been in a position to turn down four walls and a roof.

There's freedom that comes with giving up. Wearing all of those masks Dr. Love convinced me to wear was exhausting. Working menial jobs for practically nothing, stressing myself just to pay the bills—to afford a studio apartment that was barely bigger than this bloody cell.

Fighting to deny my urges and be a *good guy… It was a lot of work.*

Letting go and just being *me*, degenerate or not, has rid me of that heavy burden. And now I'm just… breathing.

Manuel Blanco gave me my own cell in general population, a few halls down from the others, meaning it's a bit more secluded. It's still a prison cell, so it's boring as all get out, but the bed is actually more comfortable than the cot I was sleeping on in Bangkok. So… that's something.

One thing they haven't relayed yet is whether there's any sort of *commissary*, though I'm assuming there isn't, based on the state of this place. For as loud as it can be at times, it still seems like there's barely anyone here. They don't appear to have an office, or much staff. Just the guards. Which, once again, has me wondering… What *exactly* does Dr. Love do here that's so enthralling?

For my first official day in general population, I can't stop moving. My body is still achy and tired, but when I try to lie down, my limbs are too restless. I have to get up and move. I wind up pacing the entire circumference of my cell dozens of times while singing miscellaneous songs. Anything to distract from the boredom and my brain's beckoning pleas for narcotics.

Just as I'm launching into my tenth straight rendition of *God Save The Queen*, I hear footsteps. The excitement is instant because I haven't interacted with another person since a guard whose name tag read *Peters* dropped off some food for me last night. I say *food*, but really it was a bottle of water and four of those little packets of soup crackers, sans soup.

I know. I'll alert the Zagat.

Anyway, I'm looking forward to seeing either him, or C.O. Chevelle, or maybe some other Officer man-candy, because so far, they're all unreasonably good looking.

Could that be the draw? Worst prison in the world, but the guards are so hot it doesn't matter?

The clomping ends up belonging to someone else—also not ugly, thus proving my point. Equally large—as seems to be the standard—but not dressed in the same uniform that Officers Chevelle and Peters were wearing. This man is in simple black garb, yet still properly tailored. He has a bronze complexion and light hair... A stern face with a no-nonsense air about him.

Either this is a requirement of working here, or working here makes them all like this.

Regardless, I'm not paying much attention to the man, because I'm distracted by what he's carrying—a giant fruit basket. And I mean *giant*.

It's the size of a Buick.

"What's this now?" I huff as he struggles to get it inside my cell without dropping it.

"A gift," the man rumbles on a breath. "From The Ivory."

I feel a sparkle in my gaze, and a timid smile pulling at my lips. "Well, isn't that sweet..."

Advantage: Blanco.

Dr. Love never gave me a giant basket of treats.

"Enjoy," the man says, with dead eyes and a blank tone, as if he doesn't care whether I enjoy it or not. "My name is Kent, by the way. I work directly for Mr. Blanco, so if you need anything, send for me."

My brow cocks. "How? Via carrier pigeon?? How am I supposed to contact you?"

He gives me an emotionless stare, and I simply exhale.

"Thank you. Much appreciated, Kent. Can I have some liquor?"

"No."

"Cigarettes?"

"No."

"A cellphone?"

"*Hell* no."

My jaw tics. "Well, what *can* you give me that isn't in this Moby-Dick-sized basket??"

He actually thinks about it for a moment before ultimately mumbling, "I'll get back to you."

And then he leaves.

Ah, sod it. At least I have this beautiful gift from my good pal Manuel Blanco to entertain me.

And *entertain*, it does. The basket is chock-full of delicacies. Mostly food, various fruits and chocolates, gourmet cheeses, crackers, and olives. There are even two small cans of some sparkling soda-like drink.

Non-alcoholic, of course. But once I get through the edible layer, I find things that allude to this basket being custom-built.

There are toiletries, like soaps and lotions, toothpaste and a toothbrush—*thankfully, because I was beginning to wonder…*

And then I notice some bottles of nail polish. Dark colors, black, red, blue, purple, but without any of the other mani-pedi accoutrements that would make it like a bridal shower or Mother's Day gift.

Understandably… They're obviously not going to give me anything sharp.

I do find some pens, though no paper, which is frustrating. But then I stop in my tracks, eyes lighting up when I reach something *amazing*.

A pair of fuzzy socks… with the Teenage Mutant Ninja Turtles on them.

"Oh…" I pick up them, instantly giddy, like I'm a child again. Only this time, my parents *weren't* raving fuckholes, and they actually cared enough about me to give me a proper gift they knew I'd *love*.

"Papa?" I call out, glancing around.

Is Manuel Blanco watching me??

How the bloody hell would he know I love the Turtles??

And the more burning question… *Will he be my new Daddy?*

It's all rather odd, but I'm too elated to care. *This is quite the sweet gift…*

But a frown swallows up my grin. *I wonder what he wants from me.*

What he'll expect in return…

Shrugging it off, I go back to playing with my gifts like a right simpleton, eating grapes and sniffing lotions. Distracted only by more footsteps roughly an hour later. Lighter ones.

I peer up to find a female approaching my cell this time. I'm momentarily taken aback, until I remember that I've also seen her before, the day I arrived.

There are female officers? Color me intrigued…

"On your feet, inmate," she gives a command, as surly as any of the men. Maybe more.

I'm instantly swooning.

Doing as I'm told, I watch her closely while she opens my cell, but doesn't come inside. She simply nods for me to come out, which I do.

"Walk," she barks.

Alright, I'm obsessed with her.

"What's your name?" I ask while we stroll the halls. She's power-walking, and I'm striding to keep up, easily since I'm much taller than her. "Mine's Trevel."

"I know," she grumbles, but doesn't answer my question.

I check her name tag. "Officer Jameson…?" I murmur, and she peeks at me.

She reminds me a lot of Officer Chevelle. They're like Prison Guard Barbie and Ken. *I wanna smoosh 'em together and make them kiss.*

Wondering where she's taking me, but opting not to ask, since she's clearly not much of a talker, I just continue to walk with her through the halls, until we reach what appear to be the showers.

Good. I'm dying to wash my biscuits.

"Go on," Officer Jameson says firmly. "Shower time. No funny business."

I open my mouth to make a smart-ass comment, but the look on her face shuts me right up. She's a bit scary, though I'd be lying if I said I didn't like it.

Wandering into the showers, I look for a good spot. They're all open, because there's no one else in here, which seems strange. *Do all inmates shower alone? That doesn't seem practical… Or fun.*

Choosing a stall in the corner that looks promising, I strip out of my clothes, my thoughts interrupted when I recall my fancy soaps.

Bollocks! I forgot them. Or I didn't think to bring them because no one told me I'd be showering.

"I wish there was someone around to commiserate with…" I grumble, pressing the button for water while glancing around. "Maybe a certain cigarette-loving ninja bear who has a habit of disappearing when I need him the most…?"

Still, nothing.

Melancholy winds around my ribcage. I'm just so… *lonely*. I've only been here a few days and I already want to swallow a bullet. Being alone is making it infinitely more difficult to avoid and deny the miserable state of my existence.

The guards barely speak, and I'm isolated from everyone else. I have no one to talk to… Not even an imaginary best friend to keep me company. I'm left with only my thoughts, and myself. *A lethal combination.*

Just as I'm reaching a new level of wallowing, I hear voices approaching. A bunch of them. Excitement flutters in my gut as I peer around the wall separating me from the rest of the showers. It looks like a group of inmates is coming in, all moving with purpose to various locations. The way they scatter, almost on autopilot, suggests a routine.

Two more prominent voices break through the rest. I keep myself hidden and watch two lads from around the corner. It doesn't take long for me to realize they're in some sort of relationship. They're both white guys, one of whom has black hair, like mine, only more swept back. He has a real pretty boy look about him, with an *amazing* body, some tattoos. And an effervescent smile aimed right at the other bloke, who looks a bit younger—slim yet defined, with light blond hair shaved close to the scalp.

They're really giving each other *the eyes*. Blond boy is flushed and biting his lip while they stand close, their obvious chemistry pooling warmth in my stomach. But then, someone else steps into my vision, interrupting their hushed conversation. And he steals the show, along with every inch of my attention.

He grabs a bar of soap from the hand of the black-haired man, striding over to his own shower. *So they must be friends… Or at least acquaintances.*

My eyes are locked. *This* lad is different. I see it right away. Not in looks, though his skin tone is a bit more bronzed, he has more tattoos and thicker muscles, a striking jawline and facial features… A flaming orange aura dripping with masculine sexuality.

But it's in his movements that I sense a difference… His mannerisms. I can't put my finger on it, but there's *something* about him that's calling out to me.

Alright, he's just a bloke… Nothing special.

And yet I *cannot* stop watching him. The other two men move in closer, and now it looks and sounds like they're arguing. The black-haired chap is getting up in the hot boy's space, and I feel muscles tightening all over like a reflex.

"Dude, back off," the gorgeous specimen grunts.

"Why? You don't like playing with me anymore?" the black-haired one says, forcing a pout. Then he calls to the shaved-head lad. "Come on, Lex. We're showering with Byron today. Prison-style."

Byron… His name is Byron.

Hmm… I bet it sounds good being sobbed into a pillow.

"Ren, just let him use the damn soap," the one with the light hair—*Lex, apparently*—says to the loud-mouth, Ren.

The three of them continue bickering, and I'm highly invested. *It's like live theatre.*

Ren gets up in my new crush's face, and I'm preparing for my first prison shower brawl. Spine straightening, I reach to shut my water off, grabbing the nearest towel as Byron is threatening to kick his friend *in the dick*. I'm not sure what's going on here, and it's definitely not my place to interfere, but I can't seem to help myself. I'm stepping around the wall, moving closer to where they are while Byron and Ren fight, and Lex just stands off to the side, sighing and shaking his head at them like this isn't the first time this has happened by any means.

Byron whips a soap bar at Ren, and it comes sliding across the tiles, stopping only a few feet from where I'm standing. The three of them go silent. In fact, the whole place is quiet, nothing but running water to be heard.

I glance around the room. Even the inmates who aren't involved in their argument have frozen solid and are gaping at the floor in horror.

What's the big deal? Why is everyone…

Ohhh, right.

Don't drop the soap. I've got it.

And now Byron and his pals are arguing about who's going to pick up the soap. I huff out of perplexed amusement.

Fucking hell, just bloody bend over! Who cares??

Sauntering over to the soap, I bend to pick it up. *Would you look at that? Nothing slipped inside of me. Astonishing.*

Waltzing over to the three lads, my eyes take in each one. I'm able to get a better look now that I'm up close. They're all naked, which I'm not trying to openly focus on, though it's enticing to say the least. But when my curious gaze finds *Byron*, it gets stuck, an immediate buzz happening beneath my skin.

He's… *very* attractive. Again, they all are, but there's something about Byron specifically that I like. Maybe it's his eyes, or his mouth, or his wet hair and wet skin, or the way the water droplets are tumbling over his pouty lips, or the fact that he clearly has a *very* impressive—

"I believe this is yours." I hold out the soap bar and force myself to speak to him because the ogling is about to become embarrassing, and I need to stop.

He doesn't take it. He simply stares up at my face—he's a few inches shorter than me—lips parted, no words to give.

Byron has nice eyes. Byron's body is phenomenal.

I think Byron's lips are shivering…

"Who the hell are you?" a voice snaps at me, coming from his pushy friend.

Unbeknownst to this chap, however, I'm not intimidated by stubborn narcissists. So I ignore him, focusing exclusively on *Byron*.

"Are you alright?" I ask him.

Based on the way they were arguing, and how aggressively *Ren* was coming at him, it feels like someone should check on Byron. And I think that someone should be me.

This time, he looks like he might respond, but before he can, Ren grabs him by the shoulders to put distance between us. "He's fine. Don't worry about him." He snatches the soap out of my hand, glowering at me. "I asked you a question, asshole. Who… the *hell*… are you?"

Byron's eyes bounce nervously between Ren and me, so I decide to finally acknowledge his friend, who already seems like the attention whore of the group. Still, I didn't like the way he was hassling Byron. Not that I know anything about any of these blokes or their dynamic. For all I know, rowing about could be their thing.

I slide my eyes over to him, purposely slow, and murmur, "My name is Trevel. And who, might I ask, are you?"

"You new here or something?" He squints at me without answering. "Why have I never seen you before?"

I glance at Byron, who's still as stone, save for his Adam's apple bobbing in his throat—an insignificant movement that has me thrumming.

Returning to Ren, I reply, "Well, if you've never seen me before, it would only make sense that I'm new… yes?"

Ren's light blue eyes harden in clear animosity that I'm not making any better by taunting him. "Watch the attitude, Mary Poppins, or I'll slap the shit out of—"

"Hi! I'm Luthor." The third member of their group gets involved, cutting off Ren's threat by stepping in front of him. "Don't mind Ren. He's a little overprotective."

Lex… Luthor, ah I get it! That's cute.

I offer him a kind smile, peeking once more at his quiet friend, awaiting an official introduction.

"This is Kang," Luthor says.

Right, we do surnames in prison.

I blink at the speechless simmering stranger… *Byron Kang*… and rasp, "Hello."

"Hi," he whispers, dark eyes locked on mine. Never wavering.

I like it. Bollocks, I like his voice too. Even that one tiny word sounds delicious coming from that mouth.

"Okay, Trevor, run along. Back to your beanstalk," Ren snaps, inserting himself into the middle of everything, making himself the focal point. *Again.* "We need to get dressed."

"It's *Trevel,*" I correct him with a bite.

I'm used to people mispronouncing my name, but that seemed intentional.

He confirms my suspicions when he quips, "Don't care," and begins physically pushing Byron away from me, in the direction of his clothes.

He's still nattering on about something, but I've tuned him out. I'm too busy watching Byron Kang as he dresses hastily, casually peeking at me in between hopping on one leg into his pants.

I bite back a grin. *I wonder if he's…*

"Now, that's not very smart, is it?"

My face whips around. *Leo?!*

That was Leo's voice! But I don't see him anywhere…

Fuck me… Leo?! Where are you??

Clearing my throat, I remind myself to act normally in front of the prison cool kids, stowing my issues to obsess over later. Fiddling with the towel around my waist, I mumble to Byron, "Maybe I'll see you around…"

I turn and shuffle off before he can react, kicking myself inside for being a bloody oddball. I hear the lot of them conversing again once I've left, and it sets a longing in my chest… For friends. *Companionship.*

Anything to distract from how loathsome my life is.

I'm dressing, all the while peeking left and right in search of Leo.

"Just show yourself," I grumble under my breath. "I know you're here…"

Of course, he doesn't answer. It's so typical of him to behave this way. To vanish as soon as the going gets tough and make me sort it all out on my own.

Officer Jameson and another guard, whose name I haven't gotten yet—tall lad with shaggy hair and a baby face—order us all to gather up and leave the showers. And as much as I'd like to hang back and try speaking to Byron some more, I'm not in the mood to be barked at by his guard dog friend.

I'm feeling pensive as I march out of the showers behind the tall guard, practically mowing him down to get out of there. I just want to go back to my cell. *Maybe then Leo will show up.*

Gaze stuck on my shoes, I walk along with the herd, although, clearly, they don't see it that way. I'm an outsider, the *new guy.*

I'm not one of them. I don't fit in…

What else is new?

It was the same way in Kings County JDC—the juvenile detention center I was in for two years before Riverwoods. We all may have technically been "children" according to the state of New York, but it felt every bit like an adult prison. There were cells—though much bigger and nicer than these—and rules. Discipline and routine being hammered into you until it begins happening like muscle memory. And there were definitely *cliques*.

In juvie, I was able to make a couple of fair-weather friends, more acquaintances than anything. But just like on the outside, it never sticks. I'm too socially awkward to make friends. People see me and assume I'm a creep, or a weirdo. And *yes*, both of those descriptors are accurate, but there must be other creeps and weirdos out there for me to befriend, right?

If ever there was a place for freaks and losers to come together, it would be here. And yet, I'm still an outcast.

Give it time. Comic Con wasn't built in a day.

We come through the doors that lead to the rows of cells in general population, and Officer Jameson strides up, grabbing onto my arm. "You good?" She's speaking to the other guard. His name tag says *Hancock*.

He simply nods, bringing the rest of the inmates through the next door, while the stern female guard tugs me in the direction of my cell.

My eyes linger over my shoulder, watching as they all file through, searching for one inmate in particular. But Officer Jameson shoves me and barks, "Keep up."

See you later, Byron... Have a good night.

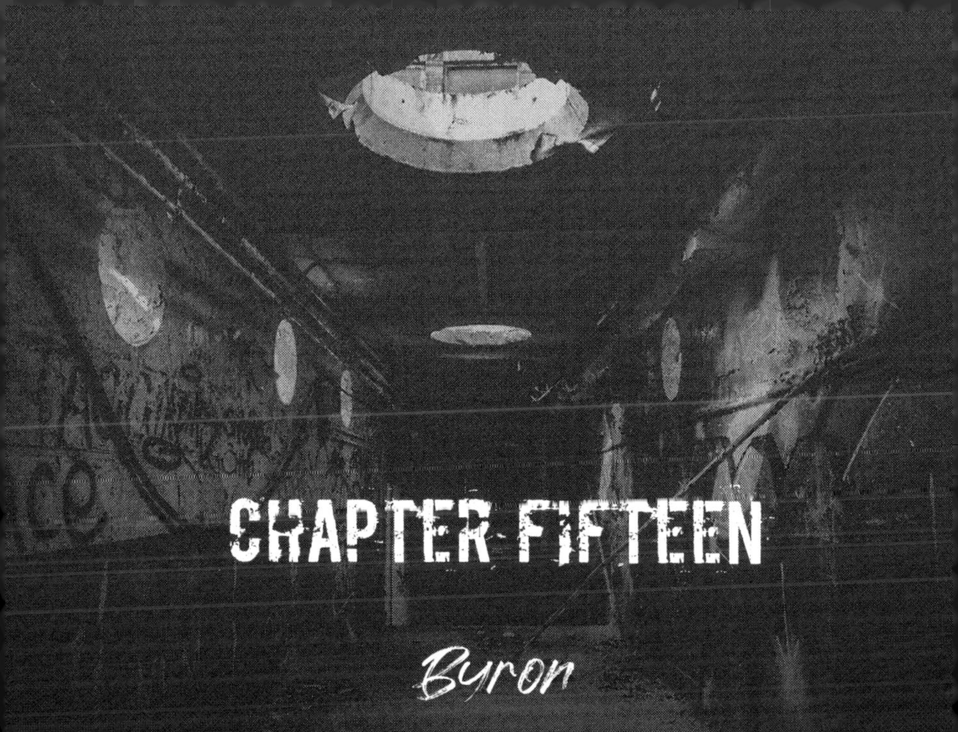

CHAPTER FIFTEEN

Byron

SAME SHIT, DIFFERENT DAY.

The official slogan of prison.

I feel like so much of my time is spent shuffling from one drab room to another. Although I will say, ever since whatever mysterious *falling out* Velle had with the Warden, it seems like we've been able to move about more freely than before.

I don't know if the lockdown has officially been lifted, but stuff is slowly trickling in again. The guards are more buoyant. Overall, it's seeming as if things have returned to normal… *I mean, as normal as they were before Dash showed up.*

To me, though, it doesn't mean dick. My cellmate is still gone, my *friend* still dead. And my other friends still don't care. So I'm walking around salty.

I refuse to admit it, because admitting weakness isn't in my nature, but for the first time in nearly three years, this place is getting to me just the tiniest bit. For once, I'd like to go somewhere, *anywhere* that isn't my cell, the caf, or the showers. I'd like to eat some different food, listen to new music. I'd like to see some new faces.

At that thought, I glance up. *I suppose there is one new face…*

Trevel Fenwick. The new guy. 102…

He's been here for a few days, and he's somehow managing to cause a stir without so much as lifting a finger. Or even looking at anyone, for that matter.

Ren doesn't trust him—*I know, right? If that's not the pot calling the kettle black.* Luthor seems indifferent about the whole thing, but *Ren* thinks the guy is suspicious. Though he's yet to elaborate on exactly *why*. Even the brain trust—*that's Rook, Velle, and Joy*—are wary of the mysterious new inmate, yet the dude's barely made a sound.

Sure, he introduced himself to us when he first got here, and then I spoke to him again the other day for all of five seconds. It was hardly a profound conversation, but still. I just don't see it... Why they all hate him so much. He doesn't *do* anything.

Keeps to himself, sits alone in the cafeteria. Stares a lot, but that's probably the *least* strange thing an inmate here could do. As far as I know, his cell is outside the first two rows of Gen-pop. It's odd, but again, not exactly evidence of any wrongdoing.

Look at fucking Darcey, for example. Apparently, he lives in some fancy bedroom off the East Wing... *And he's murdered two inmates since he's been here!* But everyone is all gaga over him. It makes no sense and is more than contributing to my growing irritations with just about every asshole in this joint.

As lunch comes to an end, and we all get up to toss out our trash, I watch Trevel Fenwick. Standing from the empty table near the front where he usually sits—by *himself*—he dumps his tray, then lines up. Waiting for Rook to give us the okay, all the while with his face aimed at the floor and nowhere else.

I'm not saying I feel bad for the guy or anything, because that doesn't sound like me. I just wish I understood what the others are seeing that I'm not.

Joy said Trevel came in *abruptly*. Not sure what that means, but she made it sound like the newest inmate since Dash might've been brought here for purposes other than simply being locked up forever.

I'll be honest, I find it all more intriguing than suspicious. I'm curious to know if any of the speculation is true; if Trevel Fenwick really is some sort of covert spy, planted among us by The Ivory. Or if he's just another poor sack of shit sentenced to life in hell and is being ostracized for it by his prisoner peers, simply because he's a loner with nothing to say.

If the latter is the case, then I could surely empathize.

"Psst." Someone nudges my arm, and I know right away who it is. "Want some?"

I peek at Joy, who's holding out a bag of Skittles. I frown at them. "Regular?"

"Listen, we all know Tropical are superior," she mumbles. "But can you really afford to be picky?"

She has a point. "Touché, asshole," I mutter, snatching the bag from her.

She chuckles while I dump colorful candies into my hand and pop them into my mouth.

Yum. Artificial fruit.

I go to hand it back to her, but she waves me off. "You keep 'em. Happy Halloween."

"Wait… is it?? *Really?!*" My face contorts in devastation.

Joy shrugs. "How the hell should I know? It's been the same year for ten years."

"Another good point that's depressing as fuck," I grunt, and she huffs.

Winking at me, Joy stomps ahead to join Rook, the two of them smiling at each other, whispering and laughing while I sullenly munch my Skittles and *try* to be fucking *grateful* for the small, insignificant distraction.

Maybe thinking about this candy will give me something to dwell on for the rest of the day… You know, other than how bored angry sad lonely depressed horny exhausted hungry moody frustrated *I am.*

The thing is, I know I should just get over the whole *Luthor and Ren sticking up for Darcey* thing. Yes, that bitch-boy killed my friend, and he's still just skipping around here without a care in the world, boning his doctor, being Alabaster Pen's resident lovable lunatic. And *yes*, my so-called *friends* are falling right under the spell of his charms, while completely disregarding *my* feelings on the matter. Still, I can't deny that life would sure as shit run a lot smoother if I just moved the hell on.

There's just one problem, though… I don't *want* to.

Because loyalty is *everything*, and friendship goes both ways.

I'm sick of being the goddamn after-thought to these people.

When's it gonna be my turn, huh??

"Taste the rainbow," a deep voice rasps by my ear, scaring the shit out of me.

I jump so hard, I spill a few Skittles onto the floor.

"Jesus…" I breathe, slapping my hand over my heart while I gawk up at the culprit.

"Oof, sorry, mate." Trevel chuckles, raking long fingers through his jet-black hair. "I didn't mean to frighten you." But the tone of his voice and the curve to his lips directly contradict those words.

Kinda makes me think he liked it…

"Sheesh. Talk about sidling up out of nowhere," I mumble, blinking at him.

He's so *tall*… He must have at least five inches on me. I guess that, paired with those piercing violet eyes, could be overwhelming if I was focusing on it. Which I'm not.

"My apologies. I hope I haven't caused you to lose them all," he says casually. My brow cocks, and he glances at the floor. "Your candies…"

"Oh. Right." I look down. "Just a couple. No biggie."

He's walking next to me now, sort of close, watching me speculatively.

I'm overwhelmed by the need to say something, so I ask, "You want some?"

An elated look sweeps over his face, only for a split second, before he ditches it and murmurs, "No, no, I couldn't. I've already cost you a few…"

My lips twitch. "It's okay. It was only yellows and greens. Those are the worst ones."

"Are they now?" He grins, and I nod. "According to who?"

"Uh, everyone in the universe with taste buds," I quip, and he chuckles. A strange heat rushes up my neck, and I clench my jaw to get away from it.

"I fancy a green on special occasions," he says teasingly… *I think*. It's hard to tell with the accent. Still, he appears to be fighting off a smirk.

"That's only acceptable if they've made the switch to green apple," I counter. "These are original, so it's lime. Bleh."

"What's wrong with a lime?" His brow creases, as if he's very invested in this stupid conversation.

"A *real* lime? Nothing." My face slopes to find him already looking at me. In fact, he's been doing it pretty much this whole time. *Not sure how he even knows where he's walking…* "Fake lime is gross."

"So you dislike lemon and lime candies?" His dark brows lift. "Yet you like orange… Isn't that pretty much the same thing? Fake citrus and all…"

"Trevel, please. Don't compare oranges to lemons and limes. They're not even in the same ballpark."

He chuckles again, softly, pursing his lips. I can't tell what the expression means, but I have to admit, chatting with him about nonsense *is* more entertaining than scowling at nothing and obsessing over bullshit.

"Does she give you gifts often?" he asks, tone growing a bit deeper, more inquisitive.

"Who… Joy?" My eyes dart briefly to where she's walking with Rook. Trevel nods. "I wouldn't say *often*… But we get along."

For some reason, I feel weird saying these words, given that Joy was one of my semi-regular hookup buddies before she went exclusive with Rook and Velle. Not that the new guy knows, or cares, about any of that…

"She's the only female guard, yes?"

It occurs to me with his question that he's still very much new here. And because no one likes him, he probably hasn't had anyone to show him the ropes, or give him the Alabaster Pen *rundown*, so to speak.

"She's the only female on the whole island," I reply.

"Hm…" He makes a small sound, as if he has thoughts about this. "That must be fun for her."

A tiny chuckle rumbles out of me. "To be honest, I can't imagine Joy interacting with women. She's like one of the guys…" I frown at the thought. "Only, you know… with lady parts."

His gaze snaps to mine, and he assesses me for a moment. I still can't tell what he's thinking, and his eyes are sort of boring into me.

In an effort to pull focus from myself, I add, "Anyway, I hate to break it to you, but she's off the market."

His lips twitch, and he murmurs, "I'm not worried about it." He seems genuine.

Entirely unaffected by the notion of having no females around.

Gazing over the sharp line of his jaw, the pointed slope of his nose, and the long, dark lashes that fan over his pale cheeks when he blinks, I wonder why people are considering him *odd* when, if anything, he looks like he could be a runway model.

Maybe that *is* why. Because someone so *striking* in appearance must've done something super crazy to wind up here…

Unfortunately, his purple eyes dart to mine while I'm mid-stare.

I look away fast, but he leans in and hums, "Willing to share?"

I nearly trip over my feet. "Huh??" Gawking at him, my muscles are all bunched up, even more heat rising into my face.

He smirks innocently, holding out his hand. "The candy."

"Oh, yea… Um, sure," I stammer, feeling stupid as I shake some Skittles into his palm. He's got an array of colors. "I hope you like those…"

"I don't discriminate, Byron," he croons, inching even closer to my ear to purr, "I enjoy *all* the flavors of the rainbow."

What the...

Suddenly, my throat is super dry, and my palms are sweating. *I hope I'm not melting my Skittles.* "Okay, um... cool," I croak, then clear my throat, distracting myself by dumping more candy into my mouth.

Trevel chuckles out a growly sound while chewing his candy. And I'm pretending my face isn't flushing from that comment, though I have no clue *why* it would be. It's just candy...

We're talking about candy.

While I'm desperately trying to think of *anything* cool to say in response, Ren stomps up to my back. "Hey, B, did Luthor tell you about his dream?"

Without a moment's hesitation, Trevel picks up speed, floating ahead of me. Like a reflex, vanishing before Ren notices him. It's unclear whether Ren missed us talking, or is choosing to ignore it, but clearly Trevel has no interest in sticking around to test the waters with him again.

My eyes are lingering on the back of the mysterious newbie's slim frame and messy, dark strands, while Luthor strides up beside me, griping, "It wasn't a big deal."

"Yes, it was! Babe, you had a dream about Batman and Superman getting it on," Ren cackles. "That's fucking awesome!"

"It was *not* a sex dream," Luthor mumbles, face flushing noticeably, which means it probably *was*.

But still. I prefer to protect him over giving in to Ren's objectives.

"Ren, cut the shit," I grumble, still subtly watching the tall dude in front of us.

"No need to be embarrassed, Lex," Ren goes on. "If I had a nickel for every time I've dreamt about Henry Cavill, I'd have enough nickels to build a life-size Henry Cavill statue with fully functioning genitalia. Ooh, Skittles! Hit me up, boo."

Ren starts trying to grab the bag, but I yank it away. "Back off. These are mine."

"Sharing is caring." He pouts. "Come on! Just a few... I only like the reds, anyway. Don't *even* try to give me any other color."

I peek at Trevel once more, before hissing at Ren, "I'm not giving you *any*, period."

"Meow." He throws me a salty look, and I toss it right back.

I know he knows I'm still pissed at him, which is obviously why he's badgering me so much. For all of his sociopathic tendencies, Ren can't stand knowing someone is mad at him and being unable to smooth it over.

Typical. He always has to be the star.

Rook opens the door to our row, motioning for us to go through. I give one last glance in Trevel's direction, and this time, our eyes meet.

"Until next time," he hums to me on his way past, following Joy to the other door. "And hey… Don't waste any of those."

He grins as he turns away. I walk to my cell with my brows zipped, unable to help how I'm overanalyzing his words.

Inside, once everyone is gone and I'm left to my own devices, I dump out my remaining Skittles onto my bed, sorting them into little piles by color. And I eat them all, one by one, savoring each flavor, until they're gone.

I found an old black Sharpie and decided to color my fingernails.

Fuck it, right? No more Dad around to scold me because "boys don't paint their nails."

I guess I'm an *emo kid* at heart, though I never fit into their cliques in high school. But I've loved the music ever since I turned fourteen and discovered Taking Back Sunday. Plus, ninety-nine percent of my wardrobe has always been black. I don't think that means anything per se, but my parents hated it. They thought it made me seem depressed.

An accurate assessment, but whatever.

I used to think guys with black fingernails looked cool, but I wouldn't have *dared* to do it myself in front of my father. Now that I don't have to worry about what he thinks, though, I'm going for it.

Maybe reinventing my look will make me feel better. *Maybe it will help me understand who the hell I even am…*

Too bad it's not real fucking nail polish, and most of it comes off in the showers.

On the way back, I'm looking around eagerly. I'm not really sure what, or who, I'm searching for. And if I am, I'm not trying to think about it. Completely unrelated, I haven't seen the new guy at all today.

Not that I care. It's just… interesting.

"So what were you and Slenderman talking about yesterday?" Ren asks in an accusatory tone, as if somehow reading my mind.

"*Who?*" I play dumb.

"You know *who*," he counters. "I saw you chatting it up with that British beanpole like you two were the best of friends. What gives?"

"Okay, you sound insane," I mutter. "We exchanged a few words, what's the big damn deal??"

"If it's not a *big deal*, then tell us what you talked about." He continues pestering me, like the most annoying person on earth.

Taking a deep breath, I let it out slowly before I answer, "Skittles."

He blinks at the side of my face. "*Skittles*?"

"That's right."

"You talked to the new guy about… Skittles?"

"*Yes*, Ren," I grunt.

"You're such a bullshitter." He huffs.

"Oh, wow… *That's* rich," I hiss.

"You guys, *please*," Luthor whines, rubbing his eyes.

"No, seriously. The fact that you can even expect me to tell *you* anything is a goddamn joke," I scoff directly at Ren, shaking my head. "Why don't you bother *Darcey* about his conversations? No? Just me?? Okay, cool. Well, I don't know what about this friendship has made you feel like you own me, but I'm not your fucking pet, *Warren*."

At the end of my tirade, I'm exhausted and wound up all the same. I can feel my blood boiling, the color red seeping into my every thought.

I really wanna hit something…

"Byron, what the fuck—"

"Simmer down, inmates," Brenner cuts off whatever defense Ren was going to make, separating us with a shove on my back, through the doorway to the row.

He drags me over to my cell, opening it and grumbling, "We haven't had a *quiet night* in a while, 62. We gonna have one tonight, or what?"

I freeze and stare at him, eyes wide.

Quiet Night… Did he just say…?

Brenner lifts his brows, like he's waiting for me to answer his seemingly rhetorical question. I'm stunned and still unsure of whether he's *actually* suggesting what I think he is.

But regardless, I immediately start nodding. "Yea… Yea, totally. We can have a… *Quiet Night*. No problem."

He winks, then pats me on the back. "Good."

Stomping away with the slam of my bars, he leaves, and I'm filled with a sudden morbid sense of thrill, effectively distracting me from that irritating argument with Ren.

Maybe it's unhealthy to crave beating someone bloody this much, but fuck it. I haven't sparred in months. Haven't fought *in even longer.*

Not only is the prospect of getting out some of this aggression I seem to have piling up inside me like a game of Tetris thrilling, but also the much-needed change of scenery. Since the lockdown, things have been next-level boring up in here.

Man, Dash really jacked things up. I love the kid, but he's like a walking earthquake. Still, I miss that chaotic little dumpling.

My mind drifts to the night of the storm, but I shut that shit down quick and refocus on *fighting*.

I decide to spend the rest of the night training. I do one-hundred push-ups, then one-hundred sit-ups, then one-hundred pull-ups off the top bunk. My muscles are straining, and I'm breathing heavily, but I love it. Not that I don't do this stuff constantly as it is, but right now, I feel like Rocky.

I'm humming "Eye of the Tiger" while I jog in place and throw practice jabs at nothing, the adrenaline inside me thrumming. I guess I'm doing this for hours, because eventually the lights go off in the row. And finally, Linetti shows up.

"Let's go, 62," he says quietly.

Fuck yes.

He brings me and a few other inmates down to the *basement*, a silent march through the darkness under strict orders not to make a sound. When we walk into the rec room, Brenner's already there, collecting cash from the other guards while inmates are fucking around, stretching and gathering up in a big circle.

Inhaling deep, I let it out slowly. *Fuck, I missed this*... The zeal that rushes up my spine. The lust for violence that sets my teeth on edge.

The adrenaline of doing something you're not supposed to wakes me up. A pungent punch to my senses, like a whiff of smelling salts.

I'm ready.

"Hey." Linetti grabs my arm before I can make a beeline toward the bags to see if Joy's and my supplies are still over there. I turn to glower at him. "This goes without saying, but if I find out you've got another cellphone stashed down here, you'll be shitting your teeth out for a week. Got it?"

I can't help how my lips twist in amusement at his threat. *That's cute.* "I have no idea what you're talking about."

He rolls his eyes, shoving me forward. "Don't disappoint tonight, Kung Fu Panda."

Bite me, asshole.

Striding away from him, I go for the tape. *Thank fuck it's still here.*

I'm wrapping my knuckles as a tall form appears in my peripheral. Glancing up, my eyes widen.

"So, underground prison fights." Trevel Fenwick sighs, looking around the room. "I suppose that's one way to pass the time..."

"What are you doing here?" I ask, baffled by this turn of events.

Why would they bring him?? Does he even fight?

"I honestly have no idea," he huffs out of amusement. "That large one over there—"

"Brenner," I interrupt, and he shrugs.

"Sure, why not. He barged in, disrupting my beauty sleep, and dragged me down here without a word." His eyes fall to my knuckles. "Should I be doing that?"

"Do you..." My voice trails, and I blink. "Are you a fighter?"

He rubs his chin. "I'm not sure how to answer that..."

My eyebrow cocks, and he grins.

"Let's just say, I've been around the block. But I don't believe that makes me *a fighter*. I simply... do what I must. To survive."

I find myself nodding. Relating in a way.

"What about you?" He steps in closer.

He likes to be close, this one.

The urge to back up is strong, but I ignore it, allowing him to push into my space. He holds out his hands, and it takes me a moment to register that he's waiting for me to tape his knuckles for him. I'm immediately smacked upside the head with a memory...

But I don't want to think about that right now.

Sucking in a secret breath, I take his hand in mine. Nerves are bunching, and I'm trying hard to pretend it has nothing to do with touching him. How cool and soft his skin is, or how long and slender his fingers are... They're very masculine and proportionate to his size.

These are nice hands...

Stuffing away those thoughts, I wrap tape around his knuckles as quickly and as *professionally* as I can.

"Yea, I'm a fighter." I answer his question. "I've been practicing Tae Kwon Do since I was a boy. I'm also into Jujitsu, Moi Tai, Krav Maga... most Mixed Martial Arts. You name it, I've done it. I was planning to become a trainer before..." My words trail, but he gets the point.

Trevel's brows lift, that glittering purple stare moving from my face to his hand. He looks beyond impressed. "Wow… So what you're saying is, none of these other blokes stand a chance?"

My mouth slopes into a small grin I can't get a handle on. It feels good to be acknowledged. To have someone focusing on *me* for once.

Plus, I like his accent, and his British words. *Reminds me of my grandfather.*

Crushing my smile, I let modesty tug me back to earth. "I don't know about all that." Returning to my task, I take his other hand and wind tape around to cover his knuckles. "It's been a while…"

"Shame." His tone goes soft, and I peer up to find him gazing down at me intently. "That you don't get to do what you enjoy…"

His fingers brush my wrist, and I shiver.

Michelangelo.

I taped his knuckles for him… That night.

Dropping his hand fast, I step back, clearing my throat. "Yea, well… Welcome to fucking prison, right? You're, uh… all set, by the way."

The way he stares is weighted with curiosity and dazed wonder. Any time his eyes are on me for more than a few seconds, I start to feel all hot and fidgety inside. Thankfully, cheers and roars give me an excuse to turn away and get my bearings.

It's starting.

Stalking over to the circle, I can sense Trevel scampering after me. "Do you have any advice for me?" he asks over the noise. "I'm really more of a lover than a fighter."

I gawk at him like he's insane. "Don't go in there trying to *love* these guys to death. You'll get your ass handed to you. And not in a nice way."

"Ooh… *saucy.*" He bites off a grin, and I just shake my head.

He is a bit of an odd duck.

I allow the violence to distract me from the warmth that won't stop creeping up my neck and into my face any time he's around.

It's not him. It must just be the excitement of the fight, that's all.

It's normal to feel awkward around such a… compelling new character.

Trevel and I stand side by side, watching two inmates, Valcic and Jermaine, beat the shit out of each other. I can tell this is something Trevel's never been presented with by the way he's sort of flinching and wincing every time one of them takes a heavy hit.

He doesn't seem affected by the blood or the pain they're inflicting, but more by the senseless violence. Fighting without purpose, I guess.

By the next match-up, he's leaning in to ask me questions. *Often.*

"Shouldn't he have blocked that?"

"Why do they call it an 'uppercut?'"

"Do you think his nose is broken?"

"Is that a proper stance?"

"What happens if you run away?"

It's actually kind of funny. He clearly knows nothing about professional fighting while being genuinely interested in my insights. Like I'm a UFC commentator or something—*the Joe Rogan of underground prison fights.* Honestly, it's more entertaining than the match after a while.

The blood is flowing, fire being fueled enough that the next time Linetti is calling out, "Who's next?" I'm stepping forward and cracking my neck.

"I'm in."

Everyone cheers, I guess because, technically, I'm still undefeated. And the bets start rolling in, cash being tossed at Brenner from all sides.

"Fuck yea!" Linetti claps, looking around for someone to pit me against.

Before he can choose, Humphrey steps into the circle, serving me a look that's *overflowing* with something to prove. "Let's go, champ."

I narrow my gaze at him. Justin Humphrey is a *big* guy. Not that it means anything per se, but he's always done pretty well down here. His last fight was against O'Malley. *And he kinda sorta whooped my friend's ass.*

Still, I'm not worried. The dude has no form, and he wears himself out too fast swinging sloppy haymakers.

"Bets in!" Brenner shouts, signaling that we're about to start.

Rolling my neck in Trevel's direction, I find his eyes rounded, wide enough that the violet in his irises is visibly shimmering. He's grinning, but it's strained. Like maybe he's… nervous. For me. *How sweet.*

Or maybe he's nervous for the other guy. Either way, he's clearly anxious about me fighting, and it sets the strangest sensation in my chest.

I don't have time to be perplexed by it, because Linetti is hollering, "Fight!"

And we're off.

As suspected, Humphrey's coming at me quick, throwing big, meaty punches like Mike Tyson's older, fatter cousin. Blocking him is easy, but when he does catch me, the pain lights me the fuck up.

Fuck yea. You want some, old man?!

My body shots are tight, head shots fast and precise. Stick and move, I'm dancing around him like Ali, in my fucking *zone*. The noise fades away, until all I can hear is my breathing. It's like I'm underwater. Everything is rippling, slow-motion helping me to anticipate his jabs.

Ducking and dodging, I work on his legs, and his kidneys, kicking and kicking, sprinkling in blows so he doesn't know what to expect.

Head, body, head.

This is where I feel at peace.

No more stressing, or obsessing…

No more doubting, questioning…

All eyes on me, because this is who the fuck I *am.*

A fucking warrior.

Sweet, simmering fury personified.

Humphrey is exhausted in mere minutes, wobbling and bleeding from his mouth. That's when I make my move.

I launch my palm at his nose to disorient, get his eyes watering up nice. Then I hit him with my signature combo… Uppercut to the chin, followed by a spin-kick to finish him. He goes down like a sack of shit.

Boom. KO.

The crowd erupts, guards and prisoners bellowing as Lucas calls it. And not that I believe in this shit, but I make the cross motion over my chest. *For O'Malley.*

"No mercy." I spit blood onto the floor where Humphrey is lying. "No fuckin' surrender, baby."

Rest In Peace, Shamrockstar.

Stomping out of the circle, I'm refreshed. My head is clearer than it's been in *months*. I've got dudes slapping me on the back left and right, calling things out. And I won't lie, it feels good, the recognition. But I don't do it for that. I don't crave attention or validation when I fight. I'm sure I would feel just as satisfied if I'd lost.

Because it's the fight itself that settles me. The pain, the adrenaline… Hell, even the fear. They remind me that I'm still *alive* when, in here, it's so easy to forget.

Striding past Trevel, the illumination on his face has me smirking.

"Byron! Fucking hell… That was *amazing!*" He breathes a laugh, following me over to the water bucket. "I've never seen anything like that!"

I give him a skeptical side-eye. "You've really never seen any boxing? UFC?"

He shrugs. "I told you; I'm a lover, not a fighter. Plus, that was obviously different from what's on television…"

Perplexed by how good his praise feels, I ignore it with a huff, focusing on cleaning myself up. But when Trevel grabs the wet cloth from my hand, I freeze.

Standing stock still, I watch in bemused unease as he brings it up to my face, dabbing my brow. I might've stopped breathing; a Byron statue, gaping up at the stranger who's gently cleaning blood off of my face.

Why is he doing this? Why am I letting him do this?

It's... weird. Isn't it? A weirdly intimate thing to do for someone you hardly know... While shirtless and... sweaty.

"I can't believe you can fight like that," Trevel murmurs, all of his attention on what he's doing while I just stare. "Do you pretend that bloke hurt your family or something? Imagine he killed your puppy or slashed your tires...? I think I'd have to do that. I'd need some motivation, or—"

"Motivation can be more than just revenge," I cut off his rambling, my voice extra raspy.

His purple eyes meet mine. "What's yours?"

Swallowing, I consider what I could share with him. If I could tell him things... About me. My life.

Ultimately, I decide against it. This guy has already pulled more words out of me than most others can. I don't understand how he does it.

Ducking away from his touch, I take the cloth back, because now it just seems like he's fussing over me, and I don't need that. I'm barely even swelling. There isn't much blood.

And I think I felt his fingers on my lower back...

Shut it down.

"So vengeance is, like, your *thing*?" I ask my own question, remembering what he said to me the other day in the cafeteria.

"You might like the taste of revenge..."

"Bit of an odd *thing* to have, I suppose." He grins. "Look, I'm no *Batman*, roaming the streets, seeking to avenge the deaths of my parents. It's just... Well, the only times I've felt the blinding need to inflict pain on someone were instances where they deserved it. They wronged me, or someone I cared for. And because of that, they had to die."

His words give me chills.

Hmm... So he has killed people.

This is my first insight into why he's here, and just like everything else about him, it's intriguing as hell. I'd like to know more...

But there *is* a golden rule of prison—you don't ask people what they've done. You wait for them to volunteer the information themselves.

Or you snoop around and find out.

I'm sure Trevel will tell me his story eventually. He's been blathering to me nonstop, odd since he's barely said a word to anyone else. But I think I like talking to him too.

How is it that two quiet loners have been gabbing away all night, like a couple of chatty Kathys? It's bizarre.

And yet…

Maybe I could do it…

Tell him… why I'm here.

The thought takes me by surprise. Even my best friends don't know the *real* reason. I've given them a version of the story, watered-down and embellished. A PG, cookie-cutter, *Lifetime* movie adaptation of what really happened.

No substance. No marrow.

No Michelangelo.

The truth is still mine. My *secrets* are only mine.

I couldn't just hand them over to the captivating stranger with the purple eyes… Could I?

"I like the feeling." I speak softly, offering him a raspy confession, though I still can't be sure *why*. "That's my motivation. It's like a high, I think."

Something shifts on his face, almost like a realization dawning.

He nods subtly. "Oh, well… *That* I can certainly understand."

This conversation, just like the one we had the other day about fucking Skittles, is twisting me up in a very puzzling way. Once again, it seems like we're talking about something deeper than the actual *words* we're using.

Roars and shouts snap us both out of it, and we glance back at the circle. Fuller and Redman are in there. And as it tends to, the fights are getting dirtier, the crowd growing rowdier as the night wears on.

"This is the type of shit O'Malley liked," I tell Trevel, cringing when Fuller jams his thumb into Redman's eye.

"Your friend?" he asks. "The one who was killed by…"

"The Carver… yea. He was a real scrappy motherfucker. No fucking mercy."

"But that's not how you fight…" I think it was supposed to be a question, but it comes out more like a statement.

"I couldn't." I shake my head. "Not with my background. I respect the art of it too much."

"I like that." Trevel grins, looking me up and down. His eyes gloss over my exposed torso, and it feels constricting. Easing in closer, his tone grows rumbly, like a tiger's purr. "You're quite the deep fellow... Aren't you, Byron?"

I swallow over a sudden lump in my throat, peering at him. "Um... maybe?"

His smirk widens, and he bites his lip. "I'd like to find out just how *deep* you go..." His breath melts into humming interest that slips into my ear from how close I hadn't even noticed we were standing.

There's palpable heat coming off of his tall frame. Or maybe it's coming from me? We're both shirtless, flesh sort of close... Either way, it's unnerving me to my core. I'm not sure if he's flirting with me, or if this is just the way he is.

Seems a lot like flirting... But then I have an overly sexual friend who flirts like it's breathing.

Maybe Trevel is... like Ren.

That thought just confuses me more.

Would it be a bad thing? If he were flirting with me...?

Blinking up at him, I consider my recent *predicament*. Sexuality hangups aside, I have needs. And I'm stuck in here, meaning my options are limited.

It's nothing more than a physical release, anyway...

Trevel is good-looking. I mean, he's actually *really* fucking pretty. Masculine at the forefront, but with these sharp angles that could certainly lure in a straight guy with ambiguous tastes.

Shifting from side to side, I wring my hands while my eyes flit around the room, searching for *anything* other than him to focus on because this shit is tripping me up. I don't know this guy. We're *not* friends, and I'm certainly not crushing on him or whatever. Yet I can't seem to stop eyeing him subtly, all kinds of whacky things piling up in my head.

Am I really that sexually frustrated??

My inner turmoil is disrupted when Linetti barks, "New guy! You're up."

Shit. I was so invested in my creepy obsessing, I hadn't even noticed the fight was over.

Trevel is wearing a deer-in-headlights expression as he gawks at Linetti, then at me. He swallows visibly, but that's really the only hesitation before he kicks into movement, weaving through bodies toward the center of the circle. Like a reflex, my hand almost juts out to stop him, because I don't think he should be doing this.

Is he really gonna do this??

"Who else needs to go?" Linetti looks around. "Bren, who do you want?"

"I don't give a fuck," Brenner rumbles, counting his money. "I think they've all gone..."

"Alright, then. Virgin's choice." Linetti aims a smug smirk at Trevel. "Pick your poison, 102."

Trevel appears deep in concentration, for all of five seconds. And then his violet eyes land on me, lips quirking as he chirps, "I'll take Mr. Undefeated Champion, please."

Murmurs are immediate, everyone else mirroring my surprise while I gape at this oddball motherfucker...

The dude I've been chatting with all night like we're besties now wants me to kick the shit out of him??

My mouth hangs open for too long, until Linetti snaps, "You heard Harry Styles! Get in there, 62!"

The crowd is cheering. Trevel is waiting, and *I'm* hesitating. *Me. The warrior.*

How the hell am I supposed to fuck this dude up without feeling like an asshole?? He literally just said he doesn't like to fight!

Stumbling into the circle, I lock eyes with Trevel. He doesn't appear worried in the slightest, which is working up even more tension in my muscles. He knows what I can do... He just watched me take down someone twice his size.

Why doesn't he look scared??

He must really be psychotic.

"Don't hold back, mate." He winks at me.

My brows zip, disturbed as Linetti yells, "Fight!"

Okay, I guess we're doing this...

Trevel and I instantly begin orbiting one another. For someone who claims to be a *lover*, his form isn't terrible. He actually looks like he knows what he's doing, which I wouldn't have guessed from the way he was prying me for details before. Our gazes are magnetized while we circle and circle, both of us refusing to make the first move.

It goes on long enough that the crowd is growing impatient, so I move in closer and start needling him. Tossing him little taps and shoves, trying to get him to hit me first.

I refuse to hit him first. This is *his* fault. *He wanted this...*

"I know what you're doing," Trevel rumbles under his breath.

"What am I doing?" I keep going, tapping him with my knuckles, advancing just enough, though he's not even backing up.

In a flash, we're up close. Close enough that I can hear him breathing. His height advantage doesn't worry me, but it *does* make it feel like he's enveloping me with his proximity.

Goading him with more light shots, I jab him in the chest, then on his abs. They're extremely firm… Not sure what I expected, but the feel of it throws me off for some reason.

"Come now, Byron," he says calmly, blocking my hits to his torso. "They won't let us stop until you do it. Just hit me."

"Why don't *you* hit *me*?" I grumble.

"I told you." He gets up in my face, crowding me until we're practically zipped. My heartbeat is popping off much faster than it should be, but I think I can feel his doing the same. "I'm not a fighter."

"Oh, right… You're a *lover*," I taunt, shoving him away.

But he comes right back. "Mhm… But we're not *loving* right now, are we?" He smirks, and I want to punch it. *At least… I think that's what I want to do to it…* "No, we're fighting. So *fight*."

I shake my head, the nerves, the tension, and the thrill all working up together, coating my muscles. "Fuck off…"

"You think I can't handle it?" he breathes out.

"I *know* you can't," I growl, my hands on his waist.

We're chest to chest, fluttering into one another. The shouts and chants, our panting in tandem… His low, gravelly voice. It's all becoming heady music, a background to this dance we're doing.

"I promise I can take it," he rasps, almost pleading. "*Hit* me."

He… wants it?

I'm in limbo, burning hotter with every lash of his firm body and smooth skin against mine. I know I need to make a move, but I'm afraid…

Afraid of how good it might feel.

"*Come*, love," Trevel whispers over my lips. "No mercy… I want your *wrath*."

And then he grabs my throat.

Instinct kicks in, and I shove him back, *hard*, launching my fist at his jaw. It was a default reaction, but still, I'm *struggling* to keep it easy. I don't think I want to hurt him…

I'm confused. This is *confusing* me.

Hard, hot body pressing into mine, sweat and dried blood in the air, mingling with the scent of *him*—sweet and fresh and masculine.

Fuck, I'm high on it all. It's frying my wires.

"Harder," Trevel snarls, coming for me again, grabbing my neck. "Like a good boy."

Ding.

It's as if a timer went off in my brain. Some bizarre Pavlovian bell.

I think I actually moan for a second, but I cover it up with a roar as I lunge at him, tackling him to the floor. I'm throwing fast punches into his sides and his face. He's able to block some of them, but still, the red is overtaking me.

This fury… It's oh-so-sweet.

"You wanted this," I hiss, straddling him, pinning him to the floor. "You want me to hurt you, pretty boy? Huh? Is that what you like??"

"I think it's what *you* like," he croaks, violet eyes sparkling up at me. "Unleash on me, baby. Make me bleed for you, *Byron Kang.*"

"I'll make you fucking bleed…" I snarl, launching a fist at his face. "You bleed for *me*, got it?! Your blood is *mine.*"

He grunts, *taking* it with a sadistic smile. A bolt of zeal fizzles inside me like electricity. It turns me the fuck on. I hit him again, and *again*, raging and *loving* it.

Trevel isn't even trying to block me anymore. He's just gripping my hips, fingers digging into me while I hit him and grab him by the throat. I might have blacked out… Except that I haven't, because I can feel *everything*.

The fury is *burning* into an aggressively erotic desire. I haven't felt this in so long. It's consuming me. I'm *alive* with sensation.

And then I feel something…

Something *hard* between our grinding bodies.

"Mmf… *Byron*, baby, tell me you feel it," he groans, eyes rolling back.

Wait…

My movements slow. *Did he just… call me baby?*

The way he's greedily squeezing the flesh of what's basically my ass… It's the way someone holds you while you're fucking them into the mattress.

The fog is lifting, and it gives him an opportunity to flip me over. In a blink, he's on top of me, using the odd sexual carnality flowing between us to his advantage. I hit him with more blows, wherever I can, mostly at his body while attempting to wriggle out from under him.

He's not bulky, but he has muscle and more strength than I'd assumed.

Now that our bodies are sort of writhing together, I can *feel* his definition, rather than just seeing it, the strain in his plump slopes and firm ridges.

He's also noticeably… *Flexible.*

"*Fuckin' hell,*" he purrs, pinning my arms down. "You are so pretty when you're mad."

H-huh…?

This bubble we're in is hazy and stifling, the fury turning sweeter with every breath and tangled motion. The fighting, our movements… They've blurred from violent to strangely sensual.

Goddamn… I can't tell if I'm pissed off or… about to shove my dick in him.

Probably both.

"Shut up," I seethe, then choke when he presses his hips into mine. "Wait… Don't…"

"Don't *what?*" His black hair is hanging in his eyes, pale skin all blushed pink.

I have to chomp down on my lip to stop from moaning, and it's *so* confusing.

God, why does this feel so fucking good??

It's then that I realize there are *two* things between us. *Both* hard as fucking rocks. *Honestly, mine might be harder…*

"Fuck you." I squirm beneath him, using all my strength to buck him off. But instead, it just feels like we're… humping. "I don't… want this…"

"Mmm… But you *need* it," Trevel drawls, dragging his stiff cock along mine.

My confusing erection pulses, and I whimper.

No no no…

Terror grips my chest, reality creeping back and reminding me that we're not alone. We're surrounded by people who *can't* know how much I like this…

Erupting with all my might, I finally overpower him, flipping him onto his back once more.

I lean over him and whisper frantically, "Tap out." I'm mortified, flaming shame rushing up my neck. *I can't do this in front of all these people…* "Tap the fuck out, *now*, Trevel, please…"

Without any hesitation, he taps on the floor. I don't wait for anyone to say a word. Jumping up, I stagger to my feet and storm away before anyone can look at me. I'm practically running.

Fortunately, the crowd is cheering, as if I just won the fight. But that's not how it feels. I don't feel like I won… *I feel like I lost, big time.*

Storming around the corner, I head straight for the locker room. I know Brenner and Linetti will come after me, but I just need a second to clear my head, away from everyone else. I need a second alone to think.

And to get my dick under control before someone realizes I'm tenting my jumpsuit pants.

Jesus, I'm mortified…

"What the hell was that??" I whisper-scold my dick. "Have you lost your mind?!"

Pacing, I palm my scalp, obsessing over what just happened. We were supposed to be *fighting*, not… whatever the hell that was.

I knew I didn't want to fight him. He just wouldn't leave it alone!

Now I just made myself look gay and crazy in front of a room full of assholes.

"Oy! Byron…" His voice startles me, and I jump, spinning around, glare intact. I really didn't expect him to follow me in here, though I guess it makes sense. He's been following me around all night. "Are you alright?"

"No," I hiss, then blink hard. "I mean, *yes*. I'm *fine*… Why wouldn't I be??"

He stares at me, head slanted to the side. "You sure?"

His dark hair is all tousled about, cheeks still pink. And he's bleeding…

"Stop asking me stupid fucking questions," I teem, chest heaving in frustration.

He blinks, lapping at some blood trickling from his lip. The sight throbs my nuts. "Don't be cross. You won."

"I'm not *cross*," I growl, and he smirks. "You just… threw me off, is all."

"Did I?" He steps forward while I glower at him, backing up. "Why?" He continues to crowd me. "Because you liked it?"

"I don't know what you're… talking about," I croak, startling myself when my back hits the concrete wall behind me.

Shit…

He has me trapped, *again*, easing his body into mine. Gazing down at me, violet eyes shining. "I think you do."

"You must have a few screws loose," I grunt, baffled and frustrated because the warmth is *still* fucking here.

It wasn't the fighting… Why wasn't it the fighting??

Fuck me, I think it was… him.

His scent actually has my mouth watering. *He smells… dangerous. And sexy. God, so deliciously sexy…*

"Maybe." Hovering over me, Trevel taps his fingertip to his bloody bottom lip. "You want a taste?"

I'm fucking *trembling*. "Huh...?"

"It's yours," he croons. "You earned it, warrior."

My head is fucking spinning off my body as my eyes covet that pouty fucking lip, all red and puffy and *so close* I can practically taste the copper already.

I gulp. "But I'm not... I mean, I don't..."

"You don't have to lie to me, gorgeous," he whispers. "I can keep a secret."

My lashes flutter. *What is this...?*

How is he doing this?

Do I need to get laid that bad??

Or is this... something else?

His hands ghost up my waist, gliding gently until those shapely fingers are wrapped around my ribcage. And I hum, because it feels *good*. Eyes tumbling over him, I watch his chest rise and fall, pale skin flushed, Adam's apple bobbing in his throat.

He wants it, that much is fucking clear. *Flirting my ass...*

I think he'd let me in him in a heartbeat.

And now I'm considering it... The things I could do with this stranger that would get me all the way off.

Push him onto his knees and pump my cock down that pretty throat...

Bend him over and fuck him rough. Bust my nut in there, nice and deep...

It's just sex, right? Like feeding your body when it's hungry...

No strings. No attachments.

Nourishment... Much-needed.

Reaching up, my hand is shaking a little as I curl my fingers around his neck and bring him to me. "You wanna make me feel good...?" I rasp into his waiting mouth.

He nods fast. "*Anything* you want to feel, hot boy. I'll make it happen."

My mind is racing, immediately overflowing with wild images and torrid fantasies.

But before I can even think of acting on any of them, footsteps clomp from around the corner, that motherfucker's voice slicing into the steamy hot tension, "62, your ass is fucking grass if you don't get out here right the hell now!"

Goddamn Linetti. Fucking cockblock.

Shoving Trevel off me, I clear my throat and blink hard, reacquainting myself with reality. He hums out of frustration, and I peek at him.

"That's a good look on you," I mumble, eyes lingering on his bloody lip.

"That's even better," he purrs, nodding below my waist.

Peering down, I frown at my visible erection, adjusting to hide it in my waistband.

Trevel laughs, and I scowl away my own amusement.

"Shut up," I mutter.

"Sure thing... *Raph.*"

CHAPTER SIXTEEN

Trevel

"TREVEL! GREAT TO SEE YOU. HAVE A SEAT, MY DEAR."

Eyeing the man cautiously, I take a seat opposite him at his desk. Large, oak, and quite ornate. But what's really caught my attention is the massive bay window behind him.

"Wow… That's quite the view," I breathe out, admiring the ocean's waves rippling below us. "I didn't know this building had windows."

"Oh, it really doesn't," Manuel Blanco says with a smirk. Then he stands, wandering over to what looks like a lavish little minibar. "Would you care for something to drink? Pellegrino? Coconut water?"

"I don't suppose you have any bourbon in there?" I lift a brow, and he cocks his head admonishingly.

"Now, Trevel… You've been given an opportunity to start fresh here, no substances. Don't squander it."

I swear, he sounds like a father. It's interesting, being that I never had parents who, well… gave a rat's tiny bollocks. So as much as I feel like a petulant teenager right now, I'm unable to disregard the warm and fuzzies in the pit of my stomach from him actually caring. Or at least pretending to.

Still more than I got from the wankers who made me.

I sigh. "Pellegrino is perfect, thank you."

The Ivory is wearing a pleased expression as he pulls out two cans, cracking them both open and sliding one over to me. He sits back down in his fancy desk chair, sipping from his drink, eyeing me as he does.

Swallowing a fizzy gulp myself, I rumble, "Also, let me just say, thank you so much for that… basket. It really was quite the gift."

He beams. "I can't imagine you've already finished it?"

"No, no," I huff. "It's enough food to last a month. But those chocolate-covered cherries… Dear *God*."

He laughs softly. "I hoped you'd enjoy those."

My smile is only partially forced. It's not that I'm ungrateful, because surely, he doesn't *need* to give me anything. Still, I'm finding it difficult not to gawk at him like a dog walking on its hind legs.

I mean, he's the *Warden* of *Alabaster Penitentiary*. I barely know anything about him, and he scares the panties off me. I can only imagine the things he's done… *The stuff of nightmares, I'm sure.*

And yet, here he is… *Smiling* at me. Offering me drinks and discussing sweet treats, as if we're old friends getting together for a long overdue lunch in between our busy schedules.

It's bizarre, to say the least. I just can't get a proper read on what it is he *wants*; why he's plying me with gifts and inviting me up to his office to chat.

I'm an inmate here, not his pal.

What is your agenda, Mr. Ivory?

"So, how are you settling in?" he asks, leaning back in his seat. "I trust that Kent's been accommodating when he can?"

Kent, of course, being the bloke he's tasked with babysitting me.

He seems like a nice enough fellow. And he has a Daddy Dom vibe about him that's rather titillating. I wonder what his official position is…

Top or bottom.

Jesting, of course. I mean his job.

I know he works directly for The Ivory… What is he, a butler? Personal security and gift basket delivery?

This place seems tragically understaffed.

"Kent is a stand-up lad," I reply. "Of course, it's *prison*… There's a certain level of discomfort to be expected."

He stares at me until I begin to cower.

"But I do greatly appreciate your hospitality, sir."

The Warden's lips curve, his eyes still lingering on my face. "What happened?"

I balk, instantly stiff. "Beg your pardon?"

"To your *mouth*, Trevel." He speaks more insistently. "You have a cut on your lip. Where is that from? Have any inmates been hassling you? If so, simply give me their names and I'll see to it that they're dealt with."

My mind instantly drifts to the other night, in the basement. Though if we're being honest, the memories haven't gone far since it happened…

The hottest fight ever with the sexiest, broodiest, most *delicious* fighter I can't seem to stop thinking about.

Byron Kang.

Fucking hell… Even just hearing his name in my head has me squirming and trying to hide it.

That boy is something else… I would let him kick my ass a hundred more times if it meant feeling that mixture of wanton rage and restless desire he keeps tucked away inside his perfectly *mouthwatering* body.

Remembering myself, I clear my throat. "Oh, no. Nothing like that. I… slipped in the shower. I can be a right clumsy thing sometimes."

It's clear from the look on his face that The Ivory doesn't believe me. Fortunately for me, he lets it go, sipping from his drink again. "As long as you're not having any trouble. I want you to be comfortable here, Trevel. You're very important to me."

A few seconds pass, wherein I stare at him and contemplate what, if anything, I should say to that remark. On the one hand, I want to stay in his good graces, because at least here, I get treats and access to his personal security. On the other, I'm not always the best at holding my tongue, especially when I feel I'm being toyed with.

"You know what would make me even more comfortable?" I sit back in my seat, mirroring his body language. "A room in your mansion with my own en suite."

The Ivory chuckles, shaking his head. But the laughter stops abruptly, and he lifts a light eyebrow. "Don't push it, Trevel."

"Yes, sir," I mumble.

It was worth a shot.

"Look, I understand that this isn't fun for you." He swivels back and forth in his chair. "The prison is no picnic. I get that. But this is where you must stay, Trevel. Make your peace with it and *don't* look a gift horse in the mouth. There are plenty of inmates, I'd say damn near every last one, who would kill to have their own private cell stocked with food, and the opportunity to wander about at their leisure—within reason, of course."

Yes, yes… within reason.

"But, sir, the thing is, I'm feeling a tad… isolated." My fingers twist in my lap. "I do relish my privacy, but I'm already going mad with boredom. I don't know how the inmates who have been here for years do it."

Once again, my thoughts go to Byron. *He said he's been here several...*

No wonder he seems desperate for someone to open up to. Bottling up his frustrations for *years* with no one to properly... *pop the top*, so to speak.

Bollocks. If I keep thinking about him, I may need to cross my legs.

The Ivory unleashes a rather cunning smirk, leaning forward in his chair. "I'm so happy to hear you say that, Trevel. Because, in fact, I *do* have a plan to get you socializing more."

I'm not sure what prompts this, but a frisson of thrill runs through me at the idea that he might give me a cellmate. *Maybe even a certain fuck-hot Asian bloke with a sinful mouth and muscles I want to lick like candy...*

I cannot even *fathom* how thirsty I am for this lad. *It's becoming worrying.*

"Color me intrigued." I scoot up to the edge of my seat.

"I've been thinking," the Warden says. "How would you feel about restarting your sessions with Dr. Love?"

My heart leaps into my throat.

Alright, then. I suppose we're talking about the other *man I found myself painfully attracted to...*

The nodding of my head becomes gradually more enthusiastic the longer that suggestion swims through my brain. "I think that's a fine idea. I could really use some... good old-fashioned therapy."

I grin, mentally sifting through all of the possibilities.

Oh, how I would love *to start seeing the good doctor again...*

"Wonderful," Manuel chirps. "I was hoping you'd feel that way."

Opening his laptop, he presses a few buttons. Then he spins it so that I can see the screen. It's playing what looks like... a video feed. "What you're seeing here is video from the East Wing."

An odd sensation settles in my gut at what I'm seeing.

Bloody hell... I'm back in Riverwoods.

"The east side of the prison was developed first," he goes on, giving me a history lesson while I'm floundering inside. "Initially, this building was slated to be an institution, called Alabaster Asylum. But ultimately, it was requested that it be made into a penitentiary instead."

"Requested...?" I murmur absentmindedly. "By whom?"

The Ivory gives me a look that says, *I can't tell you that.*

Hm... Ominous.

He taps another button, and the camera angle and location change, displaying various areas of this *East Wing*. It's very different from general population. There are rows of padded cells, occupied by inmates laced up in straitjackets, and rows of other cells, which look like a doctor's exam room from the forties—a big chair in the middle bolted to the floor, with shackles hanging off of it.

All of which can be seen at all times by Manuel Blanco, apparently.

I must admit, this is triggering me just a tad. The conditions at Riverwoods were nowhere near as bad as these, but it was still a place I detested. They would never use straitjackets... But they had no problem strapping your arms and legs down if they felt you might harm yourself or one of the staff. I know this because I spent many an evening strapped to a gurney and screaming until they stuck a needle in my neck.

Fear releases a fervent flood of adrenaline into my nervous system. I sincerely hope this isn't what The Ivory has in store for me... Testing and experimentation, *without* the laws and regulations of a place like Riverwoods.

Is that... what Dr. Love does?

Alabaster Pen's resident psych superstar, reigning over the East Wing??

The Warden presses yet another button, changing from the live feed to what looks to be recorded video. It's date and time-stamped, but I don't know what date and time it is, so I can't tell when this is from.

"You see, Trevel, the thing with Dr. Love is that I brought him here solely to examine my most prized possession, Felix Darcey. Which he certainly did, and did well. That said, it seems as if spending all of his time with his subject may be... shifting his objectives."

My forehead creases, muscles stiffening at his words. "What do you mean... And who's Felix Darcey?"

The name sounds rather familiar... But I'm drawing a blank.

"Felix Darcey is an inmate. #89. He goes by The Carver." He speaks calmly, then pauses to let his words sink in as movement on the screen catches my attention. It's Dr. Love...

The Carver... That's who Byron said killed his friend.

It sounds so familiar, but I just can't...

My confusion is set aside while I watch Dr. Love stepping into a room. He's out of sight for only a moment, and when he returns to the screen, he's... *smiling*. It's so foreign, I barely recognize him at first.

He's speaking to someone just out of view, but I can't hear what he's saying. Though it would appear that he's not just smiling… He's smiling *at* someone.

The Ivory taps a button, and sound comes through the speakers. Not crystal clear, but audible enough for me to make out my former doctor speaking.

"It's impossible not to miss you, sweet monster. Even when we're apart for mere minutes…"

What the bloody fucking hell??

My eyes are as wide as can be when Dr. Love shifts enough that the person he's speaking to becomes visible. A man, clearly younger than him, with fair skin and chestnut brown hair, wearing black-framed glasses. Lemuel's hands are on his waist…

The lad looks very fucking familiar, but I'm finding it difficult to breathe at the moment. My gut has crawled all the way up my throat and is trying to jump out of my mouth.

The young man is gazing up at Lemuel, smiling a wide, beaming expression as he toys with one of Lemuel's dreadlocks. "So… show me then, Doctor Want."

Wait…

Lem's hands slide down to cup the kid's ass, and my pulse is now *pounding* like a bass drum in my ears. He leans down, lashes fluttering. And the world crashes to a halt when he drops a kiss on the kid's mouth… So gentle, I can almost feel it myself.

Everything is falling around me. Cement bricks are cracking and crumbling, the ceiling crushing me where I sit. I can't catch a proper breath, and I *hate* it.

What sort of fresh hell is this??

Dr. Love is… He's kissing *that bloke??*

Dr. Love is gay?? Since bloody when?!

Eyes flitting up to The Ivory, I find him watching me closely, while I just sit here, dumbfounded and fucking bleeding inside.

Felix Darcey…

The Carver…

Killed Byron's friend… Lemuel is studying him…

I gasp. "Hang on… That serial killer who was terrorizing New York City??"

The Ivory simply blinks, confirming without an actual answer that this is correct. And I'm reeling so hard, I'm dizzy.

Of course, I've heard of The Carver. *Everyone* has. His case was all over the bloody news for months. I'd forgotten that his name was Felix Darcey, but it's all coming back to me now...

The reports said he died; was shot and killed by police when they were attempting to arrest him, which is why I didn't put two and two together when Byron said The Carver killed his friend.

He's not dead. He's *here*, being seen by Dr. Love... *In more ways than one, apparently!*

I stare blankly at The Ivory. *This is bloody bonkers...*

The Carver is Dr. Love's patient.

Dr. Love is sleeping with his patient?!

My head is swimming, and I feel like I could collapse. My eyes are stuck on Dr. Love, the man who'd been my *whole world*, and the doe-eyed monster he's apparently fucking.

The psychopath who stole him from me.

Felix... Darcey.

Coiled and volatile, I'm shattered and hating it. At the very least, I used to cling to the idea that Dr. Love was *straight*, and that was why we could never be... anything. I mean, I was *sure* of it.

Like the time that I arrived early for my appointment, and he was just returning from lunch with a woman. I pretended not to be subtly watching them, pretended not to overhear their conversation. But I knew it was his girlfriend.

Gabrielle... Of course I remember her name. I've never forgotten it. I'd seen her outside the building before, heard his assistant mention her.

That was who he was dating. *That* was his type...

Not this murderous, preppy twink!

"What the fuck..." I choke on the words, watching the screen with wide eyes, unable to look away.

It's blindingly clear that they're not just shagging. They look... *happy*. They look like they're in love... *Deep* love. The kind that's visible from miles away. I cannot even fathom that I'm seeing *Dr. Lemuel Love,* robot man, looking at *anyone* like that, let alone a guy.

Let alone *that* guy.

A serial killer...

He's in a relationship with a serial killer.

When the two of them finally pry apart, I'm nauseated by how obsessed they appear to be. All flushed and starry-eyed, touching each other as if they physically can't keep their hands off. My entire body is heavy, watching them display such sickeningly sweet affection, in their own little bubble, without a care in the world.

But that's not the case now, is it?

They're *not* on a relaxing weekend getaway, they're in a *prison*, surrounded by cameras and prisoners and guards… and *former bloody patients!*

"Let's get you clean, dirty thing," Lemuel says, and I'm *rippling*.

"How long has he been fucking this bloke??" I seethe, eyes practically glued to the screen as I watch Dr. Love take the hand of his smitten pal, the two of them scampering down the hall in the opposite direction. "I mean, *how* is that… Why are you showing me this??"

The Ivory's lips twitch. He slaps the laptop shut, and I'm forced to focus on him now, though it seems impossible. I feel like my organs are failing, blood rushing in my ears. My palms are sweating and my heart is racing…

I'm falling apart.

Reclining, Manuel Blanco opens his desk drawer, pulling out an orange. "I wanted you to have all of the information." He begins peeling it while speaking, "Surely, you see what I mean. Lemuel is in dire need of some perspective."

My eyes lift slowly from the orange he's dismembering, delicately and with precision, to his face. He gives nothing away in his expression, but still. I'm choosing to read between the lines. *Possibly inferring a bit…*

He's not pleased about Dr. Love and Felix Darcey's relationship.

So then why is he allowing them to have it??

"What does that have to do with me?" I ask a question I know he has to answer, attempting to rein in my frustrations.

"Well, for starters, I believe giving him another patient to focus on is necessary." Manuel's head slants. "But more importantly, you two share a history. There's a sense of *familiarity* there. If anyone under this roof—other than Mr. Darcey, of course—knows how Lemuel Love operates… it's you."

My thoughts are churning as I stare at him, like a hamster on a wheel.

"What it boils down to is that I'm allowing Lemuel to stay, and encouraging him to drop his guard. Treating you again will play a part in that." He carefully tears away one of the orange slices, examining it briefly. "Who knows what your mere presence here could do to him… Without him even realizing it."

His eyes flick to mine as he pops the orange into his mouth, chewing slow and *deliberate*, not once breaking our stare. Irises glittering like polished orbs of black onyx.

My lips part, but it takes a moment before the words come out. "Are you sure? He did up and leave me after three years." A mass of new resentments overwhelms my limbs until my fingers curl into fists and my jaw tightens uncontrollably. "He abandoned me for this job… For *Felix Darcey*, apparently." Rage tears up my throat with my words. I have to swallow it down like a jagged pill. "What makes you think he'll… care?"

The Warden croons, "Darling, you were his first." *Oh, how I loathe the way that comment makes my stomach flip.* He aims one of his orange slices at me. "Don't underestimate the significance of nostalgia. His feelings are irrelevant. In his eyes, he made you, and he trusts *himself*. It's the downfall of most brainwashing egotists, I'm afraid."

An uncharacteristic frown tugs at his lips, as if something about that statement is bothering him, but my head is spinning too fast to focus on it.

This whole thing is sort of mad.

I can't believe he actually wants me to start seeing Dr. Love again just to… What? Spy on him? Entrap him? Disrupt his flow somehow? Or maybe a bit of all of it.

Part of me wonders why he's insistent on keeping Dr. Love here, rather than simply firing, or even killing him. But this does seem more Manuel Blanco's style. He's undoubtedly a *keep your friends close and your enemies closer* type evil genius.

And if we're being honest, it doesn't seem like the relationship with Darcey is his only Lemuel-related grievance…

Letting out a discreet breath, I lean forward. "Maybe I should befriend The Carver. Get to him that way…" I suggest, trying to keep hidden my own, suddenly *rapacious* desire for revenge.

I can't help myself. I wanted it before, after Dr. Love left, then sent for me like I'm some useless object rather than a *person*. But *now*… Now that I know the true nature of what he's been up to, I'm foaming at the mouth. For the doctor *and* his murderous beau.

"Trevel, I appreciate your enthusiasm," Manuel says blithely. "But pernicious or not, Felix Darcey is extremely valuable to me. I'm not willing to part with him, under any circumstances. I already almost lost him once due to an oversight. I will not risk it again." I must be pouting, because he grins, giving me a look that's condescending, if sympathetic to my plight. "Do me a favor and focus all of that animosity on the man responsible. I promise I'll make it worth your while."

Pursing my lips, I nod in agreement.

Fine. If he wants me to infiltrate Dr. Love, I'll do just that. Felix Darcey could, through no fault of my own, wind up getting caught in the crosshairs.

Cost of business.

"Good," The Ivory chirps, smiling and chuffed once more as he pops another orange slice into his mouth. He holds one out for me, lifting a brow.

Sod it. I accept, munching on the tangy fruit with my new mate, Manuel Blanco.

This is what he wanted… The reason he's been holding me hostage here, love bombing me like he's David bloody Koresh. This was his plan all along.

I'm his Love plant.

"Your loyalty will be rewarded, Trevel," he says calmly, but with savage undertones. "Big changes are afoot, with the potential to rock the very foundation of this prison." His eyes are rounded and unblinking, prompting me to gulp down a mouthful of nerves with my orange. "A storm is coming… And trust me, you'll want to be on my side when the lightning strikes."

Leaving his office, I'm apprehensive, considering the forces that brought me here. I'm remembering Alice, and Andres… who died because of me, one way or another. I'm also thinking about who *didn't*; the person Manuel Blanco *thought* I'd killed, until discovering the truth.

Where are they now? Does he know? Are they even aware of how *significant* they are in his world?

For hours afterward, and well into the night, I'm wading the choppy waters of uncertainty, contemplating this ivory storm I've happened upon…

And all the rubble it could bury me beneath, if I'm not careful.

CHAPTER SEVENTEEN

Trevel

Today, I'm knackered, and cranky to boot.

Not in the mood for cuffs or shackles, or cold showers or grouchy guards or sitting alone at a cafeteria table, staring at the most depressing dinner ever, like Beefaroni and a juice box.

Truthfully, I should be so lucky, because that's by far one of the least disgusting meals they provide here—a fact that's sad in its own right.

Despite how unenthusiastic I am, I have no choice but to endure the miserable monotony. Though there is *one* shining beacon of light amidst the darkness…

Byron Kang. A neon color when everything else is drab.

I don't even register who else is at his table, or what they're doing… I'm too busy studying the lines of Byron's face, the downward curve of his lips, and the way the bottom one is jutting out the tiniest bit in a pout that I both love and hate at the same time.

Why is he so sad? Don't get me wrong, it looks good on him, but still. I want to choke the life out of whatever, or whomever, is making him so gloomy.

But then I notice it. The thing that's most certainly responsible for his angst… A fresh-faced and timid-looking bespectacled master of camouflage known as Felix Darcey, who's parked right across from my sexy fighter.

Not everyone *thinks that adorable freakshow is so great. At least I have one person on my side.*

Felix Darcey haters club, right here.

The others are clearly welcoming of The Carver's presence. But the hot angry boy is *not*, and I don't blame him. He said his friends—Luthor and Ren—don't care about The Carver murdering his other friend, confirmed by the way they're chatting and laughing with the doe-eyed doctor-stealer.

The rest of the meal is spent with me watching Byron while trying not to be super obvious. For some odd reason, Joy allows him and his mates to use her cellphone, and I'm quite curious to know who they're speaking to… *Someone important, I assume.*

My curiosity is overpowered, though, when I note something in the looks and smiles between Byron and Officer Jameson… I can't be certain, but it seems flirtatious, reminiscent of a possible fling.

She's the one who gave him Skittles the other day… If that isn't a sign that two people have bumped uglies, then I don't know what is.

My mood sours at the thought. I can barely even enjoy toying with The Carver by locking eyes and waving at him.

Before I know it, we're all being herded back. *Felix, the golden child,* is already gone, most likely cozying up with Dr. Love somewhere in the East Wing…

Why does he get to have unlimited prison sleepovers?? I'm *mates with the Warden, for fuck's sake.*

Meanwhile, Byron is walking behind his friends, head down, shoulders hunched. He just looks too *sad*… And while I'm certain associating with me will only ruin him *more* in the long run, I'm too enamored by him to stay away.

Inching up behind him, I whisper, "Why the long face?"

He jumps a foot in the air. It's hysterical.

"Fuck, man…" He sighs, shaking his head. "You gotta stop doing that."

"Or you should be paying more attention to your surroundings." I lift an accusatory brow. "Isn't that part of the *fighter* training?"

He glowers at me, and *mother of god*, is it sexy. "Yea, well… You're surprisingly nimble. Like a…"

"Kitten?" I grin, and he squints.

"I was gonna say squirrel, but sure. We can go with yours."

I chuckle, then bite my lip. "So, who were you speaking to on the phone?"

Byron's face goes momentarily nervous, but he covers it up. "No one."

"If you say so." I huff.

He gives me a slightly narrowed look, lips twitching. *That expression is downright lethal.*

His eyes fall to my mouth, and my dick moves. "Cut's almost gone, huh?"

"Too bad," I hum. "I kind of liked it."

He scoffs, though the grin is a little bigger this time. "Weirdo."

"Oh, Raph, you have no idea…" I sigh, and he frowns.

"Why do you keep calling me that?"

"Wouldn't you like to know?"

"Uh, I would. That's why I asked." He gives me a pointed look.

Excitement fizzles inside me at this playful banter. *God, I love it. I don't want it to end…*

Unfortunately, it does when we reach the doorway that splits us.

"See you around, *Raph*," I hum teasingly, winking at him.

He simply shakes his head like I'm tapped as I turn away, following the other guard who's bringing me to my cell. As hard as it is, I force myself not to look back. Keeping him on his toes by playing the mysterious stranger.

Hey, I have to at least try, *right?*

I've yet to figure out Byron's situation. I was sensing something between him and Joy… But then he could be bisexual, or bi-curious, although he does behave rather straight, tension and sexy fist fights aside. It's hard to tell whether he's even interested in my throwing myself at him.

Still, it's not just about how bloody *fine* he is, or how he looks at you like he could tear you apart with his teeth and you'd thank him for it. There's something buried deeper than the muscle and ink and smoldering looks.

Whatever it is, I want at it. *Desperately.*

So I'll keep digging. Keep scampering after him like the lost puppy I so clearly am, in hopes he might one day toss me a bone. *Literally.*

A big one, too, based on how it felt jamming into me. And looked, tenting his pants. I'm guessing at least twenty-four centimeters. Fingers crossed.

Back in my cell, I tidy up, then pace for a while, waiting for Kent. Typically, he comes to check on me after each meal to see if I need anything… *Within reason. Superficial requests only.*

But tonight, I'm not taking no for an answer. He's going to give me what I want. And what I *want* is Byron Kang.

Manuel Blanco's errand boy arrives right on schedule.

"All good, Mr. Fenwick?" Kent asks, peering through the bars.

I love how he calls me that… *As if I'm a guest of his boss, not an animal in a cage with no bloody choice.*

"I have a favor to ask of you, my dear friend." I lay on the charm thick, though it comes out slightly sarcastic. *Must be the accent.*

"For the last time, I'm not bringing you Peppermint Schnapps." He rolls his eyes.

"But it's basically mouthwash!" I whine. His impatient glower tells me to stop fucking around, which I do. "Will you please bring Byron Kang to my cell?"

Kent's expression shifts, his brows jumping in surprise. "Byron… Kang."

I nod enthusiastically. "I would like him to come for a visit. No supervision."

He blinks as if he's unsure whether this request classifies as *within reason*. "For how long?"

"However long is allowed." I shrug.

The suspense is killing me while he mulls this over. "I'm not really supposed to move inmates…"

"You move me… With your rendition of 'The Wind Beneath My Wings.'" I'm chewing on my lip to keep from cackling at my own stupid joke, even more so because of how disgruntled he looks. "Sorry. *Please?* It's rather important…"

He's still contemplating.

"You can ask The Ivory if you want. Tell him it would mean the *world* to me."

Kent lets out a long breath, pushing himself off the bars. "Hang on."

He stomps away, and I'm back to pacing. Hopefully, if this does work, Byron isn't upset about my dragging him away from his nighttime routine. Although, I have to figure he'd appreciate a disruption from the monotony of prison life as well… *Regardless of whether he allows me to touch and sniff him.*

Footsteps have me rushing to the bars. My heart leaps, stomach tightening in elated surprise. Kent has returned, walking behind a bemused Byron Kang. I'll admit, I'm shocked. I hadn't expected it to work, especially so fast.

Jumping back to seem less eager, I'm jittering as Kent opens the bars for Byron. He pauses for a moment of clear skepticism before ultimately striding into my cell, peering back as Kent slams the door with a clunk.

"I'll be back before lights out," Kent says. And then he leaves.

Leaves me alone with the sexy, brooding object of my obsession.

I'm speechless. *Byron Kang is actually in my cell right now.*

"So… this is weird," he rumbles, shifting his weight. "Why am I here, Trevel?"

God, I love how he says my name…

"I just… figured we could hang out." I speak quietly, losing a bit of my edge due to how awed I am that he's even in here, and we're alone, and…

Oh, bollocks. What if he ends up hating this?? What if we have nothing to say to one another?? We'll be trapped alone, forced to endure the awkwardness!

Byron nods casually, and my panic subsides. He doesn't seem physically repulsed by my bringing him in here. *So… that's good.*

He rubs his hands together, fidgeting. "Did you…" His voice trails, eyes flicking in the direction Kent just went. "Who was that guy?"

My brows knit. "You don't know Kent?"

He shakes his head. "He's not a guard… right?"

"He's the Warden's personal security," I tell him.

Now he looks even more confused. "Okay… But why would he do this for you?" He peeks behind me, at my giant rifled-through gift basket. "Is that from him too?"

Considering what to tell him, I air on the side of caution and just say, "More or less."

Byron's face takes on an intensity I haven't seen since he was on top of me with his hand curled around my throat. "Huh… I guess I didn't know you'd already started… *working the system.*"

Gaping at him like he's speaking Swedish, I tilt my head. "What on earth are you talking about?"

His jaw is visibly tight. "Trading sex for favors, Trevel. You know, the only way people get things in here…" He looks at my goodies again. "Judging by the size of that thing, you must've really… gone the extra mile."

A gust of befuddled laughter escapes me. "I'm sorry… I must be missing something. Are you saying the only way to get things in this prison is by… pleasuring the guards??"

This is news to me… *Though it would explain why inmates have things, despite there being no commissary system to speak of.*

Byron's dark eyes are boring into mine, as if he's trying to read something. I don't mind. It gives me the opportunity to bask in the beauty of his deep brown irises.

Something in them softens as his shoulders un-hunch. "I keep forgetting you're still really new here." He rakes fingers through his dark hair. "It takes a while to… learn the ropes, I guess."

"Well, thank you for the vote of confidence." I squint at him. "But no, I haven't slept with anyone for anything. Kent is The Ivory's guy, and he gives me things when he's instructed to."

"I still don't get it." He sighs, wandering past me to poke around my dross. "But you don't have to elaborate if you don't want to. It's not my place…"

Spinning, I stare at his back, lines of definition visible beneath the fitted black tank top he's wearing. His shoulders are broad, and his skin looks so *smooth*, decorated in smatterings of occasional ink. Uncontrollably—*I physically can't help myself*—my eyes slide down his frame, tapered waist disappearing into the baggy jumpsuit pants. Unflattering on most people, but on *Byron*, they somehow look just right.

Maybe it's because, shapeless or not, they're unable to hide that perfectly plump behind. *Like a firm yet juicy peach I just want to sink my teeth into.*

"Do *you*… do that?" I drool out the words. "Trade sex for—"

Turning quickly to face me, he interrupts, "Why did you really bring me here?" Effectively dodging my inquisition.

"Because I like you," I answer honestly. His eyes go round, until I add, "I don't have *friends*, like you do. I'm always alone, and maybe I enjoyed it on the outside, but in here, it feels… suffocating." I pause to gulp. "I like talking to you. I like… being around you. I don't know why, but your energy draws me in."

Once all of the words are out, I take a breath, shifting and subtly glancing around. Expecting Leo to pop up, but weighted with disappointment when he doesn't.

Byron gawks at me for a few moments of heavy silence. But then I catch a tiny twitch of his lips. "My *energy*? Are you, like, a hippy or something?"

A grin breaks out across my face. "I'm not sure what that means, but I'm a yoga instructor. Well, I *was* one."

"Ah, so you're all about *chakra* and that Namaste stuff?" He releases a full smirk that has me swooning. I nod casually, at which he breathes a tiny chuckle. "That's cool. Definitely goes hand-in-hand with most martial arts. How long did you do that for?"

"A couple of years. Would you like to sit?" I gesture to the floor.

He regards me for a moment before shrugging. "Sure."

We sit down across from one another beside my giant basket. "I'm sorry there are no chairs. I'd offer the bed, but I didn't want you to think I was hitting on you."

He huffs, and I smirk.

"That'll come later."

He blinks at me. "Are you gay…?" I can't miss how his voice has taken on a vulnerable lilt.

"Would that be bad?" I ask, itching for some clarity on what his *deal* is. I'm getting so many conflicting vibes.

My Gay-dar is all over the place with this one.

"No," he bites out defensively, then clears his throat. "Sorry… I don't know why I asked. Your situation is none of my business."

I can't help the look I'm giving him. "Well, no… maybe not. But I don't consider my *situation* to be something that requires hiding. It's part of who I am. That would be like keeping the fact I'm British a secret."

My casual chuckles fall away when I notice the way he's gaping at me. It feels *significant*. As if the concept of someone being intentionally forthcoming on things like this is completely foreign to him.

"Do you… feel the need to hide things?" I ask carefully. "About who you are?"

He becomes visibly squirmy, eyes falling to his hands as he breathes, "Everyone has secrets."

Right, well, now I'm salivating. I have to *know what he's hiding beneath that sexy, growly exterior…*

"I didn't say I don't have secrets, Raph," I rasp, almost seductively.

His gaze narrows. "I need to know why you're calling me that."

"It's from the *Teenage Mutant Ninja Turtles*," I answer sheepishly, covering it with an insecure chuckle. "Not sure if you're aware of them… Anyway, *Raphael* is—"

"I know about Raphael," he cuts me off, eyes wide. "I *love* the Ninja Turtles. I've loved them since I was a kid… Raphael is my favorite. I named my street bike after him."

I'm beaming. "See? I knew it made sense. Check it out." I show him my socks.

"Those are dope," he hums, examining them.

Oh my God, I can't believe he's a TMNT fan! I knew there was a reason I liked him.

"So I'm your Raphael…?" His lips slope into the first genuine smile he's ever shown me.

It's almost innocent; charming, and sexy, but also sweet. I think he's flattered. *Good call on the nickname, mate.*

"Uh-huh." I bite my lip. "My warrior."

The way he's gawking at me is squeezing the air out of my lungs. Call me crazy, but there's a sparkle of intrigue in his deep eyes that seems more than friendly. I could be imagining it… *Alright, I almost certainly am.* But still, it's clear that he's not opposed to this… *Us.*

Doing whatever it is we're doing.

I want to scoot closer, but I'm afraid of scaring him off. I get the impression he might startle easily.

"Which Turtle do you think I am?" My head slopes. "No, wait, don't tell me. Michel—"

"Leo," he barks over my guess. "I think you're… Leonardo."

I'm taken aback. I've *never* considered myself to be Leo, hence why my best friend in the world—*my imaginary friend who's far flakier than someone with that name should be*—is Leonardo.

Leo's the level-headed one. The *leader*. He's an amalgamation of the other three; all of their best traits wrapped into one.

I could never be Leo… I'm not good. I'm a fuck-up. A hot bloody mess.

If ever there was a time for *my* Leo to show back up, it'd be now. But he doesn't. He's still not fucking here, and because of it, my vulnerabilities are weaseling their way to the surface.

I need to change the subject. Like now.

"I'm pansexual," I grunt, raspier than I want to be. "Though, I'll admit, I haven't had many actual *relationships*…" My mind flicks to Alice, but I shake it away. "You don't have to tell me your secrets, Byron. But if you ever wanted to open up to someone…" I swallow hard. "I wouldn't mind being that person. In fact, I think it could be just the thing to breathe some *life* into this life sentence."

Into me.

His lips part, eyes locked on mine, conveying his obvious uncertainty. In this moment, I can see it, feel it, *recognize* it. His burden… The secrets he's holding on to are *burying* him. Like cinderblocks he's refusing to let go of, even though they're sinking him in quicksand.

No one truly knows you, do they, Byron Kang?

The mound of his throat dips, and he whispers, "What if I… don't know how?"

His fear is palpable, yet his tone carries yearning. As much as I'd love to shuck him open like an oyster to get the gorgeous pearl I just know is inside, I don't want to make him more uncomfortable than he already is.

After all, I understand where he's coming from. *More than he realizes.*

I've clung hopelessly to my secrets. Purposefully kept my demons locked away inside me, for fear that letting them out would show the world what I truly am.

A monster, hiding in plain sight.

So rather than pressing the matter, I grab my gift basket and begin digging through it for something to keep this night from becoming a drag.

"I have an idea." I take out a bottle of black nail polish and shake it. "Let's play two truths and a lie."

His brow furrows as he watches the bottle in my hand. "What's that?"

"Nail polish."

"No, I mean what's two truths and a lie?" He smirks.

"Oh, it's a game," I explain. "You tell two truths about yourself, and one lie. Normally, the other person has to guess which is the lie… But we don't have to do that part if you don't want to."

He's staring at me, mesmerized.

"It'll be like confessing your secrets without confessing them. Preserve the mystery." I wink.

He forces a scowl, but I can tell he's instantly intrigued by this concept. Straightening, he nods. "Okay. You go first."

I squint at his bossy command. "Fine, but only if you give me your hand."

I snatch it up without waiting for him to concede.

"Why?" He looks nervous. "What are you gonna do…?"

"I'm going to chop it off." I roll my eyes. "I'm going to paint your nails, you knob."

He frowns. "Why would I want that?"

"Well, clearly, you've been coloring them with something." I run my thumb over some faded black on his fingernail. He flinches, and I chuckle. "Hold still. I'll make you look pretty."

His mouth is set in a grumpy line that somehow makes him look even hotter. But he concedes and sighs. "Whatever floats your boat."

Scooting in closer, I hold his hand tight to keep it steady. It feels sort of shaky, though I'm trying not to obsess over why that might be.

"You have nice hands," I hum, brushing polish onto his nail.

"Oh, do I?" He scoffs.

"Yea, you do." My eyes lift to his.

His throat bobs, something of a flush taking over his chiseled face. "Is that… one of the truths? Or the lie…?"

"Those aren't the rules, Byron." I tame my smirk while he observes me. Taking a moment, I think of three things to say. "Okay, so… I was born in London. I speak fluent Spanish. And I've never been on a rollercoaster."

I can tell he's speculating as to which of these things is the lie, so I remind him, "No guessing. Your turn."

He still seems unsure, but eventually, he grumbles, "Um… I was born in Seoul. I love gardening… And I've never sneezed."

"Come again?" I snort. "Hang on, is that the lie?? I need to know."

"Those aren't the rules, Trevel," he sneers.

Lord, it is unreasonable for a bloke to be this hot and this adorable at once.

"See? I'm learning things about you already… You're a smartass." I grin, swiping more black onto his nail while he chuckles. "Alright, let's see… I never learned how to drive. I love my parents. And my favorite pizza toppings are pineapple and pepperoni together."

Byron stares at me, and I'm assuming it's because of that parental lie I dropped in there… But then he rumbles, "I hope the last one is true, because pineapple and pepperoni is my favorite pizza."

Fluttering happens in my gut. "Easy, Byron Kang. I'm trying to keep myself in check, but if you go on saying things like that, I won't be able to control myself."

Tension stiffens his hand in mine. "You're kidding… right?"

"Would that make you more comfortable?" I tease.

"No. I mean, I don't *care*, I'm just…" He's flustered, and it's *so* bloody cute. "I'm not gay."

My eyes spring to his, bringing with them an accusatory brow lift I can't hold back. "Is that a lie?"

"No…" he growls.

"So… *that* is?"

His jaw tics visibly. "Trevel… Fuck off."

I don't know why pushing his buttons is so entertaining, but it's quickly becoming my new favorite hobby. *And the way he growls my name inflates my dick like a balloon.*

"*Fine.*" I roll my eyes and bite my lip. We're both quiet for a moment before I rumble, "So you're bi then?"

"No," he hisses again, far too defensive to be a truth.

But hey… What do I know? I just work here.

"Oh, so your dick was hard the other night because of my feminine qualities?" I tease. "How sweet."

"God, let it go," he gripes. "Sometimes I hook up with guys in here to pass the time, okay?? It doesn't mean anything. I've never… dated a man."

And there's our lie.

"Who have you hooked up with here?" My interest in this conversation has been piqued. I'm practically salivating for answers.

It takes him a moment to speak up. "Ren. And Luthor. *Ow…*"

Oh, bollocks. I'm squeezing his hand too hard. "Sorry. Continue, please."

"Whatever, it doesn't matter," he grumbles, playing it off like he's unaffected, but I can tell this is a sore spot for him. And I'm dying to know why.

"Of course it does," I say firmly, and our eyes meet.

He swallows visibly, then mutters, "I mean that them hooking up with *me* didn't… matter. Because they're obsessed with each other." He clears his throat. "They've been doing this toxic dance since the moment I set foot in this prison. They're on a collision course, and anyone in the way gets crushed."

"But it mattered to you…?" I ask, trying not to sound jealous as hell.

"That's enough," he grumbles. "Can we go back to the game, please?"

"Why? Because I've got you on the ropes?" I tease.

He scoffs. "Look who doesn't know fighting. You could never get me on the ropes, *loverboy.*"

"Show me what you got, tough guy," I sneer.

The moment the final nail is done, he snatches his hand back. "Hmm. I forgot, you like to be roughed up."

A memory smacks me upside the head, and I nearly topple over.

A hand stuffing my face into the dirt…

Screams, and laughter, and pain.

And blood. Lots of blood.

"So what if I do?" Sniffing, I feel suddenly woozy.

I'm fighting to regain my witty nonchalance, but it's just out of reach. I can feel trauma oozing from my pores. Tossing the nail polish into the basket, I ignore the way he's gaping at me.

"Trevel, I—"

"I write poetry," I cut him off before he can go there. "I've never been in love. And I talk to an imaginary version of my old teddy bear named Leo."

Byron's face turns flabbergasted. It's kind of funny… How out of his element he looks. A chuckle bursts out of me, and he relaxes a bit.

Shaking his head, he scoffs while assessing his manicure. "You're certifiable, you know that?"

"So I've been told," I sigh out my amusement.

His movements stop, and he winces, pinching the back of his neck.

My brow furrows. "What's wrong?"

"Nothing. I'm still kinda stiff from the other night," he murmurs, lolling his head from side to side. I bite back a grin, and he rolls his eyes. "My *muscles*, creeper. From the fight. Sleeping on these terrible mattresses doesn't help."

My face lights up, a golden opportunity presenting itself. "I can give you a massage… If you like."

He peeks at me. "Yea?"

I nod fast. "I was a massage therapist as well."

"You were a yoga instructor *and* a massage therapist?"

"And a poetry teacher, and a bartender, and a dog-walker…"

"Okay, I get it." He grins. "I'm fine, though. It's not a big deal."

"Listen, warrior." I ease behind him, ignoring his obvious reticence. "You asked me if I wanted to make you feel good…"

His eyes widen, and it takes him a beat to breathe out, "Do you?"

Nodding, I slide my hands onto his shoulders. "Relax and let me work my magic."

"Just a *massage*, though… right?" he grumbles.

All I want is to crawl on top of him and see where things go. But I compose myself, because we're being *friendly*, and murmur, "Yes."

He peeks at me over his shoulder, wearing a rather suspicious look. "No happy ending?"

I pout, running my index finger up the nape of his neck until he flinches. "Boring, but that's your call."

Sighing, he nods with trepidation. "*Fine.* Upper body only."

"Yes, sir, Rapha." I pluck the material of his shirt. "I'll need this off, though."

Humoring me, he whips the tank top over his head. And I'm momentarily very distracted, to an almost hypnotizing degree, by just how well sculpted he is. He's like a statue of a Greek god.

And I really like his tattoos.

"Byron… can I just say one thing?"

"You've already said about five hundred things tonight," he grunts. "Not that I could stop you, but what's one more?"

Ignoring the way his grumpiness tingles my balls, I croon, "Your body is *mouthwatering*."

He goes quiet, and I can feel his nervous squirming, before he mutters, "Don't drool on me."

Fucking hell. Grouchy, a little cocky, and feral for secret gay stuff… Why is that such an unbearably hot combination??

Taking a breath, I begin working on his shoulders gently. He is stiff, but I think it's mostly because of the potentially awkward circumstances. Still, I can tell he likes it, relaxing and leaning into the sensation.

Squeezing harder, I knead his muscles, sticking to the shoulders, when all I want is to lie him down and touch every solid *inch*. But I don't. I keep it professional, though it's like mild torture, caressing him with firm force, driving down on pressure points with my thumbs.

Byron's breathing shifts and slows, as if I'm working him into a trance. He's *melting* before me, and I'm on fire myself, but for a different reason.

Wow… His skin is every bit as creamy and soft as it looks.

"Should I use some lotion?" I whisper by his ear.

"Hm…?" He sounds out of it already, barely processing my question as his head lolls back. "*Fuck*, that feels good…"

"Yea?"

We're much closer now, my chest at his back and his impeccable body between my legs. I'm holding him up, caressing from his shoulder blades to his biceps.

"I'm just saying, I give a mean deep tissue," I hum. "But you'd have to lie down on the bed and get naked…"

"Trevel… stop talking," he groans softly.

"As you wish."

In the grand scheme of massages, this one is pretty tame. I'm used to my clients being naked, covered only by a sheet or blanket, lying face down and at the mercy of my hands. Regardless, it's clearly working for him. He's releasing these little gasps and hums that are stirring my dick beyond belief. The feel of him turning to putty beneath my fingers is unlike *anything* I've ever experienced.

I still barely understand it, but since the moment I laid eyes on Byron Kang, all I've wanted is to *worship* him. To lick, and suck, and bite him. Bring him to the brink of ecstasy with my hands and my mouth… and my dick. My ass.

Any and all parts of me with any and all parts of him.

I don't have any one default *role* in the bedroom. I'm down for pretty much anything, but I do tend to gravitate toward partners who take control. On the surface, Byron seems like the type to dominate. Yet, for whatever reason, I find myself fantasizing about how he'd react if I overpowered *him*. Maybe reigned some painful pleasure over this perfect body…

Something tells me he'd *love* it. But I'm not sure he'll allow himself to admit that. *Not yet, anyway.*

"How's this… pressure?" I rasp, and he purrs.

"So good…"

"Mmm… Tell me if you want it *harder*." I brush my lips behind his ear.

Fuck, he smells so good. I wonder how he… tastes…

Without thinking, I press a soft kiss there. It just happens, and I hear him release a breath. But he doesn't pull away or try to punch me. So I do it again, kissing him ever-so-gently while massaging his shoulders sensually, but with a firm grip. The next thing I know, I'm decorating his neck with kisses. And he's *allowing* it.

I'm high in a flash. My cock is straining against my pants, balls humming as I touch this beautiful boy, kisses growing hungrier, from lush pecks to needy suction. My tongue slips out, tracing the shell of his ear. And because I have absolutely zero chill whatsoever, I take his lobe between my lips and start *sucking*.

"*Fffuck*… um, Trevel…?" He trembles my name.

"Mhm?" My hands have moved around to his front, cupping and kneading his juicy pectoral muscles while I release his earlobe to lick and bite his pulse point.

"What are you… doing?" he asks breathlessly.

Giving you a hickey, hot boy, what does it look like?

"Making you feel good," I purr.

He shivers. "But you're… kissing me."

"You like it?"

"That's not… the point."

"Are you sure?" My hungry mouth moves up his jaw, going for his lips while my hands travel down his front, reaching for his dick. I make it to the abs, and the corner of his mouth, when he stops me, diving away fast.

"Dude, come on," he pants, aiming a right foggy glare at my face. "That wasn't part of the deal."

"Fuck the deal." My fingers rush through my hair in an attempt to compose myself. "We're *alone* in this cell, Byron. We both want to feel good, and you said it yourself… You hook up in here to pass the time. Pass the time with *me*. I promise, baby, it'll give you what you need."

His flushed face is painted with frustration. "Oh yea? And what do I *need?*"

"A release." I give him a pointed look. "To clear your head and drain your fucking balls. Why are you making this a bigger deal than it has to be?"

He's chewing vigorously on his lower lip, warring with himself. Not nearly as appalled as I'm sure he'd like to be. I snatch his hand, and he lets me, eyes wide. Holding his gaze, I extend my tongue to lick a purposeful line up his index finger. And then I suck it into my mouth.

"*Mmff.*" He shifts, watching me intently with a blaze in his eyes as I suck suggestively on his finger, barely a breath separating our mouths.

Byron looks astonished, and terrified, and *so* fucking turned on. No more dancing around this. I want to fuck him, in one way or another, and I *know* he wants it too, evident when he parts his lips and eases them up to mine.

Pulling his finger out of my mouth, I push it up to his. And to my own shock and awe, he sucks it between his lips. *Sucking* his own finger, with me guiding him.

"Byron…" I whimper, and his lashes flutter. "You are *so* fucking hot. Look at you, love… so unbelievably sexy, my cock is *aching*."

He groans softly, whining while he sucks hungrily on his finger as if imagining it's a cock. *Maybe mine…*

Tugging the finger out by his hand, I lick up the length of it again, this time not stopping until I'm flicking his bottom lip with my tongue. Then *biting* it.

"*Fuck*, what are we doing?" he mewls, fisting my shirt with his free hand.

"Who cares," I rush out, shoving him onto his back and crawling over him. "Stop thinking."

"'Kay…" he sighs as he arches up to me, gaze lidded and hungry. "Please touch my dick."

"'Kay," I growl, reaching between his legs. His cock is full, hard and *huge*, and now I'm massaging *that*, palming it over his pants until he's quaking. "Baby, you're so fucking big."

"*Uhh*, shit… I think I just came a little," he whimpers, and I chuckle breathlessly onto his mouth. "This is so hot… Why is this so hot??"

"What did I say about the thinking?"

"Sorry," he rasps with his fists in my hair.

"Be a good boy and rub that big cock on me, Raphael," I breathe, thrusting between his legs.

Like the other night while we were fighting, only so much better. Deeper, hotter, *greedier*. His long, rock-solid dick is trapped between us while we move together, grinding, working our hips to dry-fuck like it's going out of style. I can't even fathom how phenomenal it feels as my hands glide around to possessively palm and squeeze his ass.

"*Ohhfuckyeaa…*" He shivers.

"You like that?" I growl, head floating off my body. "My hands on you…"

He nods fast, tightening all over.

"God, Byron… Let me fuck you, baby. I want to get you soaking wet and slide in you so *deep…*"

And suddenly, he's shuddering. "Mmfffuuck… Oh fuck, Trev… *Trevel.*"

Is he… coming??

I think he's coming!

Bloody hell… now I'm coming.

Out of bloody *nowhere*, my balls burst, and I shoot all over the inside of my pants while clutching Byron's trembling body. Holding his hips, I press my throbbing cock into his ass so that I can come on him through our clothes. Even like this, it's pure euphoria.

"Baby, I'm coming for you," I whisper, inhaling his ragged breaths.

"Jesus Christ, oh my God…"

"*Ohh…* Mmm, tell me about it."

Fluttering down from the most unexpected mutual orgasms ever, we're both panting like we just swam ten laps. Lips together, brushing. It's nothing short of astonishing.

"So ridiculous." Byron rests his forehead on mine. "That was like… some high school shit. How the hell did that even happen??"

"I don't know, but I think I wet your pants through my pants." I chuckle.

He snorts, then exhales a jittery breath. "I'm all sticky…"

"I think you're perfect…" I sigh dreamily.

Pulling back, he locks his eyes on mine, staring as if he's trying to find answers in my irises. *I highly doubt that's what he'll find…*

"We're just friends… Okay?" he says softly. Not angry, or even scared anymore.

It almost sounds like he's saying it because he thinks he's supposed to.

I'm taken aback by that comment, though I'm not sure why either. And because I don't have the brain capacity for anything else right now, I simply nod. "Of course. What else would we be?"

He bites his lip. "It's just… a release. Like you said."

"Right."

Seemingly placated by my response, his fingers brush tenderly through my hair. An affectionate gesture that swells my heart until it aches.

"Thank you for… inviting me over."

I blink at him, lips curving. "My pleasure."

Peeling off of each other, we both stand slowly, exchanging timid glances while adjusting our cum-stained clothes.

"Hey, Trevel…?" he calls out, uncharacteristically soft, and I glance up.

"Yea?"

He shifts. "My favorite actor is Jared Leto. I can't even look at frosted animal crackers because once when I was a kid, I ate too many of them and threw up…" I chuckle, and he bites his lip. "And I really… *hated* what we just did."

The timid look on his face is killing me in the best way. I take a step forward, needing to kiss him at least once because, *fuck me*, he probably tastes like candy. But footsteps approaching shut it down before I can get to him. Byron backs away fast, clearing his throat.

And although I'm not ready to give him back, I have no choice but to let him fight me…

For now.

CHAPTER EIGHTEEN

Byron

"WHAT THE FUCK IS THIS?!"

A roar that would normally stop everyone dead in their tracks is swallowed up by the noise. The sheer pandemonium is overwhelming these dank halls.

It's *loud*, echoing more turmoil than usual. Shouting and banging coming from all sides framing the clomps of an organized march… One we're not a part of.

My head flings around general population, watching on with wide eyes as unfamiliar faces stomp past us like we're nothing. I'm used to being invisible… But clearly, Velle is not.

And he's fucking pissed.

"Yo, what the fuck is going on, man??" Peters gasps, charging over with Jasper by his side. We're all just standing around—myself, Trevel, Luthor and Ren being sort of shielded by a visibly edgy Rook, Joy, and Velle. "Where did these pricks come from??"

We're *all* looking to Velle for any indication of what's happening right now. It's not even a choice; it's a reflex.

He's visibly fuming, of course, with that crazed twitch in his eye he gets when he's about to crack skulls. But apparently, this is havoc even *he* can't scowl away.

I thought it was odd that Dr. Love showed up in the rec room while we were down there, having our depressing version of "yard time." I figured he'd just popped in to see Darcey, since the two of them are *also* disgustingly obsessed and inseparable. But only a few minutes later, Rook and Velle came hustling into the room, and the four of them—the dynamic trio plus Dr. Love—huddled off in the corner for some bizarre meeting.

It was weird, and I was just about to subtly harass Trevel for more details on his history with the surly doctor, when voices came bellowing from across the room via the walkies—their cohorts hollering about some commotion up in Gen-pop.

It was immediately Defcon 1.

Like *Disaster Dominoes*. As soon as the first one fell, everything fell apart, quickly, uniforms toppling.

Rook, Velle, and Joy hustled us prisoners back up from the rec room, leaving Darcey and Dr. Love to return to The East. And we arrived to what can only be described as a *coup*.

The entirety of general population is being flooded with strangers. Not just any strangers, though. *New muscle.*

A whole-ass *SWAT team* of huge men is patrolling the halls, causing an uproar of mass hysteria. I have no idea who they are or why they're here, but I remember what Peters said over the walkie... Something about *new guards brought in by The Ivory.*

Okay. This is it.

We're officially screwed.

"He didn't say anything to you?" Jasper asks Velle, keeping his voice down while we stand still, eyes shifting nervously like we're being circled by sharks and we need to refrain from making any sudden movements.

"Is that a real question?" Velle grumbles, uncharacteristically unnerved.

As much as you want to hate the guy, when shit goes down, he's the barometer. The constant presence of stability in the form of his ever-present macho, haughty arrogance. If Velle is posted up, arms folded, lips pursed, and that damn smug eyebrow cocked, you know things will probably be alright. As *alright* as they can be, anyway.

The last time something crazy and fucked up happened, Velle was nowhere to be found. It was troubling.

But this is worse. Because he's *right here*, and every bit as uneasy as the rest of us.

"Get them back to their cells," Velle says to Rook, then turns to Joy. "Round up the rest of the team. We'll meet at the spot in twenty."

Everyone scatters in different directions, except Rook, who stays with us. I don't want to admit that I'm anxious as hell right now, but I am. I don't like this… It's not the good kind of excitement.

Glancing right, I meet Luthor's glistening green gaze, his brows zipped in worry. But I look away fast, swallowing a lump in my throat.

Yea, things are awkward right now.

Nonetheless, I might need to buck the fuck up a little. As dramatic as that field trip was, what's happening up here *now* is an epic shitstorm of glorious fuckery that makes our petty squabbling seem pretty damn childish.

I'm glad I was able to get in one last sparring session with Joy. Something tells me we won't be doing that again for a long, long *time.*

"You," Rook growls at Trevel, who points to himself. "Hands on that wall. You move, I shoot you. Got it?"

Trevel says nothing, casting me a puzzled glance before placing his palms flat on a nearby wall. Unfortunately, the rest of us barely make it a step through the doorway to the row before we're ambushed by three huge assholes I've never seen before.

One of them immediately cuffs me, without a word, giving me a hard shove to the back until I stumble. My glare goes unnoticed. He just keeps pushing me toward my cell with my hands cuffed behind my back.

Rook is yelling at them, but it's Ren's shouts that have me looking over my shoulder. They're physically ripping Luthor and Ren apart, bringing them in different directions.

Shit…

"Move, inmate." The big dickhead hustles me into my cell, cutting off my view of what's happening. He comes in with me, slamming the bars in my face, then stuffing me into the corner. "Stand still," he grunts, proceeding to raid all of my belongings.

I watch him helplessly for a moment, my face springing back when I see Luthor being dragged past my cell, with Rook following, powerless to do a damn thing. Fear coils my insides, and I inch closer to the bars. I can't see shit, but I need to know what's happening out there. It looked like they were bringing Ren out of the row…

"Where are they taking him??" Luthor cries from up the hall.

I flinch when something loud crashes next door. *Jesus, they're tearing the place apart.*

"Baby, listen to me… It'll be okay," Ren calls out to Luthor.

I don't need to see him to know he's panicking. It's audible, even over inmates screaming, metal slamming and clanging. It's fucking bedlam.

But I don't care about any of that bullshit. I want to know what's going on with *them*.

I need to know that my friends are alright.

"I'll find you, no matter what, I promise!" Ren bellows, trying to be strong for Luthor, but I can hear the distressed tremor in his voice. My heart is crumbling where it's lodged in my throat. "Lexington! I love you! *Fuck you*, you goddamn mouth-breather! Let g—"

His wails are cut off with the slam of a door, and now I'm really worried.

They're bringing him somewhere else...? Why??

What are they going to... do to him?

Leaning up against the wall, I cringe as the fucker in my peripheral throws my stuff all over the place.

This is too much... What the hell is going on??

My mind races, sifting through scattered thoughts like attempting to clean up a giant mess—*which I'm sure I'll be doing as soon as this asshole leaves.*

I'm not made of stone. Despite how pissed I was in the rec room, I *do* still care about Luthor and Ren. I brought up some shit down there that will undoubtedly be festering in their minds for a while, and I feel guilty about that...

Parker, for one. Luthor's lost cellmates, for another.

I'm really not trying to second-guess myself here. I said what had to be said. But now that our safety is uncertain, it's bringing on a wave of regret for the way I yelled at them not twenty minutes ago.

When the big douchebag has sufficiently destroyed most of my stuff, he leaves. Just fucking stomps off, slamming the bars behind him. Leaving me cuffed inside my cell, without a damn clue how I'm supposed to Houdini my way out of them to take a piss or sleep comfortably.

Prisoners are shouting these same sentiments from all angles, so at least I'm not alone. But it doesn't make me feel better. Because my nervous bladder is acting up, and I kinda have to pee.

Pacing in a small circle, on the only part of floor that isn't covered in junk, I attempt to block out the noise of these new fucking *guards*, abusing inmates, tearing things to shreds... Terrorizing the halls, and doing so with limited words, and dead expressions. Most alarmingly of all, they're doing it right in front of Velle and his team.

And Velle's paralyzed to stop it.

"Kang?!" The yelp breaks through it all, my name being called from up the row. I stop dead in my tracks. "I'm sorry! I never meant to hurt you!"

My legs give out, and I crash into a pile of clothes and broken plastic.

"You're so important to me," Luthor keeps shouting, fear and emotion trembling his words. But he says them anyway, because he wants me to listen. "You gotta know that!"

My face drops into my hands, heart splitting in half.

He sounds scared… My best fucking friend, man…

I swear to God, I can't…

Emotion is welling behind my eyes. Luthor is the smart one, the rational one. I think he knows we might not see each other for a while after this.

So he's shouting his feelings up the goddamn hall for me to hear.

A broken whimper climbs up my throat, and I push my trembling lips together to stop it from getting out.

I *want* to respond, I know I do. To yell out that I forgive him, and I'm sorry for what I said. That I don't hate him, and I never could. Things got a little fucked up, but it doesn't mean I don't love him like a brother, because I *do* and I always will.

But I don't. I can't… My vocal cords just won't work.

There's something seriously wrong with me. Why can't I speak up?? Be honest about what's in my heart to the people who matter…?

The secrets I hold are starting to feel like a *disease*, infecting my emotional state from all sides. It's not healthy, keeping so much inside that I eventually burst and need to either hurt someone or myself.

I might be detrimentally broken.

The uproar eventually fades off into the night. But I stay seated on the floor, among the ruins of stuff that doesn't mean dick compared to the shattered remains of what *should* have been an unbreakable friendship.

It's been at least a full day since the new regime showed up, and I still don't know what to think, other than that, against all reasoning, Alabaster Pen has somehow become even *more* unpredictable.

For hours, we were all left cuffed inside our cells, surrounded by the mess those dickless fucks made for no goddamn reason. No food, no showers. Just noise, in and out of my head.

Eventually, some oafish prick came by to remove my cuffs, and thankfully, it was before I was forced to piss my pants. But that was probably twelve hours ago, and we've all been in our cells ever since.

Sure, I'm starving and dirty, but more than either of those things, I want fucking answers.

What's the purpose of all this?

Is it just the Warden's way of sticking it to Velle after their falling out? Or is there more to the arrival of the Officers from Hell than meets the eye?

They've come to fuck shit up, that much is clear. And from the looks of it, they're getting down to brass tax.

I haven't seen Trevel since he was cuffed and hauled off, and I can't help the way my stomach has been bunched in concern. Not just for him... For all of them.

Luthor's voice crying out to me that he's *sorry* has been playing in my mind on repeat; a mashup with Ren's screams when they were ripped apart. I don't know where they took him, but I haven't heard his voice since that last moment of him cursing at them while he was hauled away.

Fighting or not, he's still my *friend*. It's not like I want him to be physically harmed in any sort of permanent fashion.

I just can't stop picturing the looks on their faces when I finally voiced my grievances and called them out—in the rec room, right before all hell broke loose.

It'd been a long time coming, honestly. They deserved to know how I feel... That I'm not going to sit by and let them use me anymore. I have fucking feelings too, and I *refuse* to be some sidelined, walk-on role in the *Luthor and Ren Show.*

Not anymore.

And despite what I'm sure they think, my newfound friendship with Trevel has nothing to do with it. I've been needing to get that shit off my chest since long before Trevel got here.

Okay, maybe their incessant lecturing did sort of light the fuse on the dynamite of my aggravation. And having him on my side—as someone in *my* corner for once—might have given me the courage to finally speak my mind. *Just a little.* But that wasn't the whole reason I flipped out.

Could I possibly be harboring some internal guilt over blatantly lying to their faces? *Sure.* Because I looked them in the eye and told them Trevel and I had only spoken a few words to each other... And that's certainly *not* the extent of our relationship. Not that what we're doing is a *relationship* at all. We're just friends... who sort of accidentally made each other come in the heat of a bizarre, sexually charged moment I haven't stopped obsessing over since it happened.

But that's our business, no one else's. Trevel was happy to keep what happened between us *between us*, and I've been hiding things from Luthor and Ren for years.

What's one more secret hookup to add to the book?

The truth is that despite how much I enjoy spending time with Trevel, and how unexpectedly fantastic it felt to come in my pants with him like a couple of horny teens, I still don't really *know* him. I don't know why he's here, or what his connection is to The Ivory... The true nature of his disdain for Dr. Love. Those could very well be the things my friends were referencing.

But it doesn't matter, because I do know *them*, and I don't feel like their concerns were fully genuine. Maybe from Luthor... But definitely not Ren.

The things we've done together, all the ways Ren's used me over the years... *He deserves to feel bad. I hate to say it, but he needed that knife in his chest, plunged and twisted.*

Still, that doesn't make it hurt any less now that I have no idea where he is or what's happening to him.

Eventually, after an extended amount of time and far too much stewing, I hear the door open at the end of the row. The stomping carries with it an immediate and unfamiliar voice.

"Attention inmates of Alabaster Pen!" a man shouts. I scramble up and over to the bars to peer out into the row. "This is an important announcement, so shut the fuck up and listen. You'll want to pay attention, because I'm only gonna say this once!"

It's one of the new guards. He's slightly out of view, but I can just barely make him out. Large, brown-skinned, black hair, neck tattoos. I'm picking up a slight accent... *Maybe Colombian, since that's where The Ivory is from.*

But the most distinguishing thing about his appearance is a uniform unmistakably different from the one Velle and his guards wear.

"Starting right the fuck now, we're instituting a no-talking order for general population. This means that every *single* second spent outside of your cell should be done in absolute silence."

Naturally, a bunch of people start barking back, arguing and cursing.

The guy roars, "That wasn't an invitation to open your fucking mouths! The quiet game should start the moment myself or my colleagues enter this row! When you're in the halls, showers, or the caf, *you will not speak*, you got me? That door opens, your mouths close! Anyone who disobeys will learn the hard way how serious we are."

The row is quiet for a moment before someone—sounds like Simmons—calls out, "What about other noises…? Like laughing, or—"

"You should *not* be laughing," the guy cuts him off with a stern glare aimed at Simmons's cell. "I don't know what the fuck could possibly be funny about this place, but laughter means you're not miserable enough. And we'll have to change that." He pulls a billy club off of his holster and begins walking up and down the row, banging it against the wall. "*No* talking. *No* noise. That means *not a sound*. You gotta shit your pants outside of your cell, you do it silently or your nasty ass will rot in the hole. *Am I clear?!*"

He stands still for a moment, as if he's waiting for something. And of course, some idiot decides to say, "Yea, sure."

The guard stomps over and whacks his billy club against the cell bars. The inmate—I think it was Fuller—wails in pain. I'm pretty sure the dude smashed his fingers.

God…

Without another word, the asshole storms off, leaving us all to bitch and moan among ourselves. Once the door is closed, that is.

Weighted and sullen, I drag myself back over to my bed and crash down on it like I'm full of gravel.

A no-talking order… Really?? As if this place wasn't terrible enough, now we have to spend our every human interaction in silence??

I already have no cellmate, which means no one to talk to for a majority of the day. Now I'll *never* be able to speak to anyone again.

Fucking lovely.

Many more hours pass before the door opens again. Surprisingly, everyone shuts the fuck up this time.

A different dead-eyed prick shows up outside my cell, opening the door while I stand back. "Assume the position, inmate," he grumbles.

I do as I'm told, hands and forehead on the wall. He pats me down, then cuffs me—behind my back, which sucks. *Velle rarely did that.*

He drags me out and barks, "Move."

I can't help but notice that only myself and four others from this row are going. Glancing over my shoulder, I look for Luthor.

I guess he's not coming…

As we pass Ren's cell, I see that it's still empty.

"Face forward, inmate!" the guard snaps, and I straighten.

The six of us march toward the caf in complete silence. It's highly unnerving. Granted, I was never a fan of the mindless chatter, or the loud bellows of my fellow prisoners. But this is an extreme swing in the opposite direction. *I feel even deader inside than I already did.*

When we get to the cafeteria, there are a few inmates and another one of the new guards already in here. Still, it's a grand total of ten. That's less than half the usual group size. This deteriorating room is a million times creepier when it's silent and practically empty.

My inner turmoil is interrupted when I spot Trevel, sitting alone at his usual table. My heart does this leap thing, which I won't read too much into. Call it relief, seeing a friend amidst the isolation and dismay.

Trevel looks up as I'm wandering over to the chow line, his face noticeably brighter in an instant. He smiles and waves, and I can't stop my lips from quirking as I wave back.

Jesus, you're corny.

What about interacting with this dude turns everything into fucking high school??

I take a seat across from him at his table, blinking while he beams.

"Hey," he whispers, sloping forward. "You're a sight for sore eyes."

"Shh!" I place my finger to my lips, glancing around for the guards. They're circling the cafeteria like vultures on the hunt for fresh roadkill.

Trevel frowns and shakes his head. Once he's placed them across the room, he leans in even closer, melting those deep purple eyes over me. "Are you doing alright?"

Peeking over my shoulder once more, just to be sure, I mumble, "Been better, but I guess I'm managing. You?"

He shrugs. "I haven't been here long enough to know if this is different or not."

My chest rumbles in amusement. "Oh, it's different. Velle's been in charge since this place started... Running the show for over ten years with his team. These assholes showing up must mean—"

Trevel's eyes widen as a loud *thwack!* comes from behind me; the sound of a billy club being slammed down on the table.

"What was that rule we just warned you about, inmate?!" the guard roars.

Cringing, I'm hunched and stiff with nerves, too afraid to turn around and see him glaring at me. My lips part, but before I can speak, a different voice mutters, "Um... no talking?"

My face flings, and I see that the guard is actually scolding Matthews. Not me.

Phew.

But then he lifts his arm and shouts, *"No. Talking!"*

Swinging the billy club right into the side of Matthews's head, he knocks the poor bastard out with one hit. Matthews crumples off of the bench seat onto the floor, and we all gape in horror—and of course, silence—as the guard just struts away, continuing his rotation like nothing happened. Leaving the dude bleeding on the ground.

Fuck.

After that, Trevel and I don't speak another word. No one does. We all eat in fraught silence, enveloped by a tension so eerie it's like its own presence in the room. When the meal is over, the guards bring us ten inmates to the showers where we wash ourselves in the same strained, speechless trance.

I think I'm seeing the purpose of this no-talking order. It's a way of isolating us, even with people around.

Touché, Ivory.

On our way back, I'm being suffocated by looming despondence. Nothing matters. Thanks to this new regime, even if I wanted to open up to someone, now I physically *can't*. Unless we opt to pass secret notes in the halls. *Again*, like fucking high school.

We get to the row, and I shoot Trevel an expression of reluctant *goodbye*, paired with a small wave that I just know looks pathetic, but I can't help it. He doesn't get to return it, though, because that guy, Kent, swings around the corner.

He looks to Trevel, then me, then the guard behind us. "These two are going in together."

Trevel and I are frozen, dumbfounded, while the guard cocks his head. But he doesn't argue, not the way Velle would if someone popped up telling him what to do like that.

He simply asks, "In which cell?"

Kent nods in the direction of the row. Meaning *my* cell. Then he says to Trevel, "You're moving. I'll bring your things by later."

Um, hang on... What's happening??

Trevel looks just as thrown off as I'm feeling, but when the guard ushers us both over to my cell and shoves us inside, a very visible delight washes over his face. Our cuffs are removed, and we're left alone, *together*, with the slam of the bars.

Wait, so… he's actually my cellmate now??

Trevel releases a beaming smile that shows off his straight, white teeth. The more I look at his smile, the more I notice that it's actually a tiny bit crooked. And he has only one dimple on the left side.

I like it. The imperfections somehow make it… prettier.

I gulp over a suddenly dry throat.

Oh, boy.

This might be bad.

"Byron…" He sighs my name, face alit, eyes twinkling. "I can't believe it. We're roomies!" He bites his lip, and I swallow hard again. "This is going to be so fun!"

My head swivels back and forth. I'm still too confused to process this unexpected turn of events. "Why… would they move you?"

His smile fades, forehead lining. "I'm not positive, but I *had* mentioned that I was sick of living alone… I suppose Manuel decided to listen."

Manuel…?

He calls The Ivory… Manuel*??*

"Okay, I'd really like to know why the Warden does things for you," I grumble, brushing my damp hair back with my fingers. "Do you know him or something?"

He gives me a look. "No. He expects me to do him favors, and in return, he makes my life a little easier in here. It's nothing scandalous."

I stare at him for a moment, an icky feeling weaving around my insides. "Like what? What *favors*?"

"So far, he only wants me to begin sessions with Dr. Love," he answers casually, puttering around my cell—*our* cell, I guess—poking at things.

"Why would that be a favor he'd want from you?" My consternation is evident as I watch him touching my stuff.

"You'd have to ask him that." Trevel takes a seat on my bed and bounces. "The mattress in my cell is much better. I wonder if Kent will bring it over…"

"That's *my* bed." I step up to him. "You'll have to take the top."

His already elated expression shifts to one much more wicked. "I have no problem doing that for you, Byron. You just have to ask *nicely*." He smirks, and I scowl.

I stand over him, muscles stiffening. "Let's get one thing clear, alright? Just because we're sharing a cell now, doesn't mean we'll be, like…" My voice trails as his smirk widens. I gulp. "Whatever. Just… act normal, okay? I'm happy to have you here as my *cellmate*, but that's it. This isn't gonna turn into some damn cuddlefest."

Trevel purses his lips to tone down that crooked smile. "Fine. Apparently, *you* call the shots in here, Raph," he sneers, and I squint. "I promise, I'll be as platonic as I can manage."

Exhaling a sigh of defeat, I rub my eyes, already exasperated by him. He chuckles wickedly at my expense.

I really don't want to think about it right now… But this dude is shockingly similar to Ren.

Maybe that's why Ren hates him so much. We all know Ren hates himself.

The irony of all this is tripping me out. *Every time I lose a Michelangelo, I get one back.*

Blinking down at my new roomie, I push that thought away.

He's not Michelangelo. Because Michelangelo doesn't exist anymore.

And neither does the version of me I was when I was with him.

"Get off my bed," I growl, frustrated by all of this overthinking.

I've been so bored and lonely since O'Malley left. It's been months, and now I *finally* have a cellmate again. I should be happy. But instead, I'm stressing, and I can't pinpoint why.

Well, I'm sure I *can*. But like most things, I'm choosing to bury it.

Trevel gets up and climbs to the top bunk while I flop onto my bed. I can feel him moving around up there, the rickety frame shifting as he tosses and turns.

Jeez, I forgot how much the bunk rocks.

"Byron…" he mumbles once he finally stops wiggling around.

"Yea?" I sigh.

"I'm happy to be your cellmate too." The grin in his voice is audible.

I roll my eyes, nestling under my blanket. It's pretty early, but for the first time in a while, my eyelids are heavy. I think I might actually get some sleep tonight.

"Byron?"

If my new cellmate ever shuts the hell up.

"*Yes?*" I answer impatiently.

"Would you mind if I used our toilet to make some good old-fashioned prison hooch with the rest of my fruit?"

A disturbed expression covers my face. "That sounds disgusting. I'll have to insist that you don't do that."

He chuckles. "*Fine*. I'll use the sink."

I huff, closing my eyes. *Silly bastard.*

Eventually, Trevel's shimmying begins rocking me to sleep. I'm fucking *exhausted.*

I could really use the rest.

"Byron...?" He chirps again, and I groan.

"What??"

There's a moment of pause before he asks softly, "Why is there a hole in this mattress?"

My eyes shoot open.

So much for that idea.

CHAPTER NINETEEN

Byron

WARMTH SURROUNDS ME.

Like a sheet of serenity, it wraps me up. More than just my mind… My body too. It's a heaviness, a *pressure* that mollifies me, and I pretend not to know why.

But I do.

I've been searching for this feeling ever since…

The last night I felt it. *With him.*

Easing into it, the sensation of being held down and cherished, I reach for Michelangelo. I run my hands up his frame, breathing out a soft sigh of relief because he's *here.*

I got him back.

His soft breaths brush my chest, and I hum. "I missed you, baby…"

The fingers gently grazing my hip become less gentle. They grip me possessively. My brow furrows as consciousness slowly descends on my mind, blurring away the comfort.

A voice, distinctly *not* belonging to Michelangelo, hums, "Mmm… I'd hoped you would."

Fluttering my eyes open, I see black hair, messily strewn about. But when his face lifts, I'm met with purple eyes, and I jump.

"What the fuck?!" I gasp, still hoarse, having just woken up. Yanking myself out of his hold, I scoot away and sit up. "What are you doing in my bed??"

Trevel rises onto his knees, pouting. "You just looked so warm and peaceful..." His violet eyes sharpen. "Who were you talking to?"

"No one. None of your business," I bark, crawling out of bed. Unfortunately, I'm still on the tail-end of morning wood, and adjusting my visible dick in my pants isn't really helping my cause. "I thought I said no cuddling."

Trevel slides off the bed himself, stretching before me. In times like this, I hate that he's a solid five inches taller than me. I don't like it when he's hovering over me, wearing that knowing expression, like he doesn't believe a damn word I say.

"You're awfully stubborn, you know that?" He folds his arms over his chest, drawing my attention to his shirtless torso and how cut he is. Not as thickly muscled as me, but he has that slim definition really working for him. But I'm *not* trying to notice these things, so I force my eyes to remain on his face. "Prison gets lonely, Raph. What's wrong with a bit of shag-n-snuggle between mutually attracted mates, hm?"

I'm gaping at him like he's a mental case, but I think he likes it... It only serves to widen his grin.

It's too early for this nonsense.

Releasing a relenting breath, I rub my eyes. "Whatever, dude. Just... don't do it again."

Turning away, I'm going for my toothbrush and toothpaste, ignoring him as he murmurs, "No promises," behind my back.

I have to pause my morning routine to note all of Trevel's things, which have joined mine, lining the sink. That Kent guy showed up last night to drop off his stuff while I was fighting with my mind to stop running enough for me to get just a few minutes of sleep. I only dozed off about an hour ago, but at least it was something.

Too bad I was woken up by my new cellmate, spooning me against my will.

I'm concentrating on brushing my teeth as Trevel skips over, nudging his arm against mine. I jerk away and peer at him.

"May I take a guess?" he asks. I give him a puzzled look. "About the purpose of the hole... in the mattress."

My spine stiffens while he smirks.

I spit and rinse, then mutter, "I'd rather you didn't."

"Why?" he chirps. "Are you embarrassed?"

"Why would I be *embarrassed*?" I hiss, narrowing a glare at him.

"Well, because due to its position, you would have to be the... *receiver*. And I know *hetero* blokes can be a bit defensive about things like that."

His grin is downright menacing, and it's making me want to punch him. "Mind if I use some of yours?" He picks up my toothpaste.

My jaw tightens. "Knock yourself out."

He uncaps it and squeezes some onto his toothbrush, then winks. "Cheers."

Obviously, he's being extra flirty to get a rise out of me. I'm not stupid.

So we sort of hooked up… Big deal. I've *sort of hooked up* with lots of people at this point, and none of it means a damn thing. I'm sure I could hook up with Trevel again, just for fun, no strings attached.

But for some reason, it doesn't feel as *casual* as I'd like it to be, especially now that we're sharing a cell. I really don't want to deal with him thinking this is something it's not. Honestly, he seems like the type who becomes easily obsessive and codependent, which worries me.

We already have one of those in here…

"I'm simply wondering if its purpose is for the resident of the top bunk to *feed* whomever is on the bottom," he croons, refusing to let this go. I'm shivering, but fighting against it tooth and nail. "Because I'll say, Byron, if that's the case, I can't *wait* to give you a proper meal—"

"Alright, shut up," I growl.

I really hate how warm and squirmy I am right now…

What's the problem with just telling him the truth? Why am I so afraid??

So I used to occasionally suck my cellmate's dick through a hole in his mattress… Who cares?

When I glance back at Trevel, he's frowning, amusement dried up. "I'm sorry, Raph. I didn't mean to upset you…"

I swallow hard. "You didn't upset me. I'm *fine*. It's just… whatever may or may not have happened through that hole is… done. It's in the past."

I breathe out slowly, and he slants his head. I can tell he wants to say a million more things, and it's stressing me out.

Fortunately, he nods, accepting my half-assed explanation. "Understood. I apologize."

"No apologies necessary," I mutter, moving on to washing my face.

I get in there good, distracting myself from the awkwardness of me and Trevel—*paired with the memories of slurping on O'Malley's cock through the mattress*—using some of the nice moisturizer Joy got me a while ago that I managed to hold on to despite the lockdown.

Everything is fine. Sucking your friends' dicks is no big deal.

Sucking the Warden's dick is no big deal.

You can suck as many dicks as you want, and it's nobody's goddamn business but yours.

"I knew you probably had a decent skincare regimen," Trevel says. I cock a bemused brow at him. "Your complexion is stunning."

I blink at him, baffled by the compliment. No one has ever said that to me before. No one's ever noticed such a minor detail about me, and if they have, they never cared to mention it.

But he does; this virtual stranger who seems to notice *everything*. I swear to God, when he's looking at me, sometimes I can feel him scouring my every pore. Every angle, every dip, every surface. He's all up in it, and it's only a matter of time before that scrutinizing violet attention starts seeping into my deeper places.

Gulping, I'm unable to fight the breathy, "Thanks," that leaves my lips.

"You're very welcome." Trevel winks at me in the mirror I have up over the sink, fussing with tousled black locks that fall past his ears.

It reminds me that my own hair's been growing in, and I run my fingers through, combing it back. "You can use any of my products... If you want."

He spins to face me. "I appreciate that. You can use my stuff too. Sharing is caring, yes?"

I shrug and nod. *Sure, why not.*

Having a cellmate again is interesting, especially one who's so different from O'Malley. O'Malley was a whacko, but at least you knew what to expect. As forthcoming as he portrays himself to be with certain things, Trevel Fenwick is still an enigma. A quiet, calculating monster, as opposed to a stark-raving lunatic.

It's an adjustment, having someone all up in my space again. I find myself changing my clothes frantically to avoid being naked in front of him. Not that he hasn't already seen me naked—*the joys of showering in front of everyone you know.* I just fear that lingering around the cell naked will seem like an invitation for my new roomie, the flirt with the wandering purple eyes.

O'Malley used to sleep naked, so he'd always be mulling around here, hanging brain. I mean, I'm comfortable with my body too, because I know it's sick and I work really hard on it, even in here. But that doesn't mean I just swing it around for no reason.

I do like being shirtless, though. If I never wore a shirt again for the rest of my life, I'd be totally fine with it.

I'm done changing while Trevel is still plucking clothes out of that large basket the Warden gave him, which he apparently uses to hold all of his things. And when he shimmies out of his pants, through no fault of my own, my eyes sort of go with them.

He wears briefs—rather skimpy ones, I might add—that fit him like a second skin. They look fancy, and my eyebrow cocks when I note the *Versace* around the waistband.

Are those from the Warden too?? Damn. And here I thought the ones from Skull and Bones that Ren scored for us were special.

I refuse to admit it out loud, but that underwear looks good on him. The simple black, yet obviously chic European style, with his pale skin decorated in black patchwork… He looks like a high-fashion model. I can picture him wearing only those, strutting down a catwalk in Milan.

I swear, I've never seen anyone like him in real life. He's… a different kind of beautiful.

Okay… stop. Weren't you just accusing him *of being the gawking weirdo??*

"Care to join me for breakfast?" Trevel asks, bringing me out of my thoughts.

Already dressed and digging through his basket again, he pulls out a packet of Pop-Tarts.

"Uh… sure." I answer, mouth watering and trying to act like it's not.

I'm not huge on sweets, but I do love strawberry Pop-Tarts, and I'm sure they're infinitely better than whatever we'll be getting in the caf.

"Shall we take our breakfast on the… veranda?" He arches a dark brow. "Or the terrace?"

It takes me a moment to register what he's asking me, but when I do, my lips twitch. "Veranda is fine."

"Marvelous choice." He grins, trotting over and plopping down onto my bed.

I take a reluctant seat at the edge, but he's already nestled in there, sitting cross-legged and opening the packet with obvious glee. He hands me a pastry, then holds his out.

Knowing what he wants, I roll my eyes, pursing away the grin as I tap mine against his and mumble, *"Galchae."*

His face lights up. "Is that *cheers* in Korean?"

I nod, chomping a bite that lights up my tastebuds.

"Galchae," he tries saying it, and I smirk.

"Not bad."

"Did I tell you I was in Korea?" he mumbles in between bites.

"I believe that's one of the few things you left out," I tease, recalling all the stuff we talked about the other night in his cell.

"Oh, trust me, warrior boy, there are many things I haven't voiced to you yet." He smirks, and I roll my eyes again. "But as I was *saying*, we had a layover in Seoul on our way here to New York. Unfortunately, I wasn't allowed to leave the airport… A true shame because I've always wanted to visit there."

"It's a dope place," I hum, fighting off the disparaging thought that I'll probably never see it again.

"You're so American." He chuckles.

"I've lived here my whole life." I shrug. "We left Seoul when I was a baby, and I've only been there a couple of times that I remember." He nods while we eat, and I observe him. "You sound sort of *American* yourself."

"Do I?" he gleams, pleased by that comment.

I remember him telling me the other night that he's been in the States since he was a kid too. Not as young as me, but he lived in New York for a while before winding up in Atlanta.

"I like your accent… It reminds me of my grandfather," I tell him for some reason. "He was from England."

"Really?" His head cocks.

"I think… Cambridge? But he lived in London for most of his life. Well, he split his time between there and New York."

"Have you been?" he asks curiously. "To London?"

I nod. "Twice. He took my sister and me when we were kids, and then I went back after I graduated high school. I liked it… Mostly because it made me feel… close to him."

My gaze falls to my lap.

"I take it he's no longer with us?" His voice is solemn. It sets a strange feeling in my chest while I nod. "I'm sorry…"

Shrugging it off, I sigh, "It was a while ago."

"Sure, the pain may dwindle, but the ache is always there."

I peer at him. "I take it you've… lost someone important to you?"

He swallows visibly, breaking our eye contact to pick at a loose thread on my blanket. "Haven't we all?"

There are so many things I want to say, questions I want to ask him—about why he's here, and what he's been through. Maybe as a caveat to sharing a truth or two in return…

But a loud bang interrupts it all, the door slamming open at the end of the row. The stomping footsteps of a guard approaching have me sealing my lips shut.

And now we'll have to spend the next however many minutes in absolute silence when all I want is to *scream* secrets at the top of my lungs.

Trevel is watching me the whole time we're cuffed and brought out of our cell. I can feel him *staring* at me, the weight of it bearing down on my skin. I don't look at him again until we're seated across from one another at the cafeteria table. And seeing all of the obvious questions on his face gives me the tiniest bit of solace.

Maybe he's frustrated too. Maybe he wants… more. Just like I do.

The meal goes on for hours—about thirty minutes in real time. But the quiet amplifies each ticking second, building the angst higher and higher. On our way to the showers, vexation is coiling around me with every step.

Trevel and I go to my usual shower area, but it's not the same without Luthor and Ren, yet another fact that's riddling me with tension.

This spot is home to so many memories, good and bad. They're interwoven here; the pleasure and the pain are the same damn thing…

The fighting, the fucking. The tears, the orgasms. The manipulation, the affection. The *lies*… and the *truth*.

It all came together in sweet, excruciating bliss.

Staring at the wall while I lather, I can almost feel them… The *memories*.

In my mind, I see it in flashes.

His legs around my waist, our mouths together, my cock moving in him. Licking the salty water from his throat and his chest while his hands ran all over me. Treasuring it… The *pleasure* of us.

And every time I would catch the blue in his eyes, my heart would leap forward into him, reaching out for him to be *mine*.

My pretty, spoiled rich boy…

I would kiss him and whimper because I wanted it *back*.

And he would cry, *"Lex…"*

My heart is splitting down the middle all over again, just like every time I heard a name that wasn't mine.

"Fuck," I gasp, without thinking, because it hurts too damn bad to keep it in.

To stay silent is *killing* me right now.

A warm hand appears on my back, and I peek left. Trevel is staring at me, *hard*, his brows knitted in clear concern. I bite my lip, because it's trembling, and I don't want him to see. But he does. I guess he noticed it…

He notices everything.

Reaching out, he plucks my lip from between my teeth, his thumb brushing it gently. Our eyes are locked, an unwavering gaze that's almost too intense.

But I can't break it. I can't look away. *Hell, I'm not sure I even want to.*

Trevel's fingers slip along my jaw, our bodies so close now, we're all but zipped. He lets out a breath, wide chest pulsing up and down as I swallow and lean into it—his touch and his proximity. His eyes and the fact that he sees me. He's *seeing* me…

He mouths something, and I'm not positive, but I think it's my name.

Byron.

My name, not anyone else's.

He blinks slowly, slipping his fingers under my chin. And I have no clue how, but I can hear him. I *hear* what he's not saying.

I could give you what you need… If you'd only stop fighting.

My heart is racing too fast, flesh so hot I feel like steam is coming off of me. This is too much… I don't know what this is, but it's crazy.

How is he doing this? Why does it feel like he's breathing me back to life right now?

"Two minutes!" The spell is broken with that barked warning.

"Shit." I close my eyes tight and exhale the pressure.

A growl comes from Trevel. Aiming my foggy gaze up at him, I watch as he brushes his wet hair back, visibly flustered himself. My lips want to twitch in amusement, but I push it away, biting the inside of my cheek.

It's *insane* how badly I want to speak right now. It feels like torture not saying words to him, which is also insane because I never *want* to talk to people. I don't tell them things.

Where has this gnawing need to open up come from??

My head is spinning as we get dried off and redressed, doing the silent shuffle back to our cage. But as soon as we're tucked securely inside, the awkwardness has swallowed up the lust, and we're kind of just fluttering around one another.

Now that we can speak, we have no words.

I'd really like to write in my journal, but I don't want to take it out in front of him. Instead, I crawl into my bed, and he goes up to his bunk. Neither of us saying a damn thing, just existing in the same shared space.

Lying on my back, I'm staring up at the bottom of his mattress while he shuffles around up there. Eventually, my eyelids begin to close. But they creep back open when I hear a grunt.

Then a breath. Then a *hum.*

My lips part, to ask him what the hell he's doing. But I don't. I stay quiet and wait, my pulse pumping quicker and quicker while my mind races in parallel. The buzz in my loins is still there from the showers—it never really went away. I'm still wound up, and in need, and I think he knows that.

I think he can still hear me…

Push it through the hole.

It only takes a minute or so before I feel him turn over. And then, sure enough, his long, pink dick is sneaking through the hole in the mattress. Slowly poking through, hard and thick, and shiny at the tip.

I bite my lip, nerves twisting my stomach into a knot.

This is what you wanted… You can deny it all day, but you know you love it. That's your secret. You need *this.*

Trevel rears back, tugging it away to stroke with his hand, aiming just the tip through the hole. My fingers are digging into my mattress, my own cock swelling and filling rapidly. I can't tear my hungry gaze away from it as his shapely fingers knead up and down, tugging the skin away from his blushed, swollen crown.

Saliva is pooling in my mouth now while I watch him playing with this piece of himself that's just as pretty as the rest of him. It really matches, perfectly proportionate with his frame, and his pale complexion. It's somehow elegant, if that's even something a dick can be.

Aesthetically pleasing, that's for sure.

I think it's a bit longer than mine, though mine is thicker. Honestly, Trevel's dick is almost *too* big. I have no ruler, but it has to be almost ten inches.

Imagine trying to deep-throat that…

Chills rush over my entire body at the thought.

"Stop teasing me," he croons from above my head, pushing it all the way through once more. "Come and get your meal, baby."

Fuck… A trembling breath leaves me.

Well? Go get it. You're… hungry. Aren't you?

Inching up, I watch it, lusting so hard, I'm shaking. "Is that for… me?" I whisper.

"Only you, gorgeous," he purrs. "I'm aching for that mouth…"

Fuck yea.

Slithering onto my knees, I get closer. "How bad?"

"*So* bad I'm dripping, baby," he rasps.

"I can see that…" I bite my lip again, watching a pearl of precum bead at the tip.

I'm fucking quaking. Thank fuck, he can't see me right now. It's taking away a lot of the nerves that keep this secret stowed away inside me.

That's why I did it in the first place… Made a hole in the bed. Because I wanted to do this without having to get on my knees in front of someone, like the cock-thirsty bitch I clearly am.

"Try a taste," he goads, with his erection aimed right at me through the hole.

No hands, no touching. Just a big, sweet dick, eagerly awaiting my mouth.

Parting my lips, I open just wide enough as the pearl of precum drips out. And I catch it on my tongue.

My eyes roll back in my head and my chest flutters. *Oh Jesus fuck yes…*

"Baby, *please*," he whines. "I can feel you."

"You taste so good," I groan, grabbing the bars above my head, hanging on for dear life while I ease my mouth around his eager cock.

"*Ohh…*" I hear him mewl, just barely over my blood rushing in my ears. I suck on it, just a little, and he shudders. "Fuckin' hell, *Byron…*"

Slurping off, I growl, "Don't say my name."

"Sorry, baby," he hums, sounding sincere. So I suckle at the tip until he whimpers, "*Uhhhfuck*, that's it. *Sweetest* fucking mouth ever, love…"

I'm fucking dizzy, drunk and seeing stars already, pushing up on my knees to take his dick deeper, and *deeper*, sucking up and down with fervor. I'm greedy, *ravenous* for it. But I'm going slow because I like it that way.

Fuck, I like to savor it.

"That's it, warrior," he groans. "You like how I feed you, yea?"

I nod and mumble with my mouth full, desperate for more praise that lets me know I'm doing a good job. Fluttering my tongue on his head, I swirl and swirl it around, sucking out more of his flavor until I'm going out of my goddamn mind.

Frantically, with shaky fingers, I pull my own dick out of my pants. But I don't jerk it hard or fast. Just caress it softly, palming my balls and teasing my tip while I suck the mystery dick being fed to me.

Yes yes yes…

I'm a good little slut.

"Mmm mm mmm," I groan on his solid flesh, breathing through my nose, gripping the bars above with white knuckles.

"Oh, baby, *yes*… You are such a good boy." Those words, in that tone with that accent, have my dick pulsing. "Good little whore with a perfect mouth." Fist pumping up the length of my cock, I pull out even more slickness. "Make it sloppy for me, warrior. Suck it deep into that pretty throat."

"Mmmm…" I whimper, pushing up higher—needing *more*—giving him my throat to fuck.

Relaxing as much as I can, I attempt to get him all the way back there. I gag once, my eyes watering. Then I gag again, but I don't stop. I keep going, keep chasing, spit overflowing from my mouth, my head hitting the bars.

Fuck me… Fuck my mouth. Fuck my fucking tonsils, Daddy…

I whip my hand away from my dick fast, for fear that I'll come and I'm not ready. This is fucking *amazing*.

It feels so good. His dick feels perfect inside me.

Oh, shit…

Fuck fuck fuck.

"Mmmm!" I cry a muffled moan as my dick shoots off uncontrollably.

Like a damn hose, spraying everywhere. I'm not even fucking touching it.

"*Uhhyess*… Baby…? Are you… coming?" he grunts, voice uneven with how audibly he's falling apart.

I can barely hear him through the panting in my head.

"*Mm mmm.*" I nod, sucking vigorously, gulping him back, so deep it hurts. My lips are at the fucking mattress.

God, yes. Fuck… Come down my throat. Pour hot cum into my fucking stomach.

"Good God, I'm so close, baby. Are you ready for it…?"

I nod again while slurping tirelessly, up and down, letting him slide all the way back. Rubbing my tired cock, I tease the head with slippery cum, the sensation buzzing my balls.

"I'm gonna come…" He gasps, and I slow, bracing myself for his hot load in my throat. "*Uhhhffuck*, I'm coming for you!"

The long, thick, perfectly solid cock in my throat stiffens, then begins to pulse, decorating my tongue with cum. I suck it all out, every slick throb, like the greediest of sluts. I can barely fathom what's happening right now, just sucking and *sucking*, no hands, writhing and lifting myself up to his big cock, eating cum like a fucking fiend while he sings my filthy praises.

"Good boy… fuck *yes*, that's a good, hungry boy. Swallow it all, love… Suck every drop out until I'm empty and you're *full*, baby. My sweet, sexy thing…"

Spinning, twirling and trembling, like I'm on a carousel, my pulse is racing, body *buzzing*. I'm running my hands all over myself, up to my chest to brush my nipples… Pure sensation.

By the time I finally let go of his cock, I truly am *full*. Full of cum, yes, but also just… *replete*. I really do feel like I was just fed.

What is this…? How could it possibly feel so good to be so… unlike myself?

This is the real you, Byron. Stop hiding from it.

Pulling in air, I recognize the moment the high begins to wear off. Because it's the moment I look up and see Trevel's dick, retreating back into his bed, rather than the sexy British stranger who just came in my mouth.

Tucking myself away, I glance down at the cum all over my blanket and sigh. *Goddamnit…*

"Byron, you are—"

"I told you *not* to say my name," I hiss, whipping the blanket away and curling up into a ball. Insecurities are screaming inside me. "Just… stop talking."

He stays quiet, while I feel the weight of all this nagging bullshit raining down on me like a monsoon. But somehow, I can still hear him, over all the noise in my head.

Don't be angry. You're perfect, Raphael.

Closing my eyes, I listen for his voice. Eventually, he whispers, "Goodnight."

I can still hear him in my mind, smooth and soulful, with an accent that comforts me. I see violet eyes in my dreams.

CHAPTER TWENTY

Trevel

FUNNY HOW THINGS CAN FEEL SO FAMILIAR WHEN EVERYTHING AROUND YOU is different.

New location, new circumstances, new process… And yet the simple action of sitting across from him is exactly the same as it was for three years.

Up until the moment he left.

He slants his head to the side, perfectly unreadable expression on his face. Taps the tip of his pen against the notepad he's holding. *Stares* at me, those full lips I used to think about way too often firmly planted shut. As if he has every intention of staying fully silent for the entirety of whatever the hell this is.

Just like old times.

Well, not *exactly*. Before, he would have made an attempt to get me speaking, and I would've gladly obliged. *Now*, we're locked in a stubborn and hostile game of conversational chicken. And I *won't* break first.

Mainly because I refuse to be the one engaging him when he *owes me* words, in the form of an explanation. But also because I fear the moment I do open my mouth, months of belligerent rage will come spewing out like projectile vomit.

No, no. I will continue to stew in silence, using my glare and calculated body language to convey every bit of hatred I have for this man until he chooses to put us both out of our misery.

"Trevel..." Dr. Love finally says my name, the first sound to be uttered in this room in approximately eleven minutes. *Aha! See? I win.* "Is there anything you'd like to say about why you're here?"

The aloof tone of his deep voice stirs up more anger than I even know what to do with, as does his barmy fucking question. As if it's *my* responsibility to do his job for him, despite him being the reason I'm here in the bloody first place.

My jaw clenches in a pretty obvious way, but of course it gets no reaction. Since the moment I set foot in here, I've been met with the stone wall of his indifference, and it's enraging me.

Tilting my head to mirror his, I lean forward, resting my elbows on my knees, hands clasped beneath my chin. "What do you think I'd like to say about my being here, Doctor? After all, you're the *professional*."

"I think there's a lot you'd like to say," he replies blankly. "And I think you should voice it. That is why we're here."

"*Is it?*" I hiss, frustrations bubbling over the patience-pot. "Is that why we're *here*, Doctor??"

He stares impassively, giving me that look I've seen so many times over the years. *You know*, the one that says absolutely *nothing* while *still* somehow overflowing with condescension. It makes me hate him more than even seems feasible. As does the fact that he somehow looks so much *better* than he used to.

He's just as big as he ever was; muscles equally close to bursting out of his tailored clothes. His dreadlocks are a bit longer and tied back in that half-ponytail I would occasionally imagine grabbing a fistful of. Facial hair still short and immaculately trimmed.

But his amber eyes glow with less fascination and more boredom that has me simmering on this ugly velvet couch.

Because he's not intrigued by me anymore. *And why would he be??* He has a new, more popular monster under his care. Unfortunately, I think it's this one detail that's accentuating his sheer gorgeousness more than ever. Knowing that he's sleeping with a man now—*a man who's not me*—thus making him just my type.

Bisexual and unavailable, both emotionally and physically.

I'm moments from erupting, ready to give him a taste of the old Trevel. But my mind flashes back to our early days at Riverwoods...

Strapped down to a slab after biting a nurse and spitting in an orderly's face. Roaring and screaming and laughing in such hysterics that tears and snot threatened to choke me.

"Fuck you!" I wailed until my voice nearly gave out. "Get off me! Get off get off fuck you fuck you don't touch me... Let... me... go!"

Commotion cut into my gasps and forceful yanking at my restraints. The door to the small, white-walled room opened, and in stepped the attractive doctor who'd come to observe me previously. The head nurse and administrator stood just outside with sour looks on their faces.

The doctor took one look at me and barked, "Leave us." Then he began unbuckling my restraints.

The nurse charged into the room to stop him. "But Doctor, he's—"

He aimed a stern glare at her. "Close the door, with you on the other side of it. Right now."

My screaming had stopped. My sniveling and thrashing... I'd gone completely still and silent. I was just watching him in awe as he freed my arms, legs, and neck. Even after he did, I continued to lie there. Staring *up at the beautiful man.*

"Do you remember me, Trevel?" he asked cooly, inquisitive enough that I instantly felt my heart rate evening out.

Just looking at him was like the pills they were always shoving down my throat to keep me calm, only so much better. Because with him, I was wide awake.

I nodded slowly, though my voice would no longer work.

"I'm Dr. Love," he said evenly. "I've been assigned as your psychiatrist to evaluate your progress and determine when you'll be fit to rejoin society."

I gulped and sniffled. "So... what do you think?"

My voice came out childlike, but I couldn't help it. I was barely nineteen, and despite all I'd been through up until that point, I still felt like a kid around authority figures.

Especially ones who looked and sounded like him.

Dr. Love glanced down at my wrists, all raw and blistering already. "I think I'm looking forward to learning more about you, Trevel. And don't worry... I'll make sure they never hold you down like that again."

Closing my eyes, I saw it once more... Felt it and smelled it and heard it and tasted it...

Blood and dirt in my mouth, mixing with my tears and spit. A large hand on the back of my head, keeping my face in the ground so I could barely breathe. Fingers and body parts pinning me down while I burned all over in agonizing pain. Their laughter, their grunts, and their hushed taunts.

One.

Two.

Three.

Four.

By the time the last one finished, I was numb. When they finally got up and took off, I was empty. Nothing left but the cold corpse of someone who existed solely to be used.

I reopened my eyes—just like I had that night—gazing at the doctor and remembering the one thing that had resurrected me…

Revenge.

Harnessing the fury inside, I allow it to settle, like lightweight particles of metal in my bloodstream, strengthening me. My lips quirk, and I ease back in my seat, making myself comfortable.

"You know, it *is* good to see you again, Dr. Love," I hum. "I'm glad you've taken to your new position. And so effortlessly, it seems."

Dr. Love simply stares, unaffected. No reaction. *Yet…*

"I'd assumed you leaving all of your work in Atlanta unfinished meant you were headed for bigger and better things," I go on. "Imagine my surprise when I found out you were seeing but *one* patient here… Talk about a letdown, am I right?"

I notice the slightest movement in his jaw. A subtle tic imperceptible to most. But not me.

I'm getting to him.

"Nevertheless, it appears to be working for you, and that's all that matters," I keep needling, poking and nudging, at the *one* spot where I know he holds his vulnerability. His Achilles heel… "You'd done all you could in Atlanta, and I understand that now. Coming here was like a… *retirement* of sorts. Somewhere to sail off into the sunset—alongside a pretty, young toy—and just give up…"

"Trevel, that's enough," Dr. Love grunts, with as much bite as you can expect from him, which isn't much. But still, it's *there*, and it's quite satisfying. "We're not here to talk about me. We're here—"

"Because Manuel Blanco ordered it?" I cut him off, smirking. "And he calls the shots, correct? *He's* the one in charge here, not you. I mean, you get to wield control over Felix Darcey, but that's not much of a feat, is it? He's basically a pet—"

"You're lashing out because you're still angry." He cocks his head to the other side. "It hurt quite a bit that I abandoned you… Didn't it?"

"Oh, Doctor… Trust me," I growl. "*No one* can hurt me better than I can. You know that."

"Yes, I'm aware of your habits, your coping mechanisms, and your triggers," he deadpans. "I know everything about you, which is why I know that this hostility you're holding on to toward me has little to do with you being here, and everything to do with you feeling deserted."

An unamused scoff bursts from my lips. "*Wow.* Your God complex has risen in spades, hasn't it? Is that *also* thanks to The Carver?"

At the second mention of his serial killer boyfriend, Dr. Love's eyes take on a gleam of rage. It's a thread I'm all too prepared to grab onto and *pull*.

Naturally, he disguises it very well. "You know I can't discuss other patients with you, Trevel."

"Alright, then. Let's talk about why I'm here," I counter. "Alice… I didn't kill her."

"I know. They ruled her death an accidental overdose."

"Except that it wasn't," I hiss. "Her brother and his wanker of a friend killed her in an attempt to frame me."

He blinks at me. "So you killed them."

"That's how I roll." I fold my arms over my chest.

Dr. Love tosses the notepad onto the table, leaning in to give the impression that his attention is on me. I hate that shit, because of how much it used to fill my stomach with flutters.

"Why don't you tell me why the moment I left, you decided to stop taking your medication and undo all of the progress we'd made?" He arches a patronizing brow.

"It's really quite simple," I hiss, keeping our eyes locked. "I wanted to make it painfully apparent that you'd failed."

His jaw tics again. "And why is it so important to you that I fail, Trevel?" The wrath is rising again, stiffening my muscles. My lips part, but he jumps in before I can reply. "Because I left you. Isn't that right?"

"You *freed* me," I correct him, sitting forward, putting our faces in line. He doesn't budge. "The attempts were futile, and you knew that. *That's* why you left without a second thought… Because you didn't want to face what we both knew what inevitable. There is no cure for evil, is there, Dr. Love? If there were, you'd have given it to him by now…"

Squinting at me, he rumbles, "*Evil* is not a diagnosis. It's a word used to scare people into acting right. I'm not interested in morality, or philosophical ideations."

"Says the man whose patients are running around taking lives like tickets at a deli." I roll my eyes.

"You can blame me all you want, but you chose to make those things happen, Trevel," he counters. "You're both desperate for a reprieve from the noise in your head and terrified of losing it."

My fingers curl into a fist that tightens and releases. Heart racing, the utter irritation of how *right* he always is weighting me in place on the couch.

We're both silent for a moment, glaring. It amazes me how much can flow between two people without speaking a word.

Like with Byron yesterday in the shower…

Sucking in a breath, I hold it for a moment before murmuring, "I have missed our sessions, Doctor. Hopefully, we can pick up where we'd left off in Atlanta, only now with a clearer understanding of what it is we're both looking for."

He sits back in his seat, assessing me once more. "And what are we both looking for?"

To win. "Peace." I shrug, spouting nonsense in an attempt to brush him off because I'm already over this. "And acceptance."

He's admitted that he abandoned me, and that he feels no remorse.

But he will.

"That's good to hear, Trevel," he says. "I've only ever wanted what was best for you."

My teeth grind to dust as I shoot him a grin so fake it's about to snap my face in two. "Mm… I'm sure you have."

You self-righteous fucking cunt.

"So…" He rubs his hands together. "Should I plan on seeing you in a few days?"

"Whatever you want."

It's what you're going to do, anyway.

Dr. Love nods curtly, picking his notepad back up and casually scribbling something down. Without glancing up, he asks, "By the way, how are you getting on here? I know it can be a bit of an adjustment."

Standing up, I peer around his small, drab office. "Actually, I'm fairing quite well."

To my surprise, that gets him. His eyes shift up to mine. "Is that so?"

I nod and pull another patronizing smile, this time less forced. *Ah, so he was looking forward to me struggling in here?*

How sweet.

My gaze is sparkling a palpable malevolence. "As it turns out, Alabaster Pen might just be somewhere I could truly thrive."

Shooting him a wink, I wander away, heading for the door, unable to miss the puzzled flash in his eyes at how I seem to be coming and going on my own.

My smirk widens, and I wave. "Have a *lovely* evening, Doctor."

I leave his office with the click of his door behind me, puffing out a long breath I feel like I've been holding for an hour. Closing my eyes, I rake my fingers through my hair, composing myself.

Well… that sucked.

For all of my hostility and brazen behavior, I'm still not sure that I accomplished anything of value, and I loathe this feeling of uncertainty. I didn't get any information for The Ivory, and I barely made a dent in Dr. Love. Although, let's be real, getting him even five percent worked up is no small feat.

Plus, this is a marathon, not a sprint.

Regardless, I can't deny that my body is all keyed up from being near him again, the rage swirling together with how regrettably sexy I still happen to find him.

I *despise* him for turning his back on me, then gaslighting me into thinking it was no big deal. *Oh, it all worked out, didn't it? Look, we're back together. Why are you so bent out of shape??*

Bugger off.

I *will* get my revenge on Dr. Lemuel Love, regardless of how long it takes or what I have to endure to get it. And in order to do that, I'll need to disobey Manuel's wishes just a tad.

Spinning on my heel, I stride up the halls of the East Wing. Kent informed me that Manuel has some new people working in his control rooms, and that they've been instructed to let me move about freely—*you guessed it… Within reason.*

It seems as if many things are changing here at Alabaster Pen, with the arrival of the new guards, who apparently were brought in with the express purpose of undermining the former team—*Officer Daddy and Mommy, also known as Velle and Joy, and their band of merry menaces.*

I'm not surprised by the restructuring. The Ivory said as much during our last meeting. It doesn't affect me, seeing that I had no real attachments to the former crew. But I will say, the no-talking order is a buzzkill, especially now that I have Byron. Figures, as soon as I'm no longer alone, we're ordered into silence.

These new guards seem to be all business, no pleasure. Boring.

I can't complain, though. I have much more freedom than the average inmate, lucky boy that I am. What I choose to do with that freedom is where I'll leave a lasting *impression*.

Skipping up and down the corridors, I'm snooping, because why not? Peeking into every padded cell, observing the lonely, mistreated lumps of sadness who reside here in the prison's asylum. When I look inside the cell on the end, I freeze.

It's Warren Xavier. *Ren*. He's sitting on the floor, laced up in a strait-jacket. Eyes closed, head tipped back against the wall. I'm not sure if he's sleeping or just resting his eyes while contemplating the clearly grim state of his existence. Either way, I take a moment to grin wickedly at his misfortune.

Even if he wasn't such a wanker to me during our every encounter, I'd still revel in his discomfort. *Because he's Byron's ex-fling, or whatever they'd chosen to call it, and that makes me hate him.*

Petty and jealous are two things I've never hidden about myself.

Byron claims that he and Ren fooled around casually, but clearly, it happened often enough that Byron formed some sort of attachment to Ren, the thought of which has been driving me a bit mad.

Why is he able to hook up with Ren so freely, yet with me, *it's like pulling teeth? What does this* Ren *character have that I don't?*

Is Ren easier than me? Is that it??

I can be what he needs... Even if it destroys him in the process.

"Always projecting your issues onto others..."

The voice snaps my face around in search of him. *Leo??*

Fuck, where are you??

Sighing out of defeat, I give one last lingering look to my *competition*, who, thankfully, is down here for the foreseeable future.

Enjoy your stay, sweetheart.

Heading back in the other direction, I search for the room. It takes me a bit, since all of these corridors look alike. But eventually, I find the door I committed to memory, and knock.

A moment of quiet passes before a soft voice calls out, "Hello?"

"*Hi*, Felix." I grin at the door. "May I come in?"

He sounds closer when he asks, "Trevel...?"

"Aww, you remembered."

The distinct click of him turning a lock is followed by the door opening just a crack. And there's Felix Darcey peering through the opening at me, black-framed glasses outlining his bewildered expression.

"What are you doing here?" he asks, almost mousy in his soft-spoken passiveness.

I'm amazed that this cute little ball of terror actually murdered over thirty people *and* captivated a straight doctor of the mind. He seems far too insecure for all of it.

Is that what Dr. Love likes? Vulnerability paired with impulse control??

Because… um, hello!

Focusing on what I'm doing, I pull charm out of my bum. "I was just coming back from my session with Lemuel and thought I'd stop by to say hello."

The look on The Carver's face tells me he's unsettled by many aspects of what I've just said. *Good. That's what I was going for.*

"Oh…" He peeks out into the hall behind me. "And you just… walk around? No guards or anything…?"

I shrug. "I mean, don't you?"

He blinks and straightens, opening the door a bit more. "Good point. So, how was your session?"

"Fabulous," I sigh. "Lemuel is truly a revelation. But I don't have to tell you that…"

He stares at me for a moment. "No. You don't."

My lips twitch. *Come on, baby psycho. Get mad…*

"I missed having sessions with him greatly after he left," I go on. "He was always so helpful, you know? I'm sure he's helped you a great deal as well…"

I witness the mound of his throat dip. "I think we help each other."

My stomach bunches, and I have to fight the urge to grab him by the throat. "Of course you do. He does seem rather settled now. And that's all thanks to you, little Felix." I poke him on the nose, and he balks. Peering over his head, I observe his room—it looks like a closet someone turned into a dormitory. "Cute flat."

He glances over his shoulder. "Oh. Thanks…"

"Does it ever get lonely down here?" I ask. "Just you and Lemuel…?"

"Not really." He pushes his glasses up the bridge of his nose. "We enjoy each other's company."

"Hm. I know what you mean." I continue, rolling with the punches. *It's like improv. I'm quite impressed with myself right now.* "I was alone in a nicer cell, but I was growing quite lonely. So I asked to be switched, and now I live with Byron."

"Kang?" he grunts, and I nod. "I think he still hates me..." He chews on his bottom lip regretfully, and I squint.

He's not the only one. "I'm sure he'll come around." I wave him off. "He's a sweet lad. Honestly, I'd like it if we could all be friends."

Darcey's face lights up. "Really?"

"Yes, darling! We might as well; we're all going to be stuck in here together forever, right?"

He nods. "I would like that. Maybe you can... put in a good word for me? With Kang?"

Oh, honey... I'll put in words, don't you worry.

"Consider it done." I wink at him.

"Hey, could I ask you something?" His gray eyes sparkle with curi osity behind his lenses.

"Ask away."

"Did you ever... meet Lem's ex?" He fidgets noticeably. "Gabrielle?"

This is too good to be true.

I can't believe this bloodthirsty madman is practically tying himself up and hopping into my trunk right now!

"I did." I nod, preparing to spout nonsense. "Quite the lady. Accomplished, affluent... Poised, but with an air of secret sexuality about her. The whole package, really."

Felix's forehead lines, his lips pursing in displeasure. It's bloody *perfection.*

"Why do you ask?"

"No reason..." His bespectacled gaze falls.

"Oh, sweetheart." I squeeze his shoulder. "Listen, you have *nothing* to worry about. Lemuel is enamored with you. It's obvious."

"I know, I'm just... thinking about the future."

I grit my teeth. "By obsessing over the past?"

He blinks at me, a small smile tugging at his mouth. "You know what? You're right. Thank you, Trevel. I'm really... glad you're here."

Something peculiar happens in my chest at hearing that, the sincerity in his voice and his stormy eyes. But then I remember that he's a psycho-path, and if *I'm* faking this shit, then he most likely is as well.

So I pull the most realistic fake smile I can and murmur, "Me too, darling. Me too."

Footsteps alert us to someone coming up the hall, and Felix ducks back inside his room, preparing to slam the door. But the unmistakable form of Dr. Love comes from around the corner, and he reemerges.

Dr. Love gapes at me, a protective glare casting over Darcey briefly before he grunts, "What are you doing?"

"We're just chatting," Felix answers him blithely with a twist to the lips, likely to pacify his man's suspicion.

Lem's eyes bounce back and forth between us, and he looks beyond skeptical. But I don't care. *I got what I came for.*

"Well, I should be going." I smile and wave at Felix. "See you around, love." Then I peek at Dr. Love. "You too… *Love.*"

I giggle at my own stupid joke, which, more than anything, is for the purpose of making them both uncomfortable. Then I strut away, forcing myself not to look back.

I won't get my hopes up that this one interaction will mess with their relationship. But a girl can dream, right?

Following the long halls through the prison, my mind is playing back everything that's happened today. And yesterday, and in the weeks leading up to right now. Where I *am* as opposed to where I *was* the last time I saw Dr. Love professionally is like night and day.

My eyes scan over the crumbling walls and ceilings, streaked with leakage stains and mold, literal cracks in the foundation. Based on the conversation I had with Byron the other day, this prison is sparsely maintained to say the least, and although it's allegedly government-funded, said funding either doesn't cover repairing and upgrading, or it's not being used for such things.

It takes me a while to find my way back up to general population. This building is a maze, and I just don't understand why there isn't, at the very least, the occasional sign indicating where the hell you are. Frankly, it feels intentional. Disorientation is clearly a part of it.

Finally, I make it back *home*. The bars open the moment I push them—*Thank you, Daddy Ivory*—giving the illusion that I'm *valued*, though I realize that beneath Manuel Blanco's coddling words, he's using me.

It's fine. It's what I'm here for, after all. If someone actually wanted the real *me, I wouldn't know what to do with myself.*

"You'll never guess what just happened!" I chirp to Byron as I strut inside the cell—free as a bird who gets to let himself in and out of his cage.

Byron is sitting on his bed, back propped against the wall. He spares me a brief glance, but doesn't respond. He barely even reacts to my presence.

But I keep talking. "After my session with Dr. Love, I decided to pop in for a visit with our pal Felix Darcey." I breathe a chuckle, though Byron isn't sharing my excitement. "Apparently, Murder Baby is a tad insecure about his relationship."

I go for a bottle of water, cracking it open and taking a sip.

Byron's eyes jump to mine for a split second again, and he mumbles, "Sweet." Zero enthusiasm.

I narrow my gaze at him. *That "sweet" didn't sound so sweet...*

"Are you doing alright?" I step up to the edge of the bed. "You seem grumpier than usual."

He scoffs. "I'm not *grumpy*. I just don't care about Felix Darcey's fucking problems..."

The scowl he's wearing is purely adorable, but I choose not to upset him further by voicing such things.

"Byron, what's wrong?" I continue to prod, taking a seat on the edge of his bed. "Tell me—"

"*Nothing* is wrong, Trevel," he snaps. "Leave it alone. I'm *fine*."

Flopping over onto his side, he grabs his pillow and petulantly covers his head with it.

I sigh and pinch the bridge of my nose. *He's too cute for real life, but this needs to stop.*

We didn't speak about the blowjob through the hole in my mattress. I was fine with it, being that the bliss from that experience was so strong, even *I* had nothing to say. But my timorous new roomie seems to have come out of the experience even more withdrawn. Barely able to make eye contact, speaking in one-word grunts. Much to my dismay, the fooling around may have regressed our relationship.

Fine... So I may have crawled into his bed this morning to watch him sleep again. But I barely even realized I was doing it! I'm not *trying* to be creepy or anything... With the nature of my troubled sleep, having him nearby is a comfort. I suppose I got carried away.

Regardless, I simply cannot fathom why he's able to hook up with his other friends so easily, but with *me*, it's a big fat problem.

We're well aware that my toxic trait is being tragically attracted to people who want to use me, and a saboteur of anything *genuine*, or *healthy*. *Prime example... Andres Alvarez.* His sister was perfect, and we had the makings of something truly special. But I squandered it the moment an atrocious human being with tattoos and a big dick showed me a hint of sexual attention.

It's a sickness, I'm telling you. Red flags make my pussy wet.

That's not to say I think Byron is a horrendous plonker like Andres was. In fact, he's a smart, loyal, if wildly misunderstood, catch. But it doesn't take X-ray vision to see that he's hiding his true self. Shields up sky-high and fighting to keep his demons tucked securely beneath his surface.

Naturally, it just makes me like him more.

See? Infinitely more attracted to the science projects.

Crawling over to him, I place a hand on his waist, feeling him stiffen beneath my touch. I roll my eyes because, despite how good his body feels to touch, all soft skin and plump muscle—*he rarely wears a shirt, and I'm living for it*—he's driving me mental with his *alleged straight-boy* problems.

"Byron, for the love of God... *what* is the issue?" I can predict his response before he even starts, so I add, "And don't say *nothing*!" He slowly lowers the pillow from over his face, peering up at me. Those chocolate-brown eyes stuffed full of glistening distress. "What on earth is so bad about giving head?? Honestly, I cannot with you... So you sucked some dick. Big deal! Believe me, there are much worse things than enjoying a cock in your mouth on occasion..."

"Fucking kill me now," he groans, rubbing his eyes.

Taking a long breath, I release it slowly. *Centering my chi, because this beautiful, stubborn bloke is testing me a bit.*

"Talk to me," I hum, gliding my finger along the waistband of his jumpsuit pants. "Tell me what's going on inside you, Raph. I promise I won't judge anything you say. Of all people, I'm the *last* person who could ever judge anyone. Trust me."

Byron finally allows his eyes to melt with mine. That feeling of him even considering lowering the mask and letting me truly *see* him is like a high from some designer drug I've been given to sample. And I'm instantly addicted; craving more of *him*, and all his messy issues.

He props up a bit on his elbow, eyeing me carefully. "You don't... You wouldn't understand."

I cock my head. "Try me."

He chews on his lower lip before muttering, "It's... complicated. The reason I'm here, and the things that led to it... I didn't... I never got the chance to..."

I'm vibrating, at the edge of my metaphorical seat, awaiting his words with bated breath. Whatever it is that's choking him up must be serious. I can see his stiffness, *feel* him grappling like a visible change in his chakra.

He's afraid...

Terrified to step out of the shadows.

Cupping his jaw, my hand caresses his face. And he actually leans *into* it. "Tell me your secrets, Byron. I promise, I can keep them."

I'm bloody good at it, after all.

"I'm not... supposed to be here," he finally whispers. "It was... a mistake."

My heart is beating faster and faster as my fingers trail over his throat, onto his chest, feeling his do the same. "You can tell me anything, Byron. You can trust me."

He looks like he's weighing this for many heavy moments. But at last, he says, "I don't speak it out loud..." And before I can tell him it's okay, he adds, "I write it."

CHAPTER TWENTY-ONE

Byron's Book of Secrets

"Tell Me Lies."

I'd been in prison a few months the first time it happened. When Ren came to me with his plan.

He called it a proxy job. Something he'd apparently thought up after taking one of many rides on Velle's dick.

"Come on, Byron," he crooned, that pesky finger gliding lower, where my happy trail disappeared into my baggy jumpsuit pants. "You wanna get off, don't you?"

Well yea was my knee-jerk reaction. But I couldn't say that. I couldn't admit that I was such an easy sell It didn't fit the image I'd been showing these people—the Byron from before, *pre-Michelangelo*.

I so badly wanted to be him again. *He'd* never had his heart ripped out of his chest mid-pump

But I fought it, because fighting was less scary. "Yea, but I'm not—"

"Save it." Ren fought back. He was a better fighter than even me. "We've been flirting since you got here "

"We have??" My brows jumped.

He nodded, stuffing his hand into my pants. I gasped as his fingers grazed my rapidly firming flesh. I could've sworn it was flaccid, but the second his hand was in there, my dick turned to goddamn granite.

It was bad, all of it. Because I knew right from the start that hooking up with Ren would never be as simple for me as it was for him. After all, Luthor had become my best friend—the kind of friend I always wanted, but was too much of a loner to have. He was a shining beacon of trust and hope in this dreary hellhole we call Alabaster Pen. I couldn't possibly betray him by secretly and weirdly lusting after his sort of ex.

Ren grinned, deviously victorious at how clearly my body

was betraying my words. "See? No reason to fight it. This dick *needs* some love. Doesn't it?"

Unfortunately, the haze in my brain was dizzying, temptation clouding my judgements, as it does. I could barely remember any of the reasons I'd been opposed to this before he started stroking my cock. They'd all evaporated. Except for one.

"Luthor... is my... f-friend," I grumbled, eyes closing, head tipping back while his tight fist worked up and down, his wicked mouth on my throat.

"Yes, he is." He licked my Adam's apple.

"I don't wanna... hurt him," I gulped when his left hand crept in to play with my balls.

"You're such a good friend," he purred.

The next thing I knew, we were kissing. I'll admit, this part is a bit foggy. The memories are like a strobe light, flashes illuminating what happened in the dark. I remember the sensations, the intoxication of being with a guy again, in secret. The thing I'd *thought* was bad, but felt *so* fucking good.

In minutes, Ren was on his knees, with my dick in his throat and his dark hair in my fist. I can still hear the panting and groaning and slippery wet suction, but I can't be certain it was all from that time. Because it happened *many* more times after that.

Not every day, not even every week. But frequently enough for me to warm up to it. For me to look forward to it. To *rely* on it. As fucked up as I knew it was, I'd begun to crave it—the insatiable hunger for a new sexy spoiled brat with dark hair and topaz eyes, who wanted to be roughed up. Opening himself for me to fill, because he *needed* it.

Because, as we know, so did I.

Despite him being an obsessive, psychotic, murderous pyro, Ren had qualities that weren't all bad, and those were the reasons why being around him hurt sometimes. Because the *good* in him reminded me of Michelangelo, and I was still so desperate to have it; the life I'd been right on the cusp of before Governor Russo cut the string I was holding, and it flew away.

I fucked Ren consistently, but it was always on his terms. *He* came to *me*, because he wasn't Michelangelo, and he wasn't mine. That was the only way I could justify it.

Luthor knew, and it wasn't my fault. *I* had an excuse, and that excuse was that Ren was using me. If they knew I was using him too, that might have changed things.

The problem was that Ren was much better at it than I was.

He was a pro when it came to casual sex. It was his *job*, after all. Acting *Lying*. He's a superior liar, which in turn, made him a superior actor—again, similar to Michelangelo, yet wildly different. And as our salacious rendezvous continued, my body got confused. Thus confusing my mind a little, too.

He would say things when we were fucking that really started to encourage my own proxy

"God, you feel so good. Your dick is the only one I want, you know that, right? Fuck my little hole, baby. It's yours. All fucking yours. You own me Fuck, own me harder. Harder harder harder, right there right there, yes yes yes, I belong to you. This cum is yours I'm coming for only you."

I feel stupid. For falling so easily under such an obvious spell. But what can I say? He really is that good.

Once, Ren ended up in the East Wing for weeks. I was relieved, honestly, because I needed some space. It would be a good thing Some distance to get my bearings and reacquaint myself with reality. But like any addict, it was easier said than done.

I was jonesing, while trying desperately to stuff it all down and go about my prison life, forgetting the deliciously feral sex with the hot, beautifully deceptive dark-haired creature of temptation.

But then he came back. And my excitement, while hidden from my friends, felt *excessive*.

We were in the showers when Velle came clomping into the room, hustling along an exhausted and jittery Warren Xavier. I remember how my heart jumped. It leapt right up into my esophagus, and like a reflex, I glanced right. At Luthor. Maybe to see if he was having a similar hopelessly overjoyed reaction, or to make sure he hadn't noticed that *I* was having one.

Of course, he was. He always gets this flash of relief and yearning when Ren shows up, but he makes sure to disguise it fast. Especially back then, when he was still in pain from the heartbreak Ren had caused him and using anger to disguise it.

My emotions made me feel like such a scumbag, I couldn't look at either of them. I focused on my showering, eyes stuck on the crack in the floor by the drain while I struggled to ignore the sounds of Ren's chains being removed.

"Ren are you alright?" Luthor's voice came from my side, and I cringed.

"No " Ren mumbled, his tone slipping into my ear and

wrapping around my brain. "I'm not okay. I've never been okay Never, not once."

At those oddly honest words, spoken in such an even, if lethargic tone, I couldn't help myself. I peeked at him.

He looked distraught, mentally and physically torn to shreds, most likely from whatever they'd been doing to him in the East. But still, something about him was off, more than the physical. It was as if his usual confidence was gone. The bravado he uses to bury his insecurities wasn't there. I could tell just from looking at him, and hearing him, that something was wrong.

For the first time since I'd met him, he was vulnerable, his truth exposed, and it wasn't pretty.

"Jesus what did they do to you down there?" Luthor's eyes glistened, the affection he gave his friends turned up extra high for Ren.

"Lex " Ren gasped, reaching for Luthor's face. "I love you. You know that, right?? I need you to know, *now*, while I'm still telling the truth "

"*What?*" Luthor dipped away from his touch. "What the hell, Ren?? What are you doing "

"I'm sorry, baby," Ren whimpered, reaching again. "I'm so sorry for what I did to you "

"Ren, stop," Luthor barked quietly, face flushed, though his green eyes were hardened in frustration of the overwhelming emotions he clearly didn't want to give Ren the satisfaction of feeling.

"I'm serious," Ren said on a heavy breath. He almost seemed fucked up Like he was on something. "You're the only one—"

"Dude, I can't," Luthor grunted, turning his shower off and grabbing a towel. He whipped his face in my direction and shot me a pleading look, as if he wanted me to say or do something.

I blinked. "Ren, just stop talking."

"I can't!" He flopped against the wall. "I can't hold it in. The drugs They won't let me."

"What's his deal?" Landon stepped over, wrapping a towel around his waist.

"I think they gave him sodium pentothal." Luthor rubbed his eyes.

"Ding ding ding! We have a winner!" Ren croaked, shoving his pants down. "You're so damn smart, baby. I don't deserve you. But I want you—No, I *need* you. See?? It's true!"

"God, this is gonna get bad," I mumbled, chewing the inside of my cheek.

"What's sodium pent-a-something?" Landon asked.

Love the kid, but he was kinda ditzy.

"*Sodium pentothal*, airhead Barbie," Ren snickered. "The truth serum."

"I gotta get out of here," Luthor sighed, dressing hastily.

"Don't put clothes on " Ren whined, launching himself at Luthor.

Luthor ducked away from him, and I stepped in between them, grabbing Ren by the waist. "Okay, bro That's enough. Just take your damn shower and shut up before you really incriminate yourself."

"Parker's dead," he sniffed.

At that, we all froze. Gaping at our friend, the unbridled sociopath, our collective mood fell in an instant. From slightly amusing to full-on despair with those two words.

"Why " Landon whimpered.

"Why the fuck would you say that?!" Luthor hissed, dropping a supportive hand on Landon's shoulder.

Parker was still a sore subject, after all. Ren's cellmate, a guy we considered like a brother to us, especially Luthor and Ren, had contracted life-threatening pneumonia a few months back, and had to be air-lifted to a hospital. That was the story, anyway.

I think we all knew, deep down, that he was most likely dead. But none of us were ready to admit it out loud yet.

Knowing and *accepting* are two different things.

"Because it's true," Ren croaked, face contorted in obvious hurt. "I couldn't save him I *tried*, I swear to God, I did!" He squeezed my shoulders, locking his sad blue eyes on mine. "You believe me, don't you?"

I didn't know what to do or say. So I just nodded.

"Fuck this," Luthor growled. "I'm out. Come on." He grabbed Landon, guiding him out of the showers, casting me a look on his way. "Stay with him. Please."

My lips parted to protest, but they were already gone. I tried to swallow it down and *focus*, but my stomach was tumbling with unease.

Because Ren was back, and now, we were alone. *Naked* and alone, his hard body draped on mine.

"I'm sorry I'm so sorry ." He cried softly into my neck. His flesh was cool and mine was scorching, and when he pressed into me, I broke out in chills.

"Ren stop apologizing," I muttered, voice gravelly.

I'd never been given the truth serum before—*thank God*—so I didn't understand what Ren was feeling. But he seemed like he could barely hold himself together.

His lies made up most of his anatomy, and without them, he was too weak to stay upright.

Collapsing into me, his soft lips brushed my wet skin, fingertips dancing across my shoulders.

"What are you doing?" I shivered when his hips moved, his dick brushing mine.

"Fuck me," he pleaded.

The shift from misery to ravenous desire was quick. One moment, he was crying, and the next, he was begging. Squirming against me, shivering and *unfathomably* hard. I wanted to resist, I really did. I didn't want to do this I needed to fight it, because giving in to him was tearing me apart, I *knew* it was. But I couldn't stop the way my body was reacting. The way my heart was reaching, just as needy as he was.

Ren's cheek brushed mine as the control slipped from my grasp. His lips hovered over mine, our breaths mingling as our eyes met. Pupils blown out from both sides.

Grabbing his thighs, I hoisted him up, his legs instantly wrapping around my waist while I growled and pinned him to the wall. I pumped conditioner into my shaky hand, slathering it on him and me as his head tipped back, the mound of his throat dipping.

"Give my body what it needs," he panted.

"What does your body need ?" I drawled, lost in the haze of hidden desire with my dick in my fist, aimed between his cheeks.

"Dick," he groaned, relaxed enough that I was able to push in right away. "*Fuuuck*, I need dick in me."

"You love it, don't you?" I watched, *transfixed*, as my inches disappeared inside him.

"No " he mewled.

My eyes sprung to his.

"I don't. Not really." He bit his lip, the pleasure on his face betraying his words. "*Harder*, baby "

"But I " My thrusts slowed to a stop, taken aback by what he was saying.

Why would he ?

"Keep going," Ren begged. Apprehensively, I began to move again. "It feels good "

"It does ?" I couldn't help the insecurities clawing from inside my chest.

He nodded fast, subduing my panic enough for my hips to pick up the pace. Until he moaned, "Even if I don't want it to "

"Ren *Jesus.*" I stopped again.

But this time, he grabbed my face, forcing me to look at him.

"It's fine. It's good " he breathed over my lips. "This isn't real, remember?"

The sincerity in his eyes split me down the middle. It felt like my heart was literally being hacked in half with a meat cleaver.

"It's not ?" I shivered, and he shook his head.

"You don't want me right?" He wiggled his hips to work the friction his body wanted, but that *he* didn't, apparently.

My trembling lips hung agape for way too long. It felt like *hours* of gawking at him in pain before I was finally able to mutter, "No "

It should've been the truth But it felt like a big, fat lie.

"Mmm good," he moaned. "And I only want you when I'm pretending you're Lex. It's not bad, B It's *good.* Being honest feels good."

The ache had spread well past my chest. It was all over, pulsing like a fresh cut. My hips were moving because they had to. I was on autopilot, fucking him because it *did* feel good, the insanely tight hold his body had on mine.

But the other one The one he had on me *inside* was agonizing. It was awful. It hurt so badly in that moment, I could barely keep myself from breaking down.

Tucking my face into his neck, I hid my truth while I fucked him, harder and *harder.*

"Fuck yes *Lex,*" he sighed. "I only want *you,* Lex I want you back."

A sob tried to escape my throat, but I swallowed it down. Kissing and biting his neck to distract from my sorrow, the spray of water absorbed my tears.

"Baby, I love the way you fuck me "

Not me.

Never me.

It'll never be me.

"I I love fucking you," I sputtered, my voice a wallowing hurt.

He was my proxy, too. I knew he was But as I fucked him and wept, I was tormented by the way it had become a lie.

"I'm yours," Ren breathed, coming alive in his honesty.

The truth brought Warren Xavier to life.

But I was dead inside.

CHAPTER TWENTY-TWO

Byron

THIS IS UNREAL.

I can't believe it.

I can't believe I'm actually doing this!

My stomach has been in my throat for *minutes* on end while I pace around and around, wearing a damn hole in the concrete floor. I'm trying not to look in his direction, but it's difficult.

He's too quiet…

Trevel is rarely quiet when we're alone. That's something I've come to realize. He likes talking to me—*almost too much.*

But right now, he's been effectively shut up by what's currently holding his attention, and it's freaking me the fuck out.

Peeking across the room, I watch Trevel where he's seated on the top bunk, face buried in a book. *Okay, not really a* book *per se…*

My journal.

He's reading my fucking journal.

And the real kicker is, I'm letting him.

I've been ping-ponging back and forth between glaring confidence in this decision, and a nagging doubt—*like buyer's remorse*—since I moved aside the loose piece of concrete to reveal my stash spot.

It's as if those purple eyes can see right through all of my masks and my shields. Since day one, he's been able to read me the way he's reading my secrets right now. To *him*, it's been clear that I've been hiding my true self beneath a layer of fury, disguising pain and confusion, and vulnerability… The way it never was to anybody else.

When he promised that I could confide in him, and that he could *handle* it, this sudden wave of yearning crashed over me, pulling me under. I've been dying to open up to someone for *so* long… To release my demons and let them dance freely. Maybe even… with someone else's.

The thing is, I don't need him to open his vault for me to open mine. This isn't a *quid pro quo* situation. After everything that's happened recently—my friendship with Luthor and Ren imploding, after already losing people, and the general misery that is Alabaster Pen—I'm *desperate* to drop my defenses and finally let someone in. Because life is too fucking short, and I don't *want* to take my secrets to the grave.

Trevel just so happened to be there, begging for it.

"What's that?" he asked, oozing curiosity, though he was clearly trying to downplay it.

"It's where I hide my stuff," I told him, about the hollowed-out space in the wall. "There's a… um… a journal in there. And it contains all of my truths."

He blinked at me, a baffled shimmering elation in those peculiar eyes.

"It's all in there." I stepped aside, fear and thrill vibrating through my extremities. "The reason I'm here, the things I've done… That journal is basically everything about me that no one knows."

"Why… are you showing me where it is, Byron?" he asked softly.

I took one last breath to search his vibrant irises for any sign that this was a bad idea, before finally whispering, "I want you to read it."

That was nearly a half hour of pacing and self-doubt ago, and he's still reading. Still nestled up in his bed, with my journal in his lap, violet frantically scanning the pages as if he's entranced.

I don't know how to feel about that.

"You know, you don't have to stare at me while I'm reading it," he hums, gaze never leaving the book.

"What am I supposed to do?" I scoff. "Go to bed?? I might never sleep again…"

He chuckles, finally prying himself away from my journal to peek at me. "Byron, I just have to say one thing."

Oh, God… "What's that?" I cover my face with my hands.

"You're a very talented writer."

Huh? My face snaps in his direction.

That's… not what I expected him to say.

"Honestly, this is really good," he awes. "You're not simply writing down what happened to you. I'm feeling it, alongside you. That's the mark of a talented writer. Evoking emotion and all…"

My chest warms, tingles of heat spreading up my neck and into my face. "It's just a journal… Nothing special." Gaze dropping to my shoes, I kick invisible rocks.

"Learn how to take a compliment, warrior."

When I glance up, he's smirking at me. I roll my eyes for show.

"Whether it's a journal or not is irrelevant. This is no *'Dear Diary, today we had Eggos for breakfast and the guards beat a man unconscious.'* This is *real*, deep stuff that you've bled onto the page. It's palpable how honest you're being within these pages."

I have to gulp, flustered and hiding it as best I can. "Yea…?"

He nods animatedly.

"Well, that means a lot coming from you. Since, you know… you're an *actual* writer and all."

He huffs, shaking his head. "I write *poetry*. There's a big difference."

"Yea, poetry is a lot more complex than just writing down your experiences. Doesn't it have to, like… rhyme?"

Trevel releases a rumbly chuckle, his brow cocking at me. "Who told you that? Dr. Seuss?"

I bite back a smirk. "No… I'm depressed. I like Edgar Allan Poe."

He laughs again. "Okay, I'll excuse that because Poe is one of my favorites. But no, it doesn't always have to rhyme." I give him a questioning look, to which he grins. "You want me to stop and give you a poetry lesson?"

"Not right now," I mumble, the smirk pushing its way out. "What kind do you write?"

"Anything. Everything." He shrugs. "I just write what I feel… Kind of like you."

Inching closer, I stand on the edge of my bunk, pulling myself up by the railing to watch as he dives back in. I've never considered myself a *writer*. In fact, I never wrote a damn thing before I came to prison. My interests always revolved around the physical; training, fighting, exercise and nutrition.

Apparently, I've tapped into something with this journal… A gift from The Ivory.

Disregarding that odd sentiment, I ask. "Can I read something you've written?"

He peeks at me, lips sloped. "The only thing I have written down in here are some random scribbles on the floor of my old cell."

"Well, hopefully I can check it out one of these days…"

Trevel's head slants, deep, interesting eyes skimming me over in that way he does… So fucking *different* from the way everyone else looks at me.

"You're going to regret encouraging me, Raph," he breathes. "I'll be writing you poems nonstop."

I'm trying hard to fight the awkwardness I've felt around him since the blowjob. It doesn't make much sense. I've hooked up with my fair share of people I consider friends over the years in here, carrying on afterward as if nothing happened. I never had any problem looking them in the eye…

I mean, it's the whole reason the mattress has a fucking hole in it.

But I don't know, something about Trevel Fenwick chokes me up more than anyone else. He's this mysterious presence who showed up out of nowhere, flashing that crooked, taunting smirk and restless longing in his purple eyes.

Whatever the reason, I'm *sure* we can continue fooling around without it meaning anything too serious for either of us. Because if the alternative is not doing it anymore… Well, I'm not confident I can pull that off.

"Byron, I have to tell you…" His voice pulls me out of my thoughts once more. "This book is extremely enlightening."

My lashes flutter. "Like how?"

"Well, for starters, it directly contradicts your whole *I'm straight outside of prison* defense," he sneers, and I scowl.

"What's your point?"

"You had a boyfriend." His smirk widens.

"Michelangelo was *not* my boyfriend," I grumble. "We were just fucking."

"Doesn't read that way…" he sings.

"Yea, well, I guess I'm a better writer than I thought," I grunt.

Trevel sighs, slapping the book shut and turning to face me. "Look, I'm not here to pull anyone out of the closet. It's none of my business, other than that I happen to consider you a friend, and I could tell from the moment we met you were begging to finally let *yourself* out."

"That's bullshit," I scoff. But I know he's right, and I hate myself for the knee-jerk defensive lies that pour out like a reflex.

"Byron… This is not a coincidence," he says firmly, but with an air of encouragement. "What are you so afraid of?"

Frustration builds inside me, a rolling discomfort in my gut that travels up into my chest. "I'm not afraid of shit."

He leans in closer, until barely an inch separates our faces. I gulp, gripping the railing with white knuckles. "Then tell me the truth."

This reaction is so familiar, it's baked into me at this point. The fear… I know it so well, and I hate it. I *despise* that he's right… They all are.

Everyone who looks at my behaviors and says, *"Why can't he just be honest?? What's stopping him?"*

Because they're all right. I have no reason to fear the truth anymore.

I'll never see my parents again. Losing what little love and support I had from them in the first place doesn't matter. Let's not pretend they weren't already disappointed in me, queer or not. And honestly, the feeling of being with Michelangelo was good enough that I would have gladly sacrificed their approval to keep it.

They've never given a fuck about me. Who I want to be… Who I *am*.

Might as well be the best damn disappointment they could ever disown, right?

So what if it's not what I expected? Doesn't that make it better?

Being surprised by yourself…

"You can do it, Raphael," Trevel whispers, his hand sliding over mine where it's holding on to the railing for dear life.

Swallowing hard, my grip loosens. My lips part, and I summon all of my inner strength to just… *stop*. Stop fighting for lies, and start fighting for *me*.

The real me.

My fingers slip through his, squeezing his hand as I take a breath.

"I… I think I might be…" I croak, shakily coughing up the word, "Bisexual. I mean, I'm… I *am*… bisexual."

Trevel is twinkling from head to toe, his pink lips sloping into a smile that's just… *overjoyed* for me. He sinks his teeth into the bottom one like he's trying not to overwhelm me with his obvious glee, as he croons, "There it is."

Huffing, I shake my head, rolling my eyes because I can't not. But I'm *grinning*, and I can't stop that either. I physically can't make myself stop smiling right now. It's ludicrous.

I don't think I've ever smiled this big in my whole life.

"How do you feel?" he asks quietly, dark eyebrow arching.

Amazing. "Good," I downplay it. But then I clear my throat. "Really good, actually…" A long exhale brushes past my lips, becoming a soft chuckle on its way out.

Wow… I'm fucking bi. I said it, because it's true.

So this is being honest, huh? It's not bad…

Trevel pinches my cheek. "You look good." I force a frown, yanking away and making him laugh. "You have a terrific smile, by the way."

"Shut up," I grumble, pursing my lips.

Straightening, Trevel stretches his arms over his head and sighs. But I can't stop staring at him…

Where did this guy even come from?

How is it possible that he just showed up here, in prison, and became my greatest confidant??

Inherent cynicism tells me to remain skeptical. My mind flashes to Luthor and Ren, and how suspicious they were of him. Were they on to something? Or just determined to keep me in the shadows as the lovable sidekick?

I can't deny that Trevel's connection to The Ivory seems strange. I'd be stupid not to be wary of him. But then… No one's ever opened me up like this. No one's ever been dedicated to *me*.

Maybe he really is my Leo…

"Are you a witch or something?" I ask teasingly, but also dripping with wonder. "It's a little alarming how you've managed to weasel this stuff out of me…"

"Maybe I am." Trevel shrugs, grinning. "Or *maybe* I'm just the first one to show genuine interest." The truth in that statement showers me in despondence. Of course he recognizes it immediately. "We're very much alike, you and I. Even when surrounded by people, we manage to feel alone."

My head cocks. "You feel that way?"

He nods. "I've always been alone. So much so that I…" His voice trails, and he glances away. "I was desperate for someone to confide in. As much as I hate to give him credit, Dr. Love helped me immensely." Before I can inquire any further about this remark, he changes the subject back to me. *Yay.* "So, *bisexual*, you say?"

I rub my eyes. "Yes, Trevel…"

"I'm the only person who knows?"

"Officially?" I peer at him, and he's bustling. "It would appear so…"

"You mean to tell me none of your mates had any idea?" He looks and sounds skeptical of this.

Rightfully so, because it's a little crazy.

I sigh out loud. "Where are you going with this?"

"I'm just curious how even your nutty pal O'Malley, who apparently made this hole in the mattress for the express purpose of allowing you to suck his dick whenever the mood should strike wouldn't have at least *suspected—*"

"You really don't understand how prison works, do you?" I grumble. "The whole point of the hole was anonymity. Obviously, he knew whose mouth it was, and I knew whose dick it was, but we were pretending we didn't."

He blinks at me, eyes rounded in fascination that's heating my cheeks something fierce. "Like a glory hole?"

My head falls back as I groan, "*Yes*… Like a glory hole."

"That's wicked." He claps his hands together in excitement. "Is that why you insisted that I not use your name when we—"

"Please, God, stop talking," I grunt, finally slinking back down to my own bed, mainly to hide my obviously flushing face.

Of course, he doesn't let up.

Trevel's head swoops over the edge of the bunk, and he continues his pestering upside down. "Was O'Malley bi?"

I shrug petulantly. "How would I know?? He insisted he wasn't, but who can tell around here? It's hard to differentiate between those of us who were already questioning things, and those who are really just bored as fuck, passing time with whatever hole is closest." I remember what Luthor used to always say… "Lines get blurry in here."

Trevel is quiet for a moment before he asks, "Did you and O'Malley ever…" I glance at his upside-down face, much more serious than a moment ago. "Go further? Than just the mattress glory hole?"

I shake my head vehemently. "If we had, it'd definitely be in the book." Trevel looks relieved, and it does something weird to my gut that I choose to ignore. "O'Malley was a complicated dude. He had a lot of issues."

"Don't we all," he huffs.

"I mean, like, undiagnosed mental problems," I add. "He used to fly off the handle at practically nothing. Had night terrors… He'd scream and throw fits in his sleep, and it was impossible to wake him." I can't help but scoff at the memory. "I could beat the shit out of him in his sleep, and he'd just keep freaking out, totally unconscious."

"Wow. That's… bonkers."

"I know, right?"

"No, it's bonkers that you've now wound up with two flatmates who suffer from trauma-related night terrors."

My brows zip. "What?"

"Yea," he chuckles. "I have night terrors myself. They're not always that… aggressive. Sometimes, I find myself seeking comfort…" He pauses to bite his lip, face taking on some vulnerability. "Other times, it's a bit scarier."

Wait… is that why he keeps coming into my bed at night?

Why I keep waking up with him… next to me?

The curiosity is back, only this time it's paired with empathy. "Is it because of… something from your past?"

He breathes out, "It would certainly appear so."

I know I said I didn't need anything from him in return for my sharing, but I do kind of want it. I'm extremely intrigued by him, and I want to know more.

"I'm… rather fucked up." He swallows visibly.

Before I can ask him if he wants to tell me about it, he vanishes, pulling himself back up to his bunk. Shutting it down.

Whatever he's been through must've been painful…

Something he doesn't want getting out.

We stop talking for a while after that, until the lights go off in the row. I know he's not asleep, though, because I can still feel him moving around up there.

Eventually, I curl up and close my eyes, attempting to get some rest. But his smooth, raspy voice, with that accent I'm beginning to rely on for comfort, comes back. And he speaks into the dark…

"Deep inside. Locked up tight… Far beyond the realm of fright.

Past the past, and dark of night… Farther down than seeker's sight,

Is housed a perilous plight, yearning calls, surrenders fight.

It isn't wrong, but not quite right,

For pleasure's pain, and pain's delight."

Too hot.

I'm too… hot.

It's stifling, the dense heat surrounding me. I don't understand it…

It's never hot in here. Freezing cold is the permanent temperature in this prison.

Shifting, I try to move; kick the blanket off. But it doesn't work. I'm being pinned down by something…

A body.

Awareness takes over, and my eyes shoot open, blinking again and again to adjust. I have one arm, but the other is tucked underneath something… Or should I say *someone*.

Sighing, I rub my eyes with my free hand. "Dammit, Trevel…"

He's in my bed again. Lying on top of me, drooling on my chest.

Attempting to pry myself out from under him is difficult. He's like deadweight right now. This must be part of his night terrors… Very different from O'Malley's.

O'Malley never climbed into my bed to cuddle, that's for damn sure.

Looking him over, I brush my fingers through his jet-black hair, slicked with sweat at the temples. Apparently, our bodies being pressed together is what's creating this inferno right now. It brings my attention to his skin, soft and flushed, dewy where we're connected.

We're in only our underwear, which is how we both tend to sleep. I prefer being shirtless as often as I can, but at night, I usually slip out of my pants and just rock the boxer briefs. I guess Trevel does the same, except that his underwear is definitely more… *brief* than *boxer*. And not that I want to think about it right now, but I'm sort of amazed those skimpy things can contain him. His dick is… not *small* by any stretch of the imagination.

A shift of his body brings an involuntary hum from within my chest, along with a sheet of tingles across my exposed flesh. He's curled around me like a vine, and what's worse, our crotches are sort of mashed together. Even the slightest movement demonstrates how up close and personal our dicks are getting.

Fuck me…

I've been trying really hard to push past my obvious attraction to him and just be *friends*, because it's what I thought would make the most sense. But I can't deny that I'm drawn, like a moth to the flame of his striking beauty, severe features and long, limber body. I'm attracted as fuck to Trevel Fenwick, and I have been since the moment we met.

He's pretty, and he has a hot voice, limber yoga body with perfectly taut muscles, and hands that can work you into a trance. Those facts never seem to be far from my mind.

Something *huge* happened earlier. I was trying to keep the pressure off of it, but in the middle of the night, alone in this dark cell with him lying on top of me, I have no choice but to confront it.

I'm bisexual. I finally came out, to someone else, *and* to myself. It's crazy, but I told Trevel the one thing I've always been afraid to even say in my own head.

There's no use hiding it anymore… I like his dick, and I like his body, and it's all *right here*, lying in my bed with me. Like forbidden fruit that's not so forbidden anymore. Ripe for the plucking. Sweet and tight and tempting.

And *mine*.

"Trevel…" I whisper-whine his name, brushing my fingers through his hair and down his neck, onto his shoulders.

I allow my curious fingertips to graze and explore, burning more and more with each pass. A timer has gone off, and suddenly I *need* him to wake up so I can get my fix.

God, I want it… I want more.

"Trevel, wake up." I squirm beneath him, rocking my hips into his, my erection filling rapidly. I'm already rock hard, and I can feel him too; stiff and hot, aching me down to my core. "I want…" My voice is gruff as I swallow. "I wanna play, violet eyes."

He makes a soft, peaceful noise, out like a light. I'm actually jealous, because I can't remember the last time I slept so soundly. But I'm burning alive with frustrated desire, too strong to ignore just so he can get his beauty sleep.

There's something so salacious about waking up this way, fully *ravenous*. Shrouded in darkness, curiosity piqued. It's when I can truly set myself free. Let go of my hang-ups and be real and raw and fucking hungry.

I'm fucking *starved* right now, and I need something… *Someone* to devour until I'm full.

Gliding my hand down the length of Trevel's back, I reach for his ass, cupping it and squeezing. Gently, because he's asleep, and I don't want to be a total weirdo, groping him while he's unconscious. It's a *really* nice butt, though. Firm, but still plump and juicy enough that my cock is jumping beneath him from the lascivious thoughts swirling at all the things I could do to it.

"Baby, I wanna fuck you…" I whimper, the sound of my own voice saying those words driving me even crazier. "*Please?* Will you… wake up?"

My index finger traces the crack of his ass through his little panties. *Jesus, I'm dying here… I need need need.*

Trevel mumbles something, then he flops off of me, onto his back, nestling his face in my pillow. He's still asleep.

Dammit.

My eyes scan over his body, now all splayed out. Long limbs and lines of definition making up his chest and stomach. So *masculine*, yet there's this elegance to him; a dazzling beauty so alluring, I can't stop looking. The glow from beyond the bars gives just enough for me to see his complexion, the pinkness of his nipples and his lips. It reminds me of how pink his cock is… And I bite my lip, coveting the outline of it through his underwear.

"Trev…" I mumble, hesitantly reaching over to trace it with my fingertip. "Can I… kiss?"

He writhes, but doesn't respond or open his eyes. Or do really *anything* to allude to him waking up. I should shake him or something. To make sure he's cognizant. But I can't deny that I'm hypnotized by the idea of toying with him in his sleep.

It's so much hotter this way…

Easing over him, I palm his big cock, tenderly caressing it while dropping soft kisses on his jaw, then down his throat. "Your body is so sexy," I whisper, kissing his chest. Licking his nipple.

Peering up, I watch his unconscious face, serenaded by panting while I tease his peaked flesh. That sweet, pink point is now covered in my saliva. I kiss down his abs, his happy trail… Pressing one on the exposed tip of his cock, where it's poking out of his underwear.

It's *so* arousing, my own dick leaks into my boxers. "Mmm… *fuck yes.*"

Running my lips up and down his inches, I get lost in just that; kissing and licking his cock through the material until it's wet and I'm dizzy. In my head, all I can hear is his voice, and that poem he spoke to me earlier. Those hushed, silky words that lulled me to sleep…

"I know you want this…" I purr, grinding my thick cock into the bed while I nuzzle my face between his thighs. "You want to come in my mouth again, don't you?"

My entire body is tight and hot everywhere, my brain so fogged with devious desire, I can't think. I just need to feel this. I want to feel *him*…

Lying here like my plaything, breathing soft breaths and murmuring words I can't understand.

Fuck it. He's mine.

Going for my stash spot, which is still open, I grab some lube and pour a bunch onto my shaky fingers. Shoving my boxers down, I grab my cock in my slick palm, stroking up and down while I watch the sexy black-haired boy in my bed, like he's my own personal porn.

"You're so pretty," I slip my fingers inside his underwear. "Can I play with your little pussy?"

My cock pulses again as I glide a curious finger between the crack of his ass. It brushes his rim, and my head is spinning.

Biting my lip, I push slowly, gently probing him with one wet finger. He's *tight*, way too tight. I can barely get in. I don't want to force it because that's crazy… *Right?*

It'd be super fucked up, wouldn't it? To shove inside him while he's asleep…?

Trevel's legs part wider, opening up for me. But then he mumbles a slurring, "Don't…"

I gulp. *Don't…? Did he just say,* Don't*??*

But his body, his position is betraying the word. He's spreading himself, with my hand stuffed inside his underwear, middle finger playing with his small, scorching hot hole.

"You don't want it?" I hum, applying a little pressure, until it slips in. Just the tip.

His head wobbles, eyes still closed and his chest pumping. "No… don't…"

My finger enters him deeper, and he groans quietly.

"Don't… what?" I rasp.

"Don't… *make it feel good,*" he mewls, head tipping back.

Freezing with half my finger buried in his ass, I gulp roughly, like my throat is closing.

I can't do this. I can't fuck him in his sleep… It's completely fucked up.

Even if he probably wants it in real life, in his sleep, he might not know it's me.

"Trevel," I hum. "It's me. It's… Raphael."

"I want… Rapha," he sighs, wiggling his hips against my finger. "I want *Byron*."

Relief washes over me, my dread retreating. "I'm here."

I can't help remembering how it felt with Michelangelo. How deliciously depraved it was when he'd cry and sob for me to *stop*, though his body told me he loved it. *Trevel might want the same…*

And so, I slide my finger into him deeper, as deep as it'll go.

"Uhhffuuck…" Trevel gasps, legs spreading, hips lifting.

"You like it?" I fuck him slowly with my finger, only a few times before adding a second.

"Mmmm…" he whines, and I'm soaking through my boxers.

"Can I put my cock in, baby?" I plead, working my fingers, stretching him and knowing with full certainty that whether he's aware of what's happening, I *have* to push my dick into his ass right now.

It's barely even a choice.

Pulling my fingers out, I sit back, slowly sliding off his man-panties. Biting my lip, I take them down his legs, tossing them away. He's fully naked and laid out before me as I position myself between his thighs, stroking more lube onto my cock. I take a moment to revel in the feeling of this, and the way he looks, fisting his erection. Jerking it slowly, I pull the skin away to tease the swollen tip with my thumb. He's leaking for me, and I lean down to lap it up with my tongue, eyes rolling back at the salty taste of him and how purely naughty it is to be licking his pretty cock while he sleeps.

"Are you awake yet, violet eyes?" I shiver.

He responds with only breaths, eyes still closed, lips parted and quivering. He's panting like he's just as ready as I am, but I don't think he's fully awake. If he were, there's *no way* he'd be able to keep his eyes closed. I know him well enough by now to know he'd have to engage.

I've never had sex with someone in their sleep before, but I can't lie… The idea of it has my balls thrumming harder than they ever have before.

Easing between his legs, I grab Trevel by the hips, nudging my cock between his cheeks. With the eager crown of my dick brushing his hole, it feels too tight. I'm not sure it'll ever go in, but even the act of coaxing is enough to have me pulsing precum like no one's business.

"Fuck… *baby*," I groan, jamming against the resistance of his body. "I'm already coming in your ass…"

"Ummfff…" he moans nonsense.

"You're *so* fucking tight, beautiful," I hum, pushing and *pushing*. "You wanna let me in? Or you want me to force it…"

"Make it feel…" he mumbles in a pleading whine, just as I'm finally breaking through. *"Uhh!"*

"God, that's it." I melt over him, breathing his breaths. Giving my hips a gentle flick, I drive in deeper. "So so *sexy*, baby… taking this big dick in your hot little cunt…"

He arches up to me, hole clenching, gripping me so damn tight. Feeding my cock in more, I watch between our bodies as I finally make it all the way in and just shudder in pure sensation.

"Trevel… God-fucking-damn, you feel so good."

I'm in another dimension. No clue what I'm doing, but it feels *amazing,* and I never want to stop. I could fucking *live* inside of him.

"This is the best thing I've ever fucked," I growl as I finally begin to move, pulling back and fucking in, stroking my cock in him until I'm seeing stars. "Best pussy, best ass… *The* best hole on the *planet*, baby."

"Yours…" he hums sleepily, his body jostling with my movements.

"All mine." Our chests are slick with sweat, and I lick the salty flavor from him while our bodies glide together. "Your hole's nice and wet for me, huh, pretty thing? Slippery wet and oh-so-soft… Gonna suck all my cum out."

"I'm… so… *hard,*" he whimpers, and I take that as instruction to fist his dick, stroking to match the tempo of mine stroking in his ass.

Unfortunately, as soon as I curl my fingers around his long, stiff cock, something in me snaps.

Uh oh…

Oh no oh no oh… no…

And I start coming. *Hard* and *fast*.

The spaceship is blasting off, *long* before the astronauts reach *One*.

"*Fuck,*" I grunt, going cross-eyed while my dick shoots in him. "Fuck fuck fuck, I'm coming… God, I'm coming in you, Trev, oh… *fuuuck*."

He's moaning with me, unintelligible words as his body clenches on me. But his eyes are still closed. One of his hands is fisting the blanket, but otherwise, I think he's *still asleep*. It's *insane*.

But then I remember how O'Malley used to literally fall off the top bunk and take beatings from me and still not wake up. Trevel clearly has similar sleep issues… Only this is much more erotic in nature.

The fact that I'm coming inside of him, throbbing my hot, slick orgasm deep in his beautiful body while he's fucking *sleeping* has my entire anatomy rippling with pleasure shocks for entirely too long.

"Baby, take my cum," I whisper, kissing and sucking on his throat, hands rushing all over him. "Feel me flooding your perfect ass with cum, violet…"

I can't even finish the thought. My balls are tingling, and I'm gasping for air.

Holy motherfucking shit fuck…

I think I might be dead.

When I finally come back to life, I glance down to find a small puddle of precum on his abs. It's very satisfying. At least he got some pleasure out of that, despite how fast I came…

Breeding my sleeping friend… New porn category.

Pulling out of him slowly, I run my fingers up and down over his hole, playing with my cum as it seeps out, and leaning down to lick up what's on his abs. I'm still so out of it. I barely even notice that I'm kissing his cock over and over, swirling my tongue around the skin and suckling at his wet, swollen tip. It's so beyond arousing, my dick perks up almost instantly.

I've always had decent stamina, but I'll usually need at least a few minutes between orgasms. And yet, with Trevel lying here asleep, dick all hard and pulsing in my mouth while my cum leaks out of his ass…

I could go again. Like, *now*.

Hm…

A thought pops into my head that has me shivering, my body lighting up with an even stronger mischievous torrent. I bite my lip.

In the spirit of exploring…

Since he's still asleep…

Wriggling out of my boxers the rest of the way, I get fully naked with him. I pour out more lube onto my twitchy fingers, stroking it onto his erection this time. Then I swipe some between my cheeks.

"You better not wake up," I mumble, heat racing up my neck as I spin to face away from him. "I just wanna see… how it feels."

Chewing my lower lip, I straddle him backwards, leaning forward on my knees, and taking his cock in my hand behind me. I aim and sit back until the slippery crown nudges between my cheeks, and an instant wave of chills washes over me from this position. I'm nervous, dripping in *shame* and *need*… But my dick is already full and heavy between my legs again.

Fuck… I want this.

Why do I want this so bad??

Why does it feel so damn good already??

Bearing my weight, I push my hole down on Trevel's dick. Working it like he's nothing more than a sex toy, and I'm a curious little bottom-virgin, desperate to find out if he likes this as much as he thinks he's definitely going to.

"God… *fuck*, don't wake up," I choke, relaxing as much as I can. "I should've done fingers first… Whatever, just don't… wake… up…"

The rounded curve is nudging and *nudging*, and I'm rocking and *rocking* against it, wanting it *so bad*. But I'm too far up in my head and it's making things difficult. This position is for detachment, so that I can pretend it's just a dildo and I'm fucking myself with it from behind.

But I also think if it *were* a dildo, I'd be wishing it were a real dick, attached to a *real*, hot guy.

Who's fucking me from behind, because I'm his good little slut.

Jesus, what's wrong with me?

I think I want to see his face…

Still, I'm afraid that if I turn around, I'll see purple eyes and a devilish smirk… And I'll come, *again*, before he even makes it inside me.

"Fuck me…" I breathe a plea, closing my eyes. Opening my hole just enough… "Fuck my ass, Leo…"

A soft sound comes from him, and I quake as the smooth head of his dick *finally* slips in.

"*Unngghhh…*" I groan, then bite my lip. Because that sound was far too loud and entirely too slutty.

Dropping my ass back, I focus on the *burn* and *stretch*, because *God*, it's intense, but I think I really like it.

I take another inch. Then another… And *another*. Whimpering, "*Fuuuck*, Trevel. *Baby*, that's a *long* dick…"

When my cheeks make it to skin, I release a quavering sigh. Seated on him, full of cock… and goddamn fucking *loving* every inch of it. Eyes creeping open, I peek down at my own dick, sticking up straight again. *Huge*, swollen as fuck and dripping everywhere.

Jesus…

Just as I'm about to palm it and just jerk off with him inside me because it feels *incredible*, hands wrap around my hips. And a smooth, raspy voice with a British accent croons, "Ride me, warrior."

Oh, no…

Oh God, oh fuck… what am I doing??

He's awake. Holy fuck, I'm such a slut.

What's wrong with me?!

I hate myself.

Tightening all over, I'm frozen in sheer awkwardness. The only sliver of positive is that I don't have to see him looking at me right now.

"*Baby*… bloody hell," he croaks. "I didn't think you could get any tighter…"

"Shh-shut up," I hiss, eyes falling shut, because as humiliating as this is, *Goddamn,* it feels fucking *euphoric*.

"Be hostile if you want, sexy boy." His hands run up my sides then back down to my ass, treasuring my scorching hot flesh, holding my cheeks open, no doubt to ogle the sight of his body inside mine. "You know you want to ride this big cock... That's why you're on it."

Fuck, I do...

I do want to ride it.

Why do I want to ride it??

Surrendering to the situation I've put myself in, and the sensation of being fuller than imaginable, I lift, drawing a jagged groan from my lips. Then I press back down, eliciting a coarse gasp from within him.

I try it again, rising up, then swooping down. Up... then down... Up. Down. Up. Down. Gradually gaining speed until before I know it, I have my hands braced on his thighs and I'm fucking *riding* him.

Riding his dick.

Trevel's dick is inside me, and I'm... riding it.

Who am I??

"I'm n-not a bitch," I grunt.

"Hmm?"

"Just because I'm d-doing this..." I pant. "Doesn't mean I'm... *uhh-fuck*... I'm not a fucking *bitch*, okay?"

"God, you're so cute," Trevel hums, still cupping my cheeks and holding them apart.

"Ffuck you." My eyes flutter shut at how stupefyingly good this feels.

Whether I understand it or not.

"There he is," Trevel croons. "I've seen you fight, remember? You're a fucking beast, baby..." He pushes up into me, and I grunt out a raspy sound, my face still burning red-hot shame.

But I glance down at my cock, biting my lip while I watch it, bobbing and slapping into my abs with my rampant bouncing. The way I'm riding the *guy* beneath me, hole working on his dick because I *want* it.

"You're a warrior," he goes on, "with a sick body and a big, *thick* cock... A sweet, tight ass, taking this dick like a *champ*."

My jaw clenches. But I gulp as the humiliation fades into what it's been all along. *Deep*, longing desire.

Fuck yea... I am taking it like a champ.

My ass is so full of dick right now.

"Am I... doing good for you?"

"So good, baby," he purrs, one hand slipping around to tease my cock and knead my balls. "Look at you, taking it *so* deep your first time... Riding slow and steady. You can feel every inch of me, can't you, beautiful?"

"*Fffuck...*" I choke when his dick kisses a spot inside me that sends vibrant shocks through my loins. I've never felt anything like it… I'm practically crumbling, my own giant erection spilling precum everywhere. "Don't—*uhhfuckyes*—don't tell anyone about this…"

"Please," he growls. "*This* is all mine. No one else is getting you, baby. *Ever.* Not even in their thoughts."

Something about the possessiveness in his tone, the scary rumble of his words in between his panting and clutching me to him like I'm *his*… It's lighting me up just as much as his dick dancing on my prostate.

"Tell me it feels good," I whisper hoarsely, bouncing a little harder, *faster*, chasing the good feelings. I can't believe I'm doing this… Grinding and swiveling, while his dick slides in and out of me. Even more unbelievable is that I can already feel my next orgasm looming. "Tell me I'm fucking you right…"

"Baby, you are *owning* my cock." He runs a finger down my spine, the sensation hardening my nipples. "No one's ever fucked me like you do, sweet fury."

The motivation of his words—that *nickname*—has me humping the life out of him. And as crazy as it is, part of me wants to see his face. For some reason, I want to turn around and see those violet eyes shining up at me, dark lashes fanning in his state of lust drunk and about to explode. I want to… kiss his soft mouth and moan into it every time I take his dick as deep in me as it'll go.

I can't *believe* I have a dick inside me… And it doesn't even hurt.

It burns, but I like it. I *love* the blazing fullness.

I can't even comprehend it, but I really *love* having this sexy British dude's dick in my ass.

If you tell anyone I said that, I'll fuck you up.

"Uhh, *fuck*, I never thought I'd… like this… so much."

Or I could say it myself, to the sexy British dude in question…

The words just spill out of my mouth as my head spins and spins. I can't control it.

"You can like it all you want, but as I said… *No one* else is getting this ass." He grips my cheeks hard, and I gasp. "Understand?"

I nod fast. "Okay, baby…"

"This sweet, hungry little hole swallows only one cock…" His voice is becoming uneven, and it's the hottest thing I've ever heard. "Mine. *Only* mine… Say yes, Byron."

"*Yes*… yes yes, only yours," I mewl, about to collapse and come and cry all at once.

"Say it dirtier…"

"Only your big dick gets to… fill my ass."

"More," he hisses.

"Only you get to feel my wet, greedy hole… stretching around your… *oh*, oh oh *fuuuck*, Trevel, I'm getting so… close…"

"Come here." He pulls me backward, reclining me until my back is flush with his chest. Lying on top of him, knees bent, legs wide open. He holds my thighs apart and grips me tight, fucking up into my ass. "You're so needy, aren't you, my beautiful warrior? You just couldn't wait for me to turn you out…"

"*Uhh* no, I… couldn't." I'm digging my feet into the bed so that he can slam his hips up to mine, pumping me full with salacious sounds of wet slapping. "That's why I… fucked you. Then climbed onto your cock… 'Cause I need it, baby. I need it so bad…"

"Mmm… you do, don't you? Leaving my ass worn out and gushy before getting yours…"

I hum, dizzy and shaking. "Y-you… like it?"

"I fucking *love* it," he groans. "God, you're filthy *perfection*, Byron Kang. I'm gonna breed you like the good boy you are. Drain my balls in your sweet ass just like you did to me while I was fucking *sleeping*…"

"Fuck!"

"*Fuck* is right. Get me off with this hole, baby."

"Come in me…" I plead, and he snarls.

"Beg for it."

"*Please*… Please fill me with cum. I wanna know how it feels…" I have no control over my words right now. All I am is hot, clenching sensation.

"You're going to feel it, love. You ready…?" His hand caresses my cock.

"Yes yes yes!"

"Here… it… *comes*."

I think I've blacked out.

I don't know where I am, or what's happening. All I know is that this can't be real life. It just *can't be*. No one has ever made me come this hard… *Not even Michelangelo.*

Oh, he's definitely Leo, alright. Only a leader can make you come this good.

Writhing, whining and purring, panting and growling. Coming coming *coming*.

Trevel is coming in my ass, and I'm coming all over myself. He's biting me and licking me, palming and rubbing my wet cock while I convulse and he bucks every last drop of his orgasm into the depths of my body.

It's fucking *insane.* And all I can think is that *this* is my first night being openly bisexual.

First. Fucking. Night.

Quite the celebration... Yea, I think it's clear I've been suppressing it for quite some time.

Not sure how we end up like this, but eventually, we're lying on our sides. In my bed, face to face, just staring at one another. Sweaty, fucked raw and spent, cocks tired, asses wet and used... Fucking *high,* on all of it.

Trevel is tracing the tattoo on my chest, and I'm watching his eyes. I've never felt this before, and I want to tell him that... But I'm afraid.

Coming to terms with my sexuality, and the fact that I really like dick in and around my body, was one thing. But this closeness I feel with him... That's something entirely different.

This connection... It scares the living shit out of me.

I can't do it again...

"Sweet fury..." he whispers.

My heart is thumping steadily against my ribcage. Right in his direction. "How... did you..."

"It's in your book." He grins. *Oh... right. I wrote about Ken giving me this tattoo he's touching.* "I think it's perfect... Because that's exactly what you are. The *sweetest* fury."

I force myself to huff, despite the out-of-control carnival ride that is my thoughts.

This is too much right now.

Too heavy... getting too deep...

So I shut it down. Shelving it all, I simply yawn and scoot in closer. *Future Byron's problem.* "Will you tell me another poem?"

He stares at my mouth, flipping my stomach because I think I really want him to kiss me...

But he gives me lush and tender words instead.

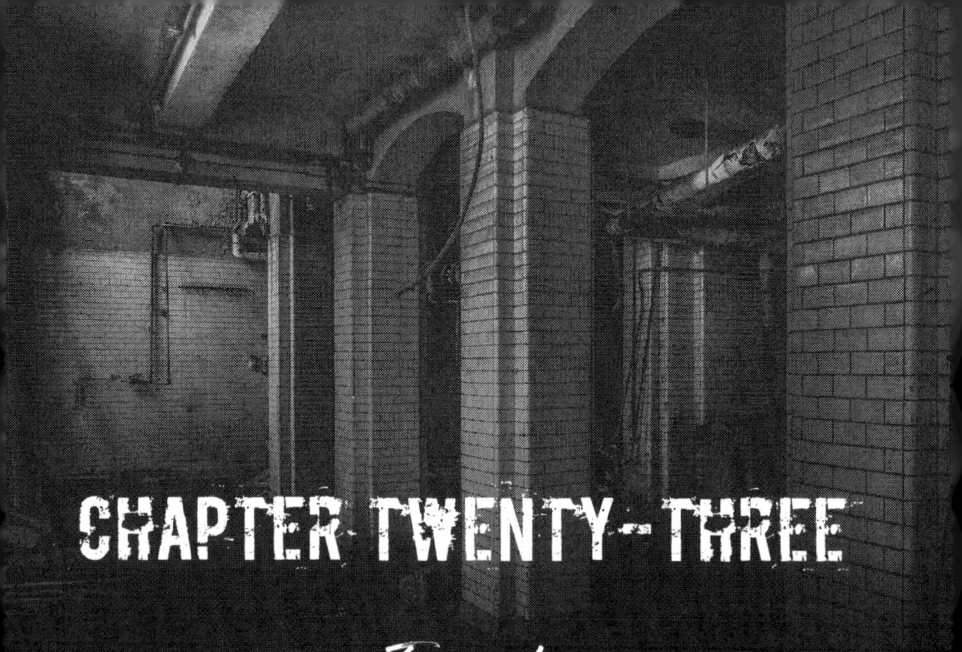

CHAPTER TWENTY-THREE

Trevel

"Him"

By Trevel Fenwick

Counting breaths, and the thumps buried beneath muscle and skin soft like velvet.
Each represents a moment of afterglow I'm basking in.
Could this be a dream? I'll accept death over waking from it.
Sated, I lie in wait, and watch, and breathe. Gazing, enchanted.
Bound by the way he looks, and our beats like a mirror.
Slowed, we are calm now. Nourished, we've been fed. Cool water to the scorching tongue.
The way we moved was a wicked dance. A tango of muscle strain and primal chase. Searing licks of flames laid in the wake of greedy fingertips.
My temple offered as his sanctuary, on a silver platter of tangled sheets. We were consumed, from deep inside. A stretch, a burn. Push, pull. Cry.
Come.
Magic made in a bed of truths set free. On the outside, and within… I see. I feel, everywhere. I fall prisoner to that body and those eyes and this draw, while the tempo of my heart echoes but one word…
Him. Him. Him.
Him.

THERE'S THIS PHRASE I HEARD ONCE, FROM A *COLLEAGUE* OF MINE WHEN I WAS a teen working on the street.

I always worked alone, but I was aware that many of the kids my age were under the wing of someone—*or an organization of someones.* A *union* of sorts, I suppose... Still, I knew better than to ask questions, or get involved.

You tend to look out for one another on the streets; a bond formed in similar circumstances. To this day, I consider those kids the only real *friends* I've ever had, despite barely knowing anything about them.

One of them, a boy who went by Stitch, used to say this thing... *"Check yourself before you wreck yourself."*

At the time, I didn't know what it meant, but I knew I liked it, mainly because it rhymed. Rhyming has always entertained me, hence my love of poetry—*and no, poetry doesn't always have to rhyme, but it's fun when it does.* I like music with rhyming lyrics, rhyming jokes and limericks. I remember loving the *Mother Goose* stories as a child.

Anyway, I was thoroughly entertained by Stitch's words of rhyming wisdom. And it didn't take much thought to figure out the premise...

Check yourself before you wreck yourself.

Stop and think about what you're about to do, lest your actions become your ultimate undoing.

Over the years, this advice has popped into my head many times. I'm a reckless person, always have been. It's rather difficult for me to see *consequence* as a reason not to do something, and I'm quite stubborn. Once my heart is set, it's virtually impossible to talk myself out of it, no matter how glaringly obvious the inevitable downfall.

So you see, whether or not I check myself... I still manage to wreck myself.

Right now is one of those moments.

Without a doubt, I should slow down and think about what I'm getting myself into before I wind up destroying myself, or more than likely *someone else.* But I just love the feeling of diving in headfirst, far too much to worry that there are jagged rocks beneath the surface.

Last night with Byron was single-handedly the best experience of my entire life, and that's not an exaggeration. *Good stuff has been in short supply in my life...*

There are no words to adequately describe what occurred. Here I'd thought I was dreaming; having one of those vivid unconscious dalliances I experience often, wherein my terrible memories merge with my deepest desires, and I wake up sweaty and sticky and flustered. But as it would happen, I was *actually* being fucked by my hot newly-out bisexual friend I've been obsessing over since my arrival in the Pen.

Byron Kang fucked me in my sleep and was apparently so hungry for more that he immediately climbed onto my cock and humped the living daylights out of me. *That's right. I got to be the first person he's ever come out to, and I took his bottom virginity! In the same night!*

Check myself? After *that??*

No, sir. I'll be accepting every single bit of this wreckage, thank you very much.

I expected Byron to pull his usual denial act—*that whole, "I'm not gay, it just feels good" rigamarole.* But on the contrary! He's good. A bit quiet, sure, but that's his default setting. Much less hostile and skittish than after the mattress-hole blowjob. In fact, the only thing he seemed worried about was penetrating me while I was unconscious.

Naturally, I shut it down posthaste.

"Byron, there aren't many things you could do to me with your dick that would upset me," I told him while we drifted last night. "If anything, I'm mad I didn't get to fully experience getting that dick for the first time. Being that I was asleep and all."

He grinned with his eyes closed, face nestling into the crook of my neck. My heart felt like a hot-air balloon.

"Well, then… I guess we'll just have to do it again when you're awake, won't we?" He said with sleepy movements and kisses on my pulse.

I was prepared to drag my reluctant self back up to my own bed. But then he whispered, "You can stay… if you want."

I know. I'm fucking doomed.

Usually, *Leo* reminds me to *check myself before I wreck myself.* He's the voice of reason in situations like these, where I find myself ready to throw all caution to the wind in a way that could potentially ruin lives. Then again, he also disappears during my most trying times, further proof that he's a manifestation of my inner *responsible* voice.

I'm an impulsive, self-destructive lunatic when he's not around, which is why I don't stand a chance of playing it safe here. When it comes to Byron, I have zero bloody chill.

No clue where it's gone, but it must be far away.

I like Byron too much, and it's beginning to feel reminiscent of Alice…

There's just so much about him that draws me in. Yes, his emotional makeup may be a bit wonky, but when he's being honest, he's actually rather emotionally stable. *Just like Alice.* He's broken, but not more broken than me. That's my sweet spot.

Depression is sexy, especially on Byron. And past trauma? *Rawr.*

There's something so irresistible about a hot boy with baggage.

Something about him has been calling out to me since the moment we locked eyes in the showers. He makes me feel like a *Leo*, and I both love it and fear it.

What are the chances I don't screw this up?

Rhetorical.

Waking up in Byron's bed isn't new, since apparently my sleep issues have been bringing me down here almost every night, one way or another. But this time is different. Because *this time*, he doesn't seem appalled by me being here. Since he invited me and all.

"Good morning," I say to his back as my eyes flutter open, but he doesn't respond. Stretching out my sore muscles, I hum, "Fucking hell… Did last night really happen?"

Byron is still quiet, and it puts me into an abrupt and immediate tailspin of dread. Grabbing his arm, a gust of relief breaks from my lips.

He's warm. *Thank God.*

Rolling over, he faces me, his drowsy expression inquisitive. "What's wrong?"

"You weren't answering…" I mutter, swallowing the lump of bad memories in my throat. "And I just… I thought…"

His brows lift, and I sigh, "Never mind. Sorry."

I know I *could* tell Byron about Alice. Easily. In fact, he'd probably be the *best* person to tell, about all of it. He's so calm and nonjudgmental.

But I can't. Whether I can see him or not, Leo is still *technically* here, within the walls of my fearfully marred mind. And I can't ignore the truth behind his precautionary advice.

There are certain things about you that no one will ever understand, Trevel. It's best to keep those things to yourself. Because when you're vulnerable with people, someone always ends up getting hurt.

There's a curse on your heart; like Pandora's box. The only way to protect yourself and those around you is to never, ever *open it up.*

"You thought what?" Byron asks, interested, and much less prying than I was with him, which makes me feel like a real knob.

Forcing a gentle smile to ease his mind—and hopefully change the subject—I brush my thumb along his perfectly angled jawline. "I just wanted to make sure you were alright. After last night…"

I think it's worked. Because his eyes widen, indicating that his attention is refocused on our sexcapades.

"I *feel* alright," he murmurs, chewing on his lower lip. "I'm not sure if that means I *am* alright…"

"Well, that's better than feeling *not* alright," I hum. "Don't you think?"

He stares at me for a moment, dark eyes softening as his lips twitch. "Definitely."

Without another word, Byron scrambles out of bed. There are so many things I want to say to him; questions I want to ask, words I want to speak and hear in return. But I'm distracted from all of it by the sight of his naked body strutting around the cell. Hard slopes and contours of muscle draped in creamy skin I could eat like butterscotch—*my hands-down* favorite *ice cream topping, by the way*—adorned with splashes of black ink that give him just the right amount of edge.

It's remarkable to see something so physically stunning surrounded by rot and decay. Like a flower, sprouting up between a crack in the weathered pavement.

I mean, look at his ass… Look at it! All high and round, with those dips in the sides… He must do a lot of squats.

I still can't believe I got to creampie that booty last night. Best DNA swap ever.

Byron grabs his pants and hops into them quickly, much to my dismay. He seems a bit dodgy, which is to be expected. This is new for him, I suppose—not just the bottoming, but admitting that he's having sex with a man because he *wants* to, rather than pretending it's out of prison boredom. Just because we crossed another line, I don't for one second think he's going to abandon his aloofness.

He's going about his morning business while I'm still in his bed, blanket draped over my waist, staring at him. Eventually, he grumbles, "Are you just going to lie there all day?"

Flopping back, I grin. "Come here and help me up, then."

He rolls his eyes, though his lips are quirked. I'm *desperate* to kiss that cocky, hesitant little smirk off of his mouth, but I know he'll likely need some more warming up to it.

Don't ask me why we can fuck and suck each other dry, but kissing *is considered too intimate. It's an odd notion, but on some level, I get it.*

Byron picks up my underwear and tosses them at me. "Put your panties on. I don't want to find out what these guards do if you're naked in my bed when they show up."

"My guess is absolutely nothing." I sigh, crawling out with little enthusiasm.

"Must be nice to be you, huh?" he rumbles while I slip on my underwear, clearly forcing his eyes away from my nakedness as he goes on with his routine.

"Possibly," I hum as I sidle up to him. "I'd say it's pretty bloody *awesome* to be me right about now..." Wrapping my arms around his waist from behind, I seal my front to his back, making sure to rub my dick on his perfect ass. *Just a bit.* He stiffens while I pout on the nape of his neck. "You don't like my knickers?"

He peeks at me over his shoulder. "They're cute. You always wear skimpy little undies like that?" He arches a cocky brow.

I may swoon myself into an early grave.

"I prefer the European style," I tease, and he huffs. "I think you'd look even more irresistible in some *skimpy little undies.*" My lips graze his ear while my fingers trace his immaculately sculpted abdominals, leading down that carved V-shape in his pelvis. "Perfect body... perfect dick... *perfect* ass."

Byron shivers, his breathing changing in a flash. I love how much I can affect him. Despite being a brooding grump who gets supreme enjoyment out of beating people senseless, he can't help but purr and tremble and melt for this pernicious trainwreck of a person.

I'm the luckiest demoralized outcast on earth.

And yet, he seems hellbent on keeping us both from floating away.

Byron pries himself out of my hold and spins to face me. "Trevel, listen... I just want to make sure we're on the same page."

I cock my head. "Which page should we be on?"

"The one where we both understand that we're not a couple," he says pointedly.

I narrow my gaze at that word. "*Both* of us...?"

He nods. "We're both responsible for keeping ourselves in check."

Meaning, this isn't just about me being clingy. He's worried that he *might start to...*

I'm fluttering.

Check yourself... before you...

"I'm just saying, we have to stay casual," he rumbles on.

"Relationships… love." He clears his throat. "They make people weak, and stupid. Not me, man. Never again."

His cheeks are blushing as he rakes fingers through his hair, vehemently protesting the idea of falling for someone again, and I can't say I don't get it. I'm willing to bet my fancy knickers that this has *everything* to do with *Michelangelo.*

It may have a bit to do with Ren also.

Ignoring my obvious jealousy regarding those two, what he's saying makes sense. After what he went through—hell, after what *I* went through—it's in both of our best interests to remain casual.

But again, my stubbornness has me folding my arms over his chest and popping out my hip. "Are you laying down the law right now?" I cock a brow at him.

Byron huffs a small chuckle that I wish didn't make him *so* bloody attractive. "Yea, I am. Hopefully, this isn't a deal-breaker for you…" His soft voice is hurting his cause. "Because I'd really like to keep hooking up." He bites his lip. "Casually."

My lips twist. "Right… *Casually.*" I slink closer, vibrating with the exact things I'm supposed to be fighting off. "What about the cuddling?"

I bat my lashes at him, and he grins, clearly trying to tame it.

"The cuddling is fine. So long as it doesn't make you fall in love with me…" As he purses his lips into this cocky smirk, the desire to bounce on his dick is instant.

"I'll try real hard, sweet fury."

Reluctantly, I put some space between us, and we go about our tasks. Prison cellmates, casually hooking up and forbidding ourselves from becoming anything more… *Whatever you do,* don't *press that button.*

We should really be knocking on wood…

This will almost certainly end in tears and bloodshed.

Well, this is an exciting turn of events.

Byron and I are currently strolling through the halls of Alabaster Penitentiary, *alone.*

I've gotten used to walking to and fro by myself, but tonight, I asked Kent if Byron could tag along. And to my surprise, he said yes.

Sure, it's just *walking*, but when you sit in a cell for eighteen hours a day, and spend every moment outside of it in silence, you learn to relish the little things.

Like going for an after-dinner stroll through a crumbling prison with your casual sex partner.

I have to appreciate such things, though I do wonder what Manuel thinks about the obvious bond forming between Byron and me…

I'm sure I'll find out soon enough.

I read what Byron wrote about The Ivory in his book—the blowjob in his office. *And that other thing, in solitary…*

His relationship with Manuel Blanco is equally complicated, and it's just another source of my ongoing jealousy where Byron Kang is concerned.

At least the Warden's never propositioned me. *Not yet, anyway. Though I wouldn't put it past him.*

I also wouldn't put it past me *to graciously accept, being that he's sexy as hell, twice my age, dangerously Machiavellian, and oozing big-dick energy. In short, he's not just Daddy as fuck, but* formidable *Daddy as fuck. The best kind.*

All signs point to him being hung like a porn star and capable of fucking you into another dimension.

Regardless of all that toss, I'm at his mercy. Trapped on this island because he wants me here.

Might as well be the villain's errand boy… At least this way, I'm getting something out of this otherwise miserable experience.

As if almost hearing my thoughts, Byron asks, "Aren't you worried about being under the Warden's thumb? About… *owing* him?"

Peering at him while we walk side by side, my gaze narrows. "Trust me, there are worse people than Manuel Blanco within these walls. At least he's upfront with what he's about."

"You're talking about Dr. Love, aren't you?" He shoots me this knowing smirk. "Man, he really messed you up, huh?"

It doesn't sound like he's pitying me per se, but still. Giving Dr. Love credit for any of my issues is enraging.

"I wouldn't go that far," I mutter.

"But he did fuck you over." He lifts a questioning brow.

I purse my lips. "Well, yea. He left me to my own devices, then sold me out to The Ivory for his own selfish reasons. *That said,* if it weren't for *Felix Darcey*, none of that would have happened."

Byron peeks at me in between subtly watching the camera watch us. "I feel you. Felix Darcey is a bitch."

I grin. "Such a bitch…"

"Right?" he commiserates. "Why is everyone so obsessed with him?? I don't get it… Just because he's a maniac who happens to be adorable? So what?? I'm telling you, I can't stand these *holier than thou* murderers. They act like they're killing for some grand purpose, but really they're just psychotic and desperate for attention."

The way he's mirroring my exact sentiments warms my chest. "I couldn't agree more."

I've decided to take the long way to the east side, which goes around solitary. I think it's part of the prison Byron's never seen, because his face is flinging all around, part nervous, part amazed, while also visibly on high alert. As if he's expecting a guard to burst through a door any moment and shoot us both in the face.

"This is fucking nuts," Byron murmurs in fascination. "I can't believe we're just… walking around. Alone."

"Pretty cool, isn't it?" I smirk, only partially teasing.

He rolls his eyes, though the excitement on his face is vivid, and infectious.

"You've barely been here two months," he grumbles. "Once you hit *years—plural—*you start to forget what it's like to do certain things."

Unfortunately, the melancholy in his voice is also contagious.

Just like with Alice, I want to know all about Byron's pain. I'm not saying I want to heal him, because I'm fully aware that I'm incapable of such things. I just want to feel it alongside him. Curl around him and endure his every single ache and twinge; suffer through it as if it's my own.

"Like what?" I ask softly, and he peeks at me. "What have you forgotten?"

He looks like he doesn't want to answer at first. But I see the very moment when his initial defenses slip away, and it's mesmerizing. To think that in such a short time, I've become the one person he can confide in… The *only* one who gets his secret truths.

I could not possibly feel more special… *Or more undeserving.*

"How to behave around people, I guess," Byron finally answers. "Like, I think if I met someone who *wasn't* crazy or dangerous, I wouldn't know how to act."

I chuckle. "That just makes you sound fun and interesting."

He grins, but bites it away. "Even just this, though… Walking around *free*. I can't help feeling like I'm doing something wrong, just for *walking* without chains on, or supervision. Isn't that crazy?"

"It's certainly messed up," I mutter.

"A few weeks before you got here, I had a cellphone," he tells me.

"O'Malley got it taken away being a hot-head idiot, as usual. But when I still had it, I stared at the thing for like ten minutes. Blankly. Just trying to remember what the hell to even *do* with one..."

"I was never a fan of smartphones," I remark casually. "I used the one at my flat more than anything."

Byron stops and gapes at me for a moment. "You mean, like a... landline?"

I grin at the look of appall he's giving me. "Sure. We can call it that."

He blinks a few times, seemingly mortified. But then a laugh bubbles out of him, and I think it's the first time I've ever actually heard him *laugh*. Not one of his rumbly little chuckles, or a puff of mild amusement. An honest to God haughty *chortle*.

It may be the greatest sound I've ever heard in my entire life.

And how delicious does he look when he's doing it... My God. Be still, my rotten little heart.

"You really are a freaking weirdo, you know that?" He sighs out his laughter, smile still resting comfortably on his pillowed lips.

"Why thank you," I jeer, and he peeks at me, a bit more flirtatious this time.

"I like it," he whispers, breeding butterflies in my stomach. "So you... what? Went to libraries and pulled out the Encyclopedia instead of just Googling things?"

He smirks, and now it's my turn to give him a look. "I never said I didn't *have* a smartphone. Of course I did. I used it for Tinder." He laughs again. *Fucking hell, I'm going to collapse.* "And DoorDash."

"Mmm... Too bad you lived in Atlanta," he rasps. "If you were still in New York, I could have delivered you your Sunday Roast."

"Ohhh, *wow*," I croon and chuckle, to which he beams with pride. "Look who knows what things are called in England."

His grin widens. "I *have* been there before, after all. Two whole times."

"Well, I'm glad one of us has happy memories of London..." I sigh, then balk at the way that just tumbled out.

I can feel him looking at me as he asks softly, "You don't?"

Glancing at him, I take a moment to consider what to say. "No, I'm sure I *do*... It's just that my home life wasn't... the best."

In fact, it was the absolute worst.

Byron looks enamored by the details I'm sharing, like measly scraps being tossed to a starving animal. I have to swallow down the guilt, and it tastes horrendous.

He wants more…

But he doesn't press. Simply gives me a nod of empathy, which has me wondering if maybe he *doesn't* care whether I open up to him or not.

He wants this to remain casual. And that's what you should want too…

Anything deeper won't work, for either of you.

Brushing off the festering doubt and insecurity, I ask, "What about you? Were your parents wankers?"

His mouth forms a line. "They weren't that bad. They just… didn't care. They didn't understand me, and they didn't want to." He goes quiet for a moment, in thought. "When I was younger, my father used to make me stand in the corner. If I was acting out, or if I'd gotten bad grades in school… He would literally make me stand still in the corner of the room, completely silent. I'd be watching them having dinner, watching TV… chatting and laughing. They would just go about their lives with me *standing* there. As if I didn't even exist. I was invisible to them… It was so easy for them not to see me."

I can't believe how badly I'm aching for him, down to my bones.

"What could you have possibly done to warrant something like that?" I whisper.

"Probably the same thing you did to warrant whatever you got," he sniffs, and I freeze. "Parents are bullshit."

My head is spinning as I mumble, "They don't deserve to know us…"

His despondence fades, lips twisting as if he likes that. "Agreed. But I would *love* to see the looks on their faces when I—" His voice cuts out abruptly, eyes dropping to his feet.

My brows lift. "When you what…?"

"Never mind."

"Byron…"

"It's nothing, okay? Forget it," he grumbles. "I'm in here forever. I'm never going to see them, or anyone else outside of this place, ever again, so it doesn't matter. Can we just let it go, please?"

There's depression in his aura now. It's palpable, seeping into his movements, in every line of his face.

I don't want to push him… He's already given me so much of his honesty. I should be grateful for that. And I am.

But now I'm wondering what else he's holding on to, aside from secrets.

Feelings for the love he was ripped away from…?

I don't believe Byron hates his parents, like I do. He only wants their love and acceptance.

But what about someone else… Someone who's wronged him?

"This place gives me the creeps…" he says when we reach the East Wing. "They had O'Malley down here for weeks before he was killed. Doing God knows what to him…"

"The experiments, yea?" I ask, and he nods. "Poor lad…"

I suppose I'm lucky. Riverwoods was bad, but it was nothing like this.

"Yup. That's the beauty of Alabaster Isle." He sighs. "Miles outside of any jurisdiction that would put a stop to the blatant human rights violations. Not to mention, rich fucks like Governor Russo backing everything…"

He immediately has both rage and despair in his eyes. My thoughts circle back to his vengeance.

Would Byron Kang take a taste of revenge if it were offered to him?

Before I can consider it too much, he changes the subject. "So you've wandered around down here a lot?"

"Not *a lot*…"

"Have you… seen Ren by any chance?" he asks, brown eyes sliding up to mine. I stare at him for a moment until he looks away. "I know he's a shithead and everything, but still… If he's down here, strapped to some chair like a mental patient—"

"He's not," I cut off his obvious pain with a blatant lie. His brows knit. "I mean, I haven't seen him down here. They must be keeping him… somewhere else."

Byron looks relieved, accepting the utter horseshit I just fed him.

Sure, I could've told him the truth. *But then what??*

I have him now… Yes, it's selfish, and manipulative—the exact things he was accusing Luthor and Ren of—but still. Unlike them, I would never take him for granted. I will not let him sacrifice his own happiness for people who wouldn't do the same for him. Not anymore.

"Want to see something?" I grab him by the arm, tugging him along. Away from the row of cells where his so-called *friend* is being held.

Bringing him back up another long corridor, I walk swiftly, threading my fingers through his. And he lets me. It's purely titillating.

I'm certain he's about to complain, but thankfully we reach our destination before he can.

"This is it?" He gives me a look. "A closed door… Ooh. *Thrilling.*"

I purse my lips at his sarcasm, and he smirks. "This is the room Felix Darcey lives in."

Byron's eyes widen. "What??" He gawks at the door. "Really??"

I nod. "This is his private bedroom… Not a cell. A bloody *room*. Where he gets to come and go as he pleases, like he owns the place."

"You come and go as you please…" His lips quirk smugly.

I frown. "*No*, I have to ask The Ivory's permission to breathe. Meanwhile, The Carver has his own bloody *chalet*, stocked with goodies. A desk, a bookshelf… A comfy bed."

"How do you know it's comfy?" He shoots me another skeptical look.

I'm becoming annoyed that he isn't sharing my frustrations here.

"Trust me, it is. Dr. Love wouldn't sleep on one of our measly cots."

"Dr. Love sleeps in there with him??"

"Of course he does," I gripe. "They're bloody inseparable."

"Shit…" Byron mutters, growing shifty. "We should go. What if they hear us?"

"Who doesn't love an unannounced visit?" I wink, then knock on the door.

"What are you doing??" He gasps nervously.

"You know, for someone who gets off on beating blokes bloody, you're a bit of a wimp," I sneer.

I may be intentionally pushing his buttons a wee bit… Only because it's *so* bloody hot when he gives me the look he's giving me right now.

Like he wants to smack me in the face with his dick.

"Don't test me," he growls, jaw visibly clenched.

"What's wrong?" I keep poking the beast. "Are you *afraid* of The Carver?"

"Seriously?" he hisses. "That preppy fuck is the one who should be afraid."

I grin wickedly at how easy it is to rile him up. *And fun.* "Then let's go inside…"

I witness the mound in his throat dip. It's obvious that his natural inclination would be to leave it alone, but there's a flicker of curiosity in his eyes. *That's the flame I want to throw petrol on.*

The deviant desire to fuck shit up. To be *bad* and cause some mayhem.

More specifically, to cause mayhem for Felix fucking Darcey.

Leaning over his mouth, I whisper, "I know you want to."

He shivers. Then he straightens, taking on a much more confident repose.

Twisting the doorknob, he smirks devilishly. "It's open…"

My face lights up, a malevolent grin sloping my mouth. Byron bites his lip and slowly pushes the door open.

Part of me expects Felix and Dr. Love to be in there, doing something we couldn't hear through the door, like reading side by side, or cuddling like sappy heart-shaped fruitcakes.

On the contrary, though. The room is empty.

Shoving Byron inside, I follow, closing the door behind us.

"This is… weird," he hums, looking around. "Why aren't they here? It's late…"

"Maybe they're in his office." I shrug, wasting no time snooping.

Wandering the room, I touch everything that belongs to Felix Darcey. His books, his clothes, his toiletries.

Byron snorts in derision, and I turn to find him shaking his head at some clothes scattered on the floor. A pair of yellow boxer briefs with bees on them. And matching socks.

"Fuckin' dork…" He scoffs.

I smile, returning to my snooping. I want to ransack his belongings, maybe steal an item or two, but I'm not sure how much time we have. Not only that, but there isn't much here. Certainly nothing interesting to take.

The room is sort of barren. Sure, it has furniture, which is what transforms it from a broom closet to an actual *bedroom*. There's a bed that does appear light-years more comfortable than ours, a desk littered with pens, a notebook, an MP3 player with headphones. More clothes stacked in a wash basket. But in terms of actual *items*, it's pretty sparse.

I don't need an MP3 player. Byron already has an iPod and he lets me use it whenever I want.

"The lad's a bit of a slob…" My mouth twists. "Dr. Love must *hate* that."

Imagining the compulsively neat Dr. Robot grimacing as he steps around the messy state of his serial killer boyfriend's bedroom is immensely satisfying.

I wonder if he does the wash for him… That would be hilarious.

"No offense, but I highly doubt he hates anything about that bratty shithead," Byron grumbles. "Did you *see* them together that day in the rec room?? He was looking at Darcey like a damn work of art. Like he sneezes rainbows and shits gold." He rolls his eyes. "I think it's clear he puts The Carver on a fucking pedestal."

My delight slips away, and I scowl. "Oh, *yes*. Let us all fall to our knees and worship the great *Felix Darcey*. The most fascinating specimen on the whole bloody planet…"

Irritation sets my jaw as I petulantly explore the books on the shelf.

They're mostly psychology texts, though I do spot a copy of *Mindhunter*, which I remember Dr. Love having on his shelf back in Atlanta.

Tugging out a random one, I look it over…

Beneficial Brainwashing by Dr. Melvin Strange.

I'm flipping through the pages when I realize that Byron isn't moving, and I can feel him staring at me. I turn to find him standing beside the bed with his head cocked.

"Yes?" I mutter, arching a brow.

He purses his lips and shrugs. "Nothing. You just…" His voice trails, on purpose. He's wearing this smug expression that's irking me even further.

"I just *what?*" I growl.

"You seem a little jealous." He plops down on the bed and reclines, propping up on his elbows.

My frown deepens. "I am not," I hiss, though my tone is proving his point. "I think it's pathetic. Leaving an entire *life* behind to come here and fall in love with a serial killer…"

"*Or* you're mad because Dr. Love never showed any interest in dick when he was treating you." He smirks.

"False," I grunt, petulantly stuffing the book back in its place. "I don't care about that. I am *mad* that he deserted me, knowing he could turn around and sell me out to The Ivory. It was all part of his plan, because he's a raging wanker."

Byron's gaze narrows in suspicion. "Just admit you were into him. It's not a big deal…"

"Bugger off," I seethe, snooping some more to distract from the resentment simmering in my gut. Stepping out of my shoes, I pick up a toothbrush from the shower caddy and use it to clean them.

His accusations are getting to me, and it's bothersome. *It reminds me of the way Leo used to hassle me about this shit.*

"Are you *still* into him?"

My gaze returns to Byron when I notice *his* tone has shifted. It's no longer jeering, and his eyes have gone dark, mouth set in a firm line. He looks indignant. Resentful…

Jealous?

"No…" I murmur quietly, and he blinks.

"Are you sure?" His voice is low, fit to smolder, just like his gaze. "Or is *that* why you hate Felix Darcey so much? Because he stole the guy you've been crushing on for years…"

Tossing the toothbrush into the caddy, I step over to him. "And what if it was?" I witness his jaw tic. It zips a chill up my spine. "Would that be a problem?"

Byron's expression is unreadable, but I can *feel* that he's fuming, keeping it locked up tight. That he might be jealous of my latent feelings for Dr. Love is purely titillating. Part of me wants to keep pressing him, to see how far he's willing to take this.

Mr. I Don't Do Feelings…

Casual hookups only.

Great story, James Patterson. Tell us another.

"I just think the least you could do is be honest with me," he rasps, hitting me with something I didn't expect. A guilt-trip. "After I've poured all of my secrets out to you…"

Unease rolls through my stomach. He has a point there as well… *Very perceptive, this one.*

Inching closer, I take him in. Lying there, peering up at me, a delirious twinkle in his dark eyes. I pause at the edge of the bed, watching his throat dip. It's unbearably hot, and the tension in the air has turned thicker than smog in an instant.

Dropping onto the bed on my hands and knees, I cage him in. I give him a studious once-over, running my index finger up his inner thigh.

"Fine. Let's put it this way…" I rumble, watching his full lips part. "I have the same residual feelings for Lemuel that you have for Michelangelo."

Byron's gaze narrows as he stands his ground. "That's not the same…"

"Could be." I shrug, gaze stuck on his mouth. "Which would mean that Felix Darcey is like my Governor Russo."

His features shift at my mention of the awful man who stole everything from him. I can practically feel him vibrating. And I'm *feral* for it.

There's a current flowing between us, gazes locked in shared scorn, some rather powerful chemistry snapping like a live wire.

"Want to taste some sweet revenge, Raphael?" I hum. "I'll feed it to you…"

His eyes are coveting my lips as he nods. Subtly, but still. He's on board. My limbs are quivering with thrill.

"We're inside the bedroom of the fucker who killed your friend," I murmur. "Let us not squander this opportunity."

His eyes sparkle, a smirk forming on his perfect mouth to mirror my own. "They could show up any minute…"

"Mmm…" I bite my lip.

Both of our chests are suddenly moving quicker with heavy breaths as Byron arches up to me… And my heart stops beating.

Intentionally or not, he's been teasing me since we met. Taunting me with his proximity, giving me a taste and then pulling away—really toying with the addict in me. And on some level, I think he likes it; being my dealer *and* my drug. Knowing I'll do *anything* to keep getting my fix.

I've been aching for his hot mouth to overpower mine since the first time I saw him. I want his lips bruising my own, his tongue in my mouth, his teeth biting me… I'm dying for the passion I know *he's* dying to unleash on someone.

But just when I think I might get it—as my lashes flutter and I lean into the brooding fighter, whose hungry gaze is zeroed in on my waiting mouth—he abruptly flips me. In a flash, he's on top, pinning me to the mattress.

"That's what you want, isn't it?" He curls his fingers around my throat. "Doctor Daddy finding *you* in his boyfriend's bed…"

I arch up into him, eyes lidded. "That's not all I want…"

His body is blazing, ridden with fiery tension and about to erupt. "Just admit you're jealous…"

You first. "Why do you *care*, Byron?" I taunt, gliding a hand between his legs.

"I don't," he growls, though it turns to a hum when my fingers brush his erection. "I want to fuck with that preppy bitch boy…"

"Right." I rub on his cock, feeling it grow beneath my palm. "So do I."

"Good," he croons, deep and raspy, dragging those unbearably soft lips over to my ear. He nips my earlobe, and I gasp. Then he sits back, leaving me squirming and needy. "Turn over."

Without a breath of hesitation, I obey, rolling onto my knees and giving him my backside. No shame in my game. I've been *dying* to get him back inside me since the other night—*preferably while I'm awake this time.*

I want to experience it fully. Especially while he's being all jealous growly-boy possessive and pretending he's not.

Casual fuck-friends don't get a thumping vein of rage in their neck when they demand to know if you have feelings for your hot doctor. Just saying.

I think my eagerness is pleasing him, because I catch a satisfied smirk on his luscious lips before he lifts my shirt over my head. Then he shoves me forward, so that I'm bent over on all fours. I'm trembling as he yanks my pants and underwear down, surprised when he rips them off my legs completely, leaving me fully naked in seconds flat.

Bare ass up and ready for him. In Felix Darcey's bed.

Positively wicked.

Peering over my shoulder, I watch him lift his own shirt off, then slither out of his pants. The moment his dick is out, my ass clenches like a reflex.

Fucking hell… I missed that thing.

Such a thick, pretty cock, and those heavy balls I want slapping against mine…

"Oh, hello…" I purr, reaching back to fondle him.

"Hi," Byron whispers hoarsely, running his hands up my sides. "Wait, are you talking to my dick?"

"Maybe…" I hum, and he chuckles.

Smacking my hand away, he shoves me forward, the *rough* of this already driving me wild. He cups my ass, spreading it open. "What do you think your Dr. *Love* would say about this…?"

His fingers run up and down over my rim, and I'm trembling, *burning* already. Dizzy with anticipation of all the things he could do to me.

"Probably something about how I enjoy being used…"

"Do you?" he rumbles, kissing a line down my spine.

"Uh-huh…" I whimper, the closer his mouth gets to my behind. "And I'm not the only one."

"Who, me?" He breathes out with an audible grin on my lower back, nipping the flesh of my ass cheek until I flinch.

Why is he so adorable and sexy?? It's not fair.

I nod fast, lashes fluttering. "But the best part is that *I'm* the only one who knows it."

Humming, he holds me down with a hand between my shoulder blades, burying my face in the bed. And then, without a moment's warning, he *licks* between my ass, feathering his warm tongue over my hole.

"Uhhh… *fuck*, B-Byron…" I'm coming apart in seconds.

I have to say, I did not expect this.

I wanted a kiss on my mouth…

But I suppose this is just as good.

"*Wow…*" He sighs in between making out with my b-hole the way he never has with my mouth. *Frustrating boy.* "You are *so* sweet right here."

"Baby, your tongue feels… *mmff*… bloody *amazing*."

"But you're clenching." He pouts. I can feel it, and I'm swooning and sweating at the same time. "Open up so I can fuck your tiny hole with it…"

"*Oh*… sweet *mmm* fury… Anything for you."

Relaxing my muscles, I present my hole for Byron Kang—*my bisexual dream come true.* And he eats me slow and sloppy, lapping and sucking and stuffing his tongue in me until I'm going cross-eyed. Devouring me like his favorite sweet, slutty dessert.

Fucking hell… He eats ass like he's eating pussy. Such a former straight boy, I love it.

Hips writhing back against his face, I'm wiggling to get him even deeper. But he holds me still with a firm hand on my lower back.

"Keep still, *Leo.*" Now I feel him *grinning* in my ass. "You're not the leader right now…"

"Mmm*fuck*, Raphael. Eat me up, baby…"

"We might be ruining the Ninja Turtle legacy," he croons teasingly, swiping a line from my nuts up to my hole and back.

"Please," I huff. "I'm sure they sit on each other's faces."

He chuckles, and I groan from the vibration of it. "Side note, if there's TMNT porn out there, I totally wanna watch it."

"Baby, for someone who doesn't talk much, you're awfully chatty while your mouth is otherwise occupied."

"I'm sorry, you're right," he hums. "Let me fill it with something…"

He sucks my balls into his mouth, and I'm *pulsing*.

"Jesus bloody Christ…"

Only a few more minutes of him licking and sucking at me desperately, in between kissing my balls and teasing my cock, and there's no way I can keep myself from squirming.

He growls, directly into my body, "I said keep still. You're gonna have to learn to follow orders…"

"Or what?" I hiss, purposely defiant, because it's who I am.

He pulls his mouth away, and I whine. "Or you won't get what you want."

"And what do I *want*, sweet fury?" I grin, stretching my arms out. My hand grazes something under the pillow.

"For me to open you up and unleash this *sweet fury* on that greedy little hole…" He smacks my ass.

I yelp, then purr, distracted from the sting when I pull an object out from under the pillow. It's a bottle of lube, and a pretty big one, at that.

"Those sluts," I grumble, and Byron chuckles, taking the bottle from me. Rolling onto my side, I palm my cock lazily. "Mm, this is perfect. Let's have wet, gushy sex in The Carver's bed. *Please*, Raph…"

Byron is quiet, still staring at the bottle in his hand. A devious smirk crosses his lips as he opens it, pouring lube onto his fingers. He strokes it onto the *many* inches of his cock, and I'm momentarily hypnotized by the motion of his fist—up and down, pulling skin away to reveal that plump, juicy crown.

Fuck, I want that inside me. I want it as deep as my body can handle…

"Get up," Byron commands. "On your knees."

"Yes, *sir*, baby Daddy," I purr, doing as he says, quaking when he slides wet fingers between my cheeks.

Easing up behind me, he grabs my hips, sealing his chest to my back. "You really wanna defile the bed Felix Darcey shares with *Dr. Love…*?" He kisses the nape of my neck, and I shiver.

"So bad…"

"Cool."

Gripping my hip with one hand, he uses the other to guide the tip of his slippery cock up to my waiting hole. I'm shivering almost violently, so hungry for his dick, I fear my ass will suck it in like a vacuum.

"God, baby, I want you…" I whine while he swirls the wet head all over my hole, still dropping featherlight kisses on my neck.

"Yea, you do…" He's pushing against the resistance of my body, and I relax for him right away. "That's it, danger boy. You don't have to play hard to get… I know your ass wants every inch of this thick cock."

I tremor as he begins to slide in, *so* bloody *slow*, it's driving me mad. "*Ummfff*—I'd be offended, but my dick is leaking like a faucet, so whatever."

He growls a sexy chuckle, following it with a heavy thrust, barreling in until I'm *shaking*. We both groan, probably too loud.

"*Fffuuuck*." Byron drops his forehead onto my shoulder. "That's a tight pussy, baby… *Goddamn*."

"*Uhhh*… B-Byron," I whimper. "Fill me. *Deeper*."

"Whatever you want, gorgeous…" he croaks, feeding me inches while I'm falling apart at the seams. "You can have *anything*, Trev, as long as I get to fuck this sweet ass."

My heart is opening like a bloom, while everything beneath my waist is searing. His dick is *much* thicker than I remember for some reason. *Or I don't remember it stretching me so wide last time because I was asleep.*

Regardless, I love it. I can't even pretend I don't. My dick is standing up straight, harder than I've ever seen it before. Veins bulging, head all swollen and shiny as beads of precum leak out.

My chest is heaving through labored breaths while Byron stuffs his big cock into my body until he's up to the hilt. When his pelvis taps my cheeks, my head lolls back onto his shoulder, and he kisses a line up my throat.

"You feel so good." He caresses my ass and my hips, fingers trailing up and down my sensitive flesh, as if he can't get enough touch. "*Sweetest* damn body I've ever fucked..."

"*Oh*... baby. *Byron*..."

"You're *so* warm, Trev... I'm never taking my dick out of you. Ever."

I'm dazed, too busy adjusting to his size to notice that he's not actually moving. He hasn't moved at all since he made it all the way in. For at least a full minute, we're just kneeling on the bed, quivering and breathing heavily, my weight resting against his frame behind me.

Still, it doesn't take long for my body to recognize what it wants... *Friction*. The itch of desire has my hips wiggling. Chasing more of the delicious burn.

"Hold still," he scolds, digging his fingertips into me.

Confusion pulls my trembling lips into a pout. "But I want—"

"Don't care. We're gonna stay like this... until you come," he says, matter-of-factly.

Huh...?

"Right, but I'd come much quicker if you—"

"I know that," he cuts me off with a grunt, sticking to whatever it is he's doing. Staying completely *still*.

His entire body is stiff and unmoving, *especially* his cock. He's so hard, it feels like a carved hunk of marble is inside me. And yet, I think I can feel his erection swelling even *thicker*... I'm not sure if it really is, or if my muscles are just squeezing him to death. Either way, it feels miraculous, and all I want is for him to bloody *move*.

Pull out, then drive back in. Stroke, thrust, pump. *Anything* to get the friction going. The primal instinct to fuck in and out of a tight, waiting hole.

This isn't fucking. This is penetration with no end in sight.

"Byron," I gripe. Sweating, muscles straining. "I wanna *move*..."

"I know," he pants. "My dick is so fucking hard in you, baby..."

"Then just... *Fuck* me. Please..."

"Uh-uh."

"Why not??" The frustration building inside me feels like liquid magma.

He chuckles deviously. "Because it's more fun to play." I feel his grin on my sweat-kissed flesh as he nips my shoulder, resting his chin on it. "Look at how big your cock is right now, Trev... Is it aching?"

I nod fast. "Uh, *yea*."

"Is that precum dripping out?"

I nod again.

"Mmm... *So* hot." His voice is tauntingly wicked. "You're not in charge anymore, are you, Leo?"

"Clearly... not..."

He huffs, licking my earlobe. "What if I touch you... like this?" His fingertips graze around my waist, brushing through the lines of my abs, down to my pelvis. My cock bobs, and he purrs, "Oh, baby... Look at you..."

Gently, he caresses the length of my cock, barely ghosting over my hardened flesh, all swollen and engorged.

"Look at how swollen it is," he sighs, running his hand down to palm my nuts.

I mewl. *"Byron..."*

"Is my dick touching your sweet spot, baby violet eyes?" he croons while playing with my balls.

"I... I..."

"Hang on, let's check." He shifts his hips, barely an inch, and my eyes roll back in my skull.

"Unnghhhfuck." I groan out garbled nonsense as a wave of sizzling euphoria crashes through my loins.

"Yea, that's it," he hums in cocky amusement. "I wanna stay on it."

"W-what the... *fffuck,*" I croak. Everything is spinning. Hazy and hot and bunched up. It's bonkers, but I think I could actually come, just from this. "Could you...?"

"Could I what, gorgeous?" he whispers in my ear.

"Could you come... like this? Just like this..."

"I'm sure I could," he tells me, scraping his nails up and down my thighs.

Every single touch is starting to feel like a hit. A shot of the best drug, flooding my system with dopamine. It's frustrating, having his cock just resting inside me. But the more he touches me and whispers in my ear, rubs his firm pecs on my back... The more I feel like his every *other* movement is a deep, *brutal* thrust.

"I wanna watch you come first, though..." Byron croons, playing with my fingers.

"Why?" I slowly slide my own hand up to my cock. Even just curling my fingers around it lights me up.

He reaches for something. "Because I want you to shoot every single drop inside here."

Handing it to me, I take the object in my right hand. I don't even realize what it is until I glance down and find myself holding the bottle of lube.

I cast him a puzzled look over my shoulder. "Pardon…? You want me to come… in the lube bottle?"

He smirks and nods. "Mhmm. That way, when your *doctor* fucks his little boyfriend… he'll be doing it with your cum."

An earthquake of thrill runs through me as his devious plan warms my ear.

"*Your* cum, Trevel… all over them. *Inside* of them."

A shivering groan leaves my lips, lashes fluttering as I rest my body weight on his strength. Melting into how truly *depraved* he is.

This man… He's a freak. A deliciously twisted kinky fuckboy…

He's bloody perfection.

"Byron…" I tremble out his name, peeking at him with bleeding hearts in my eyes. "You're unwell, baby, and it's *so* fucking sexy. I've never met someone so…" I gulp, attempting to control myself before I say something mad. "Perfect."

A lazy grin rests on his lips, which he brushes over mine. "Stroke your dick, baby. Get that sweet revenge."

My eyes fall to the bottle in my right hand again, as my left begins to pump on my cock, working up a gradual stroke.

"You want… this?" I stammer, kneading my throbbing inches, heart racing in my chest.

"Mmmyess so bad," he groans quietly. "That's it… Jerk off for me, baby. Work the cum out of that big dick while I'm stretching you open…"

My knees are wobbling, and clearly, he's feeling the burn too. Holding this position is driving us both insane—that much is apparent. But I can't deny that the frustration feels otherworldly. Like edging, in a way.

Byron's hands come up to my chest, and he cups my pectorals, thumbs flicking tenderly over my nipples. It lights me up, driving me to stroke harder.

"Good boy, *Leo*," he rasps.

Hearing him call me that sends a shiver across my skin, perking my nipples even more beneath his hands.

If he only knew…

Glancing around, I look for Leo.

You like to watch, don't you?

Sit back and observe while I fist hair and spill into hot holes…? While I'm spread open and fucked to tears, like a dirty little toy…

"Am… am I yours?" I breathe out, fucking my fist harder, *faster*, as Byron bites me and pinches my nipples.

"My what?" he growls. "My sex toy?"

"*Fuuuck…*" I grip the bottle, keeping it close because I'm getting close.

"You're so good at getting me off, you know that?" His hips shift, and tears are streaming down my cheeks. "I swear to God, I could come just looking at you…"

"Byron… *please*," I don't even know what I'm begging for, but the pleasure of tugging roughly on my cock, mixed with him stretching me and resting on my prostate, his filthy sweet words in that salacious tone… It's almost too much.

"Shh," he shushes me. "I'm not gonna fuck your hole, Trevel."

I whine, "Why not?"

"Stop talking and make yourself fucking come, baby." He covers my hands with his, taking the one with the bottle of lube and pouring some onto my cock. Then he uses the other to guide mine, stroking *with* me.

"*Uhh*, that's so good," I cry hoarsely. "If you come in me, I'll come harder and faster."

"Yea?"

"Fuck yea… Baby, you breeding my ass will set me off."

"Okay, good, because I'm so close," he groans, helping me jerk myself harder. But not much faster.

Honestly, it feels euphoric like this. Slow and steady, the *rough* movement of our hands—with his hips still, pelvis pressed hard into my cheeks. Our breaths are echoing off the walls of the small room.

Eventually, I let go of my dick, and he takes over, pumping it in his tight fist, growling into the crook of my neck.

"Fuck, *Trevel*, tell me you're almost there," he whines hoarsely. It nearly bursts my balls, just hearing him like that.

"Uh-huh," I mewl. "I am… I'm about to—"

"M-make sure you don't… spill a drop." He shivers. "I want it all… in that… bottle—*fuck*, I'm gonna come, baby…"

"Ohh… Byron! *Baby baby yes*, fffucking… come in me!"

I have no clue how this keeps happening, but we're coming *together*. The second I feel him throbbing warmth inside me, my dick begins to shoot, *uncontrollably*. Byron aims my cock, my jittery hand holding the opening of the lube bottle so that I can come into it. Some dribbles over the side, but I use my fingers to push it in.

I'm surprised I'm even able to hold still enough to do this, or that he's able to aim while we're both shuddering, tightening and releasing. Moaning and breathing…

Coming. Together.

Bollocks… I'm obsessed with him.

There's nothing else to say.

He's… the one.

"How could you possibly *know something like that already?"*

Fuck you… Don't try to distract me while I'm basking in this.

"Fuck yea." Byron sighs, coarse and audibly sated as he runs his free hand up into my hair, petting me. "That was awesome."

My hips wiggle. I feel all gushy inside, and I *really* like it. *More than I should, I'm sure.*

"Without a single pump," I rasp. "Like a holiday for your hips."

He snorts a laugh, taking the bottle from me and screwing the cap back on—*all the while still inside me, by the way*. Then he shakes it around.

"I can't believe you actually did it," he sneers.

"Can't you?"

"Okay, I can." He chuckles. "I wonder if they'll be able to tell…"

"Doubt it," I scoff. "I bet they're so swept up in one another, they'd reach for just about anything."

"I guess I can… understand that," he says softly. I peek at him over my shoulder. "I'm just saying, if there was no lube around, I'd… find something to use."

He seems to be getting fidgety all of a sudden, which has me grinning up a storm.

"Would you?" I grasp his jaw, turning over my shoulder.

He feels like he's warming to it, awaiting the soft, hungry kiss I'm about to give him.

But he catches himself and pulls away before I can, clearing his throat. "Should I just… pull out?"

Despite the disappointment of him apparently not wanting to kiss me, my grin widens, and I shrug. "Fuck it. Let's leave cum all over his bed."

Byron gawks at me for a moment, a shy smirk taking over his lips in return. "You're twisted."

"So are you."

"I know," he hums. "I kinda like it."

The feeling is mutual, gorgeous.

He pulls his softening dick out, leaving me feeling empty. After having him just resting in me for so long, not having him there anymore is unsettling. Like when you finally get a cast off. The loss feels unnatural.

I'm keeping my legs together like an instinct, until I remember myself and let it spill out… Onto Felix fucking Darcey's nice comforter.

Cum-forter. Ha!

Take that, golden boy.

"Wow… we really just jizzed all over his room," I grumble, and Byron laughs.

"Do you think they're coming back?" He asks cautiously.

"Doesn't seem like it."

"Isn't that weird? I mean, if Darcey doesn't sleep here, then where the hell is he?"

Realization dawns. It smacks me right upside the head.

"Holy mother…" I gasp.

"What??"

"The Ivory Mansion…" I whisper. "That's where Dr. Love lives…"

He lifts a brow. "So?"

"So… He must bring the bloke home with him. To the mansion."

Byron looks bewildered. "You're saying Dr. Love brings a serial killer out of the prison and back to the mansion? Where the Warden lives??"

"Bloody hell…" I shake my head, sifting through all of this. "He is brazen, I'll give him that."

Is that why Manuel doesn't trust him? Because he so clearly can't follow orders? Or is it because Dr. Love thinks he's above everyone and everything.

I can see that, too. Easily.

Byron gulps visibly. "That's completely fucked."

"Simply covering his room in ejaculate isn't enough," I mumble while getting dressed. "We need to up the ante."

"What are you talking about?" he asks, stepping into his pants.

"It's our time, Raph." I take his face in my hands. "How long are these two going to get away with everything? They think they own this place, but we can prove them wrong. We can get our revenge."

He blinks at me before murmuring, "What… did you have in mind?"

My wicked grin is practically Cheshire. "Oh, sweet fury… Just you wait."

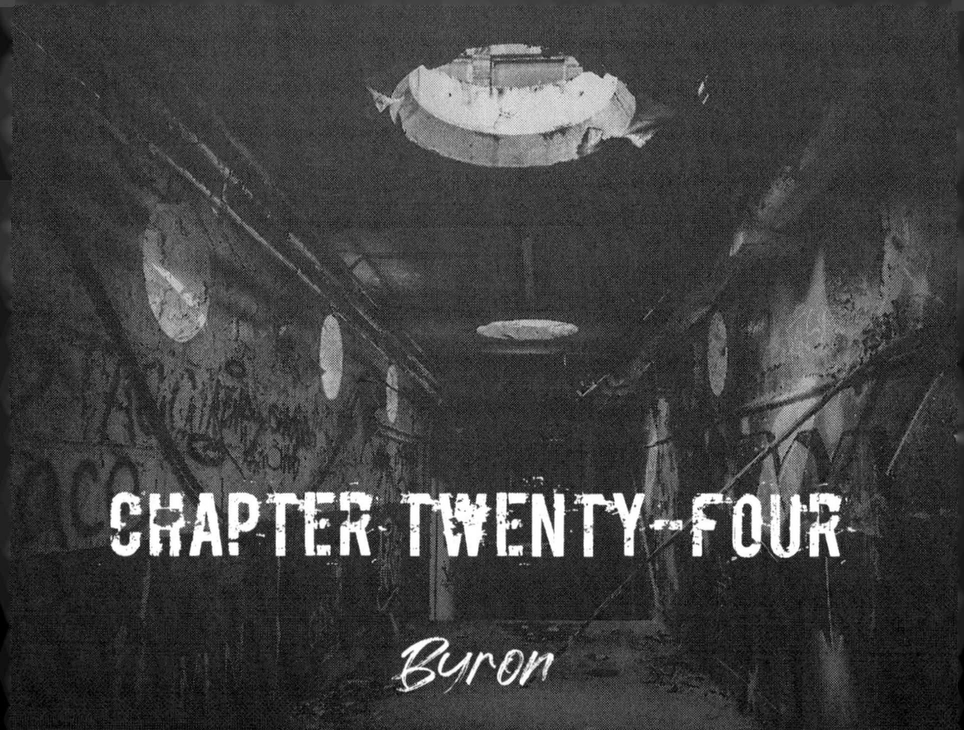

CHAPTER TWENTY-FOUR

Byron

THEY'VE SUCCEEDED IN REPROGRAMMING ME.

I hate the idea that Alabaster Pen has effectively housebroken me in any kind of way. But right now, feeling so epically *anxious* while doing what I'm doing—something as simple as *walking*—I feel very little like my old self.

Not quite like Inmate# 62… But not like Byron Kang either.

Existing here lately has felt like one long test with no conclusion in sight. I've always known The Ivory likes to play games—*he's certainly had his fun toying with me over the years.* But I have to say, right now, I could not *possibly* feel more like a mouse in a maze, being observed while hunting down a piece of cheese that might not even be there.

Some words from the past come into focus…

"Just remember that who you are in the shadows is also who you are in the light."

Shivers run through me at the memory of that day with The Ivory, in his office. But I don't think it's because I'm *ashamed* of what happened anymore. This is more like a morbid sense of elation. *Because I think he was right.*

Despite him being the most evil master of manipulation ever invented, I have to give Manuel Blanco credit where it's due. He's pretty damn wise, and extremely good at reading people. *It's what he chooses to do with what he reads that worries me.*

Like right now, for example… Allowing me to walk down to The East to meet Trevel after his session with Dr. Love.

I still don't understand how or *why* Trevel and I have been allowed to wander around alone on occasion—and sneak off into rooms for spectacular, if alarming, secret fuck sessions. And being the inherently skeptical, control-freakish lone wolf that I am, an inability to decipher someone's intentions makes me itch.

I don't know what to think about it all… Moreover, I don't know what to think about the man whose sudden, overwhelming presence in my life has brought all of these questions to light.

Trevel Fenwick. My new shadow accomplice*, apparently.*

Maybe it's just because we spend almost every waking minute together, but lately, I'm struggling to stick to our agreed-upon label of friendly fuckbuddies with a shared disdain for Felix Darcey.

Something about him has gotten *way* under my skin. It's unsettling, to say the least. But Trevel Fenwick makes breaking the rules feel *so damn good.*

Once in the East Wing, it occurs to me that I don't actually know where Dr. Love's office is. I've never been there before, and fortunately for me, I haven't spent all that much time in the East. So I find myself wandering the halls slowly, like a child in a department store who's lost his parents.

Coming up to a door, I peer through the small window at the top. On the other side is a row, sort of like the ones up in Gen-pop, though I'm sure these cells are of the *padded* variety. I press on the door, but it won't open.

Peering up at the camera, I find it aimed right at me. *No surprise there.*

I try the door again, and it still won't budge. *Okay…*

Whoever is watching me doesn't want me going in there… Which naturally has me kitten curious.

Guards or no guards, cuffed or not… On this island, freedom *is a farce.*

"What the hell??" a deep voice booms behind me, and I jump.

Velle is stomping in from another door, glaring at me, with Rook by his side.

"Oh, shit," I breathe out of relief for a second, until I register how pissed he looks. "Hey…"

"*Hey?*" He cocks a dark, studded eyebrow. "Really? That's all you have to say??"

"What are you doing down here by yourself?" Rook asks, as usual, far less hot-tempered than his menacing counterpart.

"I'm, uh… Going to Dr. Love's office," I tell them, choosing not to mention Trevel, since he has a tendency to set people off.

It's bizarre, this wave of comfort at being in their presence again. I never thought seeing Velle's surly resting bitch face would bring me any type of reassurance for anything. But I can't help it. I associate them with simpler times. And after being stuck with the Warden's new army of robot zombies for weeks, the lesser of two evils is a sight for sore eyes.

Although, the way they're oozing hostility in my direction right now, I don't think the feeling is mutual.

"Is that right…?" Velle stares suspiciously. "Just strolling down to the East for some therapy?"

I shrug, because I don't know what he wants me to say. He seems… tense. Looks more exhausted than I've seen him before, severity practically oozing from his pores.

I can't say I don't get it. The few times I have seen them since the new guards showed up, it's been nerve-racking as fuck. A nonstop pissing party between the OG rabid animals and the quiet, arrogant newcomers.

I'd be fucking fuming too.

Velle scoffs, deep blue eyes boring into mine. "I thought *loyalty* was important to you…"

My brows knit. "What's that supposed to mean?"

"Velle…" Rook places a hand on his back.

But Velle shakes it off, stepping in closer to serve me more of his piping hot glower. "You know damn well what it means. This place is in shambles and you're strutting around here without a care in the world."

"I have no idea what you're talking about," I grumble, resisting the urge to recoil under his glare. "So they let me walk down here myself, big fucking deal. What do you want from me?? I've been locked up for *three years*, being dragged around in chains by you motherfuckers. If you think I'm gonna turn down any opportunity to get away from the bullshit, even for a few minutes, then you're dumber than you look."

His agitation must be contagious.

Why is he acting like I'm the enemy?? I didn't do anything.

Whatever is happening here isn't my fault.

"Little piece of advice, 62…" Velle growls, practically vibrating his words into me. "Selling your soul doesn't work. Because the devil *never* pays up."

My mouth opens to keep arguing, but he storms away before I can even attempt it. *Motherfucker has to have the last word.*

Looking to Rook, I find his mossy irises alight with sympathy, but I can't tell if it's because he feels bad that Velle just chewed me out, or because he thinks *he* should be doing it, too.

"Why the fuck am I always the scapegoat?" I rub my eyes. "I'm not allowed a win? Like, *ever??*"

"Kang, seriously… You've got it easy right now." Rook sighs quietly, nodding toward the door separating us from the row of padded cells. "I mean, look at your—"

"Heads-up," Joy's voice chirps over his walkie, cutting off his words.

She says nothing more, but apparently, it's all Rook needs to kick back into action.

He hustles after Velle, shouting at me on his way out, "Don't forget what's right, 62!"

As soon as he's through the opposite doorway, I release a long breath. I don't know what the hell that was about, but it has my gut all twisted.

What's right…*? What the hell would they know about what's fucking right??*

This isn't my fight. I'm just another prisoner here… *Freely scampering around the place.* But still, it's not like I did anything to earn it.

I'm not The Ivory's rat…

I just happen to be screwing someone who is.

Giving the door before me one last shove, I curse when it still won't budge. Up the hall, I try a different door, which opens with one touch.

This is the way they want me to go. See? I'm still being herded. Nothing fucking matters…

I follow another long corridor, and just as I'm about to go for the door at the end, it opens, almost nailing me in the face. I jump back, half expecting to see Trevel, since he was supposed to meet me down here for our *evening walk*, as he so ridiculously put it

But it's not him. It's his doctor.

Dr. Love gives me a puzzled look, glancing behind me. In a half-second, he's assessing the situation, wondering if I'm a maniac prisoner on the loose, if he should call someone…

But that's not what he does. Instead, he cocks his head. "Byron Kang, right?" He speaks my name curtly. My brows jump. "We met in the rec room a few weeks back. Well, not officially…" He stops after that, withholding said *official* introduction, as if he doesn't find it necessary.

I would say I agree.

He clearly knows who I am… And I *definitely* know who he is.

Expanding on that, I murmur, "Dr. Love… I've heard a lot about you."

"Ditto." His slightly narrowed gaze is stuck to mine like glue.

I get the impression that he wants me to speak first, to explain what I'm doing here while he gets to just stand there and study me. But I'm stubborn, so I stay quiet.

"Where are you headed?" he asks, peeking up at the camera in the corner.

"Actually, I was on my way to your office," I tell him, pleased by the way his face shifts the slightest bit in surprise. "I'm meeting Trevel."

That gets even more of a reaction. His eyes go a bit squinted as he says, "I'm looking for him myself. He was due in my office an hour ago."

Huh?

Confusion and worry have my lashes fluttering.

Where's Trevel? Is he alright?? Why didn't he show up for his session?

"That's strange." I shift on my feet.

I could not *possibly* feel more out of place than I do right now. Standing here, an unchained prisoner, while this intimidating doctor grills me, fumbling over fact that I know so *little* about Trevel Fenwick, I don't even know where he *is.*

Dr. Love's expression darkens with some sort of realization, and he shoots another glance at the camera. "I think I know where to find him."

He's already striding past me, in the direction I just came, before I can process or question anything.

"Wait up…" I scamper after him.

His amber eyes slide to mine while we walk. "So, you and Trevel have become close…" He asks—a question that's not a question, because he obviously already knows the answer.

"We're friends…" I reply, slipping on my best mask of indifference.

I'm not a therapy guy. I've never been involved in any variation of it, because *clearly,* I'm doing *extremely well* bottling everything up inside. *In case you couldn't tell, that was emphatic sarcasm.*

But even if I'd wanted to—which I think I definitely did as a young adult, on more than a few occasions—my parents wouldn't allow it. Therapy, counseling, or anything of the sort is not tolerated by my father. It's seen as showing weakness; accepting defeat. Proving that you're not *strong enough* to handle your issues on your own.

Everyone should be made of steel inside.

Swallow your pain and never think about it again.

Dealing with any shrink, let alone one who's apparently the best of the best, and knows every inch of my *hookup buddy's* emotional terrain, feels like welcoming disaster.

As expected, Dr. Love sees through my mask like it's made of Saran Wrap, and presses on. "Just friends… Nothing more?"

"Why does it matter??" I know I sound defensive as hell, but I can't help it.

This interrogation of what I'm *doing* with Trevel is shining an even brighter light on the anxiety I've been feeling since the moment I fucking met him.

Dr. Love's lips twitch in smug satisfaction, further vexing me. "Do you care about him?"

"Do *you??*" I bark, immediately regretting it.

Fuck… That wasn't supposed to come out.

He isn't affected, though. If anything, it seems like he's loving this.

"Trevel is a very important patient of mine," he offers, impassively. "He's a very special person."

My animosity softens, an annoying flutter attacking my gut.

"He is…" I bite my lip.

"He's also very troubled," Dr. Love adds, and I frown. "But I'm sure you've figured that out by now."

"Not necessarily," I mutter like a reflex, kicking myself once more.

Why am I letting this guy get in my head??

Jesus, either I'm in desperate need of some therapy, or Dr. Lemuel Love is just that good. Probably both.

Without asking me to elaborate—*again, because he doesn't need me to*—he says, "Regardless of the label, you've certainly made an impact on him. And I think it's clear that he's made you comfortable in his presence."

His words cinch my chest. Comfort or not, the truth is that I don't know shit about who Trevel Fenwick *really* is. That's where most of my uncertainty is coming from these days—the notion of developing feelings for a total fucking stranger.

Lately, though, I'm seeing his enigma more like a puzzle.

One I might really *enjoy solving…*

We approach a door, and Dr. Love opens it, stepping through and holding it for me. But I stand still. Obviously aware that I'm not following him, he turns, lifting a confident, perfectly arched eyebrow.

As much as I hate to admit it, his presence demands attention. It's difficult *not* to stare at him, what with how large and attractive he is. Flawlessly put together, oozing so much swagger in his movements and his looks, it's like watching a tiger prowl around in front of you.

"Look, I know you're supposedly this famous PhD, like the Tom

Hanks of psychiatrists or some shit," I snap at him, and he blinks. "But I'm not in the chair, *Doctor*. I'm not interested in your diagnosis of what Trevel and I mean to each other. And after what he's told me, I wouldn't let you near my mind with a ten-foot pole."

Dr. Love's expression remains virtually unreadable. It's *infuriating* how unaffected he is. *I swear to God, I don't know how Trevel does it...*

I'd end up bashing his pretty face in.

And yet, there *is* something of a shift. As if maybe he's the tiniest bit impressed that I'm standing up for myself... *And Trevel.*

"Are you coming?" He nods toward the adjoining hallway, the amber in his eyes alight with mild amusement.

And despite my little tirade, I'm forced to continue after him sheepishly.

Ugh.

"All I'm saying, Mr. Kang, is that some people deserve to be locked up." He goes on with the lecturing I didn't ask for. *Man, he really loves listening to himself talk, huh?* "They need to be kept under glass. Studied and observed, yes, but also held *away* from society, for their own safety as well as others. But that doesn't mean they're not special. In fact, it's the opposite. They're the rarest specimens. Unique, to an almost mystifying degree."

I swallow a growing lump in my throat.

"Trevel is one of those people," he says pointedly. "He's fascinating, and I can fully understand being swept away by him, despite his misgivings. But you should know that he's also very dangerous. Maybe not physically, not to someone like you or I. But to the parts you can't protect. He's too smart for his own good."

The irritation I was already feeling has risen over the course of his monologue, until I'm ready to burst.

"What about Felix Darcey?" My head slants. "How *dangerous* is he?"

Dr. Love purses down a visible smirk this time. "Extremely."

All I can do is roll my eyes. "Trevel is just as misunderstood as the rest of the sorry souls in this place. We're all here for a reason..."

"Well... Not you."

My face jumps. "What?"

"I've seen your file, Byron," he hums.

I'm gaping at him when a door opens, a young man I've never seen before striding through. He walks past us, his eyes meeting Dr. Love's as they share a look, exchanging the subtlest of nods.

A noise draws my gaze up to the camera on the ceiling. It's following the guy.

What the fuck?

Something is going on here.

Things have been changing in the prison, more than just Trevel and the new guards. The shift is palpable. Ever since Dash escaped, it's been one thing after another… The calm of a green sky with dark clouds and havoc on the horizon.

Trevel was right about Dr. Love. After that meeting he had with the brain trust in the rec room, I totally see why The Ivory might want to have someone in here snooping around for him.

The secrets in this place are spreading. They're not tiny spores anymore… It's a full-on airborne virus, multiplying and infecting every breath of life as we know it.

It's not until Dr. Love stops in front of a new door and knocks that I recognize where we are. I hear hushed voices from inside, the door opening to reveal the dangerous individuals in question. Trevel Fenwick and Felix Darcey.

I'm unable to hide my confusion as Darcey peers at us from inside his bedroom, where Trevel and I had our little *liaison* the other day. Though I'm not sure why he's back now…

"Trevel," Dr. Love grunts at my friend, who's standing behind Felix Darcey, smirking. "Why are you here? You were supposed to be in my office for a session."

"My apologies, Doctor," Trevel says blithely, not sounding *sorry* in the slightest. "I stopped by to say hello to Felix, and we got to chatting. The time must have slipped away from me." Mischief shimmers in his purple gaze as it meets mine, and he grins. "Hi, Raph."

"You told me to meet you…" I mutter reticently. "I didn't know where you were."

"I'm sorry, love." He pouts. It's entirely patronizing. "I haven't worried you too badly, have I?"

My gaze narrows at him, and he bites his lip.

What is he up to…?

Seeing him in this room reminds me of what we did in there. I have to force away the memories to keep myself in check.

It also reminds me of how Trevel reacted to me questioning his feelings for Dr. Love. How he said that Dr. Love is like his… Michelangelo.

I still don't think that's an accurate comparison.

After all, I don't *hate* Michelangelo. If anything, I see him as someone who represents both blinding happiness and mortal dread in my life.

Maybe that is how Trevel feels about Dr. Love...

"Felix, are you alright?" Dr. Love asks Darcey. When my eyes shift, I find him staring at me.

"Hm?" He blinks, peeking at Dr. Love. "Oh, yes. Fine. We were just talking."

"About what?" I growl.

Trevel licks his lip.

Darcey shifts, awkwardly fidgeting in place. "Um... you." I don't think I could glare harder if I tried. The little shit catches on and clears his throat. "*Both* of you, I mean. Everyone really... You guys, Luthor, Ren..." His voice trails.

"Casual conversation." Trevel smirks.

"Alright, let's move this along," Dr. Love grumbles impatiently. "I don't have all day."

"So sorry, Lemuel. I remember your policy on no-call-no-shows," Trevel rasps, pushing past Darcey and Dr. Love, taking me by the arm. "Just put the fee on my tab."

Dr. Love is simmering, but his attention is stolen effortlessly by his murderous boyfriend. He steps into the room with Darcey, dropping a hand onto his waist, the other cupping his jaw as they share hushed words. Before I can eavesdrop, though, Trevel tugs me away.

"What the hell are you doing?" I whisper, scowling up at him. "You didn't tell me you were gonna have me going on some wild goose chase around The East looking for you."

"I know, baby, I'm sorry," he croons. "But I promise it was worth it for the plan."

"What *plan*?" I grumble. "And don't... call me that." My eyes dart nervously to Darcey and Love. "Not... here."

Trevel hums and bites his lip. "You're so bloody delicious, I can't handle it..."

"Trevel..." I growl, and he feigns seriousness.

"Right. Sorry. The plan involving a certain couple of wankers..." He nods in their direction. "The Carver's guard around me is way down. Pretty soon, he'll be inviting me over for tea and biscuits." He cackles, softly, but still.

"What does that have to do with me?" I grit out through clenched teeth.

"You got to have a nice chat with Lemuel, I'm sure," he whispers, dark brow cocked. "Was it... enlightening?"

I blink at him, fully flabbergasted.

He planned this…?

He sent me down here, knowing I'd find Dr. Love, not him. He wanted *me to get stuck talking to that blathering know-it-all? Why??*

Trevel leans down, brushing his lips on ear. "He's a right self-righteous prick, isn't he?"

Peering up at him, our eyes meet, and his devious destruction washes over me. His danger… His *revenge.*

It's kind of sexy.

Without a shred of control, my mouth slopes into a small smirk. "You're a menace, you know that?"

"Mmm… I think you're right, sweet fury." His finger dips beneath the hem of my shirt, running along my abs. "You like it?"

"Maybe." Pursing my lips, I grab his hand to stop its roaming. He gasps. "Don't push it."

"Trevel," Dr. Love barks, cutting into whatever this game is we're been playing. "Let's go." He drops a chaste kiss on Darcey's forehead, then stomps away, nodding for Trevel to follow him.

Trevel's hand slips down my hip. "See you back at home." He winks, releasing me to scurry off with his doctor.

Dr. Love casts me one last look that I wish I couldn't read before they leave, around the corner and out of sight. *Off to have their* therapy, *I guess.*

Gulping, my face slopes back in Darcey's direction. He's just standing there, still mostly in his bedroom, looking all cute and sweet and fucking stupid. My lips almost quirk, remembering the mess we made in his bed.

Did he even notice? Or is he so simple, he's literally sleeping in our dried cum?

I'm not sure which result tickles me more.

Darcey waves at me, and I scoff, rolling my eyes. I stalk away without another glance, back to Gen-pop.

Our row is quiet when I get there, and I immediately notice that many inmates are gone, likely in the showers. Stopping in front of my cell, my gaze slides farther down the row. I peek at the camera, and instead of entering my own cell, I continue walking quietly to the end.

I look through the bars of the last cell, holding my breath. Luthor is in there, sitting on the bottom bunk. His back is to me, and he doesn't notice me standing here, because he's clearly very invested in what he's doing. It looks like he's messing with some device—*must be the computer thing he's been rambling about for months.*

A small smile tugs at my lips. *Fuck, I miss him.*

Existing in here, not by his side, doesn't feel right.

I'm still mad at him and Ren. The things I said to them during our fight—*the last conversation we had, which was weeks ago at this point*—are all still valid. But it was never supposed to mean I don't want them in my life.

Just because they piss me off, it doesn't mean I don't love them.

Luthor is my best friend. He just so happens to be hopelessly drawn to the problem.

I don't *hate* Ren... *I can't.*

Sometimes I wish I could. *Things would be so much easier...*

Either way, none of that is Luthor's fault.

Grabbing onto the bars, I'm about to call out to him. But someone grabs me by the waist, meaty hand slapping over my mouth as I'm pulled away.

"What do you think you're doing?" Officer Pedroia growls in my face when he puts me down. I purposely keep my mouth shut. *I'm not supposed to speak, remember, asshole?* He gives me a displeased look, shoving me up the row. "Move. *Now.*"

Still, I can't stop myself from glancing back, wondering if I'll ever get a chance to speak to my best friend again.

I just want to explain... So we can make it right.

I want him to know I don't blame him for any of this. It's not... him.

Pedroia hustles me along, pushing me past my cell. My brow furrows. "Where—"

"I did *not* just hear a word come out of that pouty mouth..." he snarls.

Zipping my lips together, I swallow down my rage for this prick, and my confusion about where the hell we're going.

We end up in the cafeteria, which is a real bummer because I've gotten used to eating with Trevel. Despite not being able to speak, I like having my meals with him. I guess Dr. Love was right... About me feeling comfortable in his presence.

Not that I want to give him credit for anything, since he's an entitled asshole, but the guy is *really* fucking smart. I can see why Trevel got along with him so well for so many years...

My stomach rolls while I pick apart my stale bread.

I wonder what they're talking about... What they're... doing.

This jealousy is unnecessary and ridiculous. It makes me feel like a fool because he's *not* my boyfriend. He's not my *anything*. We're just friends who are hooking up, sharing a cell, and have a severely unhealthy attraction to vengeance. *Nothing more.*

When the meal ends, I'm brought directly to the showers, and based on the sounds of running water and nothing else, I guess there are already people in here. I wander inside, going for our spot in the back. Lifting my shirt over my head, I come to a full stop when it comes down and my eyes land on Trevel. Beneath a spray of water, running long fingers through his black hair.

What is he doing here?? He must have come straight from therapy…

I'm not trying to stand here gawking, but it's hard not to. I think I'm glad to see him… Here, with *me*, and no one else.

Really fucking glad.

So many varying emotions bubble up when I see him, but I'm having trouble processing any of them right now, because he's naked. And *wet*.

His back is to me, meaning I have the perfect view of his smooth skin and the sinews of his back, leading down a tapered waist to a fully *delicious* ass. He's so *tall*. His legs and torso go on for miles.

But that booty is just…

I swallow. *Mouthwatering.*

He's *bad* for me… *So everyone keeps saying.*

He's dangerous, untrustworthy. *Troubled.*

But that's not all I see. I don't see some fucked-up creature who will use and abuse me to get what he wants. I don't see the serpent slithering around the garden.

When I look at him, I see a hot fucking dude. A purely gorgeous guy, with purple eyes that see the *real* me. A quirky, maddening weirdo who has somehow captivated me in record time.

I see the only person in the world who knows all of my deepest secrets, and who's holding on to them for me. Trevel Fenwick grabbed my baggage without a second thought, carrying it for me so that I don't have to.

Chivalrous of him, I know. Such a gentleman…

This thing has become so convoluted, *so* damn fast. And despite what I said, what I made him agree to, the truth is that every second that ticks between us feels like a glaring indication… I'm not sure it *can* be just casual between us. It's too potent.

Foolish or not, I think I trust him. I think I want to… walk with *him in the shadows.*

Taking lithe steps, I move closer, and he spins around, as if he senses me right away. Head tilting, pink lips twisting at their corner to give me that crooked smile that's contagious.

I release a breath and shove my pants down, with the boxers. Like an admission, or an offering. And he takes it, eyes dipping shamelessly, gliding over me with a fast and furious hunger in his vibrant gaze. I can tell he wants me closer, and even if I didn't have to go that way to get into the shower, I'd be moved there by the call of those irises.

"Come here, Byron."

"Come closer, baby."

I'm still afraid to drop the shields again. *It nearly destroyed me last time…*

But with him, I don't think I can stop myself.

I'm here, violet eyes. Come and get me…

Turning on the water beside him, I've barely submerged myself before he's grabbing me by the waist and pulling me under his. I gasp, and he growls. Shivering, I glance around to check for any guards.

We're not alone by any stretch of the imagination, but so long as we stay quiet, there's no one close enough to pick up on what we're doing. *Probably.* They might be just around the corner, but *fuck it.*

I'm gonna make this count.

And I'm instantly hard from the potential of getting caught.

Trevel's touch is fast and greedy, yet sensual in the way he's biting down on his lower lip, like he can't get enough. Knowing that we *can't* speak is making this experience even deeper; *hotter* and headier than it usually is any time we're close like this. Sexual chemistry on steroids. I've never felt anything like it.

His hands run down my hips, and mine come up his chest. I whimper softly, and he breathes a near-silent, *"Fuck…"*

"Don't make that noise," I hear him saying in my mind. And I *love* the idea of turning him on so badly with something as simple as a *sound.*

My eyes fall below his waist, coveting the sight of his *long* dick. Not even fully hard yet, but still so severely impressive. My heart is racing as I reach down and grab it, and he purrs.

Mm, baby… Fuck yes.

Our eyes connect, the water cascading at his back while he presses me up against the cold concrete. Violet shimmering lust, and something more…

It's that *danger.* I do see it. But it's mixed with other things. His yearning for closeness and affection. *Devotion.* It's fucking *crazy* how much I want to give it to him.

How badly I want to bend and break for him.

"Squeeze, baby…" he says to me with his eyes while I caress his big cock. *"Stroke nice and tight for me."*

Of course, I do. My chest is fluttering as I touch him slowly, pulling up and down on his inches while our gazes stay draped in one another's. His skin is like velvet, sliding up and down the rigidity of his dick, my thumb playing with the smooth head every time it pushes out.

Fuck me... This is so hot.

Knowing that people are so close has me quaking, nipples pert and sensitive, wet flesh quivering and on display. Anyone could see this, could watch me pleasuring a man and how needy I am for him.

Just him. Only *he* gets it.

Trevel leans down to lash his tongue over my lower lip, and I shudder.

"Fall apart for me, baby. I know this is what you want."

My jagged panting tells him that he's right.

I do want it. Tear me to pieces, danger boy.

We're practically melded together as my hips shift, our tips kissing his while I pump his cock up and down in my fist. Trevel digs his fingers into my ass, spreading me rough and teasingly between my cheeks. I'm *crumbling* as I wrap my other hand around my own cock, giving it a rough stroke.

"Fury..." he moans on a whisper, dropping his lips to my neck, licking my flesh like melty ice cream.

God, fuck, that feels so good...

His possessive, hungry mouth, kissing, sucking and biting. Leaving a mark, no doubt. But I want it. I love the idea of him *owning* me. This feels like what I've always wanted... Someone to *possess* me.

One sneaky finger eases deeper between my cheeks, taunting my rim with little brushes and rubs, and pokes. I'm clenching, yet aching for him to just push it in because I *know* it'll feel so damn good. But he doesn't. He's playing with me, and I think I like that just as much.

Shoving our cocks together, I use both my hands to stroke them side by side. Our hips are moving in tandem, as if we're fucking *each other* at the same damn time while chasing the wet friction.

My hooded gaze drifts, and I think I catch sight of someone watching us... One of the guards, at least a few prisoners. But I'm too hazy to fully process it, and too high to care.

There's a buzzing in my balls from doing this for a silent audience of hungry eyes. My pulse is pinging, nervous chills rushing over me. *Thrill* in my loins, lighting me the fuck up.

Let them all watch. Let them see us...

I'm not in the shadows with him. We're out in the fucking open.

Trevel's left hand runs up to my chest, cupping my pectoral muscle, squeezing and massaging it. His hungry mouth dips, and his warm tongue circles my nipple. Then he takes it between his lips and sucks, *hard* and sloppy.

My eyes roll back. *Fuck, that's it… Suck it, Daddy.*

At an almost identical pace, his finger is teasing my hole while his tongue teases my nipple. Pawing at my chest, he's suckling my peaked flesh, growling as he does, as if he's growing hungrier the more he feasts on me. It has me fucking *opening* for him, because *fuck*, I want more.

I want him in me… His every fucking part, as deep inside as he can get.

I want him to push my legs apart and slide that big cock in me while he sucks and bites my nipples like candy.

My whining is almost too loud. Sealing my lips together, I arch up to him, giving him my body. This feels too fucking good to care about anything else. The sky could be falling right now, and I wouldn't be able to stop.

Trevel just… distracts me. From *everything*.

With my cock in one hand, and his in the other, I push them together, tip to tip. When I rub them together—our exposed crowns, silky with arousal—it's like a bolt of lightning strikes me in the balls. Jerking slow and tight, I press our dicks into one another. His body trembles from the sensation, and it fills me with helium. I'm weightless and floating, knowing that he likes what I'm doing.

I mean, so do I… It feels fucking awesome.

"Best… dick… ever…" Trevel breathes out in between brutalizing my chest with his ravenous mouth. "Feed it, sweet fury."

"Shh…" I scold, and let go with my left hand, just long enough to grab the back of his head.

Fingers burrowed in his wet hair, I stuff his face into my chest to keep him quiet. He rumble-moans, but obeys the instruction, sucking my nipples fucking *sore*, moving from one to the other. Still gripping my pec, fondling while nipping all over viciously.

Apparently, I only need one hand to keep our dicks together, like one of those fleshlight toys that's open at both ends. The thrusting works like rippling waves, my dick fucking into his while my fist keeps them connected at their heads. I'm so unleashed, so *greedy* for pleasure and pain, I barely realize how far I'm going… Until the tip of my dick slides inside, his foreskin covering my cock. *Deep*.

Trevel chokes out a mewl that pulses precum from my cock. Then, like a seesaw, his head pushes mine back, my wet skin welcoming him in. It's agonizing, almost painful, but not enough to reduce such a *fierce* pleasure.

I'm quaking, mashing our slippery cocks together so hard, if they could swallow each other up, I'm sure they would.

"Fuck my cock, Byron…" I hear him. I can't tell if he's saying it or if I'm hearing him in my mind, or if it's the same damn thing at this point.

We're becoming *one*, our bodies absorbing one another, our pleasure blooming and growing the more we move. Panting, purring, and groaning surrounding us with the rush of falling water.

My chest hurts from how hard he's biting and sucking me. My nipples are raw, my dick is *throbbing*, and my foreskin is sore. And I'm so drunk on it all that I don't even notice his finger is in me until he's up to the knuckle and touching my prostate.

Oh, fuuuuck… Fuck fuck fuck yes, baby, fucking touch it more…

It's active work to not cry his name out loud.

Trevel groans while bucking his hips, pumping his cock into mine. Our tips are soaking wet and gushy with precum flowing between them, making sounds so obscene, it has me on the verge of a colossal orgasm. Which gets me thinking…

I want to come in him… Inside his cock. And I want him to come in mine.

God, come in me, Trev. Come anywhere… everywhere *in me.*

Apparently, this desperate need for cum has been slowly rising in me. Since Michelangelo, and in every interaction with a guy since, I've become hungrier and *hungrier* for it in secret. But *now*, it's no longer hiding.

I'm out as fuck right now, and I want Trevel Fenwick's cum.

All over me, inside me.

Fuck it. Fuck everything *that isn't this.*

I want you, violet eyes. I want you to…

"Come with me…" I breathe by his ear, shaky and ready to erupt. "Come *in* me."

"You're so needy, baby," he whispers, lifting his face to lock our eyes. He looks out of his mind with lust. "My big, sexy cumslut."

"You w-want mine t-too…" I shudder with our cocks slipping and sliding. "Thirsty bitch."

He huffs, the sexiest, raspiest chuckle as his middle finger swirls in my ass. "No talking, bad boy." Barely lubed, another stuffs inside, and I grunt, abs clenching. *Fuck, I'm so fucking close…*

A quiet moan flees my mouth, and he swallows it. My tongue peeks out to lick a droplet of water from his upper lip, and he swipes his tongue over mine. I lick him back, and the next thing I know, we're just fucking *licking* each other's lips and tongues, and it's so fucking weird, but so *hot*, and *fuck me, I'm gonna come so fucking hard…*

Despite the water running cold, we're surrounded by steam. Dripping wet, grunting and gasping. Our skin is burning, and I'm *falling…*

Trevel's hand works hard in my ass to get me there, my legs spread to welcome him finger-fucking my needy hole while I fuck his dick and he fucks mine. I feed my cock into his foreskin so deep, I can't tell where he ends and I begin. He crumbles into me, sobbing into my mouth, and I think I'm hurting him. Until I realize that he's coming.

He's *coming*, all the fuck over my cock.

It's the most incredible sensation of my life, and it immediately sets me off. I'm overpowered by a typhoon of an orgasm. *Fast*. It incapacitates me, and I fucking *erupt*. Gloriously. Painfully. Spiritually.

Unlike *anything* I've ever felt before.

"Uhhhffuuck… *Trevel.*" I cry his name, because I have to. He's my god, and I'm singing hymns right now. "*Fuck me fuck me fuck me,* oh God, Trevel, *Baby,* I'm fucking coming in your… *big… fucking… cock.*"

"Shh… quiet, baby… *Jesus bloody Christ*, it's never felt like this." He's collapsing into me, wrapped around me like he's melting all over my body, taking all of my hot, aching orgasm inside his cock while he shoots his into mine. "How does it… feel so… *Mmm, Byron*, sweet furious boy… Milk it out… Just… like… *that.*"

My hand shakes as I hold us still, and we pulse and throb, twitch and convulse. Filling his skin, flooding his dick with my juicy seed. I'm barely done as he's pushing his hips forward to stuff mine with both of our cum. I hold tight, keeping us joined while we slip and slide, working all that slickness around both of our swollen heads. It's spilling out, dribbling everywhere. A big, sloppy, kinky mess. And I *love* it.

I fucking love this.

So filthy, so *depraved*. The sweet, furious sex we make together is so far beyond what I ever imagined having… It's rearranged the makeup of who I am.

It's never been like this. *Not with anyone.*

This is what I've always needed… And only the sexy British boy with the purple eyes gives it to me.

Trevel sighs and shivers, smooshing me against the wall. His fingers slide out of my ass, and I hum at the loss. Both of our eyes open slowly, dark lashes fluttering at one another as he lifts his hand and sucks on his fingers… The ones that were just in my ass.

I have no words.

There's nothing that could ever express how this man makes me feel. It's baffling. Amazing. But terrifying.

This is bad…

I think I'm getting… attached.

"I want to keep you in me," he breathes, forehead on mine.

"I don't think that's hygienic." I grin, and he chuckles.

"Shh… Quiet, Raph. Don't ruin it."

The water running frames my steadying heart rate. And I bite my lip, watching his mouth.

What is this…?

When I finally release our dicks, I pet his, giving it a gentle caress that makes him smile. Then my other hand trails up his throat.

Who are you, Trevel Fenwick?

The connection hasn't been severed yet. It's weird… Usually, the moment the orgasm high wears off, all the insecurities sneak back in. The rampant doubt and questions.

But right now, I feel nothing but *alive.*

Trevel inches, hovering his mouth over mine. "Byron…"

He wants to kiss me. I can feel it.

But we… don't really do that.

Do we?

"Let's go, inmates!"

The barking of one of the guards startles us out of our moment. Trevel still doesn't seem like he wants to lose this—whatever the holy fuck we're doing. But I duck away first, because I'm nervous, and I don't want him to see it.

He always sees.

We pull apart and rinse off, peeking at each other all the while. Dazed and high on the confusion of *us.*

Who are you, Trevel Fenwick?

And how the hell will I ever recover from you?

CHAPTER TWENTY-FIVE

Trevel

He knows why I'm here. Why I've come for him…

He's frightened.

As he should be.

Inside his bedroom is dark, but my sight sets on him immediately. Lying in his large, lavish bed, the twinkling view of a midnight city from the windows surrounding him.

New York is watching on with playful eyes and a wicked grin.

Go get him, Trevel.

He's yours.

Movements stealth, steps light, I traipse over to his bed and climb in gently beside him. He's tied in an instant.

Sitting astride him, I cover his body with mine, watching him languidly regain consciousness. My lips twist.

This is what I've been dreaming of… Seeing his face. Forcing him to look me in the eye while I take his life.

I'd like to do it all with my bare hands, but I've never tried before…

So we shall see.

As soon as he becomes aware of what's happening, his eyes widen, and he croaks, "What… what the f—"

"Shhh…" I place my finger on his lips. "Hush now, Number Four. It'll all be over soon."

My hands circle his throat, and his subtle squirming turns to bucks beneath me. "What are you—"

"You remember my eyes… don't you?" I growl, grip tightening. "You must. After all, you turned my face and made me look at you. While you were…"

My voice trails into a hoarse sound of pain; an aggrieved chuckle, sadistic and hollow as I dig my thumbs into his windpipe. I'm in *agony* inside, the deep bruising and infected wounds on my soul causing me to wince.

The rage in my veins chugs thick like hot tar, putting me into a trance. He's really freaking out beneath me, but the sounds are echoing. My vision tunnels, and I think I'm crying. All I can hear is my heart knocking throughout my body, as if my pulse is synching with his. It's pounding in my hands, pleading for a reprieve.

But I will not stop, no matter how much it hurts.

"You're *giving me* your last breath," I snarl, sputtering and whimpering above him. "It's the *least* you could do after all you've taken from me!"

"S-stop… p-please…" he croaks.

I can't recognize his voice.

I don't know why… he sounds… different.

Soft.

Helpless.

Innocent.

He's *not* innocent. *He fucking ruined me!*

They all did! They turned me into something I never wanted to be… Something I've been running from my whole bloody life!

"Trev… Trevel…" The hoarse voice is suddenly familiar. "You're… h-hurting me…"

Despite knowing where I am and what I'm doing, certainty is melting away. Reality is falling, like the tears tumbling down my cheeks.

Manhattan, the penthouse, the soft linens… They're fading into something else. And the body between my legs is no longer that of a pathetic rapist in his thirties with a beer-belly and a stupid fucking shamrock tattoo…

It's one much stronger, wider and firmer. Smooth skin beneath my fingers that my lips remember kissing and sucking.

The feel of it brings me back fast. In a few flutters of my lashes, I'm *awake*, and I can *see*…

Byron.

Oh, fuck, Byron.

"Fucking hell Jesus Christ," I rush out, ragged and dripping with regret as I immediately release his throat.

I see the dragon tattoo. And the hickeys I left on him yesterday in the showers.

Oh God, what have I done?!

"Vi-violet…" he coughs out in between hauling deep breaths, his bare chest jumping.

Fuck me, my sweet fury…

What the hell is wrong with me??

Blinking and blinking, I claw back from the pit of my nightmares. My hands run tenderly down to his chest, tracing more purple marks from my mouth.

"I'm… s-sorry," I stutter, choking back sobs the way he's choking for oxygen. "Baby, I'm… I didn't mean to…"

Collapsing on top of him, I tremble with guilt and residual fear. I'm in his bed, in prison. Starchy fabrics on a stiff mattress give me such an intense wave of relief and comfort, I can't hold back my cries.

I'm not there… I'm here.

With Byron. My sweet, furious warrior… My Raphael.

"It's okay…" he rasps, his voice even sexier after me nearly choking him to death. "You're okay."

His hands run up my thighs, brushing a pacifying touch over my ass and onto my hips as he clutches me to him. The feeling registers between my legs—where his hard body is resting—bringing attention to the stiffness trying to burst out of my skimpy knickers.

Sniffling, I graze my lips over his clavicle. "Byron… *Fuck*, why didn't you stop me?? *Jesus…*"

He's clearly stronger than me. And unlike the sadistic wanker from my memories, his hands were not bound in the slightest. He was barely trying to fight me off…

Byron's throat bobs. "Um…"

It's then that I notice it. My erection… It's not alone.

Shifting my hips, I hiss when I feel him, thick and throbbing against me. He whimpers, and I lift my head to lock our eyes. Of course, it's dark in the room, with nothing but a dimmed light coming from out in the row. But I can still make out his flushed cheeks. I'm sure it's partially from how hard I'd been choking him, though the timidity in his deep eyes tells me there's more.

I hum over his lips. "You're… so *hard*, love."

He nods sheepishly.

"Am I still dreaming?"

He shakes his head, so adorably my heart is softening to mush. Rocking my hips, I give him a slow, decadent caress of my cock along his, our solid inches of arousal rutting together. The sound that escapes his plush lips sets my loins on fire.

"I don't know…" He digs his fingers into my ass, lifting his hips and opening his legs. "*Why*. I don't know why I let you…" His eyes close and he bites his lip. "Why I… *liked* it."

"I do. You've told me before…" My fingers rake through his silky hair. Grabbing a fistful, I tug it hard, and he whines. "Because you like the feeling, the *hurt*, whether you win or lose the fight."

"N-no, I—"

"You don't need to hide from me, Byron," I whisper, brushing his quivering lips with mine. "Remember? I see you, baby…"

"You do," he says on a breath, as if maybe it was supposed to be a question, but it's not. And I'm glad it's not.

I need him to understand that I think he's perfect. That no matter the arcane inside of him, he can show it to me. *Open* wide, split himself down the middle and spill it all out, for *me*. Because I think it's beautiful, his despair, his depravity, his *darkness*.

I love the Shadowman.

"I like it too," I assure him with my tone and my ravenous movements.

"Yea?" His head slants to give me his neck.

I kiss his tattoo, sensually running my teeth over it. *God, he smells so bloody delicious…* Like masculine dominance wrapped in eager, trembling flesh.

"Uh-huh." I lick him, and he groans. "I like to be the hunter, and the prey."

I'm about to go for his lips, because I've had enough of this nonsense. I think he knows that we're more than just empty sex, our connection deeper than where our bodies can reach. It doesn't matter if we know it'll end in disaster; I'm *desperate* to be the one he kisses out in the open. Because he's *mine*. Nobody will tend to his needs the way that I can.

But he pulls away from it before I get there, glancing up at me. "Are you sure?" There's something sparkling in his eyes, like inquisitive doubt. "You're *sure* you like it… rough?"

"Yes, baby." I grind into him. "It feels good… being used." *By you.*

"I know, but it seems like—"

"No more thinking, Byron." I get the sense that he's becoming bogged down by his thoughts. Fixating on something serious that I can't get into—like the *reason* I was just choking him in my sleep. So I distract him the best way I know how. "Turn your brain off for me, baby…"

I make my request while kissing down his throat, then his chest. I'd love to make a pit-stop at his nipples and suck on them until his dick is leaking like the last time. But I force myself to avoid the detour, licking through the immaculate lines and swells of his abs and his pelvis.

"Umm…" he purrs when I run my lips along the shape of him through his boxers. Tugging them down, I free his thick cock, and he sighs, "Mmmkay…"

I grin. "Good boy."

And then I slide my mouth over him.

Byron's head tips back and he melts, fingertips on my face. "*Oh fuck…* Mmm, *baby…*"

Sucking deeper, slow and wet, I lose all semblance of who I am. The brokenness that lives inside of me, the anguish of the past, the uncertainty of the future. He makes it all seem so far away…

I forget it all and just worship this big, beautiful cock with my mouth. Writing poems in my brain about the sounds of his bated breaths and the treasuring sifts of his fingers through my hair.

I'm falling, even faster and twice as hard as the last time, and it is terrifying. Because I don't think I would survive losing him too.

I've already hurt him… But I can't make myself stop.

How can I keep him while still protecting him from my destruction? There has to be a way…

Giving him this slow, lush head is almost like an apology for hurting him the way I did. Sure, he may want his *body* to be used. But that's not the same as what will undoubtedly happen if I keep poisoning him with my curse.

"Uhh… Trev. *God*, baby, suck my dick…" he mewls, arching to me and spreading his legs.

I suck off of him with a pop, holding his ass in my hands to lift his hips higher. "How I would *love* to slide inside you right now…" I rumble mindlessly while nuzzling his balls, sucking at them almost viciously.

He shudders. "Mmff… maybe you should."

Glancing up from between his legs, I watch him biting his lip as his eyelids droop.

"I'd probably come so fast…"

"Is that so, warrior boy?" I lick lines up and down his shaft. He nods. "You want me in your hole again? Filling your hot body with dick until you can't help but—"

"*Fffuck*, Trevel, put me back in your mouth," he whines, grabbing me by my hair. "I'm gonna fucking bust, baby."

I have to chuckle as I suck him between my lips once more, bobbing and throating him, chasing those orgasms he gives up so bloody easily. It's like he can't control himself, and I *love* it. I love how effortlessly I can turn him inside out. It makes me want to spend hours getting him off in every way imaginable, until his balls are empty and he needs to seek medical attention.

All mine.

My *sweet fury.*

At least, I hope it's me he's affected by in this way, and not just circumstance. *Us sharing a cell, him feeling alone, me burrowing into his life while he's finally attempting to own his sexuality…*

The blazing jealousy of knowing I'm *not* the only one who's done this for him has me fucking him with my mouth, harder and more greedily than I've ever sucked a dick before. Like I have something to prove. And maybe I do… I want to be the best he's ever had.

I don't want him thinking about the others.

In a matter of seconds, he's bursting on my tongue, crying softly while he shoots cum down my throat and I swallow it like a fiend.

"Trev… Trev Trev Trevel, God-fucking-damn, baby. I'm coming for you… So hard… *yes*. Swallow, violet eyes… Suck it out and fucking *swallow*."

His big cock is barely done twinging before I'm sitting up between his legs, pulling out my dick and beating it hard.

"You're so fucking hot," I whisper, gazing down at him, all flushed and squirming.

"Come on me," he pleads on a hoarse breath, chest jumping.

"Where?"

"Everywhere."

"Are you my greedy little cumslut?"

"Uh-huh."

"Say it."

"I'm your greedy little cumslut," he mewls, writhing up to me. Ready and waiting for it.

"Good boy," I rasp, then moan, my hand slowing as my cum begins to flow, throbbing out onto his perfect body. "*Ohh* fuck, baby, take it like a good boy."

He whines, catching cum on his dick, and his abs, all the way up his chest. I'm showering him like a wicked baptism. "*Uhh yea*... Soak me."

"You look so fucking good," I breathe out, milking out every last drop. Then I drape over him, smearing my cum between our hot, writhing bodies. "No one has ever been as fucking sexy as you."

Rubbing our wet cocks together, I feel him twitching, hypersensitive and loving it. I move back and demand, "Lick it, baby... Clean your cum off of me."

"Yes, sir, violet eyes," he croons, pushing me onto my back.

He crawls over me and goes at it with dedication, licking up every trace of my cum, from my chest, and my stomach... and my dick. Before I can even process it, my softening cock is in his mouth and he's sucking aggressively. It's so sensitive it almost hurts. *Naturally, I love it.*

"Thirsty baby..." I shiver. "Byron, *Jesus*... you're... ruining me..."

"Mmmm..."

He doesn't stop. Keeps sucking my cock until it stiffens again, and somehow, my balls contract and I release another aching orgasm, pulsing it all into his sweet fucking mouth.

"What am I supposed to do with you...?" I gasp when I stop quaking.

He's still down there, kissing my inner thighs, up my pelvis and my abs. "Whatever you do... don't... stop."

And for my sweetest, most furious boy...

I won't.

"I've missed walking with you," I hum. Only mildly sarcastic.

Kent peers at me, but says nothing.

I release a petulant breath. "That said, I don't understand why I couldn't come up here myself..." My lips purse. "After all, I've grown accustomed to a certain standard of living. Mulling about this shithole on my own is the only real luxury I've been given."

Well, that and Byron.

My internal swooning is interrupted when Kent stops in front of the door, and knocks.

"Come," the voice growls from inside, and I balk a bit as we enter. He already sounds much grouchier than the last time I was up here.

Yay. I'm sure this will be fun.

Kent and I waltz into the Warden's office, and I'm immediately on alert. Mainly, because he's noticeably edgy. But also, because there's a stranger among us.

Manuel Blanco is leaning back in his chair, scowling at his phone screen while typing furiously, and I can't help but notice how he looks more disheveled than usual. Don't get me wrong, his suit still probably costs more money than I've made in my entire life, and he wears the open collar and sleeves rolled up his forearms shockingly well. But it's apparent in his golden five o'clock shadow, prominent frown lines and the way he's brushing back strewn locks of silky white hair with his fingers, that something is up.

Eyes flinging to the big leather chair to the right of his desk, I observe the unfamiliar face. A much younger man, maybe about my age, is sitting cross-legged, also typing away on his phone, paying Kent and myself zero attention. He has a bronze complexion, short, dark hair, obviously professionally faded, with two hoop piercings in his nose. Stylish, I'd say his clothes are equally as expensive as The Ivory's, though he's dressed a bit more casual.

While I'm just hovering in the middle of the room, waiting for *anyone* to say *anything*, Kent gestures to the chair in front of the Warden's desk. I take a slow seat, but he remains posted up by the door. *Like a good guard dog.*

The young mystery man breaks first, releasing a breath and glancing up at me. He offers a kind smile, almost as bright as his eyes, which are a vibrant teal color.

"Hi there," he chirps, lowering his phone, though it's still clutched in his hand like a part of his anatomy. "You must be Trevel. I've heard a lot about you."

I can do nothing more than blink, gaze flitting briefly to Manuel Blanco, who's still invested only in some heated texting.

"My name is Yari. I'm Mr. Blanco's assistant."

Oh… Alright, then.

Assistant…

"Pleasure to meet you." I shift in my seat. Doing my best to portray confidence, but I'm reticent as to *why* this person is here.

"Likewise," he says politely. His lips part, as if he's going to say more, but a snarl and a thunk draw our attention.

The Warden just tossed his phone down on the desk, cursing in Spanish under his breath.

"All good, sir?" Yari asks.

He simply waves him off, dark eyes settling on me. "So, Trevel… How've you been?"

"I'm all—"

"How are things progressing with your sessions?" he cuts me off, getting right to the point as he pins me with a severe look that shrinks me into my seat. "With Lemuel…"

I think back to my last session with Dr. Love. As expected, when the Warden put me up to this covert manipulation game, the sessions haven't yielded much. Dr. Love is a rock, and I *knew* that going in. He's virtually impossible to crack.

Despite numerous attempts, he has yet to reveal anything to me, and it's horribly frustrating. Mainly because I don't enjoy being bested, but also because I'm still not positive what *exactly* The Ivory wants. So I decided to try another approach.

After my session, I was skulking around the East Wing, keeping myself hidden. I waited for Dr. Love to inevitably leave his office, which he did. And I followed him…

"Well enough," I answer the Warden blithely. "I rather enjoy speaking with him. I suppose I always have…"

His gaze narrows. It's obvious he's not placated by this response. "Everyone *loves* speaking with the doctor, don't they…" His tone is dripping with sarcasm.

I clear my throat. "He *is* one of the few people I get to interact with…"

The Ivory's expression shifts. His lips quirk and he sits back in his chair, head sloping to the side. "Ah, yes… You have a cellmate now. How is Byron doing? I understand you two have become quite *close*, is that right?"

Swallowing all the words stuck in my throat, I force myself to remain impassive. "He's a friend."

"Trevel, please. Spare me the coquette," he sneers. "I don't care who you're fucking. But I will remind you that, above all else, you belong to *me*. As does Byron Kang."

My jaw clenches, fingers digging into my thighs. "Believe me, I'm aware of that."

"Good," he grunts, standing up slowly, eyes on mine as he does. "I'm sure you're also *aware* of how much leeway you've been given. You and your *friend*…"

My teeth are about to crumble to bits. "Yes, sir…"

He shows me an evil smirk. "*Splendid*. So then, if you'd like to continue flitting around this prison with 62 like it's your own personal playground, I suggest you start making it worth my while."

Sighing, I rub my eyes. "Look, I'm trying, alright? But I told you it wasn't going to be easy… Dr. Love doesn't trust me. He doesn't trust anyone." *Rightfully so.* "Except The Carver…" My face scrunches in displeasure.

All traces of amusement fall away, and The Ivory gets this deranged look in his eyes. It's alarming how he goes from zero to one hundred like that—from charming garden party host to Hannibal Lecter in seconds flat.

Rounding the desk, he comes to stand in front of me. I'm tense all over. "These sound like *excuses*, 102."

I blink up at him.

"Perhaps I should find out where *your* loyalties truly lie…"

"What does that—"

"You know, I don't like to make a habit of interfering in relationships on this island." He leans up against the desk, folding his arms over his chest. "That said, it can be a very useful tactic, and an entertaining way to pass the time."

Brow furrowing, I gape up at him.

"Byron has been left in quite the vulnerable position, hasn't he?" He goes on, watching me carefully. "What with being separated from his friends… The people who *fulfilled* him for so long." He cocks a light brow. Jealousy churns my stomach like indigestion. *Exactly what he wants, I'm sure.* "But *now*, all he has is you. Twenty-four-seven, just *you*… and *him*. It's amazing what simply keeping people apart can do in here…" He sighs, and I struggle to keep my emotions in check.

If he thinks he can take Byron away from me, he better watch his fucking back.

"Say the word and I'll move onto The Carver, then," I tell him firmly. "If you want Dr. Love, that's the way to get him."

The Warden rakes fingers through his hair, seemingly flustered again. The seesaw of his emotions is bringing on this palpable manic vibration. Like an earthquake rumbling the foundation beneath our feet.

"I grow weary, Trevel," he murmurs. He actually flinches when his phone chimes on his desk. "I'm becoming so very *tired* of people's inability to follow orders. You all seem to forget that on this fucking island, *I* am the goddamn *King*."

Growling, he's teeming with visible rage as he leans over me, hands gripping the armrests of my chair. I'm just gawking up at him while he seethes in my face, "Do I need to slaughter every last one of you to make my point?" His voice is barely audible, minty breath brushing my face.

He's unhinged. I wouldn't put it past him to do something *drastic* right now. *Like kill me...*

My eyes dart to Yari, who's just sitting there, buried in his phone again. But his gaze lifts in between typing to watch his boss threatening everyone—*even him, theoretically*—like it's no big deal.

I won't pretend to understand what kinds of things are happening behind the scenes, but I know that *something* happened between the Warden and Officer Chevelle. A disruption in the flow, some major rift that caused The Ivory to bring in his new team of guards. And I'm beginning to think flitting around in my own little world, obsessing over Byron and stewing in my hatred for Dr. Love won't be a sustainable way of life for much longer.

"Dr. Love has been meeting with Officer Chevelle," I blurt out. "I've seen it a few times... Velle and his partners having hushed conversations with Lemuel in private."

The Warden doesn't look particularly shocked by this. But he seems mildly placated by my contribution to his cause.

"And have you *heard* anything?" he asks quietly. "From these conversations...?"

I gulp. "No... But I'm *sure* Felix Darcey has."

The Ivory's lips slope into a tiny, satisfied grin that is fully terrifying. He taps me on the cheek, straightening up. "Good boy, Trevel. I believe your loyalty will keep you protected. Just make sure our shadow prince is on the same page, hm? We can't have him running back into the arms of certain lying arsonists, now can we?"

Shivering, I'm chewing the inside of my cheek to keep myself in check.

Byron is mine, goddamnit.

He will not *be leaving me for* anyone, *especially not that selfish slag, Warren Xavier.*

Over my dead body.

While I'm freaking out inside, Manuel Blanco's head lolls in Yari's direction. "*What?* I can feel that you have something to say, so just spit it out."

Yari shifts, finally tucking his phone away. He gives The Ivory this sort of doe-eyed expression that has me wondering about the nature of their relationship.

Is it strictly business?

Does The Ivory just entice this type of Daddy-me *subservience out of everyone??*

"I told you my feelings on this when you brought in the team from Medellin," Yari says cautiously, yet still getting his point across. The Ivory leers at him. I don't think I'm breathing. "Do I feel your actions are justified? *Of course* I do..."

The Ivory lifts a light eyebrow at him. "But...?"

Yari exhales. "*But* I wish you would've at least *spoken* with him first. Now everything is a big mess. We all knew Lemuel had grievances—"

"He can shove his *grievances* up his ass," the Warden barks, then rubs his eyes, hard. "I've been nothing but accommodating to that blowhard. *Maybe* if he'd spent a little more time playing the game, and a little less time fawning over a goddamn serial killer, we wouldn't all be dealing with the repercussions *months* fucking later."

An uncontrollable snort bursts out of me, and they both stare. I clear my throat. "What is Dr. Love's problem, anyway? Doesn't he have everything he wants?? Free room and board in a mansion, which I'm only *assuming* is massive and extremely fancy..."

"It is," The Ivory croons with smug amusement.

"His dream job examining psychopaths, and his *perfect*, precious monster to worship him like the god he believes himself to be." My eyes roll to the heavens. "That he even has the nerve to be dissatisfied is infuriating."

Manuel Blanco gives me a studious once-over, lips curved as if this pleases him. He grips the edge of his desk at his sides while leaning back against it, tapping his foot a few times on the floor.

"He may still be a bit salty over some things that happened while he was away..." His voice trails, and my forehead lines. "When he was supposed to be fetching *you*. Yet another job he half-assed." He glances at Yari. "I'm beginning to think his talents were slightly exaggerated."

Curiosity ripples through my thoughts. *What happened while he was away...?*

Yari shrugs. "Either way, he's not the problem."

"He's not?" The Warden hisses.

"*Okay*, he's one of them. But I still think things need to be rectified with Jonathan."

The Ivory is visibly stewing in petulance, tapping his foot over and over again. "I don't want to talk about this anymore..."

Man, I'm confused. Jonathan who?

"Jefe... please. Over a *decade*..." Yari shakes his head admonishingly, *prodding*, and I'm shocked at his audacity. *Brazen thing.* "That's longer than I've been around."

"I'm well aware of that," The Ivory teems, pinning Yari with a heated glare. "Which means you're just as disposable as he is. So watch it."

Yari isn't even fazed. "I'm just saying, why not at least try to be civil?"

"Have you forgotten who I am?" The Ivory scoffs while Yari continues to stand his ground. "I'm not in the business of coddling people. Especially those who refuse to play by the rules. I demand nothing shy of unwavering dedication." His dark eyes glide to me. "*Loyalty* is everything."

A chill zips up my spine.

"But you never even *attempted* to explain—"

The Ivory slams his fist down on the desk, effectively shutting Yari up. "I don't need to explain shit! This is *my* goddamn world! He's just existing in it, for *my* entertainment. *My* needs, not his!" He stops to breathe out slowly, jaw visibly tight. "He knows who I am, and I know who he is. *Period*. If my guard dog wants to bite the hand that feeds him, he better have jaws of fucking steel."

Despite my blood rushing in my ears, I'm able to make out the sound of footsteps clomping in the distance. Growing louder.

Manuel Blanco straightens. Yari's eyes widen, glistening with concern. I turn in my chair to face the door, noting Kent's hand slipping onto the gun on his holster.

The steps are approaching the door as The Ivory motions for Kent to stand down, which he does, reluctantly.

Bang bang bang!

Three loud knocks—or rather *slams*—from a fist against the door cause me to jump, despite knowing it was coming.

"Who is it?" The Ivory calls out patronizingly.

No answer. Just an audible growl before the door bursts open, and Officer Chevelle storms in.

"His ears must have been ringing," The Ivory murmurs, I'm assuming to us, though his eyes are stuck on Velle. Smirk intact.

In fact, we're *all* staring at Velle. I can practically see his already short fuse sizzling up.

He stomps into the room, making quick note of me, Kent, and Yari, before settling his deep blue eyes on the Warden.

"Get rid of them." He hisses a *command* at the Warden; the low rumble of an animal about to strike.

The Ivory folds his arms over his chest again. "Anything you have to say to me, you can say in front of my staff."

Wait… I'm *his staff??*

Velle's eyes drop to me once more. But he quickly gives up the request for privacy, likely knowing it'll go nowhere. He stalks closer to Manuel Blanco, and Kent pulls his gun. But again, The Ivory lifts a hand.

All focus in the room is on the two men who are breeding so much tension-wrapped hostility, it's becoming difficult to breathe.

"I've had enough," Velle snarls at the Warden's face. So quiet, it's barely audible.

"Are you ready to apologize?" The Ivory croons.

Velle looks to be near boiling point. "*Thirteen* goddamn years… And this is the thanks I get?!"

"I told you what would happen if you disobeyed me, Jonathan…" The Ivory hums, and my eyes widen.

Oh, shit…

Jonathan.

John Chevelle. Duh. Wow, I feel thick.

"Don't fucking gaslight me," Velle hisses. "You started this. I want them *gone,* or so help me—"

"So help you *what?*" The Ivory snarls.

Velle pushes in closer to his face. "This island is as much mine as it is yours. I built this fucking place, and I can tear it down just as easily. Don't *fuck* with me."

The Ivory's jaw tics. His eyes harden, black as death and just as ominous. He steps forward, getting into Velle's face until they're barely a breath apart. The rest of us are frozen solid while they stare one another down, rage crackling between them like electricity.

"Watch your fucking tone, Officer," The Ivory simmers. "I'm very aware of your Achilles *heels*… Both of them."

"Your threats don't mean shit," Velle grunts. "I. Want. Them. Gone. Or they'll all end up six feet under, starting with that prick Pedroia."

The Ivory's fist tightens and releases at his side, and Velle looks like he's seconds from lunging. I should probably get out of the way, lest I inadvertently wind up in the middle of a brawl.

"You don't give orders in this building anymore, Jonathan," The Ivory utters, deadly soft, right over Velle's mouth. "You lost that right when you forgot your place at *my fucking feet.*"

"Fuck you!" Velle spits. "This is your last chance… *Manuel.*"

"I swear to God, I will end you!" The Ivory roars, grabbing Velle by the throat.

Velle rips his hand away, launching into The Ivory, backing him against his desk. The Ivory smacks Velle across the face.

Velle makes another move, but I can't see a thing anymore. Their limbs are flying around, curses and bellows of rage bouncing off the walls. Kent is instantly between them, wrenching them apart.

"Enough, both of you!" Yari wails, on his feet while I slink out of my chair, shuffling across the room. "Can't you just calm down and have a *rational* discus—"

"Stay out of it!" they both bark at him in unison.

Velle rips out of Kent's hold, chest heaving. He eyes the Warden, pure wrath seeping from his pores. Manuel Blanco pushes his hair back into place, attempting to compose himself. I've never seen him so angry, but also so… affected.

I could've sworn he was made up of pure evil, but I don't think evil has to force itself not to care.

"I told you, I'm not your pet anymore," Velle breathes out. "I meant it. But I promise you this… I'll be the worst mistake you ever made."

The Ivory cocks his head. "You could've had it all. I gave you a life, a home, a *purpose*. And in return, all I asked was that you serve me, faithfully…"

"Fuck you," Velle snarls. "You don't own me—"

"*Loyalty*, you ungrateful fucking shit," The Ivory snaps. "It's *everything*. But you spit in my face." His glower is baleful, tone chilling. "Now, as far as I'm concerned, you, your men, your *partners*… You're already dead."

Velle's eyes are narrowed to slits as he grouses, "Not yet."

Turning, he storms out of the room, not without first casting a glare right at me. I'm uncertain what it means, but I *do* know that he doesn't care much for me. He must be even more suspicious of me now that he's seen me by The Ivory's side…

As soon as the door hurls shut, we all release a collective breath. Everyone but Manuel Blanco.

He stomps over to a different door, whipping it open and stalking inside—it looks like an attached en suite. He slams the door so hard the walls rattle. I glance at Yari, who's chewing on his bottom lip. Kent is staring out the window.

What in the bloody hell just happened??

Apparently, there's a lot more to the discord between Team Velle and Team Ivory. History, manipulation, bad blood…

I swear to God, being on this island is like being in The Godfather.

A loud, guttural roar startles me, and I look at the door. Yari flinches when something crashes, things banging and smashing in there.

"Can I go…?" I whisper to Kent, who shakes his head.

A moment later, Manuel Blanco emerges from the loo, straightening his collar and smoothing back his hair. He strides calmly to his desk, taking a seat.

We're all just gaping at him, waiting for some indication of what he wants us to do as he picks up his phone, fingers working quickly on the screen. The only sounds to be heard are the clicks of his typing.

Many tense moments later, he finally speaks. "I want Officer Chevelle and his team removed from the mansion." His gaze lifts to Kent. "They're being evicted. Effective immediately."

Clearing my head feels necessary.

After that bizarre, highly tense visit with The Ivory, I decided to take a walk, since it's the only thing I can do, shy of returning to my cell and burdening Byron with this rubbish.

Still, it's hard to feel grateful for *anything* when every inch of leeway seems like another foot of rope forming the noose currently around my neck.

I've become quite familiar with the maze of these hallways over the last few weeks, exploring the ins and outs, the corridors that connect from one area to another. I've learned how to avoid being seen by the occasional guard, doctor, or orderly. And I've perfected my spying. *Although, is it really spying when someone is always watching you…?*

Glancing up at the camera on the ceiling, I wonder who's on the other side. Which of The Ivory's men are following my every move… What they must think. What he's *told* them…

Stopping at the sound of yelling, I peer around a corner. There's a man in a white lab coat—*I'd assume he's a doctor, but then who would know*—exiting one of the exam rooms, rather quickly. Fleeing from the aggrieved bellows of whoever is in there.

When I'm sure the coast is clear, I slink over to peer inside the room. There's a form slumped over in an exam chair, looking exhausted and utterly tormented—burn marks all over his exposed skin, dark hair hanging in his face. His head slants, and I gulp.

It's Ren.

Not only are they holding him down here… They're experimenting on him.

I'm not surprised, but still. Seeing the state he's in gives me a strange pang in the gut. *I'm familiar with such agony.*

My mind flashes back to that day in the rec room…

"Don't try to pretend you care about anyone else…" Byron seethed at Luthor and Ren, his resentment masking obvious pain. "Especially not me. Because we all know it's a fucking lie."

The Ivory made it sound like the things that happen within these walls are all very intentional, and I'm not surprised by that either. We're all pawns in his game, from his spy, all the way down to the lying arsonist, who is apparently enough of a threat that he needs to be strapped to a chair and tortured.

Byron deserves to know about all of this. I should tell him the things I've heard, what I've witnessed…

But The Ivory was right. We're all one another has left. If I were to tell him, then it goes back to being all about *them*. But what about *me?*

I know Byron doesn't really need me… But I need him.

As long as we have each other, we don't need anyone else.

"Keep your secrets, Trevel… Don't rely on anyone to fix you…"

Ren lifts his face, but I'm gone before he can see me.

I'm rushing down a different corridor when I'm stopped by a voice.

"Is he okay?"

I peer around, because I can't tell where it's coming from. It's muffled, as if someone is speaking to me from inside one of the cells, but I don't know which one.

"Does it matter?" I respond, checking each window. "No one is *okay* in here…"

"Fair point," the voice croaks.

It sounds male, raspy yet smooth. Tired, though that's to be expected.

Who is that? It doesn't sound exactly like him, but…

"Leo…?" I murmur, stopping at a door that has no window, around a corner and set apart from the other cells.

"Sorry, no," he responds.

He's definitely inside this room, and now that I'm a bit closer, I can tell it's not Leo. This is a real person, a young man.

"Are you… a friend of The Ivory?" he asks me.

I'm taken aback by the question at first, though I don't know why. I suppose that's exactly what I am; a part of his team. On his *side*.

Beholden to the devil.

"It would appear so, wouldn't it?" I lean against the door, my mind swimming.

"You've put your trust in him?"

I purse my lips. "I wouldn't go that far…"

"So you get it, then," he goes on. "That in order to be on his *side*, you have to accept that you'll never come first. Your wants, needs… They'll all take a backseat to his. Because he is *all of it*."

I swallow hard, reeling from his words. "You sound like you know this from personal experience…"

"In a way."

Turning to face the door, I tap my knuckles on it gently. "Why are you in there?"

He's quiet for a moment before he sighs, "Revenge."

That one word… It sets my teeth on edge. Thumps my pulse in my neck.

"It's… important," I tell him, though my voice trails and I add, "Right?"

"Yes," he answers with certainty. "It is."

I breathe out of relief. But then he says, "I heard once that the best revenge is living a healthy, happy life."

"What the hell does that mean?"

He chuckles. It's a nice sound; melodious and pure. *Who is this mystery person?* "I guess it's like *rising above* or something. The best revenge is not needing it, you know?"

I frown, picking at some chipped paint on the door. "I suppose… But getting it just feels *so* bloody good."

The lad laughs again. "You're funny, bad guy. I hope you get your revenge."

For the sod of it, I try the handle on the door. It doesn't open.

But it doesn't matter, because voices up the hall alert me that it's time to go.

"You too, stranger," I whisper, my chest aching with a memory. Of Alice. "Stay safe."

I think he's mumbling something in Spanish, but I can't hear it, nor can I stick around.

Darting away, I rush back toward general population, all the while plagued by that voice, and those words. Everything that's happened today, and yesterday, since my arrival at Alabaster Pen, and even before.

Revenge has led me to a lot of places, some good, some not. But I can't deny that if it weren't for the terrible things I've experienced, I wouldn't be here right now…

In this dingy, awful prison. With the most intoxicating person I've ever met.

The lights are already out in the row as I'm entering our cell, slipping inside quietly. Despite the darkness, I can see the lump that is Byron Kang, who's curled up in his bed.

My exquisitely damaged shadowman.

Stepping over to the bunk bed, I pause with my hands on the ladder. But it takes only a moment to decide, and then I'm crawling into his bed.

The flimsy mattress dips at my weight, and Byron shifts, his eyes gleaming up at me. "You're back..."

I don't respond, simply nestle up beside him. And to my surprise, and delight, he doesn't ask why I'm in his bed, nor does he gripe at me to leave. He spins to face me.

Letting out a soft breath, I stare, riveted, losing myself in the depths of his gaze. There are so many things I want to say to him, so much I'd love for him to understand.

He deserves to know who I am... How I feel about him.

But I'm... so very afraid.

Grazing my thumb over his full bottom lip, I whisper, "Don't stop me."

And he doesn't.

My mouth covers his, and I kiss him, softly but insistently enough that he releases a small whine. It sets me ablaze, the darkness melting away.

I can't even fathom it, but there are torrents of light behind my eyes as I fall to pieces with his lips on mine.

Nothing has *ever* felt as good as *finally* kissing him.

"Oh, *Byron*," I purr, sucking on his perfect mouth like candy. "My taste of decadent fury..."

He opens for me, giving me his tongue. I give mine back, and they stroke while our lips brush, suck and bruise.

"Trevel, *baby*," he whimpers, sliding a possessive hand up my chest, then my neck, into my hair.

This is unlike anything else, somehow hotter than our hottest sex. All the deliciously dirty things we've done together were just that—carnality, above all else.

But *this* is passion. A fervent yearning for something deeper than just our bodies craving pleasure. God help us... But this is far from casual.

Dooming our fate or not, Byron and I are *kissing*.

We do it for so long, our mouths go numb.

CHAPTER TWENTY-SIX

Byron

A STORM IS COMING.

We've been hearing about it, bits and pieces of conversation from the guards. It reminds me of the last big storm we had here… The night the power went out.

To think that used to be a secret… Something that existed only inside my brain and my journal.

Not anymore. Now all of my wild experiences, my *truths*, are also floating around inside the pretty head resting on my chest.

My fingers absentmindedly sift through Trevel's dark, messy hair. It's tickling my skin, but I like it. I like how quiet he is right now, half conscious and unburdened by whatever it is that gives him those awful night terrors.

I think it's clear that he's been through some shit, the extent of which has marred his otherwise brilliant mind. The dude is seriously smart as hell. I'm sort of amazed by him in a lot of ways… I just wish I understood it more.

I wish I knew him more.

He knows *so* much about me, and yet I don't know dick about him. Aside from his dick, that is. *I know that thing pretty damn well at this point.*

I've been holding back from asking Trevel about himself and his past. Trying to keep my distance, because I felt like it would preserve the mystery, and keep this thing casual.

The less I know about him, the more I can keep telling myself it's just about the sex.

But lately, it's been shifting. The sex has been coming to life; growing a heartbeat. It's real now, a living, breathing organism bred between us. I don't know what that means, but I can't help feeling the tiniest twinge of excitement amidst the fear.

Last night, we kissed. And I mean, *kissed.* A lot. Deep and hot and... *God, so good.* A makeout session that led not to sex, but to us falling asleep tangled in one another. And it's freaking me out, because if the physical stuff is changing... what does that mean for the rest of it?

What are we doing? Are we really just cellmates in prison who fuck and cuddle and make out? Is that even a thing??

And if we're becoming more, shouldn't I know more about him? *Like why he freaks out and chokes me in his sleep?*

It's later in the day, and we've yet to be brought anywhere, so we're kind of just lounging in bed. *My* bed. Trevel is curled around me, and despite knowing I should probably get up, I can't make myself break this spell. It's too warm, too comfortable, too... nice.

It worries me how good this feels.

A chuckle rumbles into my chest from his, which obviously means he's no longer dozing.

"What?" I ask, still playing with his silky black strands.

"Nothing," he breathes peacefully. "Just remembering your whole *'this won't be a cuddlefest'* speech."

I pull a scowl to disguise the grin. "Fuck off."

"Such a sweet talker," he growls, suddenly shifting. He rolls over, pinning me to the mattress, his hand rushing up my bare chest. In an instant, my heart is flying. "Tell me more about how this is just to pass the time, needy boy..."

A whimper leaves me, against my will, as he drags his crotch between my legs. And again, like a reflex, my legs are spreading for him.

It's absolutely wild, but he brings out this yearning in me I never knew was there. Buzzing for the hurt, desperate to be overpowered and controlled, while still being able to control him... *Is that a thing?*

I guess we're just versatile, in our sex and our kinks. And I like it.

I like our back and forth. *The power struggle is... exhilarating.*

I don't think I stand a chance of resisting this. I wanted it outside of prison... Inside? I'm fucking *feral* for it.

Trevel's lips fall to my throat, peppering it with kisses accompanied by the word *mine*. I'm all too prepared to get slutty, when a noise up the row signals someone, most likely one of the Warden's guards, coming in to cockblock.

Trevel whines, dropping his face into the crook of my neck, "Fuckin hell..." Chuckling, I rub his shoulders. "They may not make us stop if we're mid-fuck." He lifts his head to peek down at me, cocking a dark brow.

"As tempting as that sounds, I think we gave more than enough of a show in the showers the other day," I hum.

"You liked that," he croons. "I know you did."

I can feel a flush creeping up my neck into my cheeks as I squirm beneath him. "Shut up. Get off me before I knee you in the balls..."

"God, baby... I love your hostility," he sighs, pecking my jaw once, twice, thrice, before he reluctantly pulls off of me.

I roll my eyes at him, but my body is proving his point when I have to wait a few seconds to stand up because my dick is rock-solid.

We play innocent when one of the robot minions shows up, not that he cares what we were doing. He just drags us out for another silent excursion.

Making the trip I've made hundreds of times over the last three years, I'm up in my thoughts. Considering how much it's all changed and wondering if this is the new normal.

Is this how it's going to be... forever?

Anxiety is thrumming in my bloodstream as we approach a couple of the other new guards. They're herding a small group of inmates in the direction we're coming from, and my heart clunks aggressively when I see Luthor, shuffling along by himself.

Fuck. He looks so sad. It's awful.

I've seen Luthor sad before, more often than I wish I had. But there's a new level of misery in this... Because unlike those other times, now we're moving in opposite directions.

Our eyes meet as we pass one another, the silence seeming to stretch and warp the air of the dank hallway. It lasts only a few seconds, but the sorrow in his luminous gaze still manages to slice me deep. Not anger, nor malice.

Just brilliant green regret.

I'm...

Luthor, I'm...

My lips are parted, but it's too late. He's already gone.

Not that it would matter... *We can't fucking speak anyway.*

I'm up in my thoughts the entire time we're showering. Being in here, just like everything else, is so different now. I can't lie and say I don't enjoy showering with Trevel—it's sinfully satisfying in the best fucking way. But being in this spot *now*, where so much of our time was spent over the years, attacks my heart with longing for the way things *were*...

The way Ren used to fuck around, always flirting and messing with us. How Luthor used to scold him and pretend he didn't like it. *I guess we both secretly did.*

I *miss* it. I miss Joy's sarcasm and quick wit, Rook's kindness and empathy, and the giant douchebag himself... Believe it or not, I actually *miss* John Chevelle. His loud barking orders, and his cocky abrasive tendencies, but most of all, his stability. I miss being able to count on him. Whether it was good or bad, he was always there.

And now he's gone. They all are.

Technically, they're still *here*. They're no longer a part of everyday life in this life sentence.

Jasper, Hancock, Peters... Hell, even Linetti and Brenner. I haven't seen them in weeks, and it's fucking crazy, but I miss them all. To get so used to people at the forefront, only for them to fade into the background, is jarring. *No wonder people hate change so much... It sucks.*

I just hope they're finding some way to get by, too.

On our way back, Equino stops us before we can enter the row.

"Jefe says you're to see the doctor," he grumbles at Trevel.

Trevel looks surprised. I can practically hear him thinking, *Right now??* But he covers it up quickly and nods. "Fine. But he's coming with me." He juts his thumb in my direction.

Equino glares at him for a moment, but eventually concedes with a curt purse of his lips. He glances up at the camera, then back to us. "Bueno. Just don't forget... They'll be watching."

"Yea, yea. *Big Brother.* We got it," Trevel mumbles, tugging me along.

We move through the corridors, heading in the direction of the East Wing. Since Trevel walks around here nonstop, he's apparently found some shortcuts he likes. And as seems to be my default lately, I'm just following his lead.

"Isn't it weird to be coming down here so late?" I ask, sort of thinking out loud. "Something seems... off."

"I'll say," Trevel glances around. "Do you hear that?"

We stop walking for a moment and listen. He's right. The winds are whipping outside, an audible storm raging just beyond the walls.

"Shit..." I murmur. "I wonder if we'll lose power like last time."

"Hmm... Right," he grumbles, giving me the side-eye. *"Last time."*

"What's your problem?" I grunt, noting a darkness in his purple eyes, and a sudden intensity framing his features.

"Nothing," he bites out. But doesn't elaborate. *As usual.*

I can *tell* he wants to say something, but he always forces himself not to. I can't say it's not annoying, because it definitely is. I've given him as much information as you can give a person.

If he refuses to do the same for me, then fuck it. I'm not gonna beg.

I guess he doesn't trust me... The way I trust him, despite him doing very little to actually earn it.

The mood between us has flipped in an instant. My despondence from earlier is mixing with the insecurities that follow my relationship with Trevel around like a shadow, until we're both simmering and restless.

We come to a spot where the corridor splits. Trevel moves up to one door, but I hang back.

"Isn't this way faster?" I nod at the other door.

He blinks. "No."

My gaze narrows. *I'm pretty sure it is.*

Before we can argue about it any further, the door beside me bursts open, startling us both. Joy creeps through, pausing when she sees us—just standing around, visibly agitated.

"Oh... hey," she mumbles suspiciously, eyes flicking between me and Trevel.

"Hey," I sigh. I can't even help it; I'm lighting up in her presence. "You're a sight for sore eyes. How have you been?"

Joy's clearly edgier than usual, glancing at Trevel like she's hesitant to speak in front of him. It's keying up my frustration even more.

I'm forever caught in the middle of this bullshit I didn't ask to be.

Trevel must catch on to Joy's distrust, because he scoffs and rolls his eyes, going for the opposite door. "Why don't I just give you two some privacy..."

His tone has a serious bite to it, but he's gone before I can say anything, leaving me staring in the direction he disappeared.

"Wow, so Velle wasn't exaggerating, huh?" Joy shakes her head. "You and emo Mick Jagger are an item now? Just flitting around, free as two little lovebirds while the rest of this place is a blazing goddamn dumpster fire??"

I narrow my gaze at her, irritation causing fidgets in my limbs. "What the fuck is wrong with you guys?? I'm not *doing* anything. We're down here to see Dr. Love. It's not like we're having a fucking party..."

"Dr. Love's not here," she mutters. "He's gone for the night."

I give her a puzzled look. *Why would The Ivory tell us to come see him if he's gone?? Maybe he doesn't know...?*

"Whatever. You're proving my point," I grunt. "*Felix* fucking *Darcey* has been freely strutting around this place for *months*. His sketchy boyfriend is *technically* still on The Ivory's roster, but they're treated like the goddamn president and first fucking lady of Alabaster Isle! You know he sleeps in the mansion, right? Darcey?"

Her brow arches. "Who told you that? Benedict Arnold Cumberbatch over there?"

My scowl deepens. "What difference does it make?! You guys are all butthurt that Trevel works for The Ivory... Well, guess what?? We *all* work for The fucking Ivory! Excuse me for finding someone who likes me for *me*... For the first time since I've been here, I'm someone's main priority. And my *friends*, the people who supposedly care about me *so much*, are out here trying to make me feel bad about it! *Fuck* that."

Growling, I rake my fingers through my hair, pulling in breaths while attempting to calm myself down before I really flip the fuck out. "Side with Darcey and Dr. Love all you want, but at the end of the day, they're here for *themselves*, just like the rest of us. They'll dime on you to save their own asses, I guaran-fucking-tee it. There's no honor among thieves, *jeulgeoun*."

By the end of my tirade, I'm exhausted. My heart is jackhammering, and I just want to lie down. I never thought finding someone who makes me happy would require this much fight.

Is that really what Trevel is...?

Someone who... makes me happy?

How can I tell? I guess if thinking it is a reflex, it must be true...

Blinking hard, I shake the thought away. Joy is chewing on her lower lip, looking all manners of distraught. I didn't notice it as much before, but she's visibly exhausted, and rigid with obvious stress. Maybe she was those things before, but never this noticeably.

"I'm sorry," we both say at the same time, then chuckle. And sniff.

We're so similar in so many ways, which is why we've clicked since day one. I truly love her as a friend, and it *kills* not to be as close as we once were.

"I don't want to fight," she murmurs. "Not with you."

"Funny, considering how many times you've kicked my ass," I tease, and she grins.

"Hey, you got your licks in." She wiggles her brows, and I scoff.

"Pervert."

"Seriously, though," she says. "How are you holding up? Better than your boys, I'm sure…"

My forehead lines in obvious confusion, the twinge of guilt that's been living in my gut since my fight with Luthor and Ren growing rapidly into a churn of acidic remorse. Naturally, it makes me defensive.

"I'm just fucking breathing, like I've been doing since the moment I got here." I struggle to tone down the hostility. "What do you want me to say? They separated us… I haven't seen either of them since that day in the rec room."

The look on her face is worrying, and I'm bracing for impending pain. She has something to say, I can feel it. But she's holding back too, and it's gutting me.

So she doesn't trust me either now??

Joy scrapes hands over her face, those black tactical fingerless gloves she always wears lingering on her eyes. "Listen, I love you, but you'll have to forgive us for being skeptical of your new boyfriend. I'm fucking exhausted… We all are. I haven't slept in days… *weeks*, who fucking knows anymore. They kicked us out of the mansion last night, so it's been—"

"They kicked you out of the mansion??" I gasp.

I had no idea…

I've been so wrapped up in my violet-eyed stranger, I've barely noticed that everything around me is deteriorating. And I'm momentarily awed by how much he's distracted me. How *deeply* Trevel Fenwick has sunk inside me and filled up all those vacant places.

"If you think Trevel had anything to do with it, you're high," I mumble. "He wouldn't…" My words trail off, and I swallow.

Would he…?

A noise pings—like a phone chime. Joy straightens, and my brow furrows.

"Gotta go." She squeezes my shoulder. "Keep your guard up, *gwi-yeoun sonyeon*."

"I… will." My words are left fluttering in the air as she darts through a different door.

I'm frozen solid for minutes, recoiling at the fact that I clearly don't know shit anymore.

What am I doing??

I'm a stalker, for fuck's sake. I'm best at falling back and observing details. How could I have been so blind to all of this?

Maybe because someone covered my eyes…

Finally forcing my legs into motion, I wander, distracted, in the direction Trevel went, all the while obsessing over the events of the last few months.

All of my friends, either leaving, or dying, or betraying me. And I'm left with only one person—the mysterious stranger who arrived just in time to pick up the pieces.

It seems… almost too perfect to be a coincidence.

I spot Trevel up the corridor, propped against the wall, staring blankly at the floor. He notices me right away, uncoiling as I approach him slowly. I peek at the door he's standing beside, a nameplate on it that reads *Dr. Lemuel Love, PhD.*

My gaze flits to Trevel, and the first thing I see in his eyes is an uncharacteristic flash of guilt. But it vanishes quickly enough, replaced by a forced indifference.

"He's not in there… is he?" I blink at him.

The mound of his throat dips visibly. "Doesn't seem to be."

We stare at each other in silence for a moment. There are a lot of things I want to say… Questions I want to ask. And I think he can sense it.

Trevel turns and knocks on the door, sort of jittery as he presses his ear up to it. I don't hear anything from where I'm standing, and I assume he doesn't either because he grabs the handle and whips the door open, striding inside the office.

As I peer up and down the hallway, something feels off. It's *too* quiet. There's a vibe in the air I can't explain that has me tensing all over, like a fight response lying in wait.

Reluctantly, I follow Trevel inside Dr. Love's office. As expected, it's empty.

"Joy said he was done for the day," I rumble.

Trevel pauses his snooping to glare at me. "Did she, then?" I nod. "What else did she have to say?"

I'm taken aback by the severity on his face. "Why does it matter?"

"So you're keeping secrets again?" He looks both hurt and enraged.

"I'm not the only one…" I whisper.

His jaw clenches visibly. "I'm going to look for Felix Darcey."

He brushes past me, out of the office. Of course, I follow him.

Why am I always blindly following him…?

"Why do you need to find Felix Darcey?" I power-walk after him while he strides swiftly up the long corridors, toward Darcey's room.

"Because this is all his fault," he seethes, barely audibly.

"*What* is…?"

"Everything, Byron!" he snaps, screeching to a halt and whipping in my direction. I almost crash into him. "Bloody *everything* is his fault, you know that! I thought we were on the same page. But now… I'm not sure *what* you want."

My lashes flutter up at him. I have no idea what he's talking about, but I'm tense and overflowing with apprehension. "I don't know… what you want me to say."

"Yea, no shit," he grunts, spinning away from me to resume his storming up the hall.

What is his problem??

If anything, I should be mad at him…

I should be… fucking suspicious of him, goddamnit! Just like everyone else is. Not allowing him to fucking own *me without a single shred of hesitation.*

It makes no sense to be so happy… out of fucking nowhere.

It can't be real.

I mean, look at me! I'm chasing *after him… It's fucked!*

He's not *Michelangelo.*

I can hear the wind thrashing against the building, even stronger than before, as we stalk the halls. The faint sound of pelting rain is accompanied by the occasional rumble of thunder shaking the walls.

The feeling is mutual.

We reach Felix Darcy's room, and Trevel doesn't even knock. He just bursts inside.

"Aha!" he shouts, frowning when we find this one also empty.

"*Aha*? Really?" I snort.

He looks like he wants to grin, but he's stopping himself. It's cute, and that's annoying me even more.

Trevel folds his arms across his chest. "Your friends don't trust me."

My head cocks.

"I know it's true. You and Joy couldn't even talk with me around…"

"Do you blame her?" I retort. "You *work* for The Ivory. I mean, you're here as his spy, for fuck's sake. Did you think they'd just welcome you with open arms??"

"That's not why I'm here..." he grumbles, tone deep and containing his frustrations.

"How would I know??" I bark, getting up in his face. So close, I can see his pupils dilating. "I don't know *shit* about you, Trevel. You could be a figment of my goddamn imagination for all I know!"

Something about those words flips a switch. In a flash, he's no longer containing his rage. It's lit the hell up, sparking his violet gaze and illuminating his sharp features.

"Could a figment of your imagination make you come *crying*?" he growls in my face, wicked amusement dancing on his lips as they hover over mine.

"Maybe," I hum out of stubborn agitation.

The lights flicker, and we both glance up at them before returning to our stare-down.

"You think I'm lying to you, Raphael?" he snarls, dangerously quiet.

"You wouldn't be the first liar I—" My voice dries up, and I gulp. "Do you know where Ren is?" I'm unable to mask the accusatory tone.

His blazing gaze narrows. "Why would I?"

"I don't know..." I'm stiff, but my eyes are pleading, *desperate* for it not to be true...

I really don't want to believe he'd lie to me about something like this. But I can't shake this gnawing feeling...

"Why would I keep that from you, Byron?" he growls.

"Because... maybe you were trying to protect me," I stammer. His eyes soften. "Or maybe you're jealous..."

"Oh, I'm most definitely jealous," he bites out, and my brows jump. "I mean, you've really spread yourself around in here, my sweet fury."

What... the... fuck.

Fast, wrathful indignation sweeps me up, and I seethe, "Fuck you. Are you calling me a fucking slut??"

His hand curls around my throat. "If the mask fits, baby..."

"Shut the fuck up!" I rip away, shoving him hard in the chest. "What the fuck do you know anyway?? You're a fucking *stranger* to me."

Pain flashes in his eyes, filling my mouth with remorse. But I hate it because I'm *right*. It's true...

I *don't* fucking know him.

"You don't know who I am...?" Trevel hisses, getting back in my face. "Is that right?"

"Fucking *correct*," I growl.

He goes for my neck again, but I keep fighting him off. "Well, maybe you should just think that through, warrior… Because if you don't *know* me, then who's been draining your balls all these nights? Huh??" He's coming at me quick, grabbing my shirt and my face while I block him and shove him away. "Who have you been letting inside your sweet little pussy, Raphael?!"

"Fuck you!" I roar, vision splattering red. Without hesitation, my arm cocks and I slap him. *Hard*, right across the face. *Like a fucking bitch.* "*Fuck you*, you goddamn head case fucking cunt!"

I slap him again, even harder. His face flings, and he stumbles, clutching his cheek. When he turns back to me, he's grinning, his lip split and bloody. Licking it, he lets out a deranged cackle. Like a fucking psychopath.

I swallow a mouthful of unease.

This dude is insane. Am I gonna have to beat him into the ground right now?? I don't want to…

We're staring at each other, chests heaving, for no more than a few seconds, though it feels like hours.

"Hit me again…" Trevel whispers, tone low and more sinister than anything I've heard before.

My eyes widen, forehead lined. "What?!"

He lunges forward, and I back up. "You want to, baby, I know you do… I deserve to bleed for hurting you, sweet fury…"

"What the fuck…" I breathe out, ducking and stumbling away from him.

This feels like the last time we fought, only way worse. Because *he's* making this happen, and I don't fucking get it… Why he'd rather take a beating from me than just be *honest* with me.

"*Please*, Byron…" He grabs my arm, eyes alight with anguish I just don't *understand*. This teetering scale of misery and rage is too much for me.

"You're unbelievable." I scoff, spinning away from him.

Storming up the hall, I'm quaking, fists balled at my sides. Just praying that he lets me go…

"Byron, wait," he grunts, coming after me.

So I take off running.

I've gotta get away from this…

"Oh, you're running from me now??" he growls from behind me.

"Screw you, *Leo!*" I snap, sprinting up the hall and barreling through the door. "You don't want me to see you?? *Fine*. You're invisible."

The music of a vicious storm is audible through the cold concrete, winding me up even tighter. I'm riddled with heavy thoughts and bustling emotions, and it's more than I'm equipped to handle. Running is easier.

Running, I'm used to.

I don't know where I'm going, but I'm barely paying attention, and I don't care. I just need to get away from Trevel fucking Fenwick. Away from the memories in this goddamn building, the feelings I'm too afraid to confront and all of this psycho shit—how *unhinged* he makes me feel.

Fuck it all.

Racing the halls while the lights flicker, I'm heaving for breath. I grab the next handle and turn, slamming my weight against the door. It whips open… And my entire body goes still in shock.

It's outside.

The door opened to… *outside.*

I'm gaping in disbelief. Staring at… *out.*

A gravel path leading out to a small road. Trees off in the distance. Wet dirt and leaves. Raindrops.

I can *smell* it all, and it's the most overwhelming sensation I've ever experienced. Smelling the ocean air and rain and wet earth for the first time in *three years.*

"What the fuck…" I gasp, blinking over and over.

Am I hallucinating?? How is this happening right now??

"Well… bollocks," Trevel mutters from behind me, pausing his pursuit to marvel at this crazy shit with me.

Slanting my face, I gape at him. His eyes are also round and mystified, though there's a shade of nervousness to them.

"How is this possible?" I shiver from nerves and the cold air hitting my skin. "Why would they… let us open this door?"

"They wouldn't," Trevel rumbles suspiciously.

He glances up at the ceiling, and I follow his line of sight. The camera is slumped downward. No red light to indicate that it's *on.*

I squint at it. "Do you think… the storm knocked out the servers?"

I'm fizzling with a sudden thrill, peering out into the world beyond these prison walls.

"This is…" Trevel's baffled, breathy words cut off when I step through the doorway. I'm half out when he grabs me by the wrist. "Wait!"

"*Wait?*" I grunt. "Are you kidding me?!"

Lightning illuminates the sky, catching my attention.

"Byron…" He slides his fingers through mine, filling me with warmth.

I peek at him, his violet irises much calmer than a moment ago. It's not placating… But it *is* electrifying.

Thunder rumbles.

"You want me, Trevel…?" I whisper. His head cocks as his tongue slides over his bottom lip. "Then you'll have to catch me first."

Slipping out of his hold, I'm outside and sprinting in a flash.

Holy shit…

Holy fucking *shit!*

Feet pounding the dirt, cold rain hitting my face, my pulse rocks my insides. I can't believe I'm doing this. I can't believe I'm *out*.

I'm fucking outside!

I have no idea where I'm going or what I'm doing, but I can't deny that just being out here feels incredible. Even if I were to get caught right now, it'd be worth it for five minutes of jogging outside in the elements.

"Byron!" Trevel roars from somewhere behind me. I nearly stumble over my feet. "Get back here, you sweet little twat!"

A morbid smirk tugs at my lips as I huff, running faster, toward the forest. Based on the sound of his footsteps, he's probably less than twenty feet back. A chill sweeps through me, like a current of the electricity crackling in the sky.

The fear and adrenaline… the *arousal*. I can't fight it; how enticing it feels to be running from him. To be *chased* by him.

I wonder what he'll do if he catches me…

Once in the woods, a bit of anxiety lessens. There are trees surrounding me, which means plenty of cover. My mind races as fast as my feet, but the farther I get from the prison, the less worry I feel.

I just need to get away from there.

That place is the problem. It's been the fucking problem for three goddamn years.

Out here, I'm free of chains for real. *Not just an illusion made by Manuel Blanco as some favor to Trevel.*

I don't care what I have to do, I'm staying out here.

Obviously, I've never been out here before. I've never seen anything on this island outside of Alabaster Penitentiary. But I know there's a mansion, and I know it's on the other side of the island. I also know that the entire island is only a couple of miles across, and while my cardio is pretty rusty, I know I can run two miles in less than fifteen minutes.

Regardless of what's happening in the prison, despite knowing what The Ivory could do to me if he finds out, *right now* I'm free.

Finally... I'm fucking free.

"Byron!" Trevel hollers again. "You'll regret running from me, baby, I *promise.*"

I don't understand it, but my balls throb.

I'm higher than I have been in years. This rush... *Fuck, I missed it.*

The stalking. Breaking into his rich-boy townhouse to tie him up and fuck him like a possession...

Rain is soaking into my hair, and I'm panting. Slinking behind a tree, I pause to catch my breath, peeking around it for any sign of Trevel. But I don't see him.

The mansion is visible up ahead, just through the trees—probably less than half a mile. There's a cluster of stone buildings and structures leading up to it. And along the shore, a baroque monstrosity of luxurious alabaster.

The Ivory Mansion. That's it.

Wow... It's breathtaking.

A twig snaps, and my pulse pops. *He's close...*

"Warrior..." Trevel sings. "Come out and *play.*"

It's so difficult for me not to snort at that reference to one of my favorite movies. But I force my lips together and slip, quietly, around the other side of the tree.

Yea, great. So we happen to like a few of the same movies and bands. Like *The Warriors*, and *The Princess Bride*, *The Used* and *Northstar—weird that almost all of them start with "The."*

I *do* know things about him, but it's all superficial, and that was the point I was trying to get across... *Though our argument has seemingly taken a backseat to him chasing me through the woods like The Big, Bad Wolf.*

"You can run, but you can't hide!" he bellows.

I mean, come on.

Dashing as quickly and quietly as possible, I weave between trees, with the Ivory Mansion in my sights. There's something of a house just ahead. Not part of the mansion per se, most likely staff quarters or something. I creep closer to get a better look.

There are vines and strange flowers crawling all over the exterior of the building made of weathered stone, interesting, being that it's technically winter. I have to say, it doesn't feel cold at all right now... *Maybe it's because I'm running.*

Either way, it's a beautiful sight, in spite of the decay. Reaching forward, I run my fingers over the wet rock.

But then I'm tackled to the ground.

In an instant, Trevel is on top of me, pinning me to the forest floor.

"Did you really think you could escape me, sweet fury?" he hisses, holding my arms down while I fight against him. "I'm not like the others. You can't just flutter your pretty self in front of me then yank it away. You're *mine*, Byron."

My heart thumps wildly, chest heaving to match his. Black strands of wet hair hang in his eyes, his white t-shirt soaked through and clinging to his muscles. He looks manic. Psychotic.

Sexy… so so sexy.

I swallow, writhing beneath him as he leans over my face to breathe, "Only. Fucking. Mine."

A soft groan leaves me, but I growl to cover it, using all of my strength to fight him off. He's stronger than he looks, and despite my training instincts, I'm not overpowering him.

Because I'm not really trying to…

I think I like this.

"You like when it hurts…"

We're burning so hot, puffs of steam drifting from our ragged breaths. Raindrops tumble over his lips, falling onto mine. I lick them.

I wanted him to catch me.

He's my *stalker… Chasing what he wants in the dark.*

"You gonna be a good boy for me?" he growls, thrusting his big cock between my legs. My own dick is pulsing at the sensation.

"Fuck you," I spit, eyes hooded as I gaze up at him.

"Fuck me?" he rumbles, pinning my wrists with one hand while the other runs down to cup my cock.

"*God*, fuck you…" I whimper, then snarl, "Get off…"

"You're so fucking beautiful," he groans, then kisses my lips hard, forcing his tongue between them.

I'm still fighting him, and I don't even think it's an act. I'm split down the middle, between wanting this and knowing with full certainty that as good as it feels right now, it'll most likely rough me the fuck up in the end.

"I'm not yours," I grunt hoarsely. "You don't own me, Trevel."

"Please," he scoffs, flipping me effortlessly onto my stomach. "Just wait until my cock is in your fucking stomach and you're *begging* me to breed you nice and deep… Then we'll see who you belong to, won't we, sweet whore?"

God, what the fuck…

My balls throb so hard it hurts, precum leaking from my cock at his degrading words paired with that… treasuring touch.

Trevel tugs my hands behind my back, and I whine from the pain. But my dick is *aching*, trapped between my body and the mushy, saturated ground. He rips my pants down quick, exposing my ass to the cool air, my face flushing so hot I'm melting. I try to push back, but he stuffs me harder into leaves and dirt.

Turning my face, I glimpse him pulling out his cock and spitting into his palm.

"W-wait…" I sputter, nerves bunching me up all over.

"Nope," he hisses, pressing wet fingers between my cheeks. "Don't fight, furious boy. If you open up, it'll hurt less."

Fuck… fuck fuck fuck.

My head is spinning. I'm panting and purring and… arching up to him. But pretending I'm not.

Fuck, what is this?

I feel like… Michelangelo.

Longing to be chased and cherished, and hurt. To ache with the pleasure of being fucked like a possession.

His possession.

Trevel slams his cock into my ass, without any priming or warming me up. The force of it crushes air from my lungs, and I choke, "*Ffuck…* Jesus…"

"Uhh… *yes*," he mewls above me, voice cracking as he shoves in me deeper with a powerful thrust. "Fuckin' hell, baby… *Take* it."

A guttural groan escapes my shivering lips at the intense burn. No lube, no easing me into it. Just some spit and a *huge*, hard cock tunneling its way inside my body.

"*Unnghh!*" I whine when he drags back, driving in again, *deeper*. So deep his pelvis is on my cheeks. "Fuuuck… ummfff…"

"You sweet, perfect hole…" Grabbing a fistful of my hair, he yanks my head back. "You like when I ride it raw?"

I nod, tears streaming down my cheeks with the rain and salty air as he pulls and pushes, pumping me full of cock from behind. The burn and stretch are almost insufferable. *So much more intense than last time…*

But my dick is engorged beneath me, arousal seeping out in pulses. *Fuck, I think I'm already coming.*

Trevel releases my hands to hold me by the throat, hauling my hips back so that I'm on my knees. As soon as I'm in this position, he's fucking into me rough. Not a moment to adjust, brutal thrusts driving my body back into the ground. I can't hold myself up, arms shaking, knees sore.

He whips his shirt off, then pulls mine off, melding his wet muscles to my back while he licks and bites my nape.

This sex is feral. We're wild animals, fucking in the forest. Grunting, skin slapping as he takes me from behind like a menace. A beast. A wicked, insatiable fiend.

"You don't belong to me?" he hisses as he viciously bucks his cock into my ass.

I nod, but croak, "N-no… I d-don't…" He bites me, and I whimper, "Fuck… you… Uhh*fuuuck* me."

Trevel hums, covering my mouth with his hand. "Now who's lying? I think it's the bitch on his knees taking a big dick."

God… damn…

God damn god damn god damn.

I can feel myself winding, racing to an orgasm that's *oh-so close*. I reach for my dick, but Trevel rips my hand away.

"Uh-uh." His voice is as uneven as mine from the way he's pounding me. "You come when I say you come…"

"You don't… own my… *ohhfuck*." My mumbling beneath his hand fades as the fat crown of his cock jams at my prostate.

Over, and over… *and over.*

"Mmm, I think I do." His forehead drops onto my shoulder, and he groans. "Look at you… Taking this raw cock, clamping on it like a slut."

"Unleash on me, baby…" I plead, eyes rolling back in my skull.

Everything below my waist is going numb, loins coiled up tight, ready to erupt.

But just as I'm about to get my reward for enduring this rough pounding, he pulls out. Pulling the rug out from under my climax.

"Ffuck… w-what…" I whine as I melt into the ground.

Trevel chuckles sadistically, and I really wish it wasn't *so* damn sexy.

He flips me onto my back, ripping my soaking wet pants off all the way off. Then he slithers out of his, leaving us naked and panting in the forest, succumbing to the storm.

"Let me show you just how *mine* you really are, sweet fury."

CHAPTER TWENTY-SEVEN

Trevel

"FUCK... YOU..."

Pain, searing through my chest. Aching and bruised.

"God, yes... Take it."

The winds whip rainfall at my back. My heart is flying, leaping so aggressively that I'm dizzy.

Or it's this fucked-up situation... Making it so I can hardly see through the fog.

"N-no..."

Pushing his legs open, I pin Byron down in the sopping leaves and dirt with my body weight, wedging myself between his thighs. It's dark, but I can still see him, the moon's glow and some nearby light from the house bathing him in dull orange.

He's flushed, trembling and... nervous. His body wants it, as evident by the way he's writhing into me, eyes hooded with lust, dick solid and stretched up to his navel, leaving a puddle on his abs.

But he's fighting me, because he knows I might hurt him. Sure, he likes the physical pain, but he's afraid of what I could do to him *inside*, and that's valid. I knew all along it would come to this...

I'm going to lose him if I don't... fight back.

Fight to keep him.

The last hour is a haze. I barely remember what led us here. All I know is that when he ran from me, I was overcome with the primal need to chase. To capture him, pin him down, and prove to him that no matter how badly it destroys us both… He'll never escape me.

I won't allow him to.

Spitting into my hand, I rub more sorry excuse for lubrication onto my cock, guiding it up to him. He's clenching, squirming in faux-protest, moist lips parted and quivering as I lean over his slick muscles to keep him down.

"Hold still," I breathe out hoarsely, giving a nice shove.

Despite his resistance, he swallows me right up, welcoming my body inside his.

Byron's back arches, eyes rolling. *"Nngghh…"*

"That's it." I drop my forehead onto his. Pushing in deeper, we groan in unison. *"Fuck*, baby, *so good*… Open up and swallow it. Every inch…"

"Uhh!" he gasps, fingers digging into the wet leaves while I pin his arms at his sides, drilling my whole cock into him with fervor. "Fffuck, I… I'm… *Mmfff*."

My heart swells at the way he's not making any sense, subdued by the pleasure he's trying so hard not to accept. He loves it, we both know that. Despite how cross he is with me, I just don't understand why he *refuses* to admit that he's mine.

Is it someone else?

Is that what this is??

He likes how we fuck, but he wishes I were

"Say my name," I growl, working in and out of him, thrusting between his legs like *I'm* his man, because that's *exactly* who the fuck I *am*.

I won't accept anything else. Fucked up or not, Byron Kang is mine.

"Mmm…" His head tips back and he bites down on his lip

Grabbing him hard by the face, I force him to look at me. *"Say it."*

"Fuck you," he gasps.

Pupils dilated, there's the purest intoxication on his face from the sensation of my cock teasing his sweet spot. His dick is huge and hard and soaking wet between us.

I know he loves this…

I slap him across the face and snarl, "Don't fuck with me, whore."

He purrs, blinking slowly as his chest heaves and his cock leaks. Blissed out from the degradation—the *pleasure* of the pain.

"You don't have a n-name…" he croaks. "You're nothing to me but a great—*uhh* fuck."

Jaw straining, I slap him once more and he mewls. "A great fuck, hm?"

"An *amazing* fuck." He shudders, body jostling with my savage thrusts. "The best *fuuuck*… of my… life."

"Then say… my… *fucking*… name," I seethe over his lips, gripping his throat.

Reaching up, he grabs a fistful of my hair, yanking it back hard. The sting has me squeezing his throat even harder.

"I don't name my sex toys," he purrs.

Squeeze. Harder.

His face is turning pink.

"Run that pretty mouth all you want, Byron… But you and I both know who owns this cunt." I bite his bottom lip, and he whines. "Admit it. None of them give you what you need… *No one* fucks this pretty pussy but me."

Pumping him with all my strength, I can tell he's close to breaking. His muscles are tense, abs clenching. He can barely keep his eyes open.

"You're *uhh*… so *jealous*. Aren't you?" His grip on my hair loosens, his fingers are suddenly brushing sweetly through my damp locks.

"Baby, I will fuck you to death if it means no one else can have you," I hiss.

Our eyes connect, gazes locked until his falls to my lips. He arches up to me and whimpers, "*Trevel.*"

And then he kisses me. It's surprisingly soft, considering how hard we're fucking; how aggressive and angry, and fucked up this sex is. Somehow, despite the *roughness*, his lips feel warm and delicate. His tongue is silky, and he tastes *so fucking good*.

The fury has turned so sweet, from nothing more than his hypnotic kisses.

Bloody hell, I think he *owns* me.

"God, I want you under me all the time," I croon into his mouth. "I want to watch your face while I fuck this hole the way no one else gets to."

"Vi…" he cries softly, cupping my jaw. Legs open wide, he's spread-eagle, with my cock sliding in and out of his hole, hips grinding to meet my thrusts. "V-violet… *eyes*… *Mm*baby, you're gonna… make me…"

"Can't hold on, can you, gorgeous?" I release his throat to kiss down it. "Is your big dick ready to burst?"

He nods fast as I grab his wrists, pinning them forcefully above his head.

"How's this feel, love? Tell me…"

"*Uhhhhsogood*. Trev… fuck me. R-right there."

"Here?"

"Oh God, fuck *yes!* There there right there!"

Biting his chest, I hum, "Not bad for a sex toy, yea?"

Byron is choking as I lean down enough to capture his nipple between my lips, sucking viciously. His dick is twitching, visibly jumping every time I buck into him.

"I'm going to fuck *all* your cum out, fury love," I hiss, working harder on his nipples, bruising his flesh. "I'll fuck orgasms out of your pretty cock until you have nothing more to give…"

"P-please…"

I'm lost somewhere between lush dominance and complete bloody subservience to this man. Wading through murky memories as my own climax winds and winds in my loins. My balls are bound tight, smacking into Byron's ass so hard, they're sore. Our bodies, slick with rain and dirt, sweat and precum, melt together beneath the moonlight and a hazy sky.

Byron sobs, then stiffens. "Oh fuck, oh shit, Trevel… I'm gonna come…"

"Good," I pant, lacing our fingers. "Moan for me, baby. I wanna hear you…"

"Uhh*fuuuck!*" Byron sobs, then groans out loud, splatters of cum hitting me fast, in the abs and chest.

I watch it happening in awe, my pace easing up. Slow and steady, my hips flick, like I really am fucking his cum out. Every pulse of cum that shoots from his cock rides on the tail-end of a shallow buck.

"*Wow*, By… Look at how sexy you are. Coming so sweet… *so furiously* for me…"

"I'm coming for you," he repeats, delirious and shuddering. "I'm c-coming so hard for you, baby…"

"I see that." I kiss his mouth, swallowing his moans, because they might be a bit too loud. "Mmm, my whore's tight hole is squeezing on my big cock…"

"Come in me," he pleads as his dick finally stops spraying.

"Ask nicely." I bite him.

"P-please… *Please*, Trev…"

"Am I the only one who gets to fill your big, sexy body with cum?"

He nods fast. "Yes."

"You're a slut for my cum, aren't you?"

"Uh-huh…"

"God, I'm gonna breed you so deep…" Sitting back, I lift his hips, holding him up while my fucking slows.

Chills wash over me. My head drops back as I shudder and cry.

When the orgasm overtakes me, it's unlike anything I've felt before. Holding Byron's hips still, I keep myself in him as deep as possible, barely moving. His body clutches me tight while I throb and buck into him. Filling him up *all* the way up.

And he takes it. *Like a good boy.*

"You feel that?" I'm hoarse as my hands rush over him, kneading his ass, petting his slippery cock. "Mmmm… *fuck*, it's in your stomach, isn't it, hot boy?"

"*Oh…* oh fuck *yesss*." His fingers trailing through the cum on his abs, smearing the slickness onto his chest, rubbing his own cum onto his nipples. The sight keeps my orgasm going on far longer than I thought possible. "C-come… so… deep in me…"

"Fucking hell, Byron, you're bloody perfect." I drop down to lick up the length of his tired cock. It jumps up to my mouth, and I groan. "Mine, mine, all bloody mine."

"Mhmm… okay, *yes*. Whatever the fuck you say, baby," he croons, panting for air. "I'm… yours."

Yay, I win.

Grinning, I'm fuzzy and calm. Practically sedated. Despite the chill and the cool rain hitting us, warmth seeps from my pores. The opposite of how worked up and wrathful I was not minutes ago.

It's him… His power over me. Fighting or not, we're enslaved to one another.

This is all I wanted… To catch him.. And now I have. So I can relax.

Blinking down at him, I watch him gazing up at me while we both catch our breath. I tug my softening cock out of his ass, scooping him up onto my lap. It's easier than it should be, despite how bulky he is. Because he comes with me willingly. Just curls up on top of me.

Mine.

Slipping my fingers between his cheeks, I press them up to his hole.

"Hold it in," I demand gruffly, stuffing a finger inside when I feel the wetness wanting to seep out. "Keep my cum in your gushy little hole, sweet fury."

He forces a scowl that's far too dazed with wonder. "Fuck off…"

"Hmm… is that any way to speak to your baby daddy?" I tease, and he growls over my lips.

"Ha ha," he sneers. But he kisses me, and I kiss him back. "You know I can kick the shit out of you, right?"

"But you won't," I murmur. "Because you're my bitch."

Byron snarls, pushing me onto my back. "Pretty sure I fucked you first. Which would make you *my* bitch."

I chuckle, and he beams down at me, unable to fight off the smile. "Fine," I sigh. "I'm your bitch, Byron."

He looks elated, until I add, "But you're my prison wife."

He narrows his gaze, though he's still grinning. He looks radiant. As refreshed as I feel.

"Shut up, prison husband," he croons. "Or I'll kick you in the balls."

"They're empty anyway." I shrug, and he laughs out loud.

I can't stop staring. He's filthy, covered in leaves, hair all tousled, with smears of dirt on his smooth skin. He looks… *unreal*. Too extraordinary not to be a figment of my imagination.

But he is real. He's here, and against all odds, he actually wants *me*. I can barely fathom it.

Whatever we're doing, *whatever* this is, I can't give it up. *I won't.*

Impending tragedy or not, I'll die before I let this one get away.

"That felt…" My voice trails, and I swallow.

"I know," he hums. "Pretty fucking awesome."

"N-no… please. Stop!"

I cringe at the flash in my brain.

The way I held him down in the dirt and fucked him raw, like an animal…

"God, that's good… Shut up and take it, whore."

Words, deep and hushed, panted on hot breaths by my ear…

I gulp. "I didn't… hurt you…" I take his chin in my fingers, looking him over. "Did I?"

He cocks his head. "Only the way I… sorta wanted you to."

I slowly pull my finger out of him, using my hands to cup and massage his ass tenderly.

He purrs, then bites his lip. "You were right, Trevel. I like when it hurts too. I don't know why, but I like to own *and* be owned."

"Me too," I whisper. "Like… partners."

His lips twist as he nods. But it fades into more doubt.

Swallowing hard, I gape up at him, while he stares down at me, like he's trying to make sense of everything he's feeling. I'd love to think that he's growing as attached to me as I am to him, but then I can't stop remembering his words from earlier.

He needs… more. More from me.

More of me.

And I want to give it to him, I do, *but…*

Byron looks like he wants to say something. *The feeling is mutual.*

My lips part, words climbing up my throat. I'm terrified, yet desperate to finally *say it* to someone real, who isn't my bloody doctor.

I want him to know…

"Byron, I… need to tell you—"

"Bad move, mate."

The voice ripples on the edge of my consciousness. Jaw ticking, I ignore it, because *no*… I'm not falling for this again.

He's not *there.*

Byron blinks, his eyes sparkling anticipation. "Tell me."

"I, um…"

"We've been over this," the voice speaks again, and my heart lurches into my throat, blocking the words. *"They'll never understand, Trevel. Your past is best left in the shadows."*

Closing my eyes, I take a deep breath.

It's not him. It's not…

But then I hear a noise. Footsteps. Voices… *More of them?*

Byron and I both turn, peering between the trees. I see two shadowed forms, off in the distance, but I can't make out their features… Until the lightning strikes.

"Holy shit…" Byron whispers, sitting up slowly. My eyes widen.

It's Dr. Love and Felix Darcey.

"What are they doing out here…?" I mumble, reaching for my clothes as Byron does the same.

"Well, looks like I made it just in time."

No bloody way…

My stomach twists as a different form steps out of the shadows. Tattered and torn, a deranged teddy bear with a mask and two swords… *Alive* and smirking at me.

I swallow, and he waves.

He's back.

Leo is back.

CHAPTER TWENTY-EIGHT

Leo

THE FIRST ONE WAS MESSY.

We'd never done it before and were much more *enthusiastic* than we were prepared. Wrath clouded our ability to think rationally and play it smart.

We ambushed him in the parking garage at his office and stabbed him twelve times, leaving behind a plethora of evidence.

It's fine. I didn't care much about getting caught. Neither did Trevel.

So long as we had enough time to do the other three.

Number One only wet my whistle. *Got my motor running.* Trevel was still hurt. He was *scared*. But I was there for him—as I always have been—making sure he understood that he had no choice. *We* didn't.

They all had to go. It was imperative.

Number Two kicked me into second gear. We'd snuck into his birthday party, where I slipped cyanide into his Macallan while Trevel stayed nearby and inconspicuous. *It was important that he not be seen this time around.*

Two died painfully; choking and convulsing, his organs failing as he threw up blood in front of his friends and family. It was brutal.

Fucking *brilliant*.

Oh, please. Stow your judgements. He deserved every second of it and then some after leaving my best friend in the state he had.

Trevel still had the stitches to prove it.

The high was exquisite, for us both. Despite Trevel's prior uncertainty, he was drunk on the revenge, an intoxication stronger than the cocktail of drugs in his veins.

Poor thing… He's always been *so* broken. Used and manipulated by so *many* people who deserved to be slaughtered, painfully and publicly.

He needed this. Needed to know that he was strong—*still is*. That *no one* would ever take from him again without being taken from in return.

And it worked. My nightly pep talks. My *support*.

He likes to think I'm not supportive of him. That I sometimes *disappear* when he needs me the most. That I don't *care* enough to save him from such acts of depraved savagery he's unfortunately suffered at the hands of many awful humans.

Still, deep down, we both know it doesn't work that way. I'm no more capable of stopping terrible things from happening to him than he is, and he knows that. Often times, he's just looking for someone to blame, and I don't mind. I'll gladly be a martyr for him if that's what he needs. He's always been infinitely smarter than most people, even at that age—the first two had proven as much.

Fifteen years old, and he had the remaining two cowering and shitting themselves.

Unfortunately, our lack of finesse meant that our time to complete the final two was limited. As much as I wanted him to savor it, we had to work quickly.

Only two days later, we came for Number Three in his office. Trevel pretended to be his private masseuse—*he wore a wig and everything. It was fantastic.*

Anywho, I caved in his skull with an award from his shelf, which he'd apparently received for his pro bono work with children.

I know. Rather symbolic.

At last, it was time for the grand finale. *The best saved for last, I suppose.*

We gained access to the penthouse of Number Four through some connections and a few sexual favors given to his pathetic excuse for security. It was necessary to do it in his home, being that he'd been holed up in hiding for days. The brutal slayings of his cohorts were all over the news.

Four was on edge. Paranoid.

Rightfully so.

We waited until we were sure he was asleep to come out of hiding. Each step closer was a new buzz of thrill. Though I'll admit, it was bittersweet, knowing this would be the last one.

I rather enjoyed myself over the weeks we were at large; the process of seeking revenge, from start to finish. More than that, though, I enjoyed working alongside my best friend. Helping him do what he needed to regain his control—to feel his true power, and reign vengeance over those who thought they could ruin him and get away with it.

Together, we were unstoppable.

The backdrop of the city that never sleeps splayed out before us as we approached the bed, the sleeping form awaiting us in the middle.

Trevel looked at me, our gazes locking in the dark. And I nodded, giving him the go-ahead. *This one was all his…*

"What are you doing here??" Trevel whispers to me now, eyes flicking to his pal, *Byron*, who's redressing quickly only a foot away.

"I thought you'd be happy to see me." My head cocks. And now I'm watching them both curiously. "Clearly, you've found a way to keep yourself entertained in my absence…"

"Shut up," he huffs. "I'm not—"

"Are you alright?" Byron Kang asks Trevel, likely noting his shiftiness, and the fact that he's talking to *himself*.

Trevel peeks at me once more, then sniffs. "Yea. Fine. Sorry, I'm just… surprised. I didn't expect to see them out here."

Ah, yes. Dr. Love is mere meters from where we're standing. Talk about an entrée…

Unsuspecting wanker.

I fold my arms over my chest, watching my best friend and his new *pal* as they watch one another closely. There's an obvious connection between them. I can feel it myself, which is interesting, being that I rarely feel such things. *Good* things… *Electric chemistry that crackles like the lightning strikes above.*

Byron glances back in the direction of Dr. Love and his butchering boy-toy. "What do you think they're doing?"

"Who cares?" I huff. "This is it, kids… Bloody *kismet*." Trevel peers at me, and I give him a pointed look. "Now's your opportunity. Get that *revenge* we love so much."

He blinks at me before returning to Byron. The way his gaze softens when looking at him is reminiscent of Alice. How he was with her…

Trevel was purely smitten with the girl, and I'm seeing the same sort of behavior now. He's always had a thing for people who have overcome their brokenness, who have found a way to be strong and *fight*, despite being served multiple shit sandwiches in this cosmic circus of fuckery humans call *life*.

Not quite as broken as him and stronger than he thinks he is.

Regardless of everything we've been through together—decades of friendship and being one another's entire support system—he still doesn't realize that *he* carries my strength within him.

He knows that I'm him… *He's not tapped*. But for some reason, he refuses to see the full scope of it.

Trevel Fenwick *is* Leonardo.

The strength it took to overcome his past—his *curse*, as he often sees it—to exact his revenge on the four worthless maggots who raped and brutalized him… Hell, even killing Andres and his stupid friend for what they did to Alice. That was all him. *Us*, together.

He possesses all the courage of a leader; he just doesn't want to see it. Because as far as Trevel is concerned, being broken requires fixing that he can't do himself. Hence, his recent yearning to unburden himself to someone other than a pompous, narcissistic shrink. He wants to be truly *seen* by another person. Someone who will take his baggage and carry it alongside him, in a way I never could.

He wants love. He's desperate for it, in fact.

But I'm here to remind him that he doesn't *need* it. He doesn't need anyone but me. *Together*, we are still unstoppable.

His trust should not be placed in other human beings, because humans are fucking tragic.

"They don't know we're here," Trevel says to Byron, easing up to the side of the house for some cover. Byron appears skeptical, but he follows. "Now's our chance."

I can't help but grin. *Good. He's seeing things clearly.*

"Chance for… what?" Byron asks hesitantly.

I don't know what to think of this *Byron Kang* person. Clearly, he means something to Trevel. I'd like to think it's just a physical attraction, but I know it's more than that. He does remind me of Alice in a way… Maybe a grumpier version, but still. *That's exactly Trevel's type.*

I want to give my best friend the benefit of the doubt. But it's my job to make sure he doesn't get carried away. To keep him from blindly following his heart, like a real Michelangelo.

It might sound odd, since… *well, ya know.* But I'd like to keep him grounded in reality as much as possible. His existence isn't a curse… It's *life* that's fucking cursed. *For every human, not only him.*

A relationship won't fix that. Alice, Byron… Even Dr. Lemuel bloody Love. They can't heal the wounds in his heart that have been there since birth.

It's in his best interest to stay hidden. Remain in the shadows with me, only popping up now and then to get—

"Revenge," Trevel tells Byron with confidence. "Show those egotists that actions have consequences… Even for them. They fucked with the wrong psychos."

Byron swallows visibly. Potentially nervous, but not *appalled*, which makes me like him a bit more. "What did you have in mind…?"

Trevel glances at me again, and I chuckle, rolling my eyes. "You sure you want to date this bloke? Seems like a proper sprog to me…"

Trevel's eyes flicker with the frustration of not being able to argue with me the way he normally would if we were alone. It's quite comical.

"Let's start by following them," he says to Byron, cocking his head. "You know how to do that, yea?"

Byron narrows his gaze at my friend. "Yea. I do."

"Good," Trevel chirps, kissing him on the cheek. "When they're least expecting it, we'll pop out and yell surprise." He grins, and Byron rubs his eyes.

"Uh… okay."

"Are you unsure, Raph?" Trevel frowns, rubbing Byron's shoulders. "What's wrong? Talk to me… Don't you want vengeance? On behalf of your mate?"

"Well… *yea*. But—"

"Then what's the problem?" Trevel goes on, working his magic.

He's rather brilliant at… *I don't want to call it manipulation, because that's not the right word. But he can be quite persuasive when he turns on the charm, and the massage is an added bonus.*

"I've seen you fight, baby," he croons, laying it on thick. "You can take Lemuel, I know you can…"

"That's not what I'm worried about," Byron rumbles firmly. *Cocky lad.* "I just didn't expect to be doing this…"

"Byron, maybe *this* is the reason we're out here." Trevel shifts behind him as we all watch Dr. Love and his serial killer beau, playing with flowers at the entrance of what looks to be an enclosed garden. Pops of color sprinkled between the death and decay of crawling vines and barren trees. "We were supposed to see Lemuel, and would you look at that… We've found him." He leans in to whisper in Byron's ear, "It's *kismet*, sweet fury."

Suddenly, Lemuel drops onto one knee. And if I had lungs that filled with air, I'm certain it would all gust right out.

Oh, bollocks.

I feel Trevel stiffen. I *hear* his crippled heart gasp.

"What the *fuck??*" Byron hisses. "Are they—"

"No…" Trevel whimpers as Felix Darcey drops onto his knees as well, grasping Dr. Love by the jaw. Both of them kneeling together in the wet soil, kissing fervently through smiles so bright, they're fully visible from where we're standing. "No no no no *no…*"

A bolt of lightning splits the sky. The two men are still kissing as Trevel covers his face, gripping his hair in fistfuls and yanking until it stings.

"This can't be happening…" he growls.

Thunder rumbles beneath our feet, shaking the foundation so thoroughly, small pieces of stone fall from the house beside us.

"I told you he was a tosser," I tell Trevel, attempting to rein him in. "Not worth your time or attention."

His face tips in my direction, and we lock eyes.

"Seriously… *fuck him*. Make him pay."

Byron is no longer watching Dr. Love. He's watching Trevel. I see things happening in his deep eyes, like confusion and hurt. Jealousy, even. All things I *know* Trevel is feeling… Only Byron is directing them at us.

"Let's fucking go," Byron hisses.

Trevel blinks at him, sniffling and bemused. Dr. Love and Felix Darcey are back on their feet, assessing the storm as it rages. Winds are picking up, rain pelting the surrounding structures. That must be their cue to leave, because they head into the garden.

Byron doesn't wait. He takes off, immediately trudging in their direction. *He's* now leading the charge. And we're following, stalking quietly between the trees, hurrying toward the greenhouse.

Lingering back, I feel I should say something. My best friend is coming apart; I can feel it.

"I'm sorry, mate," I offer. "I didn't mean to abandon you when you needed me the most…"

"But you did," Trevel scoffs quietly. "You always do."

"Hey, now. That's not exactly fair," I mumble. "I'm never really *gone*, you know that—"

"Doesn't matter," he grunts. "Byron and I have been getting on just fine without you."

He shows me a sneering smirk, and I roll my eyes. "Right. And once again, I've arrived just in time to save you from yourself." Trevel appears put-out, but I continue. "Do you really think this bloke can handle you? Do you think he'll stay once he finds out what you are—"

"I don't want to hear it right now," he whisper-barks to cut me off. "Just do what you do best and help me get my revenge. *That* is all that matters right now."

I simmer inside while watching Byron Kang stomping along with purpose. I wonder how much he truly wants this revenge for himself… Or if it's evolved into something else, the same way I'm sure it has for Trevel.

We sneak into the enclosed garden, following a long stone walkway that leads through the vast space. It's quite beautiful in here—dark and dreary, but fascinating, nonetheless. Old-world, almost gothic design, with an ambiance that shifts from elegance to evil rather effortlessly.

A secret garden of tainted reverie.

We cross a stone bridge over a contained pond, with what looks to be an aviary off in the distance. Broken bird cages and statues.

"This place is… creepy," Byron mutters, at the same time that I hum, "*Stunning.*"

The path leads us to something of a courtyard, and then an atrium, complete with furniture, a grill, a bar, all surrounded by flora and fauna. The ceilings seem miles-high, and the rain pattering on the skylights drowns out our footsteps.

Eventually, we reach a doorway that brings us inside the mansion. As we walk nimbly through a foyer that leads past a study, then a kitchen, it's difficult to stay focused, even for me. This mansion is a marvelous monstrosity. The architecture, the opulent decor shrouded in darkness… It's the kind of place you read about in storybooks.

"Power must be out," Byron whispers, then comes to a fast stop, huddling us behind a corner at the sound of footsteps and voices.

Peering around it, we watch Dr. Love and Felix Darcey padding their way, hand in hand, across a floor of checkered tile, over to a giant marble staircase. Once they're out of sight, Byron checks that the coast is clear before following them. *Stalking.*

"He's good at this," I tell Trevel, who purses his lips to disguise a prideful grin.

We climb the stairs quickly, keeping our steps as lithe as mice. I feel Trevel's zeal, the adrenaline coursing through his veins at being able to do this again. Stalking with a purpose. But he also seems elated at the notion of stalking with a *partner*, visibly buoyant as he sticks close to Byron.

They both have a few leaves in their hair, traces of dirt on their clothes and exposed skin. Of course, I know what they were doing before I showed up. What they've been doing pretty much since we arrived on this island…

"I hope you know what you're doing with this *Raphael…*" I say, not wanting to sound like a parent, but then… *If the shoe fits.*

He glares at me and mouths, "Enough."

I lift my hands, conceding. "Fine *fine*. Who am I to rain on your parade? I've only been by your side since you were six…"

"So long as we're playing by *your* rules, right??" he hisses.

Byron turns over his shoulder. "Huh?"

"Nothing," he grunts.

I chuckle and shake my head.

We stop on the second floor, though the stairs continue up to a third. The corridor is long and dark, housing many doors. But there are voices coming from a room at the end. Following the noise, I believe it's my turn to sneak ahead.

Spots of dimmed yellow are popping up as I creep to the doorway—*they're lighting candles.* The room is spacious and elegant, with decor similar to the rest of the mansion; blood reds and black silk, erotic artwork giving even more of a seductive feel, especially with the flickering candlelight, rain and thunder outside the windows.

Inside, Dr. Love is removing his dress shirt, and Felix is emerging from the en suite in only his boxers and an oversized hooded sweatshirt that reads *Johns Hopkins* on the front. I turn to Trevel and nod him over.

"Stay close," Byron commands on a breath.

He slips inside the room while they're distracted, going for the en suite. With one slick, effortless movement, he's in. *I hate to keep admitting it, but damn… The bloke* is *very good.*

Trevel and I scurry after him. As soon as we're all inside the en suite, Byron leaves the door open a crack so we can hear them.

"What's the plan?" he asks, confident but breathless with exhilaration, despite his *strictly business* demeanor.

"Tie them up," I say.

"We wait until they're… preoccupied," Trevel whispers. "And then we grab them and tie them up."

Byron nods, glancing around the room. "We'll need something to tie them with… And maybe a weapon."

They're both searching for only about a minute. Byron removes the silk ropes used to tie back the crushed velvet curtains, while Trevel's eyes set on what mine are seeing.

Ooh. Shiny.

At the large clawfoot tub, he picks up a straight razor from the side table. "You take Lemuel. I'll take The Carver."

He grins wickedly at Byron, who still doesn't look happy. *Does he ever?* He seems invested, although I'm still not positive if it's for his own sake, or the benefit of Trevel.

Would he really go along with this… all for Trevel?

Why?

The voices from the other room are rumbling laughter and light conversation. What you'd expect from two people who just got *engaged*, I suppose. Byron peers through the crack in the door. Whatever he sees prompts him to shoot Trevel a look over his shoulder.

"What are they doing?" Trevel steps forward.

Byron doesn't speak. He just stares.

Based on that, and the audibly heavy breathing coming from the bedroom, I think it's quite obvious what's happening in there.

Trevel slowly steps closer to where Byron is blocking the doorway with his body. My head tilts. But rather than trying to catch a glimpse, Trevel simply grasps Byron by the jaw, planting a soft kiss on his lips.

Rolling my eyes, I busy myself with sharpening my swords, all the while casually peeking at them as their kissing intensifies and they paw at one another. Eyes closed, jaws straining, tongues fluttering. It's deeply ravenous, with forced quiet keeping them in check. *Like in the showers…*

Anxiety overwhelms me. Not *necessarily* because I feel like I'm losing him… It's not that. *At least, I don't think it is…*

It's just that I *can* feel their connection through Trevel. I don't want to, but I can. That's what he tends to forget. Whether or not I've been visible to him, I'm always *there*… Experiencing it all alongside him. And this connection with Byron is a hell of a lot stronger than it's been with anyone else. The infatuation is there, yes, but it's deeper still. Hungrier and more *devil may care*. I fear that if he's not careful, he'll give himself—and in turn, *me*—over to this lad. *Fully*, because Trevel doesn't do half-measures.

And if Byron Kang can't *handle him, we'll all wind up torn and tattered.*

"I want to taste it," Byron hums onto his lips. "Your sweet revenge. *Show me*, violet eyes."

I'm surprised at his dedication. He's so very close to diving off the deep end blindfolded, and it's rather astonishing. I suppose it's possible he could be the warrior Trevel's been searching for. The one person *truly* strong enough to handle Trevel Fenwick…

Though it's still a gamble I'm afraid to see him make.

"Partners in crime?" Trevel grins, and I'm stunned again when Byron chuckles.

That seems pretty rare. Sort of special, I think.

"Like Bonnie and Clyde," he hums.

"Mmm… I'll be your Clyde Barrow, baby," Trevel beams. "You are my prison wife, after all."

Byron shoves him playfully.

They give one another a final lingering look, and a kiss that's too bright for the shadows.

Trevel peeks at me, and I wink. "It's showtime."

CHAPTER TWENTY-NINE

Trevel

LOOK AT THESE TWO…

Lemuel and Felix are in bed, wrapped up in one another. Kissing and rubbing their dicks together like two randy sluts.

See, if they weren't so busy fingering each other, *maybe* they would've noticed that there are actual *intruders* in their bedroom. *Watching them and waiting to make our move.*

But of course, they don't notice. Because they're in *love*… And *engaged*, apparently. *Bleh.*

"Focus," Leo whispers, and I snap out of it. Focusing instead on Byron.

He's… *incredible*. My shadowman, lingering in the darkness, stalking his prey. *Like a predator who takes dick extremely well.*

I bite my lip, containing my breaths and keeping still. I've always enjoyed stalking, but Byron is a pro. For someone so vibrant, he sure is able to blend into the background effortlessly. I admire that.

I also resent the rest of the world for not seeing him the way they should. The way he *deserves* to be seen.

Oh well. Fuck 'em. More Byron Kang for me.

Just as Lemuel is lifting the shirt over Felix's head, Byron lunges, stealthy like a jaguar. He hooks a fast arm around Dr. Love's neck, yanking him backward with force.

While they're struggling on the floor, I make my move, going for

Felix Darcey. Jumping on top of him, I pin him to the bed, immediately holding the blade of the razor up to his throat.

"Easy now, sweetheart," I rumble with a grin. "Wouldn't want you getting *carved*, now would we?"

I hear Byron fighting Lemuel behind me, but I don't dare take my eyes off of Felix. The fear in his irises gives me life. Gray storm clouds of worry behind his preppy glasses that melt into rage in seconds flat.

"If you hurt him, I swear to God…" he snarls, tone calm, body still. Hell, his heart rate is barely accelerated.

It is truly frightening. *I love it.*

My grin widens. "*What?* What do you *swear to God…?*"

Felix arches up, pushing his throat harder into the blade. "You'll spend every waking moment of the rest of your life wishing I'd had the mercy to kill you quick."

My tongue slides over my lower lip. "Such an adorable bloodthirsty monster."

Grabbing him, I haul him up quickly, turning us both. I stand behind him, sealing his back to my chest, with the razor pressed firmly above his carotid artery.

"Lemuel," I sing his name, loud enough to get his attention.

Dr. Love freezes from the floor, where he was fighting against Byron, eyes widening in sheer dread.

"Don't fucking move," I hiss at him. "Or you'll get to watch your *fiancé* bleed out."

I can see him weighing his options, the wheels of his mind turning while giving away very little emotion. He's extra smart; we know this. Calculating enough to read every situation and play out the angles that'll get him what he wants. But I see it… His fear, his anger, his helplessness.

It's bloody *intoxicating*.

"Right," Dr. Love breathes out as Byron stands him up slowly, twisting his arms forcefully behind his back. His chest is heaving, eyes locked, not on mine, but on Felix fucking Darcey's. "Whatever you say, just… don't hurt him."

My jaw strains while I watch them, *staring* at one another. Communicating without words. But then I glance behind him, at Byron.

"Hold still, *Doc*," Byron whispers in his ear, winking at me.

My stomach flips, a distinct flutter in my chest.

God, he's sexy.

We're just as connected as those wankers. I think maybe… he's my *grumpy counterpart.*

When Byron begins tying Dr. Love's arms behind his back with the silk rope, Felix squirms in panic. "No, no… Please," he gasps. "Don't do that—"

"Baby, look at me," Lemuel says in a hushed, comforting tone. "I'm alright. Everything will be fine."

"Wouldn't bank on it," Leo scoffs while poking around in their things.

"I wouldn't bank on it," I sneer at them.

"Why are you doing this??" Felix barks.

"I refuse to believe this prissy little twit killed thirty-something people…" Leo mutters.

"I'm sure your *doctor* is well aware of why this is happening," I grunt at Felix. "But if you'd like an explanation, I'll give you one word… Retribution."

Byron has Lemuel's wrists bound behind his back. Our eyes lock, and I purse my lips.

"Use his belt," Leo says. My eyes fall to Lemuel's waist.

"Raph," I hum. "His belt."

Byron looks like he wants to smirk, but is keeping himself professional—*I sort of love how he acts like this is a job.* He removes the belt while I slowly bring Felix back to the bed.

"Trevel, listen to me," Lemuel rumbles, robot-mode barely breaking. "You don't have to do this. Whatever you think is—"

"Shut up," I bark, glaring at him. "Not another word."

Byron brings me the belt, and I hold Felix down while he straps his neck to the wrought iron bedpost.

"Make sure it's nice and tight," I tell him, grinning wickedly at Lemuel.

"Trust me, I want this to hurt," Byron seethes, his wrathful gaze on Felix Darcey as he tugs the belt, digging it into Felix's throat.

"Ooh, I like his angry side," Leo beams.

I use the razor to keep them both at our mercy while Byron ties Felix's hands and feet. Once he's done, he stands posted beside Lemuel with his arms folded over his chest. Relaxed, fearless… *Hot as fuck.*

My warrior.

Pacing slowly in between them all, I address our hostages. "You see, you brought this on yourself, Lemuel. All you had to do was *admit* what you'd done. Show even the tiniest bit of empathy for someone other than yourself and your bloody monster… But *no*. You've proven that you're a snake, and you can't be trusted. Now, I'm not afraid of snakes. How about you, Byron?"

I glance up at him, and he shakes his head slowly. "Not even a little."

"What about sociopaths with a murder kink…" Felix croaks.

I chuckle. "There's nothing you can do to get out of this, muffin. We're all too ready to find out just how *weak* the two of you truly are when you're on your own."

The look Lemuel is giving me is titillating, I won't lie. Burning flames of amber blazing at me to betray his stone-cold outer shell.

I'm getting to him.

This is perfect.

Spinning, I stride up to Byron, taking his jaw in my hands. His eyes widen a bit, shifting to the others in the room. It reminds me that he's never really done this before—a public display of affection with a guy. *Or maybe anyone…* Either way, it's adorable.

"You stay here," I hum, swiping my thumb over his lower lip. "Keep an eye on our toy."

He looks like he wants to ask me questions, but I kiss him before he can, effectively short-circuiting his brain. I'm weightless myself.

I will never get over how amazing it feels to kiss him…

"Don't take too long," Byron breathes.

"The lad is smitten," Leo huffs. *"Unbelievable."*

I shoot him a look, kissing Byron once more. "Don't start without me."

Releasing him, I go for Lemuel, yanking him along, razor at *his* throat now.

"Wait, no… Please," Felix begs, but I'm not listening.

I'm too busy admiring the flush on Byron's face, and the twinkle in his deep brown eyes.

"I'll be back for you, baby, I promise," Lemuel says to Felix as I haul him away.

"Lemuel! I—"

Byron backhands Felix, effectively shutting him up while I laugh, shoving a snarling Dr. Love through the door and into the hall.

Dr. Love is surprisingly cooperative, allowing me to drag him along, out of the mansion. *Unsurprisingly*, though, he doesn't utter a word.

I would assume because he's smart, he figured out almost instantly that we're heading for the prison. But once it becomes visible up ahead, through the swaying trees and sideways rain, he pumps on the brakes and finally decides to open his fucking mouth.

"Trevel," he utters my name, and even that manages to annoy me.

"What?"

"I just have to tell you that if you harm Felix in *any* way, I'll kill you," he says calmly. "I promise you that."

"Right," I huff. "Is that a promise, then… *Doctor*?"

"Yes. It is."

My blood instantly boils over. I was hoping to at least keep my cool until we got into the prison, but no such luck.

Stopping short, I hold the razor up to his throat, to the jagged skin of scars I've spent *hours upon hours* wondering about over the last three years.

"And what would you know about a *promise*, hm??" I snarl. "You're the least trustworthy bastard I've ever met! And that's saying something, by the way…"

"Look, I know you're pissed." He does that doctor thing; dripping with condescension that makes *me* feel crazy… *When we all know he's a fucking nutter himself!* "You have every right to be. I understand why you're so upset—"

"Oh, do you?!" I bark, getting up close. "Do you *understand*, Lemuel?? Then why don't you fucking elaborate for me. Why am I so *upset* with you?"

"Because I left you," he replies, blinking rain away from his eyes. "Because I used you to get back here."

I scoff, shaking my head. Fury is making my blood burn like acid. "You're unbelievable." He gives me one of his inquisitive looks, and my teeth grind. "Three years, Doctor… *Three* goddamn bloody *years*! And you threw it away like it was nothing! Tossed me aside like garbage to come here and fall in love with a *guy?!*"

Dr. Love's gaze shifts. His eyes actually widen, expression falling ever so slightly. I should probably stop, but I'm already wound up to full tightness.

I think I need to unravel a bit.

"And not just any guy," I growl. "No, if he were some normal bloke, I think I could wrap my head around it. I mean, a *regular* relationship seems boring, but *hey!* Maybe that's what you wanted… But no. He's a bloody *killer!* A murderer without remorse, just like you always knew *I* was! Despite the meds and the therapy and that bullshit optimism you'd plaster onto your face every time we were together, you *knew*, deep down, that I was sick. That I was capable of terrible, atrocious things, and incapable of ever changing!

"I thought it fascinated you. I thought… you understood me." I pause to sniff and wipe the rain from my face. "You *did*, I know you did. You always have… But then you left me for him. Like you were… trading up. Like I was… a *lesser* monster."

Dr. Love is completely silent, but for the first time since I've known him, it doesn't feel like a tactic, to assert his dominance or superior intellect. It's not the silence of him observing and cataloging me in his head.

He's… stunned.

"Trevel…" His voice is uncharacteristically soft. Pitying.

It makes me want to retch.

"Piss off," I snap, dragging him to keep moving. "Spare me the fake empathy. We both know you don't care."

He yanks himself out of my grip, standing still. "You're right. I don't."

My brow cocks.

"You want an apology? Well, guess what… You ain't getting *shit*. I can't tell you *I'm sorry*, because I'm not, and there's no point in lying or faking it. You're too smart. It's a waste of time."

My gaze at him narrows.

"I don't regret coming here, Trevel. Despite all the bullshit that's happened over the last however many months. I'm not sorry for leaving or using Manuel's sudden obsession with you as my ticket back. And I think you know why…"

I swallow a painful lump in my throat. "I know. But I don't fucking understand it," I grit out through my clenched jaw. "*Why* him? What the *fuck* is so special about Felix Darcey??"

He stares at me for a moment again, the lines of his face taking on some vulnerability. It's not much, but it's there. And it's making me feel even sicker.

"For me?" he whispers. "Everything."

My fist tightens around the handle to the blade. And for a second, I think I might actually slit his throat.

"It's the sort of thing you'll never be able to comprehend until you feel it yourself. I know I didn't," he goes on, tone gentle, normal. *Human*. "I spent most of my life believing such things were frivolous and unnecessary. I mean, human beings can survive, even thrive, without attachment. Romantic love doesn't contribute to science. We don't… *need* it. But then

I met him and... all of that went out the window. Because I wanted it so badly that it *became* a need."

He huffs, tipping his chin toward the ground and shaking his head. It's so very unexpected, for a moment, I think I'm hallucinating.

"Did he just... laugh??" Leo gasps, and I subtly wave him off.

"The point is, I didn't choose it." Lemuel continues. "I didn't plan it or anticipate it. In fact, it came out of nowhere and really fucked me up." He tilts his head, bronze eyes set heavily on my gaze, holding it. "When it happens, it changes everything. It erases everything else... It didn't matter that I was leaving things behind, screwing people over, or being selfish. It sure as shit didn't matter that I was *straight*. Like a rebirth, you start fresh. Nothing from before them matters. No regrets, no apologies. You'll do anything and everything for them, no qualms or hesitations."

My heart is racing, hair brushing in my eyes from the wind. A bright flash lights up the sky, and I jump. The thunder is immediate, crackling and booming so loud, it's as if the sky just split open.

Lemuel glances up at something behind me. "That's how you know my promise is sincere, Trevel. Because Felix Darcey is the other piece of me... And I don't let people hurt me without retribution. Just like you."

"That's..." My voice dries up, as do my words. I have nothing to say.

I can't even think.

All I have are my thoughts, as loud as the thunder.

I think I might know that feeling...

"Is that why you killed Alice's brother and that guy?" he asks me. Not like a doctor, but like a *person* who's curious. Like my equal, both of us soaking wet and... considering it. Fucking *love*. "Because you felt that way for her?"

My mouth is hanging open. I should be able to say yes... But it's not working.

This time, I'm not... thinking about Alice.

Another bolt of lightning strikes, accompanied by an even louder *crack!*

Lemuel hip-checks me into the nearest tree, and like an instinct, I huddle up to it, praying we won't be struck.

"What the fuck..." I hear him grunt, but his voice is being drowned out by another sound.

A slow crackling, rumbling and tumbling, and then...

Boom! The loudest, most roaring crash I've ever heard, a reverberation beneath our feet like an earthquake. It's as if the lightning splintered the ground in two.

I'm afraid to reopen my eyes, and when I finally do, I feel like minutes have passed. Really, it's no more than a few seconds.

Lemuel and I are hugging the tree for dear life.

"What the hell was that?!" I gasp and cough from the dust in the air. "Did something explode??"

I've never seen, nor could I have imagined seeing Lemuel this way. Honestly, he looks scared.

Inching between the trees, we look up and see it. *Destruction.*

A giant structure has broken in half… And smashed right into the side of the prison.

Bloody fucking hell, what the fuck…

"Holy shit…" Lemuel breathes.

Gaping at the ruins, my limbs shiver with fear and adrenaline. I'm blinking and blinking, willing it away. But it won't go.

This isn't a dream, or an illusion concocted by my twisted mind. This is real.

Alabaster Penitentiary has collapsed.

"Come on." Grabbing Lemuel by the arm, I tug him closer to get a better look. But he's pulling in the opposite direction.

"I have to get back to Felix." He stands his ground.

"The mansion is fine. We're going this way," I growl.

"Not a fucking chance," he snarls. "I'm going back to him and making sure he's okay. If you think you're stopping me, you're not as smart as I thought you were."

"Let's get this show back on track, yea?" I see Leo up ahead, on his way toward the prison, cutting debris out of the way with his twin swords.

Lunging at Lemuel with the razor, I seethe, "I must've forgotten the part where I said *you* were calling the shots." He's obviously irate, thinking up ways to overpower me despite the weapon. So I don't give him the chance. I grab him harder, razor up to his throat. "I'm sure the mansion is a million times more structurally sound than the prison, since The Ivory lives there. It'll be fine. Now *walk*, or I'll cut your head off and give it to the love of your life as an engagement gift."

"You better pray nothing happens to him…" he seethes, and I roll my eyes.

"Yea, yea. His life is in Byron's hands now," I sneer. "Let's hope for your sake, *my* partner in crime is less reckless than Bonnie Parker."

Grinning, I haul a furious Dr. Love toward the prison.

Or… what's left of it.

CHAPTER THIRTY

Byron

VENGEANCE, AM *I* RIGHT?

Weird shit, man.

I guess I always thought about it in abstract terms. When I caught Michelangelo fucking my girlfriend, I had this urge inside me—a brutal antipathy. *Animosity,* like venom in my veins I couldn't recover from. That bitterness called for action. *Retaliation.*

Something to tip the scales back in my favor.

I think the act of seeking revenge is like trying to control karma. Ultimately, you're supposed to rise above, and let the universe work it out for you. But the emotions—the hurt, jealousy or rage—become a blinding hatred you just can't shake. And if you're like me, someone who needs control to keep yourself from spinning out, well... Simply *letting go* and *moving on* is much easier said than done.

You fixate on what happened, cause and effect, allowing it to consume your thoughts like a flesh eating bacteria, until eventually, you develop a hardened layer of spite, just beneath your surface. And the only way to get rid of it is to take back control.

I had every intention of making Michelangelo Russo pay for what he'd done to me—unknowingly or not. But even then, it was an objective ideal. Vindication would depend on the person's *reaction* to your malice.

The enemy has to play into your plan for revenge. And if they don't... It can muddy the waters a bit.

We all know what ended up happening with Michelangelo.

This part is about Felix Darcey.

"Storm's getting bad…" the timid, yet calm, voice rasps from the bed.

I cock my head.

Sitting in a large, ornate maroon velvet chair across the room, I stare at him. Gaze narrowed in the same speculative glower I've had aimed directly in his direction, and nowhere else, for minutes on end. Just watching. *Observing*. Lips firmly zipped.

I haven't taken my eyes off of him, nor have I spoken a word since Trevel left with Dr. Love twenty minutes ago. There's a lot I could say to this asshole, and yet none of it really seems necessary. He already knows how I feel about him. He knows I hate his fucking guts for what he did to my friend, and that I'd love nothing more than to spill his blood as payback for him spilling O'Malley's.

I told him all of that when I confronted him in the showers that day. And in the same way that Michelangelo Russo threw his complicated wrench into my plans for retribution, Felix Darcey has taken some of the satisfaction away from this revenge plot… By being a complete and utter sociopath.

But it's like Trevel says, there are other ways to get revenge. Violence is *my* forte, but he's much more calculated—not quite apparent in this hastily organized plan we've embarked on.

There was no discussion about where Trevel was taking Dr. Love, or when he'd be back, and that's making me itchy inside. What I *do* know is that Trevel wanted to separate Dr. Love and Felix Darcey. It's a smart play because they're obviously very codependent. Wrenching them apart is definitely the best way to expose their weaknesses and subtly poke at them until it starts to drive them both nuts.

Darcey is clearly uncomfortable; neck strapped to the bed, wrists and ankles tied. His glasses are sliding down his nose, chestnut hair strewn about, pale complexion flushed, most likely from the tightness of the belt and the overall stress of the situation.

His fingers wiggle where they're resting over his lap. At first, I thought he was trying to wriggle them free from the rope, but after a while, I realized it's just a nervous tic. Something to show me that, despite his apathetic demeanor, his brain is working overtime. Rushing through thoughts of what might be happening to his man, concocting plans or schemes to free himself from this vulnerable position.

It's *very* satisfying.

"Did the power go out in the prison too?" he asks me.

I don't answer him, confident glare unwavering.

I've got you right where I want you, asshole.

Darcey puffs out a breath, frustratedly attempting to blow his hair away from his eyes. It brings an uncontrollable twitch to my lips.

"You know, Lemuel's never spoken a bad word about Trevel..." He keeps going with the inane ramblings, meant either to fill the silence, or get me to crack. Or both. "And he thinks you could be good for him. Someone to make him feel safe."

My eyebrow arches subtly. I can't really help it. *The audacity of this nerdy twink and his charlatan fucking boyfriend, I swear to God...*

"Independence isn't a bad thing," he says with a small shrug. "Lem and I are both loners. Or, I mean, we *were*..."

You mean, before you absorbed one another?

"Sometimes it can be a coping mechanism, though," he murmurs. "Keeping people at a distance... Never letting anyone know the *real* you."

My jaw clenches. *Interesting. I didn't know bending over for a shrink makes you a fucking expert, you unbearable fucking twat.*

"Personally, I'm glad you found Trevel." He just keeps fucking *talking*. Tuning him out *was* working fine... But the moment he uttered Trevel's name, my fingers slowly curled into fists. "Despite all of this, and what everyone else was saying, I think you guys are cute together. If he's someone you can be yourself with... then it's a good thing, right?"

He shows me a tiny smirk that I can see through like glass. I can *hear* what he's saying, in between his bullshit, in that one stupid, shit-eating grin...

I killed your friend. I loved doing it.

I don't feel bad.

My boyfriend let me do it. He's stronger than you. And smarter than you.

Your friends are now my *friends. I'm The Ivory's favorite.*

I'm everyone's *favorite.*

And your boyfriend is in love with my boyfriend.

Standing up slowly, I crack my knuckles. Darcey's smirk falls away, and he tilts his head as much as he can, a curious expression covering his smug face. I step over to the bed, our eyes locked the whole time. He doesn't look scared, which is infuriating, but I know it's his thing. He's a fucking psychopath. If anything, I'm brimming with fast rage because, even tied up at my mercy, he *still* thinks he has me by the balls.

I crack my neck and lean over him. "What are you gonna do?"

His brows zip together, like he's not sure what I'm talking about. So I elaborate.

"When he's gone…"

That gets him. It's the first flash of fear I've seen since we tied up Dr. Love.

"What *ever* will you do with yourself… when he's *dead*, and you're all alone again?" I hiss quietly. "Because that's what you deserve, isn't it? You know it as well as I do… I don't have to do shit to you, neither does Trevel. We don't have to lay a finger on *you*…"

With my index finger, I push his glasses up his nose. He flinches.

My lips slope into a smirk of satisfaction. "I've thought a lot about breaking your bones, you know that? I've fantasized about how it would feel… Using my bare hands to make you bleed. How it would *sound*… breaking your jaw or your nose, cracking your eye sockets. What it might look like… to leave you lying in a pool of blood, like you did to my friend."

Darcey's throat dips.

"I know it'd be satisfying as hell." I sigh. "I mean, how could it not? These are my weapons…" I hold up my hands. "I don't need a knife to fuck up your face, *Carver*. I can do it easier than breathing, and it'd feel fucking *great*." I stop to shrug. "But the point is that I don't *have* to. We can ruin your life while you lie right here in this bed, like a scared, helpless *victim*." I hover even closer to his face. "And then you'll be all by yourself… Like you *deserve*."

Fury flickers in his gray eyes; *his* hatred, *his* malice. It mirrors my own, and it gives me chills.

"What makes you think Lemuel won't kill Trevel??" he snaps. "How confident are you in his skills? Without you… You think your man's wrath is stronger than mine's?"

His chest is jumping, pupils dilated with his obvious surge of adrenaline. *Finally*, I'm getting the serial killer, rather than his fucking disguise.

This is what I wanted. I don't give a fuck about Felix Darcey. I could crush him with my thumb.

I want into the ring with The Carver.

"My man isn't just *my* man, though," I rumble, ignoring the confusing flutters at referring to Trevel this way. "He's also *The Ivory's* man. So… sure, Manuel Blanco will keep *you* alive. But Lemuel?" I pull a very condescending shrug, and his jaw tics.

"You mean, you're willing to side with The Ivory… After everything he's done to your friends?"

"I have no fucking friends anymore, thanks to you," I growl.

A bit of his anger wavers, eyes glistening up at me. "Trevel is all you have left…?"

Okay. That's it.

A roar leaves my lips as I jump on top of him. *Fuck playing it coy. I'm going to tear him to shreds.*

"You think you own this fucking place?! You think you're invincible, you psycho bitch?? Well, guess what?? You're not! You're *weak*." My hands wrap around his throat as I snarl over his face, "You gave the doctor all of your power, and now you're nothing! The Carver is *dead!* You're just Felix fucking Darcey."

I shove off of his throat with a scoff, and he grunts in pain.

"Byron…" he gasps. "I'm… sorry, okay? I'm *sorry* about Kieran—"

"Shut the fuck up!" I snarl, backhanding him across the face. "Don't fucking say his name to me!" I grab him by the collar. "*You* don't feel shit like *sorry*, so don't fucking patronize me! You're embarrassing yourself…"

"No, wait. Listen," he croaks. "I'm not sorry I killed him… He was a piece of shit, you know that."

I glare down at him, heaving with unfettered wrath.

"Come on, man. You can't tell me he didn't deserve to die…"

"So do you," I teem.

"Yea, I know," he breathes out. "But I killed Kieran, okay? I did it, and I don't feel bad about it. What I *do* feel bad about is upsetting you. I didn't mean to do that…" He swallows. "I'm sorry."

What in the holy hell…?

The look I'm giving him is one of sheer perplexity.

My gaze narrows. "Why in the *fuck* would I believe that you're sorry for upsetting me when you don't feel sorry for taking someone's life? Do I look like an idiot to you?"

"No." He shakes his head. "But you seem like a cool guy. Like Luthor and Ren. You guys are all… really nice."

I wonder if he'd still be saying this if he knew what we did to his bedroom…

"I'm not nice," I grumble. "If we're being honest, neither is Ren. Luthor's the only one who's kind-hearted, and even he has his issues…"

"I know that, but I like hanging out with them," he murmurs. "And you. If I'd known killing Kieran would make you hate me, I might've… reconsidered."

My mouth is just hanging open. I have no earthly motherfucking *clue* what to say to something like that.

Is he fucking with me?? He has to be. Serial killers aren't… thoughtful? Considerate of people's feelings?

"What the fuck are you even talking about?" I mutter, releasing him and sitting back. "You're a goddamn lunatic…"

That makes him smile.

Okay, I'm sufficiently disturbed at the turn this is taking.

"Yea, that's a fact." He huffs. "Listen, like I said to you the day you broke my glasses… You can fuck me up if that's what you need to do. I get it, and I'll take it. Not that I think I could ever take you in a fight…"

"You couldn't," I grunt.

"I'm just saying." He chuckles. "I respect the vengeance, trust me, I do. But one thing I will *not* allow you, or Trevel, to do is hurt Lemuel. That's where I draw the line."

My brows lift while I consider his wacky words. I hate that he's getting through to me, but I can't stop recognizing the *reality* in all this.

This path of revenge we're on… It's a vicious cycle. As long as people keep getting hurt, someone will always feel the need to avenge them.

If either of them hurts Trevel, I'll fucking hurt them in return. And then they'll hurt me… *When does it end?*

I'm suddenly very tired. So *very* exhausted by all of this.

More than anything, I just want Trevel to come back. I actually glance at the door, praying he'll come striding through right *now*, alive and well. Tall and pretty, with those peculiar eyes and puffy pink lips sloped into one of his smirks. His deep voice with that accent talking so much nonsense, but purposefully excluding the real stuff. The stuff I want…

Bright white flashes outside the window, thunder rumbling with it, like the roar of a thousand lions. It rattles the walls.

I despise not knowing what Trevel's doing, and if he's okay. I'm antsy about it, feeling like a piece of me is missing and I don't know where it is. It's ludicrous… But apparently, we've become sort of codependent ourselves.

Jesus, how and when the hell did that happen??

Most of all, in the back of my mind, I truly *hate* how he jumped at the chance to take Lemuel. To be alone with him…

"I'm getting really worried." Darcey squirms beneath me.

I roll off of him with a sigh, getting up and sauntering over to the window. "That was sorta the point…"

"Byron, I know you're worried about Trevel," he says, ignoring the glare I shoot his way. "They're both out there in the storm—"

"Trevel knows what he's doing," I mutter, gulping down my uncertainty as I watch the trees thrashing.

"I saw your face..." he hums, and I peer in his direction once more. "When he kissed you. There's no hiding that look. I've worn it myself, way too many times."

"You have no idea what you're talking about," I argue, and it feels defensive. Heat is rushing up my neck.

"It doesn't all have to be a fight, Byron," he rasps. "Resigning yourself to the fucked-up reality is freeing. Believe me..."

I'm gawking at him, lips parted. This little shit is making sense, and it's making me want to beat his ass even more.

Because he has a point. Maybe accepting what Trevel *is* to me instead of focusing on what he *isn't* will help us... become something *real*.

A bolt of lightning interrupts my thoughts, so bright it flashes white into the room. There's an immediate *boom* louder than any thunder I've ever heard; a crackling rumble, like a rift in the sky.

Gazing out the window, I take a step forward. But a crash has me stumbling back. A great thundering *blast* so significant it shakes the foundation beneath us. The walls rattle, things tipping over. A painting actually falls, smashing on the floor.

Okay, that's not thunder... It felt like a missile launched right outside.

"What the fuck was that?!" Darcey gasps.

"I don't know." I'm not trying to seem affected, but my heart is racing wildly in my chest, adrenaline quaking my extremities.

"Did something blow up? Like a... transformer, or...?" Darcey keeps asking questions, as if I'm not stuck in this room with him, working with all the same information he is.

My gaze is stuck out the window as I approach it hesitantly, looking around for any sign of what might've happened. But all I can see are trees.

"It wasn't loud enough to have happened here," I mumble, mostly to myself. "It was... farther away..."

Maybe... from the prison.

"I gotta get out of here." Darcey is yanking at his restraints, really spazzing out, rocking back and forth like a nutcase. "Lem could be hurt. I have to go find him!"

"You're not going anywhere," I hiss. "Calm the hell down."

"I can't," he huffs, out of breath from wiggling around to no avail. "He's out there. Something is happening... I can't just fucking *sit here!*"

"Well, that's not your call, now is it?" I fold my arms over my chest.

He stares up at me helplessly. It gives me some minute satisfaction that's not really placating me right now.

Shouting from outside distracts me, but I still can't fucking *see* anything through the damn window.

This room has a shit view, man. It's not high enough.

I bet if I went upstairs, I could see everything...

"You go then." Darcey's voice recaptures my attention. "Please, Byron... Go check on them. I need to know that he's okay—"

"I'm not doing shit for you," I growl.

"Not for me!" he whimpers. "For Trevel. He's with Lem... If they're in trouble, you could help them. *Him...*" he corrects, noting the look on my face. "You care about Trevel, Byron, I know you do. Whatever you guys are doing, it doesn't matter. You care..."

My jaw is tight, muscles straining all over. Because he's fucking right, *again*, and I fucking hate it. I am freaking out a little...

Trevel could be hurt. Whatever that was came from the exact direction he was headed...

There's a sinking feeling in my gut I can't ignore. Fighting off the reality isn't working anymore.

Something is wrong.

Giving myself a few more seconds to weigh the options, I inevitably give up and stomp over to Darcey, checking his restraints. I double-check the area around him to make sure there's nothing he can grab to get himself out.

I can't believe I'm about to leave him alone...

But I have to. *I need to make sure he's alright.*

"Shut the fuck up and stay fucking put," I grumble. "I'll be right back."

"Thank you," he breathes out, voice uneven with fear.

"I'm not fucking doing this for you."

Leaving the room, I have honestly *no idea* what I'm doing or where I'm going. But I head for the stairs. *'Cause why not?*

I figure getting up higher will get me answers faster than running out into the woods. Plus, who knows where The Ivory is... His men could be searching for me and Trevel, being that we technically *escaped* and all.

I need to find Trevel before they find me. I assume they'd be less likely to shoot on sight if I'm with him... Right?

So far, this night feels like a manic dream. From the doors to the prison opening out of nowhere, to leaving—being *outside*, for the first time in years—to the sex with Trevel, the *chase*, and then the *capture* of our enemies… *Man, a lot has happened in the last hour.*

Typical Alabaster Pen… Years of nothing and then bam! A lifetime of exciting shit happens in a few minutes.

Climbing the large white marble staircase, I keep quiet, in case I'm not alone. It seems almost unfathomable that I would be. The place is absolutely gargantuan. It's like three mansions in one. But I haven't seen or heard anyone other than us since we've been in here. Still, that doesn't mean much. It's spread out enough that I doubt you can hear what people are doing in other areas.

I'm jacked up to the max right now, terrified that The Ivory is going to pop out from around every corner. It's fully plausible that he could be here… And as soon as I reach the third floor, I stop to gulp. Because it would appear that I'm now on his floor.

Great. Just wonderful…

So this is where I die.

It's immediately obvious that this is where he resides. This floor isn't divided up the same way the second floor is, with bedrooms one by one. This level is its own mansion, and the whole place just screams *Ivory*; from the sheer excess of space, furniture, and lavish accoutrement, to the walls, adorned with erotic artwork and what looks like some kind of mural made of feathers and barbed wire. I can *feel* him up here… And it's freaking me the hell out.

Keeping close to the walls, I use the lack of power to my advantage. Remembering my stalking days, I'm stepping lithely, breathing shallow. Staying in the darkness to avoid being seen.

I pass room after room—a gym, an office, a study. There's a separate, smaller staircase, which appears to go both down and up. *Maybe to the roof?*

This building was clearly designed by the same person who designed Alabaster Pen… It's a fucking maze. *By far the most peculiar home I've ever been in.*

At the end of a long corridor, I come face to face with the primary suite; a bedroom so large, it could fit three of Dr. Love's rooms inside of it.

This is The Ivory's bedroom.

Fuck…

I know I shouldn't go in. It's suicide. *If he's in there, I'm dead.*

But I can't help my curiosity. Furthermore, I have to assume he has windows with a great view—like his office in the prison does.

Tiptoeing closer, I peek through the open doorway. *I don't think anyone's in here...*

Stepping inside carefully, I glance around in awe. It truly is the King's chambers. That's exactly how it looks. *Regal.*

Royalty rests its evil head here.

There's a set of French doors at the far side of the room. *Bingo.* Jumping into action, I forgo snooping and head straight for them. I can see right away that they lead out to a large balcony.

The winds are so strong, I have to grip the handle tight and pull toward myself to keep the door from flying open. It's brutal out there... Rain pelting and stinging my face. I can barely see through it, but I manage to gaze out into the storm, at a view that literally steals my breath.

Wow...

Despite Mother Nature's fury, I'm astonished. From up here, everything looks so picturesque. *Stunning* in its misery. Skies of dark gray tinted green from the storm oversee a beckoning obsidian ocean. Trees like skeletons performing a ritualistic dance.

It's so mesmerizing, I almost miss it. But when my eyes focus, they widen, despite the pelting raindrops.

"Holy *fuck*..." The words gust from my lips.

Alabaster Penitentiary... has a fucking hole in it.

A large structure, what looks to be the guard tower—I remember passing it when I was running from Trevel earlier—has broken off near the middle. And apparently, it fell right onto the prison.

That's what that sound was...

"Oh my God. What the... shit," I gasp, wiping rain and disbelief out of my eyes.

The destruction is staggering. I have a bird's-eye view from way up here, and it doesn't even look real. Like a photograph taken by a drone for some *National Geographic* magazine type shit.

I'm just gaping and balking at the damage, unable to move. Nearly half the prison is just... *gone.* Nothing but rubble. The guard tower clearly hit the East Wing, and the impact took down the rest because of its weak goddamn structure.

"Fuck..." I shiver as time speeds up, panic sweeping through my entire body.

Shit shit shit. Trevel was going there... At least, I think he was. Dammit, why didn't he tell me where he was going?!

Fuck! Luthor and Ren...

Joy, Rook, Velle…

People were in there! People I care about…

"Shit. Fuck," I mumble to myself, mind racing, limbs buzzing with a need for action.

I gotta go. Now now right now.

I need to go check on my friends.

Finding Trevel and making sure he's okay is even more urgent now.

I won't be able to handle it if he's… not.

Gulping down the dread crawling up my throat, I dart back inside. But before I can close the door and run, something stops me. Yet another loud *bang!* It scares shit out of me, and I jump.

But this sound is very different from the others. It's instantly recognizable.

Fireworks…

I'm back out on the balcony in a flash, catching the tail-end of green fizzling off in the distance. Barely ten seconds later, there's another *thunk*, followed by a *whoosh*, then an explosion of blue, embers falling like a waterfall of color.

Definitely not a flare gun. These are fucking *fireworks*, like the ones you'd watch on the Fourth of July, coming from the other side of the island.

It dawns on me as a third pops off, a shower of sparkling white…

Luthor and Ren.

They love fireworks. It's one of their very few shared interests, and they talk about it all the time.

Fireworks over the ocean…

Fuck. That's them. It has to be.

Either one of them, or both.

Maybe it's a signal.

I have to go.

Shit, but what about Trevel?

There's too much going on. This is all so fucked.

Either way, I have to get the hell out of this mansion and go in that direction.

Leaving the Warden's bedroom, I'm struggling to stay quiet when all I want to do is barrel through this fucking place. The prison is on the other side of the island, but it's no more than a mile and a half from here. *It's dangerous, but fuck it. I have to go.*

I'm on autopilot as I move, leaving the mansion the way we came, through the garden. This place is really something else… It's almost unfathomable. Ominous, creepy as hell, but somehow beautiful.

Just like Manuel Blanco.

The mansion almost feels like an extension of him, emphasizing the sensation that he's *everywhere*, even when you can't see him.

As soon as I'm in the woods again, I'm on even higher alert. There are voices coming from all around. The last thing I want to do is stop, but I can't risk being spotted by The Ivory's guys, so I take cover behind a tree, listening while people run around, clearly in distress. Up ahead, I see that stone house, remembering how Trevel fucked me into the ground just outside of it only about an hour ago.

I swear to God, I'm lucid dreaming…

People are coming in and out of the house, guys rushing off in different directions, yelling at each other in Spanish. I can't understand much of what they're saying, but one word stands out above all the others…

Jefe.

They're looking for The Ivory.

Jesus fuck, was he inside the prison when it fell??

Could The Ivory be… dead?

No time to think about that. As soon as the coast is clear, I take off running once more, zipping in between the trees, sticking to a separate path.

What I wouldn't give for a compass right now…

Based on where I know the East Wing to be, I'm just heading back in the direction we came. Since the fireworks came from somewhere along the shore, I'm straying farther east, peering through the trees to get a view of the coast. But the rubble from the fallen guard tower is blocking a direct route. I'd have to either go all the way around to check the shore for Luthor and Ren, or head more inland to go for Trevel.

I come to a full stop, looking left, then right.

Luthor and Ren are one way. Trevel, the other.

My heart is leaping so hard, I'm dizzy.

Soaking wet, I'm shivering from the cold, and from the uncertainty in my chest. Raindrops tumbling from my hair, running over my trembling lips…

Without thinking, I take a step, my foot crunching on a fallen branch.

"Don't move!" a voice barks.

My hands fly up when a shadowy figure comes out from around a tree, aiming a gun at my face. Blood is rushing in my ears as I try to make him out… It's so fucking dark and my vision is obstructed by the rain.

He approaches me slowly, two more people emerging behind him.

"Byron?" Trevel says my name, and I exhale, releasing the breath I'd been holding.

He's here. He's… still here.

Thank fuck, he's alright.

Trevel rushes to me, warmth blooming in my chest the closer he gets, and the more I'm able to verify that he's *actually* here and unharmed. I have just enough time to register who he's with—Kent, who's lowering his gun, and Dr. Love, arms still tied behind his back—before Trevel is wrapping himself around me. Hugging me. *Holding* me.

And suddenly, he's holding me *up*; keeping me upright because I feel like I could collapse. I'm just so glad to see him… I hadn't even realized how scared I was until right fucking now.

I didn't allow myself to feel it… The fear of losing him. But with his arms around me, his firm body pressing into mine and the crook of his neck like the perfect place to rest my weary head, I can't help it. I melt against him, locking my arms around his waist as the stress of everything going on falls away.

"I'm so glad you're alright," he hums, fingers combing through my wet hair.

"I… I had to come find you." I shudder the words, my lips brushing the soft flesh of his throat. "I was… worried."

He pulls back, forcing me to untangle from him, taking my face in his hands. He's… *smiling*. "That's incredible, my sweet perfect fury."

I'm trying to scowl, but I'm sure it's not working. No matter how uncertain things are between us, I have to acknowledge how much more *right* everything feels when we're together. I'm not sure if it is, but it feels that way, and right now, I need that comfort.

A throat clearing cuts into our moment, and I look up. Kent has his gun on Dr. Love now, who's glaring at Trevel and me, studiously curious yet *full* of animosity.

"Where's Felix?" he hisses at me. "Is he alright?? You better not have "

"Shut up," Kent barks at Love, then nods, addressing me and Trevel. "Come on. We can't stay out here… It's not safe."

"What happened?" I ask, hoping to gain some more information on what in the holy hell is going on here. "I heard the tower fall…"

"The walls are down," Kent says, motioning with his gun for Dr. Love to walk. "We have to keep moving. You're lucky we found you before the others did. Instructions are shoot on sight."

I gulp, falling into step beside Trevel as we follow them at a brisk pace. "Shoot… who?"

He doesn't answer me, but Trevel and I share a look of understanding.

Prisoners.

They're going to be shooting any prisoner who's found outside of the Pen. And now that there's a hole in the side of it, I'd imagine that will be at least a few.

Glancing left, I swallow hard. *Luthor and Ren are out here somewhere… I know they are.*

"We have to go back," I whisper to Trevel, who peeks down at me. "I need to find—"

"No one is going anywhere until we reconvene with The Ivory," Kent barks. "Stay close and quiet. That's an order, inmates."

Tension weaves through me once more as I walk with them, back toward the mansion. Away from the prison.

I don't know what any of this means… For any of us.

I just have to hope with everything in me that they're okay… *My friends.*

The fear and concern in me are eased, however, when Trevel slips his fingers through mine.

CHAPTER THIRTY-ONE

Byron

WE'VE BEEN SITTING IN THIS ROOM FOR *WAY* TOO LONG.

It's actually gorgeous. A den just off the atrium, opposite a robust library. All large, rustic leather furniture, a lit fireplace keeping us warm and the room illuminated. I guess the power's still out, but that's really the least of our problems right now.

Just as we were arriving back at the mansion, the gunfire started. And it hasn't stopped. Not continuous or anything, but every so often, a loud pop causes us to jump in our comfy seats.

Each shot bringing with it a question…

Which of my friends are dead?

That's not to say I consider everyone in that prison a *friend*. Some of them are assholes. Most are just faces I've grown accustomed to seeing day in and day out. But a few of them I'd rather not see killed… Mainly, Luthor and Ren.

I can't get it out of my head… The last words we said to each other. Well, the last words *I* said to them, since I was the one throwing all of the hurtful accusations their way. At the time, I meant every word of it. But now that things have taken this serious, even *deadly*, turn, I can't help feeling like none of it was really that big of a deal.

I guess the threat of losing people you care about will do that to you. It makes you forget the pain, the stubbornness, the jealousy… The hostility that seemed so important at the time now just seems petty and inconsequential.

I know I was hurt when I was saying it, but I can't find any of that now. It's all just… fear. Worry. Regret.

If those are the last words I ever speak to them… I'll never forgive myself.

And it's not just Luthor and Ren, either.

The Ivory's guys have been storming around the mansion since we got here, walkies blaring. Based on the bits and pieces of conversations I've overheard, the potential of escaping prisoners isn't their *primary* concern.

That would be Velle.

It's no secret that tensions have been high since the Warden brought in his new team of guards to take over. I'm not sure what I expected to happen, but over the last few weeks, it's become painfully clear that the plan was never to simply fire Velle and his men—*give 'em the old pink slip and send them on their merry way.* I refused to think about it until right now, but that definitely doesn't seem like The Ivory's style.

It's unclear what his plan *was*, but it probably wouldn't have been good for the *former* head asshole in charge and his pack of morally bankrupt guard dogs. And after what Joy told me about them being kicked out of the mansion, it seems like this storm was pretty *perfect* in that it gave Velle an opportunity to strike.

If we're being honest, going quietly doesn't seem like John Chevelle's style either.

Now, they're in the prison, holed up somewhere the Warden doesn't want them, making them a much bigger problem than a few escaped convicts who haven't seen daylight in years.

The unknown is weighing on me. What could be happening at any given moment to people I've been existing alongside in mutual misery for so long. Attempting to understand why *I'm* here, and they're not.

Is it just because I'm boning one of The Ivory's spies? Is that really what it comes down to?

I'm safe and toasty warm because of my relationship with Trevel's dick?

A familiar voice booms from somewhere up the hall, and I flinch.

Or maybe the Warden wants me dead too, and was just waiting to for me to let my guard down…

Trevel's hand slides onto my knee, pausing its rapid bouncing. "Relax."

"*Okay,*" I scoff, shaking my head. "This is *fucked*… you know that??

What's going on out there? How long is he going to keep us sitting around with our dicks in our hands, and not the slightest *clue*—"

The clack of dress shoes on a marble floor brings with it an angry voice that instantly cuts off my complaining. Kent stands fast, pistol still in hand as he nods at us. I guess that means he wants us to stand up too, because Trevel and Dr. Love both get on their feet.

I'm not as familiar with this shit as they are, apparently... *All rise for the dishonorable judge, jury, and executioner, Manuel fucking Blanco.*

"I don't give a fuck what it costs, you get them here *now*." The Ivory is barking at someone as he rounds the corner. Once he's in sight, it's clear that he's talking on the phone, though there is a guy I've never seen before following after him. "*Escuchame* now means fucking *yesterday*. Do it, and don't bother me with nonsense. I want that boat *bustling, comprende*? Figure it out."

He ends the call, on what looks like a satellite phone. *Interesting... Is cell service out?* Then he immediately pulls a walkie-talkie off of his belt, pacing as he holds it up to his face. "Carlito? *Esta bien*?" He goes quiet while someone responds in muffled Spanish I can't make out. "You barricaded the doors? Good... Good. Whatever you do, don't let them out of your sight. Especially Carson. I mean it, *soldado*. Guns on them at all times, whether they're eating, sleeping, taking a piss... They don't move an inch without you there, *si*? Okay, I'll be in touch when the reinforcements arrive."

The person on the other end is saying *ten-four* as The Ivory secures the walkie, stalking over to us. I'm instantly so tense, it's like my muscles are seizing.

I haven't seen Manuel Blanco in a while. He comes and goes, that's for sure. But ever since Dash escaped and the prison went on lockdown, he's been much more elusive. I can't say I've been necessarily bummed about it... Being that every time he's near me I feel like nothing more than a pawn in his human chess match.

Standing here now, in his home, mere feet from him with a war on the brink of breaking outside these walls, has me recoiling even more than usual in his presence.

I don't belong here, and he knows that.

The Ivory scans our faces; Trevel and me first, then Dr. Love. His gaze narrows at the doctor, who, by all accounts, is standing his ground. Which is crazy since, from what I can tell, he has *zero* fucking ground to stand on right now. He's practically six feet under.

He must know something I don't. In fact, I'm *sure* there's a lot about their relationship I don't understand. Just like there's a lot about The Ivory's relationship with Trevel I don't understand…

The whole thing is making me feel like even *more* of an intruder here.

He's gonna fucking kill me. I'm sure of it.

The Warden shifts, dark eyes settling on Trevel. "I don't have time to get into what was happening before the tower fell, but let's just say I'm glad you were thinking on your feet."

I witness the mound of Trevel's throat bob before he says, "I told you it was the right move."

The Warden exhales, rubbing his eyes. I have to note that he looks much more disheveled than usual, his expensive dress shirt all rumpled and unbuttoned at the collar, snow white hair strewn about. It looks like he has blood and soot on his clothes, cuts and scrapes on his visible skin.

Jesus… Was he inside the prison?? When the tower fell??

"And you," he pins me with his charcoal irises, and I straighten. "You're here now, hm? Meaning you dodged a bullet… Literally."

My lips part, but I have no mother-loving *idea* how I would ever respond to that statement.

"I'm happy to allow you and Trevel to stay, so long as everyone's clear on what that means." He cocks his head. We're just staring at him until he blinks. "There will be no leaving this side. You know how I feel about loyalty…" His eyes slide to Dr. Love, and he growls, "*Es todo.*"

The room is deathly quiet. Just the crackling of the fire and the shouting of men off in the distance.

"Yari," The Ivory says to the young man who came in with him. "Be a lamb and fetch me Johansson, please."

"Yes, sir." The guy nods and scurries off.

The Warden moves in closer to Trevel and me, his eyes bouncing between us. "I must say, I'm pleased that you're here… With Trevel. With *us*. They made a mistake leaving you behind, but it's their loss, honestly. I don't expect they'll get far…"

My forehead lines. "What… *Who??* Who are you… talking about?"

His lips twitch. "Our very own Lex Luthor and his firestarter, Warren Xavier. They managed to slip out amidst all the chaos." He pauses while I gawk at him. "They're *gone*, Byron. They left. Stole a goddamn rowboat and set sail… Right into the mouth of a deadly storm."

He puffs a condescending chuckle, peeking at Kent, who shakes his head.

What the… fuck?

Conflicting emotions are flash flooding my system. I'm relieved, momentarily, at hearing that my friends haven't been killed. But it's swallowed up quickly by the reality of the situation.

They… left?

Luthor and Ren are… gone?

Like, gone *gone??*

I'm having a hard time processing this. It must be clear from my bugging eyes and mouth slack in stunned silence, because the Warden reaches forward, grasping my chin between his fingers. I feel Trevel stiffen at my side.

"I wouldn't worry about it, my fighter. You're so much more important here and now than you ever were by their side, tagging along like a permanent third wheel. They never appreciated you. Not like I do. They'll never *want* you… Not like he does." He nods in Trevel's direction.

My eyes shift to Trevel. The look on his face is serious, violet eyes searching mine for something. It seems like the same thing I'm searching for in his, which is confusing me down to my bones.

What are we? What is this??

The Ivory releases me as the young guy returns, followed closely by an older man with a vaguely familiar face, carrying a black briefcase.

Oh, crap… That's one of the doctors. From the East.

A chill zips up my spine.

Trevel shifts beside me, and I glance up to find him watching Dr. Love, who's practically snarling at the old guy. Pure wrath is coming off of him in waves. But even if it wasn't already palpable in the air, it'd sure as shit be visible in the flames of raw *hatred* Love is shooting at the other doctor in the room.

The Ivory snorts. "Not very pleased with this turn of events, are we, Lemuel?"

Dr. Love is vibrating.

I'm gonna go out on a limb and say those two aren't besties.

The Ivory sighs. "Being that I'm allowing you three to stay here, in *my* home, I'll need to utilize some… extra security." I peer at him in between watching the doctor, who steps over to us. "My men have their hands full right now, I'm afraid. As do I, meaning we won't be able to keep an eye on you at all times, surveillance or not." He gestures to the man, who sets his case down on a nearby table and opens it. "Dr. Johansson here has something that will put my mind at ease."

The guy—Johansson—removes a device from inside the case, bringing it over to me first. A black circle, maybe plastic or rubber. But when he unfastens and opens it, I realize what it is and back up.

"Wait, what the fuck??" I grunt.

"Hold still, please," Johansson instructs me, voice meek, with a discernible accent, maybe German or Norwegian.

Doesn't seem like the type of dude who'd be attempting to fucking *collar* me. *But I guess that's the point.*

"No way." I shake my head. "You're not putting that on me."

"Oh yes, he is," The Ivory says sternly. "You see, I would love to trust you, Byron, but the fact is that I don't feel I can trust anyone these days..." His voice trails, eyes hardening when they drift from us to Dr. Love. "You give an inch, but they need fucking *miles*."

"You know what you did..." Dr. Love growls at him.

The Ivory stalks over until they're chest to chest. "And you know what *you* did. After everything I allowed... Everything I let *slide*. Selfishly and thoughtlessly siding with yet another ungrateful *puto* who could've had it all." His tone is frighteningly low as he spits his words like venom.

I'm not afraid to admit it... The Warden has always been a purely terrifying dude, despite his prim and proper attire and mannerisms. But right now, in this dimly lit room, with gunfire and mayhem in the distance, his composure is slipping. Beat up and bloody, with that manic look in his charcoal eyes... He's giving off the vibes of someone who has very little to lose, and that makes him a thousand times more frightening, and dangerous, than before.

Johansson uses the fact that we're distracted to fasten the collar around my neck.

"Fuck you!" I choke, grabbing at my throat. "What the hell even is this thing??"

"*That* is a prototype of an invention we'd been working on," The Ivory says, still glaring at Dr. Love, lips curving into a sinister smirk. "I'm quite proud of it. A collar with the ability to immobilize a subject, should they leave the designated area. In your case, that would be the mansion."

Johansson moves to Trevel next, fastening a collar on him. His eyes drift to mine, etched in frightful discomfort.

"When you say *immobilize*..." Trevel mumbles, touching the device curled tightly around his throat.

The Ivory's eyes shift to Johansson.

"The inner band of the collar consists of a sensor and a series of needles, which are laced with a paralytic sedative," Johansson explains.

"If the sensor leaves the programmed *safe space*, or if it is tampered with, the needles are deployed."

What… in the actual… fuck??

I can feel the shock on my face, mirroring that on Trevel's. Both of our hands drop away from the collars fast, and The Ivory chuckles.

"Yea, I would *not* try to remove them." He grins wickedly. "It's like when you try to remove one of those security tags they put on clothes in department stores… Only the ink that ruins the clothing is an extremely powerful tranquilizer that will cause immediate muscular paralysis lasting about twelve hours. And the pretty little garment being destroyed is *you*." He turns a wink on Dr. Love.

My mouth is filling with saliva, pulse jumping aggressively in my neck. I swallow slowly and fearfully, suddenly very *aware* of my Adam's apple sliding beneath this deadly device.

"How do we know it won't, like… go off by accident?" I ask, resisting the urge to fidget in place.

The Ivory shrugs apathetically. "We don't, really."

Tentatively, Johansson steps closer to Dr. Love, dripping with unease. He honestly looks like he's about to shit himself based on the angry glare Love is shooting at him. He's shaking in his lab coat.

The Ivory thrusts out his hand impatiently, and Johansson hands him the collar. The Ivory leans in, grinning as he grazes his index finger over Dr. Love's throat.

"You wanna end up like the last asshole who put something around my neck?" Love hisses a quiet threat.

"Oh, please, Lemuel. I'm not going to *scar* you like Uncle Stephen did," The Ivory hums, wrapping the collar around Dr. Love's throat. "No, no. The plans I have for you are much more *permanent*." Once the collar is secured in place, The Ivory whispers, "You should've killed me when you had the chance."

Moving back, he pats Love on the cheek. "Bring him to the tombs. Lemuel's had enough luxury in this mansion for one lifetime."

Kent storms over, grabbing Dr. Love.

"You boys can sleep anywhere you like tonight," he says to Trevel and me. "There are plenty of empty rooms now, but that will change very soon. Feel free to roam, but remember, one step outside and it's lights out."

Striding away from us, he pulls the walkie off of his belt again, holding it up to his face. "Whoever brings me Felix Darcey gets an extra million. Still breathing is the only stipulation." He peeks over his shoulder at

Dr. Love. "Oh, and make sure he has both of his hands… I want to take one myself. Call it a *gift* for someone special."

He sneers in Love's direction while he's being dragged out of the room, hollering and cursing The Ivory's name. But The Ivory is already gone, presumably off to go threaten another room full of people.

Jesus, what the fuck am I doing here??

Deadly collars, threats, gunshots, missing people, a dark mansion… revenge. It's all too much.

Once The Ivory is gone, Johansson awkwardly scuttles off, followed by the young guy, who gives us a sympathetic smile and wave on his way out. "Goodnight, Trevel. Goodnight, Byron."

He's gone before I can even react. Not that I can process *anything* right now. I'm too busy stressing over being potentially paralyzed at any moment.

"Who… who's that?" I ask, stunned and jittery, distracting myself from the urge to fuss with the collar.

"Yari," Trevel says, waiting a beat before creeping to the doorway. "Ivory's assistant." He peeks around the corner, then motions for me. "Come on."

"Where are we going?" I follow him reluctantly, because part of me doesn't want to move.

I just want to sit in this room, maybe stare at the fire for a few hours in silence while I contemplate my bleak existence.

"We have to go check on Darcey," he whispers. "Clearly, they haven't found him yet…"

Oh, shit. He's right.

The Ivory's looking for him…

Together, we head for the stairs. It's good… I need to keep moving. I feel like if I stop, even for a second, I might fall apart.

I hate relying on people, because people suck and they can't be trusted. But in this moment, I'm desperate for some solace from the chaos. I'm craving some fucking *peace*, even if it's fleeting.

I think… I just need his arms around me again.

On the second floor, we head to the end of the wing. To Dr. Love's *former* bedroom. We race through the door and come to a full stop.

Fuck… My stomach drops.

"Well… That's not good." Trevel sighs, wandering up to the bed where I left Felix Darcey tied up, now empty.

Nothing but a belt and some rope left behind.

He's gone.

"Fucking little rat chewed himself free," Trevel scoffs, picking up the belt before tossing it down.

"Great." I rub my eyes. "Fucking perfect."

"He's The Ivory's problem now." Trevel steps up to me, resting his hands on my shoulders. "Truth be told, I wasn't sure what to do with him, anyway."

"No shit," I grumble, and he frowns.

"Are you upset with me?" His head slants in this almost innocently bemused way that makes me want to laugh.

But I'm far too restless right now to find his lunacy adorable.

"*Yes*, Trevel, I am upset with you." I puff out the words on an exhausted breath. "If you'll recall, I was upset with you before we even left the prison! And now, everything is all fucked up... I mean, *Jesus*, how much chaos can happen in one night??"

I make a weak attempt at pulling away from him, but it doesn't take. He holds me in place while rubbing my shoulders gently, yet firm enough that it's easing some stress in them almost instantly. My eyes flutter shut.

God, the way he works those fucking hands...

I'm still pissed, and worried, stressed and anxious, and exhausted, and scared. But the massage is helping, too much to attempt fighting it.

"Shh... I know, baby," he croons, pressing on some spot at the base of my skull that instantly alleviates the tension headache throbbing my temples. "Things have gotten a bit wonky, and I'm sorry for the part I've played in it."

"Watch the collar..." I mumble. He breathes a soft chuckle, and my eyes open slowly, latching onto his purple gaze. Exhaling, I drop my forehead onto his. "Whether I want it to or not, my life revolves around this stupid island. And now it's all been turned upside down. In the span of one night, *everything* has changed."

I gulp when I think about Luthor and Ren, and what the Warden said. About them leaving...

This situation feels insurmountable.

"I know it seems like that, love, but trust me, things have been changing for a while," Trevel says calmly. "Maybe you can't see it, because it's been built around you for so long..."

I think he might be right, but I don't want to accept it. I loathe the idea that I'm so easy to break now.

Alabaster Pen tore me down.

I'm not a fighter anymore… I'm weak.

I'm nothing but… a prisoner.

Lifting my face, I blink at him, remembering how we stood in this exact spot only a few hours ago. Partners in crime, working together to exact our *revenge*. That's how it seemed, anyway.

I remember how he kissed me in front of Darcey and Dr. Love…

It felt real in the moment. But how can I be sure it was? How can I be sure I'm not just another part of his plan?

A pawn in *his* game…

"Was this what you wanted?" I ask quietly. His forehead lines. "Turning Dr. Love over to The Ivory… Like he did to you?"

He stares at me for a moment before murmuring, "Karma *is* a bitch…"

"Right… And now we're on his side," I breathe. "For better or worse."

Our eyes remain locked, those words hanging in the air.

"Well… you are my prison wife." His lips twitch.

I huff, then shake my head. "Trevel, this is serious."

"I know, baby…" He pouts, continuing with his massaging that feels intentionally distracting.

"What happened?" I mumble. "With Love… when you were out in the woods?"

"We were almost to the prison when the tower fell," he answers. "It was bonkers how loud it was. Felt like a bloody bomb had been dropped."

"I mean before that," I rasp, trying to force the vulnerability out of my tone. "What did you two… do?" I clear my throat. "Did you talk to him about anything?"

Trevel gapes at me, as if he's momentarily stunned by my question. It's as endearing as it is infuriating, because I can't fathom that he *still* isn't processing how one-sided this whole thing is.

I'm not Bonnie Parker… *He* is. I'm Clyde Barrow… And that's not a good thing. Clyde was a doormat for Bonnie, doing anything and everything to please her. And she just kept stringing him along, giving him just enough to keep him on the hook.

Joke or not, the metaphor stands. I never noticed how much of a fucking follower I am… How much my existence relies on the people who use me.

I am a fucking sidekick… A desperate fucking groupie.

Trevel's eyes glisten with something I wish like hell I could read. But then he glances left and frowns, blinking himself out of it. It's strange, but he just started doing that tonight, after we fucked in the woods. Almost like he's talking himself out of something.

He brushes my hair back with his fingers. "I think it's quite sexy how jealous you are, my sweet fury."

I frown, but he kisses it off my lips.

"I don't want you to worry, baby. Our plan worked. The Ivory has Dr. Love, and soon, he'll have Felix. They'll get what's coming to them, and we'll be safe here."

My shoulder slumps a bit in defeat. I can barely hold myself up anymore. The weight of all this shit is crushing me.

"Hey," Trevel whispers, grasping my chin and forcing my gaze back to his. "We have each other. That's all that matters, yea?"

I blink at the promise in his eyes, nodding slowly.

"Good," he purrs, kissing me softly. "Now, come here, warrior." He brings me over to the bed. "You're awfully tight. Let me work all that stress out of your big, sexy body."

I don't have it in me to resist right now. As much as I can't shake the feeling that I'm being used or manipulated, I can't deny that some part of me finds comfort in it. Especially right now. The relief of not having to think is pretty satisfying.

If playing the part of his toy gets me pleasure, for now, I'd be a fool to turn it down while the state of everything else is so grim.

So I crawl into the giant bed with my violet-eyed partner in crime and get naked. I let him work those magic hands on me until I'm blissed out, and then we spend hours tangled in fancy sheets.

It's surreal, being here with Trevel. Fucking and cuddling in a luxurious king-size bed. Using lush sex and slow kisses to mask our realities.

From a prison to a mansion, but I'm still confined.

From one body to another… and I'm still in the dark.

CHAPTER THIRTY-TWO

Byron

I WOKE UP THIS MORNING IN A BEDROOM, IN AN *ACTUAL* BED, FOR THE FIRST TIME in three years. And I immediately thought I was dead.

The bed in Dr. Love's room is insanely comfortable, like a complete one-eighty from the flimsy mattress on my rickety old bunk bed in the Pen. After the massage and multiple orgasms from Trevel last night, while the rain hit the windows like quixotic music… I was out cold.

Unfortunately, sleeping in wasn't an option. Dawn brought with it a long-awaited break in the storm, and the harsh reality of the state of Alabaster Isle.

Last night wasn't a bad dream… It really happened.

The prison has fallen. People are missing… Dead, or gone, or both. Velle is still over there, with his men, doing God knows what. Prisoners who attempt to flee are being gunned down like animals.

It's chaos, plain and simple. Death, destruction, devastation.

And I'm just… *here*. Inside a lavish mansion, surrounded by people I don't know, feeling more out of place than an earthworm among pythons.

Trevel and I have been sitting around for hours, quietly blending into the background as much as possible. Just trying to stay out of the way, because there's so much going on, and I wouldn't have the first clue what part I'm expected to play, if any.

What am I supposed to be doing?

Why is he allowing me to stay here??

What… does he want *from me?*

All day, men I've never seen before have been storming around the mansion, yelling things in Spanish at each other and over the walkie-talkies. I've seen a few of the Warden's guards pop in, but mostly they're new faces—and more are arriving constantly, I believe coming in on the ferries.

Men in uniform. *Soldiers.*

He's bringing in backup. Which can mean only one thing…

I won't pretend to know much of anything about who Manuel Blanco was before he became the Warden of Alabaster Penitentiary, but based on the way all of these men look to him like he's their commanding officer—referring to him only as *Jefe*—I have to assume the rumors I've been hearing over the years are true.

The Ivory's business is with the Colombian cartel, and this island is just one small piece of his territory. A piece that's now under *attack*, and apparently, requiring the defense of a goddamn military cordon.

Seriously, Trevel and I are the *only* ones not involved in whatever is going on outside the mansion. From what I understand, there's a staff of personal chefs, chauffeurs, and cleaning people who live in that house by the back entrance. They too have been mulling around the mansion, keeping busy while The Ivory's men turn their quarters into a fucking base of operations… And an armory.

Every single dude who stalks past us is packing some serious artillery, leading me to believe that Manuel Blanco is bringing over more than just *bodies* as reinforcements.

These soldiers are strapped, which *would* be overwhelming… *If I wasn't already wearing a collar that'll incapacitate me if I try to leave the premises.*

Time is both flying by and standing eerily still. The next thing I know, a full day has passed, then another, and I can't tell if I'm adapting, or in denial.

The echoes of gunfire still register, but I'm trying not to think about it; fighting off the need to know what's happening out there, because no one will tell me anything, anyway.

Trevel and I have tried asking Kent questions, but his answers are limited to the standard curt responses.

Don't worry about it.

Just stay out of the way, and if he asks for something, do it.

In an effort to take his advice, we decided to move out of Dr. Love's room. The mansion is getting crowded with all the newcomers, but if I'm being honest, I wasn't feeling it in there. It was one thing to fuck in their bed as some silly, stupid game of revenge kink, but actually *staying* in Dr. Love's room was bothering me, and I'm not exactly sure *why*.

Maybe I am; I just don't want to think about it.

We decided to take a bedroom on the third floor on the left side—formerly the guards' quarters. I guess it still is, just not the guards *I'm* used to. It wasn't until we started poking around, looking for clothes and toiletries to use, that we discovered whose room it'd been…

My mind is still running over all of this bullshit while I sit in the library, reading—*or pretending to*—on the big leather couch, with Trevel by my side. A fire crackling, keeping us warm and distracting from the bloodshed just outside. *It's not doing the best job.*

I've been scanning the same line of this book for minutes on end, remembering the stuff I found in the back of the closet in our new bedroom… An NYPD hoodie. A Claddagh ring, engraved with the words, *"Dílseacht agus teaghlach,"* which I think is Irish Gaelic. A framed picture of a young Velle standing next to a woman…

Don't worry about it.

Keep busy.

Ignore the fact that you're now sleeping in Rook, Joy, and Velle's bedroom, and they're trapped in Alabaster Penitentiary.

It's not completely fucking insane *that you're here and they're there.*

It's fine.

Head in the… game.

"Cold?" Trevel brushes his fingers up and down my arm, over the goosebumps that have little to do with the temperature.

I give up rereading the sentence and peer at him. He's scribbling in a notebook. My eyes fall to it, just long enough to catch a few words before I look away.

Glancing across the room, I watch Yari, who's nestled in a big chair, scrolling on his phone. *No surprise there. It's what he does ninety percent of the time.*

The Warden's assistant, Yari Estevez, is a nice guy. *Too nice…*

It doesn't make any sense. What does The Ivory need with an assistant like him? He's so… normal. He's exactly what you'd expect from a personal assistant to a celebrity or some rich business mogul. Not a cartel capo who runs a depraved prison as just *one* of his many nefarious enterprises.

Yari must sense me staring at him, because he peeks up, locking his light eyes on mine. He smiles kindly, gaze dropping to the book in my hands. He cocks a brow, but says nothing. Just goes back to his phone.

"What are you writing?" I ask Trevel, attempting to distract myself.

"A poem," he answers with a smirk, though he doesn't even pause what he's doing.

"No shit," I grumble, and he chuckles. "What's it about?"

Wet flesh and growls of thunder…

Like the storm, I felt him in my bones.

Trevel looks up from his writing, violet gaze darkened with the fire's glow. "You."

Slip between the trees with me…

Fall for me like rain.

Fight me back, sweet fury…

And I'll fight for you.

I swallow hard. "Me?"

He nods slowly. There are way too many things littering my thoughts, but he's at the forefront. He has to be… He's all I have, now more than ever.

But the thing is, I'm conflicted, between wanting to keep this, hold on to it with everything I've got… And fearing it'll smash me to pieces.

It's just another thing I've been trying not to dwell on, because it's a lot of pressure on a new relationship that I'm not even confident we're actually having. We weren't supposed to be a couple, but now it feels like we've been thrust together in this crazy fucking situation, and I don't know what any of it means.

What is this?

What are we doing?

Who are you, *violet eyes?*

Before either of us can speak, The Ivory appears at the entrance to the room. I'm instantly anxious as he stalks over to where we're sitting, stopping to peer down at us.

His dark eyes take in my book, lips twitching. "Enjoying it?"

I glance at the book I'm gripping nervously—*Beneficial Brainwashing* by Dr. Melvin Strange. "It's, uh… odd."

The Ivory's smirk widens, and he huffs. "I need to speak with you about something very important." He turns without waiting for a response, waltzing away casually. "Follow me. Both of you."

We jump up and scurry after him, apprehension eating at my insides with every step. He leads us down a long corridor I've never seen, into a large room. From the look of it, it's meant to be a dining room—there's a long table with lots of chairs, with chandeliers hanging above. Except it isn't set for dinner…

There are papers all over the place, some like blueprints. A few men sit at the far-end of the table, their conversation coming to a halt when we enter the room.

The Ivory gestures to a chair. "Have a seat."

We do what he says, sitting beside one another. As soon as my ass is in the chair, Trevel's hand is on my thigh. It's my only source of comfort, and that still worries me. *Greatly.*

But I don't have time to think about it. Because The Ivory is coming up behind me…

Stiffening, I can't stop picturing him whipping out a knife and slitting my throat. Not sure why he'd do that, but I've been waiting for the other shoe to drop since he allowed me, a *prisoner*, to stay in his home.

I feel him behind me, my skin hot and itchy all over. Fear, and memories of other sensations weave through me as his fingers brush my neck. I'm bracing myself for pain when he touches my collar. But instead, I hear a faint beep, and the collar loosens. He removes it slowly from around my throat, and my brow furrows.

Huh…?

The Ivory takes the seat opposite me, placing my collar on the table while I just stare. "I'm going to need you to do something for me, Byron," he says calmly. "Officer Chevelle and his men are in the prison. They've hijacked the armory and are… making things very complicated for us right now. I need to know the extent of the damage so we can work on repairing it, but they won't let us get close." He pauses, charcoal irises boring deep. "I need you to go over there. I need *you* to go inside the prison and speak to them."

My lips part, but I can't even imagine what the hell I would say to something like that. I have a million questions, too many responses. They're all getting caught like a bottleneck in my throat.

Trevel's fingers dig into my thigh.

The Ivory leans forward. "You've known them a long time, Byron. You have a good rapport with Officer Jameson… I'm sure you've bonded with many of the guards over the years. And of course you know the prisoners…"

"What's left of them…" one of the guys at the other end of the table mumbles, and The Ivory shoots him a fiery look.

"*Callate la boca*, Lio, or I'll do it for you," The Ivory hisses quietly at the man, who recoils. "The fact of the matter, Byron, is that you're the only one they'll allow inside. Because they trust you."

"But… isn't it… dangerous?" I croak. "We've been hearing nothing but gunfire since the prison went down. What if they shoot me?"

He makes a face like he isn't as worried about this as I am, but covers it up with some obviously forced empathy. "My men will keep you safe until you're inside the prison. After that, you'll be on your own. But I'm sure you can handle yourself." His head tilts. "You're a fighter yourself, aren't you?"

"Will he have a gun?" Trevel asks, taking the words out of my mouth.

The Ivory's gaze narrows. "No."

"I don't know…" I rub my eyes. "What would I even say to them? What's the endgame here?"

He straightens. "The endgame is you doing what the fuck I say, without question." The chilling tone of his voice sweeps up my spine like icy fingers. "If you'll recall, that was the stipulation of my allowing you to stay here. You will go to the prison, you will speak with Officer Chevelle and find out what he wants. You will get eyes on the situation in there and report back."

"What if they won't…? What if—"

"Serve your purpose, Byron," he seethes, frighteningly quiet. "Trust me, you want to have one."

I'm baffled by this. And also, not.

Here I've been sitting around, waiting for him to realize he doesn't need me. Turns out he's had a use for me all along.

He knew what he was doing, bringing me here.

I'm his rat, his spy. Just like Trevel.

Trevel is his link to Dr. Love. I'm his link to the prison.

To say I'm unsure about this would put it well beyond mildly, but there's nothing I can do. Saying no isn't an option.

This isn't a choice. *He's got me right where he wants me.*

So I sit up and clear my throat. "When?"

"Right now," he chirps, almost patronizingly.

I suck in a breath. "Alright…"

"Wonderful." With the flick of his wrist, the men in the room stand. "My team here will bring you. Once inside, you'll get a lay of the land, observe the setting… negotiate and such." My brow arches. "This is serious, Byron. The fate of this island may depend on it. I'm putting my faith in you, and I trust that you won't let me down."

My thoughts are hectic. But I nod and stand.

Trevel shoots up at my side. "I'm going too."

The Ivory gives him an amused look. "Absolutely not. They don't trust you for shit."

"You must be high if you think I'm going to sit here in this mansion while he goes out into the line of fire alone," Trevel growls. His protective tone warms me inside, but I fight it off.

"I don't need a bodyguard or a babysitter," I grunt at him, and he frowns.

"I know you don't *need* me for anything, Raph," his voice is soft again. "It's for me. *I* need it… I won't be able to—"

"This is all very romantic, but the answer is still no." The Ivory stands, glaring at us. Trevel opens his mouth to continue arguing, but The Ivory cuts him off with a snarl, "Don't push me."

In an effort to diffuse the tension, I take Trevel's hand. "I'll be fine, I promise. In and out."

He doesn't look sold in the slightest, but he doesn't have a choice, either.

And just like that, we're trudging through the mansion, toward the front door. Trevel squeezes my hand until he absolutely has to let go. Giving him one last look, I try to convey everything I'm feeling, but it's hard when I barely understand it myself.

Despite what The Ivory says, I know there will be no negotiating. I'm not going in there to collect Velle's list of demands… He's playing us.

"I'll be back soon," I whisper to Trevel.

His Adam's apple slides in his throat. "I'll save you some dinner."

I breathe out a small chuckle, and it makes him smile.

Glancing at The Ivory, I turn reticently, following his men outside.

"Oh, and Byron…" His voice gives me pause as I'm walking out the door. "If there's even a sliver of doubt as to which side you're on, then I suggest you stay there."

The journey across the island is quick. It would be quicker, but we have to make a sort of zigzag to get to the spot the Warden's guys have deemed *safe*.

They drive me along the coast in a large black SUV with bulletproof glass windows—a trip in itself since I haven't even been in a car in years. Then we get out and make the rest of the trek on foot.

I'm no soldier. Sure, I like to fight, but my weapons are my extremities, and more than anything, I like the act of hand-to-hand combat. The premise of *war*, fighting battles on behalf of turf and things like that, has never appealed to me. Neither has the idea of using guns.

But these men are talking to me as if we're brothers in arms. Assault rifles slung over their shoulders, decked out in camouflage garb, they guide me down a path, from the shore inland, through the trees.

"You'll want to enter from the South Gate," one of the guys instructs. "There's a main entrance about a quarter mile from here. That'll be your best bet. Avoid where the walls are down. That's where they have the most eyes and the fewest blind spots. The woods between the tower and the cliffs is literally the Wild West."

"We'll cover you to the gate," another guy says, lifting binoculars. "Stay hidden. Between the trees, along the walls… Anywhere that's not in plain sight."

I can't help gawking at them like they're mental. Two days ago, this island was quiet. Dangerous, sure, but only for *us*; the prisoners locked up inside the Pen. Gazing over what it's become, my jaw strains, fists squeezing to control the adrenaline in my veins.

This feels like we're in *Apocalypse Now*.

It's *insane*. Velle used to threaten to shoot us damn near every day. But the thought of him *actually* shooting me now seems so bizarre.

I guess it's not, though.

History aside, this *is* dangerous. If Velle has the armory, that means the gunshots we've been hearing haven't just been from The Ivory's men alone. There's *actually* a war going on, and I'm stepping into hostile territory.

But… they shouldn't be hostile towards me. We're friends.

I'm one of them. Right…?

I stay close to the guys as they jog between the trees, aiming their scopes all over the place before calling out, "Clear."

Part of me feels like they're being extra as fuck. I almost chuckle.

But then a loud pop has me jumping out of my skin.

"Down!" someone yells.

A bullet zips right past my head, hitting the tree behind me.

Holy shit, what the fuck?!

Everything is moving at hyper speed, yet I feel like I'm underwater. Ducking, I shield myself with a tree while the guys lay down cover fire.

I hate being afraid. I don't want to admit that I am, but I've never been shot at before. I'm shaking so hard I can barely move.

What am I doing out here??

Moments of shitting myself later, I overpower the locked muscles just enough to look around. It's hard to tell where the gunfire is coming from. But when I follow the aim of the guys' scopes, I see them.

Snipers. On the fucking roof of the prison.

Okay, this is fucking nuts.

They're too far away for me to make out who they are, but I have to assume they're people I know…

"It's too hairy," one guy barks, popping off three more rounds in the snipers' direction. "We'll have to go around—"

His words are cut off when I move out from behind the tree.

"What the hell are you doing?!"

"Get down!"

They're shouting at me, but I don't care. *Fuck* this.

I need to get over there. I need them to know it's me.

Velle, Joy, Rook… Hancock, Jasper, Peters…

They wouldn't be shooting at me, *would they??*

On some level, I know it's naïve to think this way, but either way, this is happening. If they want to kill me, *fine*. But they'll need to look me in the eye when they do it.

Slinking between the trees, I harness all of my skills at being invisible and rush closer to the east, following the trail of debris. The pops of gunfire fade, in my head and into the background. It's growing farther as I leave it behind, jogging toward the gaping hole in the prison with my blood rushing in my ears.

This is my first time seeing the damage up close. It's fucking mind-boggling. Alabaster Penitentiary, my home for the last three years, is in *literal* shambles.

The guard tower only fell on the east, but it's clear that the damage was much worse because of how old and weathered the prison is. If the building was properly maintained, I'm sure it could have withstood such things.

As soon as I'm close to the giant piles of concrete that used to be walls, I see men, at least two of them, guarding the opening.

One of them spots me, and hollers, "Come out! Slowly…"

"Show me your hands!" another voice shouts.

Sucking in a deep breath, I step out from behind the trees with my hands up. They're dressed in guard uniforms, familiar ones—clearly, these are Velle's men. But they're wearing masks, so I still can't tell who it is.

"Oh, shit... 62??" one of them rumbles.

"Are you alone?" the other barks.

"Yes," I attempt to project while stepping forward slowly, ignoring the M16s aimed at my head.

"Are you armed?" they ask, and I shake my head.

"No."

Once I'm within a few feet, they rush me, grabbing me hard and shoving me up against a collapsed wall.

"Just like old times, huh?" I grunt as they pat me down aggressively.

"He's clear," one guy announces. Then he whips his mask off, and I let out a gust of relief when I see Hancock.

He brushes his sweaty hair away from his face. "We were wondering where you were..."

The other guy finally gives up aiming his gun out into the woods, turning it on me again. "What the hell are you doing here?"

Now that I'm up close, I recognize the voice. That, and his being with Hancock, I'm sure I know who this is...

"Yo, Jasper, how about you get that thing outta my face?" I hiss, shoving the barrel aside.

He lowers it stubbornly, removing his mask. "I'm serious, Kang. Why are you here?"

"Chill, man." Hancock jabs him. "Maybe he was stuck out there. Give people the benefit of the doubt..."

"Right," Jasper huffs, glaring at me. "He's freshly showered and those are Velle's." He points at my shoes.

I mean, *Velle's* shoes.

Sue me. I needed some clean sneakers.

"Okay, fine. You win, detective," Hancock mutters, rolling his eyes.

"You've been in the mansion," Jasper rumbles in obvious suspicion. The relief I was feeling when I first saw them is definitely drying up quickly.

"Listen, man, shit's been crazy out there. I don't have to tell you that." I rub my eyes. "Just... where's Velle? I need to see him and Joy."

Jasper continues to glower at me. "Why?"

Resentment is boiling for this goddamn situation I don't want to be in, and the distrust they've all been throwing at me, since even before the fall.

I push up to him, getting in his face. "What the fuck is your problem?"

"My *problem* is that we're under attack while you're over there, tucked in and cozy with the enemy!" he hisses. "Now you wanna stroll over here, demanding things??"

My jaw clenches with my fists. *I'm gonna lay this dude out.*

"Alright, enough," Hancock sighs, getting between us. "We should move anyway. It's not safe over here."

Jasper is still mean-mugging me, looking at me like *I'm* responsible for what's going on out here... Like he hasn't known me for three fucking years.

This is some bullshit.

"Fine," he eventually growls. "Follow me. And stay close..." He shoots Hancock a look before stomping off, pulling his walkie off of his holster and rumbling into it, "Heads up. We've got a visitor."

"Home sweet home," Hancock says on a tired breath, shining his flashlight into the darkness.

Keeping up with Jasper is difficult. Not because he's moving too fast or anything, but because he's familiar with the *updated layout*... And I'm fucking *reeling*. The place is completely demolished. You'd have no idea this was once the East Wing. It's nothing but rubble now, wide-open and exposed to the elements. There are remains of some ceiling, but it's all cracked and smashed through, broken pipes hanging down with water leaking. Only dimmed red light—and their flashlights—illuminating what's left of the halls.

"No power?" I ask, taking in the destruction while trying not to trip over the large heaps of concrete and rebar.

Hancock grunts in lieu of an actual answer. "The main power supply was damaged by the fall. The generators are technically working, but it's not doing much..." He gives me a hand, helping me climb over a huge pile of debris. "No lights, or hot water..."

"Nothing like sleeping in a king-sized bed in a mansion stocked with food, huh?" Jasper sneers over his shoulder, oozing hostility. "Chef been making that roast pork stir fry, or what?"

"Fuck off," I snarl.

He shakes his head, continuing to lead the way through corridors that run around solitary. I'm guessing because solitary doesn't exist anymore...

It's been days since the fall, but dust still hangs in the air. Now I understand the need for masks. Breathing this shit in has me coughing, attempting to cover my face with the collar of my shirt.

Never in my wildest dreams could I have imagined Alabaster Pen being any shabbier, but this is next level. It's a shell.

Deep pools of water have gathered in certain spots. The smell of the ocean is a hundred times stronger than it ever was before, now combined with that of wet stone, smoke and gunpowder.

And blood. *Lots* of blood.

I'm not trying to dwell on it, but there's a faint smell in the air that I can only assume is death, blood trails on much of the floor that isn't covered. My insides feel hollow from the knowledge that people definitely died here, either from the accident, or after…

"We've been trying to locate and identify as many bodies as possible," Hancock tells me, reading the mourning on my face. "Bring 'em outside and burn 'em, but we don't have the manpower—"

"Simon!" Jasper snaps. "For the love of God, shut your mouth!"

"Fuck you…" Hancock mutters.

"No, seriously! Stop telling him things!" Jasper teems. "For all we know, he's working for that prick! And I don't want him running back there, telling him we're struggling."

Hancock is giving him a seriously strained look, reminding me that I'd heard they were in some kind of relationship. I haven't seen them in a while. *And I guess I've been distracted…*

I swallow a lump, like a dry pill made of guilt.

"Are we…?" Hancock whispers to Jasper, who slows to a stop. They blink at each other. "Struggling?"

Jasper's face loses a lot of animosity, anger fading into despondence as he reaches out, brushing some messy strands of hair away from Hancock's eyes. In just that brief touch, in that lingering look, I see something that binds up my gut.

These are just guys; *people* forced into this fucked-up situation like the rest of us. I used to forget that all the time, because they were guards, and we were prisoners. They were *above* us.

But now, we're all on the same level. If anything, I might be above them, being in The Ivory's good graces.

No wonder they're so pissed off. I know I was.

"Let's keep moving," Jasper murmurs softly to Hancock, who nods.

General population isn't as torn to shreds, but it's still a mess. Jasper and Hancock keep their guns up, moving around corners on high alert. My heart is rocking steadily, eyes jumping left and right, watching out for whatever danger could be lurking in these dark halls.

Jasper whistles, and someone in the distance whistles back. *A signal.* Once we're closer, Peters comes into view. He looks surprised to see me, but doesn't comment on it. Just nods at Jasper and Hancock.

"Any word?" Hancock asks.

Peters shakes his head somberly. He clears his throat. "Nieves made a break for it…"

The three of them share a knowing look, one that I can also read.

So, he's dead.

"Sunshine here came to check on us," Jasper tells him, eyes flicking to me. "We're bringing him to Velle. Linetti and Brenner are on lookout, but you might wanna get down to the crash site just in case…"

"Ten-four," Peters says, casting me one last glance before storming off in the direction we just came.

My thoughts are a jumbled mass of confusion and questions as we keep moving, passing a few more guards outside the cafeteria. They're all armed with assault rifles, posted up like soldiers. *I swear to God, we're in Fallujah, not New York.*

I realize that we're headed into the West Wing when we reach the stairs. This part of the prison has minimal damage. *Go figure, since it's the Warden's side.* On our way upstairs, Jasper whistles again, which is met with another whistle. Followed by a familiar female voice.

"This better be good… You assholes are flaking on guard duty."

We come around the corner and I'm flooded with relief, *much* more potent this time.

"What's the—" Joy's words cut out when she sees me, her eyes widening. "Oh, shit."

Pushing past the guys, I race over to her, and she launches herself at me.

"Thank God you're alright," she whispers, hugging me tight.

I hold her back, absorbing the feel of her. Her friendship; a support I've missed more than I even realized until right fucking now. Everything has changed *so* drastically. Being back with Joy is settling me down to my core.

"I missed you, *jeulgeoun*," I hum into her silky hair, absentmindedly playing with her ponytail without even realizing I'm doing it. "I was worried…"

She pulls back to smirk at me. "*Worried*? Do you have any idea who you're talking to?"

I chuckle, reveling in this feeling for as long as it'll last. Which isn't long at all, because she glances behind me, amusement falling away.

"Come on." She drags me into a room I recognize… The Warden's office. Except that it looks pretty damn different than the last time I was in here.

For one, Velle is sitting at the desk, not The Ivory. The room is illuminated only by lanterns and a few candles. Rook is on the loveseat, fiddling with a CB radio. He glances up at me, stress-lined eyes widening. But he says nothing, just nods, continuing on with his task.

"Look what the cat dragged in…" Velle mumbles, standing up slowly. He cocks his head. "You checked him?"

"He's clear," Jasper answers from behind me. "We're gonna head back down… Cover Peters."

Velle nods, though his dark blue eyes are stuck on me as Jasper and Hancock leave the room.

I look around the dimly lit space. "Finally got that corner office you've been vying for, huh?"

His gaze narrows, but he doesn't respond. He's grilling me, sizing me up, and I can't say I blame him.

Velle is smart. Guard dog or not, he's never been the brainwashed sheep I used to think he was. After the fall, it's become clear that *he* had a plan all along, too. Whether or not it's gone down the way he anticipated is irrelevant. He knows what he's doing as much as The Ivory does.

So the simmering suspicion in his gaze is far from shocking.

"We looked everywhere for you, ya know…" Joy says. "You weren't in the prison when the tower fell… were you?"

I gulp. "Trevel and I… got out." Rook glances up in my peripheral. "The storm… I guess it knocked out the servers or something because the exit door in the East just… opened. So we   "

"Took off?" Velle finally speaks, arching that damn pierced brow.

"We weren't going to *escape*," I mutter.

"What do you think sneaking out of prison is called?" His lips twitch.

"Whatever, man. Don't act like you wouldn't do the same damn thing if you were in my shoes. I saw my shot, and I took it. But I wasn't planning on leaving the island."

Joy is making a face I can't read. I ignore it and go on.

"Trevel wanted… He wanted revenge on Dr. Love," I tell them reticently. "We grabbed him and Darcey, and that was when all hell broke loose."

Staring at me like he's piecing it all together, Velle eventually breathes and rubs his eyes. The exhaustion and mental strain on him are visible in his demeanor, despite how well he's holding it together.

"I take it Darcey got free," he hums, and I nod. "He's out there… in the woods. Taking out the Warden's men like fuckin' Rambo." He huffs, shaking his head. "I'd be careful if I were you."

"I can handle Felix fucking Darcey," I mutter.

"Listen up, champ." Velle steps over to me. "I'm tickled you came to visit, but let's address the goddamn elephant in the room."

I peek at Joy, then Rook. They're both staring at me.

"He doesn't care about you," he states. "And I know you know that. He's using you, and as good as it feels when it's working, because trust me, I *know* it feels fucking great… It's a lie. It's all bullshit. Nothing but sleight of hand from a master of misdirection."

I blink, posture rigid.

"It's time to pick a side," he says firmly.

"You belong here with us, *jeonsa*," Joy adds. "You know you do."

My chest is constricting. "I know you're right, but—"

"No buts," Velle snaps. "You're either with us, or you're against us. It's that simple."

I rub my eyes. "What's going on over here?? How did it come to this…?"

"This has been a long time coming," Velle rumbles. "I didn't start this shit, but you bet your ass I'm finishing it. He fucked with us for the last time."

"He's been killing prisoners," Rook jumps in. "I'm sure you've heard it…"

"Yea, and don't act like you guys wouldn't have been doing it yourselves!" I bark. "I get it; he's a fucking monster. We all know that. But do you honestly think you can defeat the devil? I mean, *really*?"

"Wow." Joy shakes her head.

"He's got his claws in you too, huh?" Velle scoffs. "I never noticed until now."

"No, he doesn't," I bite. "It's not about him…"

"So it's Trevel, then?" Joy balks. "That sly piece of Euro trash is more important to you than us? What happened to *loyalty*…"

"Why are you ganging up on me??" I hiss in defense. "I'm not siding with The Ivory, okay?? We're fucking stuck over there! If we leave, he'll kill us, you know that."

"You're here right now," Rook mumbles.

I stare blankly at them. I feel like I'm not explaining myself well, and it's because I don't know what I'm doing. *If I don't even understand it myself, how can I express it to them??*

"Armory or not, he has the numbers." I sigh.

Velle folds his arms over his chest. "We're rallying the prisoners."

"How many are left?" I tilt my head.

"Doesn't matter," he grouses. "They'll fight if they have to. It's better than dying out there. And I don't give a fuck… He can bring in a thousand more cartel men. It won't stop us. We're taking back this island. It's us versus him." He gets closer to me. "So I say again, you're either with us… or you're against us."

I pause, shifting on my feet. "I would never side against you guys, you know that—"

"But you have been." His tone is deep and sturdy, calm in his accusations. "You've been on his side since the moment you fell in with Fenwick."

My jaw clenches. "No, that's not—"

"You're a traitor," he hisses, still only a low rumble. "Sleeping in our bed, wearing my clothes…" He glances at my feet and scoffs. "That's where you're staying, right? In our bedroom…"

I stay quiet, stewing in guilt so bitter it's making me sick.

"Look, it is what it is, man. I just thought loyalty was important to you. I guess it's not."

"Of course it is," I growl, closing in. "I'm here because I needed to see you guys… To make sure you were alright."

"Aw. How *sweet*." His head cocks, cavernous blue narrowed at my face. "We both know you're here because he sent you."

I can feel Joy and Rook leering.

"So I have to ask… Why'd you *really* come?"

I swallow hard. "He told me to come over here and… negotiate."

Rook scoffs out loud while Joy spins, stalking away and rubbing her eyes. Velle chuckles.

"Obviously, it's bullshit, I *know* that. He wants me to get eyes on this place and report back or some shit, whatever."

"Yea," Velle croons knowingly.

"But it doesn't fucking matter," I argue on. "You and I both know it doesn't matter what the fuck I say to him. He's never going to stand down. But if I stay here, he'll kill Trevel. That's a fucking fact. He's got these collar things—"

"So?" Velle squints. "I'd say we need you here more than we need that asshole alive…"

My eyes round, chest constricting. The thought of something happening to Trevel is painful, made even worse at knowing that these people—whose side I'm supposed to be on—don't care whether he lives or dies.

Joy stomps back over. "He's not one of us, *jeonsa*. *You* are. We need you… He can handle himself."

I'm splitting down the middle, and it *kills*. The despair in what they're saying is climbing up my esophagus like bile. Swallowing it down, I cough up indignation in its place.

"I'm not going to let him die over this," I seethe. "He doesn't deserve that."

Joy scoffs, and I bark, "He doesn't! He doesn't deserve to be on this island any more than the rest of us do! Whatever you think about him is irrelevant. None of us are here by choice, and we're all just fighting to survive."

"Because of him!" Joy roars. "The Ivory did this to all of us! Are you really gonna sit here and say you think we should surrender??"

I'm fucking shaking all over. The fury and the fear have woven together into something so crippling, I can't barely keep myself standing anymore.

I just want to get back to him.

He's the only one who's truly on my side.

They don't care about me or my feelings. They just want to win. They're using me, just like The Ivory is.

Just like everyone does… It's what I'm here for, apparently.

Glancing at Velle, I find him watching me closely, assessing me with an almost pitying glint in his eyes.

"We've been trapped in this hellhole for over ten years." Joy gestures to Velle. "We're prisoners too; I know you know that. Giving up is going back, and I won't fucking do that. Not this time."

"What do you expect me to do??" I scrub hands over my face. "I won't leave Trevel behind. I can't—"

"He's holding the control room guys hostage," Rook says. "Did you know that?"

My lashes flutter, and I look at Velle once more. He confirms this with the pursing of his lips.

"Carson, Denton, Mark…" Rook goes on. "They're trapped in the control room, being held at gunpoint by his men."

My teeth set. "I say again… what do you expect *me* to do about that?"

"Get us into the mansion," Velle hums a demand.

"I can't do that. He'll kill—"

"Then we have nothing more to talk about," he cuts me off, turning and stalking over to the desk. Effectively ending the conversation.

I'm quaking in place, surrounded by people I've known for years, though I've never felt more alone.

They're putting me in an impossible position. Asking me to choose between them and Trevel is fucked up, but they don't care. They don't care about what *I* want at all.

I'm just another body they need to win this fight. A weapon they want in their arsenal.

"Bring him down to the west exit and cut him loose," Velle grunts robotically. Emotionless as he returns to loading rounds into magazines, not sparing me another glance.

Joy is visibly upset, but she's obviously trying to disguise it as she stomps toward the door, nodding for me to follow her. I give Velle one last lingering look. But he's shut down.

It's over.

I'm not giving him what he wants, so I guess we're done here.

Following Joy, we trudge in tense silence for a bit, nothing but the sounds of our footsteps accompanying my rampant thoughts. Back in general population, I hear voices coming from the rows. My face follows the direction of the crumbled corridors.

"I'm going to my cell," I grunt, not waiting for her permission.

I want my journal. The idea of leaving it behind, all of that hard work… All those years of writing…

I can't lose it. All of my truths are in that book.

Joy grabs me by the arm, but I rip out of her grip. "Why are you being like this?! Why are you all acting like I'm the fucking enemy just because I'm—"

"Fucking the enemy?" She cocks her head.

"Trevel is *not* the enemy," I growl.

She blinks at me, eyes softening a bit. "Maybe not… But how well do you really know him, B?"

I freeze, held in place by her pervasive gaze.

The truth is that I don't know him… not as well as I'd like to.

Not as well as I should if I'm going to keep sacrificing things for him.

Shooting her a defiant glare, I stomp toward my row. And this time, she lets me. But when I get there, I stop short.

There are guards in the row, delivering food to inmates in the cells. Handing it to them through the bars.

"They're stuck in there," Joy says from behind me while I gape in dismay. "When the storm fucked up the genny, some cells were open and others were locked. The servers might have a manual override in the control room…"

"But the Warden has it," I finish her sentence, gloom riding my tone.

She's quiet for a moment while we listen to the sounds of prisoners slowly rotting, more trapped in Hell than we ever were. Tools line the floor, as if they've been trying to cut through the bars or force them open. Clearly, it hasn't worked.

My face slants, meeting Joy's eyes. "What happened… to Luthor and Ren?"

Her face is alight with stuff I hate seeing. She's supposed to be a rock. She's supposed to be empty, like me. Instead, we're both drowning in bullshit emotions, and it fucking sucks.

"The Warden had Ren in the East…" she murmurs. "Ever since the new guards arrived." There's a ringing in my ears that won't stop. "He was down there the whole time, laced up and being fucking tortured."

"W-why…?"

"Why do you think??" she grits out. "Because *he* fucking said so. I'm not sure what was going on when the prison fell… I was outside, stuck in the old armory. All I know is that Luthor and Ren got out somehow… and they made a break for it." She exhales, blinking slowly. "They took a boat. Went out into the storm… And no one's seen them since."

I'm being smothered. Concrete blocks of despair are burying me alive, and I can barely move or breathe.

"M-maybe they…" I croak, words clogging my throat. "Maybe… they made it."

"Byron…" she whispers my name patronizingly. "Wake up. They're dead."

I bend at the waist.

"There's no possible way they made it out of that storm alive."

"Stop…" I whimper, pressure building behind my eyes as I cover my head with my hands. "*Please…*"

"Your friends are dead because of that asshole!" she cries. "Because escaping was their only option! The Warden would've killed them himself…

How many times has he tried?? And he'll kill you too! He'll kill us *all* if we don't stop him, you know that!"

"*What* do you *want* from me?!" I straighten, barging up to her face. "You think I can do something about it?? I can't stop him! None of us can! He has a fucking *army*, Joy. Hundreds of cartel men with heavy artillery that could wipe out five of this fucking prison! Sending me over here was just a test... If he wanted to, he could kill us all right now with the snap of his fingers."

"So... what? You're just gonna run back over there and join his team? To survive?? Is it worth it??"

"No," I sigh, defeated. "It's not. But I need to go back for him. Trevel... cares about me. I know you can't see it, because you don't want to. But he does, and I'm not going to leave him alone over there. I'm just... not."

Brushing past her, I barely make it a foot before she grabs my arm. I spin to face her, and this time, she's in *my* face.

"Fuck you," she growls, hand dropping to her pistol. "Don't make me do this..."

I'm smoldering at her with my eyes, hardened in betrayal... Masking hurt. *Lots of it.* "If you're gonna kill me, at least have the guts to do it with your bare hands, *jeulgeoun*."

Her fury is mirroring mine. But it doesn't last long. It fizzles off into sorrow fast, and she slouches, shaking her head.

"Fuck it," she croaks, like she's giving up too.

Shutting me out, like Velle did. She storms away, and I stand here...

In this broken mausoleum of lost souls.

I'm every bit as destroyed as the prison as I weave my way through the trees. This small forest, now a battleground, was once an elusive and mysterious place I'd only heard about.

A year ago—*hell, even a month ago*—I would've given anything to be out here, frolicking through the woods at night, inhaling ocean air while waves crash off in the distance. But now, I don't want to spend one more moment out here than I need to.

The mansion, as beautiful as it is, feels like my new prison. Nowhere on this island is safe. There's no place for me, in any of it.

What would it feel like to have a home…? I'm not sure I've known the feeling of *belonging* since my grandfather died.

Heading for the shore, I keep my ears open to the sounds of threats. The Warden's men could kill me. I'm sure they wouldn't feel bad about it, whether he directly wants me dead or not. But based on what Velle was saying, I think this area of the forest is being patrolled by a different kind of monster.

The snap of a twig stops me fast, and I whip around. It's dark as fuck, and I have no flashlight. *Though that might be a good thing…*

Crossing the west side of the island, I can see the shore through the trees. I wish I knew what I was looking for. Truthfully, I'm not even sure why I'm out here. I should just go back… Back to Trevel. Let him heal me with his touch and his presence. It might not be completely pure, but it's worth something, I *know* it is.

When I'm as confident as I can be that the coast is clear, I make my move, sneaking between the trees and over to the shore. I see something right away, and my heart is already in my throat. Rushing to it, I drop onto my knees in the sand.

There's a piece of split wood sticking out. Using my hands, I dig frantically, shaking and sputtering for breath. Based on the chipped paint and the size of it, I think it might be…

My bottom lip is trembling as I lift the hunk of wood out of the sand, looking it over and cursing God, or the universe, *whoever* is responsible for this.

Because I can feel it in my heart, splintering down the middle like this piece of wreckage from a small boat…

This was them.

Luthor and Ren…

They really are dead.

Falling forward, I press my forehead to the debris, fighting back tears that are forcefully driving their way out of my eye sockets.

"No…" I cry quietly, shaking my head over and over. "No no… *please.*"

I whip the piece of wood away, punching the sand. Agony is rippling throughout my entire body with nowhere to go. It's pulling me under…

A noise has me lifting my head, aiming blurry vision toward the woods.

"Felix…?" I sniffle. I don't see anyone.

But I do see something else that's apparently washed up onto the shore… A backpack.

Crawling over to it, I open it up. The thing is soaked, but I find an unopened bottle of water and some mushy granola bars inside. An aggrieved sound leaves my lips.

This is theirs. I know it.

They're fucking gone...

My best friends in the entire world. The only real friends I've ever had.

The friends I called *selfish* and *toxic*. The friends I abandoned for a striking *stranger* with purple eyes...

"*No!*" I roar and sob and choke. "*Fuck*... why??"

My heart has split into fragments of its own wreckage. And all I can do is remember...

"So yea... That's the story of me and Ren," Luthor said, frowning at the cafeteria table with sadness in his light green eyes.

"That sounds... like a nightmare," I rumbled.

I was out of my league listening to his relationship drama. But still, it felt good just listening. Having someone confide in me.

"You can say that again." He chuckled.

I could tell he was upset, and alone. And something in me just wanted to help. To be needed.

So I said, "Hey, feel free to vent to me anytime."

Luthor's face sprung, his eyes meeting mine. "Really?"

"Yea. I mean, I just got here. It's not like I have friends or anything..."

"You do now." Luthor smiled kindly. Instantly and blindly accepting.

It wrapped me up like a warm blanket of comfort I needed so badly, after everything I'd been through; the secrets that landed me here.

"Cool," I mumbled, downplaying it. "And don't worry. I'll be on your side, no matter what. *Loyalty is everything, after all."*

Luthor chuckled, shaking his head knowingly. "You say that now..."

My brow furrowed. "What does that mean?"

"Just wait until you meet Ren." He bit his lip, fiddling with his fingers. "He's dazzling enough that you'll probably forget all about any allegiance to me..."

I squinted at him. "I think I'll be alright..."

Shuddering through the pain, I gasp for air. Seeing it all, flashing through my mind like a broken slideshow, crackling and burning away the memories. Three years... *Three fucking years.* Of laughter and camaraderie.

Blue eyes and black hair and plush lips...

Three years of passing the time together.

"Don't fight me..."

"Shut up."

"Tell me it doesn't feel good, though, Byron..." Ren's deep voice purred, playing those games so well.

Burdened with a lustful need that would radiate from him like a pheromone, too alluring to resist...

Giving up and in, my hands traveled his frame. "You're... sure? That Luthor doesn't care...?"

"I'm doing this for him," he whispered, opening for me. "To have him."

Proxy or not, he wound up deep within my chest... His flames encircled my heart as he scorched me alive.

"Fuck you..." I curl up in the sand. "Why'd you... have to..."

This ache is so very pungent, like smoke filling my lungs, suffocating me with every inhale. More than just grief, it's guilt. For so many reasons; over *so many* fucking things.

They're gone, and I never got to apologize.

He's dead... and I never got to tell him...

Something rustles between the trees.

"Felix?!" I gasp. "Just... kill me. *Please*..." Crying and wrenching in agony, I plead... "Just do it! Fucking *kill me* already, because I don't deserve to be here! I don't deserve to live and not them... I'm a terrible friend and an *awful* fucking person..." I sputter for air. "I was supposed to be... pretending. But I don't think I've ever known how..."

Lying on the shore, I'm just waiting for it. A bullet to hit me, or The Carver to pop out and slit my throat. I'm *praying* for an end to this torment.

But it doesn't come. I'm forced to lie here and confront it all...

The knowledge that my friends are dead, and I never got to tell either of them the truth.

CHAPTER THIRTY-THREE

Trevel

"Morning, beautiful…" I yawn, kissing a line across Byron's shoulder.

I know he's awake, what with his constant shuffling about. Byron doesn't seem to sleep well as it is, but with everything going on, I'm lucky if I catch him passing out for an hour or two.

"Babe?" I rumble to him when he doesn't answer me, grazing my fingers up and down his back.

He grunts by way of response. And now I'm on a mission.

Sitting up, I wince at the soreness in my back. This couch isn't the worst thing I've ever slept on, that's for certain. Still, it's not exactly one of those incredibly luxurious beds up the hall.

It's fine. I suppose I understand why Byron would rather sleep on the couch than in any of the beds… *But that doesn't mean my muscles have to like it.*

"Come now, sweet fury." I shake him, and he groans. "Rise and shine. Let's go for a shower, yea?"

He continues to ignore me, and when I glance down at his face, I find him simply staring. It rolls melancholy in the pit of my stomach.

"It'll feel good, love," I croon, playing with his hair, hoping for a miracle. "Nice warm shower… maybe an orgasm or two."

But he still won't respond, and it's beginning to drive me mad.

"Byron, I know you're upset," I murmur, a bit out of my league in attempting to talk about what's going on with him.

"I'll say..." Leo smirks, sitting casually by Byron's feet.

He reaches out and touches Byron's toe. Byron flinches, kicking.

My face pulls into a disturbed expression.

I'm losing it...

Shaking my head, I go on, "None of this has been easy on you, and I understand that. But you need to at least get up, baby."

"I'm good..." He rolls over, stuffing his face into the pillow.

"Bit of a Gloomy Gus, isn't he?" Leo comments. I shoot him an irritated glare. *"You positive this emo boy is the one for you?"* He arches a brow above his mangled teddy bear eyeball.

"Have we met?" I scoff, and he fakes a laugh.

"Huh?" Byron grunts.

"Nothing. Baby, I'm just saying... You don't have to hold it all inside." I rub his shoulders.

"I *do*, though," he says, ton softly forlorn. He sounds broken, and I *hate* it. "I lost my journal. My book? It's just fucking *gone*. Everything is... gone."

I'm not...

"You can open up to me... If you want," I murmur, trying not to sound too eager. Leo is making a face. "*Or* I could get you a new journal. So you can continue writing, if you'd like..."

"Great. I'll just start over," he huffs.

"Byron, the point is that those memories are your *truths*, and they're still a part of you. They're not gone... *You're* not gone, baby. You're still here... And so am I."

Finally, he rolls over, propping up on his elbows. His dark eyes take me in, penetrating me deep. It's overwhelming... I haven't a clue what he's seeing when he looks at me like that.

"Are you?" He whispers. A barely audible accusation.

I can do nothing more than stare back at him, frozen to stone under that pretty bronze gaze.

Byron exhales, shaking his head. He looks disappointed.

Bollocks. I hate that bloody look.

He scrambles off the couch and shuffles toward the loo. My hand actually lifts, reaching after him.

"He'll get over it," Leo mutters.

"I... have to tell him," I mumble weakly. "I *need* to tell him about everything. He deserves that much, especially now." I peer at Leo, who doesn't look pleased. "He needs to know that *I'm* here… That he has all of me."

"So you're planning to tell him every last bit, then?" he counters. *"Even the part about you knowing that his friend and former fling was in the East, being tortured…"*

My jaw strains in frustration. He has a point, as usual, and it's quite annoying.

Byron's friends are dead, and he's feeling immense guilt because of their fight—because he'll never get to make amends. He will most *definitely* be upset if he finds out I lied; that I knew Ren was in the East all along. I'm sure he'd feel that, had he known, he could have changed things.

He might be right.

"Tip of the iceberg, my friend," Leo mutters.

Ignoring him, I stalk out of the room, following my sweet, sad fury, in hopes that maybe I can heal him… *If even just temporarily.*

The thing is, despite his state of depression, Byron still needs me. I'm sure he doesn't want to, but it's the truth. And because of that, we can't keep apart.

In the shower, we entwine, absorbing one another's anguish and sorrow. It sinks into our wet flesh, and we use it to fuel the desire. He fucks me aggressively from behind, sealing my chest to the shower wall while he growls and purrs and cries onto the nape of my neck. We both reach fast, crippling orgasms, but neither of us is truly *settled* when we're done.

Out of the shower, Byron gets dressed while I sneak off into the bedroom we're no longer using. Apparently, it belonged to Joy, Velle and Rook, and after their interaction in the prison, Byron returned vehemently against sleeping in there again

Still, I have something stashed in the closet that I need to check on…

Reaching into the back, I locate the cellphone, hidden between some clothes. I found it outside after the tower fell. I was heading toward the prison, under the guise of bringing Dr. Love to Manuel Blanco, but really, I was hypnotized. Witnessing such destruction had lured me in, like a call to my inner chaos.

I couldn't help myself…

But before we got there, Kent sprung out of nowhere, urging us back to the mansion. We turned back, much to my dismay. And as we passed a small cabin made of stone, which I've heard used to be an armory, I saw it. Something shiny peeking out from beneath the wet leaves. When no one was looking, I scooped it up and tucked it away inside my pants.

Since then, I've attempted to power it on several times to no avail. The device is clearly water-logged, and I have no bag of rice to stick it in. I'm hoping it'll eventually dry out enough to power on. Not that I know what I would do with a cellphone, but I imagine it belongs to someone… *Maybe it could be of use.*

Holding down the power button, I pray for light. But I get nothing but a black screen.

Bollocks.

Sighing, I return it to its hiding spot in the back of the closet, gazing over all of the possessions that aren't mine. Things that belong to Officer Chevelle and his partners…

Byron came back from his trip to the prison both overflowing with emotions and completely empty. He shuffled through the doors of the mansion like a lifeless husk. But *I* saw what no one else could; he was gripping the bloody and battered remains of his heart in his hand, desperately trying to hold it together. To keep it beating.

He's grieving over so many things right now, and I simply don't know how to help him. I don't know how to prove to him that he can trust me, short of revealing the depths of my depravity, and unearthing the secrets of my past. And I'm still *terrified* of doing that. Not for superficial reasons… I'm certain he'd be nothing but accepting and supportive.

But I just can't be yet another thing that burdens him. I can't… lose him to my demons.

Disregarding the deranged insecurities overwhelming my thoughts, I pick up a rumpled garment from the floor of the closet. I hold it up, revealing a uniform shirt with a tag that reads *Officer Chevelle*, and give it a quick sniff.

Yum. Smells like a giant Muscle Daddy who's too headstrong for his own good.

Something falls out of the shirt, landing on the floor. It's a collar, but not the same kind Byron and I are wearing. This one is much less outwardly deadly.

It's black leather, adorned with what looks like barbed wire along the outside. Upon closer inspection, I discover that the barbed wire is actually made of silver or platinum. It appears custom-made, beautiful, and likely very expensive. A diamond-studded pendant hangs from a loop on the front, engraved with *Property of The Ivory* on one side, and *J.C.* on the other.

Wow...

"Trev??" Byron's voice calls out from outside the room somewhere. "You coming down?"

"Be right there!"

I quickly wrap the collar back up in the shirt and stuff it into the closet with the cellphone. Then I scamper off to join Byron for lunch.

Things are growing more peculiar with every second spent in this mansion, surrounded by drama and a rich, massively complicated history.

Downstairs, Byron and I attempt to eat, but it's difficult with all the commotion. The Ivory's army has been stomping around like Stormtroopers since the prison fell, and as much as we've been trying to ignore it and go about our lives as normally as we can, it's quite distracting. Their presence is a constant, glaring reminder that things *aren't* normal, and at this rate, I doubt they ever will be.

For me, it's not much of a concern. Normality was never something I've had. For the few years following my release from Riverwoods, when I was *getting my life together*, so to speak, I'd been trying it on for size. But deep down, I knew it was a pipe dream. I was desperately chasing something I knew wasn't meant for me.

And how about that? I feel the same way now, for something else. Or someone *else...*

"What's so great about being normal, anyway?" Leo scoffs.

I continue to ignore him, though on some level, I agree. *Normal* is boring; we all know that.

On the other hand, I've been fighting for survival my *entire* bloody *life*. I can't deny that it felt good to play pretend—go to work, settle into a comfortable relationship, dull the mania in my head. I rather enjoyed the serenity that comes from *routine*.

When I was young and living on the streets of New York City, I used to pray for monotony. I would dream about dull days while bouncing from place to place, with danger lurking around every corner. Fear and a forever-racing pulse, sleeping with one eye open...

What I wouldn't give for some beautiful boredom, I would think.

And I had it for a bit there. With Alice, my job at Zen, my cozy little studio apartment on Killian St... But of course it didn't last. Because I'm not meant for it.

I'm destined to be forever immersed in pure, unadulterated anarchy.

Byron, however, is struggling with this. After all, he's gone from prison—*the ultimate tedium*—to constant unrest. And because he's Byron, he's dealing with it in the only way he knows how… By shutting down.

Byron is an island. He's this rock we're existing on personified.

My gorgeous warrior has retreated into himself, returning to the quiet, sullen lump of isolation he was before I opened him up. I can't say I blame him… I just wish there was something I could do.

Something that doesn't involve infecting him with the disease of my existence, that is.

A flurry of voices and noise, more excessive than usual, draws our attention up the hall, and we rush to go see what's happening.

Bloody hell, what now??

It's coming from the study, which has been converted into something of an infirmary to treat wounded *soldiers*. I wish I was exaggerating, but bullets have been flying around the woods between the mansion and the prison for the better part of a week. Not to mention, Felix Darcey is still at large, creeping around out there, attacking The Ivory's men like some adorable rogue guerrilla assassin. Because of that, it's become necessary for the East Wing doctors to have a designated area where they can act as combat medics.

I swear to God, lately it feels like I'm living in a Francis Ford Coppola fever dream.

"Get the fuck off me!" an aggrieved male voice snarls amidst a mess of other shouting as we round the corner.

"You two, keep him still," the young doctor with the black hair—I think his name is Hassan—says, crowding around a body lying on a makeshift gurney. "I'll check for an exit wound."

"One-forty-four over ninety-five," Dr. Johansson says, attempting to read the man's blood pressure while he jerks around.

"Let me go, you pricks!" the guy hollers. *I still can't see who it is…*

"Shut up, bitch," one of the guys holding him down growls. "Or we'll leave you to bleed out."

"I have an exit wound," Dr. Hassan gasps. "Put pressure on this… Love, bring me the sedatives."

I push farther into the room, eyes widening when I spot Dr. Love. He's at their sides, as if he's supposed to be assisting them, though he doesn't look happy about it in the slightest.

"Hancock…?" Byron grumbles, the unease in his tone drawing my attention.

The wounded man *is* Officer Hancock, dirty and tattered and bleeding from his right shoulder.

Christ, this gets better and better…

He's clearly in pain, having apparently been shot. But that's the least of his worries… Because now he's in enemy territory.

Fucking hell… He's a bloody prisoner of war.

Byron appears sufficiently disturbed, and he's not the only one. Dr. Love brings over an IV drip and some other medical dressings while eyeing the bloke in concern, jaw straining tight. Hancock's fearful gaze stays with his as they share a wordless sentiment that's not difficult to read. It looks like Byron wants to say something to Hancock, but there are too many of the Warden's guys around.

And then the familiar clack of dress shoes straightens all of our spines. The Ivory stalks into the room, making a beeline to Officer Hancock, everyone scattering to make way for him.

"Hi, Simon," he croons, brushing Hancock's damp hair away from his face. "It's been a while, darling."

Hancock tries to jerk away from his touch, but he's still being held down, poked and prodded by the doctors as he spits, "Fuck off, Ivory."

Manuel Blanco sucks his teeth, shaking his head with a smugly devious smirk resting on his lips. "Now, now. Is that any way to speak to someone who's saved your life? *Multiple* times now, by my count."

"Your men fucking shot me," Hancock hisses.

"Yours shot first." The Ivory shrugs casually.

Hancock winces when an IV needle is jabbed into his arm. "Sure, Han Solo. Keep telling yourself that."

The Ivory's grin widens, fingers still sifting through Hancock's hair as the bloke's lashes flutter, his eyelids drooping. "Relax, Simon. You're back where you belong." He leans over him as Hancock visibly loses consciousness. "And you will make a purely wonderful bargaining chip."

The Ivory straightens, spinning away. "Johansson, Hassan, get him patched up. Oh, and make sure he's collared, please. Can't have this one getting away."

On his way out of the room, he drops a hand onto my shoulder. "Wait for me in my office." He tosses a brief, sinister glance at Dr. Love before whispering by my ear, "We have much to discuss."

Once he's gone, I find Byron peering at me, to which I shrug.

What could he want now? What do we have to discuss…?

Regardless, I have no desire to keep him waiting. I run my fingers along Byron's lower back. "Are you coming?"

"He didn't say he wanted to talk to me…" he mutters, forehead lined as his gaze lingers on Hancock's unconscious form. "It's fine. I'm gonna… stay with him." He swallows visibly.

I truly despise his endless melancholy, but there's nothing I can do about it right now. I'm at *The Ivory's* beck and call. We all are.

Marching out of the room with my stomach in knots, I make my way to the stairs, on a mission I don't understand. The door to his office is open, so I meander inside. He's not here yet, which gives me a golden opportunity to snoop.

Wandering around the room, I examine things on his shelves and on his walls. There are framed pictures of him with people, degrees and plaques that indicate someone intelligent and successful in walks of life *outside* of the criminal. It's quite curious…

Who is this man… Really?

Is The Ivory *just a persona he puts on? Or is that the real him, hiding in plain sight beneath the impeccable disguise of* Manuel Blanco?

His voice from up the hall startles me out of my snooping, and I creep closer to the door.

"They're weak. Exhausted and running on fumes," he says to someone. "Low on food and ammunition. Sooner or later, he'll have no choice but to come crawling back on his hands and fucking knees—"

"So the plan is to starve them out?" someone else says—*I think it's Kent*. "If so, why not pull our men out of the woods?"

"Because Felix Darcey is out there," The Ivory barks. "That little psycho is ballsier than I ever gave him credit for."

"It's a fucking slaughter every time we even creep west—"

"Listen to me. I want him *back*. I don't care what you have to do. I don't care how much blood we have to spill. I want The Carver back in chains." His voice is a low, sinister command that's obviously not to be argued with any further.

I imagine Kent nodding like the good soldier he is. "What about Russo? Yari's been holding him off as best he can, but he's becoming rather… insistent. He wants answers we don't have—"

My stomach twists painfully. *Governor Russo…?*

"Under *no* circumstances is he to set foot on this island. Do you understand me?" The Ivory seethes. "Not until I have Dascha back."

"How much longer will that take?" Kent asks hesitantly.

"You tell me," he bites back, tension in his tone. "You're the one who lost eyes on him in Mexico."

"I have my best guys on it, but he's a slippery one. We might need to call in your contact…"

"Trust me, that'll be a last resort." He sounds like he's getting closer, so I tiptoe over to a chair and take a seat, trying to act like I haven't been eavesdropping.

"One we might need to explore." Kent sighs.

"I have faith in you," The Ivory grunts. "Just get it done."

He stalks into the office, closing the door in Kent's burdened face. I watch as The Ivory crosses the room, striding behind his large desk.

"Sorry to keep you waiting," he hums as he takes a seat, settling in.

I wave my hand in lieu of a response.

Leaning in on the desk, he folds his hands, staring at me for a few seconds in silence. It takes everything in me not to squirm.

I can't put my finger on it, but something about him seems… *off*. I mean, more off than his usual foreboding persona. Yes, he's less composed than he was before the prison fell, and he's actively rocking the aura of someone who's living each day on the edge of whatever sanity he had left. But it's more than that.

There's an imperceptible difference in his demeanor that's unsettling me. He's almost glowing in a way—dark eyes sparkling and some flush in his pale complexion.

Is that a… bite mark? On his collarbone?

My head slants as I zero in on it.

He clears his throat, and I jump. "I'll cut right to the chase. If you know where Felix Darcey is, tell me now. Keeping secrets at this juncture in our relationship will ensure you, and Byron, suffer far greater than you need to."

I'm frozen for a moment before I snap out of it. "I don't know where he is… Byron said that Velle told him he's out in the woods somewhere?"

He narrows his gaze. "Don't play coy, Trevel. We both know you wouldn't have gotten Lemuel without also going for The Carver."

I shouldn't be surprised that he knows more than he was letting on initially. I'm just wondering why he's only bringing it up now…

I'm sure there's a reason. *Every move is calculated.*

"We did…" I mumble, guilty like I'm being scolded by Daddy. "I mean, we grabbed them both and were holding Darcey in Dr. Love's bedroom. But he… escaped. I'm still not clear on how…"

"He's an obsessive little monster, that's how," The Ivory breathes out, pursing his lips. "Only one thing to live for and a myriad of knowledge he's putting toward that singular objective. Which brings me to our next order of business..." He sits back in his seat, pulling something out of his pocket. It looks like a knife... "I'm putting you in charge of Lemuel from here on out."

My brows jump up to my bloody hairline. "Pardon?"

His black eyes spring from the closed weapon he's fiddling with to mine. "It's what you wanted, isn't it? Your revenge?" I'm just gaping at him in silence. "Well, you've got it. He's here, thanks to you. I've had him working for Johansson and Hassan. Boy, does he hate that." He stops to chuckle wickedly. "But I think it's time to up the ante. Make him understand just how far he's fallen."

I can feel myself gawking at him.

"*He's* the prisoner now, Trevel, my boy," he goes on. "And you're not. Might as well get some enjoyment out of this. You've earned it."

I'm rather taken aback, and I think that's apparent in my bewildered expression. "What... what do you want me to... do with him?"

His pink lips twist even bigger. "Whatever you want. The sky's the limit." With a flick of his wrist, he swings the blade out of his butterfly knife, my wide eyes stuck on it. "I've instructed Johansson and Hassan to resume their experiments, as much as they can outside of the East Wing. And I think Lemuel will be the perfect rodent for them to play with." He aims the blade my way. "But you're calling the shots. *You* get to control his torment." He grins, almost maniacally. "Have fun with it."

It's odd... After *months* of obsessively fantasizing about all the ways I could exact my revenge on Dr. Love for leaving me and dooming me to this pit of despair, I'm finally being presented with a ripe opportunity to make him pay. And I'm stuck.

I'm... indifferent. Devoid of all sadistic ideals.

Where's the passion... The twisted thrill??

I could've sworn this was what I wanted...

Moments of quiet pass until I finally ask, "Why?"

"Don't look a gift horse in the mouth, Trevel," he trills impassively, then sighs. "Maybe all we need to lure young Felix Darcey out of hiding is the right bait."

The Ivory stares at me for a moment, slipping the blade of his knife into the handle and stuffing it back into his pocket. He stands up, casting me a glance. As if he's waiting for something.

So I stand as well, and force out a gruff, "Thank you."

"Don't mention it." He winks, patting me on the back.

Striding to the door, he whips it open to reveal Kent and Yari.

Have they been there the whole time??

"Hold my calls," he says to them on his way past, moving quickly, like he has somewhere to be.

Surely, he does. He seems… busy.

Yari follows after him, as does Kent, not without first giving me a look I don't have time to decode. We all descend the stairs together, though The Ivory is racing ahead of the rest of us. At the bottom, he crosses the threshold, going for the study. Kent and Yari disperse in different directions, but I follow Manuel, assuming he's going to check on Officer Hancock again. Byron might still be in there.

But when I get to the room, I don't see him, and The Ivory is moving swiftly to the opposite door, heading toward the atrium. I don't know what possesses me to do so, but I find myself overcome with the need to keep following him. So I do.

Keeping back just enough, I trail him into the enclosed garden, around a corner, and across the stone walkway, into the back… An area of the atrium I haven't visited yet.

This garden is stunning. It might be one of the most beautiful places I've ever seen in my life. But I can't enjoy it, not right now. I'm too busy rushing quietly after Manuel Blanco, through a hidden doorway that's shrouded in plants and hanging vines.

I watch closely as he opens a door decorated with ornate bronze and stained glass, and steps inside. It takes only a moment to recognize this as the aviary.

I'd heard there was one, but I've yet to actually see it.

Wow… It's incredible.

The room is just as captivating as the garden. Trees and flowers everywhere, color as far as the eye can see, despite it being winter. It *is* much warmer in here than the rest of the mansion, which may be done intentionally—a sort of greenhouse setup.

Focusing on The Ivory, lest I get distracted and lose him, I creep after him, coming to a full stop when he pulls a key from inside his pocket. It's long, and it looks antique, like an old skeleton key. He moves up to another door that's not a door at all, rather a *cell*. It has bars like the ones in the penitentiary, except that they appear to be made of bronze, or gold. And the cell itself looks… Well, there's no other way to put it.

It looks like a birdcage. A large one—bigger than any bird, or animal, for that matter—would require.

Swallowing hard, I hug the wall, trying to get closer while staying hidden. I need to get a better look at this.

I need to see what's in there…

The Ivory steps inside the cage, closing the gate behind him with a clank. My stomach twists when another person comes into view…

A large hand falls onto my shoulder, and I jump so hard, I practically hit the ceiling.

"Jesus bloody Christ!" I whisper, slapping my hand over my heart as I spin to find Kent glaring at me.

His eyes widen, and he places his finger up to his lips in the *shhh* gesture. We stare at one another for a moment, both peeking back to The Ivory in the giant birdcage.

My lips part, because I have *so* many questions. But I don't get the chance to ask.

Kent grabs me by the wrist and pulls me away. Leaving Manuel Blanco alone with his little bird…

CHAPTER THIRTY-FOUR

Trevel

PACING. MAKING CIRCLES, *AROUND AND AROUND, AND AROUND…*

Yanking my hair in my fists.

"What's the problem?"

I'm twitchy. Edgy.

Unhinged.

"Honestly… I thought this was what you've been wanting for bloody months." I peer at him. *"And now that you've got it, you're not happy??"* Leo shakes his head. *"There really is no pleasing you, is there, mate?"*

"That's not the point," I hiss at him, rubbing my eyes hard until I see spots. Until he's *blurry*… Like he's not really there, and his voice is coming from inside *me*.

It is. You know it is.

I've always been you, Trevel.

"Just shut up and let me think, goddamnit!" I bark, whipping my face in his direction.

Except that Leo is gone. And now, *Byron* is standing there, right where my decrepit ninja bear had been. Eyes wide, etched in confusion and concern.

"Are you… alright?" he croaks, tone careful. Cautious.

Keep back. Your crazy sort-of boyfriend's gone completely mad.

Squeezing my eyes shut tight, I take a breath, attempting to compose myself. "No… *yes*. I mean, I'm *fine*, but I just—"

"Trevel, what's going on?" he grunts, wearing every moment of distress from the past few weeks on his face. "You seem like there's something you're not telling me..." He steps closer. "Something you *want* to tell me... But maybe you're afraid."

I bite my lip, staring at him. The emotion in my own eyes is palpable. I can see it, being mirrored back at me in his.

I *want* to confide in him, I swear I do.

There's so much I need to say. So much *he* needs me to say.

But will it be... too much? Will he stay once he knows how truly fucked the bloody hell up I am?? I just don't see how...

We're running on fumes as it is.

"Come with me," I sigh, walking past him.

I'm not sure that he's following me at first. But after a beat, I can feel him.

I bring him downstairs, all the while mulling over the events of the last week or so, since Manuel Blanco put me in charge of Dr. Love's fate. Let's not pretend he wouldn't have had his doctors doing whatever they wanted to Lemuel, regardless of my involvement. I think we all know how The Ivory operates by now. But bestowing upon *me* this gift of revenge...

It has felt every bit as loaded as I'm sure it was intended.

"Where are we going?" Byron asks nervously when I bring him to the stairs. The ones that go *down*.

I don't answer him. I just keep moving, taking the stone steps down into the depths of darkness.

The mansion's basement—*at least this part of it*—is reminiscent of Alabaster Penitentiary, in that it's cold, and it smells like concrete and musty ocean. *And it's currently housing prisoners.*

Dim light guides us into the dungeon—or as Manuel Blanco refers to it, *the tombs*—and I spot him right away. My chest constricts, and my teeth set.

"What the..." Byron gasps, shock and horror swallowing his gruff words.

"Yea." I stop and just stare.

Lemuel Love is slumped on the floor, his hands cuffed behind his back and his ankle shackled to a post. He's wearing the same clothes he's been wearing since the night I plucked him out of his fancy bedroom upstairs, where he was existing in a bubble of blissful ignorance and overconfidence with his sweet little psycho boyfriend.

"Fiancé," Leo's voice echoes behind me, and I cringe.

Those fancy tailored fabrics are all worn and dirty now, stained with blood. His eyes are closed, as if maybe he's asleep, or at least attempting it. But there's visible strain around them, marks on his exposed skin that tell the tale of what's been happening down here.

"The doctors have been doing things to him." I bite the inside of my cheek. "*I* have…"

I feel Byron gaping at me, so I allow my eyes to meet his. The look he's giving me only confirms all of my hidden doubts, and I don't like it.

"Trevel, this is…" His voice trails, and he shakes his head, glancing at Dr. Love. "Why…?"

"Why?" I chuckle derisively. "*Why??* Are you serious?? You *know* why, Byron…"

"I know, but this… Trevel, this is sick." He steps over to Dr. Love, whose eyes slowly creep open. There's instant rage in his amber glare, masking visible exhaustion, and some fear.

"This is what you wanted," the voice inside tells me. "Revenge. *At any cost."*

"He deserves it," I sniff, choking back every foolish morsel of remorse, because *fuck it, right?*

I deserve this.

This is mine.

"Does he, though??" Byron snaps, and I squint at him. "I mean, *come on*, Trevel. Wake up! We all know The Ivory would've gotten you here with or without him, so what's the fucking point??"

"It's the dungeon." I shrug. "And now *he's* the prisoner…"

"If you think you're not prisoners, you're in for a world of hurt…" Lemuel rasps, eyes closing again. He rests his head against the wall as if he's too tired to hold it up.

Byron gestures with his hand, in a sort of *See? Told you* motion of agreement with Dr. Love's statement.

"You shut the fuck up," I growl at Lemuel. "You brought this on yourself, you know you did."

"Keep telling yourself that," he breathes out.

"This is insane," Byron grumbles. And now *he's* pacing. "I didn't want any of this, you know that?? I only went along with that bullshit plan for you!"

"Right!" I bark at him. "You *did*! Because you agreed with me… You wanted revenge on Felix Darcey as much as I wanted it on this wanker."

"Okay, *fine*. You're right. Is that what you want me to say??" He gets up in my face. "At first, I wanted to make Darcey pay for what he did… But can't you see by now that it's pointless?? Vengeance doesn't *solve* anything, Trevel! It doesn't change the past, and it sure as shit won't make you feel any better about the future!" His chest is heaving, and I'm just staring at him blankly. *Refusing* to admit that I feel his words. "When does it end…?"

"It *ends* when they stop breathing!" I hiss at him. "You have no *idea* the kinds of things I've had to endure… The kinds of things I've had to *live with* because of other people, so don't tell me revenge is pointless! It's *all* I have, Byron."

His fury melts into sorrow so fast that I witness it. The anger in his gaze softening, slipping into vast, shining sadness.

"You're right." His shoulders slump. "I don't know what you've been through… Because I don't have a damn clue who you are."

His brown eyes glisten, and they fall to hide the emotion. That one look slices me open.

It stabs me, poisons me, chokes me…

It *kills me* the way I've done to others. *Revenge.*

Reaching for him, I mumble, "Baby, I didn't mean—"

"You're right, Trevel." He pulls away. "Revenge is all you have left…" He sniffles, refusing to look at me. Then he grunts, "This is done." His voice is shaking, though he's fighting to disguise it. Putting up a wall between us. My heart is bleeding out in my chest. "Whatever we were… It's over."

And then he walks out.

Turns and storms away from me. He fucking *leaves me,* in the tombs with my vengeance. And nothing more.

Emotion pounds in my skull, so hard I can barely see. My vision is blurring, tears welling in my eyes.

I look around for Leo… But he's not fucking there.

"You're your own worst enemy, Trevel," Dr. Love says.

Like dropping a match into a pool of kerosene, I ignite in blazing wrath.

Storming over, I launch myself at him. Shoving him onto his back, my hands are immediately around his throat.

"You think I don't know that?!" I roar in his face. "This is all *your fault!*"

"How do you figure?" He chokes a laugh that boils rage in my bloodstream, so thick it's visceral.

"All you had to do was stay," I seethe. "But you *chose* to come here, because you're just as sick as the rest of us! You're a bloody *junkie* for this shit… The depraved and the twisted. The darkness you study sets your blood on fire, doesn't it, *Doctor??*" I'm shaking as my grip tightens around his neck. "You brought this on yourself! You were too cocky, and now you're paying the price. So why *shouldn't* it be me, huh?? Why shouldn't *I* be the one to make you suffer??"

He simply gazes up at me, as stone-faced as ever. It's so infuriating, I could snap his neck right now with my bare hands.

"You'll lose him if you keep giving him reasons to go…" he croaks. "Just like Alice."

"Shut up," I snarl, my limbs vibrating.

"I've known you a long time, Trevel," he mumbles. "You're not worried about hurting him physically, like you were with Alice. Because you know he can handle you. So instead, you're destroying him *inside*. If he's too strong, he could break *you* down… And that terrifies you."

"I'm not paying you for this head-shrinking garbage," I simmer.

"When are you going to stop hiding from who you are? Sabotaging any and all chances at happiness because you don't feel worthy…" He keeps going, bloody *needling* at me until I'm overflowing crimson from my goddamn pores. "The only way you'll ever move on and feel something *real* is by accepting it…"

"Accepting *what?*"

"That you don't need to be put back together," he hums, as if it's the simplest thing ever. "No amount of revenge will ever fix you, Trevel. Because you can't be fixed. So let him love you *broken*… Or spend forever alone, looking for a partner in crime who doesn't exist."

My face pales. I feel the color drain as I stare at him in shock.

Fuck you.

My muscles stiffen. My chest *burns*.

Fuck you fuck you

"Fuck *you!*" Growling out loud, I lift and slam his head down onto the concrete floor.

He winces in pain, but it doesn't feel good like it's supposed to, and *I hate it!*

"It was supposed to feel better than this," I choke out, jumping off of him. "Where *are you*, Leo?! Stop *hiding* every time I need you, selfish bloody bastard!"

Staggering away, tripping over my feet, I race back upstairs, going straight to the room where Dr. Johansson and Dr. Hassan are working. I fly in like a bat out of hell, and they both look up, startled.

"Get down there!" I roar, wheezing and shaking. "Right now! Make him fucking *bleed*. I want him to rue the day he ever stepped into my life like he could *fucking help me*, because he *can't!*" I'm heaving, fisting my hair as I breathe out ragged, "No one can."

Their faces are the picture of baffled uncertainty, but I just growl again, "Go. *Now.*"

And they nod, grabbing their bags of supplies and sauntering off to obey my orders. But the power in it is doing nothing for me. I feel nothing but impotence and insecurity.

Storming to the kitchen, I ransack the place for *anything* that will numb me. I can't take it anymore. I don't want to feel this. I don't want to feel *anything*.

What I wouldn't give for some bloody heroin right now.

The Ivory's cartel blokes must be able to get it. Maybe I could blow one of them for a bag…

The way my brain goes to this so easily, like a physiological response, only makes me angrier, and makes me hate myself more. After several minutes of tearing through the mansion like a twister, I stumble upon The Ivory's bar. Grabbing the first bottle I see, I unscrew the cap with trembling fingers. I'm about to dump the entire thing down my throat when I feel something buzzing in my pocket.

I pause, bottle at my lips. *Huh…*

Pulling out the cellphone, I stare at it in shock. It's ringing. It's *on* and actually *ringing*.

I take too long balking at it, and end up missing the call. Placing the bottle of booze down with a *thunk*, I rush around a corner for some privacy, taking a deep breath. And then I redial the number that just called.

It rings only twice before a male voice answers. "Hello?"

My lips part. But I say nothing.

"Hello?? *Joy??*" the person asks frantically.

Well, that explains whose phone it is.

And that voice is awfully familiar…

My heart rate evens out, lips sloping into a grin. "Hello… Luthor."

I'm wading through emotional muck, waist-deep and *sinking*.

Byron… ended things. He hates me.

Dr. Love is still trying to help me, despite my having him tortured.

And then that phone call…

They're not dead.

I just spoke to Luthor on the phone. He and Ren are very much *alive*. I'm not sure *how*, or where they are. Those are questions I would have asked if I were a good person. But I'm not.

Luthor and Ren are worried about their friends, about Byron. Because *they* are good.

But me?

I'm pure black mold.

I barely remember what I said to Luthor. Just raving resentment and disdain while rippling with the need to make something happen. If anything, it sounded much more like *Leo* than me.

But the part I wasn't exaggerating about was Velle being at a disadvantage. I just can't see how he and his men could overpower The Ivory. There's no defeating the devil.

And if that's the truth, wouldn't it make sense to stay in his good graces?

I have no ties to Velle, Joy, or the others. Sure, they seem much more interesting than The Ivory's dead-eyed soldiers. But if staying on his side keeps Byron and me alive, I'll do what needs to be done. Even if that means playing the part of the enemy.

Hell, I'll be the slimy, untrustworthy newcomer. If that's what they want.

Except that it's not that simple, apparently. Those people are Byron's friends. He cares for them, and clearly, they care for him. But they've cast him aside…

Because of me.

"No amount of revenge will ever fix you, Trevel… Let him love you broken… Or spend forever alone, looking for a partner in crime who doesn't exist."

I cover my face with my hands, growling and crying into my palms

Sod it all. What am I doing??

Giving up Byron for this? I don't want *this…*

I'm not in love with Lemuel, and I don't care that he left…

The conversation with Luthor was the last straw. I told him that Byron wanted revenge on Felix… But he doesn't. He doesn't need it anymore, and neither do I. Because there's something so much *better* here…

"If it weren't for Dr. Love… you wouldn't have met Byron…"

Picking myself up is difficult. I'm so heavy with regret, lightheaded from unnecessary anger. But as soon as I'm standing, I feel sturdy once more. I'm determined.

I rush back down to the tombs, immediately hit by the sounds of my doctor being tortured. It sheets my flesh with chills.

Emerging from the darkness, I wander over to where Hassan and Johansson have Lemuel chained to the wall by his neck, wrists, and ankles. Bag over his head, he's shirtless, decorated in electrodes and burn marks. They're using hot pokers—some sort of pain measurement test that seems like overkill.

Of course it is. It's just torture and humiliation. They stand to gain nothing with this… *Nothing but revenge.*

The Ivory's revenge, not mine.

This isn't for me. I don't need this.

"You'll never come first. Your wants, needs… They'll all take a backseat to his. Because he is all of it."

"The best revenge is not needing it…"

"Hurts, doesn't it?" Hassan grins, taunting, "Where's your pretty monster boyfriend, Lemuel? If only he could save you like you saved him… From Templeton. And *me*."

Dr. Love is grumbling, but his words are muffled, most likely by a gag in his mouth.

"I was disappointed that you burst in that day… Before I could finish my experiment," he goes on, sadistic glee in his eyes turning my stomach. "If only Felix knew how much shit you've been taking because of him… He might come out of hiding."

Johansson flicks on a device and murmurs, "One-sixty."

He presses a button, and Dr. Love jerks violently.

Electroshock… Jesus.

"Let me," I grunt, stomping over with my hand out.

They both look up. Hassan steps aside, watching as I grab the long, pointed metal rod he's been using to burn and pierce Lemuel's skin.

I rip the bag off of his head. "Look at me, Doctor," I growl. His eyes slowly creep open. "I want you to see all of this…"

Our gazes lock, his amber irises housing the same rage and helplessness I've been seeing for weeks on end. And yet, *still*, he shows no remorse…

Like he said to me, in the woods. *"No qualms, or hesitations."*

And I get it now. *I do know that feeling.*

"Now we're even," I whisper.

And I spin fast, stabbing the metal rod right through Hassan's neck.

Blood squirts from the wound, his eyes wide and bulging as he falls to the floor with a thud.

Johansson's face morphs in shock and terror. He stumbles backward, attempting to flee. But tackle him to the ground. Reaching for the chain of Lemuel's shackles, I wrap it around Johansson's neck. I pull with all my might, choking him brutally, using my body weight to hold him down.

A guttural roar leaves my lips as I yank both ends of the chain. There's a distinct *crunch*. And Johansson goes limp beneath me.

Panting, my breathing echoes through the cold, damp space as I feel a weight being lifted from my shoulders. Interestingly, it's the same kind of release I felt when I killed the four men who raped me. When I killed Andres. It's freedom from *my own* chains.

I'm *flying*, higher than the best hit I've ever had.

The best revenge is not needing it anymore.

Wiping my forehead with my hand, I look over the bodies beside me… The pool of blood seeping closer to where I'm slumped on the floor. I peer up at Dr. Love. His eyes are round.

"I suppose it really was inevitable, yea?" I breathe out, stuffing my hand into Johansson's pocket and pulling out a set of keys to the cuffs and shackles.

Standing up on shaky legs, I remove the gag from Lemuel's mouth and free him from his chains. He stares down at the dead assholes, spitting out some blood right on Hassan's body.

"Thank you, Trevel," he says sincerely after a beat.

"I didn't do it for you." I pull him out of the way before Hassan's blood reaches his foot.

"I know," he hums. "But still. I owe you."

I give him a skeptical side-eye. "I'm the reason you're here in the first place."

"No. You were right," he grumbles. "I'm here because I *chose* to be. And I deserve it, just as much as the rest of them."

"You didn't deserve that." I gulp, guilt easing out in my tone. "No one does…"

"Maybe not, but it's not your fault." He stares at me until I eventually meet his gaze. "I am sorry, Trevel… For leaving you the way I did. I want you to know that I wouldn't be who I am if it weren't for you. Having you as a patient… it changed everything. You were a gift I didn't deserve."

My throat is closing, chest constricting so tightly I can barely breathe.

I'm astounded… That after everything I've done to him over the past few weeks, he's actually standing here, *thanking me*.

Giving me credit for being his first monster.

And it dawns on me. *This* is the revenge I wanted. Better than weeks of spilling his blood and inflicting him pain.

All I've ever wanted was to be *seen*.

I clear my throat, fighting off the pressure building up in my skull. "We'll have to do something with the bodies…"

"I can help."

My face springs up at the sound of Byron's voice. He's standing there, lips pursed to dampen his smile.

My real partner in crime… He's here.

Dr. Love nudges me, and I peek at him. "Share the burden. He's strong enough to help you carry it."

CHAPTER THIRTY-FIVE

Trevel

We spent all night debating our next moves—Lemuel, Byron, and myself. *Together.*

Quite the turn of events.

We've also been debating what to do about the very dead twats formerly known as Doctors Johansson and Hassan. I suggested hacking them up and inconspicuously burying one piece at a time in the garden, and while we all agreed that seemed fun, ultimately we decided it might arouse suspicions if Byron and I took up gardening out of the blue in the middle of a war.

I suppose I'm still trying to figure out which is the lie from our game all those weeks ago… It's between loves gardening *and* has never sneezed, *and I just cannot* fathom *that the latter is true.*

At any rate, our primary focus was tending to Lemuel's wounds and getting him cleaned up, since he was in pretty rough shape. We did what we could with limited options, brought him some clothes from the guards' quarters, and I must say, he's much better off. Still, there's an air of wrath about him, decorating his aura in a palette of flames.

While we were fixing him up, Lem told Byron and me about what these doctors had done to Felix when he was away—*evidently dealing with the aftermath of my killings*. As a sexual assault survivor myself, I felt a deep pang of empathy for The Carver. I can say with full sincerity that Dr. Hassan will be rotting in Hell right alongside this Templeton character—whom Felix and Lem already exacted their bloody revenge on—and his boss, Johansson, whose lack of interference makes him just as complicit, as far as we're all concerned.

The thing is, Lem's collar was removed when Hassan and Johansson chained him up, meaning he *can* escape if he wants to. But as eager as he is to find Felix, he's insistent on being patient, and smart.

The Ivory *quite literally* has eyes everywhere, his mob of cartel men scurrying to and fro at all times like busy insects. *I'm not certain they even sleep.* Sneaking out would be a highly dangerous venture, and once The Ivory realizes Lem is gone, he'll be out for blood… *Most likely mine to start.*

We weren't able to locate the remote for the collars anywhere on either of the bodies, but the good news is that few people know the tombs even exist. Nobody comes down here.

That's not to say The Ivory won't decide to pop in on Lemuel just for funzies, so we are on a bit of a timer to figure something out.

Byron and I aren't exactly itching to leave the way Lemuel is, though. After all, he's a direct enemy of Manuel Blanco, *and* he has someone out there waiting for him. Velle sees us both as enemies now, and if The Ivory finds out I killed the doctors, there goes our good graces.

I've isolated Byron in a very precarious position. The guilt of causing so much strife and impending doom for him is heavier than cinderblocks stacked on my shoulders. Whether I chose it or not, I'm indebted to Manuel Blanco; trapped in a labyrinth of calamity, and unable to see a way out.

"You'll never come first… Because he is all of it."

Those words keep coming back to me, from the hushed voice of a stranger behind a thick metal door. It makes me think about the cage in the aviary…

"So we just… leave the bodies here?" Byron asks, frowning at them.

Lem nods. "It'll make it more believable that I was the one who killed them." His amber eyes sparkle with veracity.

Apparently, he's been gunning for the doctors since Felix was assaulted, hence his defecting to Team Velle. Losing the trust of Manuel Blanco threw a wrench into his plans, but then I killed them. Unknowingly doing him a solid while also sparing him from excessive torture. And now *he's* in *my* debt—*his words, not mine.*

The fact that Dr. Love is pledging *any* loyalty to me after what we did to him and Felix is perplexing. *Alright, I did most of it. Except the cum-lube. He must not know about that…*

Still, his willingness to forgive brings warmth and fuzzies to my chest that I'm quite unfamiliar with.

Is this… friendship? Bollocks, I haven't felt it, real, *in so long…*

I'm much more familiar with obsessive infatuation and blinding wrath… And what I feel for Byron.

"As far as anyone is concerned, I killed Hassan and Johansson and got free," Lem says matter-of-factly. "The Ivory knows I've wanted them dead. It's more than believable."

Byron chews on his lower lip. "So… What happens now?"

Lem loses a bit of his visible confidence. But then I recall…

"Here." I pull out the cellphone and hand it to Lem. "I found it outside," I explain, mostly to Byron, because he's giving me that look again… The one that says, *I have no idea who you are or what you're hiding.* "You'll need it more than me."

Lem takes the phone, nodding. "I'm going to explore the tombs… See where they lead. Maybe try to get ahold of someone… But I promise, I'm not leaving until we can all get out."

Byron's lashes flutter. "Are you sure?"

"I'll be fine. Just watch out for yourselves," Lem hums, rather gallantly. Protective of *us*. "Keep your eyes open. Things are going to get much worse before they have even a prayer of getting better."

"This is headed for disaster…" The voice grates inside my skull. *"You know that, right?"* My eyes flit about in glaring frustration at my so-called *friend* I can't see, because he's just such an unsupportive wanker sometimes. *"Keep giving me that look, mate, but you know I have your best interests at heart. No one else's. You're not meant to be part of the* pack. *You're a lone wolf."*

"That makes no sense," I growl under my breath, rubbing my eyes.

When I look up, Byron and Lemuel are gawking at me. They exchange glances, and my spine stiffens in irritation. It reminds me of how people used to look at me in Riverwoods. *Like I'm an unbridled nutter.*

"Trev… let's go get some rest," Byron patronizes me with that *appeasing* tone.

"Fine," I grunt, stalking off, not waiting for either of them to say another word.

I take the stairs two at a time from the basement, rushing across and up to our floor, all the while kicking myself. *Hating* myself for not knowing how to do this. How to be *with* someone.

I know how to be alone. How to be an addict. How to seek revenge…

And most of all, I know how to demolish good things and leave them in rubble. *It's what I did to Alice...*

It's what I'm good at.

I'd *love* to give Byron more of me. *Fuck it...* All *of me.* I want him to have me in full, so that I can have *him* in full. But I have this nagging bloody voice in my head that spouts nothing but *doubt*.

"Blame me all you want, but I know what's best for you..." Leo grumbles.

I whip in his direction. "For *me! Me*, Leo! It's just me, because *you* don't exist! You are me, and you're holding me down, *suffocating* me because you're afraid!"

He looks hurt, like I've just stabbed him with one of those ninjatos on his back.

"You're nothing but fear, and I hate it," I whine breathlessly. "That's why you disappear every time I need you... Because you're bloody terrified. *I* am... and I don't want to be anymore. I want to try. Can't I *try*, at least??"

"Trevel, Jesus..." Byron's voice startles me, and I jump, spinning to face him with wide eyes. "What's going on?? *Who* are you talking to??"

I stare at him, jaw slack. I assume Leo's gone, but this time, when I peer left, he's still there. He looks just as afraid as me.

He's *afraid... Not me.*

Leave the fear with him.

"Tell me what's going on, Trevel," he whispers, *begging* me. "Please tell me *something*, violet eyes, or we can't... *I* can't do this anymore." He's in visible pain. I can tell he doesn't want to end this. But he *will*... If I don't give him something.

I have to... step out of the shadows.

I release a slow breath. "Okay. I'll t-tell you... All the things."

Byron nods and whispers, "I promise, I can handle it."

My lips twitch, a soft chuckle fleeing my lips.

Fuckin' hell, he's perfect. Such a hard shell around so much mushy sweetheart, I swear. Like Alice.

Wandering over to the couch, I take a seat and pat the cushion next to me. Byron joins me, nestling up by my side. Facing me. Giving me his full attention. I'm nervous, but also amazed by how much he wants this.

Is this all he's needed the whole time? Just... more? More of me?

I peer at Leo, and for the first time, he's not warning me against what I'm about to do. He's just watching me.

Be strong, be fearless, be kind.

Be Leonardo.

"I told you I left London when I was young because my parents were shit," I begin. Byron nods subtly. "Well, I didn't tell you how awful they truly were. My father was abusive… In just about every way one can be. He used to beat me, degraded me… The worst sorts of things, like cutting my hair uneven, making me drink his bottle of lager with cigarette butts in it. He'd whip me with things, force-feed me foods he knew I hated, put a cockroach in my bed. Real mean, mind-fuck type shit. And then… Well, I was barely eight years old by the time he started… touching me."

I pause to swallow, remembering to breathe through it; the pain and rage that's still fucking there, lodged in my chest cavity like a tumor that can't be removed.

Byron's eyes are wide, and I think he might move away… But he doesn't. He moves in closer, taking my hand in his, threading our fingers. I hear him in my mind, like all those times in the showers…

Go on, violet eyes. I'm listening.

"My mother didn't care," I croak. "She did nothing to stop it. In fact, I think she enjoyed it, for some reason I've never been able to figure out."

I'm staring into Byron's eyes, but my gaze is far away. Only for a moment, and I pull myself back.

"One day, I'd had enough. I just couldn't… bear it for one more day. Instead of going to school, I went into the city and stayed there. I began pickpocketing and stealing to get by, but I knew the longer I stayed in London, the more likely they'd somehow get me back. My plan was to save up enough to take the train to Berlin, but I wound up meeting a man who offered to bring me to America. I'd always wanted to come here because it seemed so exciting on television… So I agreed to let him photograph me in exchange for him buying me a plane ticket and pretending to be my uncle on the flight to New York."

"Jesus…" Byron whispers, appearing appalled.

I have to chuckle because this is nowhere *near* the worst part. "Anyway, there I was… Twelve years old in the Big Apple. Naturally, I had no money, no friends, no family. No place to go. So I did what I had to… I preferred stealing, and I'd become rather good at it. But it was never *enough*. Everything was so bloody expensive, and I was too young to get an apartment or even a hotel on my own. That's actually how it started… I'm sure you can… guess." I gulp.

"Prostitution?" he mutters after a beat, and I bite down on the inside of my cheek.

"I wasn't even thirteen yet… But you know some people liked that. Okay, some *men*. They were all men, at least until I turned about fifteen. And I have to say, it severely stunted my sexuality. I'd known for years I liked both girls and boys, but it was impossible for me to think of men in a way that wasn't rough and aggressive, and just… too painful."

I barely even notice how hard Byron is squeezing my hand until it starts to go numb. But I like it. It's… comforting.

"I'm not sure why this is still the hard part…" My voice shakes, and I clear my throat. "I'm not ashamed. I did what I had to… To survive. But I *hated* it. There's no shame in sex work, but I was a child. I wasn't supposed to be doing those things, and the men, my *John's*… they knew that. I carried a lot of rage because of it… I think I still do. For my parents mostly, because my being out there was their fault. And for the adults who took advantage of me and the other kids. I still hate feeling helpless… Hence, the drug use."

Byron's brows lift in surprise, because he didn't know about my substance abuse issues. He didn't know about anything…

But the look he's giving me is so utterly supportive. He tilts his head, eyes gleaming as if to say, *"It's alright. You can say anything you want. I won't judge you."*

Interestingly enough, it reminds me of the first time I told this story to Dr. Love.

"I began drinking and using hard drugs almost right away," I rasp. "I needed something to numb the pain and make it all… easier. Heroin definitely did that."

"Oh, baby…" Byron reaches out to brush my hair back with his fingers. "How long has it been?"

"Since I arrived at Alabaster Pen, so a few months?" I tell him.

"That's great, Trev. Really. I can't imagine it's easy…"

I'm dying over how sweet and supportive he is.

"No, it's not," I sigh. "Honestly, if I had access to drugs right now, I can't guarantee I wouldn't be doing them." Pausing, I recall something while Byron plays with my fingers. "I was going to drink… The Ivory has a bar downstairs. But I stopped myself because it won't… help. I know that now. But with the other stuff… I don't know, self-medicating was a distraction. And when I was using, I stopped caring and started feeling… bad. Because that's what I was, you know?"

Byron simply nods. He's not trying to help. He's just listening, and it's amazing.

I take a deep breath, glancing at Leo. He looks sad… *Because he knows what's next.* "So I was living and working on the streets, mostly alone. I'd been recruited a few times by a few groups, but they couldn't deal with me. I was too much of a wild card, with the drugs and the mental health issues… It wasn't worth it for them. But I didn't mind. Honestly, I preferred going it alone. I mean, I enjoyed being around other kids my age, but it just made me sad, seeing them mistreated…"

"You were more concerned with them?" Byron's lips twist. "Baby, you were being mistreated too…"

I shrug and bite my lip. "For me, it was inevitable. I'd been born into pain."

His amusement falls away, and he looks devastated for me. I rub my eyes.

"Either way, it was *fine*, until… that night. Until… *them*."

"Who's them?" Byron asks nervously.

"I was on my way to a mate's house… This lad I knew from Morningside," I recount, unable to stop from squirming already in discomfort. "I'd just been with one of my regulars who was nice, and he paid well, so I remember I was chuffed because I had a place to stay for the weekend and enough cash that I could take a break for at least a few days. I was walking, cutting through the park 'cause it was faster… That's when I ran into them.

"There were four of them. I knew one bloke… Not well, but I'd seen him around. He was a businessman. A Wall Street tosser who liked to bring underage boys up to his penthouse on Fifth. He was what we'd call a *Red*, meaning a John to watch out for because he was a freak known to get rough. Anyway, it was him and three other Wall Street-looking pricks, and as soon as they spotted me, it was like a game… Right away. A bloody *hunt*."

My voice goes softer in an instant. "That part of the park was empty, so right away, I was uneasy. I tried to avoid them, but the more I did, the more they came after me. The kick of it, you know?"

I pause and stare, still able to see this all so vividly, as if it just happened moments ago…

Darkness, trees lining long paths that seemed to go on for miles… No escape.

The clap of their dress shoes on the pavement.

Their laughter.

On my knees, cold wetness seeping into the denim of my jeans. My face being smashed into the grass…

Rough hands grabbing at me forcefully. Tears and snot running down my face.

The searing hot pain, and the violent smacking of their hips against my backside…

One… after another… after another.

Sniffling, I blink hard. "I realized rather quickly that fighting was pointless. There were four of them, and they were bigger and stronger than barely-sixteen-year-old me. So… yea. That was that. They raped me, all four of them. It only lasted, like, twenty minutes, but it felt like *days*." I inhale deep, letting it out slowly. "When they were done, they left me there… Bruised and bleeding in the dirt. They left me for dead."

I feel hollow inside as my eyes slink up to Byron's. They're glistening. And a lone tear rolls down his cheek.

He wipes it away quickly, but I'm thrown off for a moment.

That's not like Dr. Love…

I've never seen that type of reaction before.

"Trev…" His voice is hoarse, full lips parted and sort of quivering. He bites down on the bottom one.

It's such an adorable little pout, I find myself wanting to comfort *him*.

"I'm sure they thought I was dead." I continue quietly. Still struck by this man… "Or as good as. But I wasn't. Because you can't kill something that's already dead inside." Reaching out, I brush my thumb over that succulent lip. "I got up, dragged myself, beaten and bloody, to my mate's house… And that was when I began planning it. My revenge."

"We *did,*" Leo croaks.

"I spent the next few weeks tracking them down, following and studying them. I waited for the right time, which was difficult, since I *so* badly wanted to attack them any time I saw their pig faces, going about their lives like everything was fine. Like it was all *normal*… As if my body, my life, my *existence* meant nothing."

In a flash, my jaw is tight, heart rate picking up to a steady thump.

I still have fury in me. Whether they've been dealt with or not, I don't believe it'll ever go away.

"I harnessed every bit of patience I had, and I waited until the perfect moment to strike. And it paid off." My lips twitch. "I killed all four of them, one by one—within a span of three days? If I'm not mistaken… Lyle Ferguson, Connor Wainscott, John Beckten Jr., and Vincenzo Puglisi. Those were their names, but I just call them one-through-four. And now they're dead."

Byron is gawking. I don't think he's even breathing. He looks shocked—obviously enraged on my behalf, only slightly horrified—but relieved and impressed all the same.

I'm trying to imagine how Alice might have reacted to hearing all this… I don't mean to always be comparing them, but it just happens. They're my only two relationships. For what it's worth, I know Byron does the same with me and Michelangelo—*and maybe Ren too, but that's a whole other thing.* I can't fault him for it while I'm doing the same thing. *It's just a part of our shared baggage, I suppose.*

Sighing, I feel like I've been talking forever. *And we're still not done.* "Afterward, I didn't go into hiding… I felt prison was a small price to pay for my well-deserved revenge. I *was* eventually arrested, held as a minor while they built a case. Ultimately, there was only enough evidence to convict me of two murders, so I spent two years in a juvenile detention center. After I turned eighteen, I was sent to a psychiatric facility in Connecticut. If I'd done life… It still would've been worth it. I mean, I've grappled with feeling like I let them off too easily…"

"I don't know…" Byron hums. "Seems to me, you made them pay. With interest."

I chuckle, and he smirks.

Lifting his hand, I run my lips over his knuckles. "I was only in the Connecticut facility for a few months before they moved me down to Atlanta, to a place called *Riverwoods*. And that's where I met Dr. Love."

Saying his name now, as a part of my story, after everything we've been through… It floods me with emotions. But they're not what they used to be.

The feelings I had for him weren't real; I see that now. It was a crush on someone who helped me when nobody else did, and who saw me as something more than a deeply troubled and severely scarred individual.

Because we all know Dr. Love appreciates emotional damage.

"Trev… This is insane," Byron breathes. "It might be the craziest story I've ever heard. I mean, damn… What am I doing writing my shit?? *You* should write a book! Your story makes mine seem like an episode of Teletubbies."

I snort, resting my head on his shoulder, because reliving all of this is making me sleepy. "It's not a competition, baby. We both have our stories, and they're both valid."

"Did Dr. Love teach you that?" he teases, and I play-elbow him.

"So…. yea. Riverwoods. I was there for about two years before I was granted early release, which Dr. Love advocated for, by the way. He was the one who testified to the parole board that I was fit to rejoin society, so long as I continued outpatient treatment with him…" I snicker.

"What?" he asks. "You think he was wrong?"

"I think *he* thinks he was wrong." I chuckle. "Or rather, he knew the only way to test my monster was to get me out of captivity. And that's exactly what he did."

I can feel Byron's pulse picking up. "Do you think you belong in prison?"

I tilt my face. "I think there are certainly worse people out there…"

"That's not an answer," he whispers, and his tone, while he's touching me and I can smell him… It zaps me in the balls.

"I suppose we'll just have to wait and see, hm?" I purr. Byron bites his lip. "Does it frighten you…?"

He takes my face in his hands. "You did what you had to do, baby. I'd say that's very Raphael of you."

A wide grin captures my lips. His mouth inches over mine, and I'm longing to end this and just wrap myself around his big, strong body. But I force myself back, because I can't always jump into the physical… That's not what he wants.

"We're not done yet," I whisper, and he groans.

"Jesus, Mary, and Joseph, how is there not a documentary about you?"

I laugh, shaking my head. He plays with the hair at my nape as I pick back up. "Fast forward a year or so after I'd been released, and I had a job, an apartment… I was seeing Dr. Love twice a week, and he had me on medication for my night terrors, depression and anxiety. I was still figuring out what life looked like for someone like me… Someone broken. I was trying hard to put Trevel back together, but I think I always knew in the back of my mind I was missing a few pieces. I thought I'd gotten past my past… Or maybe I just told myself I had. Because I wanted it…"

"Wanted what?" he asks softly.

"A normal life." I feel so vulnerable in this moment. Split open for him, more than I've ever been with anyone else. "But I'm certain now that some people just aren't meant for normal…"

"Fuck normal," Leo grunts.

"Fuck normal," Byron says firmly.

A whimpering chuckle leaves me as I touch him, because he's *perfect*. All of him. *Every bit.*

"In Atlanta, I'd actually started dating," I tell him. "Casually. I mean, it wasn't really *dating*. More like Tinder hookups, but still. It was something. I could finally have sex with guys without freaking out or losing my wood, so I called that a victory."

Byron's cheeks are flushing, and I have to bite back my smirk.

"One day, on the way to Dr. Love's, I saw the most beautiful person in this coffee shop up the block from his office. She was working as a barista, and I was immediately swept away by her." I pause to gulp before mumbling, "Her name was Alice."

Speaking her name brings memories too… And they're breaking my heart… Even the good ones.

Because she's gone, and she doesn't *need* to be.

I think Byron can tell right away that the story is about to take another turn. He's visibly bracing himself.

"Alice was a twenty-one-year-old trans woman from Colombia. She'd been through a lot in her life, what with transitioning and her family's lack of acceptance. Of course, I didn't know that at the time. All I knew was that she was beautiful. Her personality was like this glowing ball of light that followed her around. I guess you could say I… stalked her. Just a little. Amateur hour compared to your stalking," I huff, and Byron smirks. "I just watched her come and go while struggling to work up the nerve to talk to her. Finally, one day, I took the leap, though, I still feel like she was the one asking me out. Which was bonkers because she was way out of my league." I chuckle.

Byron appears fascinated and wholly invested.

"We dated for only a few weeks… Barely two months. But I felt so strongly for her. I'd never…" My words fade and gulp, noting a shift in Byron's expression, the slightest increase in tension. It looks like he's feeling jealous while trying not to, and it's so unbearably sexy. *Too bad that's all going to change in a moment…* "I wasn't… good to her, though. Because I'm a mess, Byron. I'm a *curse*, baby, I'm just… awful—"

"Shh…" he shushes while my pulse pings. "Tell me why you think that…"

"Because I cheated on her," I choke out, burying my face in his chest so I don't have to see him looking at me while I say this… "With her brother."

"Oh, violet…" he whispers, stroking my hair.

"It was after Dr. Love left." I sniffle. "I was off my meds, and I started using again. Alice's twin brother, Andres, was staying with her. He'd been in prison for drug offenses, so it was just… a bad situation. I was weak, and I fell apart *so* easily." I wipe a tear onto his shirt. "I sucked him off a couple times in exchange for heroin… Like a loser junkie—"

"Hey," Byron hums. "Don't say that… Please, baby."

"I've always been a mess, By…" I grumble. "That doesn't stop. It *never* ends. I had a great girl who I actually cared deeply for. Who I might have…" I clear my throat. "And I threw it away for a hot dude with strong narcotics. You must think I'm such a knob…" I bury my face even deeper.

"You messed up, Trevel. You're only human. If there's one thing I've come to understand, it's that you can be in love with someone and still make mistakes like that. Physical ones…"

Lifting my face, I peek up at him. He bites his lip, and I can tell right away he's thinking of Ren.

"Ren did that…?" I ask carefully.

His eyes gleam with sadness as he nods. "He loved Luthor with all of himself. I know that. It was just… physical. With us… It was an addiction for him, like yours."

"I know what that's like…" I mumble, remembering being high out of my mind the night that Alice died. "I would've used anything to forget, Byron. And I still battle those demons every day." Scrubbing my hands over my face, I exhale a rough whimper. "I lost her because of it… I let her *die*, Byron… Because I was too fucked up to save her. *That's* why I'm here. I'm trapped forever as a permanent reminder of the lowest point in my life…"

Byron's face has never been more still. "You don't have to say any more if you don't want to, baby—"

"The night Alice died, I was high." I force the words out. "Andres and I… did our thing. Then he shot me up, which was weird, because I usually snorted it." I blink hard and shake my head. "I was in and out for a bit, and the next thing I knew, he was fucking me…"

Byron's jaw clenches, expression dripping with fast rage.

"I was… awake. I mean, I was groggy, but lucid. I… consented." I gulp. "But Alice… she was in the bed next to us. I thought she was just sleeping, so it was kinda hot…" A whimper flees my lips, and I slap my palms to cover myself. "I didn't know she was… she… was…"

I'm full-blown crying in an instant. Like a dam burst, I'm hysterical.

Byron tries to steady me, but I rip away from his hands. "She was dead, Byron. She *died*! Her twin fucking brother *killed* her by intentional overdose and then fucked me, knowing bloody well he was planning to frame me for her murder! Do you know what it feels like?? To walk around every day, knowing you let someone who killed the first person you've ever loved fuck you right next to her fucking corpse?!"

I'm practically hyperventilating. The guilt and agony are so strong, I can't see.

Swallowing back pain, I choke, "I killed him when I found out. I killed that waste of bloody life and his asshole friend for what they did. But it's still my fault. *I'm* the evil one, Byron. Because I had love, and I gave it up for *nothing*… That's who *I* am."

He's gaping at me, brown irises reflecting my sorrow back. "How… How did you end up here?"

"Manuel Blanco thought I killed someone else." I sniff.

His brow furrows. "Who?"

"I don't know," I mumble, exhausted from the emotional marathon I just ran, rehashing all of this. "Someone he confused with Alice, or Andres, I suppose. By the time I was already here, he'd found out he had the wrong information, but you know him… He saw an opportunity."

Byron looks like he has a million things to say, but can't manage to cough up a single word.

"So… there you have it. The whole story." I rake fingers through my hair, drained and hollow, from the pure devastation of my life. "That's what led me to where I am right now… Here with you."

I actually got through it… And he's still here.

Now let's see if he stays.

Byron bites his lip. I can't help plucking it from between his teeth again.

"Trevel…" His voice shakes with emotion. Not pity, *thank God*, but I can feel what he's feeling on my behalf, and gives me a rush of dopamine.

"I just wanted you to know, Byron. Because from the moment I met you, I wanted nothing more than to figure you out." I run my hand up his chest, resting my palm over his heart. "You *let* me, baby. And now it's… my turn. Surrendering feels good sometimes. When it's with… you."

He's quiet for many generous moments while we just stare at one another. Finally, he exhales, breaking the silence. "Why did you wait so long to tell me this? You're right, I've shared *so* much with you, and all I wanted in return was this… This deep stuff you've been clinging to. Don't you trust me…?"

"I do! I swear, I do… I just…" I pause to collect my thoughts. "I mean, Byron… Do you blame me? I'm bloody *tapped*. My life, everything I've been through, all that I *am*… It's like a disease." Tears are welling again, and I try to sniff them away. "I was scared… I'm *so* bloody scared with you, Byron, and I hate being scared. I despise it… But with you, I'm *terrified*."

His eyes are rounded as he shakes his head. "Of what?"

"Of hurting you, like I hurt Alice. Of ruining you, like I ruined myself… Of… losing you… In any way. Losing you to someone else…" My voice trails as I think of Ren. And Michelangelo…

He can obviously tell, because he breaks our eye contact. There are so many things in that one expression, so much of what we've been through over the last months. From the moment we met… until right now.

And I want it all. The good, and the bad.

"You said your feelings for Lem were like mine for Michelangelo," he starts softly. Wary, but still… *He's still here.* "Well, Michelangelo isn't the only person I've… felt that for. He was my first, yes, but not the last. I've felt those same things, *stronger* things… for someone else." His throat dips in a heavy swallow, vulnerability shimmering in his eyes. "Have you?"

I know what he's asking me… And I don't need the moment it's taking me to answer him. But I'm taking it, because I'm so afraid.

Please don't let me lose him too… I won't survive it.

I cup his jaw in my hand. "Baby, I *have*, I promise. Byron… My feelings for Lemuel were… only one tiny flicker. Barely anything. But there's a whole *world* of light out there… belonging to someone else."

His lashes flutter.

You're all of it, sweet fury…

Every single shine and then some.

"I don't want the past to matter, Trevel," he hums. "I just want to move on, but I feel like we're stuck in it."

"How can we break free?" I ask him, pleading for answers because I need them, too.

I don't know what I'm doing… In truth, I never did.

"You got your closure." He gazes up at me. "I didn't get that much. He's gone, and *they're* gone, and I never got to…" He gulps back his painful confession.

I gauge him closely, that grief he's been wearing every day since he found out that Luthor and Ren were dead…

But they're not.

They're not dead.

I just spoke to Luthor.

"It's over," the voice speaks from inside my skull. I close my eyes and

see him… *Me*, as Leonardo. *"If they're alive, it'll never be over, Trevel. He'll always be wondering where they are… Where* he *is."*

My lip trembles, and I bite it. I'm aching inside, a bloody gash within my chest that just wants to be healed. And I *need* him for that.

"With Ren gone, Byron is yours. You know I'm right."

"But I can't… I have to tell him," I whimper, maybe out loud.

Oh, Byron… My fury. My warrior. My Raphael…

You're all I want. But I'm terrified that you'll get sick of me when you realize how much work it is to love me.

My lips are parted, the words resting on my tongue…

Ren's not dead. Neither is Luthor. They're alive, baby, and they might… be coming back…

But they won't come out. I just *can't* cough them up. He's just squirming, tense, with hesitation in his eyes.

Fuck me… This is agonizing.

"Do not fucking tell him," Leo growls.

But what if they show up? What then…?

"I h-have to… tell him," I stammer.

"Trevel," Byron hums my name, taking my wrists in his hands. "Is there… anything else?" I blink at him, gagging on guilt and those pesky truths I'm holding hostage. "Is there *anything* else you want to tell me?"

"Y-yes… There is." Sitting up slowly, I take a breath, casting one more glance at Leo. "We're not alone."

CHAPTER THIRTY-SIX

Byron

LIFE ON THIS ISLAND IS BECOMING STRANGER EVERY DAY.

Every time I think maybe, just *maybe*, things are settling down, some new bizarre thing pops up. Another layer to the nightmare, like a bad trip you just can't come down from. *No end in sight.*

It's starting to feel like we're doomed. All of us. No matter which side of this thing you're on, the future is looking bleak. *I don't mean to be a negative Nancy, but hey… If the deadly collar fits.*

Thinking about how unsteady things used to be, when it was just the prison, living each day shuffling through concrete hallways, eating bland food and fighting just to feel *anything*, I find myself yearning to go *back*. Sure, I spent my days teetering between blinding fury and mind-numbing hopelessness, loathing my pathetic path of existence for leading me here; putting me in chains when all I'd wanted was to break *free*. But if I'd known things would end up like *this*… Well, for starters, I would've been less mopey about it.

It's been days, and by some minor miracle, The Ivory hasn't found out that Trevel killed his doctors. He still thinks they're working on Dr. Love down there in the tombs, with Trevel overseeing the whole *project*. And Trevel's been doing a decent job of keeping up the charade. But we're not naïve enough to believe it'll last. It's only a matter of time until the truth comes to light, and the next wave of the *fiasco* begins.

I worry about what that means for Trevel… and for me. We're

attached now, our lives entwined because of this relationship that neither of us fully understands. The Ivory has already used my feelings for Trevel as blackmail—when he sent me to the prison. What's stopping him from using me as revenge for Trevel's betrayal?

It's all very fucked up. And to top it off, I recently found out that this *boyfriend* of mine—*if that's what we're calling him*—is *way* more broken than I could've anticipated.

I hate to seem ungrateful after he *finally* confided in me and shared what he's been through; all the mayhem that led him here. I mean, I was practically begging for it—*okay, I was* actually *begging, a few times.* But when he was pouring his heart out, slicing himself open at the middle and letting his guts spill all over me, there was a brief moment where I was so overwhelmed, I seriously wanted to hit the rewind button and go back into the dark.

Things were much less complicated when I was blissfully unaware of his many, many *issues.*

I wonder if Dr. Love is open to holding a session down there in the dungeon... Because I think we could both *use it.*

I'm not talking about Trevel's *past*, per se—though listening to everything he's experienced, all at once, was a bit jarring. I mean, how is it even *possible* for one human being to endure so much hardship? It's a wonder he's even still alive, let alone as outwardly well-adjusted as he is.

I will say, learning the truth about his past made me infinitely more fascinated by him, shining a light on his strength and resilience. And cards on the table, I totally get his obsession with revenge now.

But then there's the *other* part...

My boyfriend has an imaginary friend.

Yea. That's what I'm dealing with... Hence the need for emergency therapy.

Believe it or not, Trevel is actually extremely self aware when it comes to the whole *Leo the talking Ninja Turtle-bear* thing. He knows Leo isn't real. *So... that's good, I guess.*

But then he talks to him, *out loud*. He told me he *sees* him. And I can't tell if it's just a coping mechanism, or if it's something more worrying.

The first thing that came to mind was Dash. How he used to behave when he was here, like he was seeing and hearing things no one else could.

We've since found out that it was part of his schizophrenia. But Dr. Love treated Trevel for *years* as a patient. If Trevel had schizophrenia, surely, he would've picked up on it and diagnosed him... *Right?*

Or maybe he just hid Leo... *really* well.

That's what I'm itching to figure out. If Leo is a symptom of some untreated mental illness, or if he's really just… Trevel's imaginary friend. Controlled by him and used as a way to deal with his past trauma.

I can't tell. And Trevel is no help… Because while he *did* tell me about his toy bear that he manifested into an anthropomorphized figment of his imagination, he refuses to talk about him any more than simply acknowledging his existence. He won't answer any of my questions about Leo, and gets defensive when I bring him up, accusing me of thinking he's crazy.

Let's just say, I don't *not* think he's crazy… But I care about him. If he's crazy, I want to know about it, so I can prepare myself. Because honestly… it's not a deal-breaker.

I know, I seem like a desperate hoe, but I swear, that's not what it's about. I can't lie, though. Crazy *on Trevel is… kinda cute. It's a Leonardo teddy bear, for fuck's sake! I don't care who you ask; that's adorable,* and *pretty awesome.*

Trevel Fenwick is under my skin. *Deep*, like where my bones are. At this point, I doubt something as endearing as him having an imaginary friend he argues with would drive me away. I'm not sure it *could*.

Maybe I'm losing my mind, too. Maybe this whole *fall of Alabaster Isle* has sent me into an emotional tailspin, and because of that, things that might have worried me in the past I'm now finding charming. Like a welcomed distraction from the somber state of our existence… *My own cuddly, unhinged ninja bear.*

Or maybe that has nothing to do with it… And I just love him, *because* of his quirks and emotional baggage, not in spite of it.

Gulping down a mouthful of saliva and some nausea that's making me dizzy, I grab onto the nearest piece of furniture.

Jesus Christ, did I just say that I love him *in my mind?? Is that real??*

It has to be, right? I mean, why else would I have thought it if it weren't… true?

This is getting so far out of hand, it's fucking levitating. Turns out, I was clinging to the idea that I didn't really know Trevel, because it allowed me to keep him at a distance. And now that he's told me all of his secrets, there's nothing left for me to hide behind. No more excuses to keep me safe and warm in denial…

God, I think he might really be my boyfriend.

Someone call an exterminator… I think I've caught the love bug.

Oh, God… barf times a million.

Taking a deep breath, I continue mulling around the study, because it's safe and quiet and I need some alone time to gather my thoughts.

Unfortunately, it's not as secluded down here as I'd thought, because I hear sudden voices coming from the atrium.

They must hear me at the same time that I hear them, because two of The Ivory's men swing around the corner, guns in hand. When they see that it's me, they lower their weapons, and one of them rumbles, "It's just Kang."

Yup. Just me… The former inmate having a secret meltdown about the state of his prison marriage. Nothing to see here.

"Oh, good," I hear Manuel Blanco murmur. "Send him in."

"Wait… I wasn't…" I start to protest, but give up noting their uninterested expressions and sigh, "Never mind."

Wandering carefully onto the veranda that leads out to the garden's patio, I balk at the first thing I see… The Ivory sitting on a loveseat with someone kneeling at his feet. It only takes a moment before I realize it's Hancock—practically naked, and *muzzled*, with a leash connected to the collar around his neck.

"Holy balls…" I mutter under my breath, gawking at the former Alabaster Pen guard in a position I never would have expected to see him. *And I've seen him in some pretty precarious positions. Mostly thanks to Ren.*

"To what do I owe this pleasure, Byron?" the Warden says calmly, tugging the leash until Hancock stumbles. He seems out of it, but I think he's registering my presence, eyes gleaming up at me from behind the thing covering his face.

Hancock was captured by The Ivory's men a week or so back, after some shootout in the woods went sideways. He was treated for his gunshot wound, hence the gauze pad on his shoulder. In fact, that, the muzzle, a jockstrap, and a furry tail appear to be the only things he's wearing.

Okay… Let's look somewhere else.

From what I've heard, nabbing Simon Hancock was a win for The Ivory. It forced Velle to retreat and regroup, in the interest of keeping Hancock alive. I have no idea what any of that means for the outcome of this war, but I'm finding the state Hancock is in right now troubling. He was always one of the good guys. Not innocent by any stretch of the imagination—none of them were—but much less of a bastard than some others.

Oh, Jesus. Jasper… He's probably freaking out.

Recalling that The Ivory asked me a question when he cocks a light eyebrow at my awkward silence, I clear my throat. "Uh… Just checking in. Seeing if you… need anything."

Who are you, the butler now??

The Ivory's gaze narrows, but he's still smirking, and it's wringing my stomach like a wet dishcloth. "As of matter of fact, I do need something from you. Well, *need* is a strong word. You'll do it, or you'll be dead. Sound good?"

I just stare at him with my mouth agape. *What am I supposed to say to that??*

"I'm expecting company," he goes on, watching me closely. "One visitor, and one… not. You know both of them. Anyway, I need you nearby when they arrive."

My brows crush together in obvious confusion. "Why…?"

"That will become readily apparent very soon, my darling fighter." His smirk spreads into a devilish grin, and he pats the seat next to him.

I don't move right away, not until his dark eyes sparkle with threatening urgency. Reluctantly, I step over and I sit down on the loveseat with as much space between us as physically possible. I can't stop my eyes from repeatedly flicking to Hancock, fingers curling into a fist.

"Where is Trevel?" The Ivory asks, and I stiffen.

Truthfully, I don't know where Trevel is right now. I haven't seen him since he said he was going to check on Dr. Love, and that was a few hours ago. He could be anywhere at this point.

But that answer doesn't work, so I say, "He's with Johansson and Hassan."

The Ivory shows me a pleased expression. "So he's enjoying his time with Lemuel, then?"

I nod reticently. "Yes… Seems that way."

"Good," he sighs, crossing his ankle over his knee, wrapping Hancock's leash around his fist until it tightens. "It's important to reward loyalty, don't you think?" He stares at me until I nod again. "Trevel has been vying for the good doctor since he got here, and while at first it wasn't beneficial for me to show my hand, things have obviously changed."

"That's an understatement," I mutter, then catch myself, eyes flinging to his.

He simply grins. "Felix Darcey will pop up eventually, and when he does, maybe I'll let you take the reins on that one."

I don't even fucking care anymore, man. Felix Darcey is the least of my worries at this point. But I force a grateful nod and a curt, "Thank you."

"In the meantime, I need to make sure you'll be able to coexist with our visitor," he goes on, absentmindedly brushing his fingers through the messy strands of Hancock's brown hair. "It might be a bit trying for you.

But just remember, you fought to be here, Byron. No one can take that away from you."

I have no earthly clue what he's talking about, but his words and the way he's speaking them are causing nervous chills to scatter over my body.

Movement across the room catches my eye, and I gulp. Trevel has emerged from the far end of the garden… The opposite direction from where I just told The Ivory he was. When he sees us all sitting out here, he ducks behind some trees. I glance at The Ivory, then his men, releasing a secret breath. *Thank fuck, they didn't see him.*

Trevel peers out just enough for my eyes to widen at him.

Stay where you are.

For the love of God, don't let him see you.

My heart is thumping like crazy, but I'm trying to ignore it and act normal. Clomping footsteps grow closer as Kent storms outside, addressing The Ivory. "We've got him."

Manuel Blanco chuckles, rubbing his hands together in satisfaction. "Perfect. Bring him to me."

Kent nods, pulling the walkie off of his holster and grumbling into it, "Bring him to the atrium."

"Go find Yari and let him know we're all clear," Blanco says. "I want you and Paulino up there to greet Russo when the helicopter touches down."

"Yes, sir." Kent stalks off almost as fast as my heart just sank into my gut.

Russo…

Did he just say… Russo?? As in, Governor Russo??

As in, Michelangelo's scumbag father, the man responsible for me being locked up in Hell for three goddamn years?!

I feel myself pale. Naturally, The Ivory is already staring at me when I whip in his direction, and he murmurs, "I told you it would be a bit trying."

"*Trying??*" I gasp, jumping up from my seat, panicked rage filling my extremities. "Are you fucking serious?! You expect me to be in the same room as him?? That man wants me dead… That's why I'm here, you know that!"

"Sit down," he commands, deep and warning.

I have no choice but to slink back into my seat, though my knee is bouncing rapidly. I expect The Ivory to spout some of his usual ominous Jigsaw crap, but when he isn't speaking, I allow my eyes to slide his way again.

Leaning closer to me, his dark gaze hardens in frustration. "Do you think I *want* him here? Considering the current state of this island, it's not exactly the best time for the Governor of fucking New York to show up. I've held him off as long as I could, and now he's coming. Swallow it, shadowman. It's happening."

My jaw clenches so hard I feel my teeth snapping. "I can't look him in the eye. He ruined my life."

"You can and you will," he says firmly, though his tone is much less foreboding than before. It sounds almost… supportive? That is, until his head cocks. "*Unless* you're more worried that seeing him will remind you of what *else* you lost… Aside from your freedom, I mean."

My lungs shrivel up, and my heart constricts, like everything behind my ribcage is being crushed. Of course, seeing Michelangelo's father again will remind me of him, and how we were before he caught us. It's as devastating as it is enraging.

The smallest silver lining in being here was knowing I'd never have to see Governor Russo's fucking face again. Now he's *coming here?!*

And The Ivory expects me to… what? Play nice??

Are you fucking kidding me??

The fear and anger in me feel like anchors around my ankles, pulling me underwater. Glancing behind The Ivory, I subtly search for Trevel. But I don't see him over there anymore.

The Warden straightens at the sound of footsteps approaching, joined by the familiar clanking of chains. "Don't worry, Byron. Something tells me you're about to have more on your mind than just reuniting with your ex's terrible father…"

Suddenly, two of his men come clomping up the path, dragging someone along in shackles, hands cuffed behind their back and a bag over their head. My breathing is labored as they shove the person onto their knees in front of us.

The Ivory looks purely elated, reaching forward to grab the bag and yank it off.

What…

The…

Fuck.

A gasp flees my lips, eyes bulging out of my skull. "*Dash??*"

The unmistakable hazel gaze of my friend I haven't seen in months—because he fucking *escaped*—shimmers up at me, tousled pink hair hanging in his eyes. He blinks, in just as much apparent shock to see me as I'm feeling from seeing him. Blowing the silky strands away, he peeks at The Ivory, expression hardening to a distinct hatred.

Manuel Blanco smirks and reclines. "Welcome back, Dascha."

Perfect fucking timing... Trevel comes traipsing around the corner, while I'm reeling down to my goddamn *soul*, and looks around. "What did I miss?"

My eyes are on The Ivory. Concern ripples and rushes all over me as I watch him, taking a phone call across the room. When I'm absolutely sure he's not paying attention, I lean in.

But Dash beats me to it. "Bro, oh my *God*," he sighs, an exhausted, fluttery chuckle, swirls of brown and green aimed up at me, all wide and shiny. "It's so good to see you."

"You too." I shake my head over and over. "But what are you doing here??"

"I could ask you the same thing..." His gaze narrows, shifting briefly to Trevel. I swallow hard, and we both check on The Ivory again before he whispers, "Kemper and I came back."

"On purpose??" I gasp. Trevel shoots me a *be quiet* look.

"We've been trying to call Joy for weeks and couldn't get ahold of anyone," he explains, hushed yet determined. Not a ton of worry in his tone for someone who escaped prison *and* this island, only to find himself chained up in front of the very psychopath he dipped out on. "I was sure something was wrong. I mean, clearly, I was right..." He gives me a knowing look.

Accurate. Shit is all kinds of fucked right now.

Hancock tries mumbling something beneath his muzzle, and I snap, "Shh! Not now."

"What the hell are you doing over here?" Dash asks again. "Why aren't you with Velle?"

"We were here when the prison fell, and shit got... complicated," I mutter sheepishly, gulping. "It's a long story."

Dash is peering up at Trevel again, who's studying him right back, head cocked in that curious animal way that *I* find pretty cute, but I think others might find unsettling.

"Oh, sorry… Dash, this is, um, Trevel," I rasp, trying not to sound as uncomfortable as I'm feeling. "He's 102. Trev, this is Dash. He was 101… until he escaped."

"Charmed." Trevel pulls a polite grin that's more skeptical than anything. He's getting the same thing right back.

Dash squints at him. Then at me. "Are you two a thing?"

I'm gawking and speechless while Hancock nods enthusiastically. I kick him in the back, and he grunts. "Where's Kemper?" I ask, blatantly ignoring his question. "And how did The Ivory get you??"

Dash's lips part, but the answers I desperately want are interrupted by the Warden stalking over. We all scuttle back into place, presenting as much innocence as we can.

"Sorry about that," he sighs, returning to his seat beside me. "Business as usual. Now, where were we?"

"I think you were about to take these goddamn chains off me," Dash grunts.

The Ivory chuckles. "Was I?"

"If you want me to play along." Dash shrugs.

I'm bewildered right now. I just can't fucking believe Dash is *here*, and that he's going toe-to-toe with Manuel Blanco, after escaping and turning this whole damn place upside down!

The kid's got fuckin balls. He's an Alabaster Pen rock star!

"Or maybe I could just kill you," The Ivory grumbles, then grins. "After all, Russo only wants to know that you're *here*. He doesn't care what state your sexy little corpse is in."

"But someone else does…" Dash hisses through gritted teeth.

Blanco's amusement falls away, and he purses his lips to downplay his obvious irritation. It seems like Dash has some kind of leverage I don't know about.

Who? Who *are they talking about??*

"Keep pushing me, Dascha, and I'll cut out Kellan Kemper's tongue," he seethes.

Dash doesn't budge. "Good luck finding him."

"Nice try. But we both know he would never allow you to come here alone."

"I'm not alone," Dash growls. "I've got *family* here… Remember?"

"Listen to me, you little shit," The Ivory's tone hops right over the line from controlled anger to unhinged wrath. Like flipping a switch. "You're *mine*, understand me?? As far as the world is concerned, I fucking *own* you.

So do me a favor and keep your pouty mouth shut while I handle Russo, or so help me, I will not stop until you're in bits and pieces. Your *officer* will be bringing you back to Mexico in a goddamn Tupperware container like last night's leftovers!"

My nervous eyes meet Trevel's, both of us visibly stiff. Dash is *glaring* at The Ivory, practically buzzing, though he doesn't respond to that threat. Simply sits back on his knees and cocks his head, displaying a bored expression.

The Ivory's dark gaze stays on the Russian bank robber for a few extra seconds that feel like heavy minutes. His jaw is visibly tight, and there's a tick of something extremely stabby, even more than the usual hostility over Dash escaping. I really wish I knew what was going on here…

I want details.

That's the worst part of this position I find myself in. I'm expected to sit by The Ivory's side, obey him while mindlessly nodding like, *yes, sir, Mr. Blanco, sir…*

But I don't get any intel. I'm still fully in the dark. The only real perk in all this is sleeping in the mansion and eating good food. *Is it worth it?*? I can't really tell. Sometimes I think it might be, but moments like these have me second guessing everything.

The Ivory eventually stands with a sigh, nodding at the two officers who brought Dash in. They immediately stomp toward the doorway that leads inside the mansion.

"Keep an eye on him," he says to Trevel. His eyes bounce to me, brow cocking pointedly. *This* is an expression I can read.

I'm not sure I trust you with this one.

Still, he hands me Hancock's leash. "We'll be back. Just going on a scenic stroll…"

His evil eyes fall to Dash once more before he stalks after the guards. "Scour the area! Kellan Kemper's here… I want him found."

As soon as he's out of sight, Dash breathes hard, wobbling to his feet.

Shaking myself out of it, I ask Trevel, "You still have those cuff and shackle keys?"

Trevel pauses, watching Dash as he nods hesitantly, using the keys we got from the dead doctors to unlock Dash's chains.

Dash eyes Trevel while rubbing his wrists. "Thanks…"

Trevel nods, though he still doesn't appear confident in this move. We're supposed to be on *Team Ivory*… Granted, I'm not sure I ever really saw how that would work. But if he finds out we're breaking the rules, we're dead.

"So are you siding with this asshole now??" Dash growls at me, bending to fuss with the muzzle on Hancock's face. "You remember that he's been personally responsible for all of our misery for *years*, right?"

He manages to get it off, and Hancock immediately groans, spitting on the floor. "Jesus motherfucking Mary and Joseph! That thing was *so* uncomfortable." He unbuckles the clip of the leash from his collar and grunts, "Kang, be a pal and pull this fucking plug out of my ass, would you?"

"Pretty sure you can do that yourself," I mutter, dropping the leash onto the floor, eyes springing back to Dash. "And I'm not *siding* with him. I'm just here. Not that it matters… Velle doesn't care about me, so what difference does it make??"

Dash looks like he wants to argue, but I think he realizes it's pointless. He knows damn well Velle only cares about three things in this world… Rook, Joy, and himself.

"Well, what about Luthor and Ren?" he asks, and my heart sinks like a hunk of concrete tossed into the ocean. "They must be over there, right?? How could you not be with them?"

Swallowing is difficult, as if my throat is closing up. I glance at Trevel, who's giving me a very intense look, then Hancock, whose face falls in despair.

Dash must be noting the grim expressions and the sudden mist of sadness covering us all. His shoulders drop, eyes widened with unease. "What…?"

"Dash…" I shake my head slowly. "Luthor and Ren are… They didn't…"

I physically can't say the words. It feels like knives are stabbing me in the heart every time I *think* them. Speaking them out loud solidifies it.

My best friends are dead.

Dash trembles, a knowing heartbreak instantly overwhelming his pretty face. I can see his breathing shift as his chest jumps up and down.

"No…" he whispers in a voice suddenly small and innocent, like a child. A complete shift from the confidence of a moment ago.

I finally manage to croak, "They're dead. Luthor and Ren are…" My voice cuts out in a ragged sob, and I cover my face. "They tried to escape, but they… didn't make it."

"No…" Dash whimpers, but I keep my hands covering my face. I can't look at him right now. I just *can't. I'll break the fuck down.* "No no no… *What??* That doesn't make any… *Fuck*, Byron. You're not fucking serious!"

He's crumbling, voice even raspier than usual and jagged with emotion as he launches himself at me.

"It's not true…" He sobs quietly into the crook of my neck, quivering uncontrollably.

Fuck me, I can't do this…

Tears well and fall from my eyes while Dash hugs onto me so hard, he's crushing my ribs. Or maybe that's the pain…

Slowly, the stiffness in my muscles eases, and I circle his waist with my arms. The second it happens, I fall the fuck apart.

Dash and I are holding on to one another for dear life, tears tumbling, wetting each other's skin. We're both shaking, gasping for breath, and attempting to hold ourselves together, when in reality, I think we're the only thing holding each other together right now.

No one else has been able to give me this… Not even Trevel. No one gets it. They don't understand this devastation like Dash and I do. Luthor and Ren were our *best friends* in the entire world. We've been through so much together. They meant more to us than anyone else on this godforsaken island…

It's fucking crazy to think about, but I never had real friendships until I came to Alabaster Pen. I never had this sort of connection. An almost familial bond I never even had with my own flesh and blood. We were like the crew from the *Fast and the Furious* movies. Bad guys banding together, having each other's backs, no matter what. We fight, then we make up, because above all else, we're a *family*.

But I never got to…

"I never got to… tell them I'm… sorry," I heave into Dash's chest while he struggles to breathe through his own sobs. "We had a fight… after you left. I was angry at them, and I—"

"I know," he hums, consoling me with his tone and his palm cradling the back of my head. "I get it."

"There was so much I should've s-said," I sniffle. "And now it's too late. I'm the shittiest friend ever…"

Dash pulls back, forcing me to abandon the humility of being vulnerable like this and meet his eyes. The hazel is glassy and red-rimmed, but still such a comfort right now.

I swallow past the memories trying to push their way to the surface of my mind.

"You're not," he says with quavering sincerity. "Trust me, I have my own regrets. But I'm sure they knew, Byron. I'm *positive* they knew how much they meant to you."

I'm so grateful for him being here in this moment. For trying to cheer me up and placate my unbearable remorse.

But he doesn't know the whole story…

No one does. No one but me.

And maybe…

Glancing over Dash's shoulder, I find Trevel, looking like he's about to crawl out of his own skin. He starts his pacing thing again, rubbing his eyes and pulling his hair. His distress is clear, and I have to wonder if he's really feeling all of this anguish on my behalf.

He can't be that much of a sociopath, then… Right?? If he's so distraught for me…?

"Look, I know this is a rough time. For all of us," Hancock rumbles, finally standing up again, though he's swaying and sluggish, like he might be coming down from some strong shit. "But we really can't just stand around here like this. If he comes back, we're all fucked. We need a plan."

Dash and I detach from one another, composing ourselves while looking him up and down.

"I can't take you seriously while you're wearing that," I mutter, referring to his lack of clothes.

The dude's just standing around in nothing but a jockstrap. And rather brazenly, I might add.

I never knew he had such a… great body.

I clear my throat and shift my gaze.

Oh, right… I'm bisexual.

My eyes slink timidly back to his abs. And his butt.

"Then go grab me some pants, bitch." Hancock lifts a brow at me.

I narrow my gaze. "You know I can't do that."

He simply shrugs, and I have to commend him for his apparent shamelessness.

"Guys, focus," Dash snaps quietly. *The level-headed one…*

Never thought I'd see the day.

Dash jaunts over to the veranda, peering inside the mansion—I'm guessing to check for the Warden or any of his men. "We need to do something. We have to get to Velle."

"The Ivory's expecting you both to still be chained up in here when he returns," Trevel says, radiating tension. "I hate to say it, but you may need to—"

"I'm not putting that fucking plug back in," Hancock bites.

"Yea, same." Dash purses his lips. "Think again, man. There's absolutely no way I'm chaining myself back up."

"Okay, I get that," I chime in. "But he has a point... Governor Russo is on his way here, and he's going to want to see you locked up."

Same goes for me...

"When is he supposed to be arriving?" Trevel asks. Our eyes connect, and my breathing hitches.

It feels like we haven't spoken in days. Things are still strained between us, and it's adding to my current state of trepidation. Trevel has become my constant. He's the only one who's been on *my* side all along.

Velle doesn't want me back...

Dash is only worried about Kemper, I'm sure.

If I were to leave Trevel for them, I'd be alone again.

I don't want to go back to being invisible.

"Um... not sure," I mumble, then clear my throat. "But The Ivory said he was coming in by helicopter. I guess he's on his way..."

Trevel curses under his breath, raking fingers through his messy black hair.

"Can't we just get out of here??" Dash asks frantically. "Make a run for it?"

"You got some Kevlar under your skin we don't know about??" Hancock scoffs. "You step outside, especially over here, and those assholes will turn you into Swiss cheese." He gestures to the bandage on his shoulder. "Trust me."

"Yea, not to mention, we're all still wearing these." I tap the collar around my neck.

Dash rushes to me, examining the collar. He goes to yank on it, but I back up fast.

"Yo, take it easy," I chide. "I don't feel like being paralyzed for half a day."

Dash's brows jump, morbid fascination shining in his eyes as he chews on his pouty bottom lip. "How do we deactivate them?"

"From what I've seen, The Ivory has the key... A small remote-like object he used to remove yours," Trevel says to me.

"I'm assuming he has the only one," I sigh, and Trevel nods.

"What about those fuckhead doctors from the East Wing?" Hancock asks.

"They're no longer with us," Trevel hums darkly, his tone giving me chills. "But they didn't have anything on them. Trust me, I checked."

Hancock and Dash give him an intrigued look, but they don't press it.

"Kemper's with Joy and Rook," Dash tells us. "If I can get to them, we can come back for you…"

"So you're just gonna leave us here??" Hancock shakes his head.

"What other choice do we have??" Dash points out. "We need backup. They should be able to cover us so we can all get to Velle, but you guys are stuck here until we figure out how to get those things off of you."

"You're acting like Velle is going to somehow save us all, like Walker Staten Island Ranger or some shit," I grunt. "It's a nice thought, but he's outmanned and outnumbered."

Dash and Hancock both glare at me.

"You're such a fucking traitor," Hancock scoffs.

"I'm just being realistic," I hiss. "Do whatever you want, but Velle doesn't give a fuck about us, so why should I put my life in his hands?"

Dash's eyes flick between me and Trevel, bemused hurt in them that twists my gut like a clove hitch.

"Kang… please." Dash steps over to me again. "I won't pretend to know what's been going on here since I left, but you're *family,* and you know that. It's always been us versus him…"

My heart is reaching, banging against the inside of my chest, desperate to believe what he's saying. But when I glance at Trevel, he's nothing but uncertain. He looks like he's never felt more like an outsider, and I can't take it.

He's the only one who's been here for me. While everyone else was pairing off, leaving me in the dust, he was right the fuck here. By my side, holding me up.

So I straighten, jaw clenched as I move closer to my partner in crime.

My… partner?

"You're right," I murmur to Dash. "You have no idea what's been going on since you left. You took your shot… I won't pretend any of us wouldn't have done the same. In fact, I'm pretty sure we all have, or at least tried. You were doing what was best for you, and it's fine. But don't act like we're all supposed to have each other's backs, because it's bullshit. It's every man for him-fucking-self on this island."

I swallow down a mouthful of guilt at the look on my friend's face. Dash fidgets, chewing on his bottom lip, eyes wide and sparkling with hurt.

"I… I offered…" he whispers, but his voice dries up and he blinks hard, shaking his head.

"This is great." Hancock sinks onto the loveseat, face falling into his palms. "We're all fucked."

"W-well… we should at least hide somewhere," Dash stammers, like a sad child again. "To avoid Governor fucking Russo when he gets here… And The Ivory."

I blink at him, agreeing, but not wanting to.

"I should, um… go down to the tombs," Trevel croaks to me. I turn to face him. "Check on Lem and the bodies."

I nod, eyes settling on his violet angst. Dash is scampering around the garden in my peripheral, searching for God knows what. Maybe a way out or a place to hide.

With some privacy and not enough confidence, I lift my twitchy fingers, running them up Trevel's chest. It's baffling how just touching him seems to calm me in some deep place I didn't know I could access.

I care about him. I don't want to leave him. And I don't want him to feel like I *would* leave him, even more now, knowing all the heartache he's had to endure in his twenty-three years of life.

He's… mine. And I think I might be his.

I open my mouth, maybe to tell him these things. But it dries up when I notice how twitchy he's being. Gaze flinging left and right, like he's having trouble making eye contact. There's an air about him that feels off, and it's interfering with my attempt at affection.

"Are you alright?" I ask softly, brushing his hair away from his eyes. He flinches at my touch, and I frown.

"Uh… yes." His lashes flutter, Adam's apple bobbing. "Mhm."

My face dips, trying to catch his flitting gaze with mine. "You sure?"

His heart is racing beneath my palm. I glance around.

"Are you… seeing him? *Leo…?*"

His eyes jump to mine, and I expect him to get defensive, like he thinks I'm calling him *crazy* again. But instead, he just stares, lips parted and a deep crease of distress between his brows.

"Baby, you know I don't care about that, right?" I tell him honestly, keeping my voice down. "I *love* that you told me everything. You finally put all of your cards on the table, and it makes me feel closer to you. That's all I wanted…"

Trevel swallows visibly hard again, expression taking on even more strain. "Fucking hell…" he whispers, digging fingers into his eyes.

"Trevel, what's wrong?" I ask once more, pleading for him to confide in me, not because I need it, but because I think *he* does.

He needs to just fucking tell me *what's going on inside him. It's the only way we can be real.*

No secrets. No shadows.

"I… I…" he stammers. I can see it; mere inches from freeing itself on his sweet tongue. But he shakes it away and mumbles, "I've got to go check on Lemuel. He m-might be able to… help."

The next thing I know, he's stumbling away while I stand *alone* in the garden of shadows, reaching out for his light.

CHAPTER THIRTY-SEVEN

Byron's Book of Secrets

"The Shadowman"

It was the night of the storm.

Well, *the* storm isn't really accurate, since it'd been storming for weeks already. But *that one* was the biggest one.

The loudest thunder

The longest darkness.

The power had gone out while we were in the caf having dinner, so Rook was herding us back to our cells. But Dash stopped him.

Dash is the new guy. *Inmate 101.* He showed up the day they took O'Malley, and by all accounts, sort of just slid right into my cellmate's spot.

But it's not his fault. He got tossed in here without a choice, just like the rest of us after killing Governor Russo's niece during a bank robbery gone wrong.

Carly Klatyon Michelangelo's cousin.

I wonder if he's grieving the loss. I wonder if he too hates Dascha Reznikov

Anyway, I'm sure Dash didn't intend to serve as the O'Malley stand-in for our group. After all, he didn't even know O'Malley. I couldn't blame him, just like I wouldn't blame Luthor. Dash is his cellmate now, and Luthor's been missing a cellmate for a while, needing that companionship to make things feel normal again after Landon disappeared.

No, I don't blame either of them. The only person I blame, as per usual, is Ren. Because while the others don't do things on purpose, Warren Xavier *does*. He plays games with people's emotions; tests you to see how far he can bend you before you inevitably snap.

Sounds like someone else I know. Another manipulative, self-centered, narcissistic presence on this island

And he'll pop up in this story too, trust me. He can't help himself.

Dash is a good guy, but he's already broken, so it's difficult to understand the things he does. Like O'Malley, only much less comfortable with his chaos. From my very first encounter with Dascha Reznikov, I could tell he was running from something And over the weeks we spent together, eating meals while chatting in the cafeteria, showering side by side, I came to the conclusion that his demons, like my own, weren't ones that others could see. They're on the inside.

And the thing about running *away* from something is that it usually leads you right *to* something else. *Or someone*

During the night of the big storm, Dash stopped the rookie in the hallway and started flirting with him. It was a bit of a shock, and Luthor and I were caught off-guard.

Without any provocation, Dash was rubbing Rook's dick, trying to talk him into letting us hang out for a while, rather than going back to our cells for an early, boring night.

Mission accomplished, I guess.

We had no clue what Dash was doing since he hadn't voiced any part of this plan to us before just launching into it. Plus, I'd always thought Dash was straight, though I'd heard stories. But in that moment, he didn't seem all that creeped out by having his hand on Rook's visible erection. In fact, he seemed more comfortable with his actions than he'd been with most other things.

Rook's an attractive guy, so I get it. He's not skeevy, like that douche-canoe Brenner.

Regardless, up until that point, I was under the impression that Dash wasn't interested in bribing the guards with sexual favors. And because of that, the *surprise* in seeing sweet, doe-eyed Dascha fluttering his long lashes up at Rook's face, teeth sinking into his pouty bottom lip while he caressed the guard's hardening cock, had me sort of coiling up inside.

Look, by now we've more than established that secret stuff turns me all the way on.

I hadn't noticed just how hard this sudden turn of events was making me until Velle burst through the door. And everything got much more *tense*.

The rumors are that Velle and Rook are most likely boning. Or if they haven't already, it's only a matter of time As was evident from the rapacious jealousy and possessive hunger immediately radiating from Velle when he stumbled upon us in that hallway. Not to mention Rook's instant shivering submission The dynamic makes perfect sense, and the chemistry was palpable.

Before I even knew what was happening, Rook's dick was out, Dash was on his knees, and Velle was jerking Rook off right in front of our new friend's face.

I wish I could say that I was stunned by how quickly things escalated, but it's par for the course around here. Weeks pass like watching paint dry, and then all of a sudden *You're watching people jerk each other off into another person's waiting mouth.*

I'm fairly certain they'd *all* forgotten that Luthor and I were even there. Dash didn't seem like he remembered what was happening minutes prior, and Rook and Velle were on another goddamn planet. But Luthor and I *were* still there, standing stock-still and gaping our wide eyes at the scene only a few feet away. The three of them were so invested in what they were doing, it was as if we were invisible.

Of course, I liked it.

Without thinking, I sunk my cuffed hands between my legs to rub out some of my own pressure as best I could. Like a reflex, I was being driven by urges and the ever-present arousal that comes alive inside me when I feel like no one's looking. Lost in the temptation sensation, it took me a minute before I noticed—from a shift in my peripheral—that Luthor had followed my lead and was doing the same thing.

The throbbing in my balls rocked my foundation.

No words and not a single glance were shared. It was just *happening*. Unintentional or not, my best friend and I were in-synch, moving and breathing together. Watching something new and dirty happening in front of our eyes, touching ourselves like naughty little voyeurs. And the rest of them had no idea.

We were each in our own bubbles Velle and Rook giving in to their simmering attraction, Dash succumbing to his curiosity, and me and Luthor—my best friend, practically my *brother*—in a dark corner, leaning into it.

Literally. By the end, Luthor and I were sort of *leaning* on one another, biceps moving and flexing as we touched ourselves, *together*. It was confusing as fuck, like it always is at first. But I was burning. My brain was fogging up like car windows during a secret backseat dry-hump session, enough that my thoughts began to wander mischievously to *other* things

Like giving my hands to him.

An orgasm rushed even closer as I wondered how it might feel. Trapping Luthor to the wall with my body. Grinding my erection into his.

Maybe kissing him a little. Just to see how it'd taste.

But most of all, how utterly, ravenously, mind-numbingly *jealous* it would make Ren.

I came in my pants before I could even give it a full minute of thought.

And then Luthor came by my side, shuddering through rough pants and gasps. It was hot as hell, something I can only admit here, amongst the bevy of my secrets.

I was still fizzling down from the heavens when Rook came—in Dash's mouth. And I'm pretty sure Dash came in his pants, too. I don't know why that's so sexy. In theory, coming in your pants is supposed to be humiliating.

But there's something to knowing that a person is so helplessly turned on, they can't stop themselves from erupting inside their clothes. Head tipped back, eyes shut, lips parted and quivering.

It's the ultimate unexpected loss of control.

The only one I'm not sure about is Velle. I couldn't tell if he came or not. Honestly, it wouldn't surprise me if he made everyone in the general vicinity come except himself.

He seems like that type of dude.

So, there you have it. Concrete proof that storms are sexy, and secret kinks are much easier to accept in the dark. That would have been a perfectly tantalizing place for the night to end.

But we're only just getting started.

Because in Alabaster Penitentiary, every moment of debauchery is a preface to something much more sinister.

Velle sent Dash to solitary for that little stunt. Arguably harsh, but the running joke is that Dash *likes* being in solitary. He's down there more than he's up in Gen-pop, which is disturbing to any of us who have spent time in solitary.

They don't call it *The Hole* for nothing. It's literally a hole where dreams go to die.

Wanna crush your spirit quick? Spend three days locked in a pitch-black, mold-ridden ten-by-ten tomb with no food or water and nothing but your every insecurity to keep you company.

I considered all of this while back in my cell, alone, lying in bed with the lights flickering in the row. Like living in a place where one minute, you're slurping cum out of a relative stranger's dick, and the next you're isolated to a concrete box.

I couldn't stop thinking about my friends and the forever-blurring lines of this prison. I thought about O'Malley, if he was okay in the East, and Ren, what he was doing and who he was doing it with. About Luthor—*did he feel awkward after we came side-by-side? Has he ever had even a fleeting thought about fooling around with anyone other than Ren?*

And then I thought about Dash. How effortlessly he'd slipped from angry and hostile to kneeling for a mouthful of cum.

There's a lot I don't understand about Dash. He's an enigma, and I find him more interesting because of it. Because of *them* His secrets.

Our secrets are the foundation of our true selves; the bedrock of what makes us us *Whether we choose to show it to the world or not.*

Curiosity piqued in the darkness of my lonely cell. Pulling out this very journal, I read through some of *my* secrets and fell asleep reading one about me and O'Malley, and our shared bunk bed

I awoke to fingers brushing through my hair.

On the edge of my consciousness, I could tell it wasn't a dream. Naturally, my first instinct was to fight. Because someone had broken into my cell, and they were *touching me.*

But as quickly as the reflex came on, my muscles relaxed, and I gave in

Just like in the hallway earlier, I leaned into it instead.

I was so tired of fighting. I'd been fighting so many things for so long Being here meant that I could finally stop. Being a prisoner is to relinquish control. There's no need to fight.

What's the point when my life isn't mine anymore ?

This realization felt *so* good; as comforting as the fingers stroking my hair, petting me like a precious kitten It was all I really wanted, deep down, in the place where I house my secrets.

I want to be held down and fawned over. Fucked to the zenith of pleasureful pain and wanton humiliation, then cuddled and kissed and caressed like I'm everything.

The fingers felt vaguely familiar, unnerving, but somehow hypnotizing all the same. It continued to lull me into a trance Until the rickety mattress dipped.

Someone was in my bed with me. Someone was moving over me.

Forcing my eyelids open, I froze in fright at the pale skin and snow-white hair gleaming in the dark.

"What the f—"

My words were cut off by his lips on mine.

They were uncharacteristically soft. Not that I'd ever imagined kissing him, but if I *had*, I wouldn't have thought it'd feel like *this*

The unexpectedness of it held me still, allowing him to pin me down and kiss me deeper.

What the fuck is happening? My thoughts pulsed with every thump of my heart.

Hands lying limp at my sides, my brain was running through a million questions and concerns about *why* The Ivory was in my cell and *why* he was kissing me. I just couldn't process it. My head was spinning.

But it felt good. Despite what I knew about him as *the Warden*—a vengeful being who thrives on the chaos, discomfort and the sadness of others—the kiss was different. It was *separate* from all that.

Maybe it makes me weak, or maybe I'm too needy for my own good. But I remembered the way it felt with him, in his office that day Under his desk. I remembered how *giving in* had settled me so profoundly.

When you're so used to fighting the truth, giving up can get you high with a much-needed release of serotonin.

I couldn't believe it was happening again, but against all will of my mind, my body took over once more and I arched up into it—into *him*. I gave myself over to the sensation of a softly ravenous kiss from this wickedly powerful man and *opened* for him.

Just like that, I was blooming. His tongue slid into my mouth, and the feel and taste sent a jolt between my legs, stiffening my cock. He licked deep and deliberately into my mouth, feeding me the distinct flavor of sweet mint, like wintergreen. His tongue was toying with mine in slow, feathering strokes that were scrambling my goddamn brain.

Why is he doing this?

Why am I letting him do this??

Why does it feel so *fucking good?*

Without even realizing it, I reached out, for hair or a jaw to cling to. But as soon as I had it tangibly in my hands, it stopped. He took his mouth away, and the hypnotizing kiss was over way too quickly.

The abrupt *end* to it jump-started my furious confusion. The shame of how instantly needy I'd just become—for *him* of all people—turned to fast hostility.

"What the hell was that?!" I gasped—quietly, so no one outside of my cell would overhear. I scowled up at his face, shadowed by the lack of light, only just noticing how pitch black it was around me, save for a red glow coming from up the row. It meant the power was out, the generator running only back-up lights. "Why are you why would you—"

"Shh " The Ivory pressed his long finger to my lips. "No talking. Just wait."

"Wait for *what??*" I grumbled, eyes flinging to the cell bars in sudden paranoia.

I hated how hoarse my voice sounded, how much I was shivering, and how hard my dick still was.

What if someone found out? What if someone saw me being so gay and slutty??

Oh, shit. My fucking journal.

Feeling around frantically, I located it under my blanket, breathing a sigh of relief. A humming chuckle echoed beside me

"Silly shadow pet," The Ivory spoke quietly, resounding like a bass line. "I don't want to *read* your secrets. I want to watch you make them."

It was then that I began to feel it. Something wasn't right.

I felt strange.

Blinking up at him, I tried to ask, "What's happening to me?" But my tongue wouldn't work. I physically couldn't speak.

The Ivory grinned down at me, the glowing halo of his white hair shrouded in darkness showing him to me as his true self.

The angel of light *Lucifer.*

Okay, what in the hell is going on? I thought. *Why does everything feel weird??*

"Come," he commanded, then stood up, floating toward the bars of my cell.

Once I sat up, I felt it even *stronger.* That sort of hypersensitive awareness only narcotics can provide.

I knew right away he'd drugged me. *That* was the purpose of the kiss. He wasn't sneaking into my cell to make out with me, or make me feel good because he liked me

He literally shoved drugs into my mouth via his tongue.

Typical.

Manuel Blanco peered at me over his shoulder and cocked a brow.

Oops. I said that out loud.

Naturally, he wasn't fazed. He simply stood there, waiting for me to slither out of my bed and follow him. Which I did, because I couldn't not. I felt like I was tethered to him, on a leash that he was holding.

I'm not a drug-doer. Never have been. I tried things in high school and a couple of times in college, but only enough to determine that I'm far too desperate for control to let go of my faculties and get *wasted*. It probably speaks to why I am the way I am, but I was always afraid that being under the influence would cause me to accidentally reveal some inner part of myself I didn't want the rest of the world to see.

The *vulnerable* part, where I hold my secrets.

The nature of the high was unlike any of the highs I'd felt before, from things like coke, or pills, or weed. *This* was an alternate reality, as if someone had cracked open my skull and all kinds of other things were being absorbed by my brain. Like a sponge, soaking up external sensations.

In that moment, I truly wasn't sure if I was awake or dreaming

Either way, I had no choice but to obey The Ivory by following him, wordlessly, through the long corridors. He eventually stopped in front of a large metal door. I looked around and registered where we were.

Solitary.

He peered in through a small plexiglass window.

"What are we doing here?" I tried to ask. "Why do I feel like this? What did you give me??"

But again, none of it would come out. I got the sense that he wanted me to be quiet, and what's more, *I* wanted to be. Everything down there seemed still and silent. I felt like hearing my own voice would hurt my ears.

The Ivory reached into his pocket and pulled out a single key. It was peculiar-looking, antiquated brass with a bird at the top, within the crown. He stuck it into the lock and twisted. Even the sound of the mechanism unlocking the door with a metal *clunk* seemed loud. Once the door was opened, he nodded for me to go inside.

I didn't want to. I really didn't *want* to be in solitary, especially while trippin' balls on whatever crazy drug he'd given me. But I also knew resistance was futile. He would get what he wanted, one way or another, because that was the nature of this whole thing.

We belong to him, prisoners and guards alike. He's the omnipotent being with his hand around the joystick, controlling us and this island like his own personal video game.

For whatever reason, he wanted the Byron character in that cell. So in I went.

As soon as I set foot inside, he closed the door and locked it with another *clunk*. Gulping down my nerves, I looked around the small, dark room. There were a few candles lit on the floor by the wall, melted wax pooling and hardening beneath them. The only sounds that of the storm's wind billowing from outside, and water dripping off in the distance.

Shadows danced on the jagged concrete walls, calling to me. Whispering

You belong here. You are the Shadow Man.

Standing still by the door, I felt my presence melting into the darkness. I had become *one* with the shadows.

But something shifted, movement in the room startling me. There was someone else in the cell A person, curled up on the tiny cot. Blinking through the haze of drugs in my system, I recognized him instantly.

Dash.

He appeared to have just woken up, eyelids heavy with sleep. He noticed me right away, but he said nothing. Simply stared for minutes in silence. Barely moving, the two of us watched one another, breathing to the tune of harsh winds and dripping water.

When Dash blinked, I felt something. I'm not sure how, or why, but I was overcome with a distinct notion that he didn't recognize me as his friend, Byron Kang. He was seeing someone else Someone he only saw in the dark. Someone he *wanted* to fear, though his yearning had piqued a lustful interest he didn't fully understand.

I recognized it because I'd seen it before.

In that moment, he was Michelangelo.

Striding forward, an ease of confidence filled my extremities in an instant. I was moving the way I had so many times before, inside that townhouse. Sneaking around in the shadows, like a predator on the hunt for my *unsuspecting prey*, awaiting my soothe to his needy ache.

He gazed up at me, bright eyes shining in the glow of candlelight. We watched each other for many moments more, the warmth inside me spreading to a burning blaze. I took a seat on the bed next to him, and he closed his eyes, leaning his head back against the wall. Shutting me down.

And so, it begins

"Let me touch you," I growled into his ear.

"No."

"That wasn't a request."

Things were moving faster, unfolding and unfurling before my eyes and my hands. It was *electrifying* being back with him.

In the corner of my mind, I doubted whether it was *real*. But whatever was flowing through my bloodstream was simulating the reality I wanted I couldn't make myself see past the scene splaying out before me.

I took our shirts off, then lowered his pants while he struggled and whimpered.

"I don't want this "

"Yea, you say that a lot," I hummed, pinning his wrists. "But then you purr when you come, like a happy little kitten. So what should I believe, rich boy? Your words, or your actions?"

"P-please don't "

"*Relax*."

Dazed and panting, I had him on his knees in the bed, face down and stuffed into the mattress, ass up and ready for me. Bringing down his boxers felt like the lid being lifted off of a gourmet feast. My mouth was instantly watering.

He was trembling, and I liked it. And while I didn't have anything to restrain him with, he held his wrists together behind his back for me.

"Perfect " I crooned as I spread him open. "*So* fucking *perfect*.

The next thing I knew, my mouth was between his cheeks, and I was eating him, slow and possessive. Lapping, sucking, and kissing I was fucking *devouring* him just like I always wanted to. Like I *needed* to.

My dick was so hard, it had its own pulse.

"Guhhh *Fuck*, what are you doing?"

"I'm going to make you come from eating your ass out, baby," I purred into his hole. "Is that okay?"

He nodded fast and groaned, clenching beneath my tongue. "God *yes*."

"Good. Now, relax your tight little hole so I can stick my tongue inside."

For minutes on end, I was gone. Wandering lost in a lush

forest of desire, licking and licking and *licking* until my jaw was sore and my tongue was numb.

"You like how I eat your pussy, baby?" I asked him, just to hear the way he'd cry and moan for me. "Your tight little pussy loves to be licked and sucked, doesn't it?"

"Fuck fuck fuck "

At the feeling of him tightening all over, I took my pants down and began beating my dick fast and rough. I held him open with my free hand while his fingers raked aggressively through my hair, stuffing my face *deeper* into him. He sounded like he was about to combust, and I knew I was too. The air in the room was *buzzing*.

I felt him letting go, because we were one. Holding myself up from collapsing into him, I groaned and growled along with his sobs of ecstasy. I slid my hand between his legs to feel his dick, shooting cum all over the bed, and it was too much.

"I'm gonna come, baby," I breathed to *my* Michelangelo, sitting back, hands on his cheeks, spreading him apart.

I barely recognized the sound of my own voice. But seeing his tiny pink hole, all wet with my saliva, had me *throbbing*. I wanted to fuck him *detrimentally*. In that moment, the need was stronger than anything I'd ever felt before.

Easing the slick, swollen exposed crown of my cock up to him, I brushed it over that sweet spot, marveling at how small it was compared to my girth. I was amazed that I was ever able to get inside him More importantly, that he *let* me in. It was like coming home; like *finally* having a place in the world when Michelangelo's body welcomed mine.

He made space for me inside him. I so badly wanted to fit in someplace like that again.

Craving that first, most satisfying *push* into heaven—*or maybe hell, based on how scorching hot it was*—I moved my hips just a bit, all too ready to get in him and fuck. But before I could, my orgasm rushed to the surface, and I was coming. *Hard*.

Shuddering and breathless, I pressed the head of my dick into his hole, just enough to pulse cum inside, because I wanted to leave my mark. And he opened up for me. Wanting it, *taking* it. He let me feed my cum into his perfect little hole, whimpering the sounds of his own crippling pleasure into the bed while I quaked in blissful agony behind him.

By the time I was done, tears were streaming down my cheeks.

Like a resurrection, he'd brought me back to life.

Michelangelo I *had him* again, if only for a moment Kissed by warped reality in the shadows of the dungeon.

I don't remember much after that But I woke up the next morning back in my cell. In my bed, alone, groggy and confused. And I still have no idea how I got there.

I don't know if The Ivory returned to bring me back

I don't know if he was there all along, watching me do those things with who I now know was Dash, *not* Michelangelo.

I know nothing of his intentions, or why he made that happen. Why he forced me to use yet another friend as a proxy to mend my battered heart

All I know is that I awoke with the taste of carnal deception, and wintergreen, lingering on my tongue.

CHAPTER THIRTY-EIGHT

Trevel

I HATE MYSELF.

That's what this all comes down to.

I'm an awful, terrible, atrocious bloody bastard of the highest degree.

Stalking through the mansion, I'm like a ghost. An evil spirit, slinking around corners unseen, pausing in the shadows while cartel men rush about, sparing me not one glance.

Holding on to painful truths with white knuckles, because I'm nothing but wicked, and I don't know how to be anything more.

"You did the right thing," Leo says while we head down to the dungeon. *"I know it doesn't feel like it, but it's for the best. Byron—"*

"You don't get to say his name!" I snap. "You don't want me to be with him anyway, isn't that right?? You think I should be alone forever... That's why you've convinced me that lying to him is the *right* thing to do..."

"Trevel," he breathes my name, sounding too much like *me*. Not him. *This is me, and I hate myself. "You and I both know it was your choice to lie to him..."*

"Fuck you," I spit, sniffling and whimpering with tears welling in my eyes.

I can't stop seeing it... Byron and his friend, clutching another while they sputtered and cried over the loss of their friends. Their friends who are very much *alive*...

And I could have told them. I should have.

I could have easily spared them the heartache of thinking people they care about enough to grieve so palpably died tragically at the hands of this bloody island and that life-altering storm. But I didn't.

Because I'm a monster.

A selfish, pathetic, terrified little boy, clutching a weathered teddy bear to his chest.

In the dimly lit concrete chamber that is the Ivory Mansion's basement, I look around for any sign of Dr. Love, wandering through the darkness, past the decaying bodies. Fortunately, it's freezing down here, which has delayed decomposition quite a bit. The smell hasn't become unbearable just yet. But it's certainly *present.*

The stench of death brings up so many emotions inside of me. From the past, present, and future…

Born this way.

Inevitable.

You're a killer, Trevel. You always will be.

You can't fight it, and there's no need to…

You're not a fighter. You're no Raphael.

"Lem…" my voice calls quietly as I trek deeper into the tombs. "Lemuel…?"

There's a light in the distance… Noises. Footsteps clomping, hushed voices. No gunfire, but it *does* sound like outside is just ahead.

We discovered that the tombs actually lead out of the mansion—like an underground tunnel, or *secret passageway*, if you will. But the outside is blocked by a metal gate, and last we checked, it was locked from the outside.

Adrenaline has spiked inside me as I grow closer. Despite the sounds coming right toward me, I don't stop. Because if I'm going to die down here, may as well get it over with.

Maybe I'll finally be at peace.

Byron will be sad… Until he finds out I lied to him. And then he'll be glad I'm dead. He'll have his friends, his family back, and I'll no longer be weighing him down with my evil breaths.

I'm the reason he's turning his back on the people he loves. The way he *once again* chose me over them made me so nauseated with myself, I nearly gagged. It should feel *good*, having him want me this way… But it doesn't. Because I didn't earn it.

I only have him because I've lied and manipulated him. Byron isn't weak; he's just lonely, and I took advantage of that. I seduced him, dragged him out of the closet and lured him away from his people. And go figure, now he's attached, when *he* was the one pretending to fight it all along!

It should be the happiest thing ever, because I'm utterly *enamored* by him. But that's the problem. I can't stop myself from ruining the things I love…

And I don't want to be that curse anymore. The storm that smashes him to pieces.

A shadowy figure approaches me in the dark, and my steps slow. My breathing shallows when I see the person lift their arm, the glint of a knife in their hand bringing fear, *yes*, but also an odd sense of reprieve.

"Just do it," I whisper, closing my eyes. "Fucking kill me…"

"Trevel??"

My eyes spring open.

"F-Felix…?" I tremble as he steps out of the darkness.

The Carver is here, covered in dirt and mud and… all sorts of black, on his face, his clothes. He looks feral. Like he's been living in the woods for weeks.

He tucks his knife away in his pants, wandering up to me until we're inches apart. I swallow hard as his gray eyes hold me in place.

Then he launches himself at me. Not to attack, but to…

He throws his arms around my shoulders, pulling me in tight.

He's hugging me. The Carver is… hugging me?

What in the bloody hell…??

"Thank you," he whispers by my ear, squeezing me so tightly I can barely breathe. It feels… *nice.*

I melt into him, arms slinking around his waist to hug him back because I just need it right now. I'm sick of talking to myself.

I don't hate you, Felix Darcey. I'm not certain I ever did.

"Thank you so much, Trevel," he says again with emotion thick in his tone.

"Alright…" I shiver. "For… what?"

He chuckles, letting me go to smile up at my face. "For saving Lemuel."

My lashes flutter, brows lifted in surprise.

"I mean, I know you also kidnapped us." He smirks. "But you made it right. That's all that matters."

"It is…?"

I'm very surprised by this. I figured that despite Lemuel forgiving me, Felix might feel different. But he's forgiven me too. The *monster*…

Apparently, this evil soul has more heart and emotional clarity than I do. It's alarming.

"Of course," he says surely.

So I nod. I'm not going to argue with his decision to let bygones be bygones. Especially when I know I'm still a bloody fuckhead for lying to Byron.

Reconciling with them is fine, but I still suck at life. That's what's important here.

"Is Lemuel alright?" I ask. "Where is he?"

"He's fine," he answers on a tired breath. "A bit worse for wear, but aren't we all?"

I shrug, because *not quite...* Byron and I are fine, physically. Sitting by The Ivory's side, well-fed and freshly showered, in clean clothes, while everyone else is living a dystopian nightmare.

Although I'm sure emotionally, we too resemble raggedy forest goblins.

"He's with Joy and Rook," Felix tells me, pausing to listen for sounds. He's on high alert, reacquainting me with the situation. The lad's been out there assassinating The Ivory's men for weeks. I clearly never gave him the credit he's due. *Maybe Felix Darcey deserves the hype.* "They showed up with Kemper to get eyes on the mansion and figure out how to get Dash out, and decided to take Lemuel..." He blinks at the look on my face. "Oh, right. You don't know them. Um, Dash and Kemper are these guys who used to—"

"I've met Dash," I cut him off. "And heard the name Kemper a few times. He's Dash's partner, yes?"

He nods. "There's a lot going on right now..."

"I'll say," I breathe, head cluttered.

"Well, Lemuel refused to leave you guys behind, so I told him I'd stay and help get you all to safety," he says, his wide, gray eyes capturing mine. "That is... if you're with us."

Felix goes quiet, as if he's waiting for me to make this decision. To finally admit that I'm not loyal to The Ivory. That I want what's best for myself, and Byron, and that I've known all along that Manuel Blanco will never be for us what he's expecting us to be for him.

It may seem like an easy choice, but for me, it's a bit more complex. I don't fit in with the rest of them... With Byron's mates. They all hate me. Say what you will about Manuel Blanco, but he's done alright by me—in the way a maniacal sociopath does, of course.

But regardless of everything else, the only thing that keeps coming back to me, the only thing that *matters*, is my sweet fury.

And the words he wrote in his book of secrets assault my mind…

The Ivory using Byron's mouth, drugging him and making him engage with his friend. Manipulating him, playing on his secrets. Using *him*… My *warrior.*

That's not even close to what I've done to him. Yes, I've lied, and I've hid, but that's about my issues and insecurities, not wanting to control him.

Whatever else happens, I think we can all agree I'm not as bad for him as The Ivory.

Jealousy burns up my esophagus, possession wrapped around the most potent of emotions… *Love.* I *love* him. And it sparks another familiar need in me…

The need for *revenge.*

Byron is *mine*, not his. He's all that matters to me anymore. And if I want to keep him, after all of this is over, I'll need to leave the darkness *with* him.

"You belong to me…"

"I am." I nod. "I'm with you. Byron has always been with you all… And I want to be with him. That's all I care about."

Felix grins and steeples his dirty fingers. "Great to have you on board, fellow monster."

My lips quirk, and he winks.

But a very specific sound crushes our amusement.

"Is that a… helicopter??" Felix's forehead lines.

"Bollocks… He's here," I grumble.

"Let's go. We don't have much time…" he starts, but I grab him by the shirt to keep him in place.

"Not so fast, Jason Voorhees," I rumble. "You've been out there for a while. Things inside these walls are a bit different."

He spins to face me, giving me his full attention. Ready and willing to listen, to team up. I have to admit, it feels bloody wonderful.

My eyes scan the area for Leo… But he's not here.

Because *I* am. *He's in me.*

I'm… Leonardo.

I stand taller, limbs coming alive with credence. "We need to get to the others before Russo does. But you need to stay hidden. I don't know where The Ivory is, and he's looking for you. They all are."

Felix nods quickly.

"The others are in the atrium… The garden may be our best bet, but we'll have to figure out how to deactivate these collars."

"How the hell are we going to do that?" he breathes out warily.

"I wish I had a solid answer," I mutter. "We could check The Ivory's floor… See if he keeps spare keys in his office. There's something in the garden I need to… get."

"Pajarito… You belong to only me. And I'm never letting you get away again."

"Something important," I whisper, seeing a birdcage made of gold in my mind.

"What's—"

I slap my hand over his mouth to cut him off.

There are footsteps stomping above our heads, like a march of soldiers. But they're scattering around, running after something. My determination is swept up in a cyclone of nerves.

Governor Russo is here.

"I have to get back to Byron," I say shakily, frenzied and needing to protect him at all costs. "Russo is…" I clear the panic from my throat. "He can't be near Byron."

Felix simply nods. No need for context.

Fuck Governor Russo.

The plus side of having a serial killer friend. They don't ask questions.

"I'm going back," he says, spinning quickly in the direction he just came.

"W-wait…"

"Trust me," he whispers. "I'm better out there. Go get Byron and Dash and find the keys. I'll get eyes on Russo and come for you all in the garden. If you get out before I get back, stay west and head for the prison."

I barely have time to register the plan before he's darting away, into the depths of the tombs.

They must have opened the gate that leads outside… Good to know. Still, there's so much I need to do, and not enough time.

Back upstairs, I head straight for the atrium, jogging while trying to remain inconspicuous, my pulse leaping in my neck. I take a corner fast and come crashing right into the solid frame of Manuel Blanco.

"Jesus," he grunts, visibly agitated and unkempt.

His eyes are wide, fraught and momentarily crazed. I don't think I was supposed to see that look, because he covers it up fast and with hostility.

I steady myself with a hand on his hip…

"My apologies." My head tilts.

His gaze narrows. "What are you… Where are you going?" His voice goes from a flutter to a hiss.

"Nowhere," I murmur, knowingly soft, as I pull my hand back slowly.

He looks like he wants to say something, but is distracted when Kent and another one of Manuel's personal security team, Paulino, come storming up to us.

"Sir," Kent says, appearing concerned. I notice it right away, because on him, it's rare.

"What…" The Ivory growls.

"There's a problem…"

I blink at The Ivory. His jaw tics.

"What else is new," he bites out, stomping past me.

"Sir…?" Kent shouts again, chasing after him.

"Fuck off," Manuel Blanco barks, practically running away from them.

My lips twist subtly as I rush off to find Byron. *All these years and I've still got it… Like muscle memory.*

I squeeze the skeleton key tightly in my palm. *Never underestimate a lad from the streets.*

I'm chuckling to myself, considering what I'll need to do with this key as I head toward the atrium. I wasn't able to locate the remote to our collars… *Maybe it was in his other pocket…?*

Still, I'm filled with a renewed sense of confidence. I'll get to Byron, and we can go search upstairs. Clearly, The Ivory is distracted…

The lights go out.

Out of nowhere, I'm bathed in pitch-black, coming to a stop before I crash into a wall.

The entire mansion has gone from light to dark in a split second.

Well, bugger me sideways…

So much for that idea.

Byron

"Something's wrong," Dash mutters, shaking his head. "Where's The Ivory? He's been too quiet…"

He's right, but I'm too busy freaking out about other things. Like Trevel leaving me. And the sound of a helicopter off in the distance…

It was loud at first, as if it had landed on the roof. We heard voices and commotion, but figured our best bet was to hide out in here just in case. *It's not like we can leave the damn mansion anyway…*

But the idea of being sitting ducks isn't sitting right with any of us ducks. We've been pacing around for minutes on end, wondering what's going on, and now I swear to God, I can hear a helicopter again. Though, it sounds farther away than before…

It doesn't make any sense. Why would it land and then leave so quickly?? Would Russo really get dropped off by a helicopter on its way somewhere else?? That seems ridiculous.

"If your boyfriend ratted us out, I'm gonna kill you both myself," Hancock hisses at me.

"Fuck you," I growl. "If he had, wouldn't The Ivory have come back by now??"

"Not if he's planning something worse," he grumbles.

"Stop," Dash scolds us. "We can't turn on each other. That's what he wants."

"Too late…" I grumble, pacing. I just want Trevel to come back.

I *need* him.

"Hey, I know you're hurting," Dash says to me. "I *know* that. But you don't get to just shut down because it's easy." He pins me with a look that cuts like a knife. "You're stuck with us, whether you want to be or not, okay? Deal with it."

I'm balancing on a tightrope, clinging to my anger because it's been a loyal companion to me for so long. At the same time, I'm so tired. I'm *exhausted* from running and hiding, and I just want my strength back. I want to feel like *me* again.

I need my Leo…

My lips part, the longing gaze of someone who's fucking lost aimed at my friend. But I flinch when I hear The Ivory's voice.

He storms out into garden, but he doesn't come for us. He's heading in another direction, *literally* running away from his men, who are calling after him.

"What the hell?" Dash whispers.

And then everything goes dark.

In a blink, the lights are out, *everywhere*. Not a single lamp or goddamn emergency sign to be seen. It's dark as fuck.

The dull orange glow of moonlight is coming in through the skylights, but it's not exactly illuminating anything. I can barely see an inch in front of me.

"Now!" Dash grabs my hand. *"Now now now*, come on, *right now*. Let's go!"

He pulls me and Hancock as we all stay close together, trying to find some way out. There are voices coming from somewhere in the distance, but we don't stop. We just keep moving, shuffling slowly while feeling around and trying to gauge where we are. Eventually, we make it to the veranda and inside the mansion.

"It's way darker in there," I huff. "We won't be able to see shit."

"You two know this place better than me," Dash huffs. "Where should we go?"

Hancock is silent, just breathing because I think he's panicking a little. So am I. I'm not afraid to admit it. All it takes is one of The Ivory's guys bumping into us with a goddamn M16 and it's lights out for real.

"Byron!" Dash gasps.

"I'm thinking…" I stammer, racking my brain for thick seconds chugging by slow, until finally it comes to me. "There's a panic room. It'll have backup power. Maybe even something that controls the collars."

"Perfect. Let's go," Dash breathes out as I lead the way.

It's difficult when I can't see a damn thing. And all the while, I'm freaking the fuck out.

Where's Trevel?? Is he okay?

I need to find him. I'm not leaving without him.

This adrenaline that's been coursing through my veins for minutes, hours, days, *weeks* at this point is doing nothing to thwart my feelings for him. If anything, it's clearing my vision. Like a fog light, I can *see*

I just want him, and I don't care what anyone thinks about it. I care more about him than I've ever cared about anyone else… I *feel* things for him that I haven't felt for anyone before.

Not Michelangelo… Not Ren.

This is different. It's more than a secret lust, hidden away in the dark, or a fucking proxy. It's *so* much more than physical.

I think he might really be it.

My real, true partner. Not just in crime, but in life.

"Is that it?" Hancock whispers.

There's a faint glow coming from up ahead in the distance, and now that my eyes have adjusted, I can see that we're in the library. Just beyond the study is where the panic room is located.

"Yea." I bring them with me, through the rooms, slowing down when I hear hushed voices coming from inside the panic room.

"Fuck," Dash mumbles. "This might not be a good idea…"

Swallowing, I release Dash's hand, inching closer by myself.

"Byron!" Dash whisper-shouts after me. But I'm still going.

Whoever they are, I can take 'em.

"Ha! I fucking told you I'd find it," a familiar voice rumbles.

All the hair on the back of my neck stands up.

"You're a genius, baby. We all know that. Now what?"

My heart is lurching up my throat and out my *goddamn motherfucking mouth* as I peer into the room.

Everything falls…

Heart, gut, hands, head. No air in my lungs… My knees are buckling.

"W-what…" is all I can say, eyes wide and burning with baffled emotion.

They jump at the sound of my voice.

"Oh, thank God," Luthor cries.

"Babe, *shh!*" Ren scolds him, tripping over his feet to get to me. "Byron, Jesus, you're here…"

He throws himself at me, knocking me into the wall. His entire body is coiling around me, but I can't… move. I *can't breathe.*

I'm fucking stunned, coming apart at the seams of my soul.

Is this a dream…? Is this some kind of sick joke??!

What?? How??

Luthor curls around me too, the both of them hugging onto me tight. But I'm limp, arms hanging at my sides.

"I'm so glad you're okay," Luthor whimpers.

Ren sniffs in my neck. Like he's… crying.

Jesus Christ, what is happening??

My heart can't deal with this much emotional whiplash.

"You're… you're…" I stutter, unable to catch my breath as my hands lift to touch them. To verify that they're *really here.* "I thought…"

"Kang, what's—" Dash's words come to the same frozen halt when he enters the room. "Holy fucking shit…"

"Dash?!" Luthor squeaks, his voice a broken sob of disbelief as he pries off of me and Ren to attack Dash. "What the fuck, man?? How are you here?!"

Ren finally releases me, tear-stained sky-blue eyes finding mine. "I'm sorry I left you," he sniffles, then chokes. "We had to try… You understand, right??"

He seems desperate for me to know this, but I'm too busy losing my sanity… Attempting to unlearn everything I thought I'd known for the past however many weeks.

I… think I'm… having a… panic attack.

Dash lunges, wrapping himself around Ren from behind, sobbing while Ren rumbles out wet chuckles. The emotion is overwhelming this small room, like a change in altitude. The air is thin, and it's making me dizzy. I can barely see through the blur in my vision, but I make out Luthor trying to calm Dash down, holding his face and telling him to *breathe*.

"What the hell is going on??" Ren croaks, rubbing his eyes before they slide to Hancock and his dark brow cocks. "Why is Simon dressed like a thirsty bottom at a circuit party?"

Dash snorts a laugh that makes him cry even harder.

"Funny, you dumb skank." Hancock grins, hugging Ren hard while he chuckles. "Glad you're okay, 48."

"You too," Ren chirps.

"Are you…?" Luthor asks, nervously looking over all of us. "Okay?"

"We should be asking you that," I finally find my voice again, though it's grating over the emotion in my throat. "We… thought you were…"

It dries up again, and I just stare.

Their brows pull together in matching puzzled expressions.

"We thought you were dead," Dash is finally able to croak. "Byron said you t-tried to escape and you… didn't make it…"

"We thought that too," Hancock jumps in.

"Everyone did." My head wobbles, still bewildered as fucking hell, though now I'm also fidgeting with guilt, at upsetting Dash so deeply with clearly false information. "I found the remains of your boat…"

Luthor and Ren share a look, and Ren's brow lifts. "Are you sure? That boat was made of fiberglass, man. It'd take a fuckin typhoon to smash it to smithereens."

I blink at him. *What the hell do I know about boats?! I'm not a white guy named Chad!* "Okay, well, I found a piece of *a* boat, then…"

They laugh softly, rubbing my back while I scoff and shake my head. *Jesus… All this over the wrong fucking boat?!*

"It *was* close, though," Luthor says. "We definitely almost died…

But somehow, we made it." He grins at Ren, who winks back. "And we found each other, in Cali."

"California??" Dash gasps, eyes wide. "How'd you get all the way to California?"

"Long story," Ren hums, rubbing Luthor's back. "What about you?? Why the hell are you here?" he asks Dash.

"Same reason you are, I'm guessing." Dash smirks.

"Yea, guys, this is a great reunion and all, but we might need to put it on ice till later," Hancock interrupts. "The Ivory's around here somewhere, and this place is crawling with cartel men…"

"Where's Velle?" Luthor asks.

"Prison…" I manage to mumble, my head spinning.

They're alive…

They're… alive.

Not dead. Alive!?!

"Did you guys cut the power?" Dash asks.

"Not technically…" Their conversation is coming in and out while my mind reels. "Our friends hooked us up with a helicopter… Landed on the roof… Immediately started running around, looking… for this."

Luthor holds up some clunky device, a sly grin on his lips.

"What the hell is that?" Hancock asks. "A calculator from 1945?"

"No… Rude," he grumbles. "It's LOIS 2.0.! And she's a fucking boss bitch."

My lashes flutter, but Dash asks before I can, "Is that your… computer?"

"Oh yea, baby." Luthor shimmies around. "I can disable any of The Ivory's security systems with this baddie."

"Hang on," I snap out of it. "You think you can disable these??"

I pluck the collar around my neck.

Luthor's head cocks while he and Ren assess them.

"Ooh… kinky," Ren hums.

"They're like a shock collar you put on your dog, except that if we leave the mansion, we get paralyzed. Not shocked," I tell them.

"Good times," Hancock grumbles sarcastically.

Luthor's mouth slopes into a wicked grin. "Why didn't you say so?? Fuckin' child's play. Give me two minutes! No! Ninety seconds."

Ren chuckles, hugging onto him from behind while he works. "Look at that big, sexy brain go."

I'm buzzing from head to toe. Being back with them—*all three of them*—feels like the best moment of my life. But I'm still having a hard time wrapping my head around it.

I've been grieving them for weeks! This is insane…

"Are you sure you're not dead…?" I whimper, and Ren pouts, stepping over and hugging me again. I can't stop crumbling to bits. It's every two seconds, and it *would* be embarrassing, but I don't even care. My hand cups the back of his head. "I'm… *so* sorry."

"Shut up," he mumbles. "I don't wanna hear that shit."

"I know, but—"

"We're just glad you're okay. And that you're not with that awful British ghoul."

I stiffen in his arms, pulling out of his hold. "Wait, what do you mean?"

"Fenwick," Ren huffs. "He's a fucking prick. He's the reason we're here…"

I'm giving him a bizarre look. Hancock and Dash are shifting awkwardly.

"We've been trying to reach *anyone* over here pretty much since we left," Luthor mutters while typing away on his device. "We finally got through to Joy's the other day, and Trevel answered… *God*, this thing is a bitch."

His tongue pokes out in his concentration. But I'm dizzy again.

The whole world feels like it's flipping upside down.

Wait… what?

"You… spoke to Trevel?" I croak.

"Yea. He was being an epic douche, as usual," Ren grunts.

"Got it!" Luthor cheers.

"Are you sure??" Hancock flutters.

Luthor nods enthusiastically. "You're good."

Hancock carefully brings his fingers to the collar. "Can you get it off?"

"I think you need to be putting things *on*, not taking them off," Dash teases, fiddling with the back of his collar.

"I told you, if you don't wanna look at my ass, you'll need to find me some pants," Hancock gripes.

"Hang on…" Ren mutters while Luthor comes to me, fighting to get the collar off gently. "So Trevel didn't tell you he talked to Lex?"

I swallow a mouthful of nothing that feels like gravel. "No…"

I'm shivering all over, confusion working through my muscles.

"That's fucked up." Ren shakes his head. "I told you he was a fuckface."

"Ren…" Luthor scolds, finally getting the collar off of me.

"Fuck that," Ren growls. "He let you think we were dead!"

I blink at him, then at Luthor, with my heart splintering all over again.

"When did you… talk to him…?" I ask for the information again, desperate not to believe it.

No… He wouldn't do that to me.

Trevel wouldn't…

"It's been, like, a week, fam," Luthor replies, with unease, and something else on his face…

Pity. He feels sorry for me. Because my boyfriend is a lying sociopath.

My world is collapsing all around me, *everything* I've been hanging onto for months blowing up in my hands like dynamite. And I'm fucking *bleeding*.

"He wouldn't…" I whisper, bending at the waist. "Why?? Why would he do that?"

"Because he's not good for you, Byron." Ren rubs my shoulder. "I've been telling you this since day one. He's a fucking snake."

"Guys, we have to go," Dash mutters. "Kemper, Rook, and Joy are out there. We just have to try to get to them."

"I can't… breathe…" I shudder.

Everything hurts. *It fucking kills.*

This betrayal is… goddamn *excruciating*.

"Byron…?" the smooth voice, with that accent, calls from the doorway, and I cringe.

The way he says my name… Jesus, I fell so hard for it.

I barely even noticed how effortlessly he became my world.

But he's just another liar.

Flinging upright, I turn to find Trevel standing at the entrance of the room. But I'm already stalking to him, vision doused in red. *Every* muscle in my body is woven tight with the agonizing fury of his deception. I feel so fucking stupid, and it's making me so much *angrier*. Rage clouds my vision until I can't see straight.

Ren growls, "Look who it is… Fucking *Aro*." He folds his arms over his chest, gaze narrowed. "That's the bad guy from *Twilight*, in case you didn't know."

"Babe." Luthor smacks his arm. "Not now…"

I'm not paying attention. I'm up in Trevel's face in an instant. Zero fucks given that he's taller than me. *I'm going to lay him out.*

I want him to bleed *for this.*

Trevel can't look at me. He's just trembling in place, entire body practically convulsing. I want to scream at him, but I'm afraid that if I open my mouth, I'll either throw up or start crying again.

"*Well*, bitch?? Speak up!" Ren barks. "What do you have to say for yourself?"

"Okay, stop," Luthor rumbles, and I can feel him holding Ren back.

"He's right," I snarl, barely audible, eyes boring rage into Trevel's face. My mouth is inches from his… That sweet mouth I thought was *finally* opening up and giving me the truth. But it was all bullshit, made to hurt me. "*Say something…*"

His lips part, but all I get is a weakened, "I'm… sorry, baby…"

"Wrong fucking answer."

I cock back and swing, punching him so hard in the face that he flies back against the wall. Diving onto him, I hit him with all the fury I possess. All of that anger I've been giving up is back with a vengeance, erupting with blow after blow… after blow.

He's bleeding, and I'm *shaking*. I think I'm crying, and it just pisses me off more. Dash and Hancock are using all of their strength to pry me off of him. And when I can't feel my hand anymore, I let them, stumbling back, breathless and pacing like a caged wild animal.

"Yo, we have to go," Dash croaks again.

Trevel pushes himself up on shaky arms, bleeding from the face. He coughs and spits blood onto the floor. "F-Felix…"

"I'm gonna fucking kill him!" I roar, but Dash holds me back.

"Stay… west," Trevel rasps.

He looks broken. Bruising already, swollen and bloody… He's a wreck. With only agony on his battered face.

Good. Fuck him.

But it doesn't *feel* good. It feels awful. I'm miserable as Dash hustles us all to the door.

"Why should we trust him??" Ren gasps. "He could be leading us into a trap!"

"Doesn't matter," Dash breathes out. "We have to get out of here either way. Kemper and I came up on the west, so chances are, it's still relatively clear."

They all scramble out of the room. Luthor grabs his computer, shooting me a pained look that he also aims at Trevel on his way out. "Your collar is… disabled. You can leave if you want."

Trevel just shakes his head. He still won't look at me.

"Figures," I grunt, though it's too shaky, giving away the sorrow rising like bile.

"Come on," Luthor hums to me.

But I lean over Trevel once more and whisper, "I never fucking knew you… And I don't want to."

He finally slides his eyes up to my face, *my* violet eyes, welling and spilling tears down his blood-smeared cheeks. I gulp.

"You got what you wanted. I hope it was worth it."

Stepping over him, I leave him on the floor.

Broken and bleeding and alone.

Just like my foolish fucking heart.

CHAPTER THIRY-NINE

Byron

THIS IS DANGEROUS. NOT THAT I CARE.

What's danger anyway, when you feel nothing and life is pointless?

"Shit shit shit," Dash huffs from a few feet ahead. "Watch out for whatever that is… I almost tripped over it."

"Good looks," Hancock grunts, hopping over this weird cluster of rocks that could be a boobytrap.

Maybe I should throw myself on top of it.

We managed to locate Hancock a pair of pants and some shoes before we escaped the mansion, so he's not hiking through the woods in a jock. *Kind of a bummer.* The thought of it brings on some mild amusement…

Until I remember that I'm dead inside, and I scowl it all away.

I should've known, man. I should have *fucking known* that even the most confusing of good things would never last for me. Just like always… It's ripped out of my hands, just when I'm warming up to the idea of happiness.

That's my bad. I'm meant to be forever bitter and alone.

It's just who I am. That's my identifier.

Ren's the slutty one. Luthor is the smart one. Dash is the sweet, broken boy. Felix is the lovable lunatic. The Ivory is evil… Velle's gonna win.

And I'm the lone wolf. *On the outside, looking in.*

"Felix?!" Luthor calls out in a hushed voice.

"I don't like that we haven't found him yet…" Dash murmurs.

"Don't think about it," I rumble. "Just keep moving."

The shore is visible up ahead, just through the trees. Based on where we came out of the mansion and the direction we're headed, the old armory should be close. Hancock says it's a safe spot. Apparently, they've been stashing guns and supplies there for months, using it to prepare for this uprising since long before the new guards showed up.

It's kind of amazing. There we all were, just going about our vacant lives in that prison, thinking things had calmed down a bit after Dash escaped and Darcey killed O'Malley. Sure, we were on lockdown, but after Velle came back, it seemed like the tension had cooled off. But his guard was up the whole time.

When The Ivory brought in his guys, it was technically a move Velle hadn't anticipated, but that didn't mean they weren't prepared. And now, I can't *believe* I doubted him, even for a second.

If anyone has a chance of defeating The Ivory, it's Jonathan Chevelle.

I'm not sure how it'll happen. And things might still get worse before they get better. In fact, I'm *positive* they will. But the fact that we're all still alive and back together feels like a sign.

I hate myself a little for letting The Ivory get in my head; letting him instill doubt through *Trevel Fenwick*. Maybe that was his ultimate act of brainwashing…

I should've seen this coming. After all, *everything* The Ivory does is carefully calculated. He knew what he was doing, putting Trevel and me in the same cell. Giving us *freedoms*… Giving us the means to build our *relationship*. So that when he was ready to cash in on his debt with Trevel, I wouldn't think twice about tagging along.

Whether Trevel knew, or was also being played by The Ivory, remains to be seen. But based on the gorgeous Brit with the captivating purple eyes being a world-class chameleon, I'd say it's a strong possibility that he was in on it all along.

Fucking asshole.

I hope they shoot him.

I bite the inside of my cheek to stop from backpedaling. I don't care what happens to him. He *should* get hurt, because he hurt me. *An eye for an eye…*

That's that revenge *he's so damn obsessed with.*

A distinct sound paired with whipping winds grows closer, and we all stop.

"Shit…" Hancock peers up through the trees.

"Is that your helicopter?" Dash asks Luthor and Ren.

"Uh… maybe?" Luthor's brows zip.

"How can you not know??" Hancock snaps.

"It's a helicopter," Ren grunts. "Is it supposed to have some distinguishing feature??"

"*Yes*," Hancock glares at him.

Ren blinks. "Okay, well, I didn't know that. My bad."

"I can't see the pilot from here." Luthor sighs anxiously.

"It must be ours," Ren attempts positivity. "Tauren must've told him to pick us up if we were in danger…"

Luthor frowns. "How would he know we're in danger…?"

"It doesn't matter," Dash grumbles. "I'm not getting in no helicopter without Kemper."

"Attached at the dick, I'm telling you." Ren shakes his head.

"It's at the hip, dumbass," Dash huffs.

"No. It's not." Ren smirks.

"Oh my *God*," Luthor groans, rubbing his eyes. "What do we do??"

"What if it's Russo…?" I murmur, and they all turn to stare at me.

"Governor Russo??" Ren balks.

"Why would he be here?" Luthor stiffens.

"He was on his way," Dash explains for me. "I guess he wanted to come see what was going on here or some shit. That's why I let The Ivory grab me… Sort of." He shifts and clears his throat. "He needed to show Russo that me and Byron were still here."

"Why you?" Luthor looks at me, head cocking.

Anxiety strangles my chest as heat rushes up my neck.

Do I have to tell them the truth? Look at what happened the last time I revealed my secrets to someone…

"Does it have something to do with why you're here too?" Dash asks curiously. "Come to think of it, I don't know why you're here…"

"The guy you killed for sleeping with your girlfriend?" Ren tilts his head, and I'm about to throw up. "Was he related to Russo?"

"Um…" I rub the back of my neck.

"Shit, you guys, they're landing," Dash panics.

Leaves crunch, and we all freeze. Our faces fling back and forth as we peer out between the trees. Footsteps are growing closer. *Someone* is coming through the woods, at least two people.

We're fucking trapped. This is it…

The helicopter is touching down on the shore, just beyond the trees we're hiding behind. My heart is pumping aggressively, sweat breaking out on my forehead.

"Don't move!" someone shouts.

"Fuck it," I grunt, diving out from behind a tree.

"Byron!" Dash gasps.

"What the fuck is he doing??"

Not sure, but I'm doing it. Rushing onto the shore, in the direction of the helicopter.

I'll take the heat so they can get away. If he kills me, so be it.

What do I have to live for, anyway?

The propellers hit me with rapid gusts of wind until they power down. I stand frozen as the doors open… And out hops the man I'd been hoping never to see again as long as I live.

Antonio Russo, the corrupt Governor of New York.

Followed by two big guys in black suits, he strides over to me just as the others are emerging from their cover. My face whips around and I see my friends with their hands up, Kent and Paulino following close, guns drawn on them.

Shit.

"Well, well… Look at this," Russo says with a smirk. "If this is the kind of shit going on out here, no wonder Blanco's been dodging me for weeks."

My jaw is clenched so tight, my teeth are snapping. Russo strides closer to me, and his men drop their hands onto their weapons.

He squints past me. "Dascha Reznikov… You look well. That's unfortunate."

Dash scowls, but says nothing.

Russo glances at me, head cocking. "Where's Manuel?"

"He's in the mansion, sir…" Kent answers, sounding as exhausted as he looks. "If you'll come with me—"

"I'm not going anywhere," he barks. "I've already lost nearly an hour circling this damn island because there's conveniently another chopper in our landing spot. Bring him here. *Now.*" He folds his arms over his chest. "I'll wait."

Kent lowers his gun a bit, nodding at Paulino, who turns and darts back into the woods, in the direction of the mansion.

It's wild to consider, but this prick actually seems *worse* than The Ivory, which I didn't think was possible. I always thought Manuel Blanco bent to no one. But Governor Russo is acting like *he's* El Jefe…

I wonder how The Ivory would feel about that.

Russo circles me, like a fucking shark, eyeing me all the while. I glance behind me at my friends once more, all of whom are just standing stock still, eyes wide with fright.

"You thought I'd forgotten about you… didn't you, *Byron Kang?*" he growls.

Harnessing all of the wrath inside me, I square my shoulders and grunt, "No. I'm sure you didn't."

"Hm…" He makes a displeased sound. "You know, at first, I was hoping Blanco would unleash some of that Grade-A sicko shit on you. After what you did to my son, you deserve nothing less."

My jaw tics.

"But I suppose it doesn't matter. The mere fact that you've been rotting here for years, with eternity on the horizon, is enough for me. And for Michelangelo."

Hearing his name kicks something on, like a backup power source in my brain; igniting my spinal cord, sizzling volts through my muscles and tendons. My *every* molecule is lit up with that *sweet* fucking fury.

I step forward, ignoring the men in my peripheral, guns in hand. "Is he happy?"

Governor Russo's gaze goes momentarily puzzled. "What?"

"Michelangelo…" I hum. "Is he *happy?*"

"Of course he is," he hisses. "He's a strong and resilient man. *You* could never break him."

"Well… no. I couldn't." I purse my lips. "Not in any way he didn't want."

Russo's mouth sets in a line, eyes hardening.

"Is he seeing anyone?"

"Yes," he spits. "In fact, he's engaged." Those words are a slice. A quick one. But it's nothing I can't handle, and the pain is eased when he adds, "To a lovely girl. They'll be married this spring."

My head slants. "Does *he* know about that?"

"What the fuck—Of course he knows…"

"If you say so." I shrug, inching closer. "The thing is, Governor Russo, for three years, I've gone over that night. I've replayed it in my mind *thousands* of times, wondering what I could've done differently. Contemplated all the various places along the way to your townhouse where I could have just… stopped. The opportunities I had to change my fate." I pause to breathe. "But in the end, I come up with the same result… every time."

"Listen to me, you sick fucking fa—"

"Hang on," I cut him off mid-slur. "I'm not finished. You can call me that after I say this, I promise. If I could go back, I wouldn't do a damn thing differently. Because despite how fucking awful this place is—and yes, it *is* just… terrible—it was still worth it, for even a *few* moments with him. Those last ones… they were life changing." My eyes flit behind him. "And I'm only telling you this now because I know it won't matter… He won't have to be afraid to be himself anymore. And that's a beautiful thing, because people shouldn't have to hide themselves… *ever*. Especially not from their family, the people who are *supposed* to love them, no matter what."

Russo is turning beet red, backing up while I move closer. Like he's afraid he'll catch it.

Fucking dipshit.

"Your son is gay, Governor. And I know you know that. So I just wanted to say that I don't regret any part of being with him. Even if it landed me here, even if it had to stay in the shadows, Michelangelo Russo was the first person who made me feel *real*. He's part of my origin story."

I smirk, eyes moving over his shoulder once more. "And so are you. So you can rest uneasily, Mr. *Governor*… knowing that your son will be having lots of fantastic sex with men from here on out… And *you* won't be around to lock them all up for being queer."

Just as his face is morphing into pure rage—as he's undoubtedly about to call me a *faggot* and maybe try to hit me—a hand holding a blade juts out from behind him, flicking in a quick, yet seriously *deep*, slice across his throat.

Antonio Russo's eyes widen, blood instantly spraying from the gash in his neck, splattering across my face. Like an instinct, he reaches up to grab it, but it's pumping too forcefully.

Nice shot… He got the carotid artery without even looking. That's a pro for you.

Russo falls to his knees in slow motion, slumping at my feet to reveal The Carver, who's standing behind him with his long, *super* sharp knife. We lock eyes, in the split second while time is standing still.

I nod at him, and he smiles back.

I guess he's not so bad after all.

But then it all speeds up. Back to chaos in a *flash*.

Diving onto Felix, I cover him with my body as gunshots ring out around us. People are screaming and shouting, but it's muffled and unintelligible over the blood pumping in my ears. I'm certain I'm about to be shot. There's no way I won't be...

Russo's guys were close. They've got a clear shot, and none of us have guns or any protection. The only thing I can do is keep covering Felix and shout for the others to take cover in the woods.

But when seconds pass and I *haven't* been shot, I lift my head enough to look around. The ringing in my ears gives way to a loud roar. A familiar one...

Sounds like a... motorcycle.

"Get up!" someone is shouting. "Run for the armory!"

Holy fucking shit, it's Velle.

My face whips to the side, and there he is... Officer fucking Chevelle, on his Harley—*the bike, not his boyfriend*—speeding through the sand, firing rounds from an automatic AR-15 directly at Russo's men.

Checking on the others, I see them all retreating between the trees. I breathe out of relief, peeking down at Felix, who's literally lying underneath me in the sand.

"Ready to run?" I rasp, and he nods fast, cheeks all flushed.

Okay, he's kinda cute.

Scrambling onto my knees, I grab Felix by the arm and drag him with me, making a run for the woods. Velle is laying down cover, and fortunately he's moving because there are shots coming from up the shore too.

The Ivory's men. Shit.

Running like I've never run before, I haul Felix along with me, dodging gunfire. Russo's men are shooting at us, and my heart is flying so fast I think it's actually propelling me.

Glancing left, I spot Kent, gun in hand. My stomach seizes. He has a clear shot. I shield Felix and prepare for death...

But then he turns and fires at Russo's men instead.

What the hell....?!

I can't believe it. *He's protecting us!*

I'm basking in relief when Kent falls to the ground. He's been hit.

"No!" I scream, breaking left to check on him.

He's down, bleeding from the chest. *Jesus fuck... they shot him in the heart!*

"Run! Go!" I yell at Felix, dropping to my knees in the dirt at Kent's side.

I don't even care that they're shooting at me. He sacrificed himself for us. Kent is a good man... He doesn't deserve to die over this.

Putting pressure on the wound, I get as low as possible to avoid the gunfire. "Stay with me, man," I gasp, tears welling in my eyes as I watch him… fucking *dying*. Coughing up blood. "Don't die. *Please…*"

Rapid gunfire pops closer to me, and I jump.

"You gotta move, bro!" Joy shouts.

She and Rook are covering Velle. Everything is echoing. I can barely hear them over how loudly my ears are ringing, the air rippling from all the gunfire.

As much as it hurts to do so, I leave Kent, scrambling between the trees. Taking one last look, I see that both of Russo's men are down, lying dead in the sand next to the Governor of New York. *Dead* dead.

Good. Fuck you.

The Ivory's men are still shooting at us, though. We're not in the clear, not even close.

Velle peels out, taking off while laying down cover fire.

"Retreat!" Rook calls out, he and Joy bolting in my direction.

"Get the lead out," Joy croaks, grabbing me and pulling me with them.

So I just run. Run and run and *run* some more, with my heart hammering so hard it's threatening to break my ribs. I run and I don't stop until I make it to the old armory. Before I can even knock, the door whips open.

And there's Dash, waving me inside.

Oh, thank God.

Catching my breath takes minutes. Between the adrenaline of being shot at, seeing multiple people killed in front of me, and then sprinting like I've never sprinted before, I'm worried I might collapse. I'm just pacing inside the cold, weathered stone structure for seconds that feel like hours, attempting to get my bearings. Until the haze begins to fade and real-time speeds back up.

Joy and Rook burst through the door, latching it behind them. I want to ask where Velle is, and if he's okay. But I have to assume they've got it covered. Plus, I don't have the capacity to speak right now.

I'm reeling. Rocking down to my goddamn core.

Motherfucking fucker… what the hell just happened??

Was that even real?

I know it was. I can feel it everywhere; my skin is alive and buzzing with adrenaline. I'm covered in dirt and Governor Russo's blood. *All* I can smell is gunpowder.

When I'm finally able to breathe better, I take in my surroundings.

The armory is basically an old run-down shack, except that it's made of stone and concrete, which pacifies me just enough. No bullets will be penetrating this place.

Next, I take stock of my friends…

They're all here. They're all… alive.

Dash is with someone I recognize as former Officer Kemper, though I haven't seen him in a while. But Kemper's hands are on Dash's face, and he's kissing him in between whispering things over his lips that Dash is nodding to.

Felix has Dr. Love wrapped around him, cradling him to his chest.

Luthor and Ren are slumped on a large wooden crate they're using as a seat, comforting each other, chests jumping in the same sort of recovery I'm feeling.

Even Hancock and Jasper are back together… Jasper has Hancock pressed up against the wall, and it's almost too intimate. I can't look at it without feeling a lot of things that are just… *too* much for me right now.

Back at the door, Rook and Joy are setting their weapons down, checking each other for any sign of damage. They look a lot less shaken than the rest of us, considering that they were shooting at people.

Joy sniffs and straightens. "Everyone okay?"

We all nod, murmuring and grunting responses as we look around at each other. And something just… clicks.

Family.

"Holy shit, man," Luthor croaks, rushing to me. "Are you alright?? I was so scared… You were almost shot!"

I huff, shaking my head. "Psshh. I ain't afraid of a few bullets."

"Yea, totally." Ren trots over. Then Dash and Kemper join, Felix and Lem… They all crowd me. "You're such a *man*. Grrr."

Ren smirks, and I roll my eyes.

"Tell me you didn't pee your pants just a little."

"He was on top of me," Felix chirps. "If he peed, then I'd have pee on me."

"Do you?" Dash grins.

Felix glances down, feeling himself. "I don't think so… I might be wet from something else."

I can't help the chuckle that bursts out of me.

"Yea, no offense, killer bee, but when's the last time you showered?" Joy cocks a brow at him.

Felix shrugs. "I took a few ocean baths… Does that count?"

"No, baby. It doesn't." Lem kisses his dirty hair. "Get me some hot water and I'll take care of it."

"Unfortunately, I don't see that happening any time soon," Rook breathes out, exhausted. "We're gonna be in here for the duration… Unless something pulls their attention elsewhere."

"They know we're in here. It's only a matter of time," Jasper grunts, lifting Hancock's hand to press a kiss on it.

"Well, you know what that means," Joy says, tightening her gauntlets.

"Yea…" Kemper nods. "Fight our way out."

"Eek… Uh, I don't know about that." Luthor shivers. "I'm only good with, like… virtual guns."

Ren snorts, kissing his cheek. "It's okay, baby. We'll protect you and your nerdy ways."

"Yea, I'd say that device you've got there is a win." Rook nods. "You think you can get into the servers in the prison?"

Luthor's brows shoot up. "The servers are still working?!"

"They're on the backup genny, we think," Hancock says.

"I thought you guys had the prison," Ren mutters. "Why would you need to hack the servers? They're in the prison…"

"The Ivory has guys in the control room," Joy explains. "Holding our guys hostage."

Ren's face drops, blue eyes shining with worry. "Carson…?"

She nods solemnly, and he swallows.

"Is he alright?"

"We don't know," Rook grunts. "We haven't been able to speak to them in weeks… Carson, Denton, Mark…"

"Mickey?" Kemper asks.

Joy scoffs. "Fuck that guy. He's a traitor."

For some reason, everyone looks at me. And it brings back all of my insecurities, all the reasons I'd been hesitant to defect back to *Team Velle*.

But then Joy wraps her arm around my waist, pulling me into her side. "We're really happy to have you back, *jeonsa*." She kisses my cheek.

"Yea, that was pretty badass, by the way." Dash grins at me. "That stuff you said on the beach… To Russo."

"Was it true?" Ren leans in, damn near toppling over he's so thirsty for the tea.

I have to chuckle, but I'm fidgeting, cheeks warming because they're all *staring* at me.

Sucking in a deep breath, I give up and nod. "Yea… It was."

Luthor gives me a kind, if sympathetic look while Ren blinks. "How come you never told us?"

"I never told anyone…" I mutter.

Except…

Shaking it off, my gaze lifts to Felix. "Thanks. Seriously, that was… fucking crazy." I laugh, and he grins, biting his lip. "But it was pretty damn badass."

"Yea, it was!" Dash cheers, turning to Kemper. "Babe, you should've seen it! Felix snuck up behind Governor Russo while Byron was giving him the business, distracting him and shit… Then, all of a sudden, at the perfect moment, *wham!*" Dash mimics slitting his throat, complete with blood spray and everything. "Slit his throat like fuckin' Rambo! *So* cool."

Kemper grins, nodding animatedly while shooting a disturbed look at The Carver.

"More like Rambo's gay friend, Flambo," Ren cackles.

Hancock chokes. Luthor shakes his head, and the rest of us burst into fits of laughter. Even Dr. Love is cracking a smile.

"No, for real, though," Luthor sighs out his amusement. "You guys didn't plan that?? It seemed rehearsed."

Felix and I share a look. He purses his lips over an eager smile that I can't help returning.

"I guess we make a good team," I hum.

He looks purely elated. I kinda like it. It feels good not to be holding on to that grudge anymore. I'm positive O'Malley wouldn't care.

Well, he might. Since he's most likely burning in hell right now.

Everyone disperses, going for food, water, and supplies. And I think this might be the best time…

I mean, fuck it, right? Who knows how much longer any of us have…

Approaching Luthor and Ren, I keep my voice hushed. "Hey, can I talk to you guys for a minute?"

They nod, the three of us huddling up for some privacy. Giving myself one more moment to prepare, I drop my chin and close my eyes.

Here goes nothing…

When I lift my face, they're staring at me, full attention given. It's nerve-racking, but I push past it.

"First of all, I'm really sorry," I start. "For everything. For what I said in the rec room, for disappearing on you after that. For… choosing him. Over you."

Luthor looks like he's about to start placating me, telling me it's *alright*, but Ren motions to him, and they both stay quiet. Just listening.

Ugh... God. This is gonna suck.

"I was hurt... That's why I said what I said," I go on. "Because I was just... in pain. All the damn time, for reasons I'll get into in a second. But when I thought you guys were dead, I thought I'd never get the chance to tell you the truth. So I'm gonna tell you everything right now, just in case. No regrets..."

They look nervous, awaiting what I'm about to say.

Inhaling deep, I harness all of my exterior strength, coating my interior with it, like armor for the inside. "I lied to you... A *lot*. About tons of stuff." My eyes flick between them. They're still just staring. "I'm not here because I killed the guy who was fucking my girlfriend... I've never killed anyone, actually."

"Oh my God! Samesies!" Luthor gasps excitedly.

"Babe. Shush," Ren chides.

I grin, but bite it off. "I'm here because I was sleeping with Governor Russo's son... Michelangelo. He wasn't my *boyfriend* officially or anything, but I think I really... cared about him." I glance at my shoes. "Who knows, maybe I loved him... But whatever, that's not the point. The point is that we were a thing. And one night, Russo caught us, and he threw me in here because that's the kind of man he is. *Was*, sorry. And that's why he's dead."

I glance across the room at Felix, who's gleefully eating a bag of chips while Dr. Love wipes his face with a washcloth.

"That's fucking awesome," Ren says, bringing my attention back to his bright grin.

"Yea, fuck that guy," Luthor adds. "Homophobic scumbag."

"That whole thing sorta stunted me." I rub the back of my neck. "I probably would've been fine with being bi if it weren't for that shit..."

"Are you really bi??" Luthor asks.

I nod, and Ren snorts, shaking his head. "Called that from a mile away..."

"*Anyway.*" I ignore him, scowling. "I already felt lost and alone... And then you guys came along. Parker, and Landon, and O'Malley... Dash." I peek at where he's sitting on Kemper's lap. "It was great to have friends. But you two were... *more*." I swallow hard. "I should have been able to tell you the truth, but shit got... complicated."

They're both gawking at me, waiting for me to continue. But this is the hard part.

Fuck… It's already awkward.

"The thing is… You reminded me a lot of him," I whisper, eyes flitting to Ren's in between staring down at where I'm brushing dirt around with my shoe. "Of Michelangelo. Not only do you look like him, but your personalities are kinda similar. I guess I have a type…"

When the blaring silence gets to be too much, I peek at Ren. His eyes are wide, jaw slack. For maybe the first time in our entire friendship, he's speechless. No smart-ass remarks or flirtatious jokes. It's kind of amazing, but it makes getting this out that much more difficult.

"When we started hooking up, I was pulling the proxy too," I admit. "I just… needed it. I never got any closure with him. And I couldn't let go…"

Ren nods subtly, and I can tell he understands what I'm saying. But Luthor is frozen solid. It doesn't look like he's breathing.

"It might have started to feel… different," I mutter, clearing my throat a hundred times. "I swear to God, I didn't want it to. You gotta believe me… I couldn't help it. I didn't want to have… feelings. It was just a lot of other shit… Mixing with the physical."

They're both frozen now, gaping in mild shock. But they're not yelling at me or storming off… *So I guess that's good.*

I continue before I lose my nerve. "It hurt… being just a body to you. So when you guys started up again, I felt like I was losing both of you… in different ways. I was jealous, and I *hated* myself for it… I still do, because I let it ruin our friendship. I let it tear us apart…"

The silence stretches, anxiety twisting me up. I'm afraid they both hate me and think I'm pathetic, my vulnerabilities making it hard to look at them.

But Luthor's voice pulls me out. "Fuck that." My face jumps. "You didn't ruin shit. We're *still* friends, Byron. We always will be. In fact, we're more than that… We're family. And family members fight sometimes, but it doesn't mean they don't still love each other."

"Yea, and sometimes family members bang each other," Ren sneers. I snort. "And it's beautiful." He peeks at Luthor and winks.

"What our perverted pork dumpling here is trying to say is that we would never hold any of this against you." Luthor grins. "And I'm sorry too. For overlooking your feelings and being selfish."

"You really didn't…" I shake my head.

"Okay, well, I did." Ren sighs, rubbing his eyes. "Look, B, I'm sorry. I'm *so* fucking sorry. I can never express to you just how deep it goes. You were totally right. We *were* being selfish and toxic, and that was mainly because of me. I did use you, and it's not cool. I've been sick about it, honestly. Since even before we got out… Because I care about you, hard. You're one of the most important people in my life, and I feel like I failed you…"

"No, you didn't," I fight past the emotion in my voice. He gives me a skeptical look of guilt, but I press on. "I'm serious. You did the best possible thing, Ren. You stayed true to yourself from day one. You're the realest motherfucker I've ever met, and I'm sorry I was too afraid to be real in return. I'm sorry I didn't just… I don't know, talk to you or something. I should've handled it all better."

"Me too." Ren throws his arms around my shoulders. And I slink mine around his waist, holding him tight.

Damn… Talk about a million pounds of weight off my shoulders.

It feels incredible to *finally* be honest with him. Having all of this out in the open. This is what I've been needing all along.

I know I'm not in love with Ren. Part of me will always feel *something*—between friendship and more—because of how much we've been through. But above all else, he's my *friend*, and I love that more than whatever confusing proxy shit got into my head.

"Are you still into me?" He grins on my neck, and I shove him away. "It's okay, you can tell me. I might be engaged, but I can still be the object of men's fantasies. That's not cheating."

Luthor scoffs, shaking his head.

My lashes flutter at them. "Wait, you're… *engaged*??"

They're clearly trying to dampen their luminous expressions as Ren lifts his left hand, wiggling his finger, adorned with a thin silver ring.

"Holy shit…" I breathe, mouth sloping. "Congratulations."

"Is it okay?" Luthor's forehead lines. "I can take it back if it upsets you…"

Ren gasps, smacking him in the chest. "Bitch."

Luthor chuckles. "My fiancé, ladies and gentlemen." He grasps Ren's jaw and kisses him.

And the best part is that I'm not jealous anymore. Not of them, anyway. I'm just *happy* for them because I love them. But most importantly, they love *each other*, more than anyone's ever loved anyone or anything.

There's no one more *meant to be* than Luthor and Ren.

Unfortunately, there *are* twinges of jealousy as I look around at all these couples. All happy, engaged, and moving forward. It stings like salt being sprinkled on the open wound in my chest…

Because I'd thought I was headed there, too, finally. For the first time, I thought I *had* somebody, who was more than a fuckbuddy or a friend, or a proxy.

I thought I had a real partner I could love, and who would love me back. Instead, it was just more darkness…

And now it's gone. And I'm alone again.

In a room full of couples—and throuples—with no one to call my own.

Sniffing, I fight hard to shake it off. "I can't wait to hear about everything you guys have been through since you left."

"Please, no one cares about that," Ren huffs. "I wanna hear about how bi you are. Have you hooked up with anyone else I know? Other than my fiancé, I mean."

My eyes flick to Dash, and I clear my throat. "Stories for another time."

"I'm gonna hold you to that, *Bi*-ron." He beams. Luthor and I frown. "Like with a B.I… No? Come on, that's funny!"

"Not when you're saying it out loud," Luthor argues.

"Fine, I'll text it you." He rolls his eyes.

"If you have to explain your jokes, they're not funny." I grin.

"Oh yea, like you know what's funny," Ren gripes. "You didn't even know you liked dick when it was in your damn mouth."

"I already regret this entire conversation," I rumble.

Dash comes strutting over with Kemper, throwing his arms around our shoulders. "God, I fucking missed you guys."

"For real," I hum.

"I know we're trapped like rats about to be slaughtered, but I have to say, this just feels right," Ren sighs.

"Is it weird that I agree with you?" Dash chuckles.

"Yes," Kemper teases, kissing Dash's neck.

"Did you guys know that Luthor and Ren are also engaged?" I tell him, and his face explodes.

"What?! No fucking way!" Dash grabs Luthor by the shoulders, shaking him back and forth while he laughs.

"Hang on, you're engaged too??" Felix comes scampering over with Lem, having overheard.

Ren shows off his ring, and Dash pouts. "Baby, how come I didn't get a ring??"

"Because you got a house." Kemper gives him a pointed look. "And a Ducati. And a dog."

"Spoiled bitch," Ren jeers.

"Right. Thank you, baby," Dash purrs.

"We're engaged too," Felix butts in, bouncing, with pink cheeks.

"Are you serious??" Dash gasps, excitement overload.

"Get out!" Luthor claps. "Congratulations!"

"Jesus," Joy mutters while moving things around. "It's a damn epidemic."

"You're not getting married, Joyful?" Kemper teases her.

"Not unless Velle wants to be a housewife." She grins, as does Rook.

And right on cue, almost unbelievably, the low rumble of a motorcycle engine grows closer.

"Speaking of Mr. Jameson-Samuels." Hancock laughs.

Rook darts over to the door, lifting the latch and opening it wide. Velle drives the Harley right inside, killing the engine. He's barely off the thing before Rook and Joy are attacking him with kisses and affectionate touch. It's sweet to witness, no matter how painfully single I'm feeling.

It's *Velle*, after all. He, Joy and Rook are the perfect trio. They're like Mom and Dads. Things feel *complete* now.

They were right, and I knew it all along, despite trying to fight it. We're a fucking *family*.

Is it always pretty? *Hell no.* But we've been through so much together… Denying it would be foolish.

"Daddy's home, kids." Velle sighs, pushing his hair back with a smirk, mirroring almost my exact sentiments. We all converge around him. And when he sees me, his grin widens. "Good to see you came to your senses, 62."

I scowl, and he laughs.

"Sorry. *Byron.*"

"Thanks, Dad." I chuckle, giving him dabs.

"So… what's next?" Kemper asks.

Velle looks us all over—his crew, his *team*. His Pen family.

Cocky, wicked smirk intact, he hums, "We fucking *win.*"

CHAPTER FORTY

Byron

THAT SHOULD'VE BEEN THE END… RIGHT?

If we all just sailed off into the sunset after reuniting like the badass band of warriors we are.

Come on now… That's just too easy. It doesn't work that way… *Not on this rock.*

We've got a war to win, and unfortunately, it's gonna get a hell of a lot bloodier.

The guards are on *regroup* and *strategy*. Seriously, if any of this seemed frivolous before, the way they're behaving corrects that notion *toot suite*.

Velle is drawing some kind of map in the dirt with a stick, while Joy and Kemper huddle around him, nodding and discussing *tactics*.

Rook is organizing the artillery. Apparently, this little hut is stocked with enough firepower to take on the cartel. *Oh, wait…*

Jasper and Hancock are on the walkie, communicating with the others inside the prison.

The way the six of them are moving on instinct has me wondering if any of them actually have any formal military training. Or if they're just *that* sick of Manuel Blanco's shit. I know Rook was NYPD, and I think Jasper was a detective somewhere upstate. Kemper was in the Academy. Peters and Linetti are ex-military—but they're in the prison. I have no idea what Hancock used to do…

And our commanding officer, the *former bouncer* from *Staten Island*,

Let's just say, he must have had a lot of on-the-job training over the last ten-plus years, because *damn.*

Even though there are no *guards* and *prisoners* anymore, it does sorta feel like they're the parents and we're the kids. That's not to say any of us are *without skill...*

Dr. Love is patching up those who need it, mostly Felix and Hancock, setting up a station with medical supplies in the event of further injury. Dash is using his bank robber experience to help Rook with the weaponry—he and Ren are checking guns, loading magazines, taking inventory of ammunition, and making sure everything is easily accessible.

Luthor is working diligently on getting into the servers with his device—which he calls *LOIS 2.0,* though it really looks like the first Gameboy ever invented—in order to free the prisoners who are still stuck inside their cells. Apparently, Velle's plan to rally the prisoners to fight wasn't without its challenges. Regardless, with the inmates and guards still in the prison, we have a great deal more manpower. Maybe not as robust as The Ivory's... But I'm choosing not to dwell on that right now.

According to Luthor, he can also use that thing to get a message to the control room operators who are being held hostage, and he can fuck with certain aspects of The Ivory's network inside the mansion. Overall, Luthor's part in all this is extremely important, and it's hard to feel like *anything* I'm doing is helpful compared to that. My best asset is my ability to fight, on the front lines or in the shadows.

The same goes for Felix, though he's been ordered by his doctor boyfriend to rest his weapon for now. Since the prison fell, Felix has been busting his ass harder than anyone—*maybe even Velle.* The kid has been taking out the Warden's guys left and right, giving our side a fighting chance and allowing Velle and his team to recover from the fall. The little psycho is beyond impressive.

It's funny to think I hated him so much for so long... We're actually a lot alike. *Okay, he's much sweeter than me.*

Anyway, for now, I'm busying myself by tending to Velle's bike, which was in serious need of a tune-up, and fighting to keep my mind off of things I can't change.

Like the fear of The Ivory closing in on us... And the betrayal of my *almost boyfriend.*

"Need any help?"

Speaking of my new ally...

Felix is standing beside the Harley, holding out a bottle of water for me. I accept it with a grateful twitch of my lips, twisting it open and taking a few large gulps.

"You know anything about motorcycles?" My brow cocks, and he bites his lip.

"I know that people other than me look really cool riding them," he mumbles. Chuckling, I wipe my hands on a rag. "I take it you had one?"

"I had a Kawasaki Ninja," I reply, and his face scrunches like he doesn't know what that means. It makes me smirk. "A street bike. Different from a Harley Davidson, but the mechanics are similar enough."

He nods, though he seems distracted, finger running along the chrome handlebars.

I stand up, putting us face to face. "Something on your mind?"

Felix swallows visibly, wariness in his gray eyes. He still seems reticent around me, as if he thinks I might try to hit him again if he says the wrong thing.

But then he murmurs, "I heard about what happened… with you and Trevel." My gut wrenches like the bolts I was just tightening. "That he found out Luthor and Ren weren't really dead and didn't tell you…"

"Okay…" I grumble, unable to keep the bite out of my tone. "I'm kinda not trying to think about that right now, bud…"

He blinks at me. "I just wanted to make sure you're okay…"

"Listen, this isn't a fucking reality show," I snap. "There's life-and-death shit going on all around us, which is a hell of a lot more important than some relationship drama, you know?"

Felix nods, parting his lips. But before he can offer a response, I bark, "I'm just saying… *days* of watching me grieve, knowing he could put an end to it. That's what it comes down to. He stood there while me and Dash *fell apart!* And didn't say a damn word! The dude must be a total psycho…" I pause to take a breath, because suddenly I'm fuming.

Without even realizing it, I'm pacing, and Felix is watching me.

"Okay, so he has issues… Cool. Welcome to *Earth*. *Everyone* has issues! Sure, his are… pretty diesel. I mean, he's been through more shit that I can even comprehend…" My voice trails.

Felix blinks. "Did he explain w—"

"I don't want to hear excuses," I cut him off with a hiss. "I'm too pissed. He lied to my fucking *face*… Issues or not, that's not cool. I bet he knew Ren was in the East too… Which is something I'd asked him about, point-blank, because he was being shady…" I rub my eyes. "It's just… petty. This jealousy thing… I bet that's what it is, too. Since day one, he's been jealous of my relationship with Ren… Because he knew it was complicated."

My mind is bristling with thoughts, stopping and lingering on the memories of how jealous *I* was over his crush on Dr. Love…

Like when we fucked in Felix's bed… That whole thing started because I was jealous of him being jealous of Darcey.

Ew, why is this sounding so drama?! This is some Luthor and Ren shit!

I peek at Felix, a lot of my anger fading into confusion, guilt and gloom. Because I know Trevel's not into Dr. Love like that anymore. And he knows I'm not still into Ren like that… *Doesn't he?*

"Whatever. I just don't want to be lied to, ya know? We were supposed to be… headed somewhere. I thought we were…" My voice dries up, and I swallow as Felix's brow furrows. I clear my throat and shake my head. "It doesn't matter. Because he's *too much*, and clearly, I dodged a bullet. So, I'm fine, if that was your question, honestly, I can't remember…"

Jesus. So much for not thinking about it.

"Hey…" Felix reaches out, like he might try to rub my shoulder or something for comfort, but I glare at him, and he pulls back. "I just… I understand where you're coming from. When Lem and I first started fooling around, I didn't know shit about him."

My brow cocks.

"He was my doctor, and he was extremely aloof. I couldn't get a read on him to save my life. He resisted it hard, and there was a major power shift in the beginning. It was pretty frustrating."

Mulling over his words, I'm giving him my full attention.

"All I can say is, it's not always about how it starts, or how it looks to the outside world. Where it ends up is what matters most. And how you feel about each other." He tilts his head. "I saw some very obvious chemistry between you two. We both did. And when I saw him in the tombs—"

"You saw him?" My eyes widen.

He nods. "After Lem got out, I stayed back to let Trevel know what was going on and see if you guys needed help. I met up with him in the tombs… and he said he wanted to be with you. He said that was all he cares about. Word for word."

I feel like I'm falling apart inside, while frantically fighting to stay together. I'm just *so* sick of being vulnerable when my heart keeps getting stomped.

"Maybe it's not my place to get involved…" Felix says softly. "I just wanted to tell you what he said. He seemed sincere…"

"Yea, well... He's a liar," I grumble. "A pretty damn convincing one..."

My eyes fling to Ren like an instinct.

Felix catches on and whispers, "You know what broken looks like, Byron. So you know it's not always that simple. Sometimes they're hurting so bad, they end up hurting the ones they love by mistake."

There's a significant pang of remorse in my chest. I hate it. I *hate* that he fucked me over, and *I* feel bad...

But I think Felix is right. After everything Trevel's been through in his life, he's probably entitled to be a little fucked up—*okay, a lot fucked up*—and make more than a few mistakes.

I mean, shit. He grew up on the streets as an underage sex worker. The years when you're supposed to be learning, developing and figuring yourself out, he was being assaulted, sent to juvie and institutions. He's seen so much pain...

And I punched him in the face a bunch of times.

Fuck me... This is awful.

I don't want to let him off the hook.... I'm not sure I *can*, despite how deeply I care for him. Because I do, clearly. I can't help it. The feelings are there, and they're strong as fuck, no matter how stupid they make me feel.

But the hard truth is that having any kind of relationship with Trevel Fenwick would require a fuckload of patience and understanding that I'm not sure I'm capable of giving.

My black-and-white emotions would need to discover gray for him.

I'm staring helplessly at Felix when Ren and Dash come traipsing over, holding out rifles for us to take.

"All good?" Ren asks, possibly noting the dismal look on my face.

I push past it and nod, taking the AR-15 he's handing me.

Dash gives an AK-47 to a visibly hesitant Felix. "You ever shot one before?"

"I understand the premise," he grumbles, and Dash chuckles. "I'll probably just stick with my hunting knife."

"No arguments here," Rook looks up from what he's doing to smirk.

A phone rings, and we all freeze. Mostly us prisoners, because we *never* hear that sound anymore.

Joy pulls a cellphone out of her pocket, checking the screen before answering quickly. "Hi! It's so good to hear from you..." She paces over to Rook, Velle and Kemper following closely. "Yea, we're alright. Exhausted and stressed, but hey... Who isn't, right?"

She chuckles while the rest of us exchange puzzled looks.

"He's right here. Hang on, I'm gonna put you on speaker." Joy taps the screen, holding the phone out in front of her, specifically aiming it toward Rook. "Alright, the gang's all here, Mr. Samuels!"

"Thank you, darling," the deep voice of an older man comes over the speakerphone. "And please, I've told you, call me Keith."

Joy chuckles, and Velle smirks.

"Hey, Dad." Rook sighs, an immediate calm settling over his features and a pretty adorable grin tugging at his lips. "How are you and Mom? And Kira??"

Rook's dad... How cute.

"We're fine, don't worry about us," Mr. Samuels says, sounding every bit like the stern yet polite and supportive Midwestern father we all assumed Rook was raised by. "Your mother just wants to know if you're drinking enough water. That goes for Joy and John, too. And whoever else is there."

Kemper is chuckling as my eyes glide to the guys. Felix and Dash are grinning. Ren pouts and whispers, "Aww! He sounds *so* North Dakota!"

"Shh. Drink your water." Luthor smirks at him.

"You got it, Dad." Rook's excitement fades into the serious pretty fast. "So... what's the word?"

Mr. Samuels rumbles, "There's been a new... development."

It's clear that most of them know what this conversation is about. Pretty much everyone is zoned in on the call, except me, Luthor, and Ren.

"Is it about the girl?" Velle barks, wedging up close to Rook, huddling by the phone as if this is very important to him. *Whatever* it is...

At that, realization dawns visibly on Ren. His eyes widen, and he steps over to Rook, like he's also invested in what his dad is saying.

What's going on?? I'm lost.

"Yea," Mr. Samuels sighs. "She's dead."

Velle's face falls, harder than the rest of theirs, though they're all clearly shocked by this news.

"What girl??" I whisper to Dash, who shushes me.

"Are you sure?" Velle frowns at the phone, forehead lined in confusion. He peeks at Ren.

"For how long?" Rook asks, equally puzzled.

"My guys found the death certificate and some hospital files," his dad explains. "Minimal info, but according to that, she died in Vegas a few years back of *drug-related complications*."

Velle runs his hands through his hair, while Rook and Joy watch him. "Well, there goes that theory," he mutters.

Ren is staring off into space.

"Whoever was in there disappeared during the storm, anyway," Joy murmurs to Kemper. "We haven't been able to locate anyone…"

"Unless she's in the mansion," Dr. Love jumps in, and they all glance at him.

Okay, who *the hell are they talking about?? And since when is there another "she" anywhere on this island??*

"Doesn't matter now," Velle snaps, clearly frustrated. "If it wasn't Alvarez, then who the hell was it??"

"There's more," Rook's dad reclaims their attention. "Turns out, she has a twin brother."

"A twin… brother?" Rook's brow furrows.

Velle looks even more confused now.

"Yea," Mr. Samuels says as Jasper's walkie-talkie starts going off and he staggers off to answer it. "We're still digging, but I'll update you as soon as we get more."

"Okay, thanks, Dad," Rook sighs. Velle is pacing, rubbing his eyes while Jasper stalks back over, signaling that he needs them. "We have to run right now."

"Stay safe, Harley." His father's voice is laced with concern, and it aches my chest to hear.

What would it be like to have parents who actually gave a crap about my well-being?

"I will," Rook answers. "I love you, Dad. Tell Mom and Kira I love them too."

"I can't thank you enough, Mr. Samuels," Velle hums.

"What did I say?" he teases, and Velle chuckles. "*Keith.*"

"I dunno if I can do that." Velle grins.

"You better, or I'll force you to call me Dad." The smile is audible in Keith's voice.

Rook laughs, and I think Velle is actually blushing.

Breathing out hard, my head is circling that baffling phone call. Ren is still frowning at nothing as I grab his arm. "What the hell was that about?"

It takes him a moment, but eventually he murmurs, "I got intel from Carson…"

My forehead lines. "From the control room?"

He nods. "The Ivory was holding a woman in the prison, keeping it on the hush-hush. But that's pretty much the extent of my knowledge on it..."

"So then what's all this about a dead girl and her twin brother...?" My words trail as something sticks in my mind.

Trevel's girlfriend... Alice. She had a twin brother. Andres.

He said they were Colombian...

Andres killed Alice. Trevel killed Andres.

And The Ivory brought Trevel here because he thought he'd killed... someone else.

"Velle found out about someone from The Ivory's past and thought maybe that was her," Felix tells me. "But I guess not if she's dead."

I can't help how I'm just staring blankly. This is a lot of information, and I'm not really sure what any of it means, or how it fits into our situation.

But I don't have time to think about it. Because there's commotion happening around Velle.

"Talk to me, Bren," Velle asks into the walkie. "What do you see?"

"An SUV," Brenner's voice comes in choppy. "On the east. It's headed our way.

With one nod from Velle, Rook, and Joy's rifles are immediately in hand, and they move to guard the doors. Everyone else rushes around, taking weapons and getting into position. My heart rate jacks in an instant, the adrenaline from before returning swiftly.

Oh God, here we go...

"Just one?" Velle keeps talking to Brenner, our lookout on the prison roof.

"Looks that way," he replies. "They're kinda... driving erratically. Oh, shit!"

"What?!" Velle barks, dashing to the back.

"They're off the road!" Brenner shouts. "Are they drunk?! *Jesus*... They're gonna hit a damn tree!"

Rifle slung over my shoulder, I decide to cover Velle at the back lookout point, which is really just a hole in the wall the size of a small window. Velle is aiming his scope through it to check the direction this drunk driver, or whoever the hell, might be coming.

"What the hell..." Dash grunts from behind me.

"You got eyes on 'em?" Brenner asks. "They disappeared into the trees."

"I can't see shit," Velle growls.

"They've gotta be on foot," Brenner says. "Linetti, you see anything?"

Linetti's voice chimes in over the walkie. "I think I can make someone out, but I don't have a clean shot..."

"Who is it??" Velle hisses.

"I dunno... but I think they're coming your way."

There are a few uneasy moments of suspense while we all wait for a potential attack. The whole place is silent, with nothing but breathing to be heard as we listen for *any* impending sounds of an ambush. Eventually, light footsteps come through the woods.

Velle holds up his index finger, signaling that it's just one person. I suck in a breath, attempting to calm myself down and focus. We're all ready, but the fear is palpable.

What if it's a distraction? Or a suicide bomber or something... You never know.

The footsteps approach slowly, until they're within a few feet of the armory walls. And then they stop.

"Come on, prick..." Velle grouses under his breath. "Fuck around and find out."

"Officer Chevelle?" a voice calls.

My stomach drops.

"Holy shit..." Dash says the words I can't get out.

"Jesus Christ... *Fenwick??*" Velle barks.

"Um, yes, uh-huh," Trevel stammers. "It's me."

"You got a death wish or something?!" Velle snaps.

"I'd prefer not to answer that right now," he replies with his usual brand of secret snark, carefully disguised by the accent.

Just hearing his voice and knowing he's out there is swarming me with too many things.

"What the hell is he doing here?" Joy hisses to us.

Everyone stares at me. My mouth is hanging open, eyes wide as I simply shrug. "How the hell would I know??"

Velle's glare is on me for a couple of extra studious seconds before he grumbles, "Son of a bitch," then turns back to his scope. "If he sent you, you're about to die slow. Was it worth it?"

"That's a lovely sentiment," Trevel says. "But no, he didn't send me. Though I imagine he'll be on his way when he realizes what I took..."

Velle's gaze, pressed up to his scope, narrows. "Oh yea? And what's that?"

"I've brought you something, Officer," Trevel rumbles. "Something that… belongs to him. Something that will undoubtedly help you win."

"Spill it," Velle growls. "Or I'll put a bullet in your favorite ass cheek."

"Oh, please don't shoot Byron," he whines.

Dash snorts, and my jaw clenches.

Enough.

I shove Velle aside to seethe through the hole. "What the fuck do you *want*, Trevel??"

He goes quiet for a moment. I peer out into the forest, but I can't see him. "I… I need to talk to you."

"So talk," I grunt.

He's quiet again. "Can I… Can I see you?"

"Come on out," I goad, nervous uncertainty gripping my chest when I see Velle's finger ghosting over the trigger.

"Is… Officer Chevelle going to shoot me?"

"Maybe."

"Well, tell him not to."

"I don't think I can do that," I bite out of frustration.

He sighs audibly. "Look, I promise you, I'm not here for any other reason than to see you and explain myself, and maybe apologize a few thousand times… and then deliver your bargaining chip. I suppose you can kill me if you'd like, but can it wait until after we talk?"

Falling back from the wall, I scrape a hand over my face.

"Why are we even entertaining this?" Jasper grunts. "Just shoot him in the brain and be done with it."

"Jesus, babe…" Hancock scolds, shaking his head.

"He's right," Ren says, squeezing Luthor's hand while the other grips his gun. "We can't trust that chump! He's a spy… For all we know, he's trying to steal Byron back!"

I'm chewing on my lower lip while Luthor rumbles, "Okay, that's a bit extreme…"

"Is it??" Ren snaps. "He threatened you on the phone and let our best friends think we were dead! As far as I'm concerned, he can rot."

"I'm just saying, Byron can take care of himself," Luthor argues. "It should be up to him… Right, B?"

"Yea… What do you want to do?" Dash asks me.

Trepidation seeps from my pores. I honestly have no clue what to do…

If I'm listening to my heart, I kinda want to hear what Trevel has to say… *But that stupid thing is what got me into this in the first place!*

Plus, the last time I chose Trevel over these people, they ostracized me. And I really don't want to feel that kind of rejection again. Especially for someone who lies to me and hides things like it's second nature.

"Ren's right," I gulp.

Ren's head cocks. "I am?"

Luthor rolls his eyes.

"Yea, he's basically a stranger. I don't even… know him." I hate the way my voice tremors on those words, and how much I can tell everyone else heard it.

"Enough said," Velle grunts, repositioning his rifle. "Want me to shoot him?"

I'm obviously about to say *no thank you*, when someone else joins the conversation.

"Hang on a minute." Dr. Love steps over, putting himself close to the barrel of the rifle, like he's attempting to shift Velle's aim. "You know he saved me, right?"

He says this to Velle, but then turns his amber eyes on me.

"Wasn't he the one who turned you in to The Ivory in the first place?" Jasper scoffs.

"That's irrelevant," Dr. Love replies stoically. "Officer Chevelle and I have tried to kill each other before. In fact, haven't most of you been at odds at one time or another over the years?"

Eyes are shifting around the space, considering this definitely true fact.

"I agree that it should be up to you whether you wish to speak to him or not," he says to me, then addresses the group. "Outside of that, we should still let him in. Find out what he has and give him the opportunity to join us… if he wants."

"I hate to disagree with you, Lemuel, since you're just… *shredded*, and your jawline is immaculate," Ren flutters. Hancock and Dash both cackle as Dr. Love's lips twitch. "But I'm looking out for my best friend here. The things that former patient of yours has done are questionable as fuck."

"He withheld the truth," Felix jumps in. "I mean, who hasn't?"

The way everyone's faces slowly shift in Ren's direction feels almost comical. In fact, Luthor folds his arms over his chest, presenting his fiancé with a smug look of satisfaction.

"Who… me??" Ren gasps. "I'm the most honest person here! I'm practically Abraham Lincoln!" Luthor chokes while the rest of us gawk at him like he's insane. "Wait, didn't he hide the fact that he was super gay? Never mind, I don't know shit." He drapes his hands on my chest. "Do whatever you wanna do, B. I trust you."

I let out a breath, feeling the pressure like a thousand pounds of concrete doubt on my shoulders. The only person I can look to right now is Velle.

"We all know you can handle yourself," he says with a smirk, and I have to huff, rubbing the back of my neck. But then he goes serious. "I shouldn't have turned my back on you… Back at the prison. You're just as much a part of this team as the rest of us, and we need a warrior like you in our arsenal. If you say the Brit can be trusted, then that's good enough for me."

"Aww!" Ren squeals, hugging onto Luthor's waist. "Look at Dad being all fatherly…"

"For the love of *God*, Luthor, sit on his face or something," Velle gripes.

I snort, biting the inside of my cheek.

"Oy!" Trevel hollers from just outside the wall. "The longer you lot take chatting, the less time we have until The Ivory discovers what's missing! And when he does, it'll be all-hands on deck, so to speak."

"I'll go outside and talk to him." I try to project confidence I'm not feeling, bracing myself for whatever could happen.

And believe it or not, the prospect of getting mowed down by the cartel isn't even the scariest thing out there.

I get supportive nods from all around as I make my way to the doors. Dash chirps, "You got this, B!"

Ren squeezes my shoulder, and Luthor hums, "Head in the game, bro."

All this encouragement is giving me a migraine.

Joy shoots me a wink, then opens just one of the double doors for me. The moment I'm in through, she slams it behind me and I startle, inhaling and exhaling to calm my racing pulse.

"Okay, Trev…" I call out tentatively, wandering the perimeter of the armory, face flinging back and forth for any potential threat. We haven't heard The Ivory's men this close yet, but you never know. *Technically, I'm walking towards one right now…* "You got what you want. I'm out here… Let's talk."

I make it to the east side of the armory, where Trevel had been hiding. But I don't see him.

"Trev…?" I peer between the trees, walking slowly. "Violet—"

In a flash, I'm being shoved up against the stone wall and pinned by a taut and limber frame. Gazing up at the severely beautiful face of Trevel Fenwick, I sigh out the word, "Eyes."

"Hi, sweet fury." Deep purple shines so many emotions down at me; it's beyond overwhelming.

His pink lips are sloped into a crooked smirk, marred by a cut on the bottom one, which I put there. There's bruising around is eye, his cheek is swollen, and a few smears of dried blood still mark his face. I wish it made him look worse, but of course it doesn't. He's even hotter all battered up by my fists.

Fuck me, this is gonna be unbearable.

"So… what do you… h-have to say?" I stammer, fighting the shake in my voice from how close we are and how good he smells, and how fucking angry and hurt I still am.

His eyes are still twinkling, but that overzealous grin melts into a sorrowful pout. "I hate myself."

My brows jump. *Okay… didn't expect that.*

He's still caging me in, palms pressed flat on either side of my shoulders, but his face isn't reflecting the confidence of our position. He looks broken.

"Honestly, Byron, I had to see you," he breathes out. "To make sure you know that I never meant to hurt you, and I'll *never* forgive myself for the way I have. I needed to speak these things to you, and… see your face one last time." He swallows visibly as my stomach clenches.

"Last time…?" I gust and blink. "Why… one *last time?*"

He frowns, like he's confused by my question. "Because… it's over. Isn't it? I mean, surely you never want to see me again, and I don't blame you. But I just couldn't let this… *end* without being able to look at you once more." His eyes scan over my face, and he lifts his fingers to brush my jawline. "Fucking hell, you're so pretty, baby." Heat is rushing up my neck as his eyes close and he clears his throat. "Sorry. I don't expect you to believe me, or to care, but I wanted to tell you face-to-face that I'm so sorry it's physically *excruciating*. For everything I did, Byron… For everything I kept from you, and for being the worst, most selfish, dysfunctional, horrible person in the world."

I blink, swallowing a lump of confusion. "Okay, that's hyperbolic, even for you."

Pouting deeper, he huffs and drops his forehead to mine. "Stop making me love you…"

My chest constricts so hard I grunt.

"I'm trying to let you *leave*, because I suck, Byron. I'm a mess, and you're way too good for me. Just know that the last few months with you have been the best of my entire life. And that's not hyperbole, baby. It's the *truth*. You brought light into my pitch-black existence, and for that, I'm eternally grateful."

"Hang on." I push him back so that our eyes can meet. "Did you just say…" My voice cuts out. I physically can't speak it. I'm petrified.

"That I love you?" Trevel hums. I nod nervously, and he sighs, "Yea. I do. I'm so in love with you, Byron… Far more than I'm comfortable with, and I'm sorry for that too…"

My brow furrows. "Why?"

He blinks at me. "Because we can't be together."

"We can't?" *I'm so confused.*

"Well… I mean…" He starts fidgeting. "You *hate* me… Because I hurt you. *Right…?*"

I'm frozen. There was so much on my mind before, so many things confirming what he's saying now. But as soon as he said those other words, it all just… vanished.

"Are you pulling a Bugs Bunny on me right now?" I grumble.

He chuckles, then whimpers like it hurts. "I don't know… I'm fucked up, Raph." His eyes are welling with tears. "*Do* you… hate me?"

No. My lips part, ready to cough up what I think I *should* say, which is yes. Because I *should* hate him for what he's put me through. But I don't. Not even a little.

Especially after… what he just said.

He's in love with me…?

No one's ever… said that to me before.

"No," I croak. "I don't hate you, Trevel."

His head tilts.

"Maybe I should, but I don't, and I don't understand why you're writing this off. How can you be in… *love* with me, but give up that easily??"

He sniffles, shaking his head. "You said you didn't want to know me…"

"Yea, I was fucking pissed!" I growl, grabbing his face. "Do you blame me?? You've been treating me like a fucking yo-yo for weeks! Opening me up and devouring everything inside me like you were surviving on it only to leave *me* starving for you!"

"You told me you didn't want a relationship," he cries softly. "You s-said you couldn't do it…"

"I was lying!" I roar.

Our chests are heaving in tandem, the mess of what we are so overwhelming, I'm dizzy.

"Shit, Trev, I… I think I'm…" My face is burning, my throat trying to close up on the words.

"Please don't…" he whimpers. "Baby, don't say it… I'm so scared."

"I know," I gasp, tugging his face so that I can whisper it in his ear. "I'm… in love with you too."

"Jesus bloody Christ." He collapses into me, crushing me against the wall. "You shouldn't, sweet fury. I love you so much, but you *shouldn't* love me…"

"I know." I tremble, sweating all over, knees wobbling.

But I'm… *high.*

I feel suddenly weightless, and it's the scariest thing I've ever felt, like flying through the air with no wings. I'm purely *terrified* that I could plummet at any moment, but… this soar is *spectacular.*

"This… is not at all how I expected this to go," he sniffles, wiping his tears on my neck.

I chuckle, reveling in it. Basking in this; the fact that I love him and I'm admitting it. I'm *in love* with a guy, and he loves me back.

"Yea, no shit," I mumble. "You raced over here waving a white fucking flag."

"I'm sorry…"

My shaky fingers toy with the soft, messy strands of black hair at the base of his skull. They trail his smooth skin, sloping along the sharp line of his jaw. Touching him, feeling him; feeling this.

He's mine. I get to… have this.

"You can keep apologizing if you want." I sigh. "It's kinda sexy."

Trevel laughs again, softly rumbling into me, kissing my pulse over and over. "You forgive me? For being a knob…"

I nod, taking his wrists and dragging his hands off the wall behind me, placing them flat on my chest. "I do. Because I know you didn't mean to. You weren't trying to hurt me, Trevel, I know that."

"I promise I wasn't…"

"I know. You're a wreck, violet eyes, but it's okay. I've always been drawn to walking disasters." I grin because I can feel his on my flesh. "We both lied about things and hid things. But that's done now."

"Completely done." He finally pulls back to show me those stunning eyes. "I'll tell you everything, all the time, forever."

My throat dips, and he blinks.

"Or, you know… for however long you want to…"

The way he's squirming has to be the sexiest thing I've ever seen. Because it's the real him. *At last*, the walls are down, for both of us.

Nowhere to hide. We're free.

Out of the shadows. For good.

"I don't know how this will work," I murmur.

"It'll be quite hard, I'm sure," he breathes out.

"Good thing I like it hard, huh?" I smirk at him, and he purrs.

"Byron, I love you. More than I've ever loved anyone."

I huff and shake my head, but he grips my chest harder like he's desperate for me to understand what he's saying.

"I'm serious. I told you… everything I felt before you was a flicker. But, baby, you're the *brightest* light. You're the sun, and the moon, and the stars…"

"Fuck…" I say on an exhale, tears pushing behind my eyes.

"You're not in the shadows with me, sweet fury," he mumbles sweetly. Almost innocent, he's vulnerable. *Finally*. "You light up my world. You're like… Times Square."

I snort, and he's beaming. That gorgeous, crooked smile. I brush my thumb over the split in his lip… The second one I gave him since we've met. This whirlwind of us… It's mesmerizing.

"We're so dysfunctional," I hum, pulling his mouth to mine, kissing him gently.

I feel like the ultimate asshole… For coming down so hard on Luthor and Ren, and their toxic relationship. Because I get it now.

Zero to one-fucking-hundred. This isn't normal. In fact, it's fucking weird and crazy and probably not a good idea. But every person I've felt strongly for in my life has instantly swept me away. The only difference is that this one wants *me* too. Just the way I am… Not in the shadows, but in the light.

"Are you worried?" Trevel mumbles on my mouth. "About falling for someone who's *so* bloody tapped?" I chuckle. "Are you worried about having to be strong enough for me, Byron?"

"Mm… not really." I touch his face and his chest and his heartbeat. "Because I know I am. And I know you can do this… Calm the hell down and let me love you." He grins when I pause to kiss his lips, and whisper, "Just be *mine*, Leo."

Trevel hums, holding me like he's finally *here*.

When I kiss him, everything else melts away. The past is gone… The fight is over. And it's just us. Me and my partner in crime, kissing while the world burns around us.

CHAPTER FORTY-ONE

Trevel

WE'VE BEEN KISSING FOR TOO LONG.

I hate to even think that. Because how can you be kissing the best lips in the universe for *too long*?? Attached to the man you *love*, who—*get this*—loves *you* back!

Too long doesn't exist with Byron Kang in the picture.

That said, there's a lot going on right now, and we should probably compose ourselves. After all, this isn't the ending to some sappy rom-com starring Hugh Grant.

I'm just an unhinged maniac, standing in front of a broken boy in the middle of a bloody war zone, asking him to be my partner in crime…?

Actually, it's got a nice ring to it.

But it becomes painfully apparent when a throat clears from somewhere behind us, that we won't be able to simply bask in this unprecedented new love for much longer. Not with a militia standing by, an evil menace on his way to exterminate us all, and the key to *everything* waiting patiently nearby.

The passive-aggressive sound forces my mouth away from Byron's, and I peer at the hole in the stone wall. My brow raises at the surly glare of Officer Chevelle, his wicked smirk dampening the grouchiness just a tad.

"Very sweet," he growls. "But could you please come in here? We have business to attend to."

Eyes falling to Byron, I find him flushed and fluttering, and it's almost painful, the thought of pulling away from him like this. After he just told me that he's *in love with me...*

We should be shagging until our bodies shut down, not sobering up to go talk *war*.

But I know Officer Chevelle is right. The last thing I want is for anything to jeopardize the highly dangerous work I did to get this peace offering. So I take just one more moment to touch Byron's throat and gaze into his deep eyes while the mound beneath my fingers bobs and his fists slowly release my shirt he's been gripping.

"Fuck, Leo," he sighs. "You're distracting as shit, you know that?"

I grin, quite pleased with that remark. "Thank you, Raph. You're pretty bloody hypnotizing yourself." I kiss his cheek.

"Okay." Byron shakes his arms out. "Let's go. Jesus, this is gonna be brutal..."

My grin flips into a frown as I read the apprehension on his face.

Ah, right...

I peek back up at the tiny window hole in the stone building. There are at least three of his friends gawking back at me, who scatter the moment our eyes meet.

I heard what they were saying when Byron was considering whether to come out here and speak to me—*the walls are surprisingly thin for being made of rock*. These people don't trust me. It's not exactly news, but before, I didn't care. *Now*, I'd like them to accept me... Because of Byron.

He *loves* me, and I love him. I have no intention of letting him go.

He already said he wants to be with me... No takebacks.

"Let's go, my furious love." I grab his hand, giving him confidence in my gaze.

I can be rather charming when I set my mind to it. The situation in the prison was a complex one. Things were quite tense, and much of my behavior was being guided by my stubborn disdain for Felix and Lemuel, which I now see was nothing more than a coping mechanism.

But being with Byron, building our relationship—and it *was* one from the start, regardless of how hard he fought against it—showed me that the *revenge* had been highly romanticized in my mind. It was thrilling, and kinky at times... But I didn't *need* it.

I only needed him.

Hopefully, his friends can see what Lemuel and Felix saw... That despite not having made the best first impression, I'm not actually a sneaky, traitorous plonker, and I love their friend, brighter than all the stars in all the galaxies.

If that doesn't work, at least I have the key to the Warden's surrender to offer them.

Byron and I stalk swiftly around the building, hand-in-hand, headed for the entrance. One way in, one way out. *Maybe not the best place to be when a swarm of bloodthirsty animals are out to get you…*

"Now you're starting to sound like me, mate…" The voice echoes from within the trees. *"A real* Leo *should probably be a bit less cynical."*

Glancing out to look for him, I think I catch a glimpse of his eyes—one of them mangled—his grubby gray fur and that smirk…

But he's not actually there. The visions of him have been slowly fading off, back into my mind where he belongs. And I can't tell if I'm relieved, or mourning another loss.

"Hey." Byron's voice catches me before we reach the doors. I blink down at him, and he cocks his head. "You good?"

I nod reticently, biting my lip as his eyes shift.

"You know you can tell me… if you're seeing him. I think it's kinda cool."

My lips sweep into a smile that feels far too good for real life. Leaning down, I grasp his jaw and rumble over his lips, "You would. You're a twisted little monster yourself, aren't you, baby?"

He smirks and hums, swiping my mouth with his tongue. "I can't wait for you to dive deeper into my depravity, violet eyes."

I'm growling, all too eager to say sod it all and hump him up against a tree. But the door to the shack whips open, the familiar female rasp of Joy Jameson hollering, "Come on, sluts! Get in here before you get us all pinched!"

Byron pulls me inside, and they slam the door behind us. "Really? *Pinched*?" He gives her a teasing look. "What are you, a 1940s gangster?"

She purses her lips. "Stick 'em up or I'll pump you full of lead."

Huffing in amusement, my face tips around to take in the conditions of this shabby place. The room has gone quiet, and I land on a whole slew of curiously appraising gazes, aimed right at me.

"Um… hello," I mumble to the ragtag band of ready-made soldiers, squeezing Byron's hand.

But this time, the glares don't all give off *kill the traitor* vibes. If anything, it seems more like a family's overprotective scrutiny of the *new boyfriend.*

The only person in the room I don't know is a large, unnecessarily attractive blonde man, clutching the hand of the pink-haired dreamboat I met earlier, named Dash—*this must be Kemper, then.* Byron has mentioned Dash before as his friend, the prisoner who escaped Alabaster Pen and reconnected with a former guard, Kellan Kemper.

Apparently, he and his partner came back from wherever they've been hiding to help Velle defeat The Ivory. Just like Luthor and Ren did. The notion of such loyalty spreads warmth in my chest.

These people genuinely care for each other. Whether prisoners or guards, killers or cops, from all different walks of life… They're ready to lay down their lives for one another. It's as baffling as it is remarkable.

No wonder they all hated me so much… In their eyes, I was stealing Byron away from where he clearly belongs by their sides. And it's not *not* true… I just hadn't realized until I saw them together earlier, when Dash arrived, how *strong* their bond is. And now I feel like even more of a wanker for isolating him the way I did—unintentionally or not.

Choosing to deescalate the situation in an overtly British way, I address Dash's large *Daddy* of a partner. "You must be Kemper… We haven't been properly introduced. I'm Trevel Fenwick."

Ren scoots between us before I can shake his hand. "Let's save the Alabaster Pen alumni meet-and-greet for later." He folds his arms over his chest, serving me a vibrant blue glower. "You said a lot of stuff out there, Fenwick… Was it *true*?"

"Hi, Ren. Good to see you again," I sigh begrudgingly. "Were *all* of you eavesdropping on our conversation?"

The collective group of them nods, murmuring various versions of, *duh*, *of course*, and *no shit*.

Byron huffs, shaking his head and rubbing his eyes, though he seems unsurprised by his friends' meddling.

"Did you mean it?" Dash blinks wide, hazel eyes at us. "'Cause it was… really romantic." He bites back a swooning grin.

I open my mouth to answer him, but Ren snaps, "Not now, Dascha, you marshmallow. I want to know what this young man's intentions are for my friend."

"I'm certain we're about the same age," I rumble in amusement.

"Don't talk back to me," he barks. "I'm fully serious. That dude is *family*. You mess with him, and you mess with me, plain and simple. I don't care if you've hypnotized him with your sexy accent, or your pretty eyes, or because you're like the lovechild of Ozzy Osbourne and Shaggy from Scooby Doo and he thinks that's hot for some reason. I *will not* tolerate him being used in any way, shape, or form." Ren's eyes flit to Byron. "He's had enough of that for one lifetime."

Byron is shifting at my side, his palm becoming terribly sweaty where it's engulfed in mine. The rest of the crew appear to be equally anticipating my response, and honestly, I'm not upset, or offended, or frustrated by them calling me out.

The only thing I am is awed at how much they care for Byron. I'm so bloody *glad* he has this type of support, knowing he never got it from his actual family, and I'm filled with a sudden sense of determination to prove myself. To them, but most of all, to *him*.

"Guys, can you please lay off of him?" Byron grumbles. "This isn't a job interview. It's been a crazy few weeks, but we… care about each other. A lot, so just—"

"Baby, I'm sorry to interrupt, but I feel I need to weigh in here," I cut him off, addressing Ren and the rest of them. "The truth is that I fully understand your doubts. I had them myself. You all haven't seen me the way Byron has. You've only seen me as the *villain* because, from the moment I arrived on this island, that was the role I took on. Many things from my past made me feel like that was who I needed to be… But most of all, it was because *The Ivory* wanted me to be the antihero. And at first, he was the only person I had any real connection to here. But it was all fake, and I know each of you can relate."

I witness them softening. Especially Officer Chevelle.

"He played on my weaknesses to get what he wanted, and frankly, I don't blame him. I was an easy target. I was a *mess*… I still am. But through all of the uncertainty, the resentment and disguising myself with darkness, there was *one* thing that, right from the start, felt *good* and *honest*… And that was Byron."

I glance down at him, and I'm chuffed to find him gazing up at me, a purely gorgeous, timid smile on his perfect mouth.

"I was instantly infatuated," I go on. "How could I not be? He's *fantastic*. And I'll be brutally honest… I thought you all were bonkers for keeping him in the shadows the way you had." Many of their faces fall with some visible remorse. Especially Ren. "Don't get me wrong, it wasn't all your fault. He certainly enjoyed being there." I smirk at Byron, and he chuckles. "But he didn't *belong* in the dark, and it drove me mad to see him feeling so unimportant. Because he's the most important person I've ever met. He *deserves* to be the star of the show, and now he is. And I'm just the late addition to the cast who gets to watch him shine."

Lifting Byron's hand in mine, I kiss his knuckles. "I know I fucked up along the way… A lot. And trust me when I say, I would take a million more beatings from you to prove that this is real. That I'm real, and *we're* real, and I'm never going to hide again."

Byron pouts, eyes shimmering as he touches the cut on my lip. "I do feel bad about that…"

I chuckle. "It's alright, Raph. I thought it was hot."

"Me too," Ren hums.

"Definitely scary, but in a secret boner kinda way," Dash adds.

"Not now, Luscious." Kemper covers Dash's mouth with his hand.

"Cards on the table, that wasn't the first time I've kicked his ass." Byron grins. "It happens way more often than it probably should."

"Show me a relationship on this island that isn't at least a little unhinged." I give them all a pointed look.

No one has a word of argument about that.

"Yea… I get it now." Byron sighs, specifically to Luthor and Ren. "Whether it's toxic or not, you can't fight chemistry."

"I love when he has to admit he's wrong," Ren whispers to Luthor.

"I'm sorry for what I said to you on the phone, Luthor," I address him sheepishly. "I was manic and truly despising myself… Quite literally the worst moment for you to call." I pinch the back of my neck.

Luthor blinks at me, then at Byron, observing the hopefulness in his friend's eyes. His lips twist. "It's okay. If it weren't for that ominous conversation, we wouldn't have come back. So I'd say it worked out for the best."

"Yea, thanks for luring us into extreme danger that we risked our lives to escape," Ren mutters sarcastically. "Much appreciated."

Luthor smacks him playfully.

I turn to my doctor and his fiancé, prepared to monologue to them next. But before I can even go there, Felix holds his hand up.

"Don't worry about us. We've been through worse." He grins at Lemuel, who kisses his tousled brown hair.

"The point is that I'm sorry to anyone who was run-through by Hurricane Trevel," I murmur. "But the only person I need mercy from is my Shadowman." My eyes linger on Byron's shy smile before I peek at Lemuel and whisper, "I get it now."

He grins, the first genuine smile I've ever gotten from the robotic doctor who's helped me so much over the years. I wouldn't be here without

Lemuel Love, that's for certain. But this sentence turned out to be the best thing that's ever happened to me.

I cup Byron's jaw in my hands while he holds my waist. "I love you, warrior. Thank you for fighting for me when I didn't."

And this time, he isn't afraid. He kisses me, in front of *people*. No holds barred.

"I love you, prison husband." He beams, and I laugh into his mouth.

"Never thought I'd see the day," Joy snorts.

"Really??" Rook scoffs. "I never doubted it for a second. This island's number one export is codependent relationships."

"Okay, listen." Velle claps his hands together. "It tickles my balls that you two fuckin' weirdos found each other. And I promise there'll be plenty of time for us to rub our dicks together after we win this thing, but right now, we need to focus."

Byron and I pull apart just enough to give him our attention.

"While you were outside, I got into the servers," Luthor tells Byron.

His brows jump. "So… we have the prisoners?"

Velle nods. "Everyone's locked and loaded. Peters is gathering up the troops, and they'll be ready to back us up. Because you were right…" He steps closer to me, intimidating in his size and stature. "He's coming for us. So I'm gonna need that bargaining chip. *Now.*"

I swallow hard and straighten. *Playtime is over.* "Yes, sir."

"It better be a smoking fucking gun," he rumbles, still eyeing me in a way that doesn't exactly scream trust.

But it's alright. *I'm about to make him very happy.*

I kiss Byron quickly, then jaunt toward the doors.

"Hang on…" He rushes after me. "If you're going back out there, I'm coming with you."

I can't stop the utter delight from overpowering my face. I have an honest to God *boyfriend*… It's almost unbelievable.

Bollocks… I hope I don't fuck this up.

"Oh, trust me, sweet fury," I croon as Joy unhooks the latch and carefully opens the door. "You're stuck with me now."

Byron relaxes, giving her and Rook some space to assess the immediate area for any threats while I peer in between the trees.

Ren rests his chin on Byron's shoulder from behind. "I can't believe you're *in love!* And with the British Chalamet, no less." He sneers, and Byron rolls his eyes.

"I can. He's hot," Dash hums, patting Byron on the back. "Nice work, kid."

"He's Byron's man, okay?" Luthor's arms circle Ren's waist. "Which means he's family now too."

"I'm sure I'll learn to love my future brother-in-law," Ren jeers, then motions between Byron and Felix. "I mean, if these two could squash their beef, anything's possible."

"What's a little bloodshed between friends, right?" Felix winks at Byron.

Byron grins, shifting awkwardly as he glances at Felix and Lemuel. "I should probably let you know… if we're burying the hatchet and all," he pauses, peeking at me. "We kinda sorta… had sex in your bed."

I freeze while Felix's face drops. Ren snorts. Luthor gasps.

Lemuel perks up. "Excuse me??"

"You… had sex… in our bed?" Felix mumbles.

Byron clears his throat. "And put… cum in your lube."

"Oh my God, that's fucking awesome!" Ren cackles.

In fact, everyone is laughing… Except Felix and Lem. They're standing there looking dumbfounded.

They turn to me, and I shrug. "Our bad…?"

Ren whispers to Felix, "Did you use it??"

Based on how red his cheeks are, I think we have our answer.

"No comment," Lem growls, leering at me.

"Yea, so… Now we're even," Byron gulps.

Felix blinks as Dash steps over, plucking the knife from between his fingers. "We'll just… hang onto that for right now."

"It's fine," Felix says after a breath. "Sorry, I'm just… replaying a few things in my head."

Byron snorts, attempting to cover it. Then the others join in, and eventually, Felix grins. Lemuel still looks a bit disturbed, but he'll get over it. *After all, we know he's a freak.*

"You feel those little emo boys swimming around in there?" Ren sneers at Felix, and Luthor slaps him.

But they're all laughing, and I'm grinning to myself. They seem so *happy* to be back together. It has my heart soaring for my sweet fury and his found family as Joy gives me the *all clear.*

Zoning back in on the task at hand, I whistle. "You can come on out, love. It's safe."

Byron steps over, his face serious once more. "Who…?"

But his question is cut off when we hear tentative footsteps approaching. Everyone has stopped what they're doing, gathering around as the lithe creature emerges from behind a tree. He looks nervous, and I get it. This is kind of crazy, and I'm sure he doesn't know what to expect.

Stepping forward, I grab his hand and pull him inside. His big eyes shift about the room, focused mainly on the guns in the hands of all these strangers. The guards lower their weapons, every face but mine etched in perplexity, aimed at the quiet beauty.

"Who's this?" Joy asks softly.

Velle's gaze narrows, head cocking to the side. "You look familiar… Where do I know you from?"

The lad's full lips part, but then he snaps them shut. There's a blush to his cheeks as he observes them all. But he doesn't say a word, like a shy animal you need to let sniff you before it feels comfortable.

I nudge him gently. "Go on, then. Tell them who you are."

His long lashes flutter, sparkling eyes taking in the faces staring back at him. Then he straightens.

"My name is Angel Alvarez."

Trevel's Epilogue

One year later…

"Birdcage"
By Trevel Fenwick

It's a fascinating sense of mortality…
Flying through the sky.
Amidst the clouds, up high. Defying gravity.
A bird, freed from their cage. Wings spread, a stretch of reprieve.
They were never clipped, apart from what he had you believe.
Autonomy is yours now, beautiful. Metal bars no more,
Chains asunder on the floor.
You choose, little bird, how far you will soar.
And should you wish to be confined again,
It will be for passions of love, nary pain.
For the sovereignty you claimed.
His acquiescence was for you and you alone.
A once Tartarean heart, now but a man of flesh and bone.
So remember, little bird, when you descend from the
firmament's height,
Your reign are feathers of a crown, resting atop quelled Ivory white

"HELLO? EARTH TO TREVEL." BYRON'S VOICE CUTS INTO MY PLAYLIST, AND I peer to the right.

He's literally plucked one of my earbuds out of my ear.

Grinning, I put the pencil down for the first time in over an hour. "I'm sorry, baby. I was in the zone."

"I can see that." He smirks.

"What's up?"

"The lady was asking if you wanted anything to drink, but I couldn't get ahold of you." He chuckles. "So she left."

I frown. *Bollocks. I kinda wanted a Coke…*

"I got you a Coke." He places the can on my tray table. "If you want ice, though, you're shit outta luck."

I snicker, grasping his face to kiss it all over while he fights me off.

"Alright, back off," he huffs. "We have another two hours until we get there, and I'm trying not to focus on how hard you're making me."

"Am I, sexy man?" I croon in his ear, licking the lobe until he shudders.

"Yea…" he breathes out.

"But I'm not doing anything."

"Oh, yes you are. Just sitting there quietly…"

He grins, and I chuckle.

"*Ignoring* me. God, it's hot."

More laughter bubbles from within my chest while I touch his throat and his chest. The poem I've been working on for the better part of this trip was certainly keeping me occupied. But now that I've stopped, it's right back to being insatiable for my delicious, growly boyfriend and his delicious hard body.

Byron turns fast, cutting off my tongue-assault of his ear, grabbing my face in that possessive, dominant way that certainly betrays how needy he is when I have his ankles in the air.

"Behave, violet eyes," he growls, fully serious. My balls are thrumming. But then his lips twitch, and he licks mine. "I promise, as soon as we land, I'll be so deep in your body, you'll be giving me a reverse blowjob."

I stifle a whimper, smirking over his mouth. "Because your dick will be in my throat the other way?"

"Uh-huh," he beams.

I snort, and he laughs back. It's bloody fantastic. I swear, I've never felt like this. We have so much fun together, and every day is brand new.

Being with Byron Kang is the first thing that's truly made me feel alive, as *myself*. We've been together for a year now, and it's going shockingly well. I can't believe I get to call him mine, and that he actually *wants* to call me his, after everything I've put him through.

To be honest, though, the past doesn't affect us nearly as much as it used to. Things were different back then. It's almost disturbing how much has changed…

Since my poem is done, mostly—*you know us artists, nothing is ever truly finished*—I opt to cuddle up with my boyfriend for the remainder of our flight, watching episodes of *Brooklyn 99* with a blanket over us so that I can casually feel him up without scandalizing the other passengers. And before we know it, we're touching down at Heathrow Airport, arriving for our next adventure, in a place I haven't been since I ran away from it at eleven years old.

I won't say it isn't odd being back here, because it certainly is. I have only fleeting awful memories of this place, so old they've begun to warp over time. But we're here for a reason…

And besides, Byron associates much of London with his grandfather, so this is a trip I know he's been longing for.

Traveling has become a big part of our lives, and it makes sense. Byron was locked up for three years. Once things ended and they settled down enough, he was desperate to break free for real.

We found a small but cozy flat in Astoria, moved in and began building a new life *together*. And then, as soon as we were able, we started taking trips. Naturally, funds were limited, so we couldn't simply jet-set all over the place like the heirs to some billionaire tycoon. But we managed to have fun while keeping it modest.

The first place we went was Atlanta, so that I could say a final goodbye to Alice.

As Byron and I get our luggage and get into an Uber, my mind is sorting through memories of him holding me while I fell apart at Alice's gravesite. It was difficult… Like reliving the night I lost her all over again.

I don't know if I ever won't carry guilt over what happened to Alice. I still feel somehow responsible, though I know it wasn't my fault. Dr. Love has made sure to drill this into my head.

"There's a big difference between killing someone and simply being a shitty boyfriend," he would say during our weekly sessions.

It made me smile and allowed me to breathe just a little easier. The comfort he gives me is one thing that's never wavered, in all the years I've had him as my doctor. Despite how angry I was with him for a while there, I can't discount how much he's changed my life, for the better.

I wish I was able to see him more often, but our schedules and locations don't allow as much these days. Hence, the other reason this trip is so exciting… *Well, part of it.*

Byron and I get settled into our hotel, making almost immediate use of the bed, and the shower, and the desk, and the window that overlooks the Thames. And once we're sufficiently sated, muscles sore and balls empty, we get cleaned up and head out to meet some friends for dinner.

They've chosen a place that's supposed to have excellent Chinese food, and Byron and I arrive to find them already seated at a table in the back, with privacy. *Makes sense, all things considered.*

They barely notice us at first—*typical*. Too busy kissing and smiling and whispering things to each other that are most likely a combination of sweet and filthy. As we approach, they finally look up.

"Hey!" Felix cheers, jumping from his seat to hug us both. "I'm so happy to see you guys!"

Lem stands as well, though much slower and less outwardly enthusiastic.

"Look who it is… Our cum buddies," he sneers and Byron chokes. Lemuel chuckles, "How was your trip?"

He hugs me first, then Byron, giving us each one-half of a Mississippi. Still, it's fascinating. I never so much as grazed his flesh in all the years he treated me, pre-Alabaster Pen. I was beginning to think he was a mirage…

Or an imaginary friend.

Oh, come on. Not even fair!

"Long," I mumble my answer to his question, taking a seat beside Byron, across from Lem.

He chuckles—something he's started doing much more since the wedding. Smiling, laughing, general human behaviors. Of course, they're still done in quiet, blasé sanguinity, because that's who he is. But I wouldn't want him any other way, and I'm certain his husband feels the same.

I've come to realize over the last year that I do love Lemuel, but not in any romantic sense. I think of him a bit like a father figure—*okay, maybe more of a hot uncle*. Either way, he's always been a supportive and stable presence in my life, something I never had before him. The crush I'd developed in the past was more about having someone reliable in my life, someone who listened and understood. Who *saw* me.

But now I have Byron for that, and he's much more my type—not to mention infinitely less infuriating. Byron is the perfect person for me, similar to me in ways that keep him always empathizing, but with enough differences to keep us forever bickering and laughing at each other. Truly, I cannot imagine a better partner in crime.

I love Byron Kang in every single facet of my existence.

"Please," my love scoffs at me. "Eight hours is nothing. Just wait for our trip to Seoul."

I bite off my grin, taking his hand on the table. "I absolutely *cannot* wait, sweet fury. It's going to be magnificent."

"I'm jealous," Felix sighs dreamily. "We haven't gotten to anywhere in Asia yet, and I'm dying to go."

"Honestly, I'm amazed you're traveling at all." Byron blinks. "Isn't it dangerous?"

"Yes," Lem grumbles, but Felix waves him off.

"Life is dangerous. After what we've all been through, we have to make the most of this." He smirks at Lemuel, who narrows his heated gaze in return.

But then he takes Felix's hand, kissing the ring on his finger. "What am I supposed to do with you, Mr. Love?"

"Whatever you want, Dr. Monster," Felix purrs through a sickeningly love-drunk grin.

Byron and I share a look, one of our wordless passes of relationship hubris that has us both chuckling. *Yes*, we've made it to the stage in our relationship where we think we're better than every other couple. Amazing in itself, because I never thought I'd make it past sleeping with someone, let alone to a place where my partner and I feel comfortable lofting our love over others.

But then he kisses me, and it's slow and passionate. Because we're equally bloody disgusting, so who are we to judge?

The four of us order food—actually, we let Felix and Lem choose for us since they're the Chinese food connoisseurs—and we eat together amidst casual conversation. We haven't seen them in months, so there's a lot to catch up on, most of it pertaining to what's happening on the island. They talk about their honeymoon in Belize, and we talk about Montreal, Maui, and Mexico. And then we laugh about how the last three places we visited start with "M."

We discuss our friends, and what they've been doing since we all parted ways. And of course, we talk about the reason we all know each other; the person who brought us together, for better or worse.

"No one's heard from him," Felix says, breaking open a fortune cookie. "At least, no one in our neck of the woods."

"Not even Velle?" Byron asks, surprised.

Felix shrugs. "If he has, he hasn't mentioned it."

"It's better that way," Lem adds. "For everyone."

"Did Dash say anything? When you saw him?" Felix tilts his head at Byron.

Sure, he could be asking both of us, but where the boys are concerned, it still feels like they're Byron's family more than mine. Frankly, I *do* feel sort of like a brother-in-law to them.

You can get close, spend time together, laughing and enjoying one another's company. You can love, respect, and trust one another, but you'll never have as close a bond as they do. Because they're blood.

I don't mind it, though. I'm happy to have them in my life, but more than anything, I'm happy that Byron has them in his. That's what matters most.

"He cut off contact," Byron answers. "For obvious reasons…"

Felix and Lem both nod in understanding. We all do. The events that led to where we are now were anything but simple. Still, I'd say it worked out for the best. *I hope the others feel that way too…*

"So… What's the plan for tomorrow?" I ask, because there's something *else* on my mind. My eyes connect with Felix's while I sip my tea.

"Oh, I'm ready." He grins, a sly little thing. "You give me the okay and I'm there."

I nod, dumping more oolong onto the butterflies multiplying in my stomach. Byron notices my sudden nervous zeal and grazes his fingers along the base of my skull, playing with my hair.

"Will you be… tagging along?" Lem asks, waving off the fortune cookie Felix is trying to shove at him before eventually conceding and taking it.

"I've gone back and forth," I mumble, clearly still apprehensive. "But ultimately, I think I need to be there. I think I'd regret it if I weren't."

He nods, not necessarily agreeing with my decision, simply accepting that it is *my* decision. *How very doctorly of him.* "If you're worried it will… wet your whistle, so to speak, you know what I'm going to say…" His lips twist.

I grin, slouching back in my seat. "Yes, I do. And if nothing matters, then why not make it count? Being here, this opportunity… *Life.*"

"I never said nothing matters." He gives me a pointed look.

"You didn't have to." I chuckle.

"So, it's settled!" Felix beams. "Tomorrow night… we ride!"

Byron and I laugh out loud, while Lemuel shakes his head.

"Could you possibly be more excited?" Byron snorts.

Felix's head lolls. "*God*, I'm telling you… I need this. It's been *way* too long."

"In that case, I propose a toast." I lift my glass, signaling for them to do the same. "To like-minded individuals. And to not *needing* revenge… but getting it anyway."

Byron is humming in amusement as he leans into my side.

"And to a much-needed vacation!" Felix adds, illuminated. And we clink. "What does yours say, baby?" he asks Lem after his sip.

Lemuel removes the small piece of paper from within the cookie. His face is the picture of a scientist who could not *possibly* find it more frivolous to partake in such things. He reads it, then frowns. "You're a perfectionist. Don't spoil it."

Felix doubles over.

"Hilarious," he growls, throwing the crumpled fortune at Felix. "And what does *yours* say, husband?"

Felix purses his lips to dampen the grin as he reads his aloud. "Make time for hobbies. The value of *you-time* is priceless."

It's not the same place I grew up in.

Unsurprisingly, my parents moved around a lot. Dad did some time in prison for minor drug infractions, and Mom did a few stints in rehab. Obviously, I don't know whether it stuck or not, but judging by where they live now and the state of their rental, I would wager a resounding no.

Outside of that, I know nothing about them, because I chose not to keep tabs—I only found these things out when we started planning this trip. On some level, I think I've always been afraid that knowing more about their lives would drive my ever-present need for revenge.

My biggest fear was that killing my parents wouldn't fix me… That they'd be dead, and I'd still be fucked up. And I'd be stuck dealing with what that meant.

The revenge was always a crutch. If I focused all my energy on anger, I didn't need to deal with the truth of how deeply and severely my childhood traumatized me. From the abuse, to the streets, to addiction and the assault, I was never able to just *exist* without pain. Which is why when I finally got the chance, with Alice, I didn't know what to do with myself. Naturally, I had to sabotage it. Because life without pain didn't make sense to me.

It truly is a testament to Dr. Love's abilities that I'm even able to walk around in society, let alone love and be loved.

I swear, the bloke deserves a Nobel Prize, or at least a trophy of some kind.

I was in immense pain after Alice died, struggling with my addictions, my past trauma, and the sudden loss of Dr. Love as what I'd thought was the only thing keeping my demons at bay for years. And instead of dealing with it, I dove headfirst into revenge, because it was what I knew. After all, it *was* how I'd coped with my assault. And it had been so satisfying, brutally slaying those rapist cunts. It was the only time I'd ever felt like *Leo* myself.

But it didn't undo the damage they'd inflicted on my life. Because, as we now know, revenge doesn't solve anything. And in never letting myself grieve, the pain became like an infection left untreated. It just kept growing and spreading until, before I knew it, I was shutting down.

That's the best thing about finally seeking out closure and healing now, as opposed to getting high and blowing up everything around me like a grenade of human suffering like I used to. Because *now*, I have him.

I don't need to rely on revenge anymore. I can focus on Byron, like I should've done with Alice. He's helped me move out of the shadows and into the light, in ways I couldn't back then. I wasn't ready, and I only wish Alice hadn't needed to die for me to realize these things…

But I will never forget her.

"I'm trying to forgive myself for what I did to you…" I told her through tears and sniffles while I knelt in the dirt next to her headstone and the pink dahlias I left for her. *"I'm trying hard, angel. And I don't know what happens, or where you are… But I can only hope it's somewhere good. Where you're happy and safe, and loved, better than I could ever give you."* I sniffled and wiped my eyes, glancing at Byron, hovering a few feet away. I couldn't help snorting a wet chuckle. *"He reminds me of you. Sometimes I feel like the universe gave him to me as a second chance… I almost lost him once, acting like a bloody twit. I won't make that mistake again. For you, baby, I'll be as good as I can with him. And I'll never forget you, Alice Alvarez."*

As painful as it was, I needed to let myself feel it. Let the sorrow settle over me, and just sit with it, because it's the only way to finally let the wound heal.

That's precisely what I'm doing now. Although, this excursion is slightly different.

Byron and I took the tube to my parents' current place of residence. We're lingering outside, and I'm pacing, trying to remember to breathe and not let the mere fact that they're currently sharing the same air supply as me send me into a spiraling panic attack.

"You wanna tell me what you're feeling, violet?" Byron asks. Not smothering or pushy. Just… *here*. For me.

It's my favorite thing about Byron Kang. Support comes second nature to him. He's a real Leonardo in that way.

"Knowing they're in there is making it… rather difficult not to remember things." I'm stiff all over, my skin crawling from the memories. "I hate remembering…"

He nods, then holds out his hand. Peeking down at it, I feel calmer already. From simply *looking* at his hand—*it's bonkers*. But it's a very nice hand. Masculine and strong, veins on top decorated with his new ink—*Leo* written above two swords. His nails painted black and the bracelet I made him out of carnelian and sunstone.

Reaching out, I give him mine. He threads our fingers, whispering, "You fucking amaze me… You know that?"

I blink and sniff.

"How badass you are… You did that all by yourself, baby. *You're* the real warrior."

"He's right, you know…"

I hear the voice inside my head—my inner strength and courage.

I don't see Leo anymore. In fact, I haven't since around the time Byron and I became official. But he's still here. He's always with me, except that now, he's my voice of reason, like he probably *should've* been from the start.

Leo got me through a lot of dark, lonely times, and for that, I'll always imagine him as something separate from me. Because I needed a guardian, and Leo was it. But just like me, he was angry, and afraid.

I'm not those things anymore, and I'm not lonely anymore. I have Byron.

He's my Leo, and I'm his.

In a way, aren't we all Leo? It sounds culty, but it's true!

"He got me through it…" I tell Byron, and his head cocks. "Leo. If it weren't for him, I probably would've…" My voice trails, and I gulp. "Who knows."

"It was all you, Trev." He brushes my hair back with his free hand.

"From darkness to light and everything in between. You survived a life not many people could've made it through."

I chuckle and kiss his wrist. "I love that you're totally fine dating someone who's killed eight people."

His face drops a bit. "*Dating*? Baby… we're way past dating. Aren't we? I mean, I thought we were…"

My stomach is doing somersaults. I'm swooning over how adorable he is when he's all shy and insecure, while also feeling like kind of a knob for making him think I'm not hopelessly in love and desperate to have his babies.

"By…" I whisper, considering just falling onto one knee right here and now. But a ping from my pocket stops me. *This is it…* "The signal… Hold that thought, sweet fury."

Yanking him along, I bring him up the steps and into the house. The door is unlocked, as expected. And the moment I set foot inside, I'm bombarded with treacherous memories. It's not even the same place, but my parents live here; the people who brought me into this world, and then tortured me for years out of their own sick amusement.

They made me into what I am… Not quite evil, but certainly not good.

It's the scent of them, I think. The same knickknacks triggering images of the abuse. I barely even notice that I'm having trouble walking until I collapse into a wall, clutching Byron's hand to my chest while I struggle to breathe.

"Baby, you don't have to do this if you don't want," he whispers, holding my face. "We can leave anytime, and you'll still know they're gone…"

"No," I gasp, shaking my head. "I want to. I need to see…"

He still appears concerned for me, but he nods, helping me continue on. Giving me his strength to share.

We move to the bedroom at the far end of the flat, where they told us they'd be. And when I peer through the doorway, I have to gulp.

There are my parents, tied up back-to-back, mouths gagged with dirty socks. My chin lifts, and I exhale.

"Hey," I murmur to Felix and Lem.

Felix shows me a kind smile. "Hi. How are you feeling?"

"Good," I mumble. "Nervous…"

He nods in understanding.

"I haven't seen them in over a decade…"

Lem pushes himself off the wall, stalking toward the doorway. "I'm going to keep watch." He drops a large hand on my shoulder, giving a supportive squeeze. And then he strides away.

Byron slips his fingers up into my shirt, trailing them along my lower back. "You want me to stay?"

Peeking at him, I take in his face. It's the face of someone who will do literally anything for me, and it's mesmerizing. "Only if you want to."

His lips curve. "I'm here."

"I'm… here."

I take Byron's hand once more, and nod at Felix. "I'm ready."

Felix exhales heavily, his entire aura coming alive with the energy of The Carver. He looks different, moves different. He seems lit up, and yes, it's a bit terrifying, but also sort of brilliant.

Let's not pretend he isn't doing this for himself, but it's also for me. And I'm happy to give him this opportunity.

My mother and father are fighting against their ropes, mumbling and moaning as Felix rounds them with a kitchen knife.

"Would you like to say something to them?" he asks me, gray eyes dark, yet shining with encouragement.

My mouth slopes. "Actually… yes. I would."

Positioned so that they both can see me, I cock my head, gaze narrowed. I feel a lot of things being next to them right now. Rage, pity, sadness… But most of all, I'm relieved. Because, in a matter of minutes, they'll be dead. And I'll still be alive, holding the hand of someone who loves me.

I feel victorious already.

"Hi, Mum and Dad." I smirk at the fear in their eyes. "Remember me?"

The next morning, Byron and I sleep late. We're exhausted from a long night of watching The Carver hack my parents to bits and discard them in a nearby pond.

He carved T's all over their faces—*for Trevel, obviously*—and rather than giving them even the mild satisfaction of being posed, he simply scattered their parts all around, removing their teeth, and fingers and any distinguishing marks in order to delay identification.

Afterward, the four of us went out for a few pints, got a little tipsy, and wound up singing karaoke until the sun came up.

When Byron and I returned to our hotel, we were drunk and high on the adrenaline of watching a serial killer murder and dismember my parents. We fucked until we couldn't keep our eyes open, then passed out covered in lube, cum, and sweat.

A fantastic evening of debauchery.

We came down to the hotel restaurant for greasy burgers and bloody marys to cure the hangover and refuel for more sex. And I'm just staring at Byron in between bites, watching him stuff his face in the most adorable and somehow sexy fashion.

"I've gotta say… Darcey really knows what he's doing," he rambles, pouring out more brown sauce for his chips. "The dude is thorough. If there was a serial killer Olympics, I'm confident he'd take the gold. For America, anyway."

I snort. "Who'd get silver?"

He thinks about it for a moment. "I hate to say it, but probably Bundy. The guy was an obnoxious conservative prick, but he was tenacious as fuck. *Wily*… You know he escaped prison twice?"

"That's not that impressive… I know people who've done that," I murmur, and he chuckles. Stifling an out-of-control grin, I pick up a pepper shaker. "I never knew you were so into true crime…"

He scoffs. "You definitely did. How many nights have we spent rotting in the apartment, binge-watching true crime shows?"

While he's distracted, I'm nodding, casually dumping pepper into my hand. "You're right. Hey, By?"

"Yea?"

I blow the pepper into his face like pixie dust, and he immediately starts coughing.

"Jesus fuck!" He's frantically wiping his nose and eyes while I'm cackling wickedly. "What the hell did you do that for?!"

"Two truths and a lie, sweet fury." I grip the edge of the table, staring at him in wait.

He pauses his freaking out to gawk back at me. "You're out of your goddamn mind."

I nod emphatically. "Are you really not going to sneeze right now??"

He chuckles, shaking his head. "Do I seem like I tend gardens in my spare time?"

"Hey, anything is possible." I frown. "It's a lot more believable than never sneezing in your entire life!"

He shrugs. "What can I tell you, gorgeous? I just—" His words cut out, his face scrunching.

My eyes widen in anticipation.

But he just shakes it off and takes a sip from his drink. *More pepper! There's* pepper *in the* bloody *bloody mary! I can't even right now.*

"I'm awestruck," I murmur, and he grins, winking at me. "No, seriously. Byron, I… Can we…"

"Can we what?" he hums, continuing on with his eating. "Go to the loo and shag?" Clearly proud of himself with that one, he grins wide.

I'm seriously about to cry.

"Can we get married?" I ask softly, and his face flings to mine.

I'm not sure his eyes have ever been wider. I sneeze, and he mutters, "God bless you."

"Cheers."

"Wait, hold on… *Married?*"

I nod. "You said we were way past dating…"

"Okay, but there's a pretty big leap from whatever comes after dating and marriage… isn't there?"

"We're already living together." I shrug.

"That's true…" he hums, chewing his bottom lip.

"We're hopelessly in love…" I grab his hand from across the table and suck salt and burger grease off of his finger. He chuckles. "And we have the most earth-shattering sex known to mankind."

An old lady at the table next to ours gasps and makes a face.

Byron laughs some more. "Also, very true."

"Plus, all our friends are doing it." I grin. "We don't want to be left out…"

"No, we do not," he croons, playing with my fingers.

"So, what do you think?" I bat my eyelashes at him.

He's quiet for a moment, clearly in deep thought before he says, "Well, I'd have to ask you first…" He cocks a brow. "We're not just popping down to the courthouse."

I purse my lips. "No?"

He shakes his head.

"You want it to be *romantic*, sweet fury?"

"Oh, I'm gonna sweep you off your feet, Vi." He beams. "You better be ready."

"I am so ready."

My gut is swarming with thrill as he smirks. "On your mark…"

"Get set…" I whisper, biting my lip.

Go.

Byron's Epilogue

3 months later...

IT'S OFFICIAL. I CAN'T BELIEVE IT... *I'M SO EXCITED I COULD DANCE!*

Okay, maybe not. But still, I am pretty fired up.

Trevel and I have officially moved into my grandfather's penthouse apartment! Also known as the place where I grew up, *minus* my asshole parents.

It went down like this. We were in Seoul visiting my sister when we heard the news... My parents were retiring and moving back to South Korea.

I hadn't seen them since Trevel and I came back from the island, though I did speak to them on the phone a couple of times. Apparently, I was one of very few inmates in Alabaster Pen who got a *mysterious missing person* story rather than a *death* story. Meaning, when I returned, I was able to explain my disappearance by making up some excuse about moving to Canada on a whim. And because my family has never given much of a crap about me, they accepted the nonsense without a blink of skepticism.

Ridiculous, but whatever. Works for me.

When Trevel started raving about wanting to visit Seoul, I figured it would be the perfect time to officially come out to my family—and less nerve-racking with only my sister. She could relay the message to Mom and Dad. Kind of a cop-out, but at least I was doing it.

Turns out, me being bisexual wasn't the only family bomb being dropped during the trip. My sister revealed that my parents had been planning to retire and move back to Seoul anyway, and since I was back, I could take over the penthouse. Needless to say, I was completely bamboozled.

My father has *always* wanted to sell the place and pocket the money. *The fact that he's suddenly giving up the fight and just handing it to me is a thousand times crazier than the idea of me being bisexual ever was.*

The moment we returned from Seoul, I planned to race home and talk to my dad. Seriously, the plane was barely on the ground at JFK, and I was on a mission. I needed to hear the news straight from the horse's mouth, because if it was true… Well, that meant my man and I would officially own a four-bedroom, two bath penthouse on the twenty-fifth floor of a stunning building off Central Park West that belonged to my favorite person ever. *With a doorman and everything!*

I dragged Trevel along with me, and let's just say, he had his reservations. He was more nervous than I was. *It was adorable.*

"I just think this is a private family conversation." He continued to gripe the entire way there. "Not the best moment to introduce your historically unsupportive parents to a boyfriend for the first time…"

"Trust me, the *conversation* will be the most awkward part," I grumbled. "Just stand still and they'll pretend they don't see you."

"Ugh. I'm pretty sure you told me they wanted you to marry a Korean girl from a good family… Then here comes a Brit who's never held down a job for longer than a few months and spent his formative years either having sex for money or in an institution. *And* I have a dick! Did I mention that??"

I didn't want to laugh at him when he was clearly worried, but worry on Trevel is highly adorable. I love when he gets all jittery and starts rambling like a loon.

"Um, the dude you're describing sounds like a catch. Sign me up." I smirked at him, and he forced a scowl. "You know red is my favorite color flag."

"I hate you," he whined while I kissed him.

"Liar."

We arrived at the penthouse, and my dad was surprised, to say the least. It was the first time we were seeing each other in four years, and I was just dropping by, unannounced, holding the hand of a tall British dude with tattoos and a lip piercing—*he got it done shortly after we came back from London. It goes without saying that it's insanely hot, and it makes my dick happy.*

"It's good to see you, Byron, but I wish you would've called first," my father said, his eyes shifting between Trevel and me.

"Yea, well, I just wanted to talk to you about the penthouse," I muttered, forcing off the instinct to feel like a child around him. "Jaelyn says you and Mom are moving back to Seoul..."

"You know we've wanted to return for quite some time."

No, you've *wanted to return, and Mom just does whatever you say.*

"Okay..."

"We would've liked to sell it, but I know you don't want to do that," he went on, the disapproval in his tone increasing by the second. "I assume even more now..."

His brow lifted, eyes moving between Trevel and me again. My blood was rolling to a boil.

I cleared my throat in an attempt to steady my tone. "What are you trying to say?"

"I'm not saying anything, Byron." He sighed.

Suddenly, I was ten years old again. And he was carelessly explaining why coming to my tournament was a *waste of everyone's time.* Not just his. Mine, the other kids, *everyone* involved.

"No. You're not saying anything," I grunted. "So let me do it. You're pissed off that Grandfather left your home in my name. You're disappointed that I came back, when you thought I'd died or something, which let you off the hook pretending to care about me. And last but not least, you're itching to get this process over with so you don't have to deal with me telling you I'm bisexual and introducing you to my boyfriend. That sound about right?"

Pulling in a deep breath, I attempted to steady my heartrate while Trevel gasped a chuckle at my side. He clearly hadn't been expecting all that... Honestly, neither was I. But once the words were on the march up my throat, there was no stopping them.

And no matter what happened from that point on, I could finally relax a little. Because I'd come out to my family. My identity was real, not only to me, but to them, whether they accepted it or not.

I was openly bisexual. *Everywhere*, not just in front of my friends, or tucked away on an island.

The way I felt instantly lighter soothed the sting of my father's obvious disgust, as did the feeling of Trevel's hand in mine, and his supportive presence by my side.

No, my father didn't react the way you'd hope one would when coming out. Neither did my mother, who came home right as he was berating me about my *disgraceful lifestyle*. She made sure to urge me not to *throw my life away for a phase*. And neither of them said a goddamn word to Trevel, as expected.

At least my sister had the decency to act fine with it to my face—though she should really learn to control her weirded-out facial expressions a bit better.

Lovely people, I'm telling you.

I was so angry by the time I was storming out, I think the last thing I said to my father was, "I can't wait to turn this place into the gayest gay sex club ever!"

Yea, maybe not my most mature moment, but fuck it. I've been dealing with their bullshit since I was a child. I think I'm entitled to some lashing out, especially since I don't intend to speak to them ever again—or at least for a long time.

"Fuckin' hell, Byron," Trevel had laughed the moment we stepped inside the elevator. "That was amazing! You're a savage."

I huffed, shaking my head. "Right… Now they just think I'm having a gay tantrum. That's why I can never speak to them again… Anything I do from here on out will be because I'm *gay*. Since they don't believe in bisexuality and all. *'Byron's not feeling well; he must have caught something during his gay sex orgy.' 'He never used to laugh like that or smile like that or talk like that… Must be a gay thing.'* All kinds of offensive ass bullshit."

"Baby, who cares what they think?" He moved in close and held me by the waist. "I know you don't."

"You're right, I don't."

"So… Fuck 'em." He shrugged, grinning.

I smiled up at him. "You're so cute when you get all American."

He hummed and leaned over my face to brush our lips. "And you're sexy as fuck when you pop off." He beamed while I laughed. "Seriously, though… That was the best coming out showdown I've ever witnessed. A *little too Raph*, and I'm here for it."

"Love that line," I snickered, arching up to kiss him, just once. A quick soft one to ease any leftover burden from the suckiness of people. And it was all gone, just like that. "You're lucky your parents are dead."

Trevel's head tipped back, and he cackled. It just looked and sounded so damn good, the next thing I knew, I was kissing him *more*, gripping his jaw, pulling his mouth so that I could eat him alive.

"You're so hot, baby. I love you," he whimpered, pressing me up against the wall.

Then I spun him and pressed *him* up against the wall.

I love it. I love *us… Constantly fighting for control and bending the fuck over.*

The elevator doors opened while we were mauling each other, and this super annoying conservative Wall Street guy, Richard something, stood at the entrance, staring at us with his sour puss on.

Pulling back just enough to smirk at him, I crooned, "You might wanna get used to it. We're moving in on twenty-five." Trevel chuckled, and I grabbed his chin. "That's right. It's about to get all kinds of gay up in here."

I pecked him on the lips while Wall Street bitch boy scowled.

Extremely satisfying.

Anyway, that was six weeks ago. *And now we're both officially residents of Manhattan again!*

Don't get me wrong, I loved our little place in Astoria. It was small—we liked to call it *quaint*—but it had a lot of heart, and tons of amazing restaurants nearby. That apartment was good to us, especially after having just returned from Alabaster Isle; after being locked up in a tomb with no fresh air or sunlight.

Or miscellaneous bodega cats to play with whenever we want! It's a travesty.

Even after the prison fell, things certainly were *not* easy. The war, and the confusion of what came next… It was a lot.

When Trevel and I decided to bounce; come back to the city and get a place together, we had an uphill battle. I had to go from the doom and gloom of years in Alabaster Pen to jumping back into the hustle and bustle of New York City without missing a beat. We had some help, but it still took work.

Eventually, we found a place that would rent to us without any in-depth background checks, I got a job as a trainer at our gym, and Trevel went back to accumulating odd jobs as if he were secretly three people.

Seriously, though… It's like he's trying to win some kind of award.

At the end of the day, as long as he's happy, I'm happy. And he likes variety in his work. It's safe to say neither of us are nine-to-fivers—we wouldn't know what to do with ourselves.

For now, Trevel teaches a weekly yoga class at our gym—*I know, right? The fighter and the crunchy granola hippie, it's pretty cute*. He's also a freelance massage therapist, a dog-walker, he works in a flower shop, and he manages a few Airbnb rentals for people. He could've stopped there, but because he's Trevel, he also picked up a few shifts at the Starbucks around the corner. He said he wanted to be a barista because Alice was one. I think it's sweet. And kinda sad, but that's okay.

He's working through his trauma, and I'd say he's doing a fantastic job.

Of course, all of these things are just ways to make money. Our real passion, together as a couple, is writing. Trevel has been working diligently on a poetry book for the last six months or so, and he's almost ready to publish.

As for me, I never saw myself as a writer until Trevel came along and read my journal. Once we were back in the real world, I decided to just start writing and see where it took me. Well, as it happens, it gave me an immense sense of joy. It still does. My *Book of Secrets* was just the beginning.

Last year, I wrote and published a novel based on my life called *The Shadow Man*, and I'm planning to turn my journal into a memoir. Keeping everything independent works for me, because I'm really not doing this for money. It's therapeutic, the same way writing poetry is for Trevel.

I'm not saying my issues are anywhere near his. In fact, they're light years apart. But I still carry a lot of the weight of Alabaster Penitentiary. Trevel says I might have PTSD, but I'm not sure. *Maybe I should see a shrink…*

If you know anyone. Wink.

I struggled with leaving the Isle at first. That place was all I knew for so long. But it was time to start a new chapter.

Separating from Luthor and Ren, Dash and Felix, was tough. After being basically attached, to losing them, getting them back, only to turn around and leave… It was an emotional seesaw for sure. But it wasn't just us leaving. We *all* had bigger plans.

We promised to always stay in touch, and so far, we've been making good on that promise. Trevel and I went out to Mexico a few months back to see Dash and Kemper's house and meet Dog, and we definitely plan on frequent visits to my besties, Luthor and Ren. We've also been able to see Felix and Lem, and the Velle trio pretty often.

It's been working. Things are just… good.

Traveling sustained us for a while, but now that we have the penthouse, I don't see any reason to leave for at least a bit… Until the next vacation, anyway. *But the next AP family reunion is gonna be at our place. I just decided.*

So many things have changed in the last year, it could make my head spin if I let it. But there's one thing that keeps me sane, with just the right amount of crazy... One person who swept into my life like a storm, shaking me up in the best possible way.

My partner in the shadows *and* the light... Trevel bloody Fenwick.

I can't even think about him without smiling. He's just so perfect for me. To think there was ever a time I tried to convince myself I didn't want it, or denied what we were always meant to be to each other is laughable.

Yes, Trevel is an utter and complete nutball. But he's *my* nutball. And I wouldn't want him any other way. I'm proud of him for getting help; doing weekly sessions with Dr. Love via Skype and taking his meds—*prescribed only, no more self-medicating.* But make no mistake, I don't need him to be *normal* to be the love of my life.

Fuck normal. It's for chumps.

Give me an obsessive, needy, six-foot-five filthy-talking big-dicked emo Daddy with an imaginary friend any day.

Trevel doesn't see Leo like he used to, which I am glad about, for his own sanity. But I know he still thinks about him. Ren actually drew him an awesome picture of Leo and mailed it to us. Trevel's going to have him tattoo it next time we get together.

"Cowabunga!"

There's my dark angel...

I chuckle and shake my head, leaning against the marble island while my boyfriend is across the room in the den playing virtual reality surfing in his underwear.

And yes, they're still the skimpy ones that show off his lickable ass and suckable dick print.

What a delicious, sexy, dorky giant, I'm telling you.

"Baby...?" I call to him, questioning whether he can even hear me.

He loves to blast things—music, video games, movies... You name it, Trevel has its volume all the way up.

"Yea, love?" he responds, meaning he *can* hear me. But he's shouting.

My grin widens. "As entertaining as this little performance is, I'm going to get coffee. Are you coming or not?"

"I'm almost done," he yelps, arms out, knees bent like he's actually surfing. "Oh yea! Hang ten, baby!"

"I love you, but I'm going," I huff.

"'Kay, I'll meet you down there in five minutes!"

That means twenty in Trevel-speak. *He's also late for everything.*

I'm not kidding. Yesterday, he was late to a meeting with his boss at Starbucks to discuss his frequent lateness.

Hence why I'm going up the block to Blank Street instead.

I finally manage to pry my eyes away from his tight booty and leave, heading out into another loud, chaotic, beautiful late spring day in NYC. My phone buzzes in my pocket while I walk, and I pull it out to check. It's a new message from Ren in our group chat entitled "AP Family".

We went with the normal name, rather than Ren and Dash's suggestion: *Alabastard Frienditentiary. Or was it Penitentifamily?*

I can't even remember, but it was two weeks of bickering and incessant messages culminating in Velle telling us all to shut the fuck up and naming it "AP Family." Pretty sure Ren wanted to call it "Daddy Velle's Slut Children" after that, but was afraid to send one more message and push Dad over the edge.

Either way, I'm attempting to read the bombarding texts responsibly, lest I walk into oncoming traffic, but it's difficult because Ren is spamming us with pictures of the baby.

No, it's not a human baby. Jesus… Can you imagine??

Luthor and Ren adopted a ten-week-old Boxer-Bulldog puppy last month and named him Parker. Parker Tobias Deon-Xavier. *I know, right? An extremely queer dog name.*

So yea, they've immediately become insufferable gay dog-dads, and it's massively entertaining. Ren is popping off pics of Parker at the beach, and it *is* highly adorable. So much so that I'm not paying attention to where I'm walking…

"Whoa!" a guy gasps when I crash into him.

"Oh, shit! I'm so sorry," I'm apologizing before I can even process what happened.

But then I do. And I freeze like a goddamn wax figure.

"No harm." The voice I haven't heard in over four years chirps. "You're lucky, though… This is my good Bud Light t-shirt," he teases while I'm gawking. "They don't just hand those out to any… body…"

His words roll to a stop, and then flop out of his mouth, now agape as he recognizes me. We're both speechless. Just staring while the rest of the world moves around us like everything is normal.

Like the universe didn't just decide to uppercut me in the soul.

"Byron??" he finally breathes out, bright blue eyes as round as saucers.

"Uh… yea. Hi," I croak, feeling suddenly very dizzy….

Standing in front of Michelangelo Russo.

He still looks exactly the same. Sure, it hasn't been that long, in the grand scheme, but the least he could do is have a beer belly, or a hairline that's receding even just a little. But *no*. He's still drop-dead fucking gorgeous.

Thanks a lot, whoever is controlling my simulation.

I shake myself out of it fast, because this isn't a problem. I can handle this. It's *no big deal…*

I clear my throat. "It's good to, um… see you."

He shakes his head in disbelief for a couple more seconds before his lashes flutter. "Sorry… this is just really tripping me out right now." He huffs, then swallows.

God, I can vividly remember every single time I had my hands around that throat…

Shake. Away. That. Thought.

"I mean… yea. It's good to see you too," he says, voice awed, eyes dipping over me once. Just once, but it's heavier than I expected, and now my face is burning. "You look… Did you get bigger??" He grins, but bites it off quickly. "Thicker, I mean. Just, uh… Sorry, I'm embarrassing myself." He releases a breathy chuckle and clears his throat. "You look good."

My stomach is churning. "You too."

He must notice that I'm radiating a lot more awkward tension than he is, because he backs up and fiddles with his cup of coffee. "It's been… a long time."

I nod robotically, seeing nothing but the night that changed my life. Between his legs, with his hands tied, fucking and crying with him. And then his father ripping me away and the *years* of searing pain that followed.

Governor Russo got a *hero's* funeral. I'm not sure how—what kinds of strings The Ivory had to pull, or what they even said. I purposefully never read or watched anything about it because I couldn't deal with seeing his face while people cried and mourned, like he wasn't the biggest scumfuck on the planet.

"I, um… I should've reached out sooner," he mumbles, shifting nervously. It's interesting, he was always so sweet, kind and quiet. But behind closed doors, he was an entirely different animal. "I know I should've, and I've felt awful about it for years…"

My brows zip. "Oh…?" It's all I can say.

"Yea, I mean, what happened between us was… crazy. And I was afraid…" His voice trails.

He doesn't need to elaborate. I know what he means.

He was afraid of his father.

But how is he thinking he could have reached out?? Did he not know that his father banished me to hell in the middle of the ocean? I guess he wouldn't… But that thought never crossed my mind until right now.

"I really wanted to reach out, you know?" he murmurs softly, topaz twinkling back at me, like it did so many times in the dark… "I've thought about y—"

"There you are!" Trevel's voice assaults my back, followed instantly by his hands on my shoulders, massaging me as he does, absentmindedly. "Oh good, you haven't gone in yet."

Trevel notices that I'm frozen in awkwardness, and he glances at Michelangelo, who's gaping at him. He cocks his head.

At first, it seems like he might ask who this is… But I think it's clear from one look…

The dark hair and the bright blue eyes, the pink lips and sharp jawline.

Like a Ren from another dimension.

"Hi." My boyfriend smiles, though I can see the dark stuff all over his face. "I'm Trevel, Byron's fiancé."

He extends his hand to Michelangelo, following a word that wasn't accurate, though it flowed from his plush lips like the truest thing he's ever said.

I'm gawking up at him, as is Michelangelo while he takes Trevel's hand and shakes it slowly.

"Oh… wow." He coughs. "You're engaged…? Congrats!"

It's the most forced compliment ever, but still, I'm not focused on him anymore.

How is he gonna just call me his fiancé like that??

We're not engaged!

Sure, we talked about it when we were in London, and the thought of asking him gave me the most thrilling sense of fear I've ever experienced. But life got in the way, and it slipped my mind…

Okay, that's bullshit. It's never far in my mind, but I'm scared.

I'm afraid of anything bad happening to ruin this love that lights up my soul.

Forcing down the confusion, I mutter, "Sorry, baby, this is Michelangelo Russo. The late… Governor Russo's son. Michelangelo, this is Trevel Fenwick. My…" I gulp. "Fiancé."

"So lovely to meet you." Trevel pulls a sickeningly sweet smile.

"Likewise." Michelangelo's shock seems to be morphing into something else I don't want to think about.

"I was so sorry to hear about your father," Trevel says. "My condolences."

Michelangelo just nods and stares.

Trevel turns to me. "Baby, I just remembered, I left the stove on."

I blink at him, arching a brow. "The stove?"

When the hell has he ever used the stove??

"Yea, big mess. Stove on, bacon grease… everywhere. The place is probably burning down, so we should probably—" He nods in the direction of our building. "But it was so nice to meet you, Michael."

"Michelangelo," he mutters.

"Hopefully, we get to see you around real soon." Trevel pats him on the shoulder, then takes my hand. "Come now, beautiful."

Nodding, I cast one last glance at the man who I'd *thought* for so long was my first real love. "It was nice… uh, yea."

"You too." Michelangelo bites his lip, but I don't get to see how long he watches us, because my *fiancé* is dragging me up the block.

Scurrying after him, I hiss under my breath, "Fiancé??"

His jaw is visibly tight. "Yea. So?"

"Well, for starters, we're not engaged," I grumble.

"No shit," he grunts under his breath.

I pull to stop him. "Then why'd you say it?"

Trevel glares down at me, violet eyes glowing with jealousy, insecurity, all of it. "Why not?? Because your precious *Michelangelo* was there?? What's wrong with being engaged to me, Byron? Why not me??"

I've never felt such flabbergast sprouting from my face. I have no idea what to say to that.

"Ugh, screw you, Byron," he growls, yanking away to stalk into the building.

I chase after him. "What's your problem?? Why are you being—"

"What?!" he barks. "What am I being??"

I glance at the doorman, forcing a smile to let him know everything is fine, despite Trevel's voice echoing throughout the lobby. I drag him inside the elevator, scanning the key for our floor.

"You're being fucking crazy," I hum, and his eyes burn with rage.

"Am I??"

"Yea!" I crowd him, pushing him against the wall. He doesn't back down, because he's taller than me, and way more stubborn. "You realize you just proposed to yourself, right?"

"Fuck off." He reaches to push me, but I grab his hands and pin them at his sides. When he whimpers, my dick stiffens. "I don't want you to ever see him again..."

I cock my head, gaze stuck on his fluttering mouth. "Who do you think you are?"

"Your fucking *fiancé*," he hisses, directly over my lips. "Face it, Byron... You're going to fucking marry me, because you belong to me."

"Is that right?" I rumble into him, pushing my rapidly hardening cock into his. He mewls, then nods. "You *own me*, violet eyes?"

He nods. "Uh-huh."

"And what makes you think I'd wanna see him again?" I grab his face hard.

He's shivering so hard he's practically convulsing. "Y-you l-loved... him."

"I don't know that I really did," I whisper, dragging my erection along his shape. His lashes flutter. "Not like this..."

"Fuck me..." he whines, as the elevator dings.

"You are such a stubborn, bratty thing, aren't you?" I snarl, dragging him out into the hall. Slamming him up against the door to the penthouse, I drop my hand between his legs, groaning when I feel how big and thick he is. "The best needy little psycho slut ever..."

"*Mmmff*... baby, put it in me. Right here..."

I huff, opening the door with one hand while the other continues to fondle him. "You've gotten me in enough trouble, bad boy."

Once inside, things are fast and scorching hot. Our mouths are together, tongues tangling. I stuff my hand inside his pants and fist his big cock, stroking him until he purrs.

"Fffuck yea," Trevel whines. "Mmm... I love the way you touch me..."

"Yea?" My head is twirling, shaky fingers ripping at our clothes to get them out of the way.

"You touch only me, sweet fury," he whines.

Shirts off, pants shoved down, I kneel when I pull his to his feet, gazing up at him from the floor, his cock thick and heavy, bobbing and leaking in front of my face.

"You mean I only get this dick?" I rasp, licking and sucking on it.

Trevel's eyes roll back in his head. "Fuck yea..."

Using my hand, I pull the skin back so I can work his tip over with my tongue, tasting him. "Mmm. Give me that sweet sweet, naughty boy."

"Uhhhfuck, Byron!" he cries, his cock throbbing into my mouth. I suck it out and swallow with a satisfied hum.

"Oh, baby, that's so good… Is this the only cum I get to taste?"

"Uh-huh." He nods, quivering and panting, legs parting wider.

I slide my fingers curiously between his cheeks, and he mewls.

"Forever?" I whisper as I play with his hole.

"Bloody fuckin' hell, baby, yes… *Yes yes yes*, I'm yours forever."

My heart is soaring, sweat breaking out over my flesh. I lick my fingers just enough that I can push them in him a little, middle finger sliding inside. He sucks me right in, and both of our cocks pulse.

"Whose little hole is this?" I growl, lapping at his dick, and his balls, swirling my finger in his tight ass.

"Yours, Byron," he gasps. "*Mmm*-my hole belongs to you."

"Forever…?" I purr again.

He shudders. "God… *yeessss*. Sweet fury, will you get in me? I wanna come with you stretching me open…"

"You know I can't resist you." I kiss his cock, thrusting my finger inside a few more times before I stand up. "That's why you act like such a jealous, possessive, crazy fucking brat… Because you know I like it."

He whines when I hoist him up onto the countertop, pushing his legs open.

"You fucking have me, don't you, gorgeous boy?" I palm his cock and knead his balls roughly until he arches. Then I grab the nearest thing that could be lube… Some coconut oil. "My pretty little slut wants this cock that he *owns* inside his tight pussy?"

"God, you're gonna make me come just t-talking…"

I chuckle, slathering oil onto my inches, then between his cheeks.

"I'm gonna push in, baby…" I growl. "Take all of this big dick at once, okay, violet?"

He's nodding, crumbling and heaving as I nudge, then grab his hips, and then thrust. One deep push, and I'm settled between his legs with my cock all the way in. His dick is leaving a puddle on his abs, and it's the sexiest thing ever.

"Ohh, baby… That's right. Open that warm little hole for your man."

"Unngghhfuck." He's writhing, squirming, squeezing my hands on his hips. "*Fuck* it… fuck m-my… spot."

"God, you're a beauty, baby." I pull back then press in, dragging a garbled cry out of him. "Am I fucking you right?"

"*Yes yes yes yes yes*, there there, please!"

"I love you so much, Trev," I whimper, dropping to lick the cum off of his stomach. Then, I force my tongue into his mouth, and he sucks at it greedily. "I can't believe you'd think I could want anyone else…"

"I'm… s-sorry…

"Yea, you are. Don't doubt my loyalty, tight, perfect thing." Kissing him, I'm smacking my hips between his legs, fucking my cock into his hole rough. It's so tight it's sucking me, squeezing and gripping.

"I won't, baby," he breathes out, fingers in my hair.

"You love me?"

"I—*fuuuuck*—I love you so much." Trevel wraps his legs around my waist, getting me as deep as our bodies will allow.

I'm going out of my mind, pumping him full while we groan and growl and sob. I'm getting close, and I can tell he is too by the way his thighs are tightening.

Licking and sucking at his nipples brutally, I purr, "I'm almost there, Trev…"

"Byron… mmff baby, please…"

"Please what?"

"Ask me…" His back arches. "Oh fuck, ask me to marry you, baby… And then come in me. I'm gonna *come*, sweet… fury…"

I chuckle breathlessly, teasing his dick. The feel of it hard in my hand is going to push me over the edge. "You wanna marry me, gorgeous love?"

He nods.

"You wanna be my husband…?"

"Yes…"

"You want me to breed you 'cause you're mine?"

"Uhhhfuck, *forever*. Forever, Byron… I'm coming!"

His long cock shoots cum all over him, while I milk it out in my fist. Matching his spurts with bucks, I reach my orgasm while he's still coming, the clamping of his hole welcoming my hot, thick pulses.

"God, Trevel… *fuck yea*, baby." I take his left hand in mine and suck his ring finger into my mouth, sucking and sucking on it while I come deep inside him.

"I'm yours I'm yours… I wanna be… *your* husband." He melts into a puddle beneath me on the counted.

I'm humming, releasing his finger to kiss his gasping lips. "You're my prison husband," I fizzle down, and he snorts.

"I want you to be my actual wife," he says through a yawn. I grin. "You better ask me one of these days… I'm sick of waiting."

My thoughts go to the ring in my pocket… The one I've been carrying around since we left the island.

"I promise I'll make you mine forever, Trevel Fenwick." I kiss him softly, and he hums. "I love you."

"I love you brighter than a million Times Squares." He chuckles.

"Moon, and sun…" I whisper the words he said to me, over a year ago. "And all the light between… You're it for me, baby. No one before you matters."

He blinks up at me, and whispers, "I know."

Pulling out, I ogle him for a moment, all flushed and gushy and so perfectly *mine*, it's not even fair. Sure, I have memories. We both do… But they don't hold a candle to *this*…

Psycho shit. I love it.

Bending to grab my pants, I reach inside my pocket, chest fluttering with nerves. But then my phone rings.

Trevel peeks at me, smiling and content. Happy. *I love that look.*

"It's probably just Ren calling to blab about the puppy some more," I mutter, and he chuckles.

But when I pull my phone out, I see a Las Vegas number. And my heart falls with a *thud* into my gut.

"What's wrong, babe?"

Oh, fuck…

I know I should ignore it. I should just… decline the call.

But I don't. I swipe to answer.

Tentatively bringing the phone to my ear, I mumble, "Hello?"

And the voice of Manuel Blanco croons into my ear. "Hello, Shadowman."

To Be Continued…

Here's an EXCLUSIVE SNEAK PEEK of Ivory, Alabaster Penitentiary Volume 6, THE FINALE:

Angel

WHEN I WAS THREE YEARS OLD, I MET THE DEVIL.

I didn't know it at the time… Turns out, everything they say about him is true.

He hides quite well in plain sight.

But he doesn't blend into the background. No, that wouldn't work. It would be impossible *not* to see him. Instead, he lures you in, flatters, manipulates and comforts, giving the illusion of loyalty.

He's very good at what he does.

El diablo esta astuto.

He had woven himself into the fibers of my family. Earned their trust, and he did it well. He *was* good… And my father was weak.

In the end, though, a debt must be paid. That is what I learned as a child, as I cowered and sniffled, hand clasped tightly over my mouth to keep quiet. Eyes wide with terror.

I saw evil that day, and it looked right at me. It *saw* me.

Yet I was spared. I wasn't taken… Not *then*, anyway.

I hate to admit it, but I learned a lot from him; el diablo. And anything he didn't teach me, I learned because of him. One way or another, he is responsible for so much of what my life has become. Whether that's good or bad remains to be seen, but I prefer not to give him the satisfaction of thinking he molded me…

I'm sure he'd love that all too much.

For now, I will focus on the things I've done for *myself*, what I've discovered, and how hard I've trained. How diligently I've worked over the years… It's been my sole motivation for so long, I can barely remember a life outside of *him*.

I hate it.

That's good. I need to hate. I need to loathe, and remember *why*. Because sometimes it's easy to forget… *When he's close.*

Teeth clamping together, I close my eyes, taking in a deep breath. Reminding myself to be in the present. Not to dwell so much on the things

I can't change. It's difficult for me… *Life* is difficult, and it has been since I was just a boy who lost his parents. Forced to grow up way too fast…

Again, because of him.

The ocean breeze brushes through my hair, and I let it settle me. The smell of the saltwater and the mist of it touching my skin. When I reopen my eyes, I see it. *We're close…*

I glance over myself, my body in this outfit. My hands run down the silken fabric, and I buzz inside.

I bite my lip.

"Hey," a sultry male voice comes from behind me and I startle, tipping my chin. "Are you new? I haven't seen you before."

Swallowing hard, I attempt to calm my instant nerves, and nod. "I am."

He's very good-looking, in a fair, yet defined way, like me. Though his skin is pale, and his hair is platinum blonde. A face of all sharp angles, in contrast to his full pink lips. He looks like a model.

I'm instantly insecure.

But then he smiles, a dazzling thing, though it's kind, like his deep green eyes. "I always love meeting a newbie. I'm Soren."

"Ari," I try not to stammer. I've practiced this dozens of times, but it's still overwhelming… Actually being here, so close.

"You're, like, *way* too pretty." He pouts playfully. "I'm not sure if standing next to you will make me look better by association, or worse by comparison."

I have to snort at that.

Soren leans up against the railing, facing me rather than the view from the top deck. "So what brings you here?"

Revenge.

"I like to party, and I need the money," I serve him my rehearsed answer. "What else?"

He chuckles. It's a great sound; melodious and sweet. *I think I like him.*

"You're cute, Ari." He tilts his head. "Stick with me. I'll show you the ropes." He winks, and I think my cheeks are warming.

But I don't have time to obsess over it, because we're about to dock.

We've arrived… At Alabaster Isle.

"Come on." Soren takes me by the arm, guiding me to the stairs.

Okay… I guess we're besties.

I'm not mad at it. I could certainly use a friend. Especially one who knows *the ropes…*

We disembark; myself, Soren, and a group of eleven others, by my count. Not including the staff—two large, quiet men who have been instructing us on where to go and what to do.

They're the ones who explained the rules, and handed out the NDA's for us to sign. None of it was a surprise to me. I knew what to expect going in. After all, this has been the plan for quite some time.

The rules are simple… No phones. No talking about the island. No leaving the left side of the mansion. *That's the one I might have to break…*

We're here purely for entertainment purposes, and we aren't allowed to leave until the ferry goes back to the mainland on Sunday. Not that we'd have any other way to get off the island…

The group of us are ushered into a few black SUV's, and driven up the coast of the island. And all the while, my pulse is steadily increasing, with every inch we cruise closer to the giant palace of alabaster elegance.

The closer we get to…

My fingers roll the material of my dress between my fingers as I shift subtly in the soft leather seat. I still can't tell if I'm comfortable or not, and it's bothering me. I don't like not being able to identify my feelings—something he's a true master at weaving in people. El diablo, he has this magnetic force when he's nearby that frays confidence and breeds uncertainty.

Just one of his many powers.

"Relax," Soren whispers to me, noting my fidgets, which naturally makes me even more self-conscious. "You'll do fine. Velle will love you. And if you're in with him, you won't have to worry about anything else."

My stomach twists into an even tighter knot. I don't want my new friend to think I'm unappreciative of his camaraderie, so I nod and offer him a grateful smile. But his pep talk is only making me more nervous.

Yes, I know about John Chevelle. And I would stand to agree that getting in his good graces will be helpful…

But is he… too close? If he is, it might be difficult…

That's the question I'll need to find an answer to.

The vehicle comes to a stop, and we all file out. The sun is just setting, casting a pale orange glow over the scenery. Ocean on one side, forest on the other. It's truly quite breathtaking, but the thing that steals every ounce of oxygen from my lungs is what's towering before me…

The Ivory Mansion.

"Diablo…" I whisper, eyes wide, chest caving.

"What's that, sweetie?" Soren asks, and I shake myself out of it.

"N-nothing," I stutter. "This place is…"

"Yea, it's massive," he chuckles. "Sorta creepy inside, but you get used to it."

He takes me by the hand, tugging me along with the rest of them as the security team brings us all inside through the front. Double-doors, large, black, with brushed brass fixtures. On the way inside, I sneak a peek at the ornate door knocker… In the shape of a birdcage.

I swallow a jagged lump in my throat.

"Huyes de tu jaula, pajarito…"

Once inside, we're immediately guided left, toward a large staircase. But my eyes are coveting the right. The side of the mansion we're not allowed to enter…

Still, I'm becoming distracted by the sheer size of this place. All of the research in the world couldn't have prepared me for what it would actually be like…

From the decor, to how *big* it all is; opulent, *regal* grandeur with an underlying sense of malevolence. To the naked eye, it's luxurious and majestic. But the immorality is palpable, and my heart is instantly racing, almost too fast.

This *is* him. I feel it in the air, in every square inch of this monstrosity.

What have you created here, diablo?

What did you do…

"Dios… ayúdame," I mumble under my breathe.

At the top of the stairs, the security team spouts off a warning for us to remember the rules, but no one seems to be listening to them. I think I'm the only one who's new here, because the moment we reach the third floor, they all scatter, as if they're familiar enough with the place to know where they want to go.

I'm left slowly wandering the long corridor, following Soren—*sort of*—but getting lost in studying everything. My eyes scan floor to ceiling, taking in the ambience of dimmed light from lantern sconces, accentuating the deep red paint with the occasional black accent, erotic artwork, brass and bronze fixtures… Baroque, and beautiful in its own very ominous way.

It's ridiculously familiar, and I have to scoff to myself for a moment.

Would you look at that? I'm back at the house in Bogotá…

Voices ring out from up the hall as music begins to play, soft at first, until someone cranks the volume.

"Ari!"

I'm lingering outside of a bedroom whose door is ajar, peering inside. No one's in there, but it's pretty big.

"Hey, Ari!"

People are cheering in the distance. I suppose the party is getting started right away. *Makes sense.*

I'm about to push the door open a bit more when someone grabs me, and I flinch. "Uh, Earth to Ari," Soren chuckles. "I've been calling you..."

I gulp and blink. "Sorry..."

Get used to the name, Angel... You picked it.

"Come on, party favors are out." He grins, yanking me up the hall, where I'm assuming everyone is gathered to begin their evening with alcohol and drugs.

Fluttering nerves encompass me. *Blend in... Be a chameleon. It's the only way.*

"I, uh... is there a... restroom I can use?" I ask him, pumping on the breaks.

Soren is distracted by a guy setting up lines on a bronze tray as he motions with his hand. "Yea, door on the end."

I locate the bathroom, slinking inside and locking the door. After I triple-check that it's definitely locked, I can breathe a bit easier. I step up to the vanity and assess myself in the mirror.

Combing fingers through my hair, I blink at my reflection. The person staring back at me... I smooth out my dress and adjust myself.

I look like her...

It's good. This is by no means the first time I've done this, but it still always shocks me. How easily I can look like her when I want to. How much this settles me sometimes...

I wish I could wrap my head around it fully, but it's hard, because so much of what I do is wrapped up in anger... And vengeance.

Running hands down my front, I verify that everything is securely in place. I take a deep breath, and I leave the restroom to join the party. But when I return to the hall and hear the raucous noise of my fellow party-goers, I bite my lip, chin tipping in the opposite direction.

There appear to be guards emerging from their rooms at the sound of the party, dressed in uniform. One of them is griping about the *night shift*.

When the coast is clear, I slink down the hall toward the stairs. The front door opens, and I slip around a corner, peering over the balcony of the third floor landing.

"Don't piss me off, Rookie," a male voice barks from downstairs. "I'm not in the mood."

I watch as two big guys storm inside, also in uniform. The taller guy has dark, chin-length hair, tied back in a tiny bun, whereas the shorter guy has sandy-blonde hair, and a much more *country* look about him.

"Sorry… I just thought you might—"

"No one's paying you to think," the larger, surlier of the two cuts the other guy off. "Just do your job and shut up until it's time to stop." He pauses, eyes flinging in my direction. I duck out of sight. "Sounds like the festivities are getting started…" I peek down in time to catch him slapping the blonde guy on the back, hard enough that the dude winces. "Do us all a favor… and lighten up."

That's him.

I don't even need confirmation. That *has* to be John Chevelle.

He turns toward the stairs, the blonde guy looking after him, longingly and a bit dejected. He's about to follow when dress shoes on the marble floor stop them both in their tracks.

My heart is instantly in my throat. My anatomy is sizzling, chills breaking out over my exposed skin.

"Go on upstairs," Velle mumbles, eyes fixed in the direction the footsteps are coming. "Grab a drink, do a line. Just… whatever."

He saunters away from the blonde guy, toeing the line between right and left. The blonde guy's shoulders slump visibly, but he doesn't come upstairs. He stays on the first floor, stomping off in a different direction.

But I'm no longer focused on either of them. I'm too busy gripping the edge of the bannister with white knuckles, eyes rounded in wait.

Officer Chevelle is speaking to someone. I can't hear what they're saying, and I can't *see* him, and it's driving me mental. I feel like I could crawl out of my skin.

Fortunately, they're only speaking for a minute, and then the *clack clack clack* resumes. I'm chewing my cheek so hard I taste blood, limbs tense, my entire frame stiff and sickeningly anxious. It's purgatory… It always is. *Awaiting* him.

Until suddenly there's a beam of light, like a lightning strike.

Diablo…

"Ahí estas…" My pulse is thumping so hard it's rocking my body.

The magic fades when I remember myself, jaw clenching tightly, leering after him as he ascends his staircase. As if *everything* is normal.

It's all fine… I'm the King, the ruler of this dark castle, and nothing else matters…

Yea, we'll see about that.

I'm startled out of my simmering when I realize that Officer Chevelle is on his way up the stairs.

"Shit..." My first instinct is to hide, but then I remember that I'm an invited guest.

Straightening, I take a deep breath, slinking back toward the party just as the large form is arriving on the third floor. He stomps past me without a glance, and I watch him closely, observing his rigid posture and his brooding expression.

He doesn't seem happy.

Poor thing... I get it.

Velle makes a beeline toward the room that I was peeking inside before—*it must be his bedroom*—but he stops before entering. He turns over his shoulder, casting me a brief glare, eyes sliding me up and down. Something in them makes me want to cower.

I feel like he can see right through me, and it's unsettling.

There's an intruder in our midst...

I simply blink at him, striding as carefully as possible past the guard dog and hoping like hell it won't bite.

Good doggy... nice doggy.

It's okay... I'm on your side.

Eventually, he pries his narrowed gaze off of me and slips into his room, slamming the door behind him. Releasing a long breath of relief, I place my palm over my heart. It's leaping up to my hand.

I'm *alive* here. I feel this, *all of it*, in my bones.

Stepping timidly over to the door that just closed, I lean in, and rest my forehead to the wood. I'm fighting back unexpected tears, and I don't know why. The pressure in my skull anchors my head to the door.

I'm six years old again, the smell of copper in the air. Screams, and that same damn *clack clack clack* ringing in my ears as I watch him walk away.

"Whatever he's done to you..." I whisper, seeing him stop in my mind, "lo siento."

It's not my fault, but I'm still sorry.

Because he's all over me, coursing through my veins, and I can't stand it. Every moment that he's still breathing feels like my responsibility, and I know that's crazy, but I can't help it.

I feel like I summoned him, or something. And now, on behalf of my bloodline, it's my job to exorcise him back to the pits of Hell where he belongs.

In spite of the fervent thrill, my fingers curl to a fist. "I promise, for you, for me... para la casa Alvarez... I will make him *pay*."

RESOURCES

For a full list of resources, visit my website: authornylak.com/resources

If you're thinking of harming yourself, please know that it's not the answer. You are loved, and no matter how dark it can feel at times, all life is a gift.

Dial 988, or visit 988lifeline.org if you need help.

For LGBTQIA+ resources and assistance, visit www.thetrevorproject.org - The Trevor Project for LGBTQ youth in crisis.

Find more information here: glaad.org

For Transgender resources and assistance, visit: transequality.org
For assistance with Transgender legal matters, visit: transgenderlawcenter.org

If you or anyone you know is struggling with substance abuse or mental health issues, please seek help. There is a light at the end of even the darkest tunnels.
www.samhsa.gov - Substance abuse and mental health services.

www.projecthealthyminds.com - End the stigma on mental health
www.mentalhealthishealth.us - Mental health resources

If you need an ear or a shoulder, I'm always here at info@authornylak.com. It might take me a bit to respond, but I will. Middle fingers up. Perfect is overrated. Never stop fighting.

A NOTE FROM THE AUTHOR

Well, well, well… Look who finished this EPIC TALE of dark and depraved fiction. You must feel *pretty* proud of yourself, huh? *You should!* Because you're officially one step closer to the conclusion!

I'm going to attempt to keep this brief—*she says before writing a zillion words*—because this is already close to the longest book I've ever written. It's sitting pretty at 225k words. To put that into perspective, that's about 25k more than *Fragments*, which means the books in this series are only getting longer. I have no idea how long *Ivory* will end up being, but at the rate I'm going, it'll be a 900-page paperback.

And the craziest part is that this was never even supposed to be a book! Originally, the series was planned as five books (which is why for the longest time, Goodreads was showing *Ivory* as Book 5, despite numerous requests for them to fix it. *Here's hoping it's right now, but I won't hold my breath.*) The point is, Byron Kang was always a side-character. A lovable, grumpy sidekick who was just another inmate on the roster. But as time went on, and I got to know him more, I realized there was no possible *way* I could leave him in the shadows. That boy had a story, and dammit, I was gonna let him tell it!

Well, tell it he did. *And he spared no details, clearly.*

The other half of that is our tall, mysterious British newcomer… Otherwise known as Harry Potter's drug dealer, Slenderman, aloof Jack Skellington, Sid Vicious's creepy cousin, or Benedict Arnold Cumberbatch (*that one's my favorite*). Honestly, I don't think people realize how clever my characters are sometimes.

Anyway, Trevel Fenwick was a new addition to the AP cast. After showing up in *Brainwashed*, he became another unplanned, yet pleasant surprise. And as soon as Trevel came into the fold, I just *knew* he'd be the one to bring our Byron out of hiding.

So, did you notice what I was saying in the foreword… about this being like two books in one? It is, isn't it? That might've been what made this one of the most difficult editing experiences of my life. And let me tell you, I *live* for the editing process. It's my bread and butter! But this one put me through the wringer. I was *really* trying not to have it be 8 million pages long, but there was just *so much* to cover. I needed to give Byron his time to shine, and connect you to this completely new character, while also unveiling mysteries from the existing storyline that we've been anxiously awaiting!

Eventually, I had to give in to this book being long as shit. And while we *did* get a bunch of answers we've been waiting for, there are still so many more secrets left to be revealed!

One of my favorite things about this series is how different each book is from the last. Not only do we have different couples—or throuples—falling in love and banging like there's no tomorrow, but the style of each book is also unique. This one came together similarly to *Brainwashed*, in that it took a while for Byron and Trevel to even meet—not something that's typical, or recommended in romance. But you know me... I've never been one for following rules (*wink*). And like I said, this isn't just a romance between two relationship virgins without a single clue how to be together (*hence the term I've coined: "delulu-to-lovers"*.)

It's a vast exploration into the characters, their issues, and the ways in which Alabaster Penitentiary ultimately brings them together. Not to mention covering years of backstory, the "present timeline" (the same one covered in each book), the aftermath of the storm, and the war... It's a lot! I mean, *dang*.

Speaking of the actual "timeline" of Alabaster Penitentiary, you have to expect a certain level of fictionality. The most difficult thing about writing this series has been making sure all of these timelines match up, from *Distorted* to the end. Between thirteen POVs and six total happily ever afters that need to somehow all culminate in the same ending, I was tearing my hair out more than once when things didn't *exactly* line up. Seasons are endless, years are shorter and then somehow longer... Let's just chalk it up to time being a construct on the Isle. *I honestly have no idea how Quentin Tarantino does it...*

Which is a nice segue into something I wanted to mention about inspiration. I believe I have mentioned before that I'm hugely influenced by Quentin Tarantino movies. *Pulp Fiction, Once Upon A Time In Hollywood, and Kill Bill* in particular have played (and will continue playing) huge roles in my creative thought process for this series. I'm sure I've also mentioned this somewhere before, but I also found inspiration in two of my favorite television series: *Breaking Bad*, and *The Walking Dead*.

If you're a hardcore fan of either of these shows, you might even pick up on a few of the subtle tributes... One of my *favorites* being The Ivory, who was loosely based on the character Gustavo Fring from *Breaking Bad*.

Of course, I say *loosely based* because The Ivory is very much his own entity, but I have really loved developing him into this sort of elusive, omnipotent supervillain, something I will obviously dive much deeper into when we get to the next book… Our *conclusion*, which will also be The Ivory's redemption—*sort of (lol)*.

Many of you are *convinced* you will never love him. I'm here to tell you that you will. I don't make the rules. *Oh, wait…*

Part of this book required a lot of action and suspense-inspiration; basically everything that occurs after "the fall". I'm a huge *Walking Dead* fan—I'm not caught up on any of the spin-offs, but the original series is my jiggity jam. This is another series with excellent villains, that plays with the notion of "good" versus "bad". Things like found family, survival during extreme circumstances, loyalty, betrayal, and ultimately war between two sides all come into play, and playing with them was a lot of fun for me, especially as a fan of such shows.

Another thing I *have* to mention is the abundance of TMNT references. Now, I've always loved the *Teenage Mutant Ninja Turtles*. But Byron and Trevel's obsession with them took on a life of its own. It seeped into *everything*, from the colors of the corresponding turtles (we'll come back to that), personality traits, nicknames… And of course Leo.

The concept of "Leo" as Trevel's imaginary friend came to me in the early stages of plotting this book. To go off-topic and bring up *another* TV show that I love, have you ever seen *Happy*? It was a show on the SyFy network starring Chris Meloni (aka Daddy Stabler), and Patton Oswalt as the voice of "Happy," the imaginary friend of Meloni's character, Nick Sax's daughter, which was *tragically* cancelled after only two seasons—*one of the great travesties of television history, as far as I'm concerned*. Anyway, I've always loved the darker side of imaginary friends—see also: *Donnie Darko* and for Trevel Fenwick, having this deranged ninja bear sidekick made perfect sense.

For most of the book, Leo seems like sort of a negative influence on Trevel, which is odd, considering that Leonardo is the leader and the most moral of all the Turtles. But when we get to his POV in chapter 28, we really see how much of a coping mechanism he is for Trevel. At the end of the day, he *is* an extension of Trevel, and Trevel knows that. But growing up the way he did, having such a tragic past, Trevel needed guidance he wasn't getting anywhere else. He needed a friend, a confidante… He needed a partner in crime. That was Leo… until Byron comes along, that is.

Next up, on the subject of side characters named after Ninja Turtles, we have one Michelangelo Russo. I have to tell you, the governor's son was originally supposed to be an antagonist. I mean, he *was* sleeping with Byron's "girlfriend", after all! (Side note, how cute was it that Byron actually thought Rey was his girlfriend?? I had more written about Byron's Rey obsession, but I had to cut it. Still, his stalking was a fun little surprise when developing his character.)

Back to Michelangelo, the original plan was for him to be an asshole. Governor Russo was always going to be responsible for sending Byron to AP, but when Byron began writing out his origin story, in the form of his Book of Secrets, Michelangelo just wasn't cooperating as an equally atrocious human being. He insisted on being sweet and adorable, and just the right amount of secretly kinky that allowed Byron to explore his latent bisexuality. He's basically Ren, if Ren didn't have a treasure trove of issues rolling around in his pretty noggin. Hence, Byron's attraction to Ren.

"Proxy jobs" play such a significant part in this entire series, it's almost as if Ren didn't invent it at all. *Don't tell him that, though.* But seriously, *everyone* be pulling the proxy in the Pen! And there will be much more on the origin of the "proxy" in *Ivory*, just saying.

Michelangelo *could* be the reason the *Shadowman* cover is orange! Well, maybe one reason. But color comes up a lot in this series, in things like the corresponding cover colors, characters' eyes, belongings—"Zadira", Dash's car, being purple, and "Raphael", Byron's street bike, being red. In his epilogue, Trevel mentions a bracelet he made for Byron out of sunstone and carnelian. Those stones are both orange, and they promote health and wellbeing, courage, vitality, and creativity, all of which are things that Byron and Trevel can embrace in their new lives, post-Pen.

Okay I'll shut up about the Ninja Turtles... After this: it's not lost on anyone, I'm sure, that our little "Pen Boy Posse" has a Michelangelo (Ren), a Donatello (Luthor), a Raphael (Byron), and a Leonardo (Dash). *Is Dash really a Leonardo, though??* Maybe not in *Distorted*, per se. But in *Shadowman*, when he returns to the Isle like a boss, only *hell yea.*

The found-family vibes of this series are strong by this point, and they're only getting stronger. I'm telling you, there was *nothing* more satisfying than having all of our boys reunited! Despite the grief and drama that had to go down before we got there. I really hope you guys loved that stuff, because it delighted me to my core—having Dash show up, followed by Luthor and Ren, when everyone thought they were dead! I mean, *come on*… It was what we've all been waiting for, wasn't it?!

I'll talk about the ending in a minute, but just a couple more quick things. First, I definitely need to mention Alice. That was a very significant and difficult part of Trevel's backstory, but also of the story as a whole. You might remember, in *Brainwashed*, the reason Dr. Love had to leave was because Trevel had killed again—it's mentioned that he "killed his girlfriend, her brother and a busboy." Those details have been a part of the storyline we knew was coming, which would play a big role in the storyline overall, because of The Ivory factor (we'll get to that).

So as much as it hurt to have Alice die, it was a major event, that was not at all done in vain. Of course, we now know that Trevel didn't kill Alice. Sure, he was a shitty boyfriend, but he did care for her deeply. The fact that both Trevel and Byron were recovering from significant and ultimately tragic relationships is a major part of what brought them together. And that both of their exes were great people, not evil ones, makes the whole thing a lot sadder.

Although I must say, to *me* this is significant. So many times, we see characters coming out of shitty past relationships. To have them both heartbroken after losing great people, felt unique and complex to me.

As mentioned in the foreword, certain parts of this series are much darker than others. I enjoy seeing the varying shades, from light gray to pitch black. I like to think it verifies that nothing done in this series is done for "shock value", or in order to be edgy. This isn't dark romance for the sake of being dark. It's fiction with realistic values, and that's one thing that makes this series so special.

Byron and Trevel's relationship is a unique one, that's for sure. They start out as sort of fuck-buddy confidantes, having long, elaborate bouts of luscious sex—*do I even know how to write a sex scene less than 5k words anymore?* And there's a lot of confusion and insecurity, sexual attraction fading seamlessly into reluctant feelings. But it's all these things that bring them back together in the end. It's unconventional af, and I love it.

Quick thing… *How did we like Trevel's poetry??* Personally, I was thrilled about it, because I've always loved writing poems (and songs), but I don't get to do it often. I had more of his poems I couldn't include because the book was too long as it is, but I plan to share them with Patreon, so if you're ever in that neck of the woods, check it out!

Having Byron end up as a fighter/writer was really the icing on the cake of his character development for me. *Just saying.*

Before we talk about the ending, I want to quickly mention the nicknames. There are a lot of them in this book! *It's almost as if I couldn't settle on just one because I'm indecisive as shit and so are my characters.* Trevel calls Byron "sweet fury" (based on the tattoo on his chest), and "Raph" (obviously for Raphael), and "warrior" (because it's cute and accurate). And Byron calls him "violet eyes", "Leo", and at one point "danger boy" (which is a nod to one of my favorite obscure af 90's cartoons, *Aeon Flux*). Plus, "By" and "Trev", 'cause adorbz. And doesn't it seem like The Ivory comes up with interesting nicknames for everyone? *I wonder if there's a reason for that, or if he's just Daddy asf (lol).*

The ending of this book was a tough one. I always knew it would end with the gang back together amidst a war, leaving us on a massive cliffhanger with the final reveal of a name... Meaning that giving Byron and Trevel their happily ever after and the epilogues I love using to showcase such things was complicated. The only way to do so was to go a year in the future. I know some books end that way—seeing the characters finally admitting their feelings, then sorta just ending it and jumping a year in the future. But I usually like to give my couples a chapter or two together before the end. Unfortunately, we couldn't do that with this one, so hopefully their happiness came across in the epilogues. Because they are deliriously happy. But make no mistake... There's still so much more to come!

In the interest of shutting the fuck up because I've written more words in the last two months than in the previous eighteen months, I'll wrap this up with one last juicy morsel... And his name is Angel Alvarez. ;)

Remember the knife Felix used to kill O'Malley? Engraved with the initials A.A., and a bird wrapped in barbed wire? *Yea... muy importante.* The fact that Trevel was brought in to AP because he killed someone with those same initials... Again, extremely fucking relevant. As is the conversation with Rook's dad at the end. All of these things and more—*where are Luthor and Ren now? Why did Dash end up in The Ivory's custody when he got back to the Isle? Who was that girl with the auburn hair Byron recalled following in his book...?*

Will we see more of Colson, Cyrus, and Tauren? (*Thanks for the helicopter, by the way, Daddy T.*) Who was this *mystery girl* The Ivory was keeping in the prison? Is Carson okay? (*And is Peters freaking out about him being held hostage in the control room? P.S. how cute are Hancock and Jasper?!*)

All of this and *oh so much more* to come in the conclusion, which will undoubtedly kill me. I broke down, in a few ways, writing this book. And if that's any indication of how the finale will be, then I'm in for a world of dark and delicious hurt.

I'm telling you, of all the things I've done in my writing career, *this series* is my masterpiece. You either get it, or you don't. But if you do, I cannot wait for you to experience the bittersweet end with me... *Five whole years* in the making.

I have a lot of tricks up my sleeve for this one. Everything we didn't get to cover will be resolved, I *assure* you.

In the meantime, get ready to fall for a villain... *Finalmente.*

ACKNOWLEDGMENTS

A lot of what I do gives *lone wolf*, but in this business, there's no way to do it all on your own—no matter how badly my control-freakish self wants me to. Writing this book was incredibly difficult… Coming off an excruciating burnout, not having published anything in nearly two years… Needless to say, I was stressed during basically this entire process.

But we did it. *We made it!* And for that, there are some people I need to thank…

First off, my family. Patrick, my partner in crime… You drive me absolutely insane. I'm fully confident this book would have been out a year ago if it weren't for you. So my turning into a complete goblin in the month prior to releasing this book is payback for that. I love you, despite your craziness. You're very much the Michelangelo in my life, and I'll always be grateful for all the ways you're different from me, whether it gives me ulcers or not.

To Team Nyla… My mom, Debbie, for holding down the website business and taking a massive and super annoying weight off of my shoulders. To Amber, you're not only my PA. You're my friend, my soulmate, and the person who tries to wrangle me like the wild stallion I am (LOL). And to Karie, my sweet little Tinkerbell. Thank you for all that you do, all the hype and the graphic stuff I'm not good at. It's not easy to be the assistants of a control freak who can't let go of anything, and who disappears for days at a time… So thank you endlessly for all that you do. You make my life infinitely easier, you're my squad, and with friends like you in my corner, the sky is NOT the limit, because the limit does not exist.

To my editor, Kay; darling, you had your work cut out for you with this one. The first draft of this manuscript was a literal dumpster fire, and after not working with me for almost two years, I'm sure you came back like… *fuck*. But you never complain, you never try to stifle me, and you understand who I am as a writer, which is why I'll never use anyone else. Because I don't need an *editor*, I need someone with an eagle-eye who understands the subjectivity of art. Fuck structure, fuck word count standards, and fuck what you're *supposed* to do. Rules are made to be broken. Our ride or die motto!

To Kenzie from Nice Girl Naughty Edits… GORRRLLL. Two years and I come back more chaotic than ever… I'm amazed that you haven't told me to go fuck myself yet (LOL give it time). No, you wouldn't. Because you're the sweetest person ever, the best person to have on my team, and just an overall talented, driven, amazing human. You're the organized presence that I'm not, and I love that for me (and hate it for you lol). I apologize for being a nightmare and giving you this book in three sections because I was still editing a week after we were supposed to be done. We made it! That's all that matters lol!

To Ashlee, of Ashes and Vellichor… What a year we've had together (HAHA!) Shit's been crazy, but the one thing I know I can count on is your raw, unapologetic talent. Thank you for saving me (*yes, I'll keep saying it*), for creating these stunning covers that perfectly encapsulate the series, and for being a shoulder when I need to rant about things in this community (lol). Slayyyy, kween.

To Stacey Blake of Champagne Book Designs… Thank you for formatting these books beautifully, for dealing with my chaos, and for always being there to help me on a dime. You're a rockstar!

To Hong Phi Filler, the model I randomly approached out of nowhere after a reader sent me a DM about you being the perfect Byron Kang inspo (shoutout to Dee! The real MVP of this one *wink*) Thank you for being so kind and enthusiastic about being on this cover! It was a pleasure working with you.

To Jordan Gray, thank you for taking the time to talk with me about the trans presence in this book, and for reading the dark shit and giving me your thoughts. Not only are you an immensely talented author, but you're also my friend whom I absolutely adore, so having you help me with this meant the world. I love you big, my dude. I can't wait to hang again, and get more tattoos!

To Maddie, my real-life friend who doesn't read and has no stake in the romance book world whatsoever, but who *still* took the time to talk with me about Alice, and give me thoughts on her death. You were a vital part of getting this book out into the world (and not just because you kept Patrick away from me for a week so that I could work LOL). I love you, and you are just such a special person. Never forget that.

To Corinne, my sister from another mister, thank you for being a supportive presence in my life, and someone I can turn to and bitch to whenever I need it (which is often, apparently). And to all my other author friends who have been here for me throughout my burnout, encouraging me and being positive voices when so much of what we deal with on the daily is negative af. You guys know who you are, and you're bad-freaking-ass.

Thank you to all the artists who have worked with me on this series, the narrators, Pink Flamingo, Cara (my audio liaison), and anyone else I might be forgetting because my brain is dead.

To the Flipping Hot Fandom… I would *not* be here if it weren't for you guys. Your loyalty and support means the entire world, and your enthusiasm keeps me going when I want to quit. MY LEO's!!! This book is for you…

And last but never least, to the INMATES! The empathic readers of this series, who have been sitting around patiently for TWO YEARS waiting for this book. I told you it was coming, didn't I?? And that it would be well-worth the wait?! Thank you for trusting me, and for falling as in love with this world as I have. Thank you for the edits, and the theories (and the protection of baby Dash at all costs). For the timeline breakdowns, and for picking up on even the tiniest Easter eggs… This series is your birthright.

We're BACK, baby! Now, try not to lose your shit too damn hard until the finale.

Love you all,
Xoxo Nyla

FLIPPING HOT FICTION BY NYLA K

Thank you for reading

Subscribe to my Patreon for bonus content, like The Vacation (PUSH/ Alabaster Pen, etc. Crossover), and more!

THE MIDNIGHT CITY SERIES:

Andrew & Tessa's Trilogy

(MF Forbidden/Age Gap, celebrity romance, suspense. Read in order)

Midnight City (TMCS #1)

Never Let Me Go (TMCS #2)

Always Yours (TMCS #3)

Alex & Noah

Seek Me (TMCS #4 – Standalone/Spin-off, MF Friends to lovers/Angst)

UNEXPECTED FORBIDDEN ROMANCE:

PUSH (Standalone, Taboo/MMF, bi-awakening)

PULL (Continuation novella!)

Trouble (Spinoff that can be read as a standalone, MM, gay-awakening, second chance)

Audio for the Love Is Love books available now!

To Burn In Brutal Rapture (Standalone, MF Taboo/Age Gap)

Double-edged (Standalone, MMM Age Gap, Twincest – **BANNED by Amazon!** Can be found on Nyla's website, Google Play & Eden Books.) Also available in duet narration audio! Exclusively on Nyla's website!

For The Fans (Standalone, MM, Stepbrothers) Also available is audio!

Wicked Things (Collection of 4 novellas, MM/MMM, monsters, paranormal, retellings)

ALABASTER PENITENTIARY:

Distorted, Volume 1 (MM, prisoner/prison guard, dub-con, mindf*ck)
Audio available now!

Joyless, Volume 2 (MMF, prison guards, bi-awakening, second chance, kinky)

Brainwashed, Volume 3 (MM, doctor/patient, true crime)

Fragments, Volume 4 (MM, frenemies to lovers, jealous/possessive/pining)

Shadowman, Volume 5 (MM, bi-awakening, revenge & jealousy)

Ivory, Volume 6 (The Finale) – Coming March 2026!

Alabaster Pen is available in audio!

The Control Room, a FREE Alabaster Pen short!

TWISTED TALES COLLECTION:

Serpent In White (MMM, dark romance, drug cult, age gap, foster brothers, retelling of the Brothers Grimm's The White Snake)

STANDALONE NOVELLA:

Unwrap Him by Nyla K (An Age Gap, Taboo MM) – Available across all digital retailers, and Nyla's website! Coming to audio, Christmas 2025!

Join my Facebook reader group for discussions, giveaways, and all the best Nyla K madness!

Don't forget to share and leave a review! It means the world!

ABOUT THE AUTHOR

Hi, guys! I'm Nyla K... Author of Flipping Hot Fiction, which basically means all things unique & boundary-pushing! If you're looking for the same old story, you won't find it here. I'm the... *bad guy* ;)

I'm an awkward sailor-mouthed lover of all things romance, existing up in Maine—in our dream house in the woods—with my partner, who you can call PB, or Patty Banga if you're nasty, and our fur baby, Ziggy Stardust! When I'm not writing and reading sexy books, I'm rocking out to my various awesome playlists, cooking yummy food and fussing over my kitten (and no, that's not a euphemism). Did I mention I have a dirtier mind than probably everyone you know?

I like to admire hot guys (don't we all?) and book boyfriends, cake and ice cream are my kryptonite. I can recite every word that was ever uttered on *Friends*, *Family Guy*, and *How I Met Your Mother*, red Gatorade is my lifeblood, and I love to sing, although I've been told I do it in a Cher voice for some reason. I'm very passionate about the things that matter to me, and art is probably the biggest one. If you tell me you like my books, I'll give you whatever you want. I consider my readers are my friends, and I welcome anyone to find me on social media any time you want to talk books or sexy dudes!

Get at me:

info@authornylak.com
Visit AuthorNylaK.com for Banned books, Signed Books & Merch!

The Flipping Hot Newsletter!
Patreon: Where you'll find Nyla K UNCENSORED!

Instagram:@AuthorNylaK

Facebook: AuthorNylaK

Tiktok: @NylaKAuthor

Twitter: @MissNylah
(Misc uncensored content! NSFW!)

Goodreads: Nyla K

BookBub: @AuthorNylaK

Happy reading!

Printed in Poland
by Amazon Fulfillment
Poland Sp. z o.o., Wrocław

54915866R00370